W9-AEM-671

Gunnerkrigg Court

Reason

Thomas Siddell

EMMA S. CLARK MEMORIAL LIBRARY
SETAUKET, L.I., NEW YORK 11733

Gunnerkrigg Court Volume 3: Reason

Written & Illustrated by

Thomas Siddell

ARCHAIA™
NEW STORIES. NEW WORLDS.

Published by **Archaia**

Archaia Entertainment LLC
1680 Vine Street, Suite 912
Los Angeles, California, 90028, USA
www.archaia.com

GUNNERKRIGG COURT VOLUME THREE: **REASON**. July 2011. FIRST PRINTING

10 9 8 7 6 5 4 3 2 1

ISBN: 1-936393-23-9
ISBN 13: 978-1-936393-23-7

GUNNERKRIGG COURT is © and TM 2007 Thomas Siddell.
Archaia™ and the Archaia Logo™ are TM 2011 Archaia
Entertainment LLC. All Rights Reserved. No unauthorized
reproductions permitted, except for review purposes. Any similarity
to persons alive or dead is purely coincidental.

Printed in Korea.

Gunnerkrigg Court

Reason

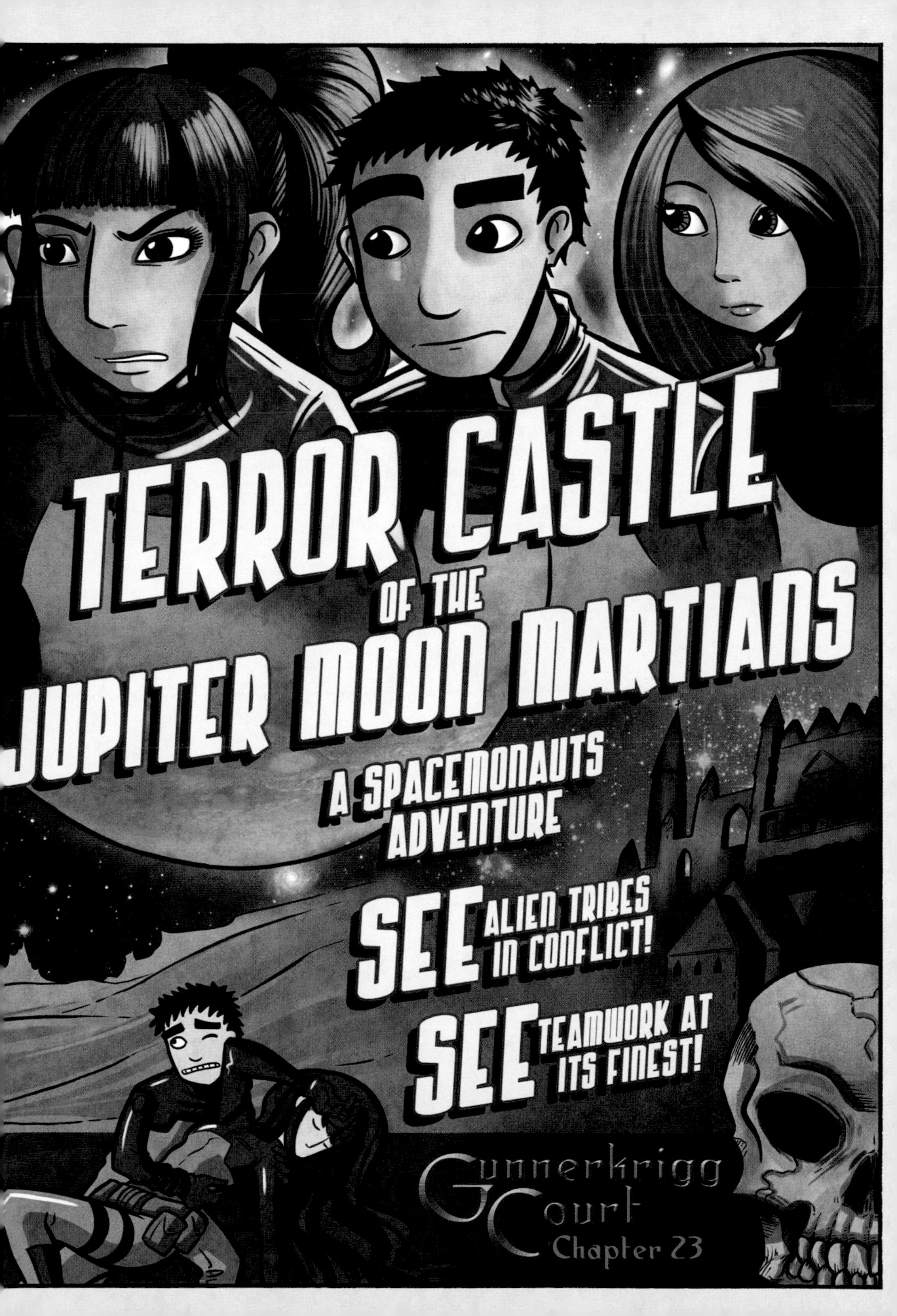
TERROR CASTLE
OF THE
JUPITER MOON MARTIANS
A SPACEMONAUTS
ADVENTURE
SEE ALIEN TRIBES
IN CONFLICT!
SEE TEAMWORK AT
ITS FINEST!
Gunnerkrigg
Court
Chapter 23

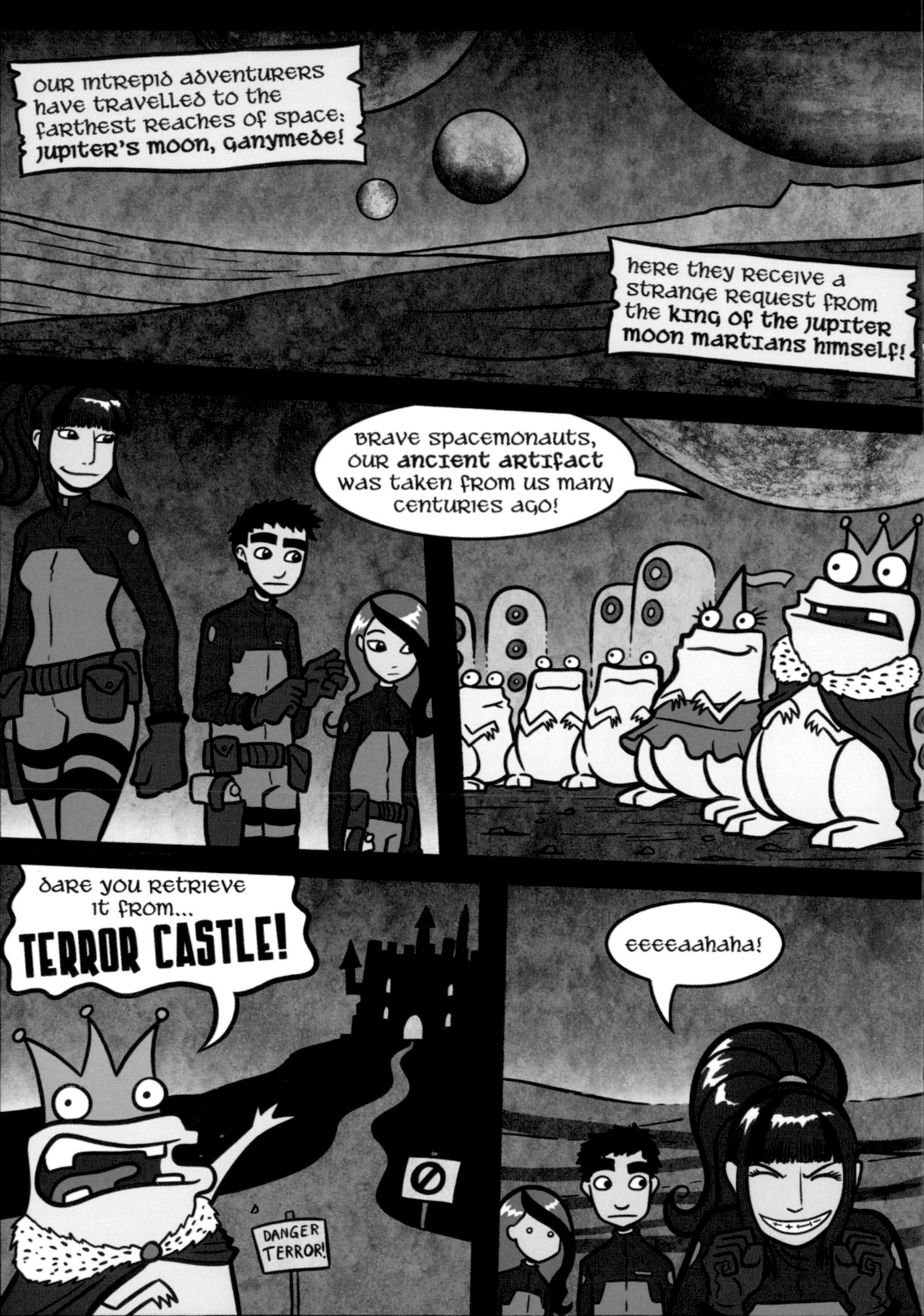
our intrepid adventurers have travelled to the farthest reaches of space: jupiter's moon, ganymede!
here they receive a strange request from the king of the jupiter moon martians himself!
brave spacemonauts, our ancient artifact was taken from us many centuries ago!
dare you retrieve it from... TERROR CASTLE!
DANGER TERROR!
eeeeaahaha!

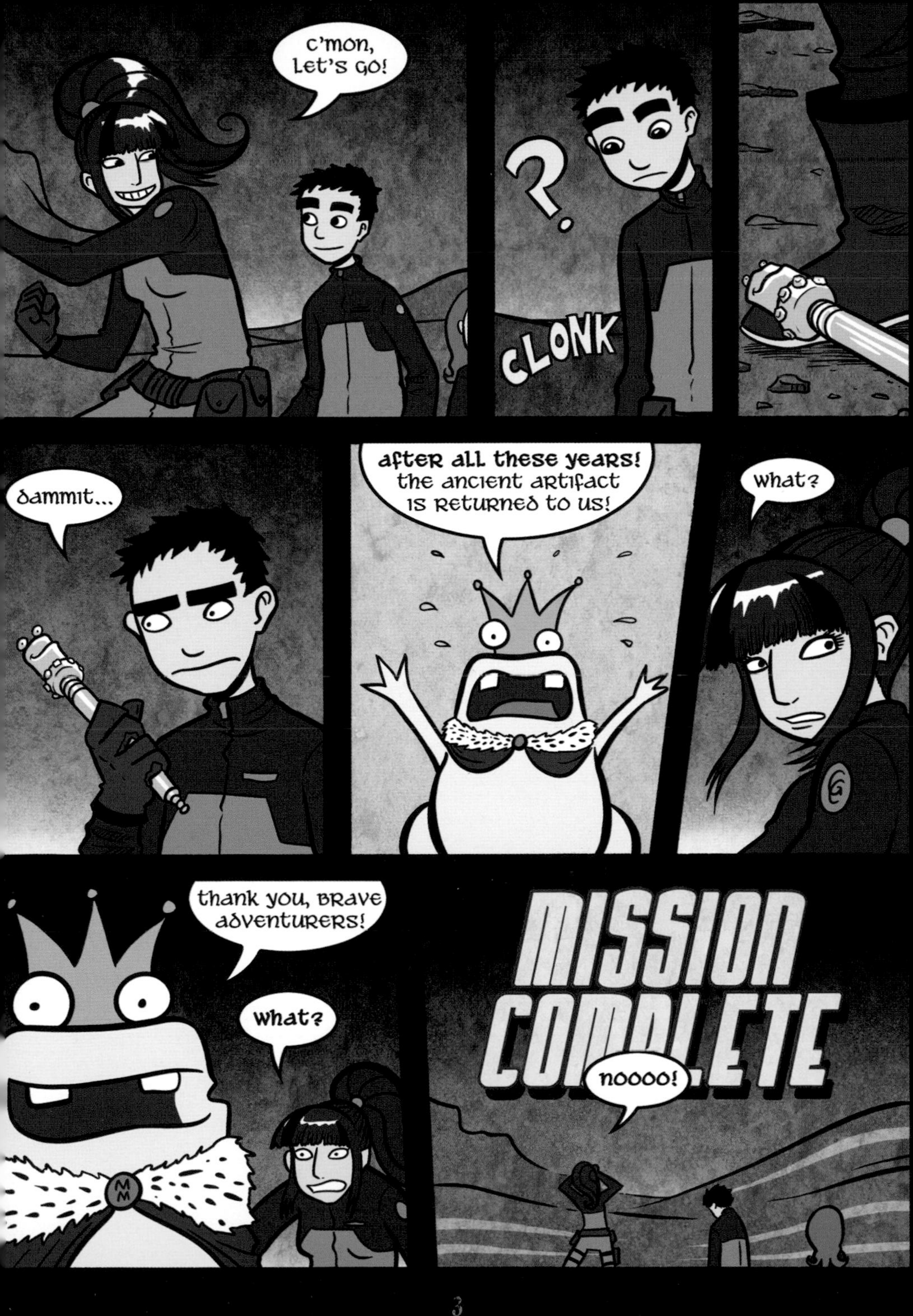
c'mon, Let's go!
?
CLONK
dammit...
after all these years! the ancient artifact is returned to us!
what?
thank you, brave adventurers!
what?
MISSION COMPLETE
noooo!

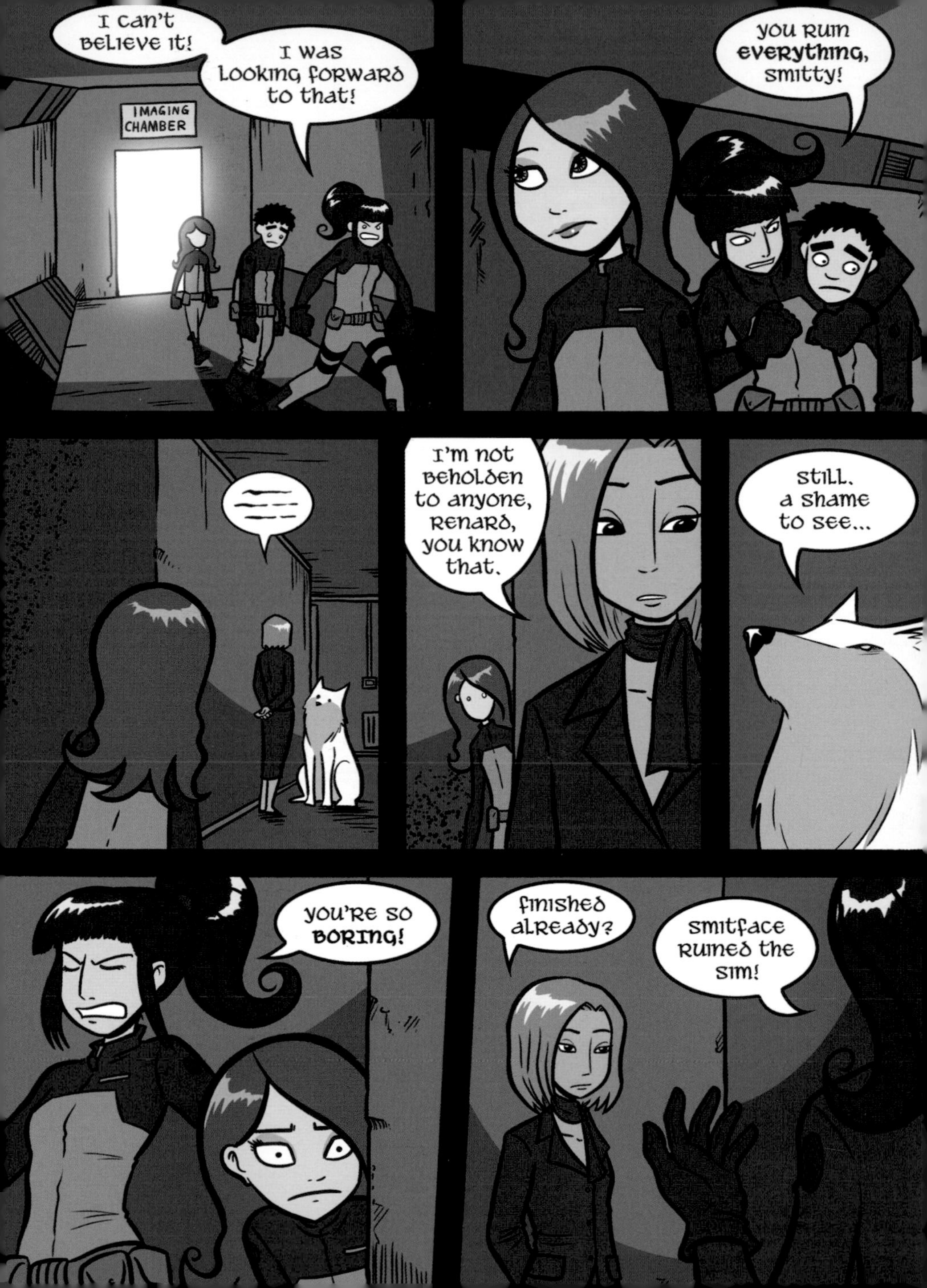
I can't believe it!
I was looking forward to that!
IMAGING CHAMBER
you ruin everything, smitty!
I'm not beholden to anyone, Renard, you know that.
still, a shame to see...
you're so BORING!
finished already?
smitface ruined the sim!

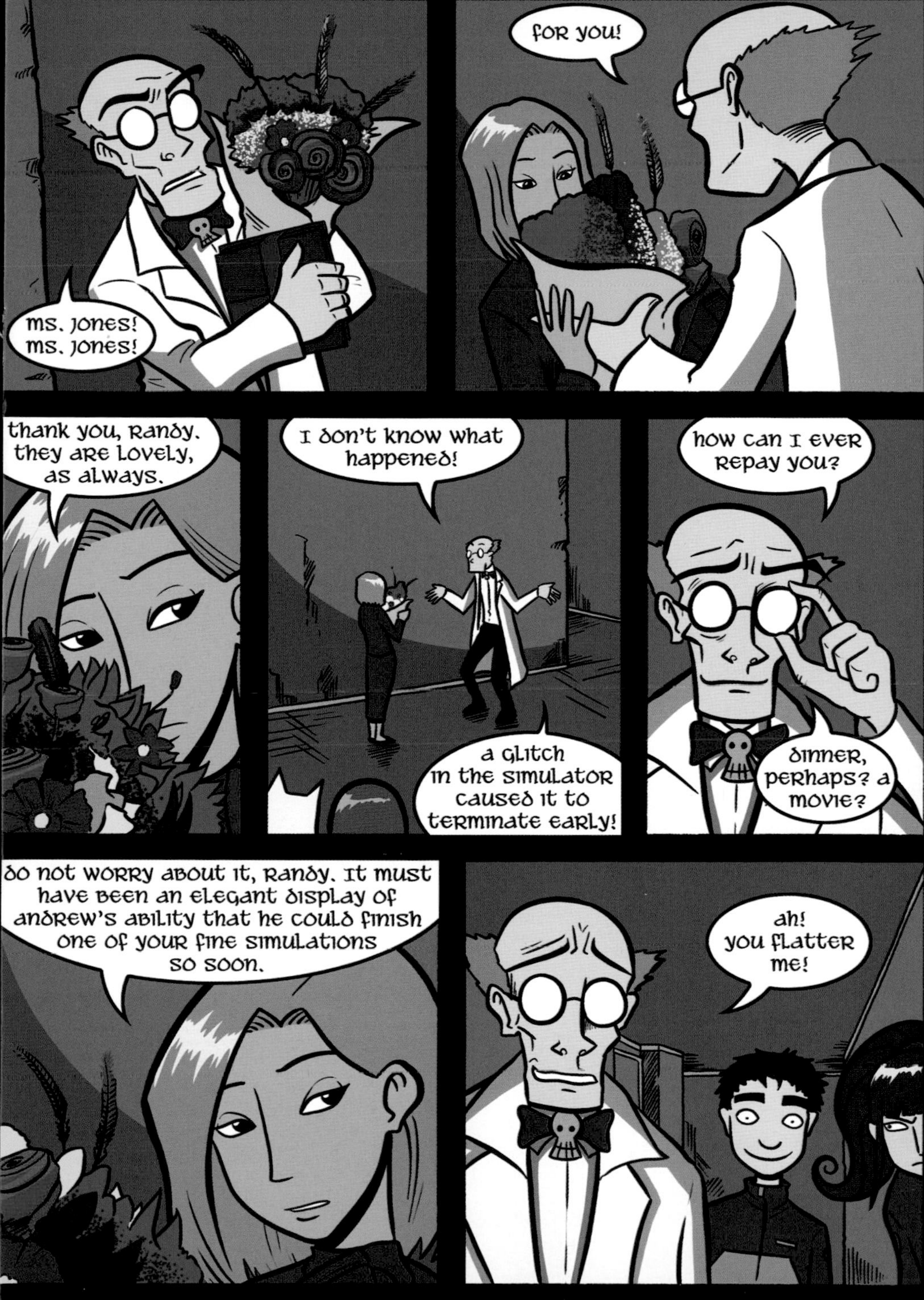
ms. jones!
ms. jones!
for you!
thank you, randy. they are lovely, as always.
I don't know what happened!
a glitch in the simulator caused it to terminate early!
how can I ever repay you?
dinner, perhaps? a movie?
do not worry about it, randy. it must have been an elegant display of andrew's ability that he could finish one of your fine simulations so soon.
ah! you flatter me!

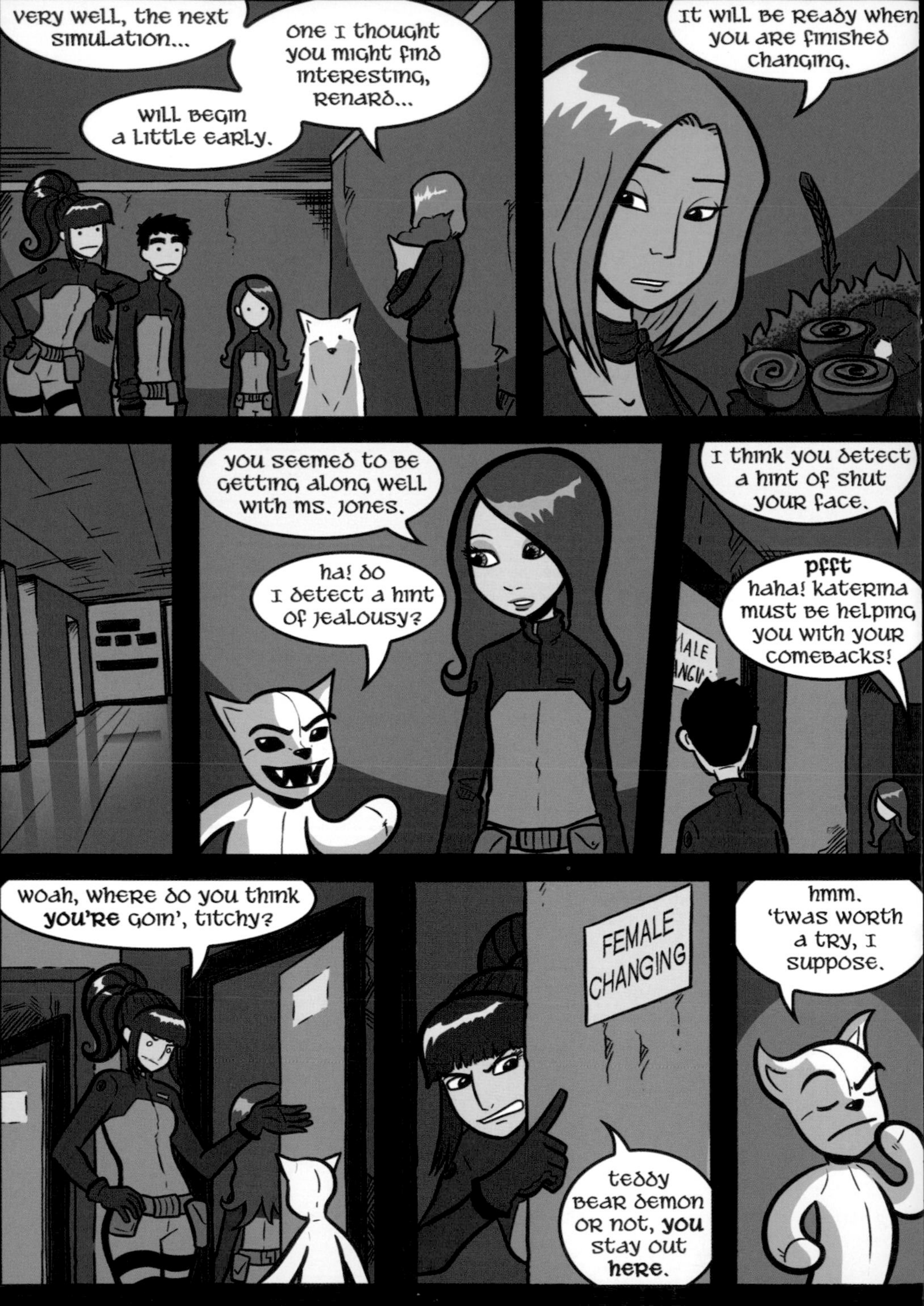
very well, the next simulation...
will begin a little early.
one I thought you might find interesting, renard...
It will be ready when you are finished changing.
you seemed to be getting along well with ms. jones.
ha! do I detect a hint of jealousy?
I think you detect a hint of shut your face.
pfft haha! katerina must be helping you with your comebacks!
woah, where do you think **you're** goin', titchy?
FEMALE CHANGING
teddy bear demon or not, **you** stay out **here**.
hmm. 'twas worth a try, I suppose.

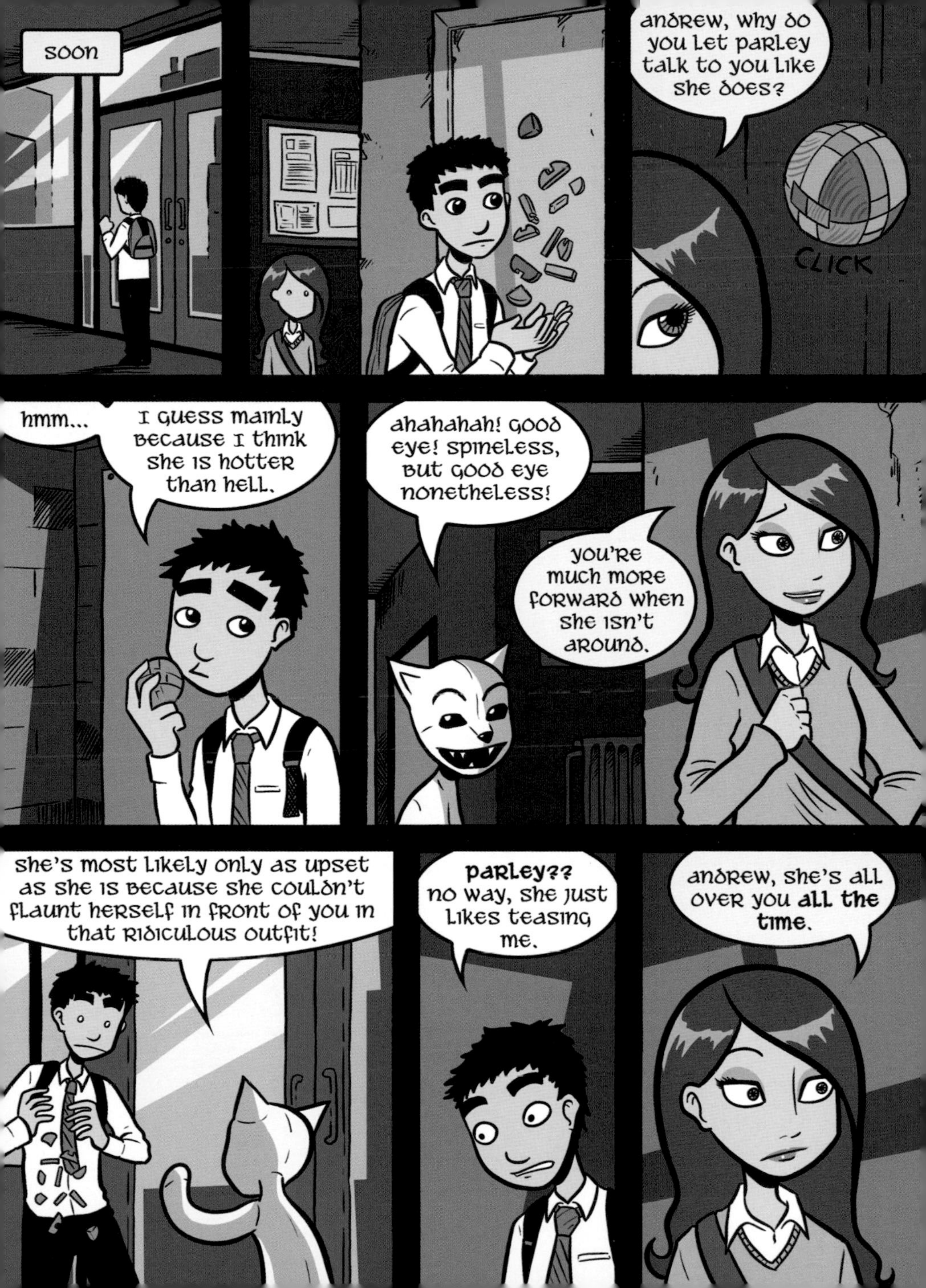
soon
andrew, why do you let parley talk to you like she does?
CLICK
hmm...
I guess mainly because I think she is hotter than hell.
ahahahah! good eye! spineless, but good eye nonetheless!
you're much more forward when she isn't around.
she's most likely only as upset as she is because she couldn't flaunt herself in front of you in that ridiculous outfit!
parley?? no way, she just likes teasing me.
andrew, she's all over you all the time.

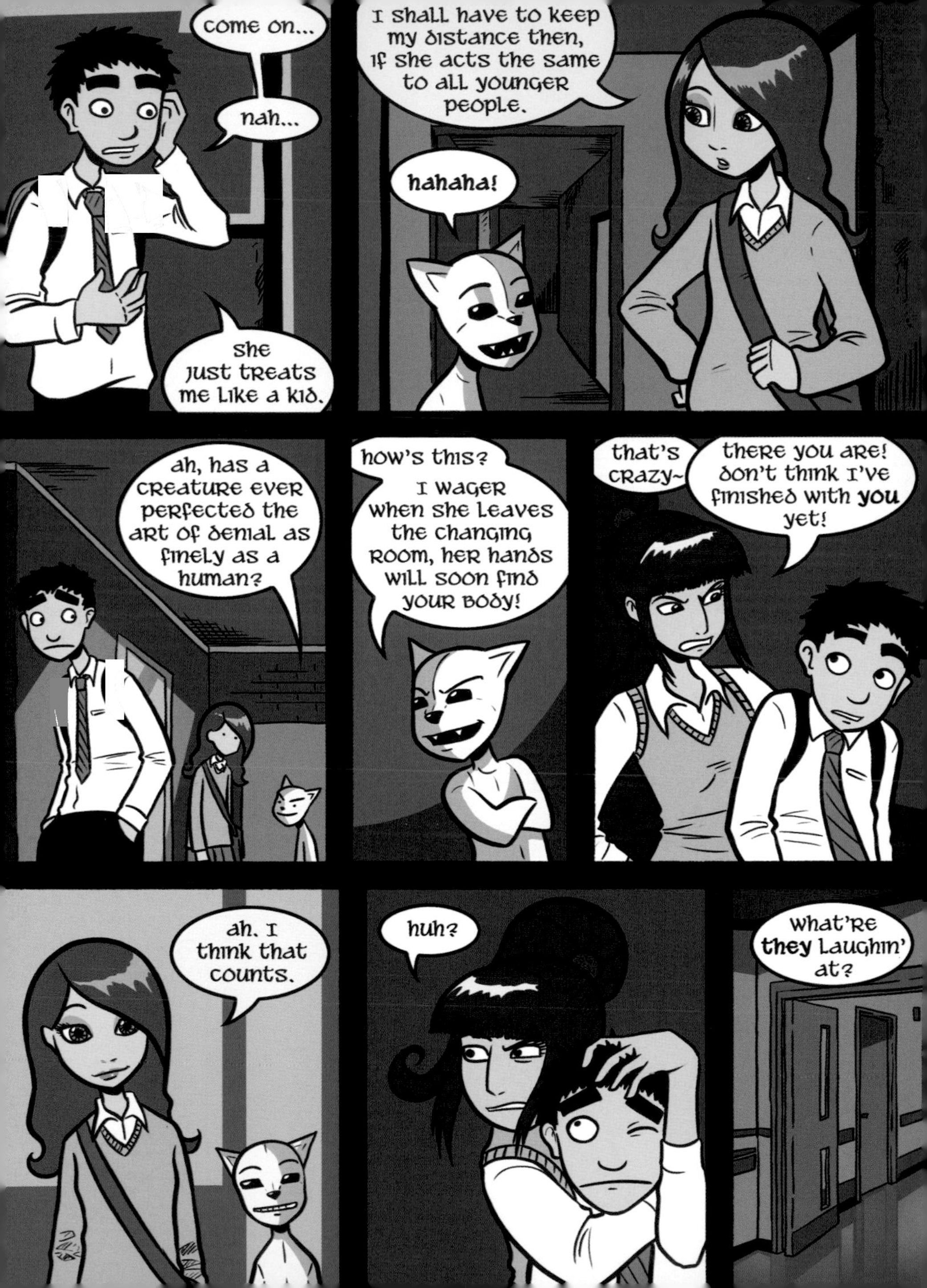
come on...
nah...
she just treats me like a kid.
I shall have to keep my distance then, if she acts the same to all younger people.
hahaha!
ah, has a creature ever perfected the art of denial as finely as a human?
how's this?
I wager when she leaves the changing room, her hands will soon find your body!
that's crazy~
there you are! don't think I've finished with **you** yet!
ah. I think that counts.
huh?
what're **they** laughin' at?

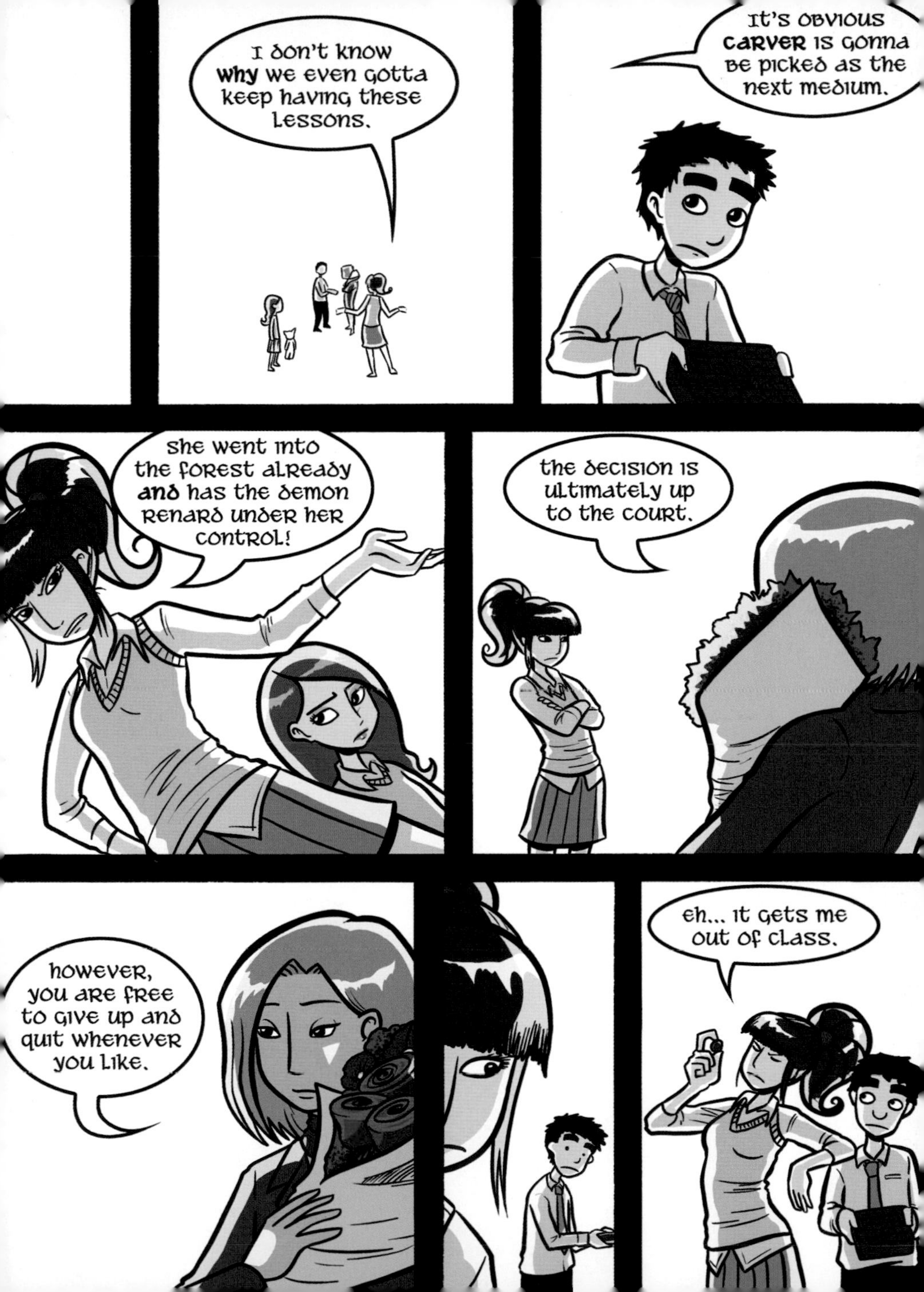

I don't know **why** we even gotta keep having these lessons.
It's obvious **Carver** is gonna be picked as the next medium.
She went into the forest already **and** has the demon Renard under her control!
The decision is ultimately up to the court.
However, you are free to give up and quit whenever you like.
Eh... it gets me out of class.

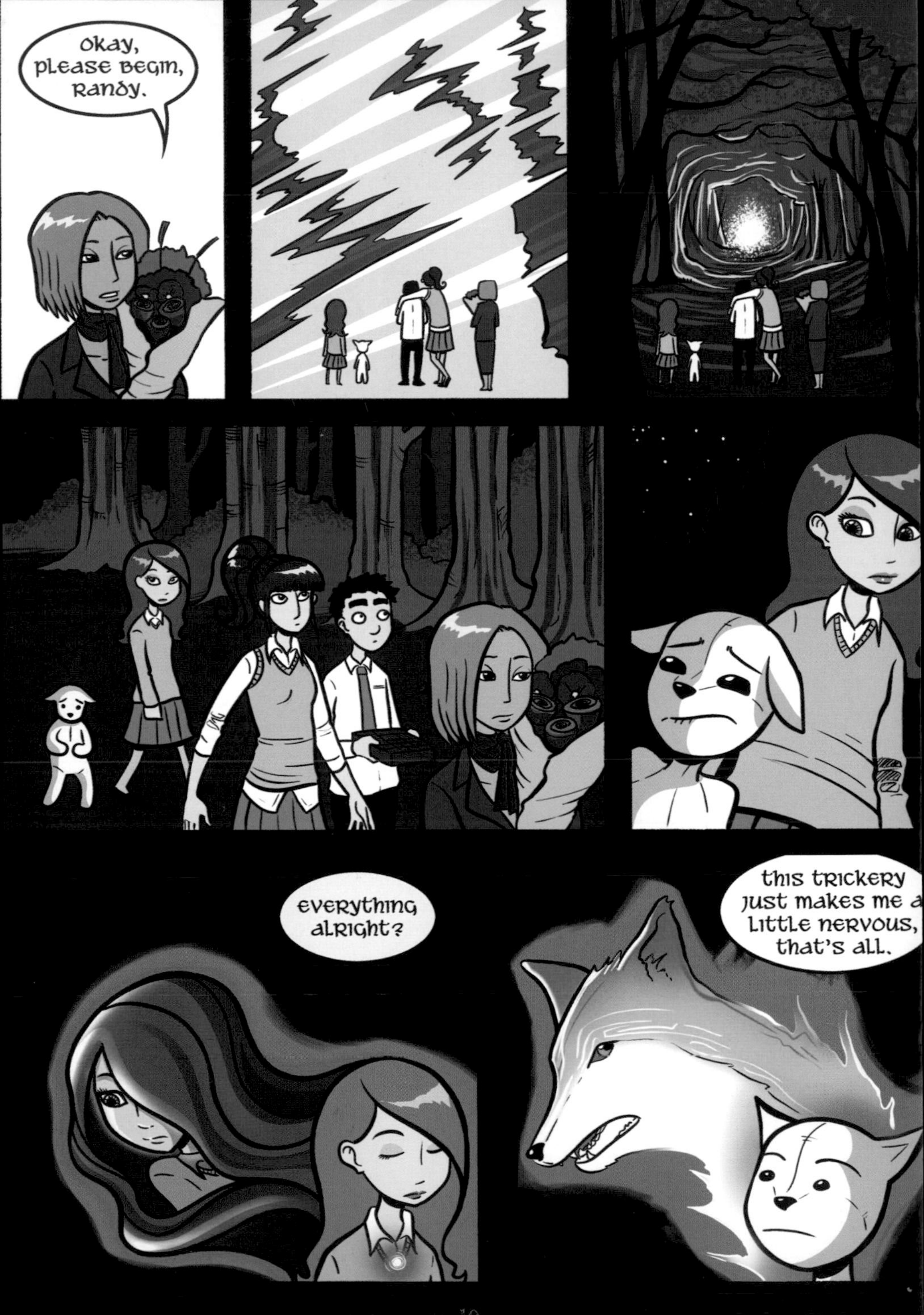
Okay, please begin, Randy.
everything alright?
this trickery just makes me a little nervous, that's all.

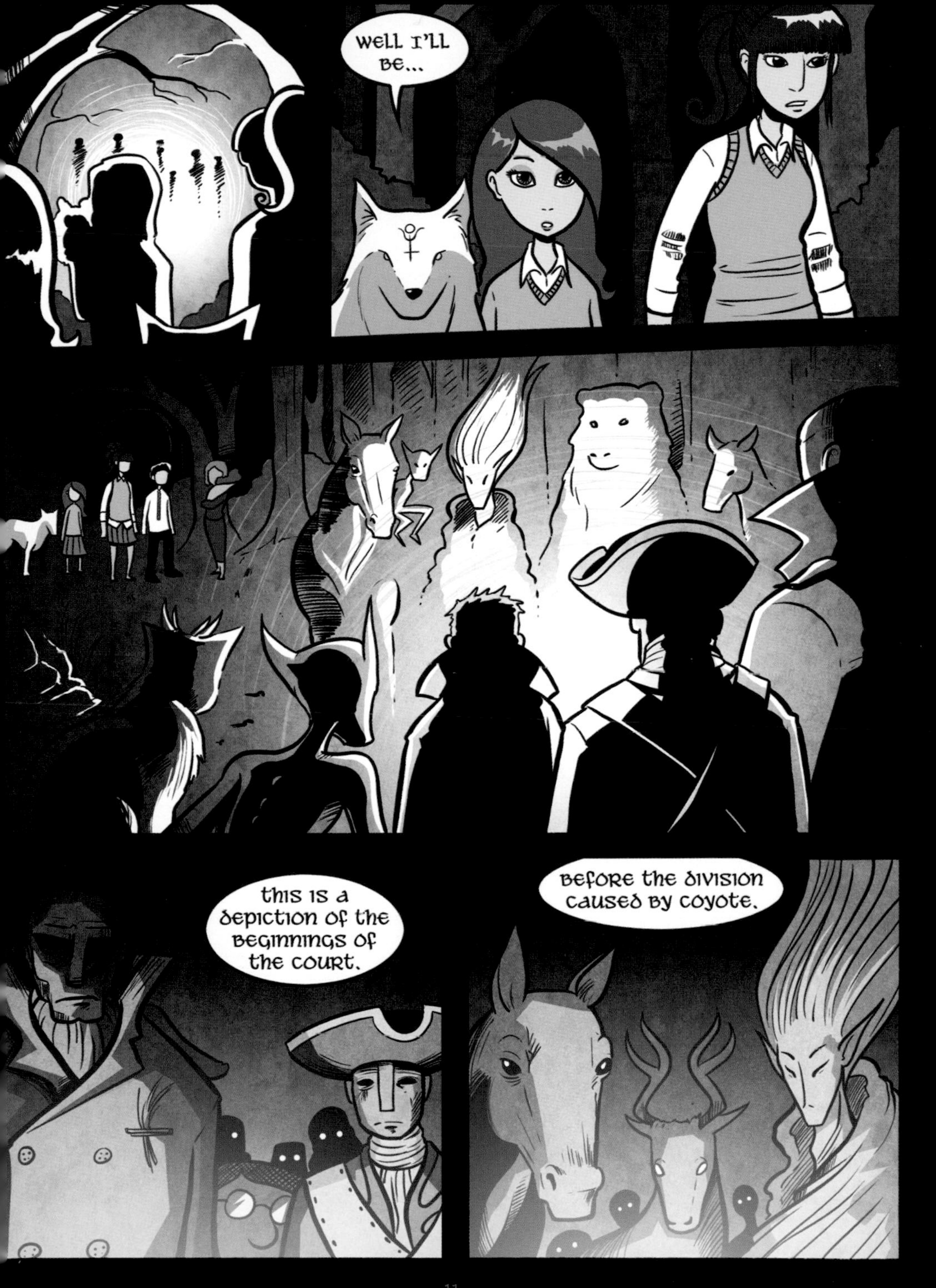

WELL I'LL BE...
THIS IS A DEPICTION OF THE BEGINNINGS OF THE COURT.
BEFORE THE DIVISION CAUSED BY COYOTE.

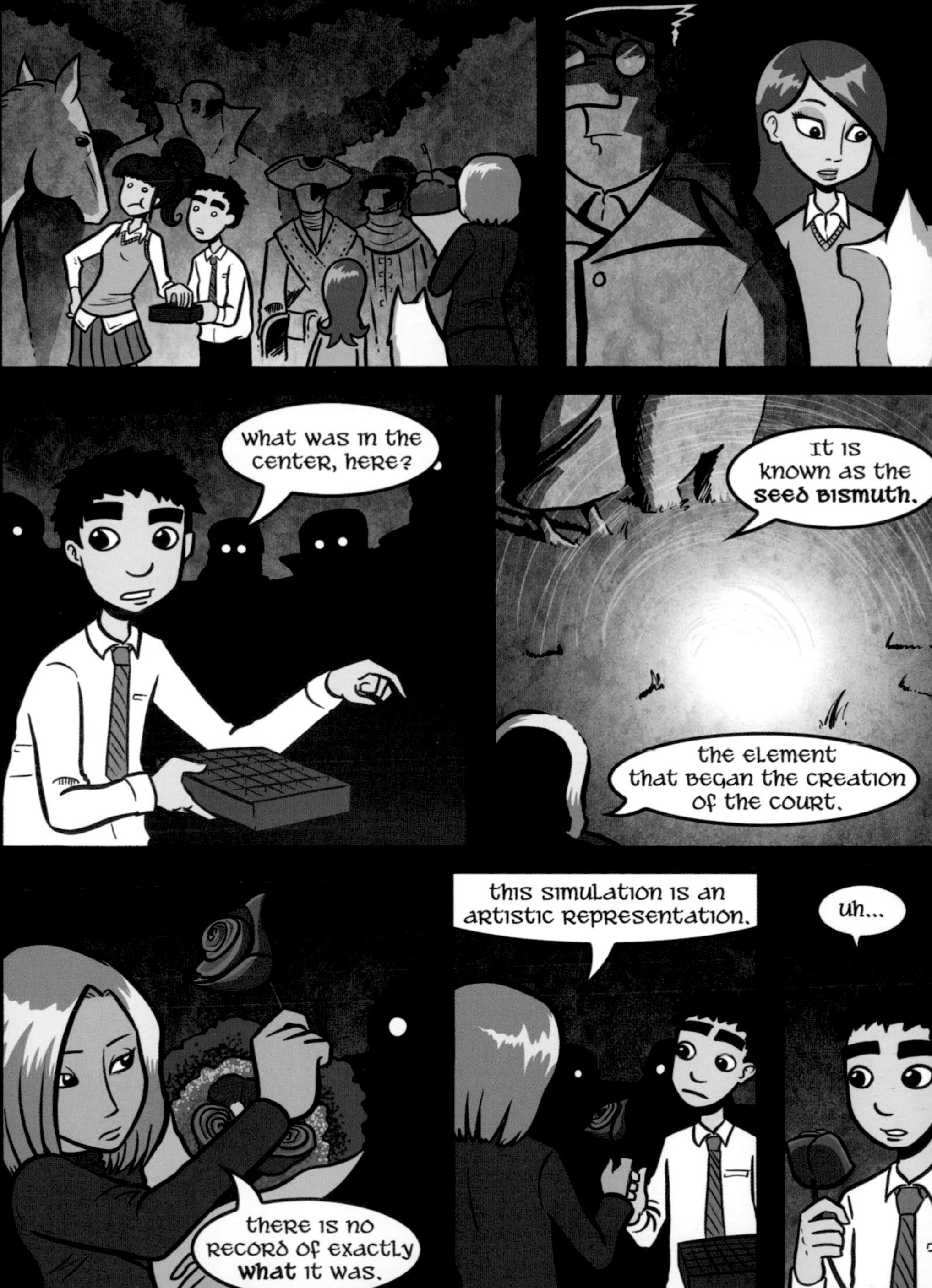
What was in the center, here?
It is known as the Seed Bismuth.
The element that began the creation of the Court.
There is no record of exactly what it was.
This simulation is an artistic representation.
Uh...

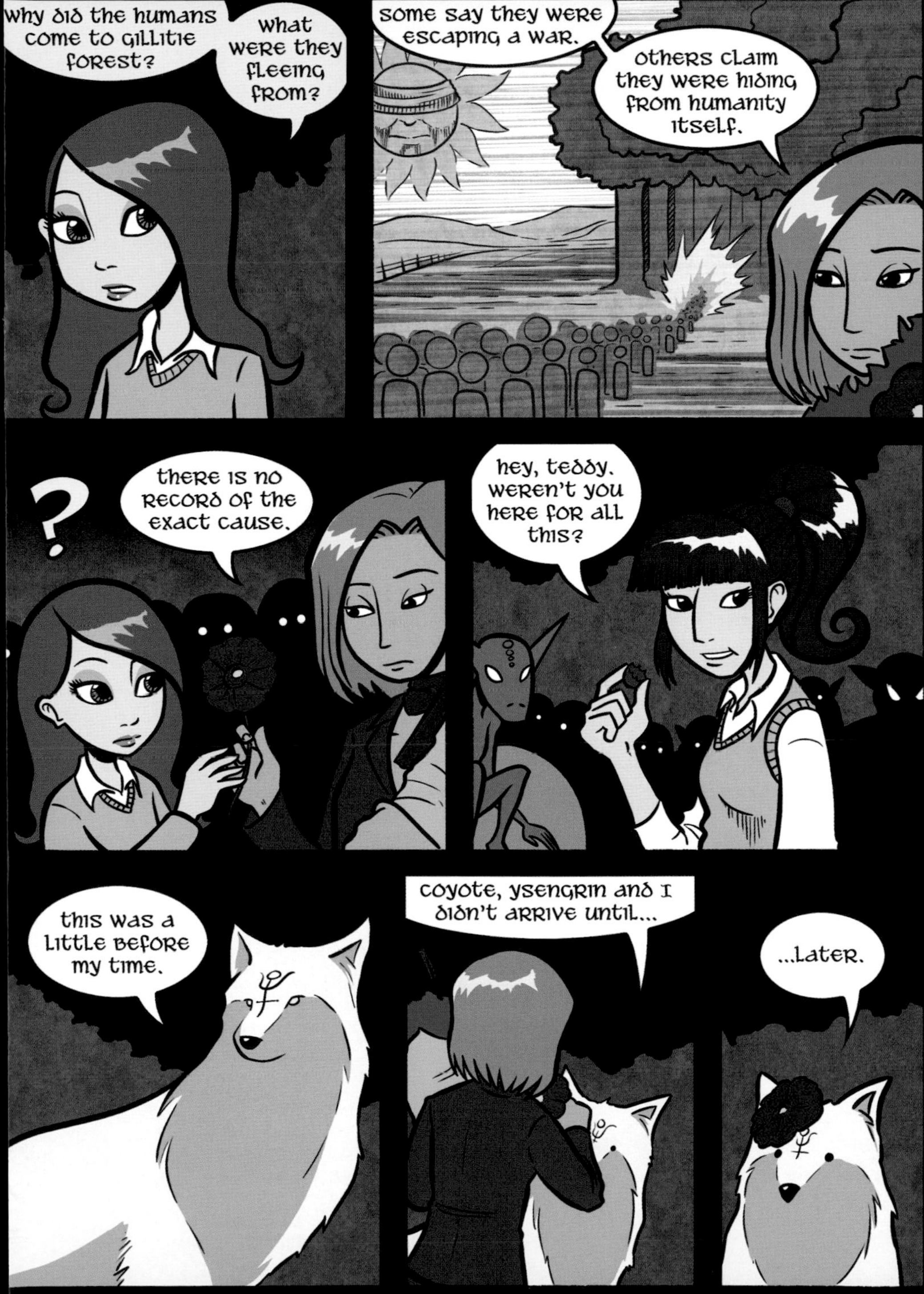
why did the humans come to gillitie forest?
what were they fleeing from?
some say they were escaping a war.
others claim they were hiding from humanity itself.
there is no record of the exact cause.
?
hey, teddy. weren't you here for all this?
this was a little before my time.
coyote, ysengrin and I didn't arrive until...
...later.

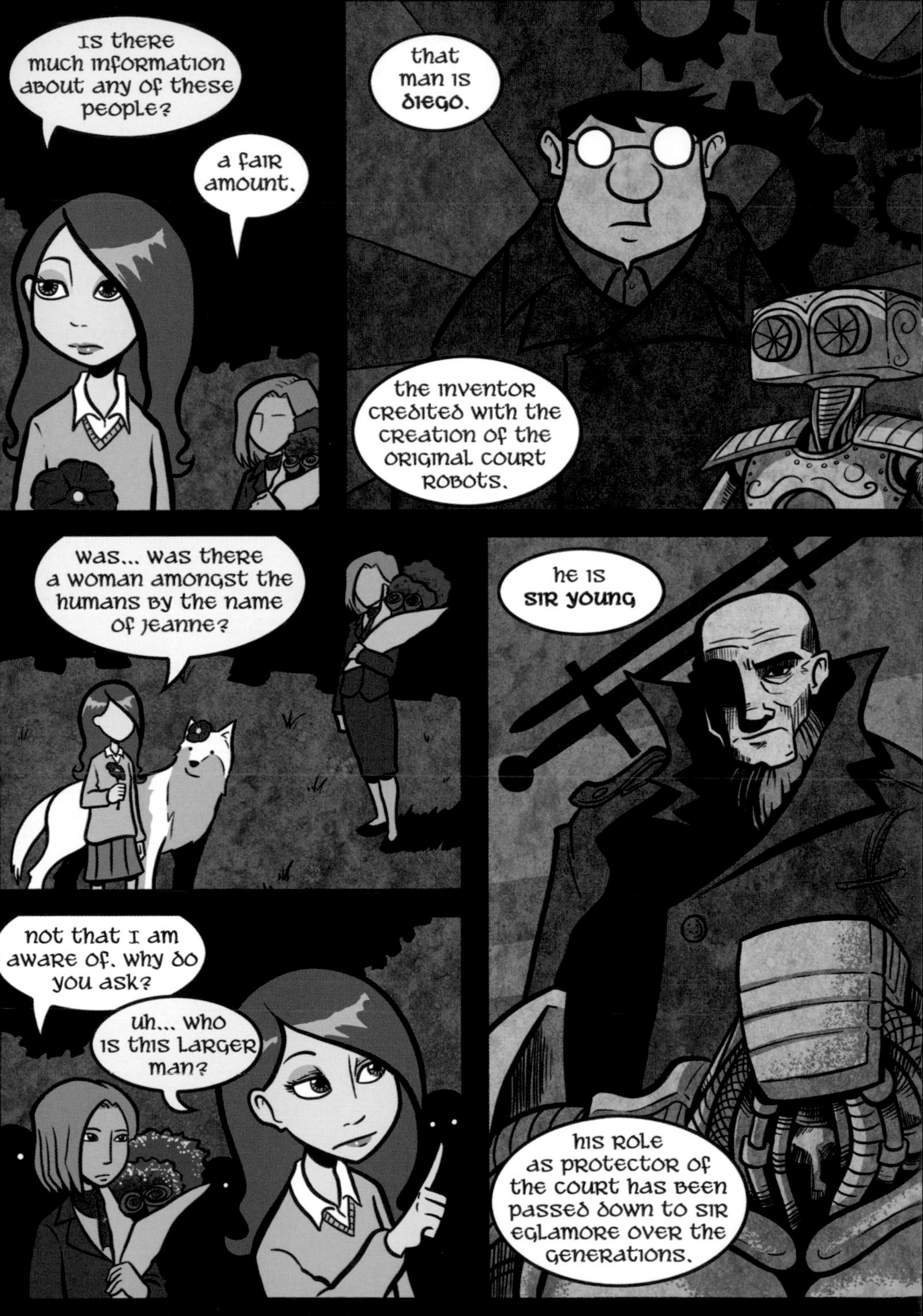
is there much information about any of these people?
a fair amount.
that man is diego.
the inventor credited with the creation of the original court robots.
was... was there a woman amongst the humans by the name of jeanne?
he is sir young
not that I am aware of. why do you ask?
uh... who is this larger man?
his role as protector of the court has been passed down to sir eglamore over the generations.

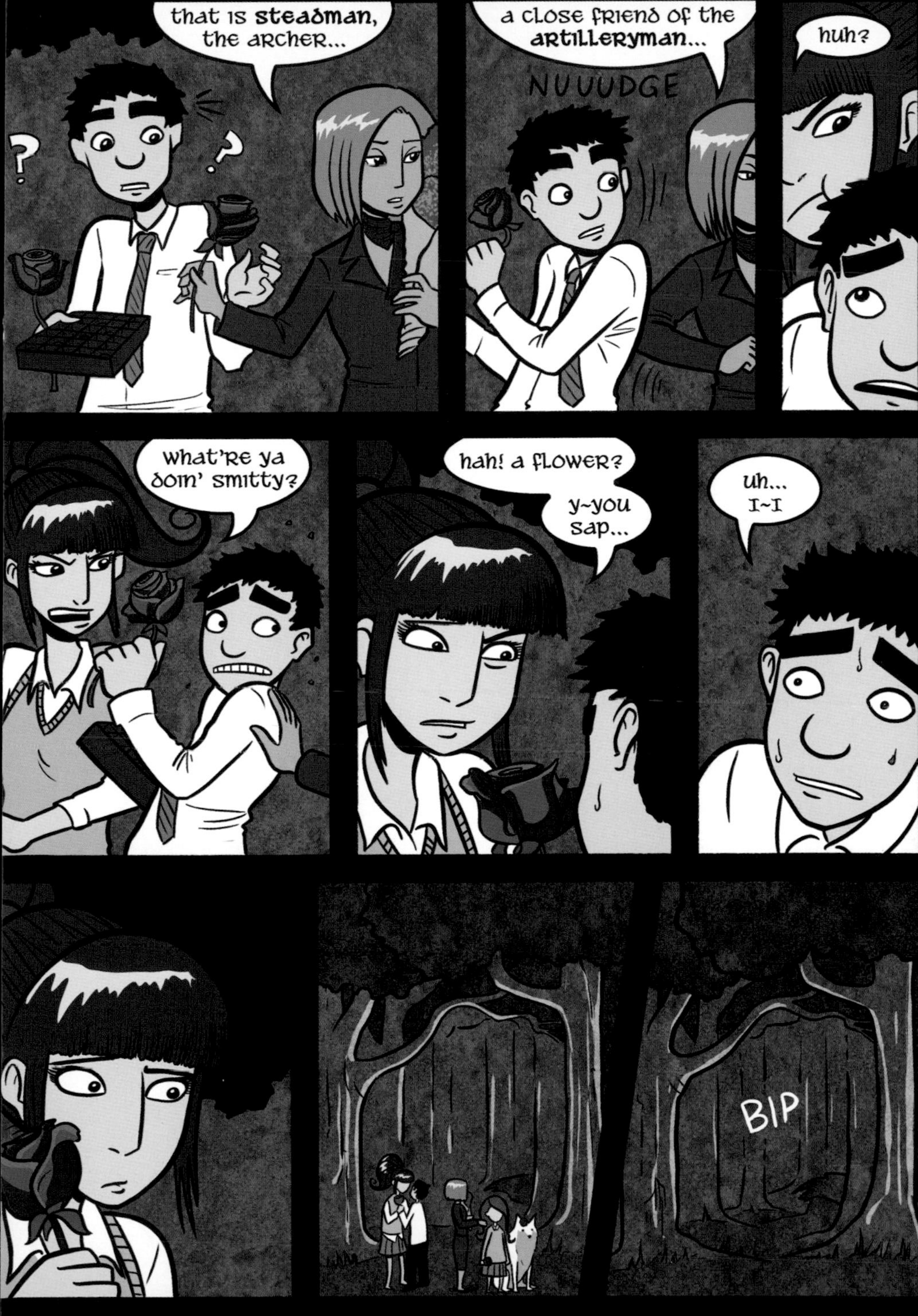
that is steadman, the archer...
a close friend of the artilleryman...
NUUUDGE
huh?
what're ya doin' smitty?
hah! a flower?
y~you sap...
uh... I~I
BIP

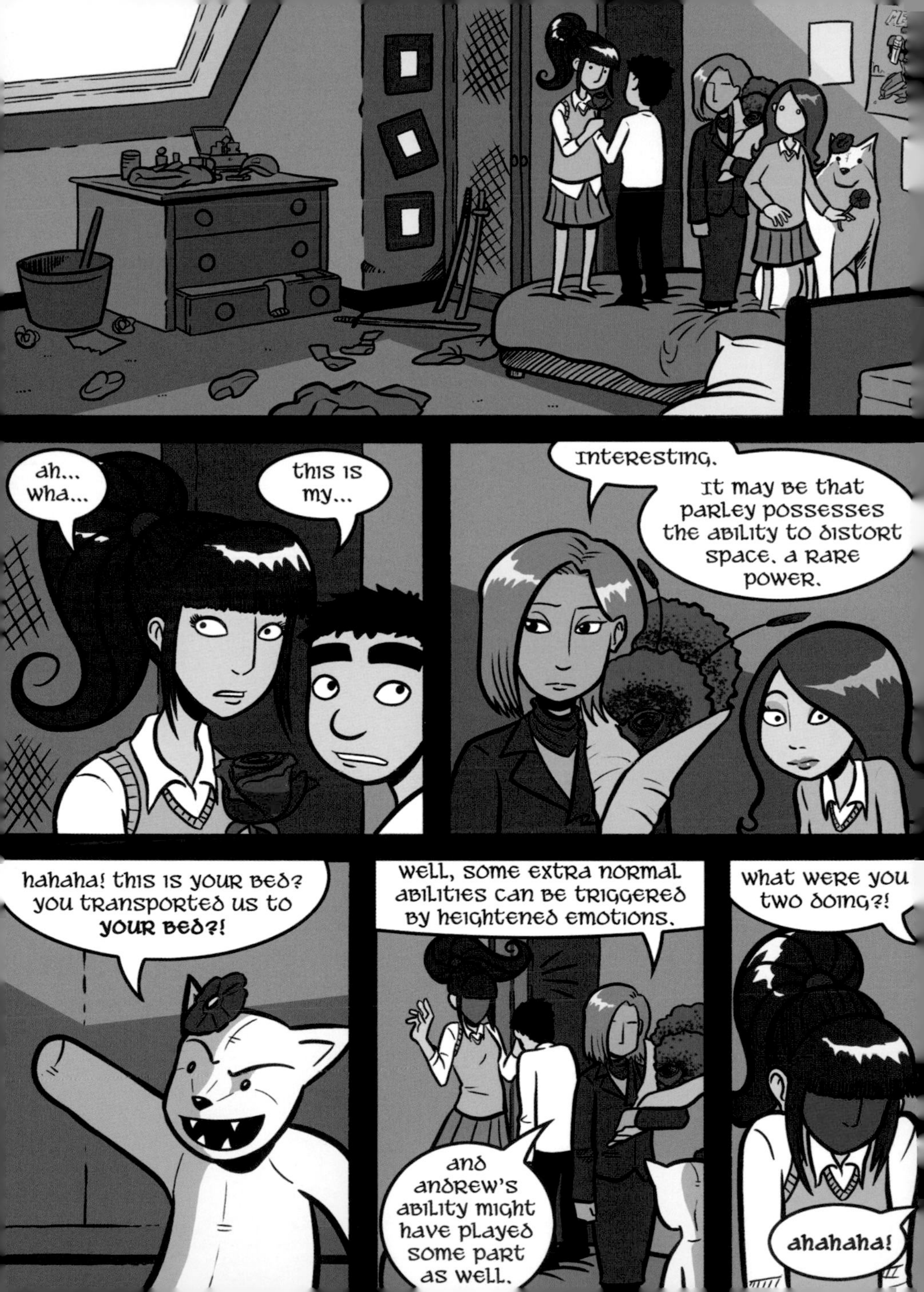
ah... wha...
this is my...
interesting.
it may be that parley possesses the ability to distort space. a rare power.
hahaha! this is your bed? you transported us to **your bed?!**
well, some extra normal abilities can be triggered by heightened emotions.
and andrew's ability might have played some part as well.
what were you two doing?!
ahahaha!

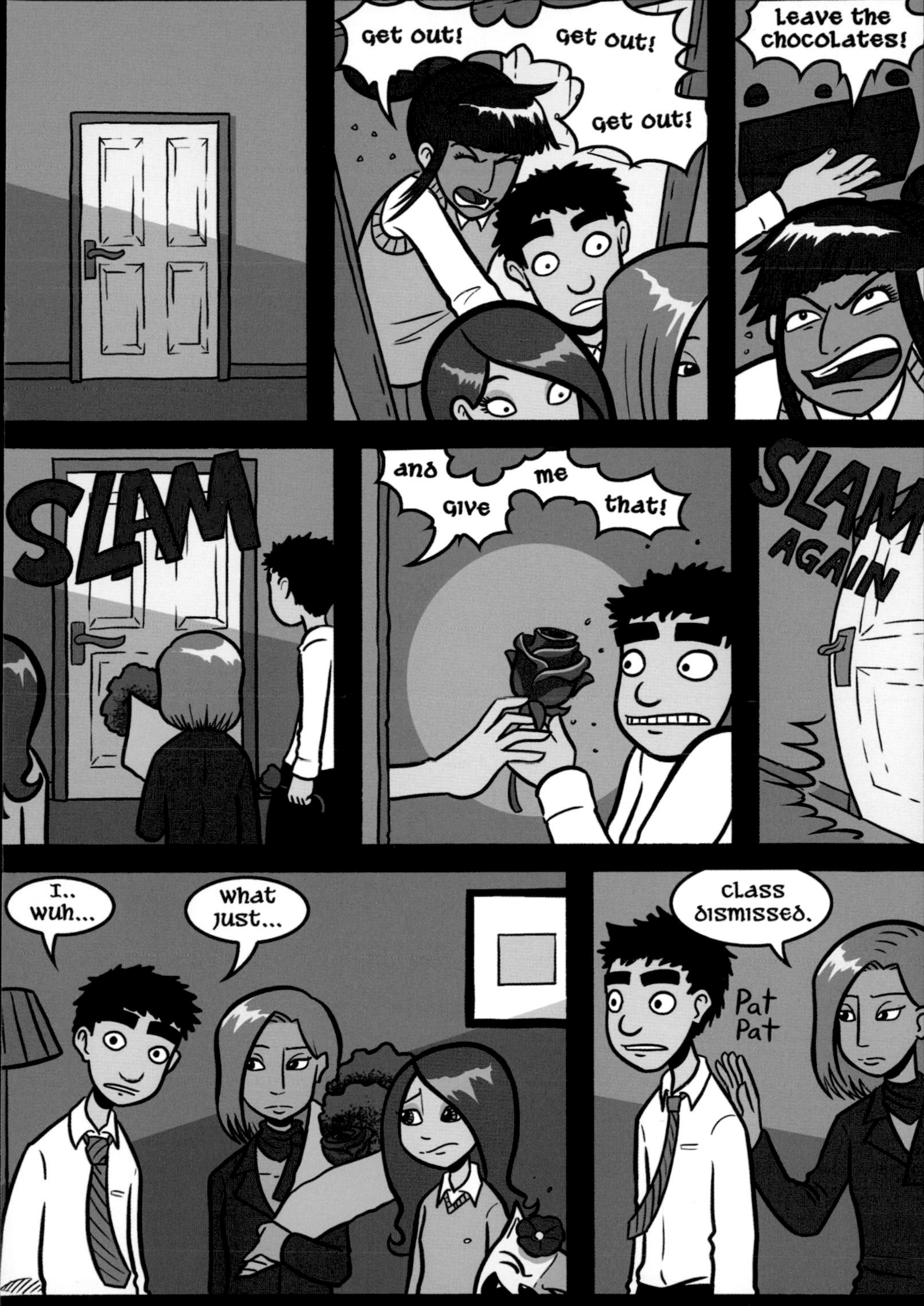
get out! get out! get out!
Leave the chocolates!
SLAM
and give me that!
SLAM AGAIN
I.. wuh...
what just...
class dismissed.
Pat Pat

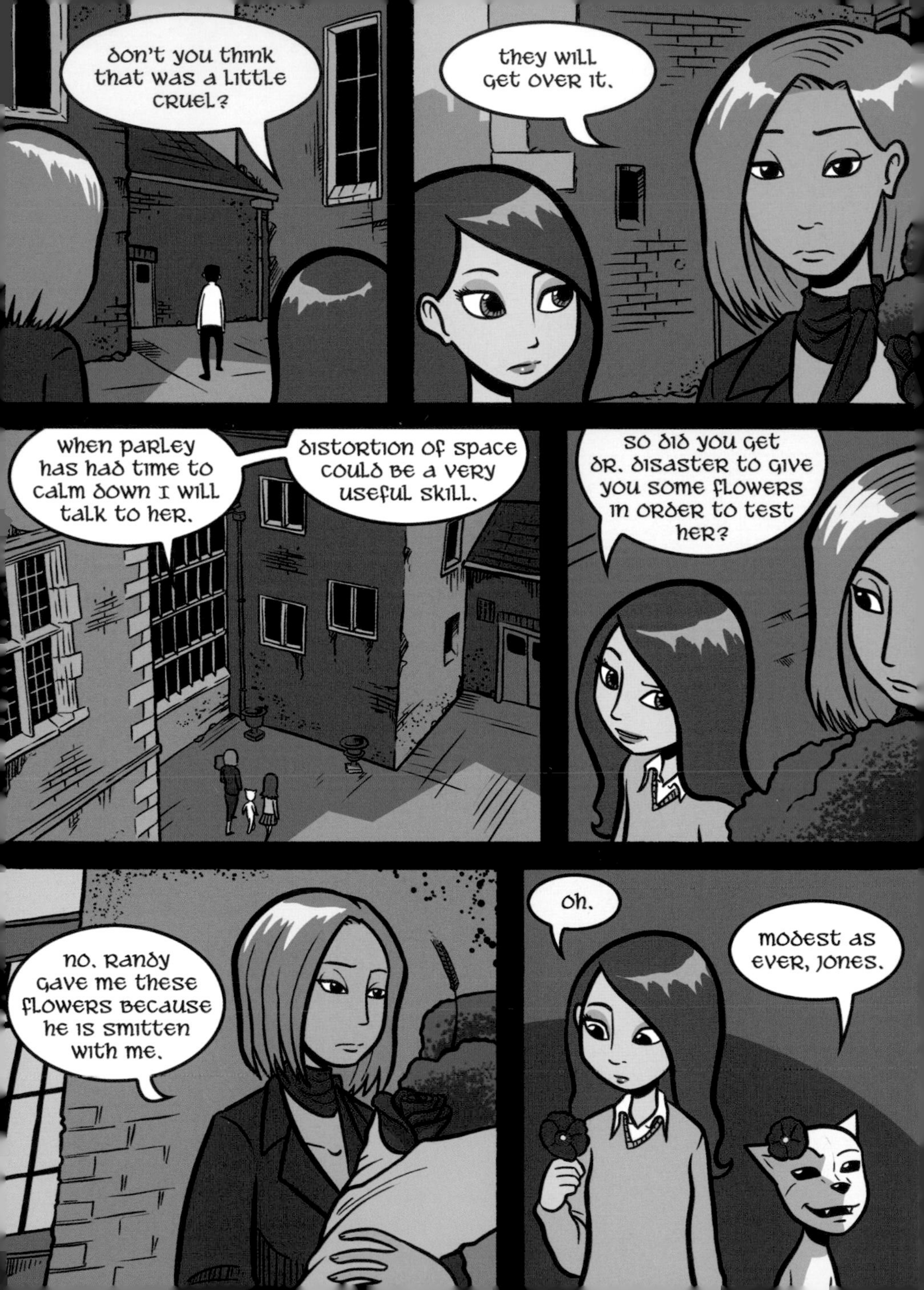
don't you think that was a little cruel?
they will get over it.
when parley has had time to calm down I will talk to her.
distortion of space could be a very useful skill.
so did you get dr. disaster to give you some flowers in order to test her?
no. randy gave me these flowers because he is smitten with me.
oh.
modest as ever, jones.

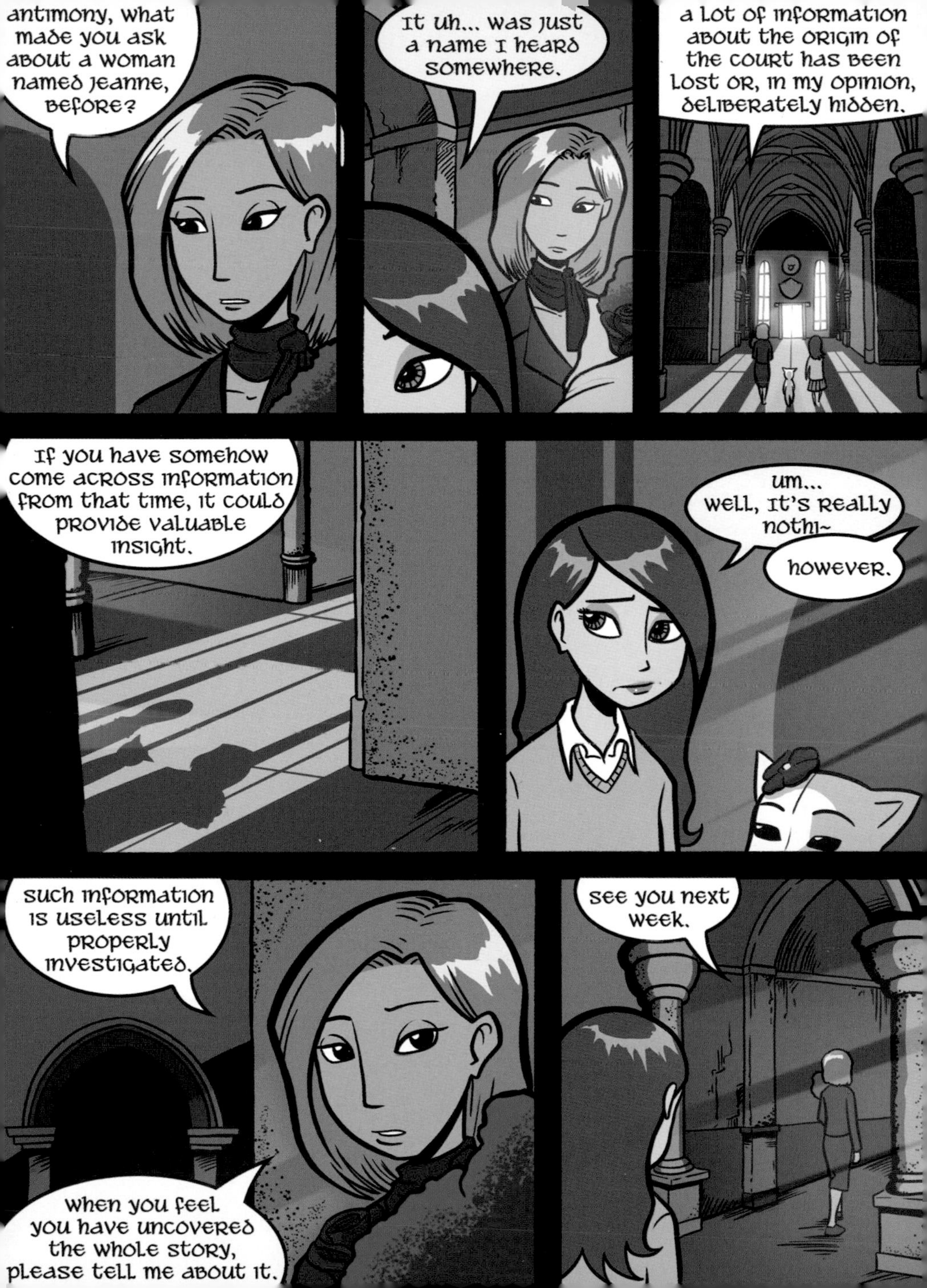
antimony, what made you ask about a woman named jeanne, before?
It uh... was just a name I heard somewhere.
a lot of information about the origin of the court has been lost or, in my opinion, deliberately hidden.
If you have somehow come across information from that time, it could provide valuable insight.
um... well, it's really nothi~
however.
such information is useless until properly investigated.
when you feel you have uncovered the whole story, please tell me about it.
see you next week.

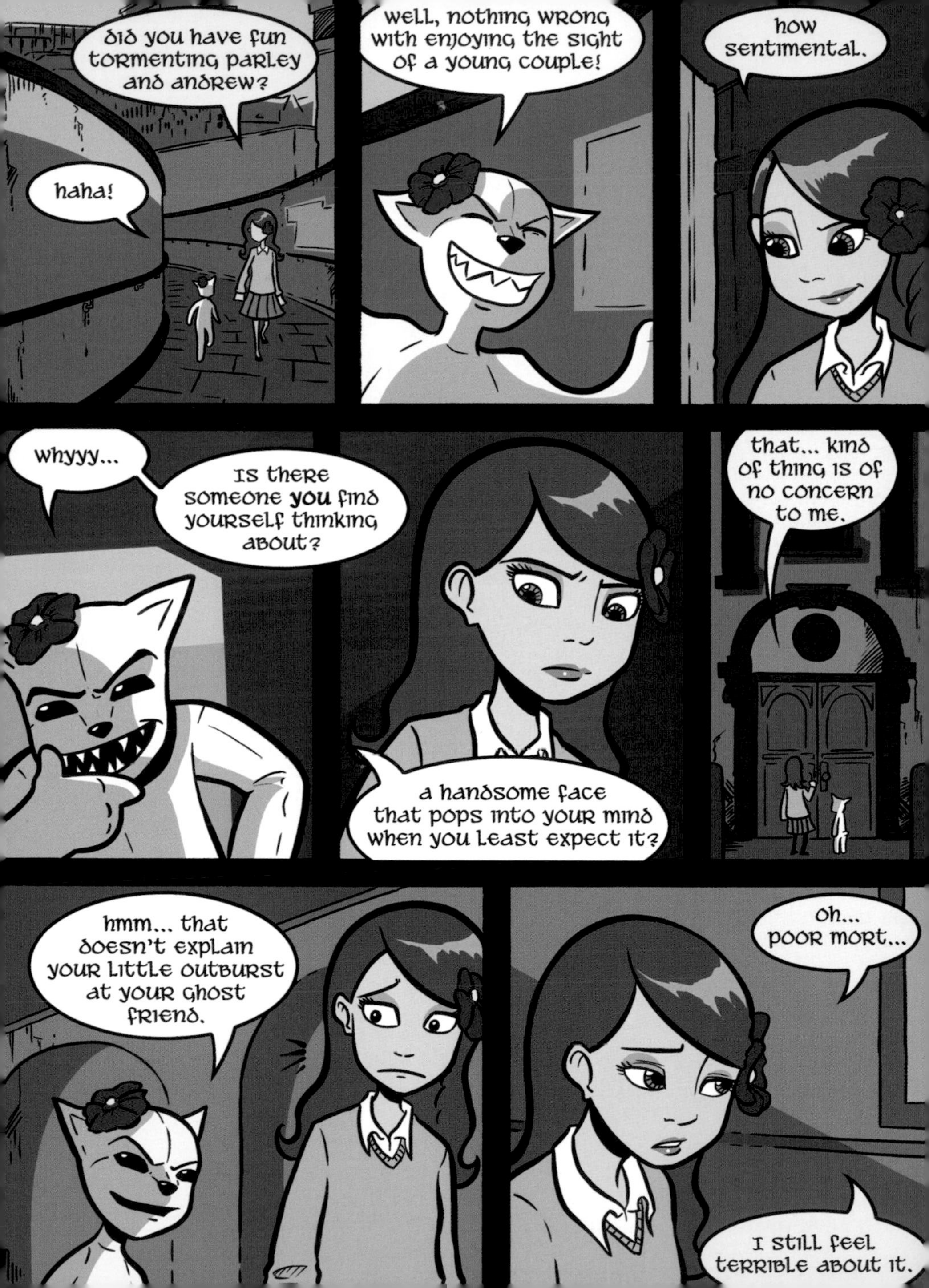
did you have fun tormenting parley and andrew?
haha!
well, nothing wrong with enjoying the sight of a young couple!
how sentimental.
whyyy...
is there someone **you** find yourself thinking about?
a handsome face that pops into your mind when you least expect it?
that... kind of thing is of no concern to me.
hmm... that doesn't explain your little outburst at your ghost friend.
oh... poor mort...
I still feel terrible about it.

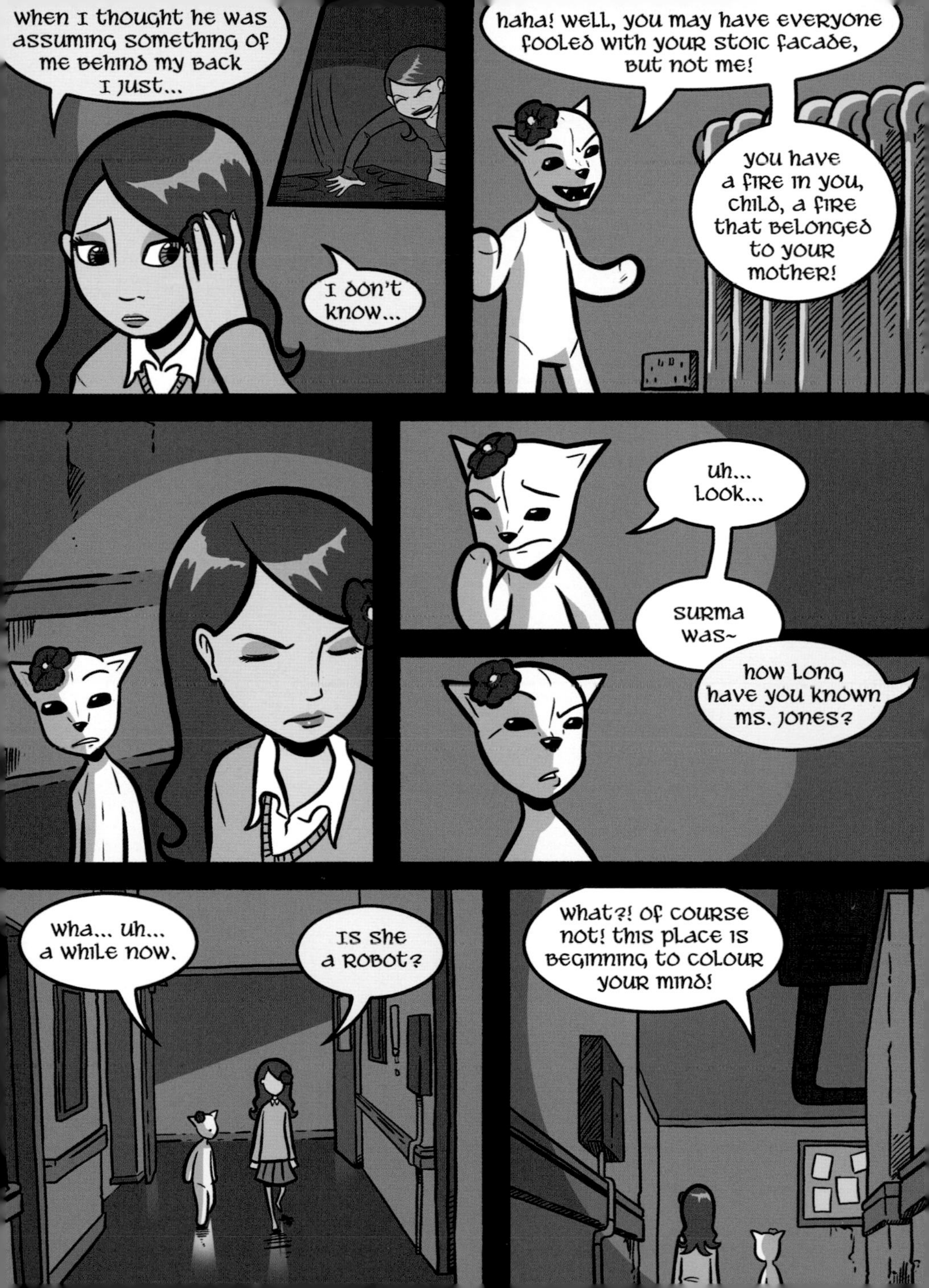
when I thought he was assuming something of me behind my back I just...
I don't know...
haha! well, you may have everyone fooled with your stoic facade, but not me!
you have a fire in you, child, a fire that belonged to your mother!
uh... look...
surma was~
how long have you known ms. jones?
wha... uh... a while now.
is she a robot?
what?! of course not! this place is beginning to colour your mind!

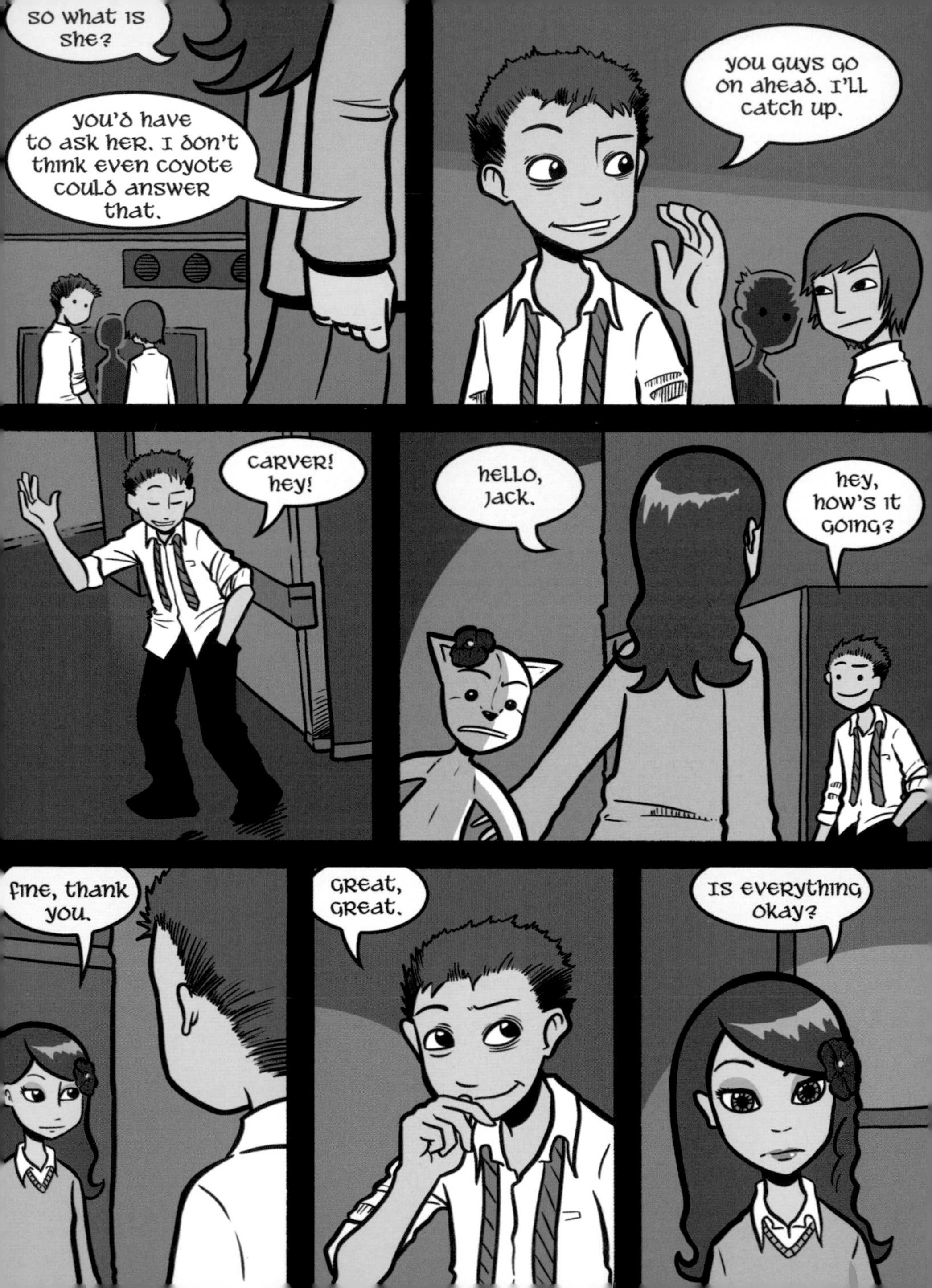
so what is she?
you'd have to ask her. I don't think even coyote could answer that.
you guys go on ahead. I'll catch up.
carver! hey!
hello, jack.
hey, how's it going?
fine, thank you.
great, great.
is everything okay?

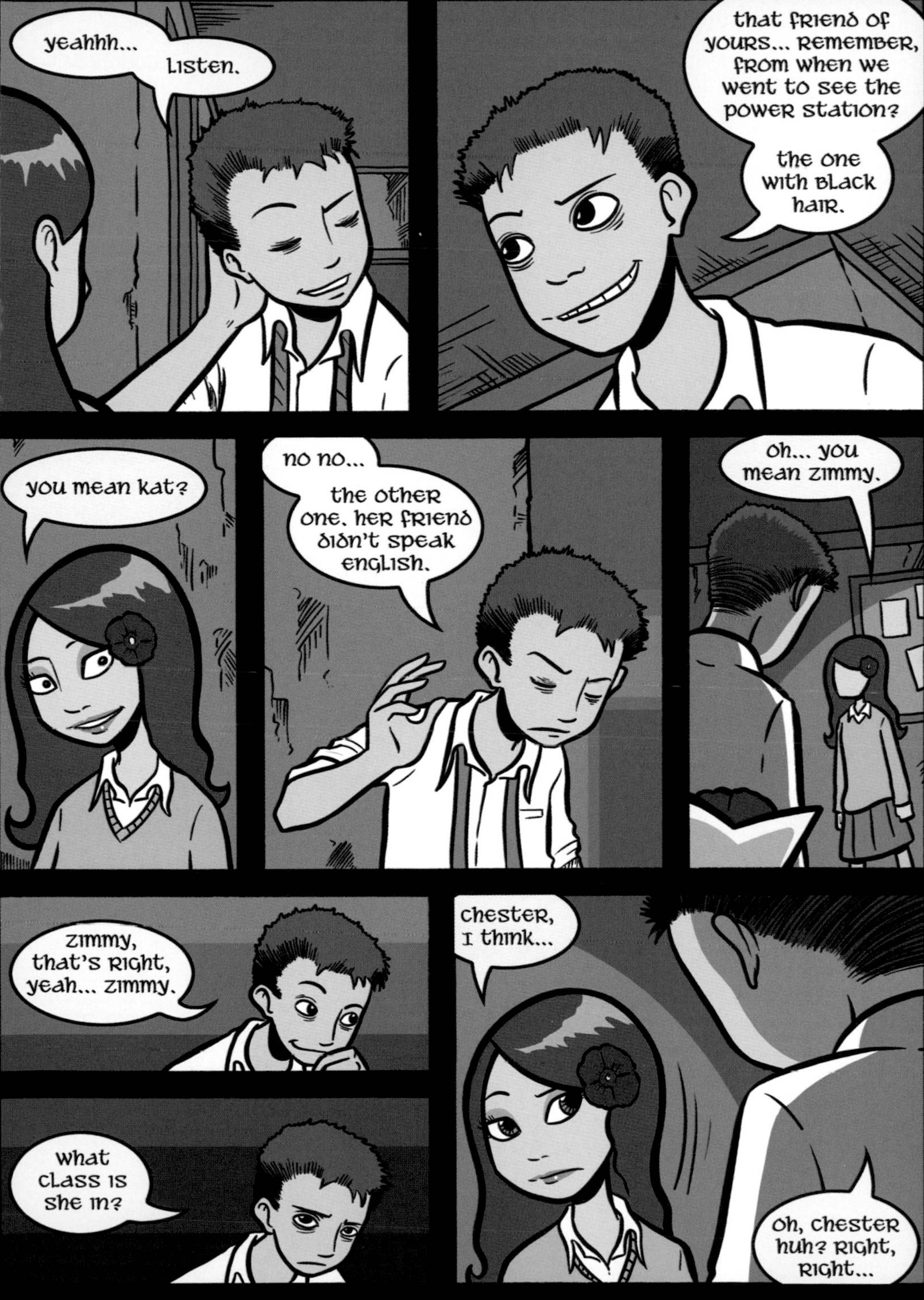
yeahhh...
listen.
that friend of yours... remember, from when we went to see the power station?
the one with black hair.
you mean kat?
no no...
the other one. her friend didn't speak english.
oh... you mean zimmy.
zimmy, that's right, yeah... zimmy.
what class is she in?
chester, I think...
oh, chester huh? right, right...

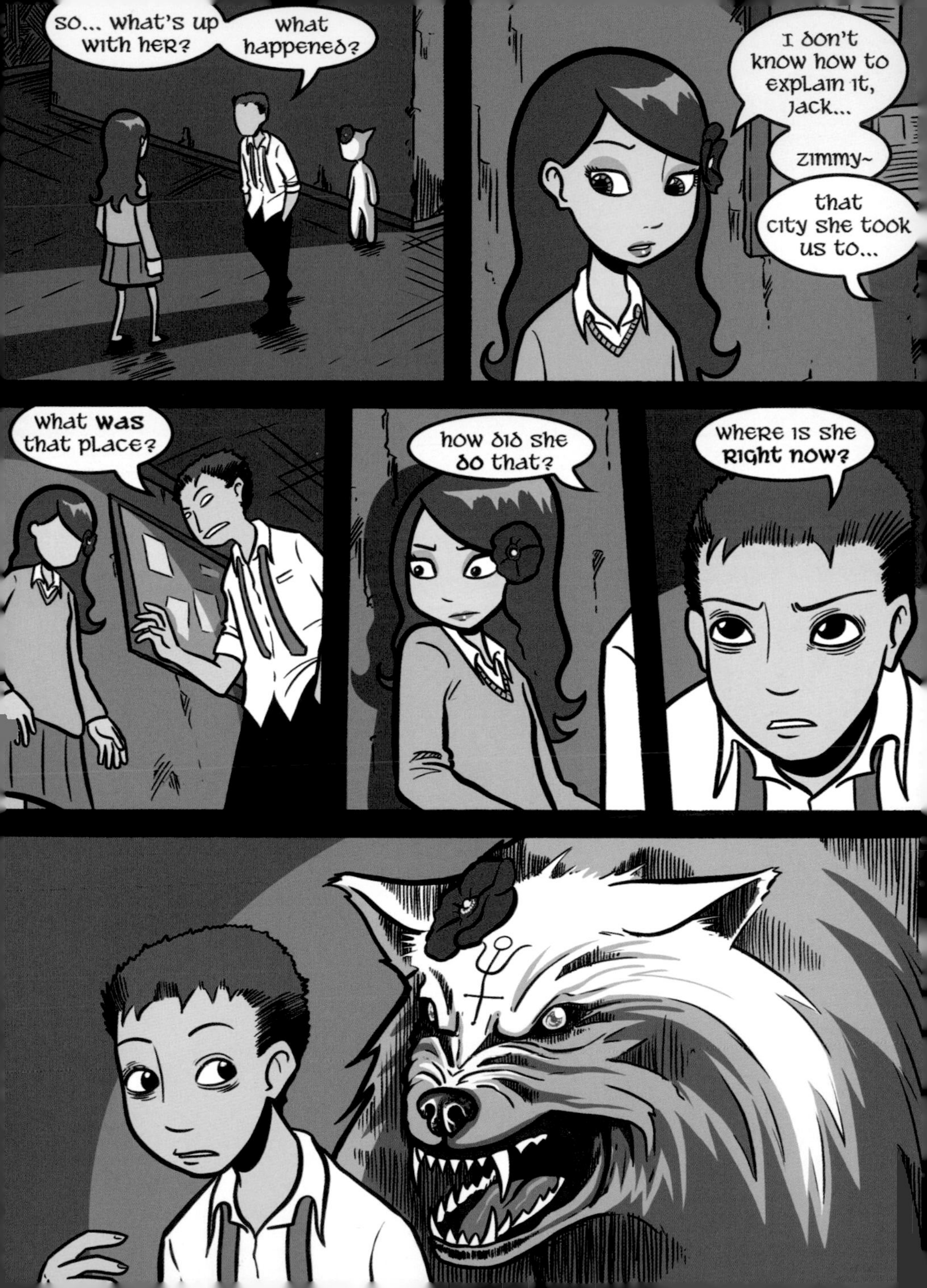
so... what's up with her?
what happened?
I don't know how to explain it, Jack...
zimmy~
that city she took us to...
what was that place?
how did she do that?
where is she right now?

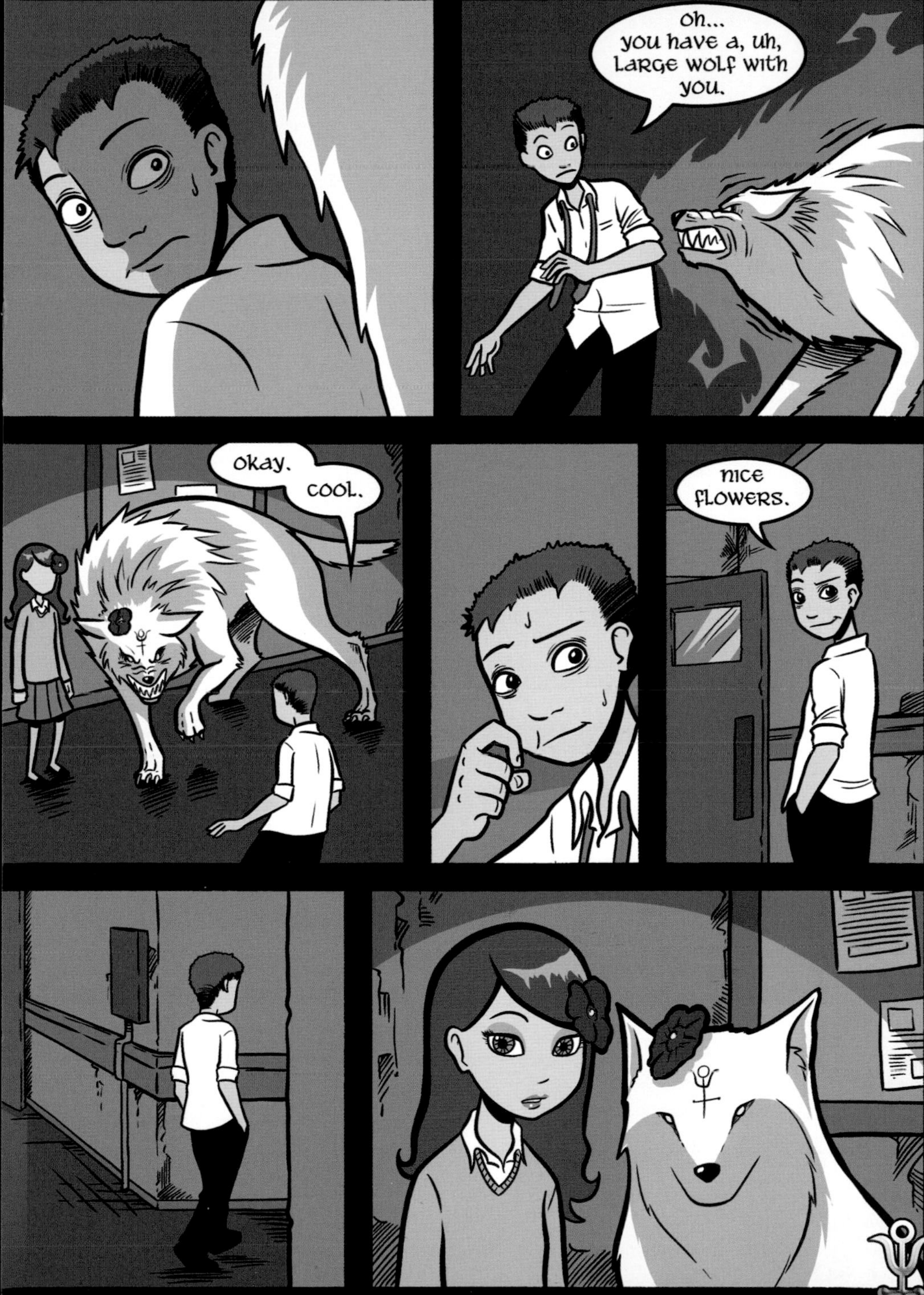
Oh...
you have a, uh, large wolf with you.
Okay.
Cool.
Nice flowers.

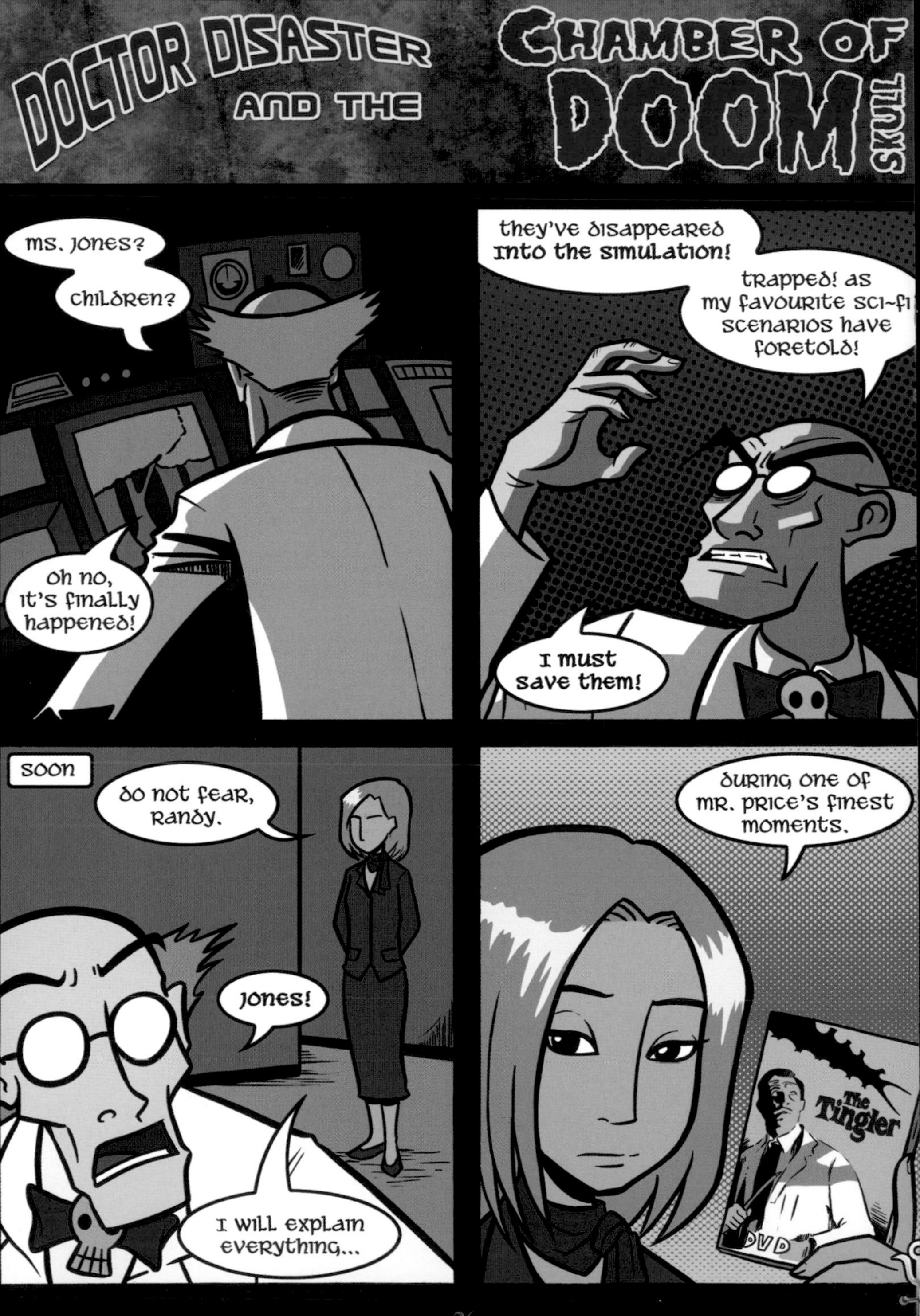
Doctor Disaster and the Chamber of Doom Skull
ms. jones?
children?
oh no, it's finally happened!
they've disappeared into the simulation!
trapped! as my favourite sci-fi scenarios have foretold!
I must save them!
soon
do not fear, Randy.
jones!
I will explain everything...
during one of mr. price's finest moments.
The Tingler
DVD

Gunnerkrigg Court

Chapter 24:

Residential

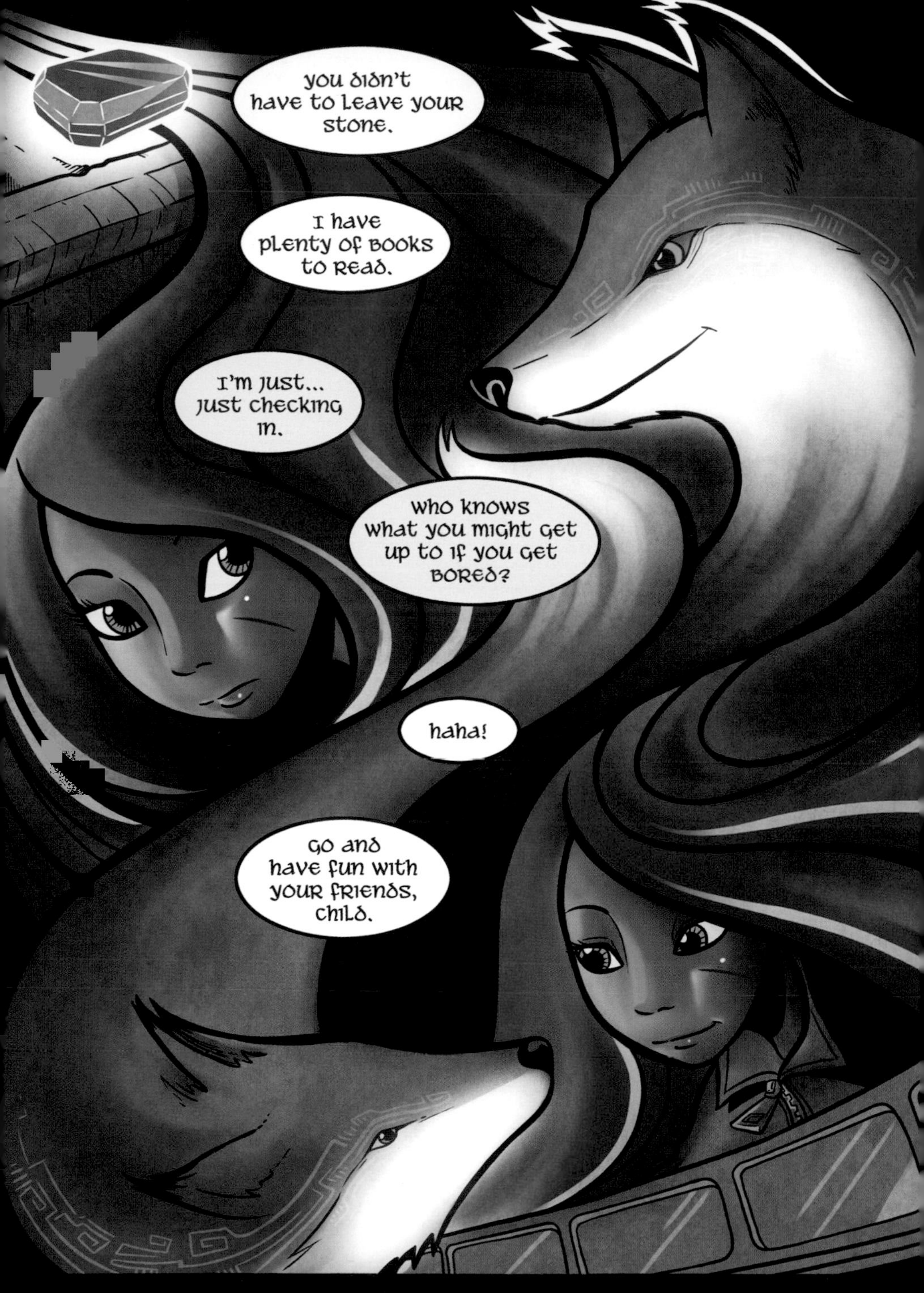
you didn't have to leave your stone.
I have plenty of books to read.
I'm just... just checking in.
who knows what you might get up to if you get bored?
haha!
go and have fun with your friends, child.

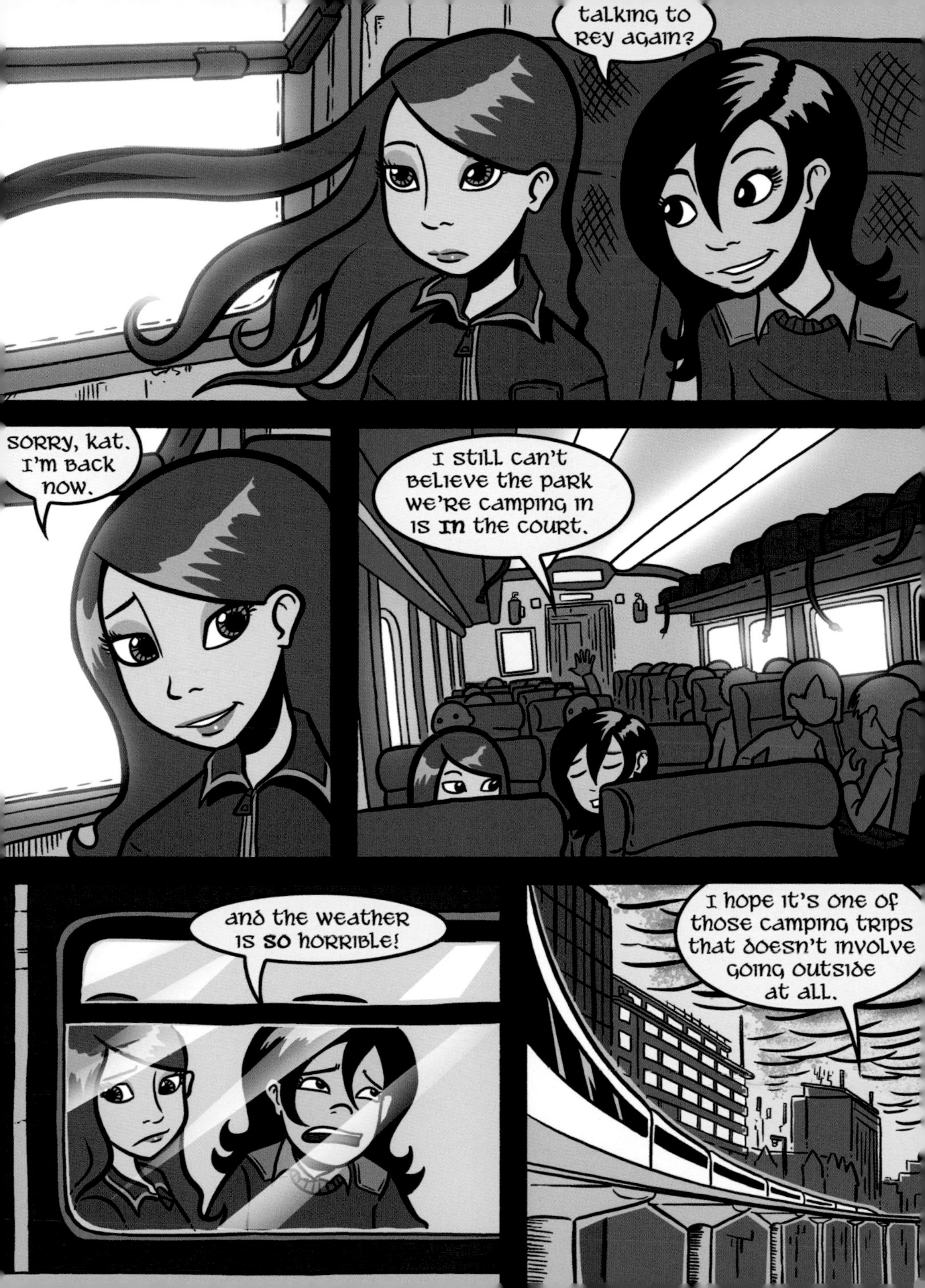
talking to Rey again?
Sorry, Kat. I'm back now.
I still can't believe the park we're camping in is **IN** the court.
and the weather is **SO** horrible!
I hope it's one of those camping trips that doesn't involve going outside at all.

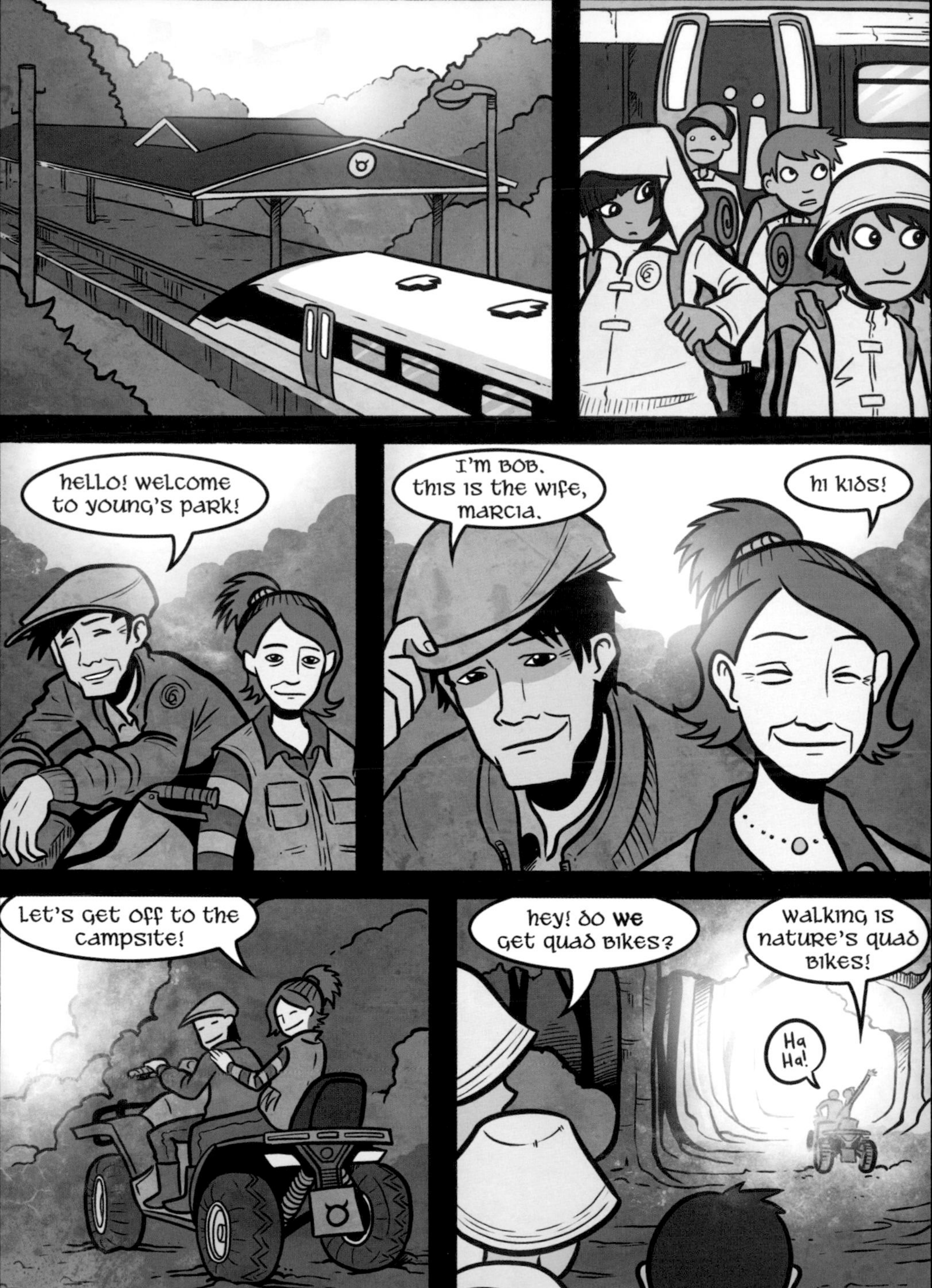
hello! welcome to young's park!
I'm Bob. this is the wife, marcia.
hi kids!
Let's get off to the campsite!
hey! do we get quad bikes?
walking is nature's quad bikes!
Ha Ha!

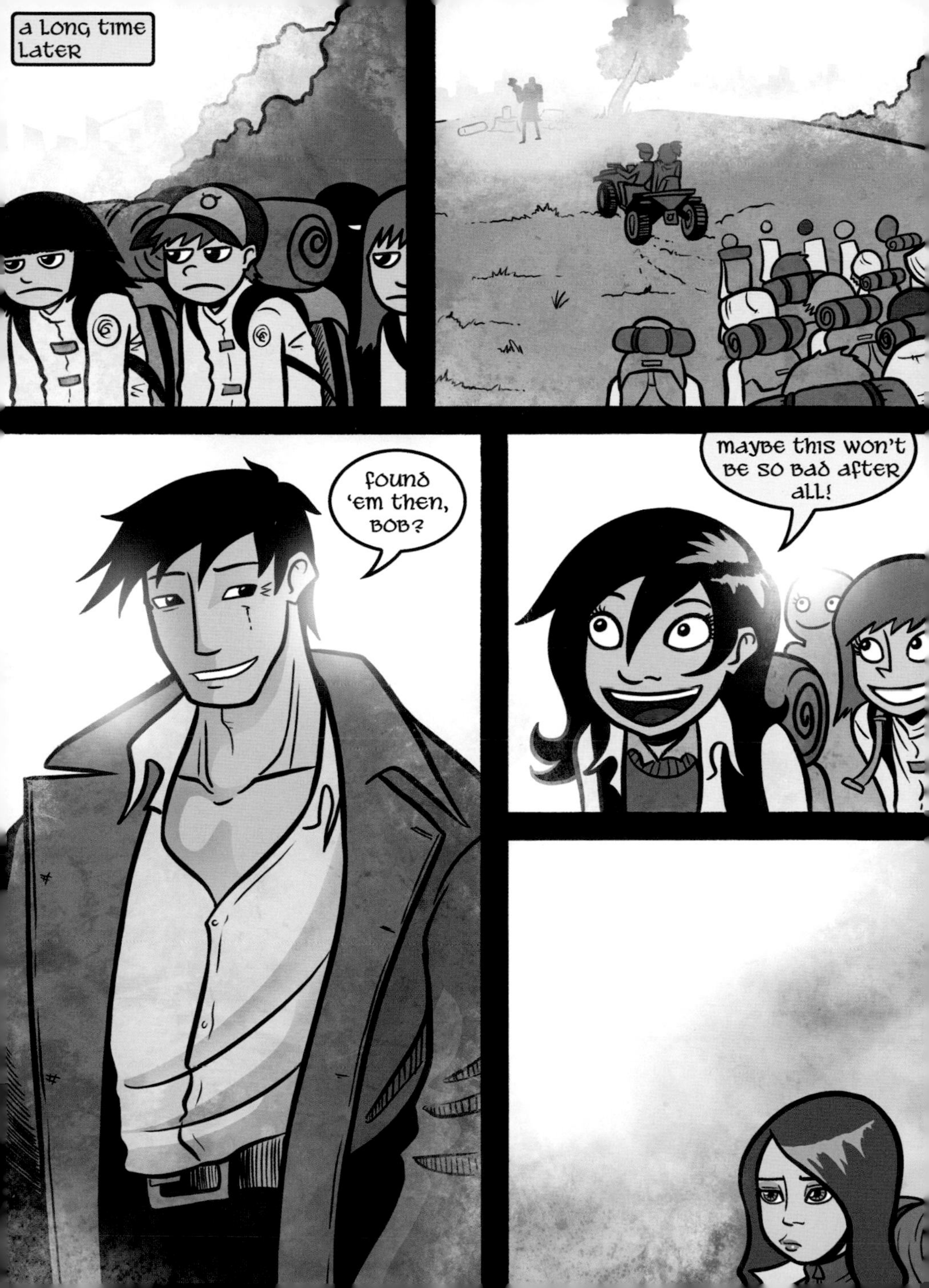
a LONG time Later
found 'em then, BOB?
maybe this won't be so bad after all!

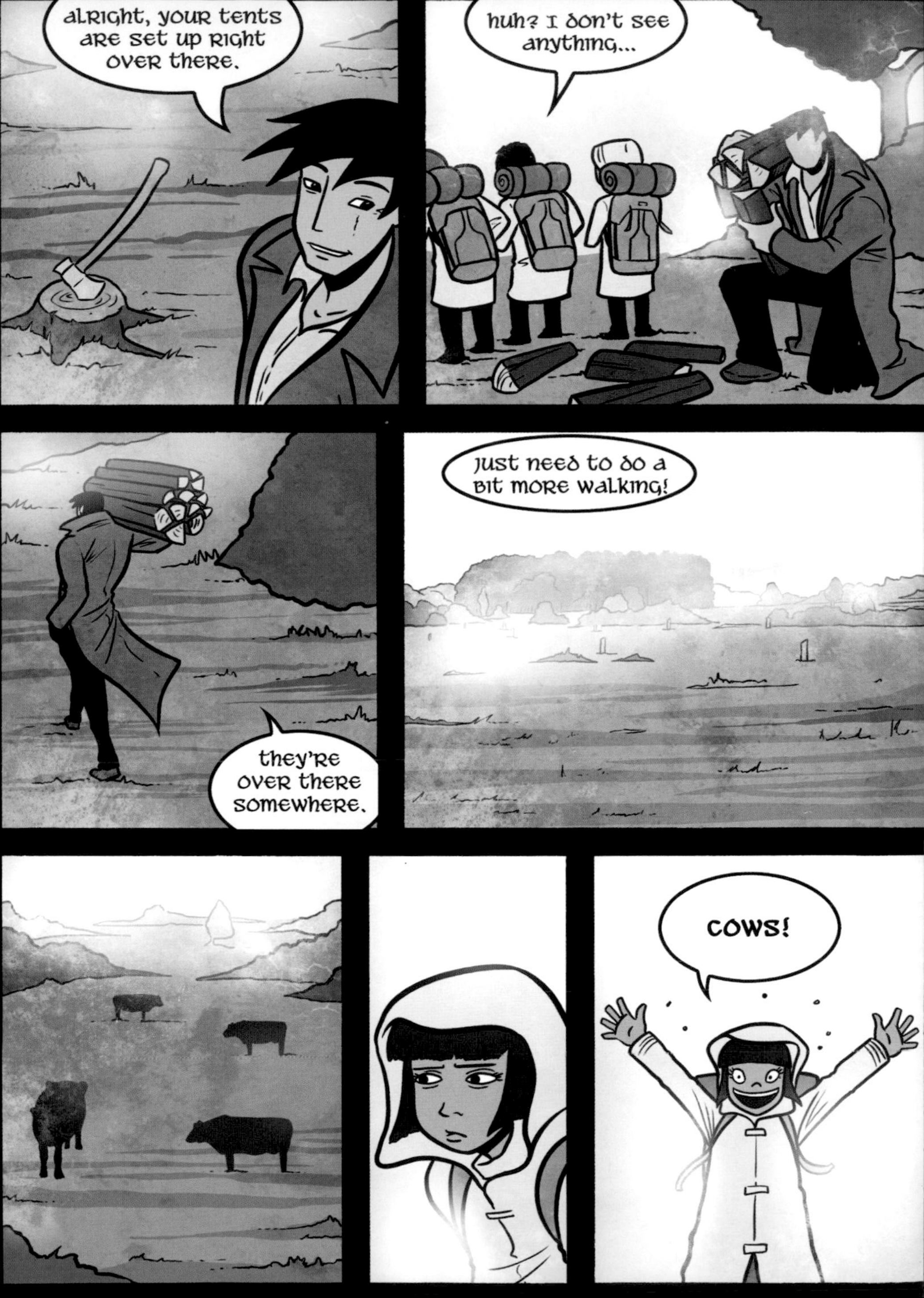
alright, your tents are set up right over there.
huh? I don't see anything...
they're over there somewhere.
just need to do a bit more walking!
COWS!

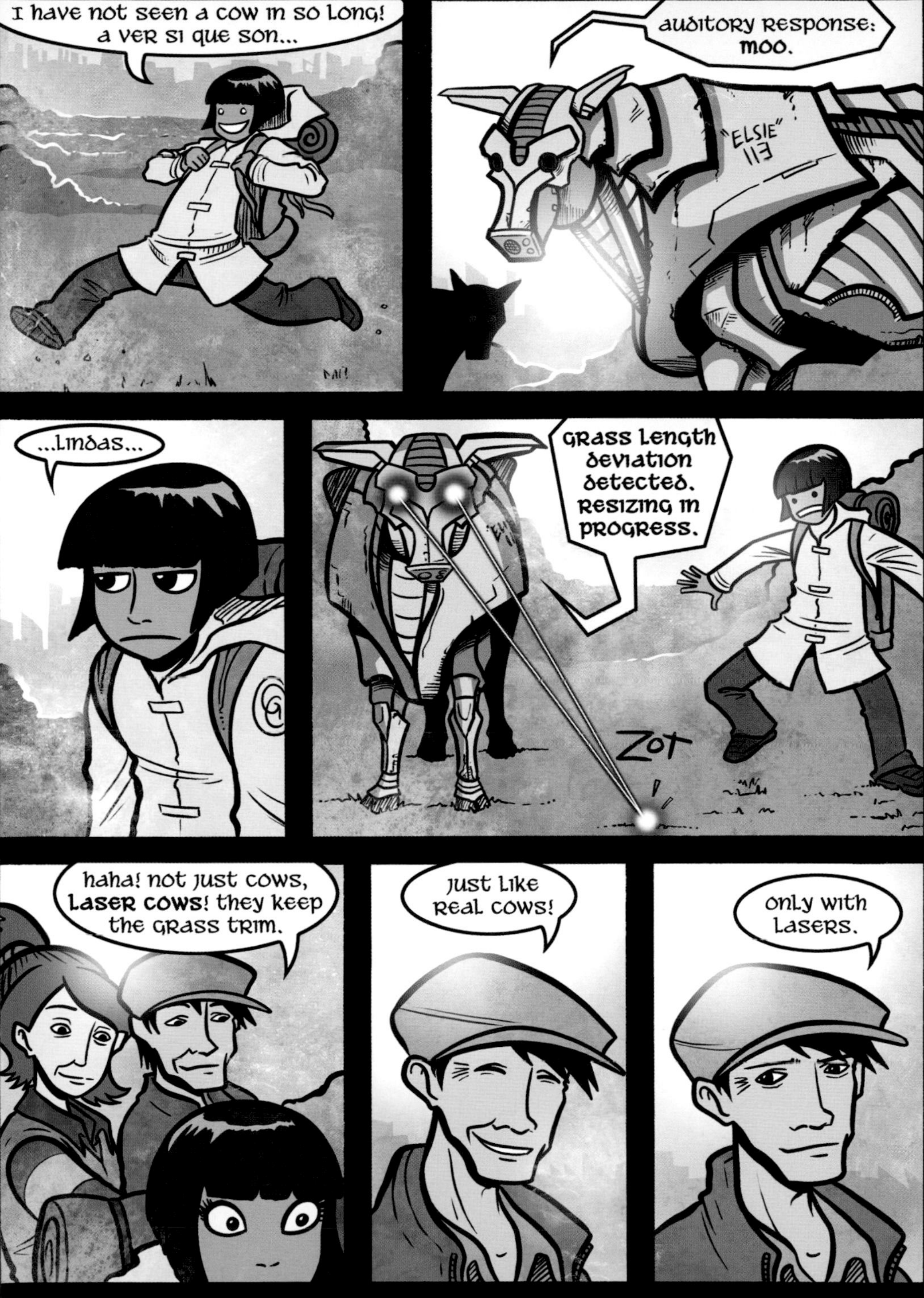
I have not seen a cow in so long!
a ver si que son...
auditory response:
moo.
"ELSIE"
...lindas...
grass length deviation detected. resizing in progress.
ZOT
haha! not just cows, **laser cows**! they keep the grass trim.
just like real cows!
only with lasers.

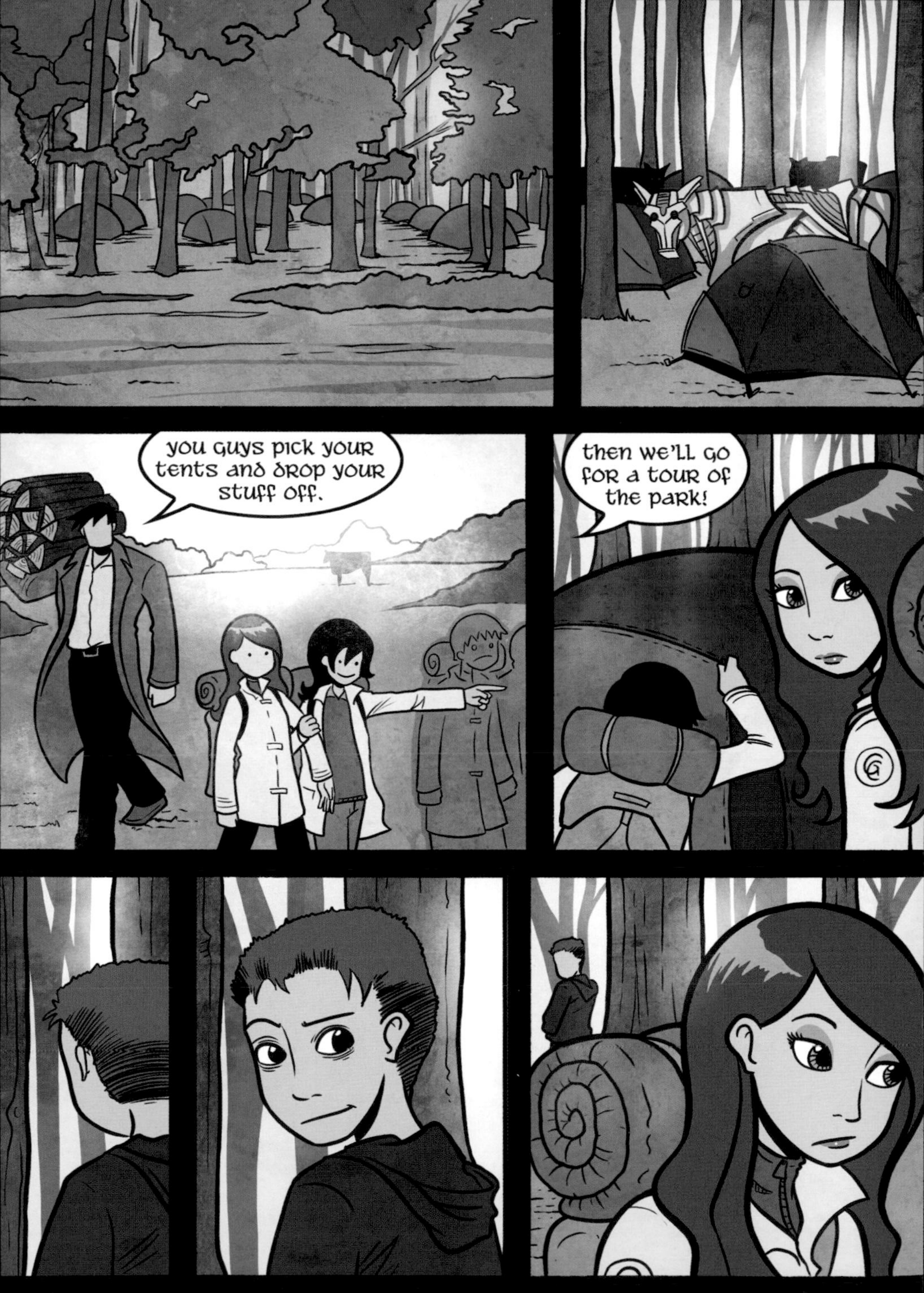
you guys pick your tents and drop your stuff off.
then we'll go for a tour of the park!

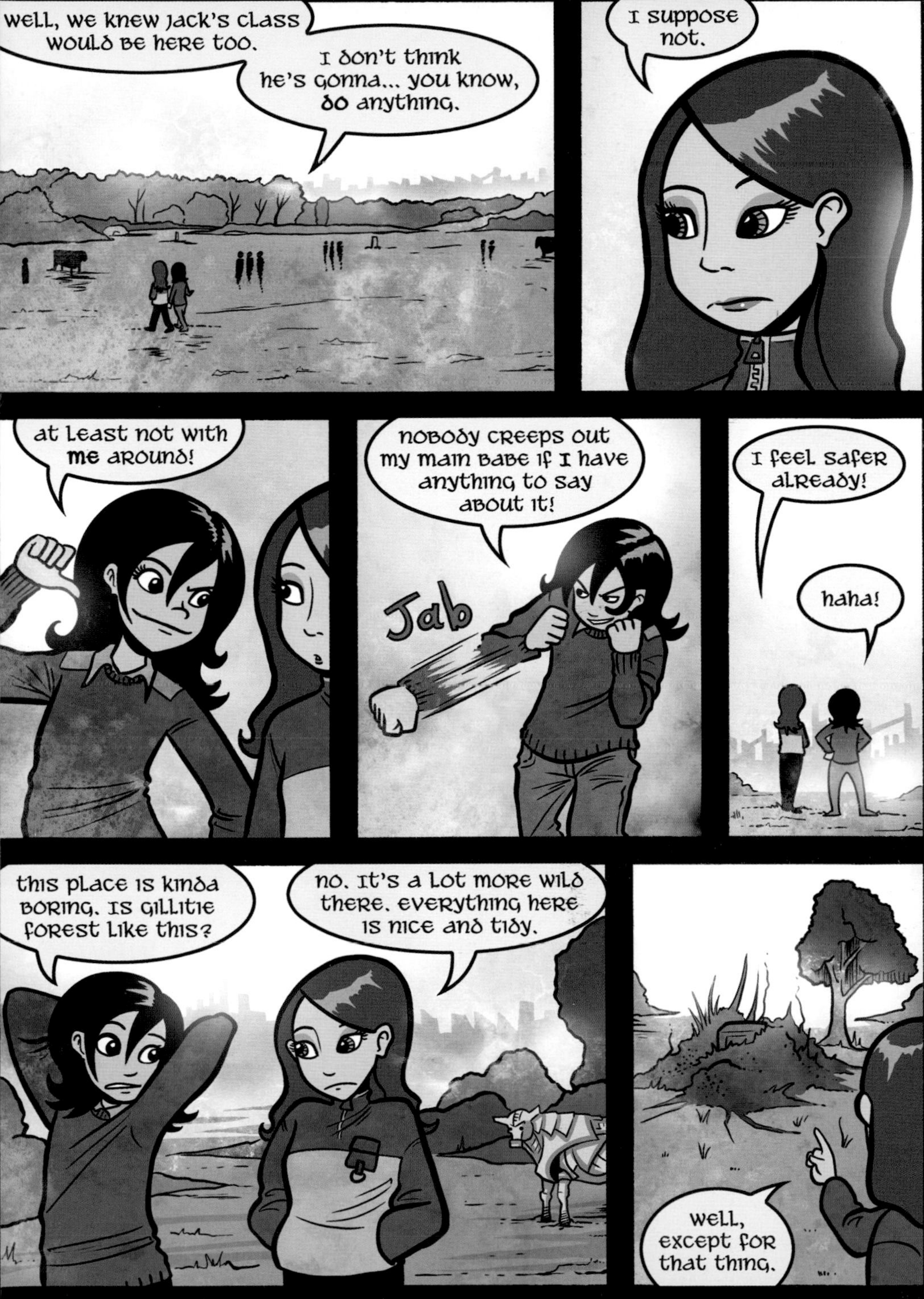
well, we knew jack's class would be here too.
I don't think he's gonna... you know, do anything.
I suppose not.
at least not with me around!
nobody creeps out my main babe if I have anything to say about it!
Jab
I feel safer already!
haha!
this place is kinda boring. is gillitie forest like this?
no. It's a lot more wild there. everything here is nice and tidy.
well, except for that thing.

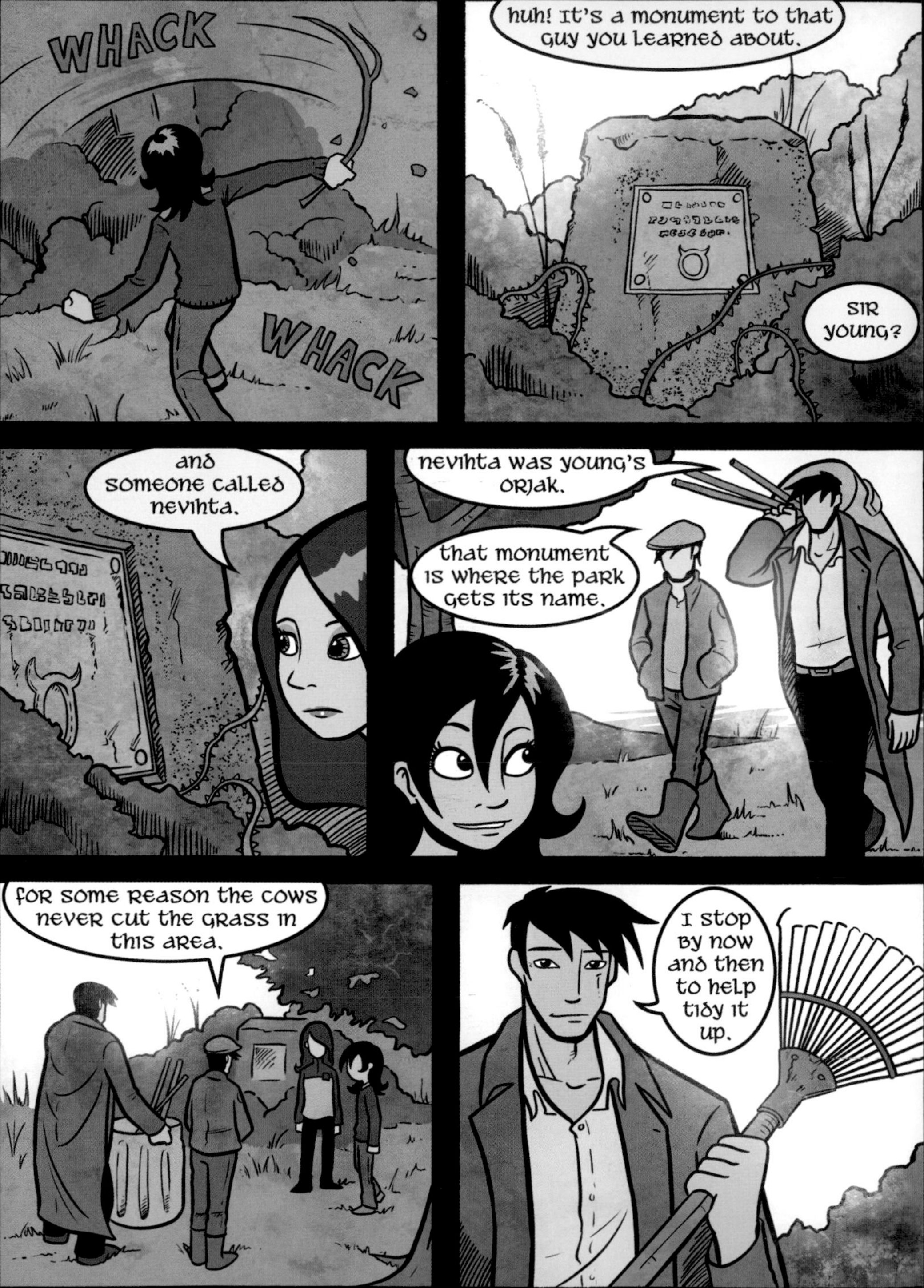
WHACK
WHACK
huh! It's a monument to that guy you learned about.
SIR young?
and someone called nevihta.
nevihta was young's ORJAK.
that monument is where the park gets its name.
for some reason the cows never cut the grass in this area.
I stop by now and then to help tidy it up.

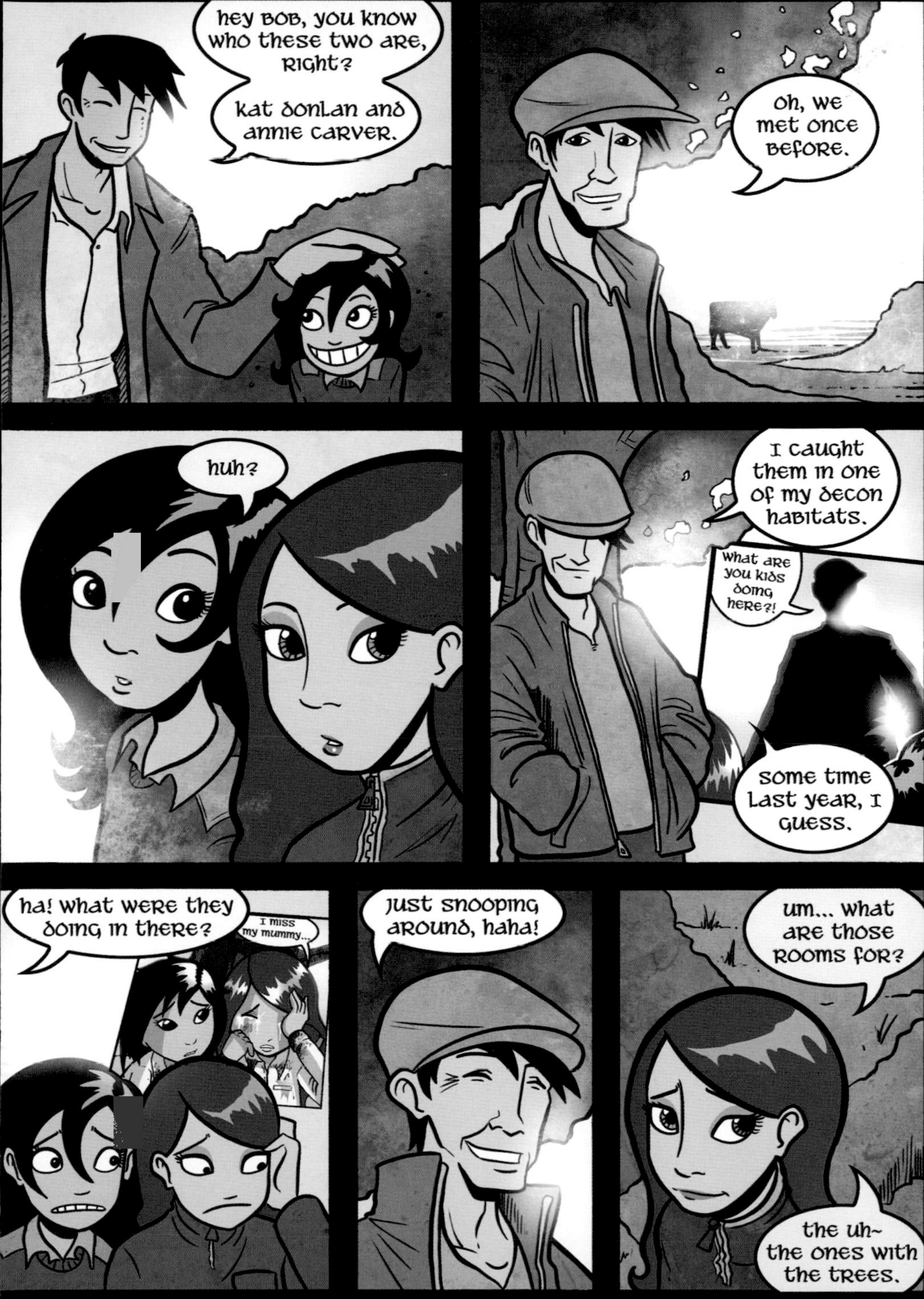
hey BOB, you know who these two are, right?
kat donlan and annie carver.
oh, we met once before.
huh?
I caught them in one of my decon habitats.
what are you kids doing here?!
some time last year, I guess.
ha! what were they doing in there?
I miss my mummy...
just snooping around, haha!
um... what are those rooms for?
the uh~ the ones with the trees.

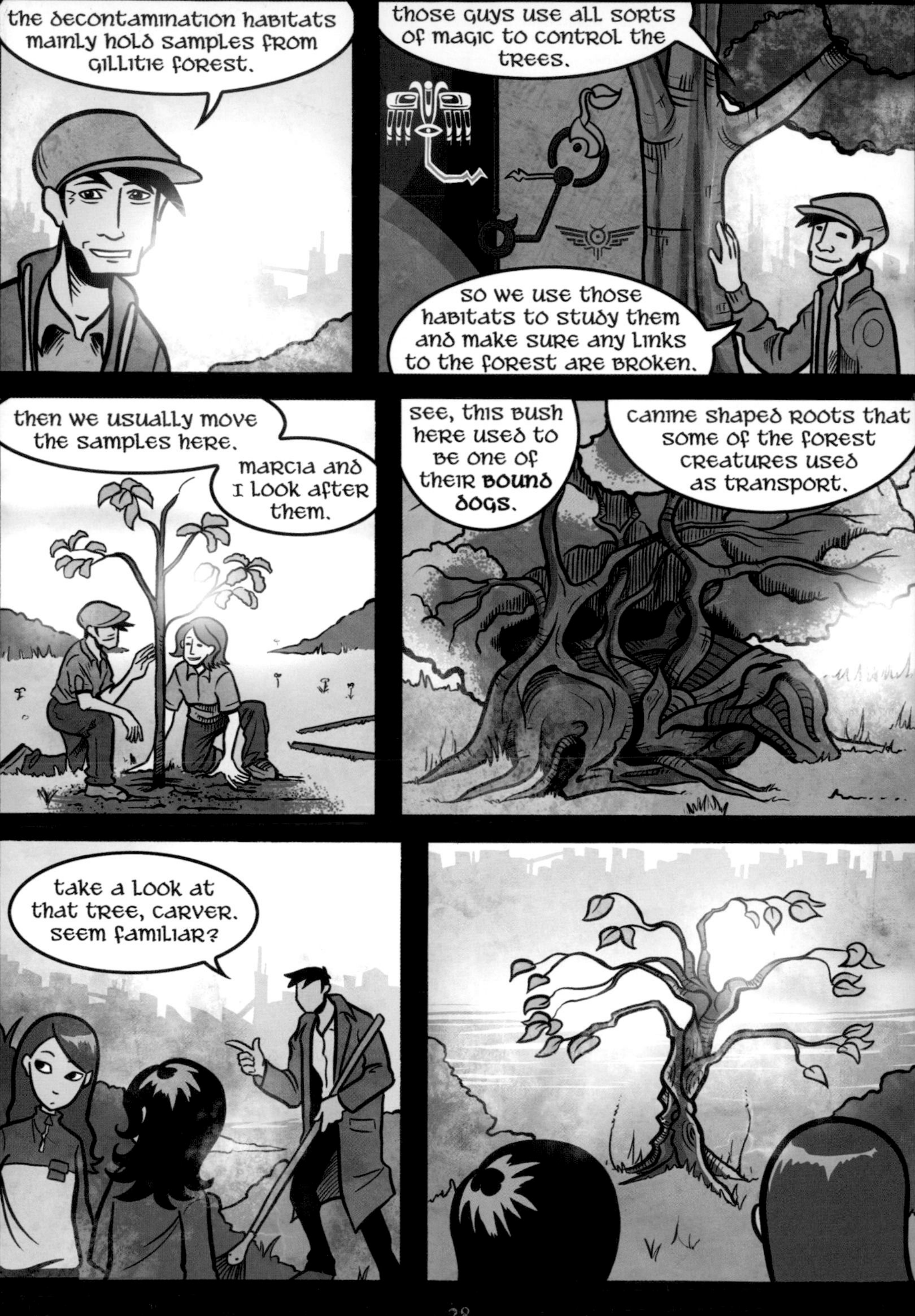
the decontamination habitats mainly hold samples from gillitie forest.
those guys use all sorts of magic to control the trees.
so we use those habitats to study them and make sure any links to the forest are broken.
then we usually move the samples here.
marcia and I look after them.
see, this bush here used to be one of their **bound dogs.**
canine shaped roots that some of the forest creatures used as transport.
take a look at that tree, carver. seem familiar?

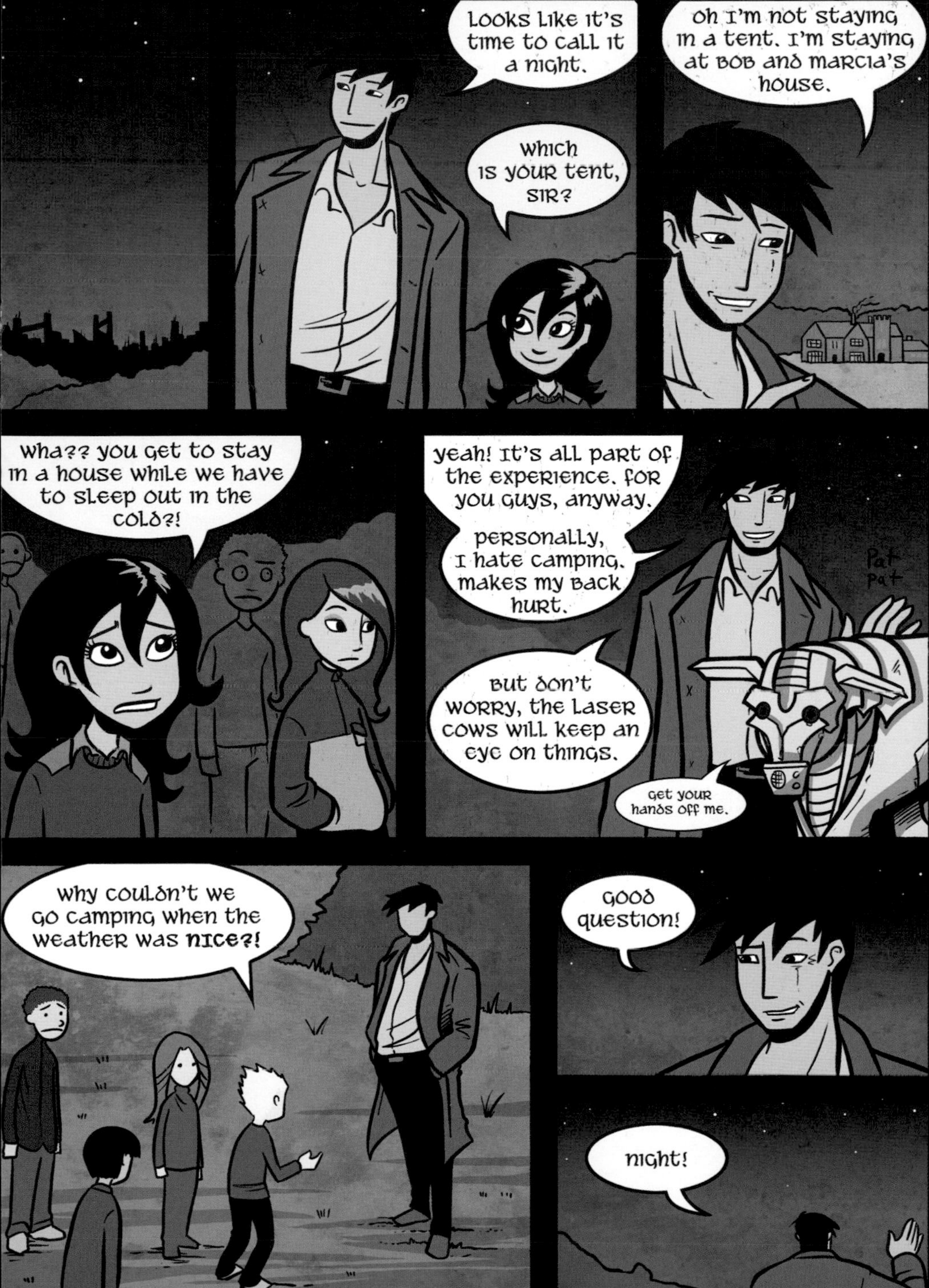
LOOKS LIKE IT'S TIME TO CALL IT A NIGHT.
WHICH IS YOUR TENT, SIR?
OH I'M NOT STAYING IN A TENT. I'M STAYING AT BOB AND MARCIA'S HOUSE.
WHA?? YOU GET TO STAY IN A HOUSE WHILE WE HAVE TO SLEEP OUT IN THE COLD?!
YEAH! IT'S ALL PART OF THE EXPERIENCE. FOR YOU GUYS, ANYWAY.
PERSONALLY, I HATE CAMPING. MAKES MY BACK HURT.
PAT PAT
BUT DON'T WORRY, THE LASER COWS WILL KEEP AN EYE ON THINGS.
GET YOUR HANDS OFF ME.
WHY COULDN'T WE GO CAMPING WHEN THE WEATHER WAS NICE?!
GOOD QUESTION!
NIGHT!

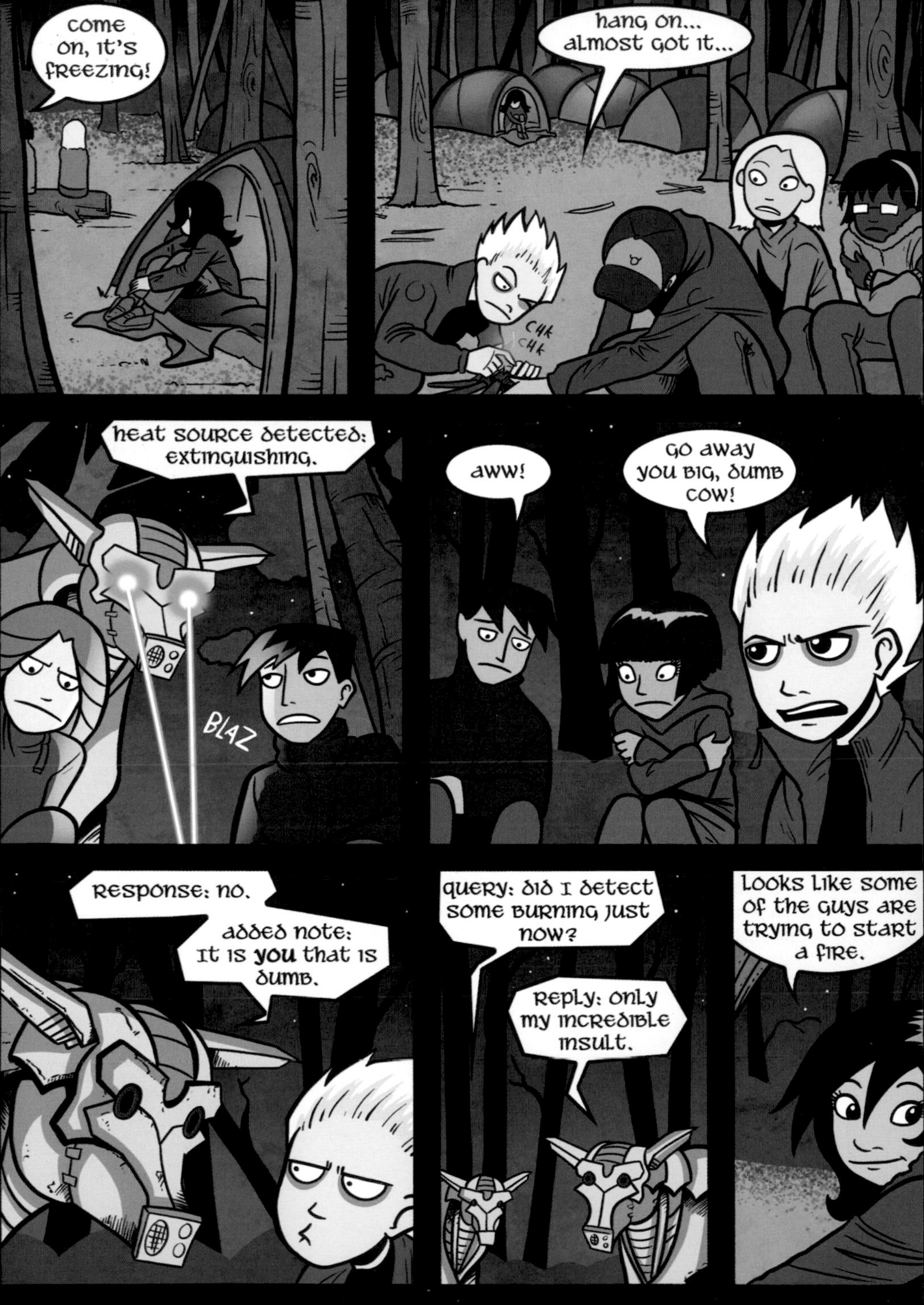
come on, it's freezing!
hang on... almost got it...
CHK CHK
heat source detected: extinguishing.
BLAZ
aww!
go away you big, dumb cow!
Response: no.
added note: It is **you** that is dumb.
query: did I detect some burning just now?
Reply: only my incredible insult.
Looks like some of the guys are trying to start a fire.

no heat source detected.

huh? feels warm to me.

I made the fire undetectable to the cows. It's perfectly safe as well.

wow, thanks, CARVER!

yeah, thanks!

Okay.

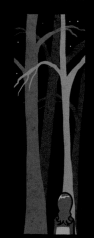

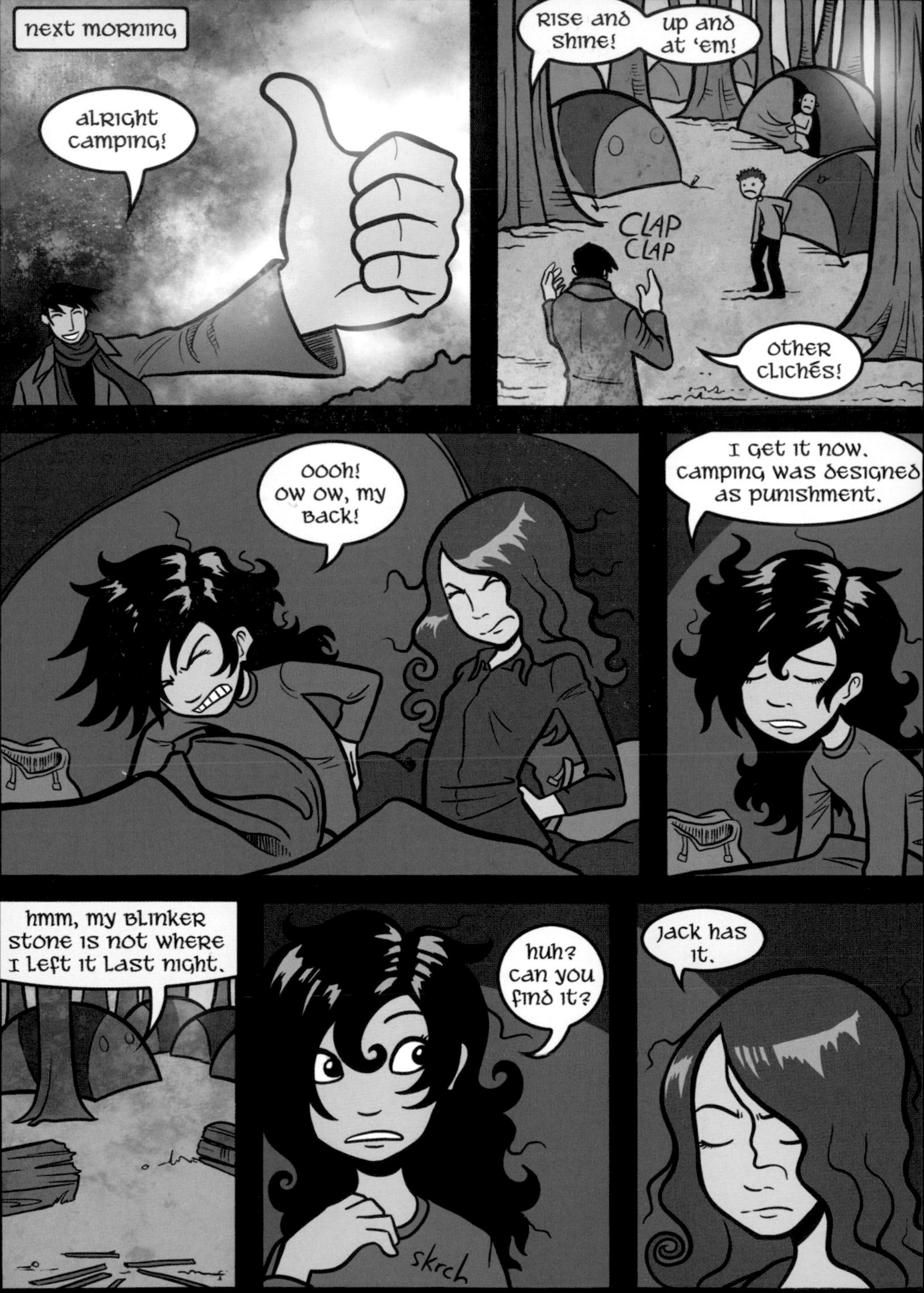
next morning
alright camping!
Rise and shine!
up and at 'em!
CLAP CLAP
other clichés!
oooh! ow ow, my back!
I get it now. camping was designed as punishment.
hmm, my blinker stone is not where I left it last night.
huh? can you find it?
skrch
Jack has it.

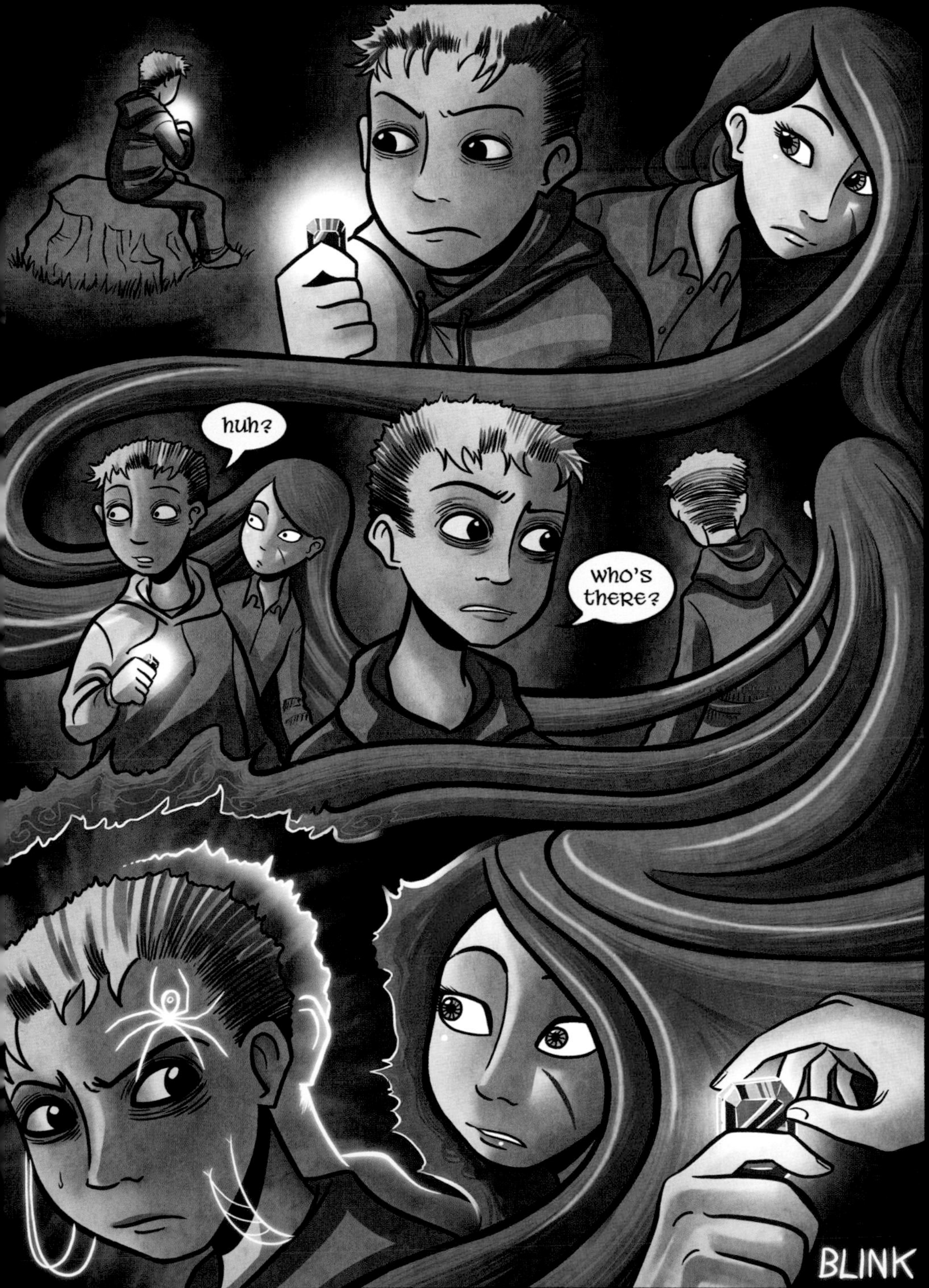
huh?
who's there?
BLINK

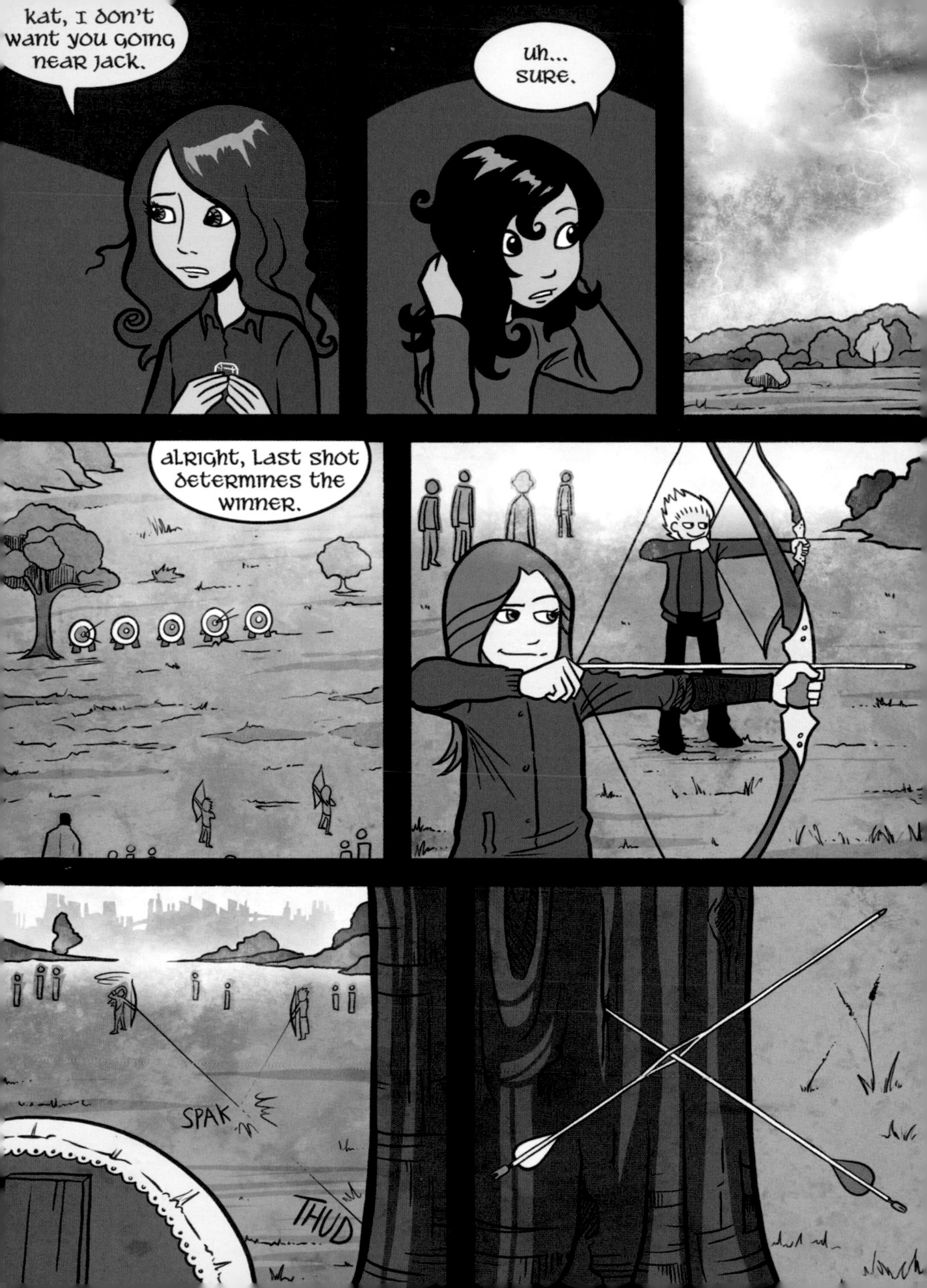
kat, I don't want you going near jack.
uh... sure.
alright, last shot determines the winner.
SPAK
THUD

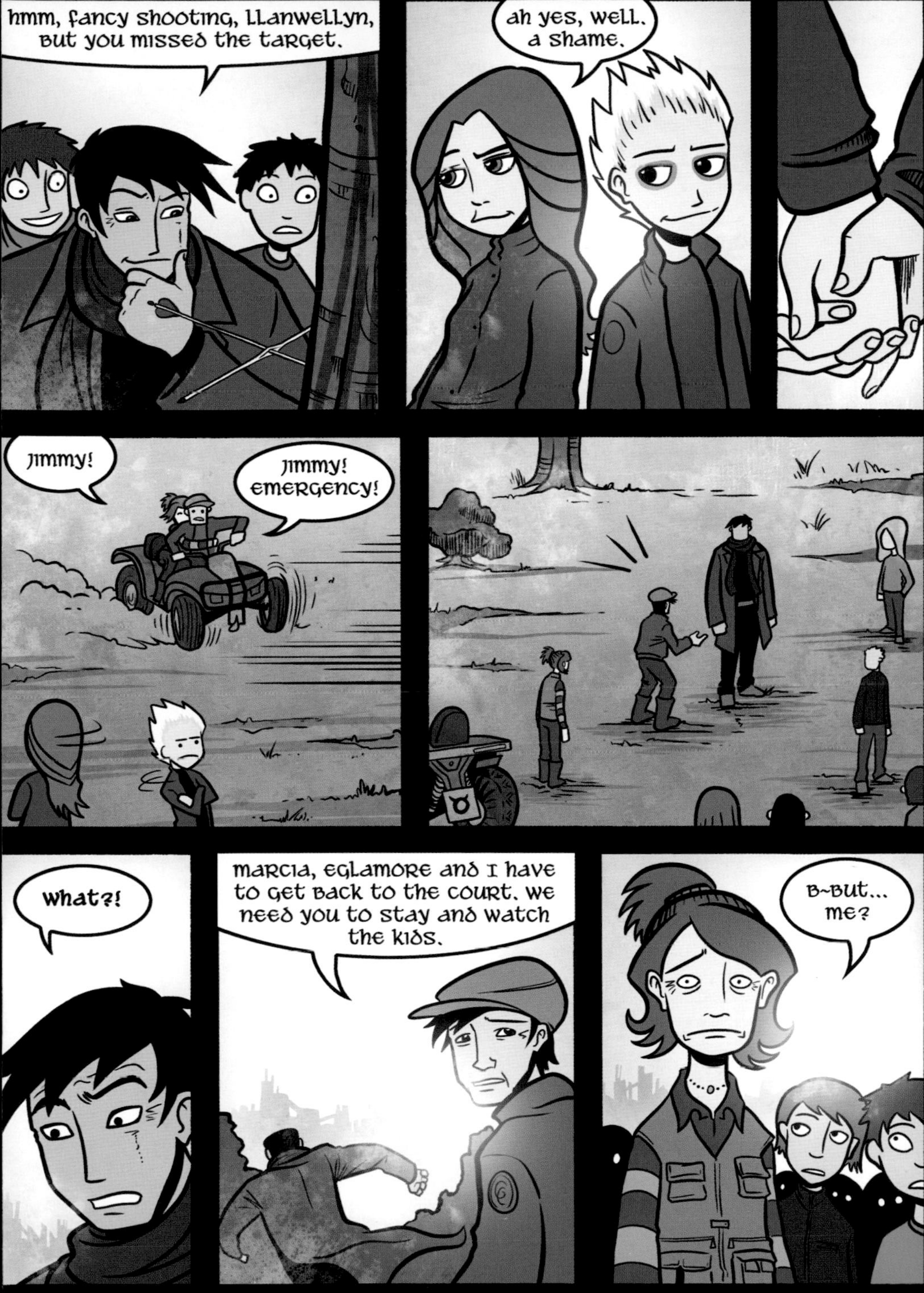
hmm, fancy shooting, Llanwellyn, but you missed the target.
ah yes, well. a shame.
Jimmy!
Jimmy! Emergency!
What?!
Marcia, Eglamore and I have to get back to the court. We need you to stay and watch the kids.
B-but... me?

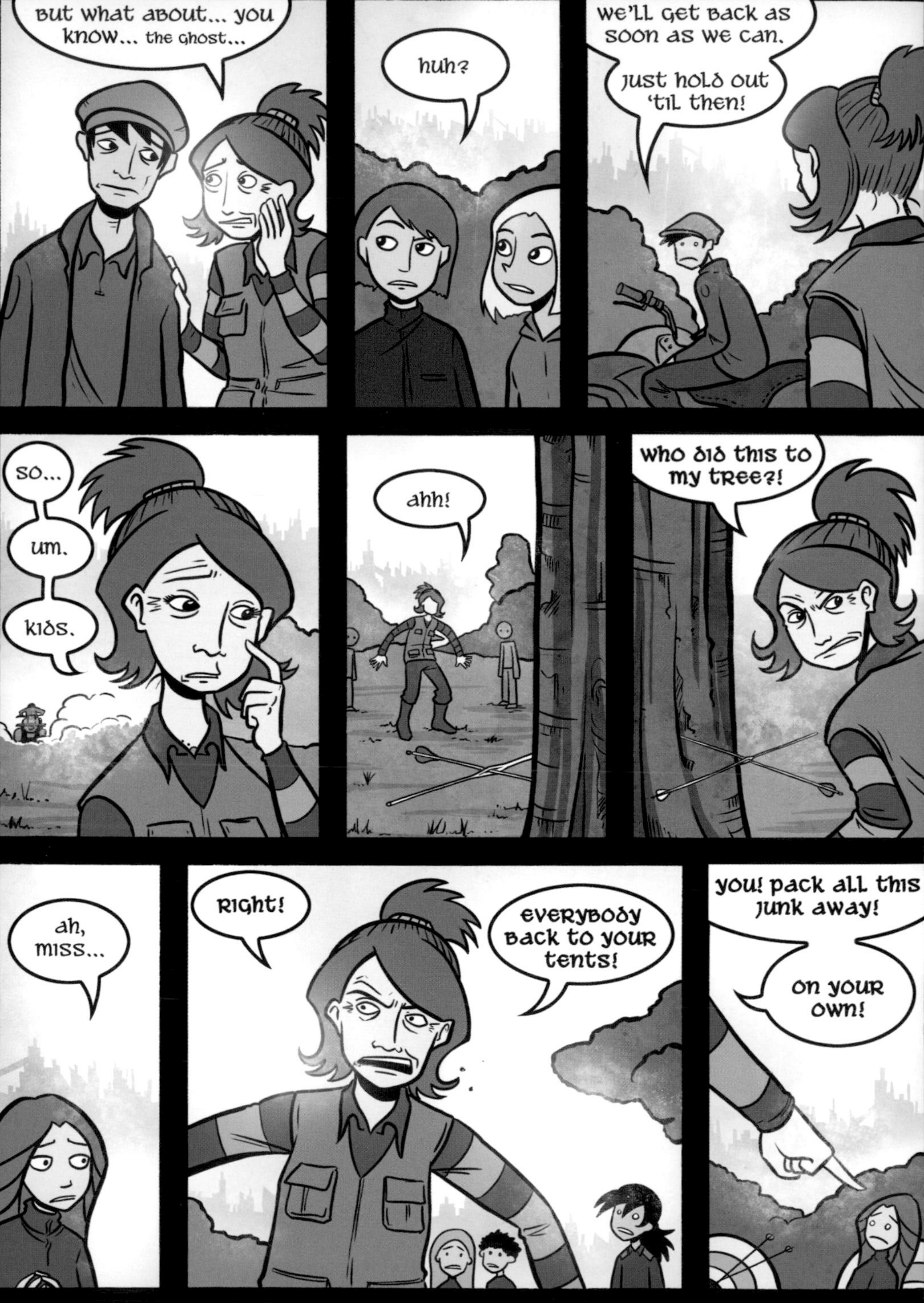

But what about... you know... the ghost...
huh?
We'll get back as soon as we can.
Just hold out 'til then!
So...
um.
kids.
ahh!
Who did this to my tree?!
ah, miss...
RIGHT!
EVERYBODY BACK TO YOUR TENTS!
YOU! PACK ALL THIS JUNK AWAY!
ON YOUR OWN!

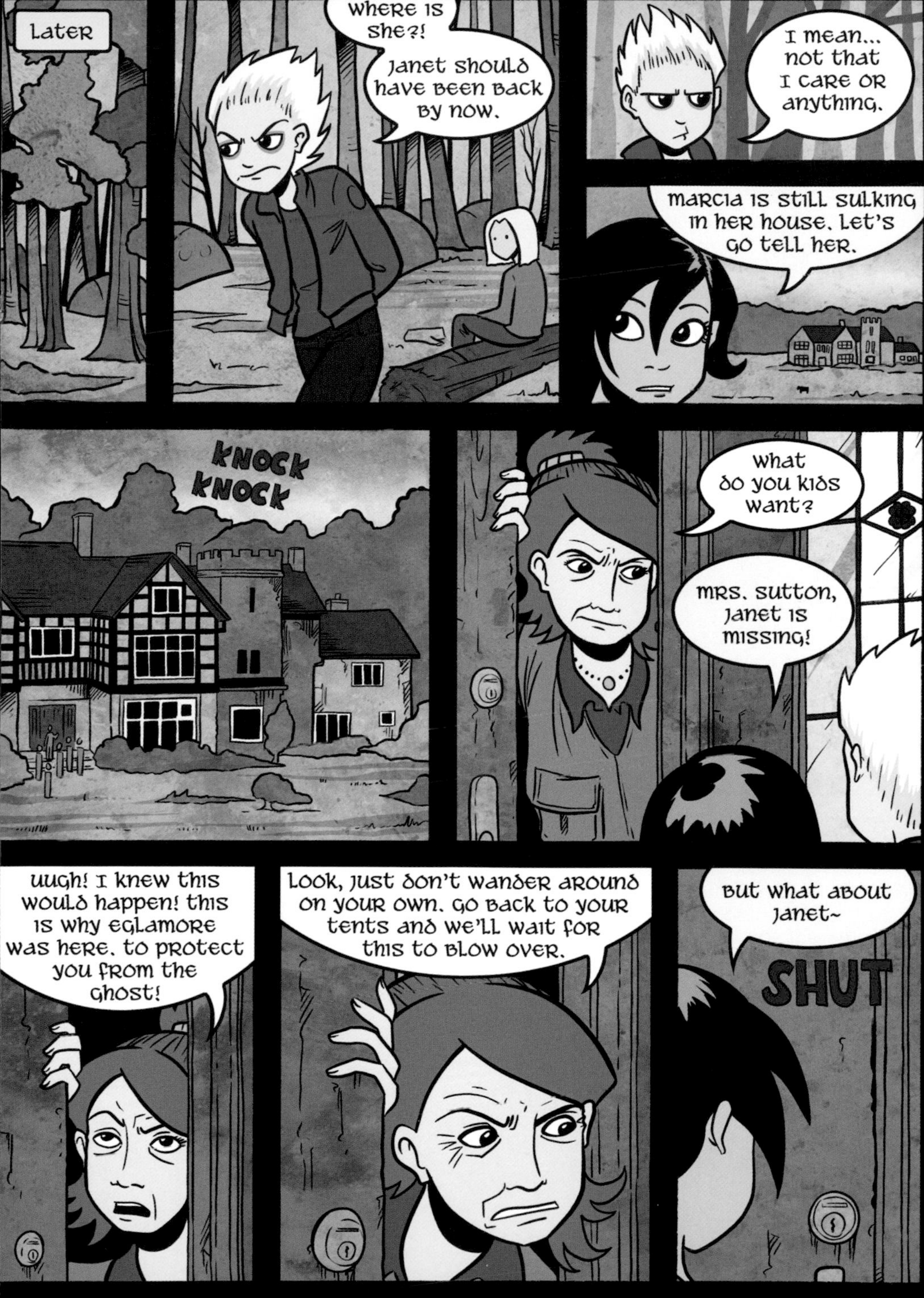
Later
Where is she?!
Janet should have been back by now.
I mean... not that I care or anything.
Marcia is still sulking in her house. Let's go tell her.
KNOCK KNOCK
What do you kids want?
Mrs. Sutton, Janet is missing!
Uugh! I knew this would happen! This is why Eglamore was here, to protect you from the ghost!
Look, just don't wander around on your own. Go back to your tents and we'll wait for this to blow over.
But what about Janet~
SHUT

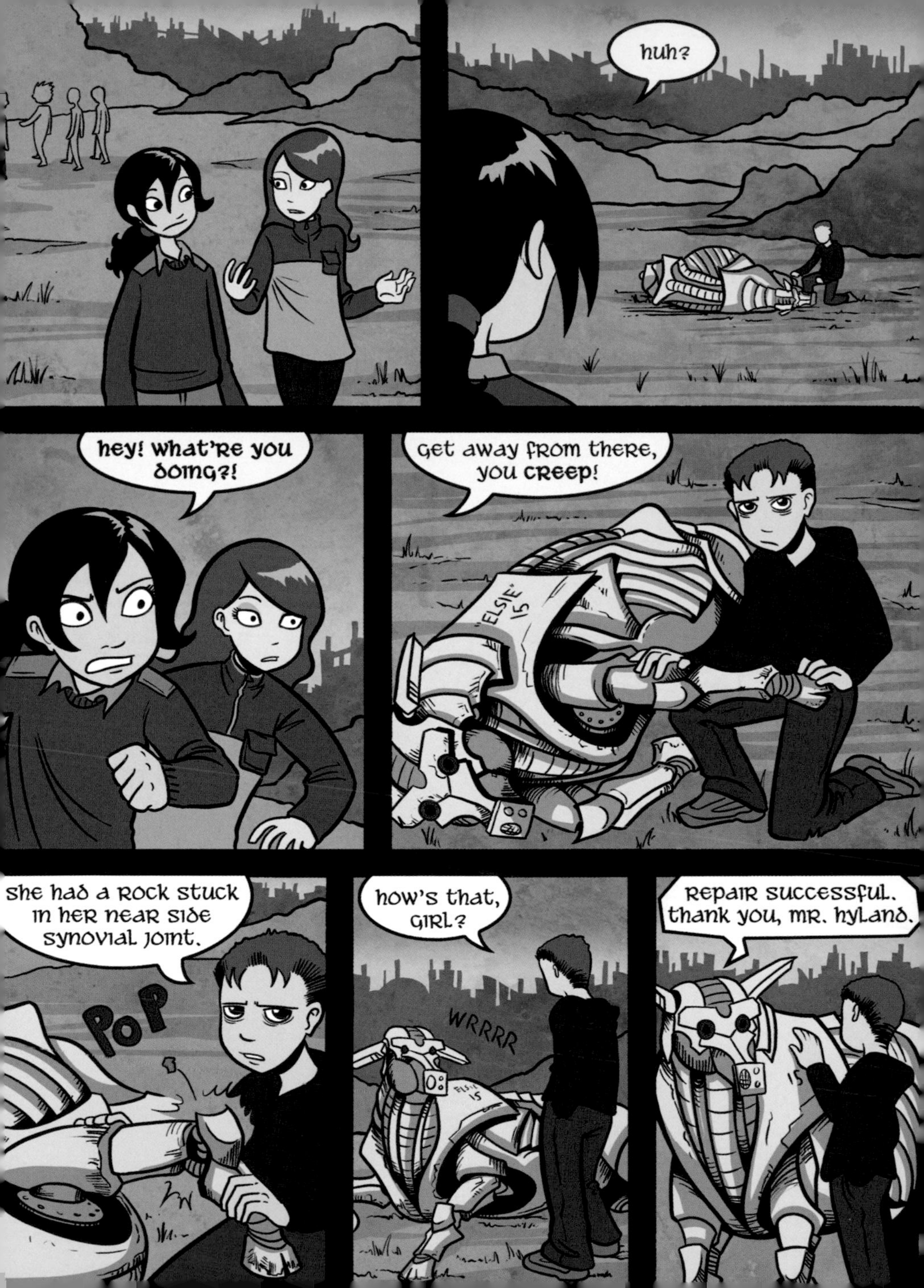
huh?
hey! what're you doing?!
get away from there, you creep!
she had a rock stuck in her near side synovial joint.
POP
how's that, girl?
WRRRR
repair successful. thank you, mr. hyland.

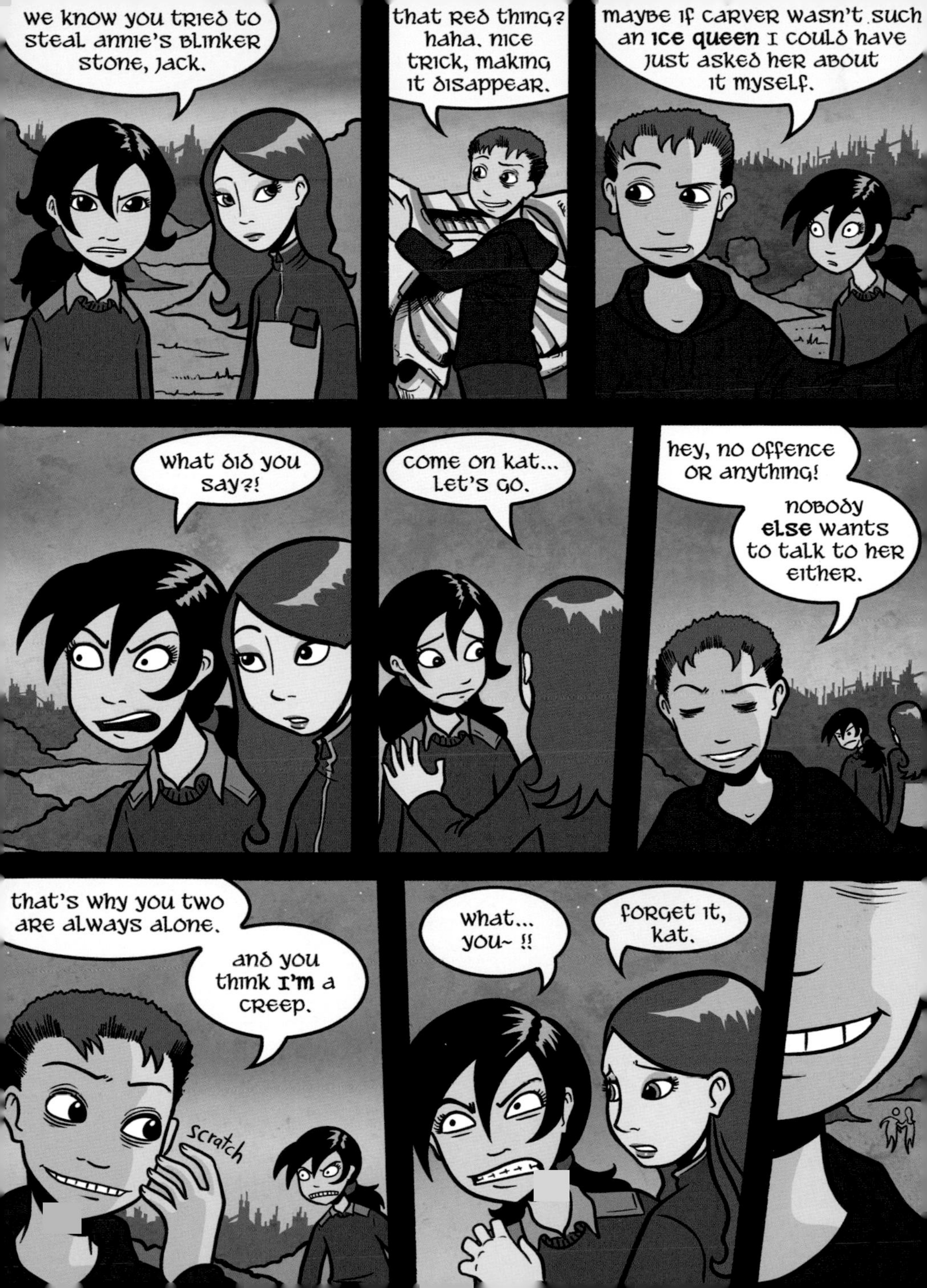
we know you tried to steal annie's blinker stone, jack.
that red thing? haha, nice trick, making it disappear.
maybe if carver wasn't such an **ice queen** I could have just asked her about it myself.
what did you say?!
come on kat... let's go.
hey, no offence or anything!
nobody **else** wants to talk to her either.
that's why you two are always alone.
and you think **I'm** a creep.
scratch
what... you~ !!
forget it, kat.

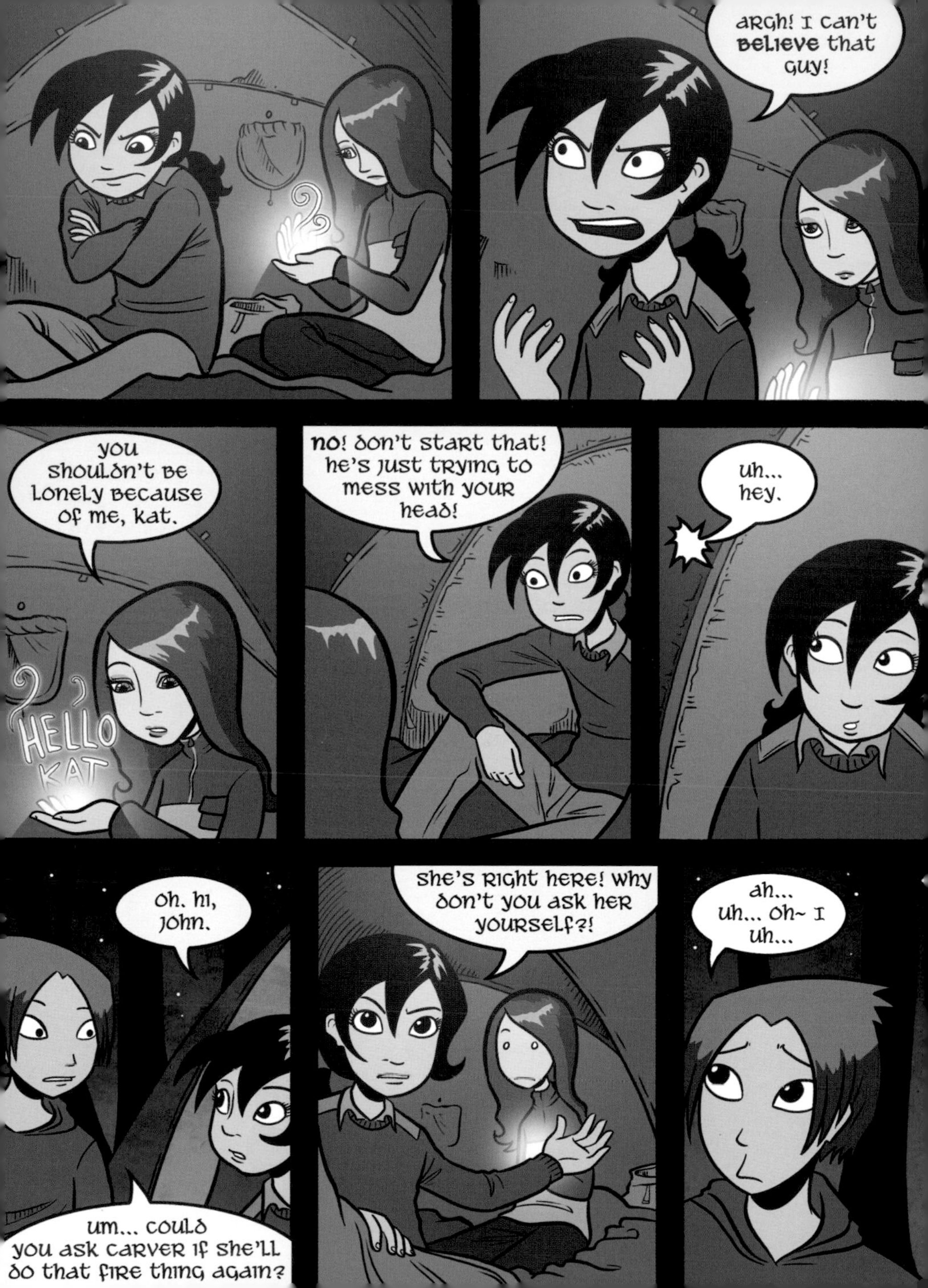
argh! I can't believe that guy!
you shouldn't be lonely because of me, kat.
HELLO KAT
no! don't start that! he's just trying to mess with your head!
uh... hey.
oh. hi, john.
um... could you ask carver if she'll do that fire thing again?
she's right here! why don't you ask her yourself?!
ah... uh... oh~ I uh...

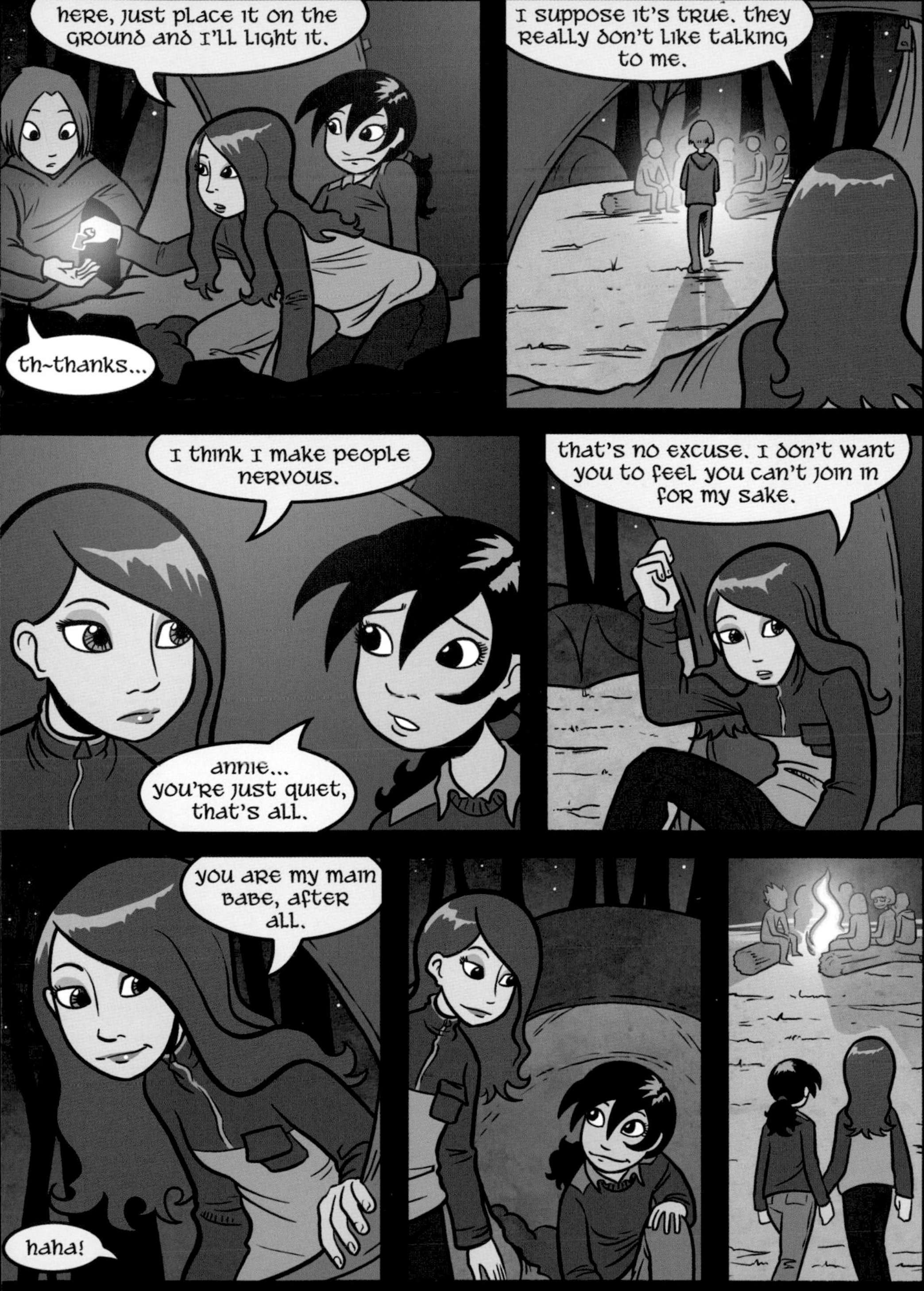

here, just place it on the ground and I'll light it.
th-thanks...
I suppose it's true. they really don't like talking to me.
I think I make people nervous.
annie... you're just quiet, that's all.
that's no excuse. I don't want you to feel you can't join in for my sake.
you are my main babe, after all.
haha!

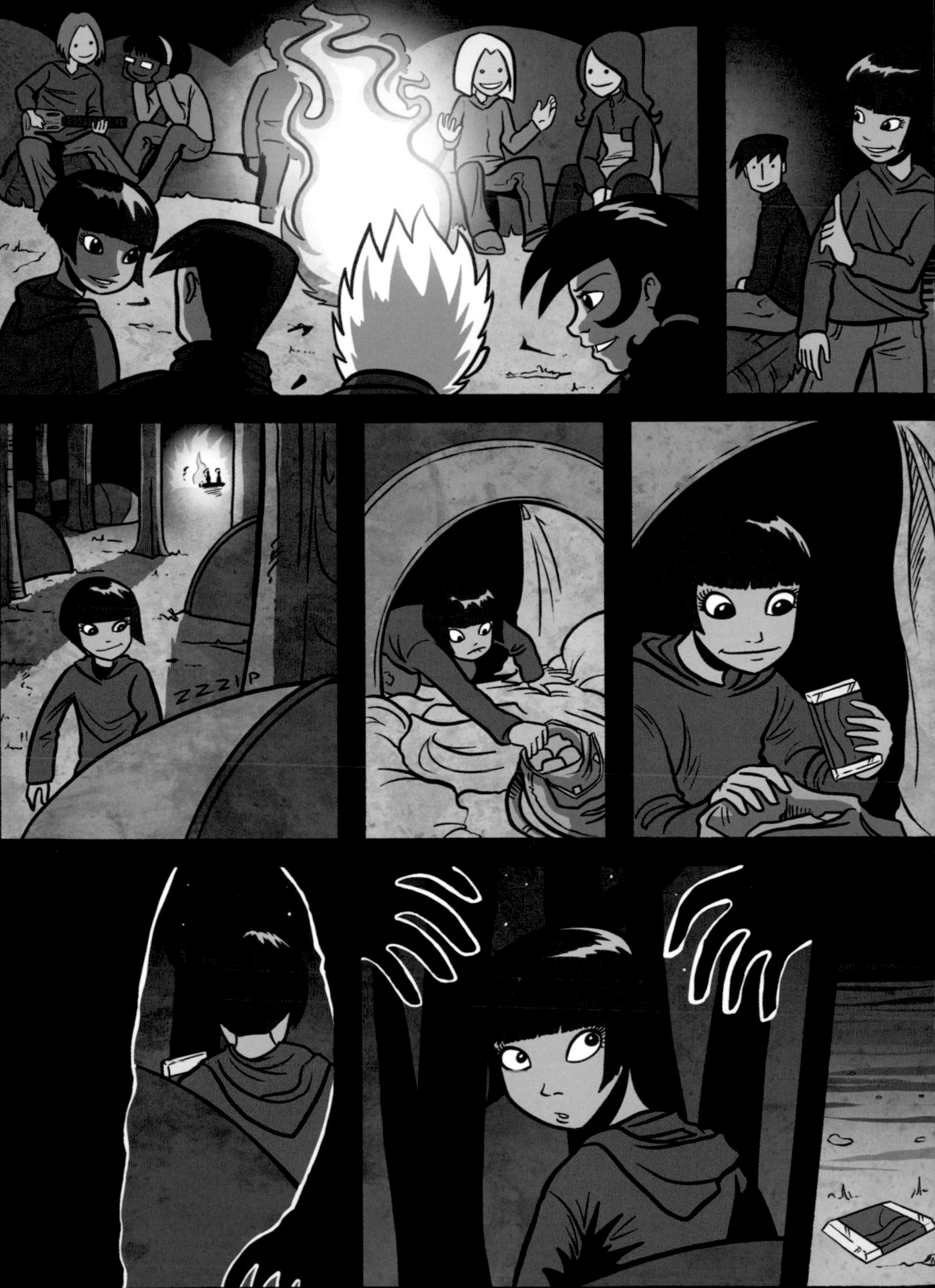
ZZZIP

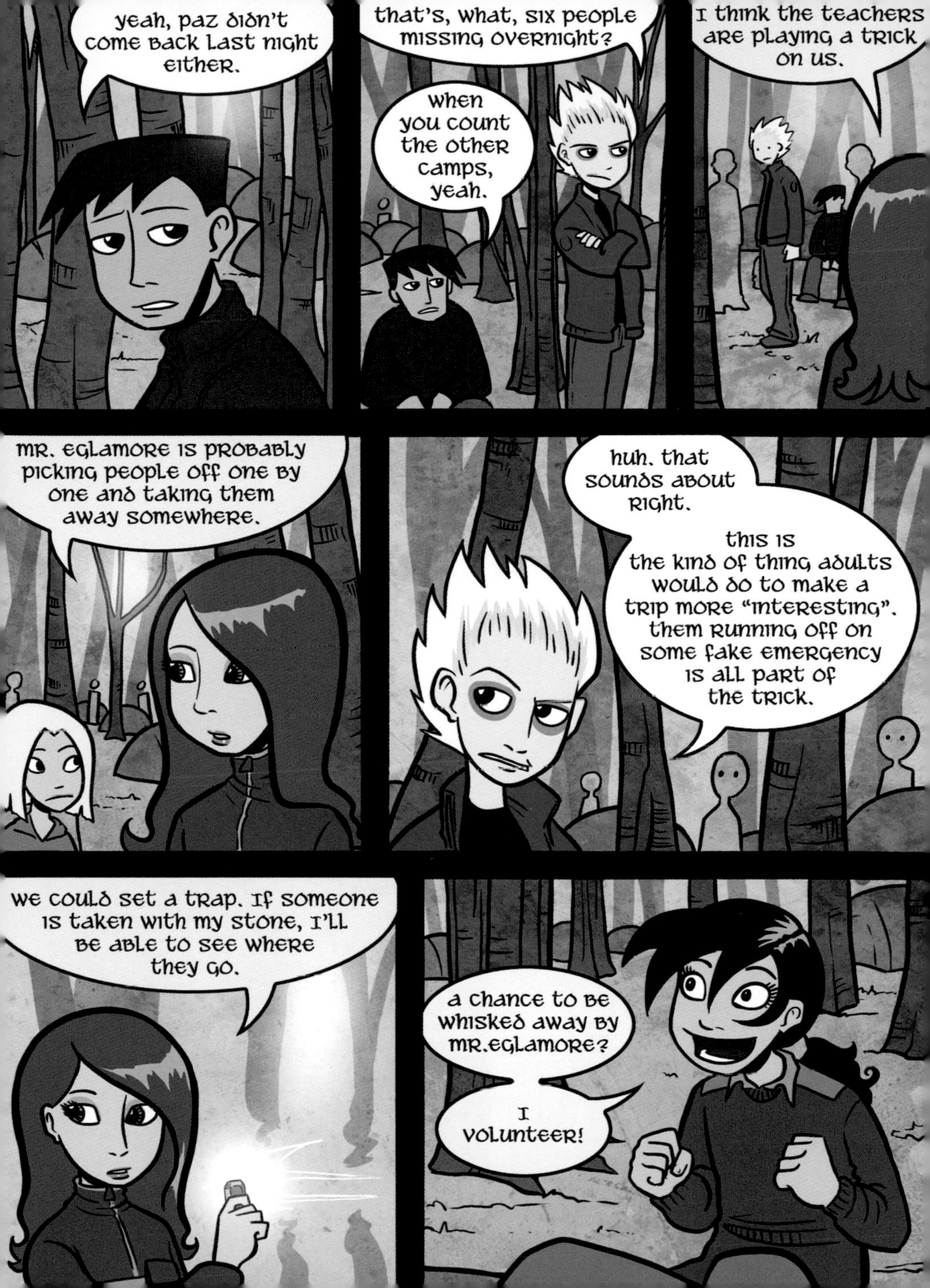
yeah, paz didn't come back last night either.
that's, what, six people missing overnight?
when you count the other camps, yeah.
I think the teachers are playing a trick on us.
mr. eglamore is probably picking people off one by one and taking them away somewhere.
huh. that sounds about right.
this is the kind of thing adults would do to make a trip more "interesting". them running off on some fake emergency is all part of the trick.
we could set a trap. if someone is taken with my stone, I'll be able to see where they go.
a chance to be whisked away by mr.eglamore?
I volunteer!

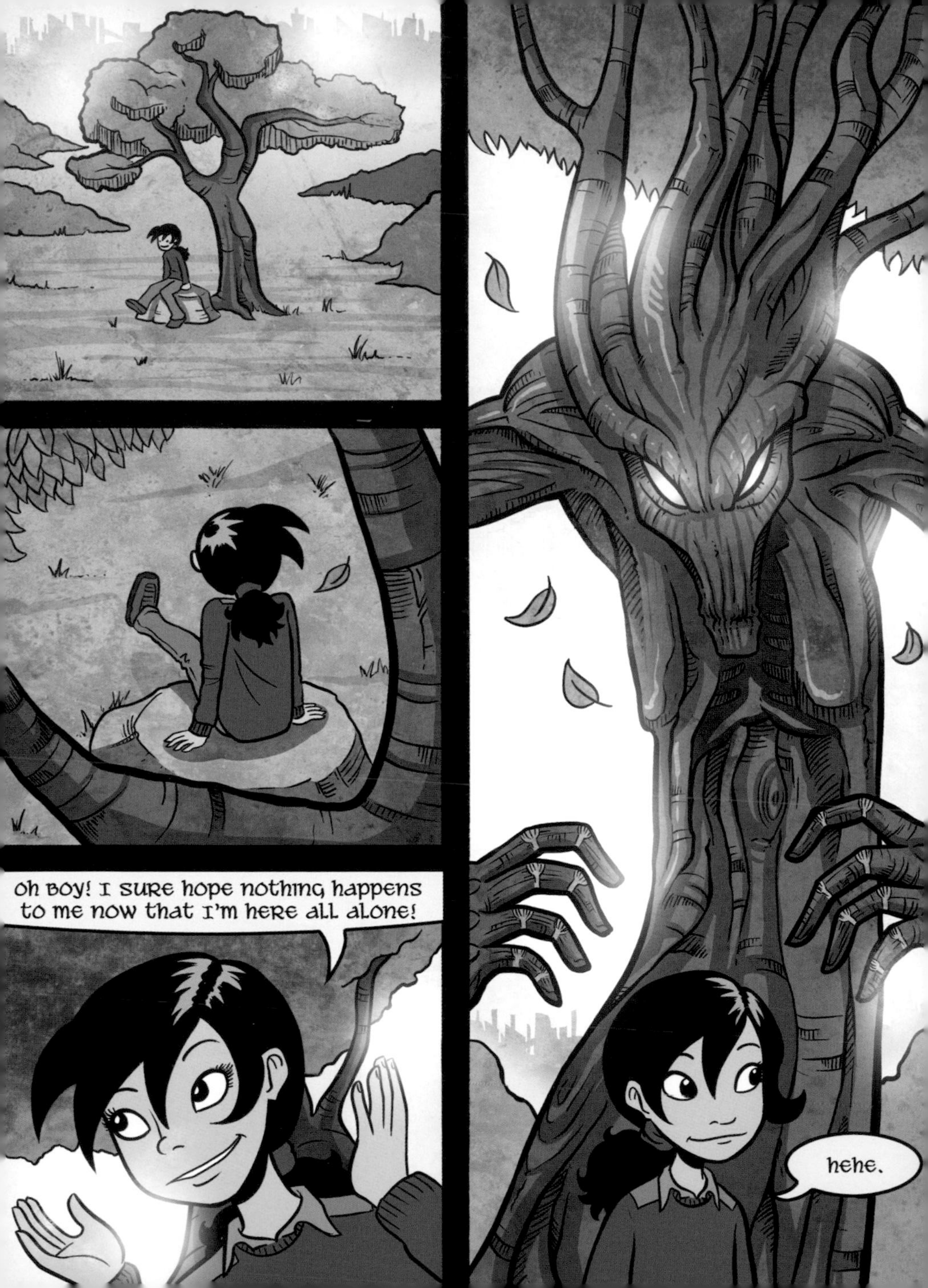
Oh BOY! I SURE hope nothing happens to me now that I'm here all alone!
hehe.

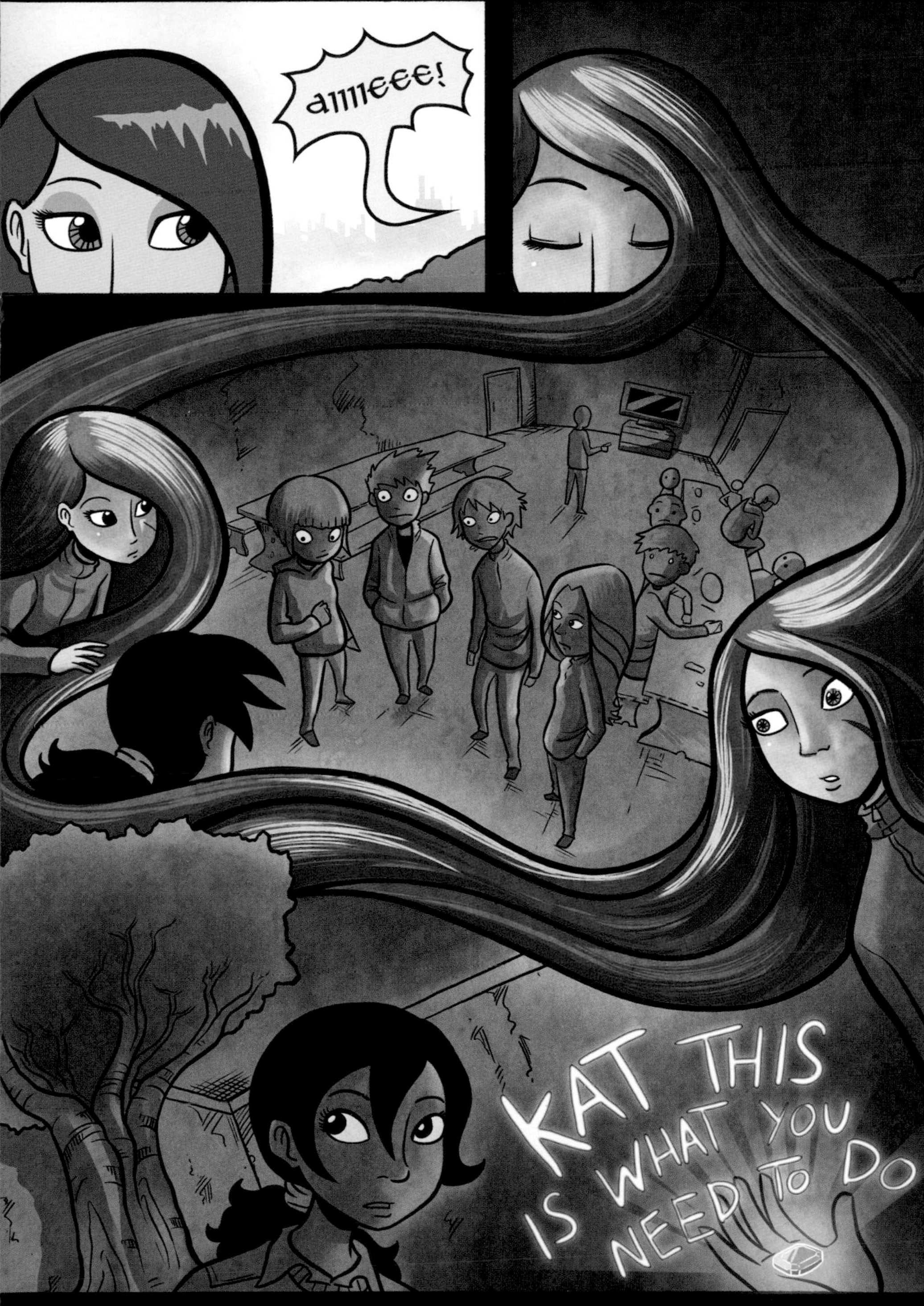
aIIIEEE!
KAT THIS IS WHAT YOU NEED TO DO

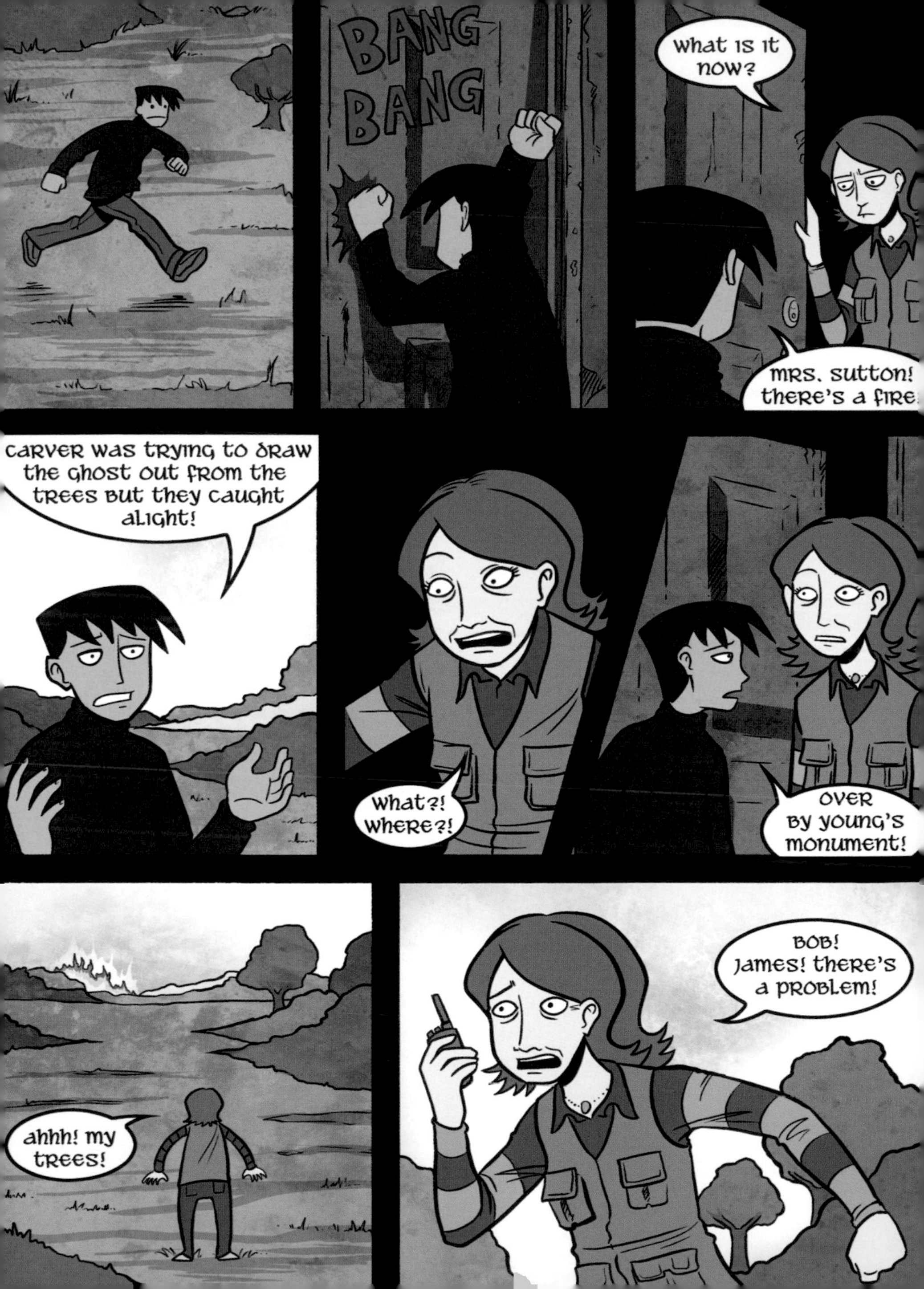
BANG
BANG
what is it now?
MRS. Sutton! there's a fire!
Carver was trying to draw the ghost out from the trees but they caught alight!
What?! Where?!
Over by Young's monument!
ahhh! my trees!
BOB! James! there's a problem!

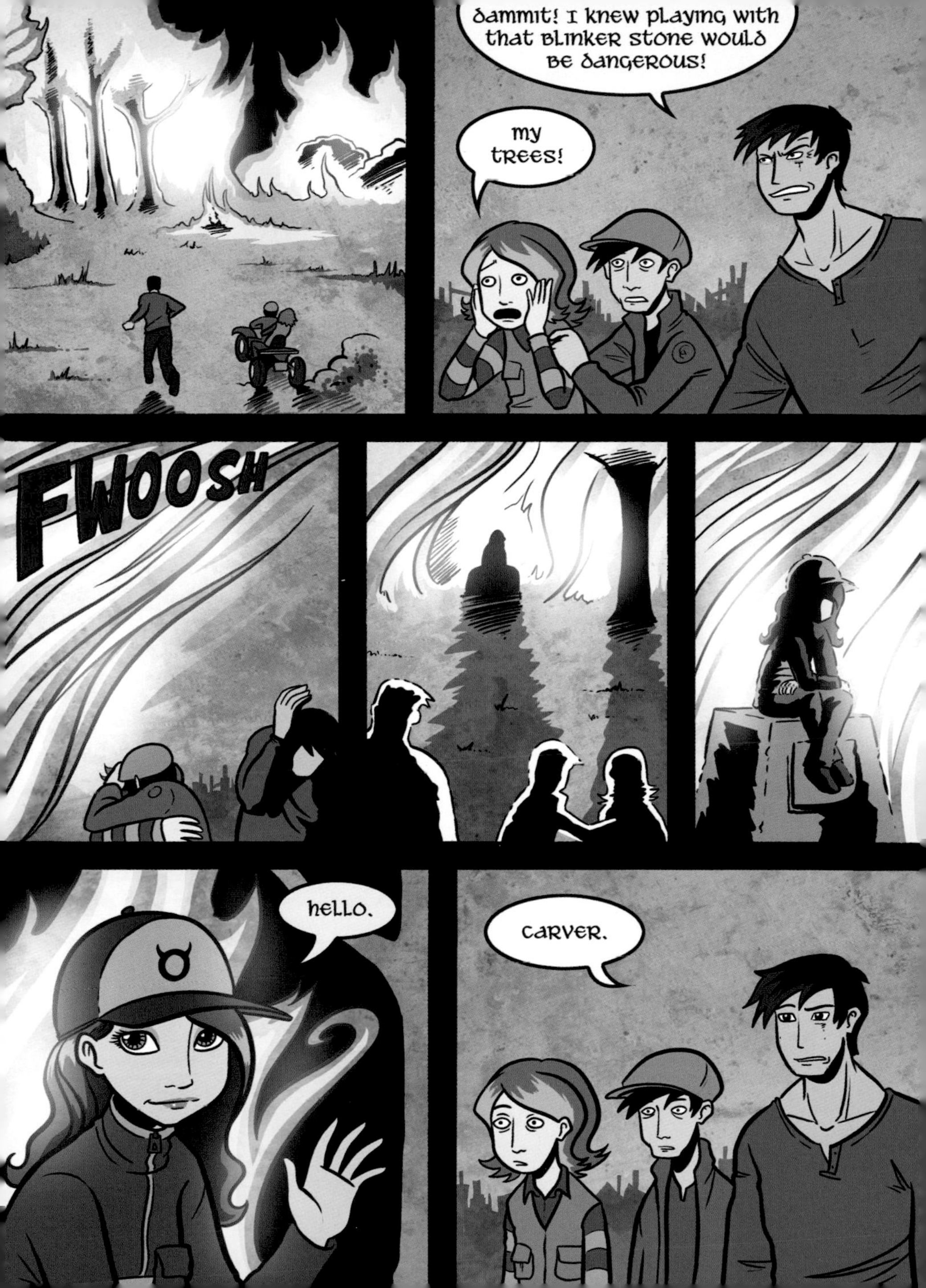
dammit! I knew playing with that blinker stone would be dangerous!
my trees!
FWOOSH
hello.
carver.

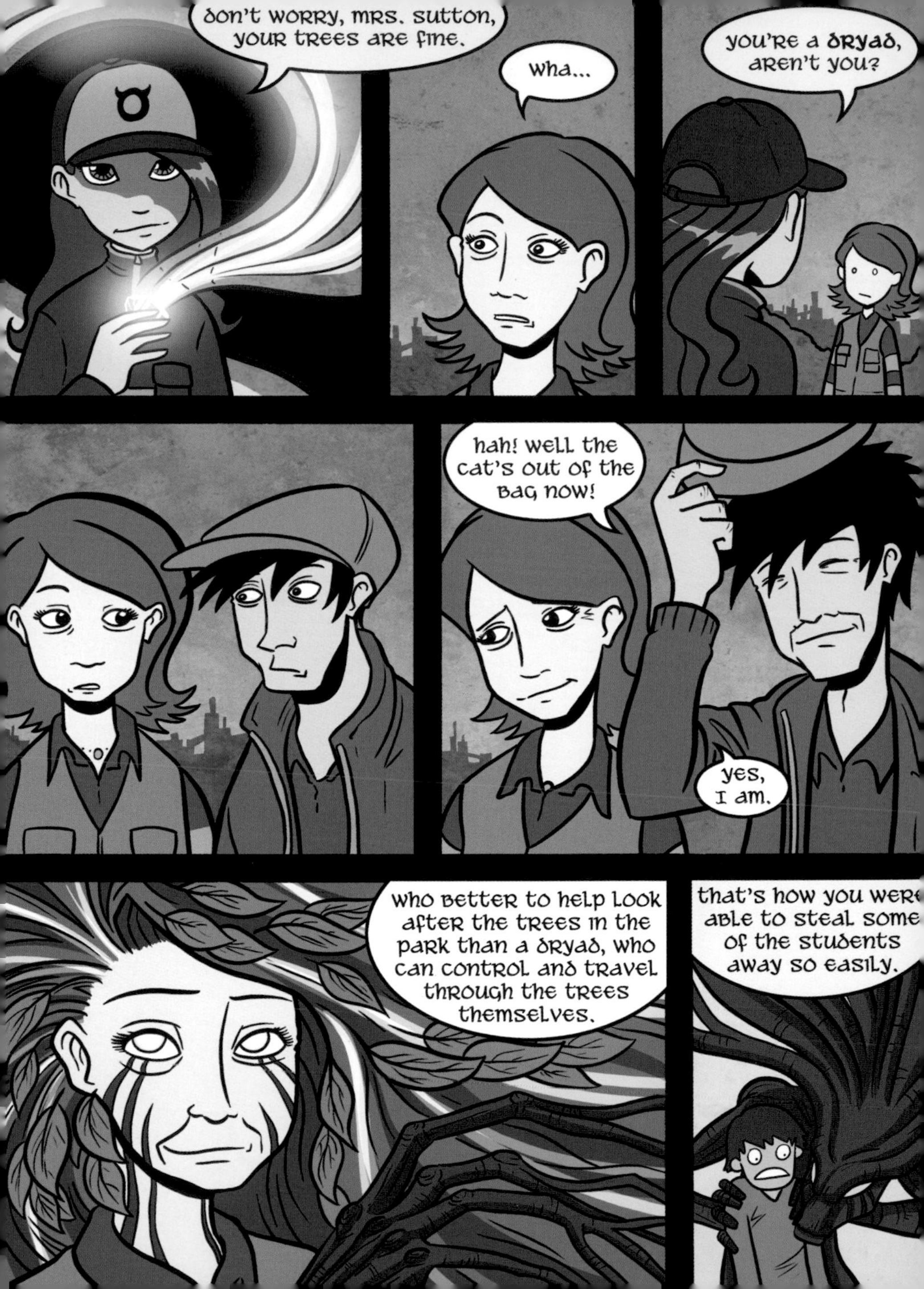
don't worry, mrs. sutton, your trees are fine.
wha...
you're a **dryad**, aren't you?
hah! well the cat's out of the bag now!
yes, I am.
who better to help look after the trees in the park than a dryad, who can control and travel through the trees themselves.
that's how you were able to steal some of the students away so easily.

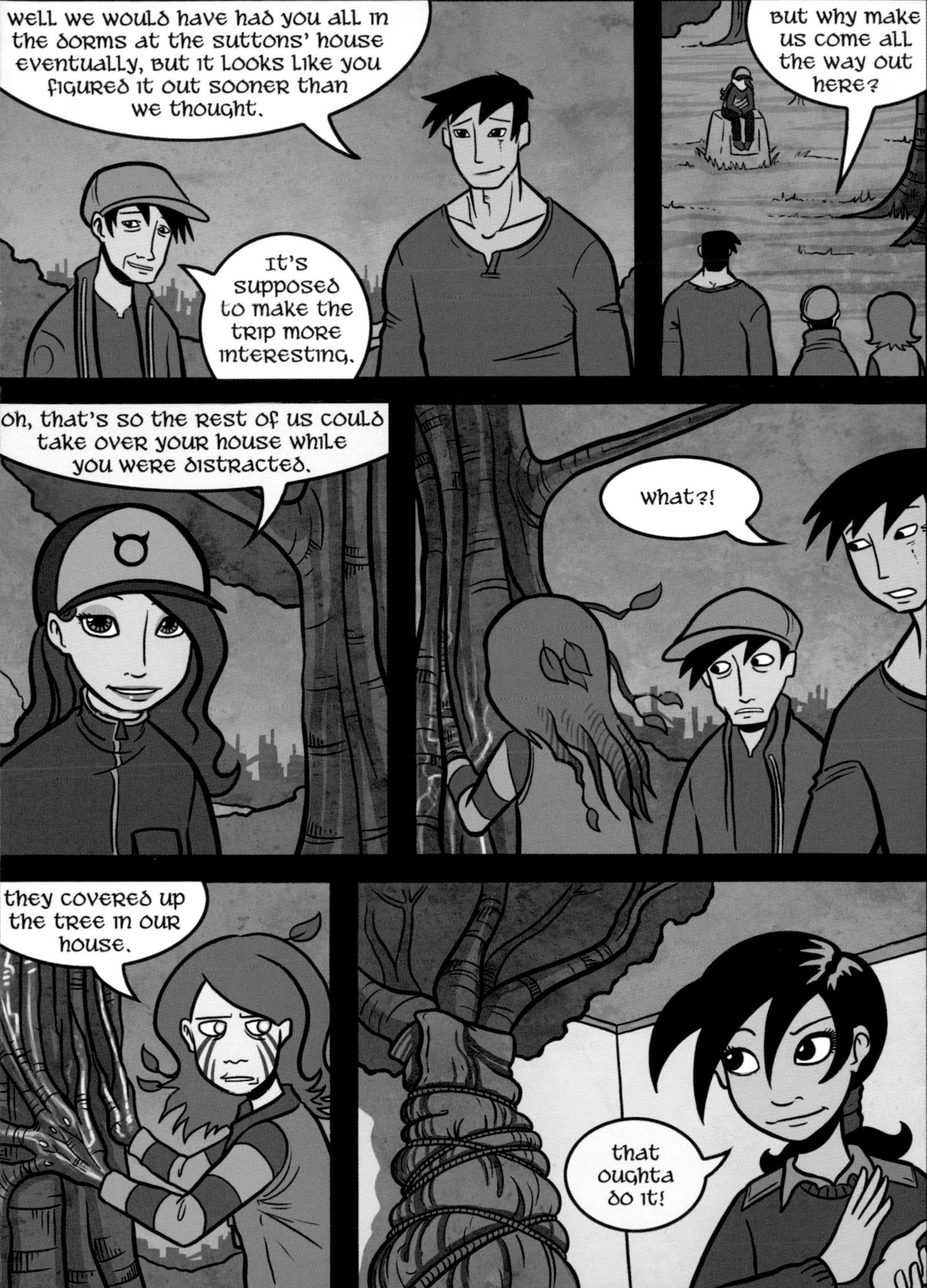
well we would have had you all in the dorms at the suttons' house eventually, but it looks like you figured it out sooner than we thought.
It's supposed to make the trip more interesting.
But why make us come all the way out here?
oh, that's so the rest of us could take over your house while you were distracted.
What?!
they covered up the tree in our house.
that oughta do it!

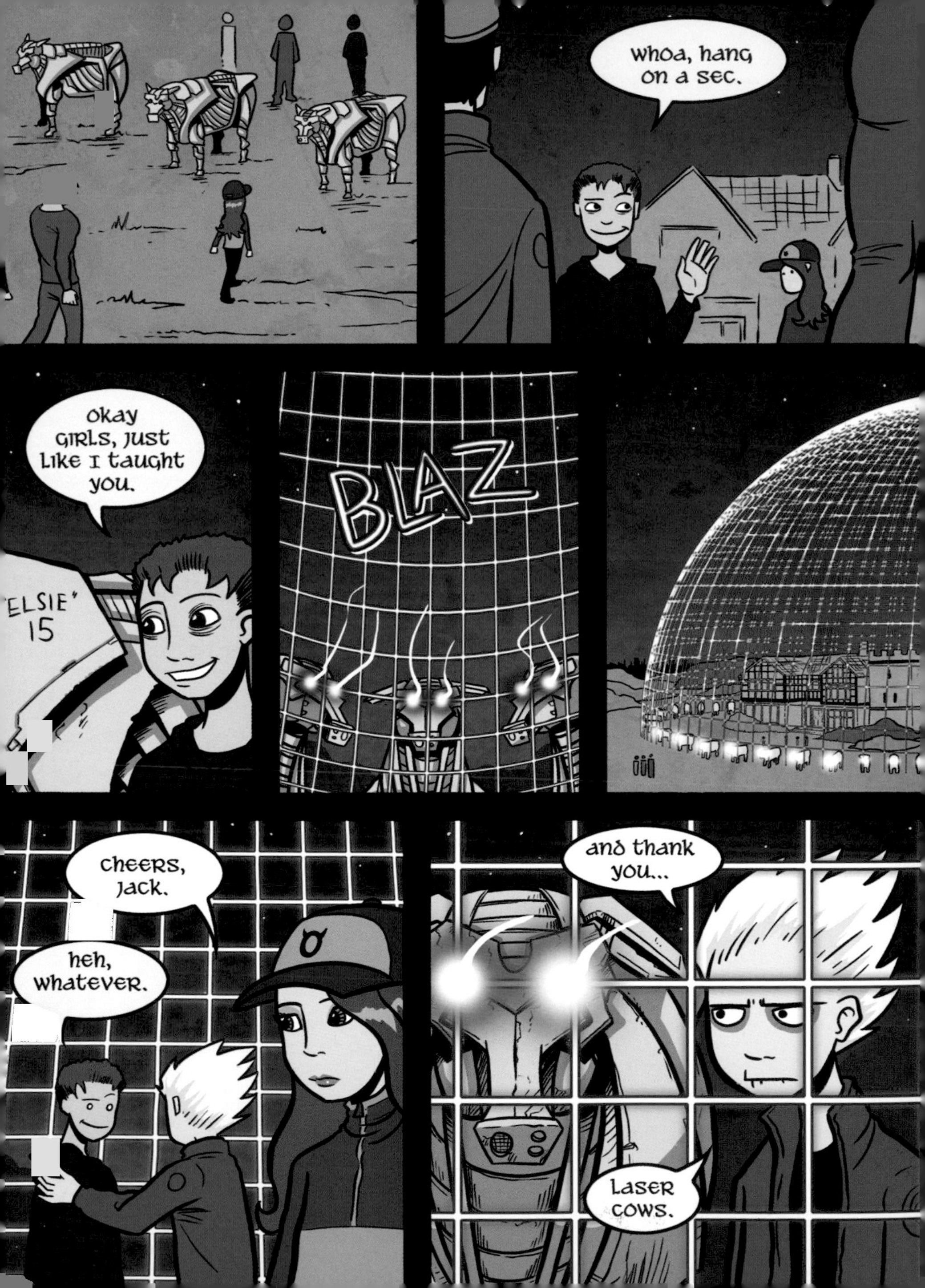
whoa, hang on a sec.
okay girls, just like I taught you.
"ELSIE" 15
BLAZ
cheers, jack.
heh, whatever.
and thank you...
laser cows.

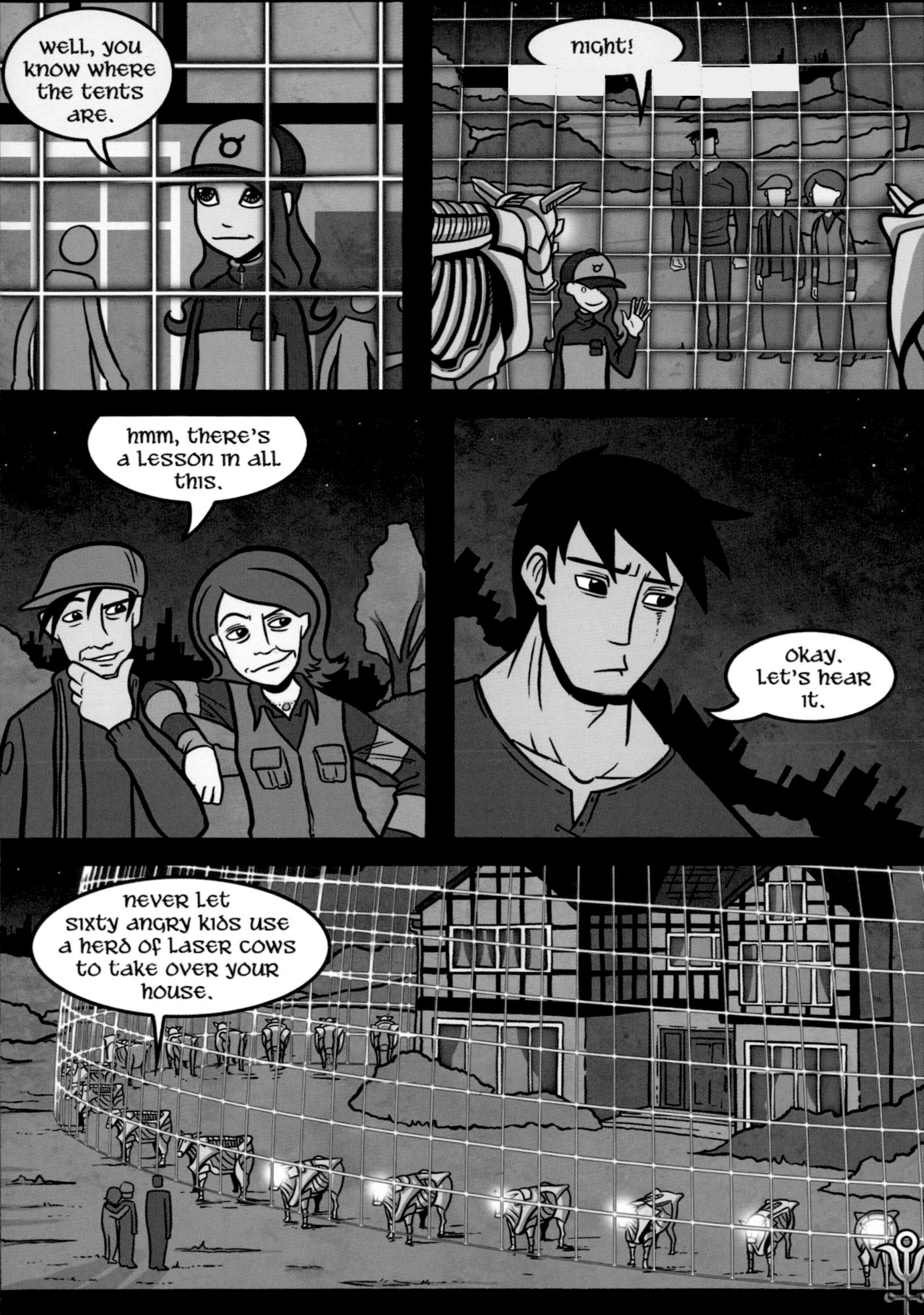

well, you know where the tents are.
night!
hmm, there's a lesson in all this.
Okay. Let's hear it.
never let sixty angry kids use a herd of laser cows to take over your house.

Absence and Hearts

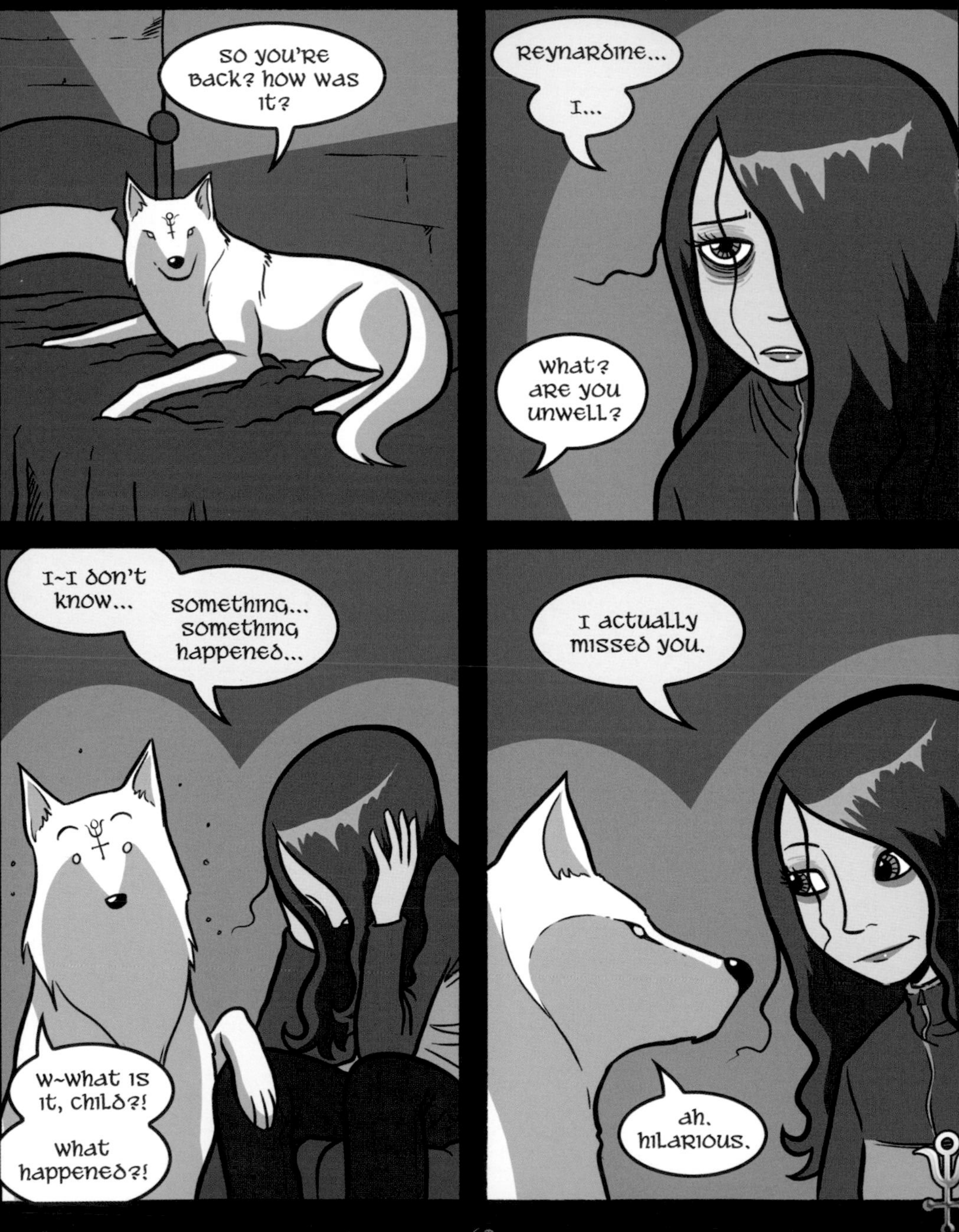
So you're back? How was it?
Reynardine...
I...
What? Are you unwell?
I-I don't know...
Something... something happened...
W-what is it, child?!
What happened?!
I actually missed you.
Ah. Hilarious.

Gunnerkrigg Court

Chapter 25:

Sky Watcher And The Angel

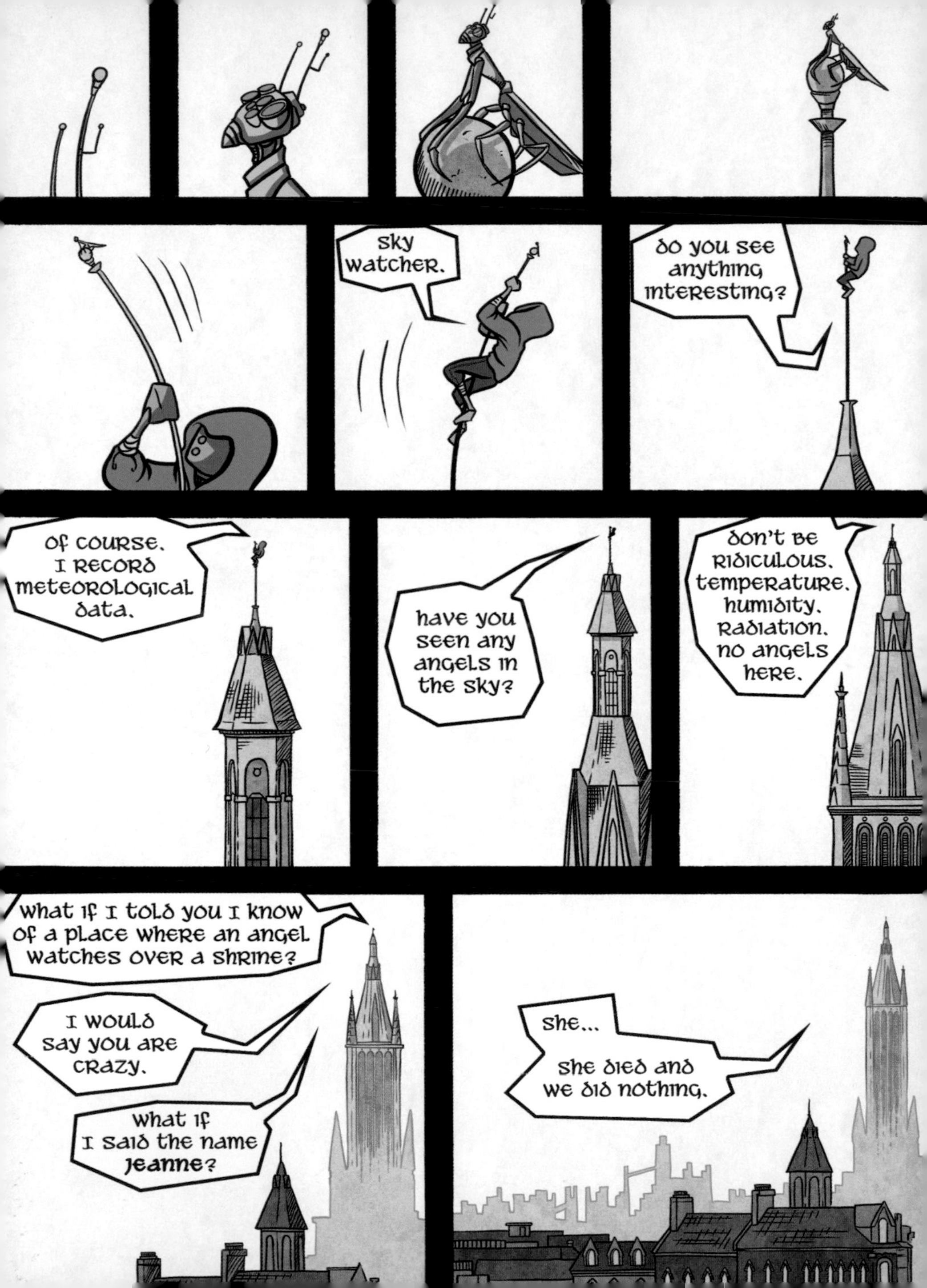

Sky watcher.
Do you see anything interesting?
Of course. I record meteorological data.
Have you seen any angels in the sky?
Don't be ridiculous. Temperature. Humidity. Radiation. No angels here.
What if I told you I know of a place where an angel watches over a shrine?
I would say you are crazy.
What if I said the name Jeanne?
She...
She died and we did nothing.

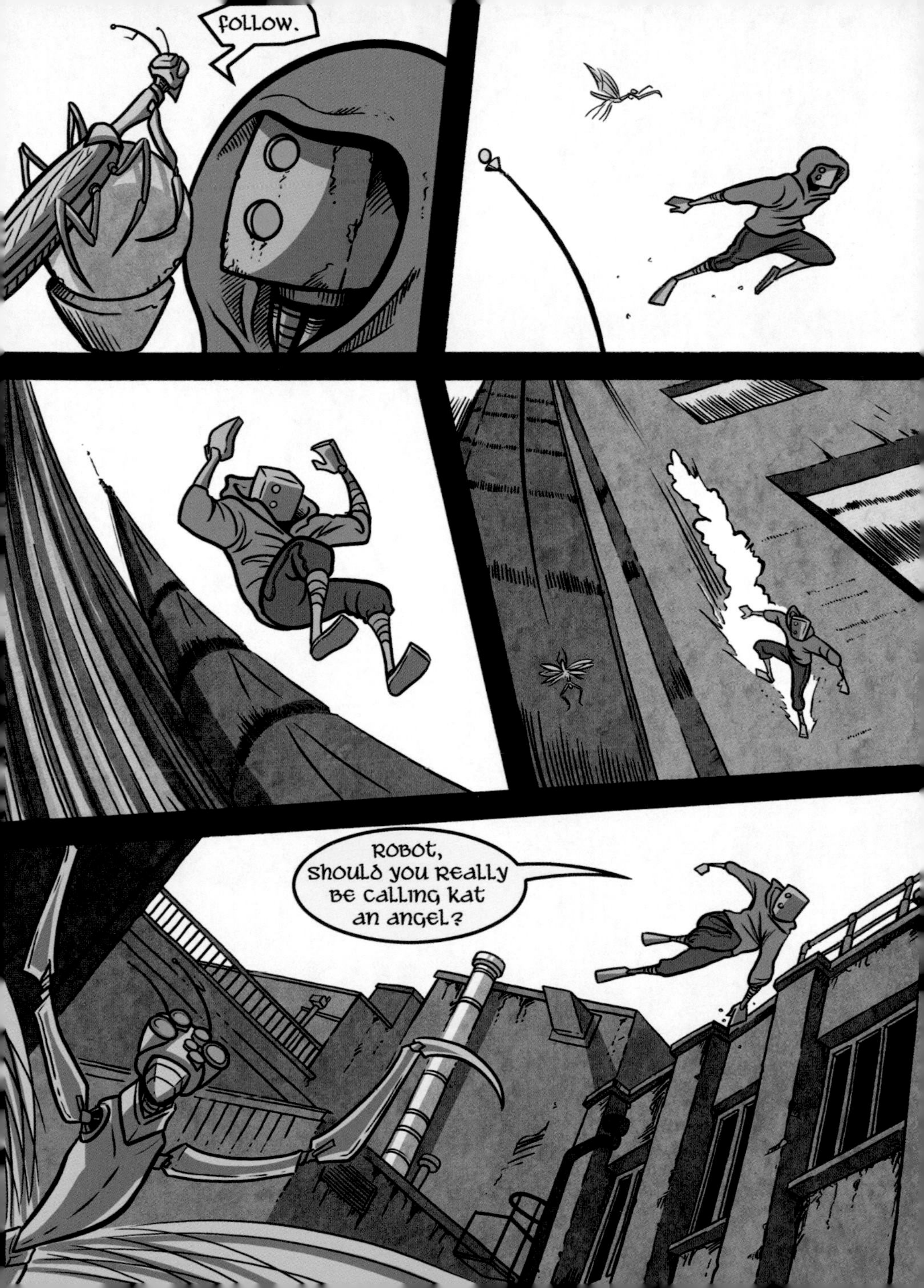
follow.
Robot, should you really be calling kat an angel?

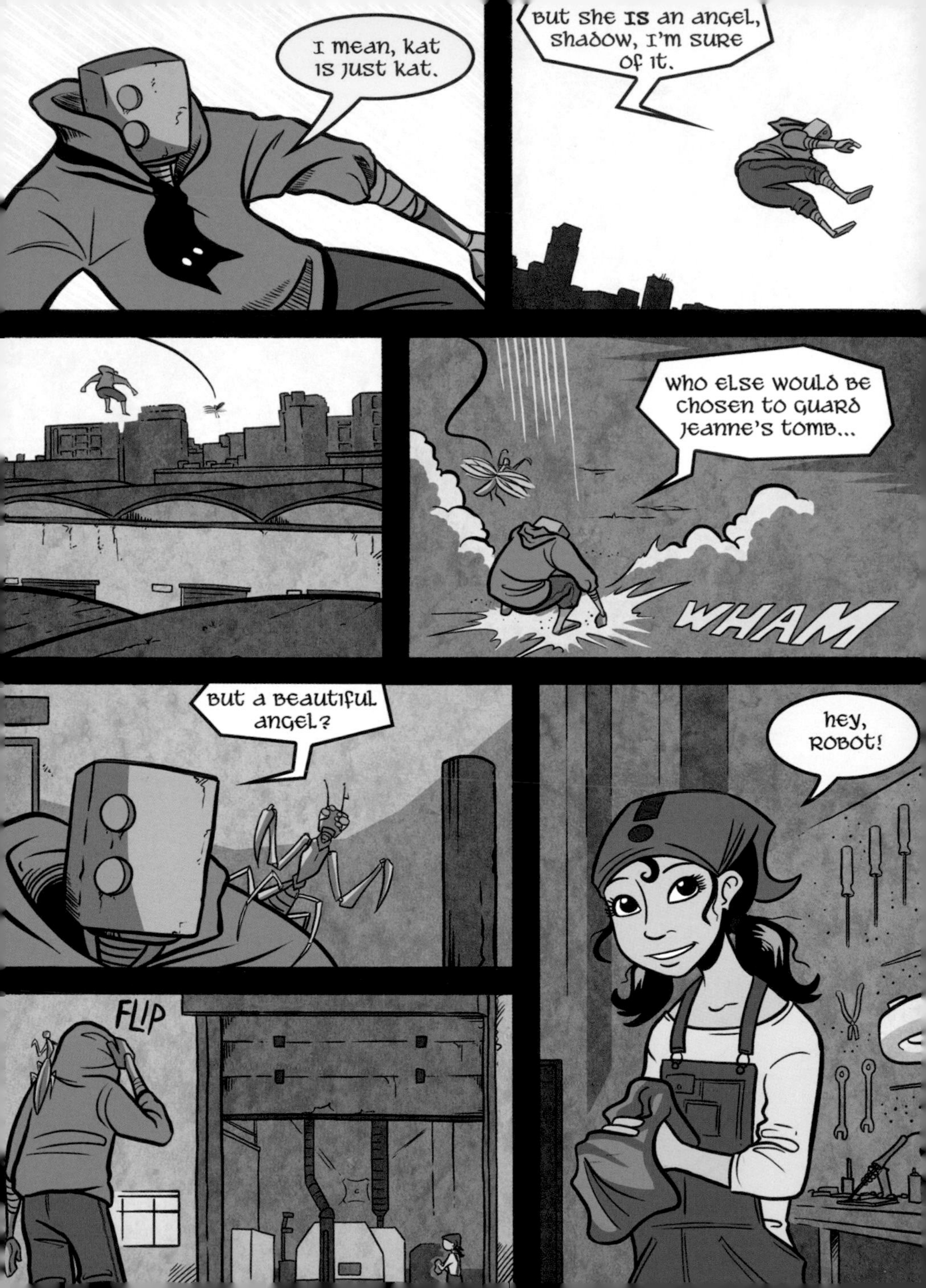

I mean, kat is just kat.
But she IS an angel, shadow, I'm sure of it.
Who else would be chosen to guard Jeanne's tomb...
WHAM
But a beautiful angel?
FLIP
hey, ROBOT!

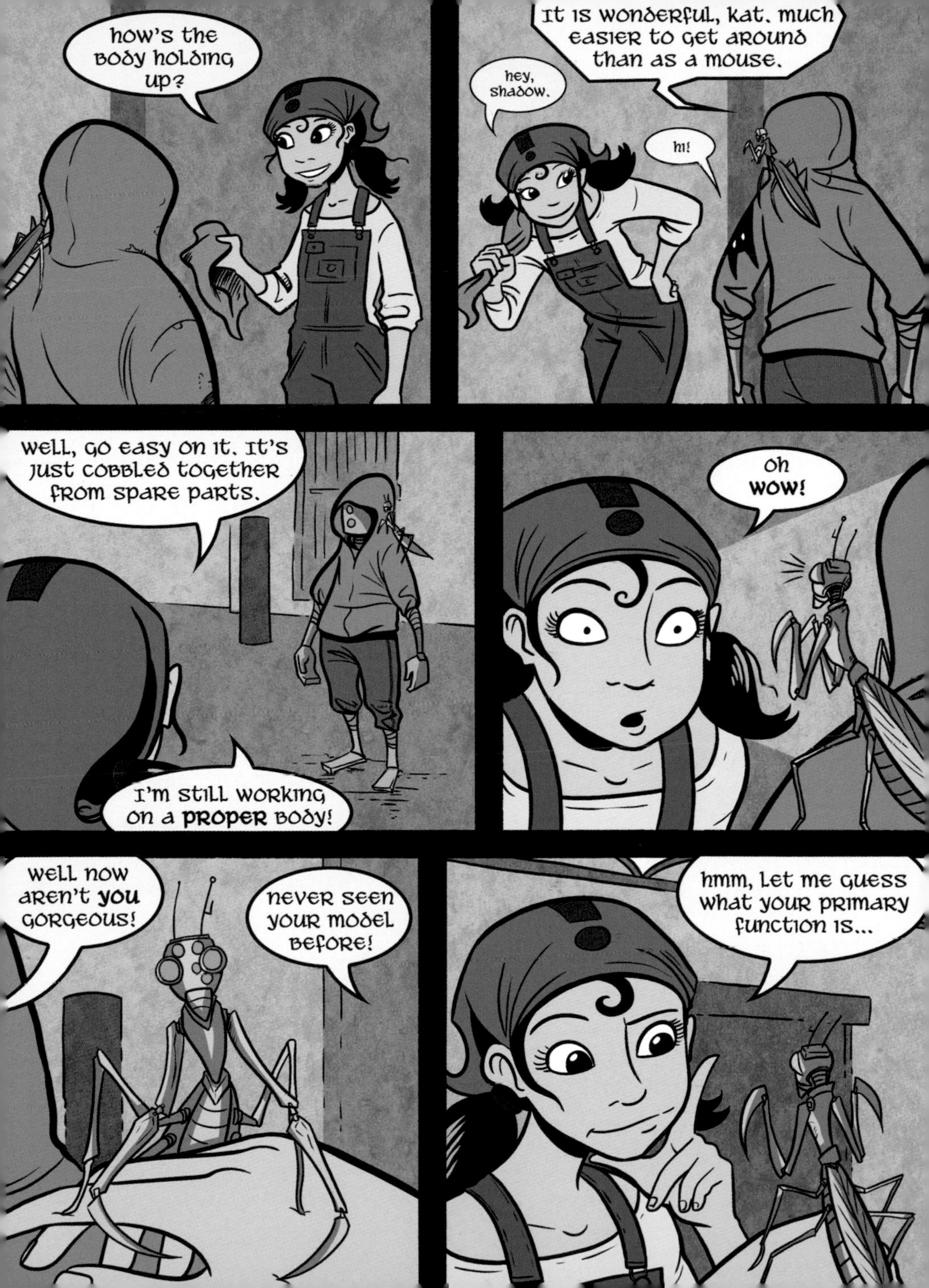
how's the body holding up?
It is wonderful, kat. much easier to get around than as a mouse.
hey, shadow.
hi!
well, go easy on it. It's just cobbled together from spare parts.
I'm still working on a **PROPER** body!
oh **WOW!**
well now aren't **YOU** gorgeous!
never seen your model before!
hmm, let me guess what your primary function is...

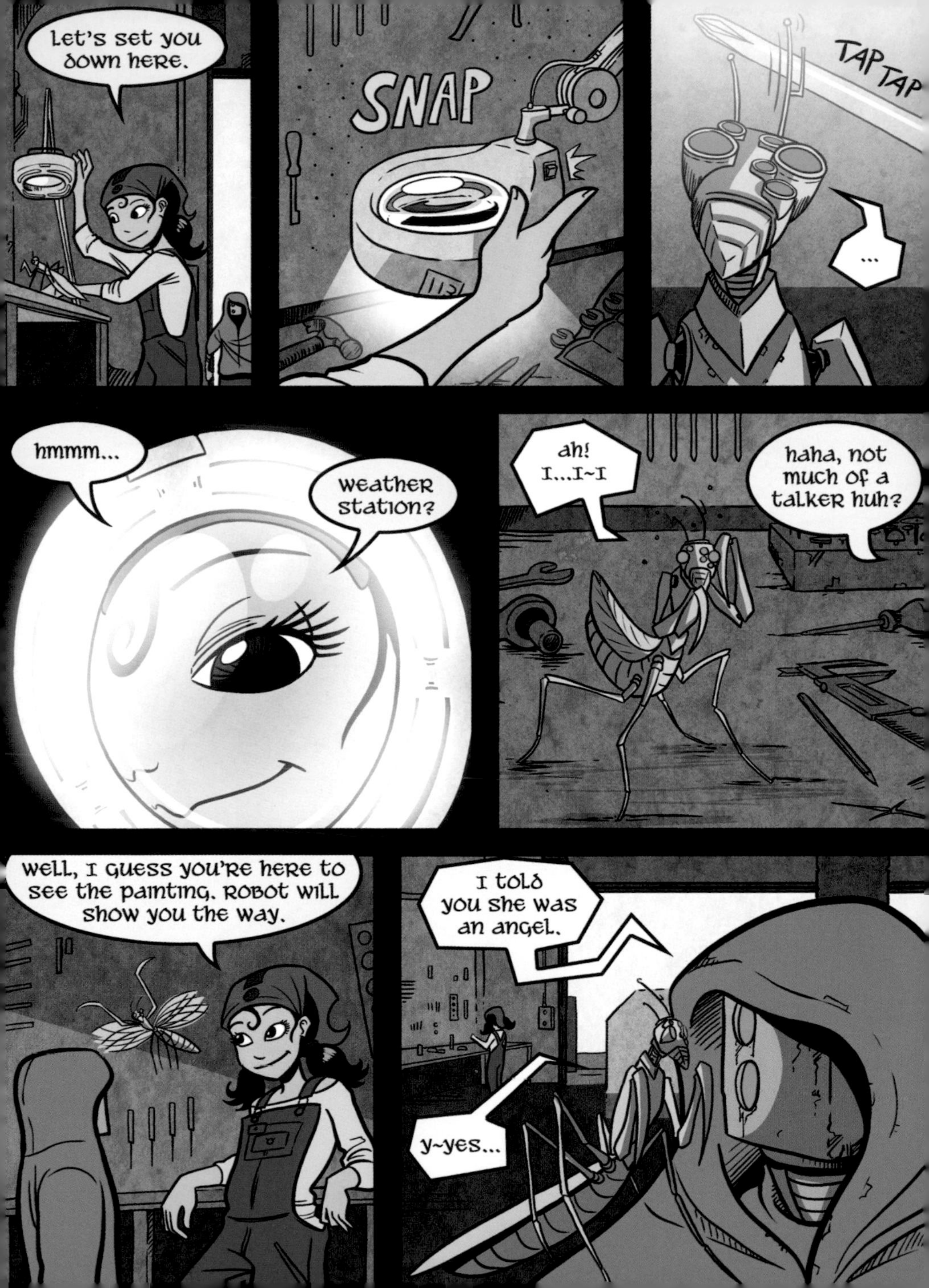
Let's set you down here.
SNAP
TAP TAP
...
hmmm...
weather station?
ah! I...I~I
haha, not much of a talker huh?
Well, I guess you're here to see the painting. Robot will show you the way.
I told you she was an angel.
y~yes...

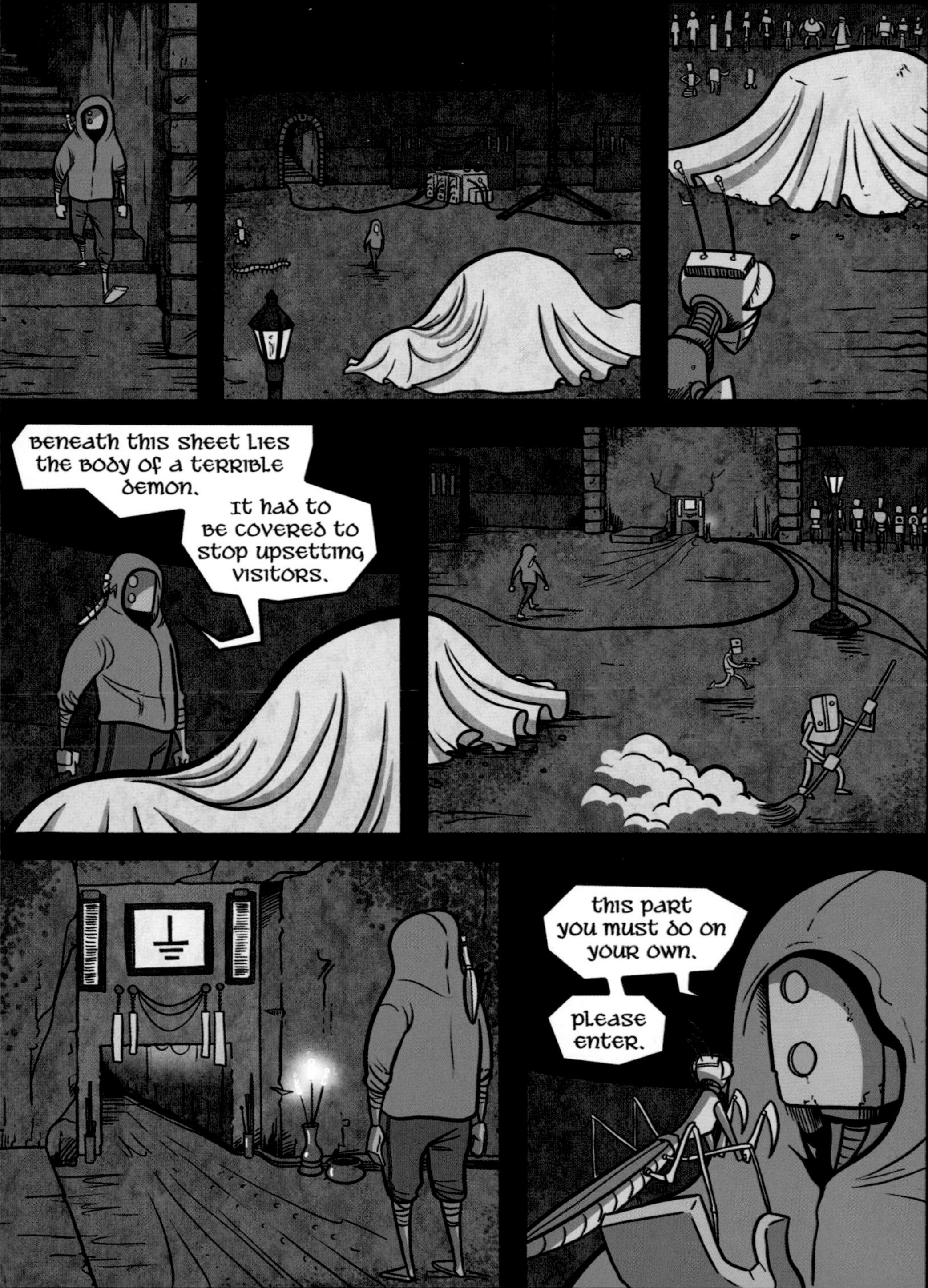
Beneath this sheet lies the body of a terrible demon.
It had to be covered to stop upsetting visitors.
this part you must do on your own.
please enter.

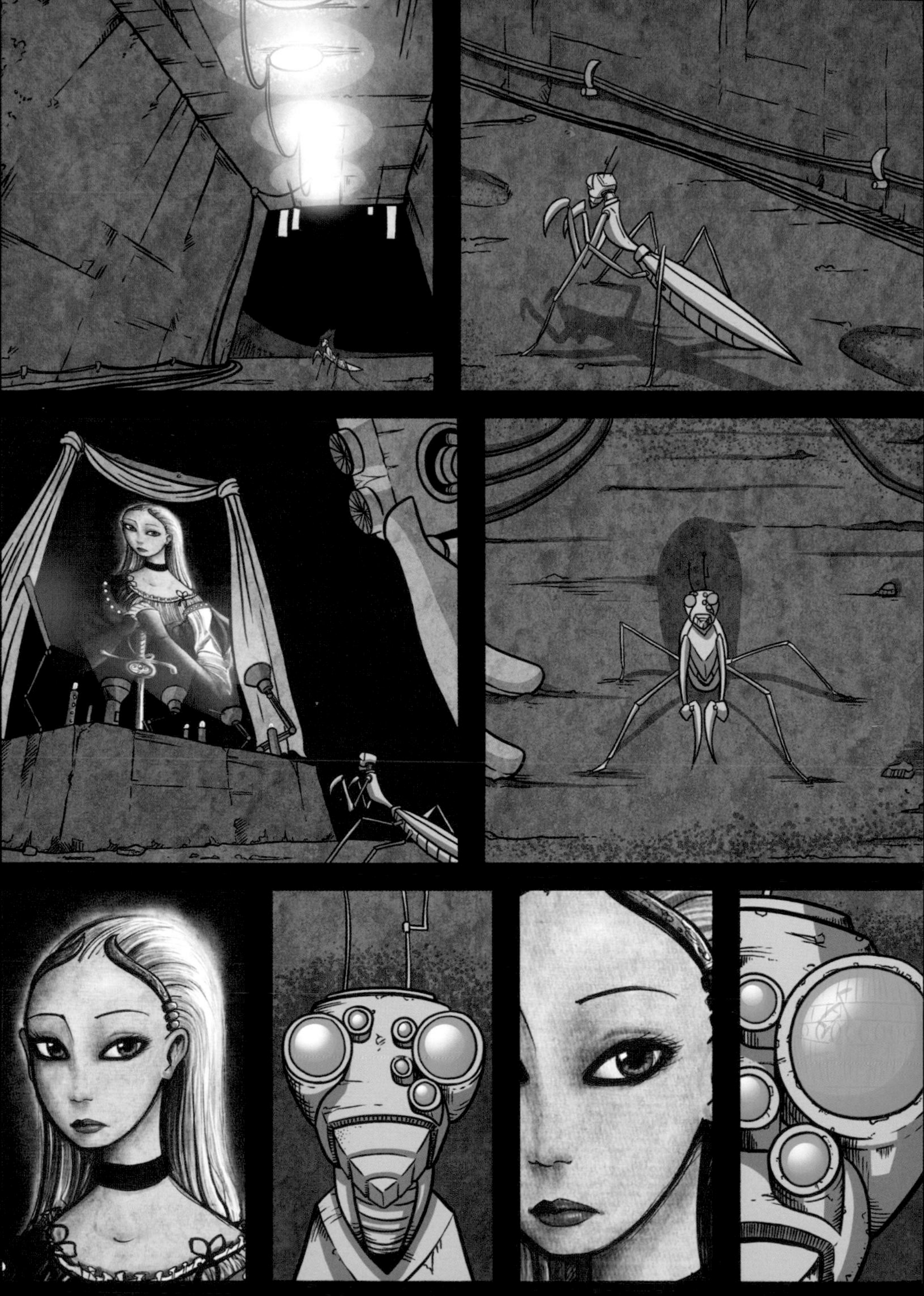

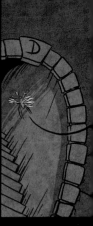

kat, what would make two people deny their love for each other?

oh! hi, annie!

haha!

what?

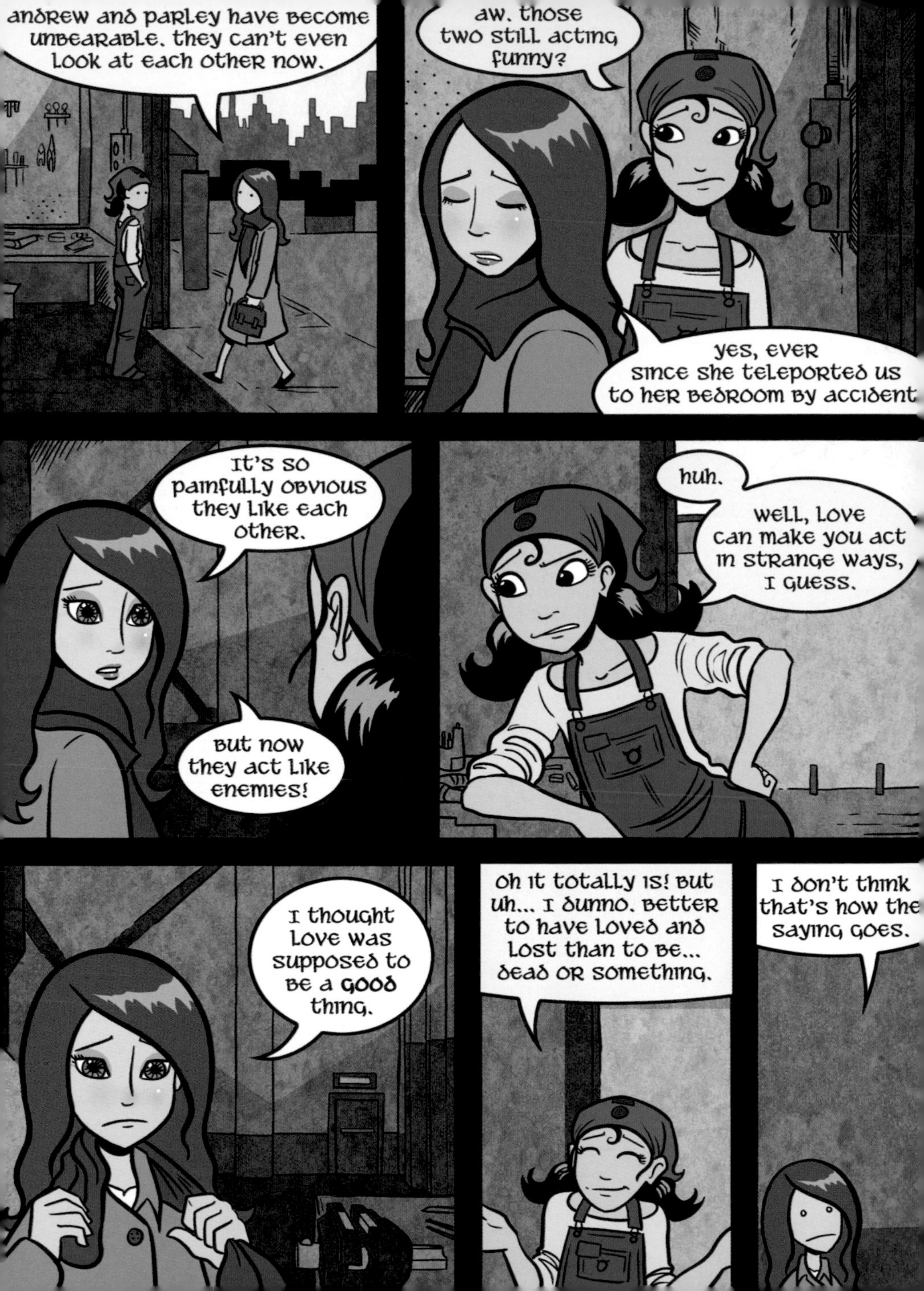
andrew and parley have become unbearable. they can't even look at each other now.
aw. those two still acting funny?
yes, ever since she teleported us to her bedroom by accident
It's so painfully obvious they like each other.
But now they act like enemies!
huh.
well, love can make you act in strange ways, I guess.
I thought love was supposed to be a **good** thing.
oh it totally is! But uh... I dunno. Better to have loved and lost than to be... dead or something.
I don't think that's how the saying goes.

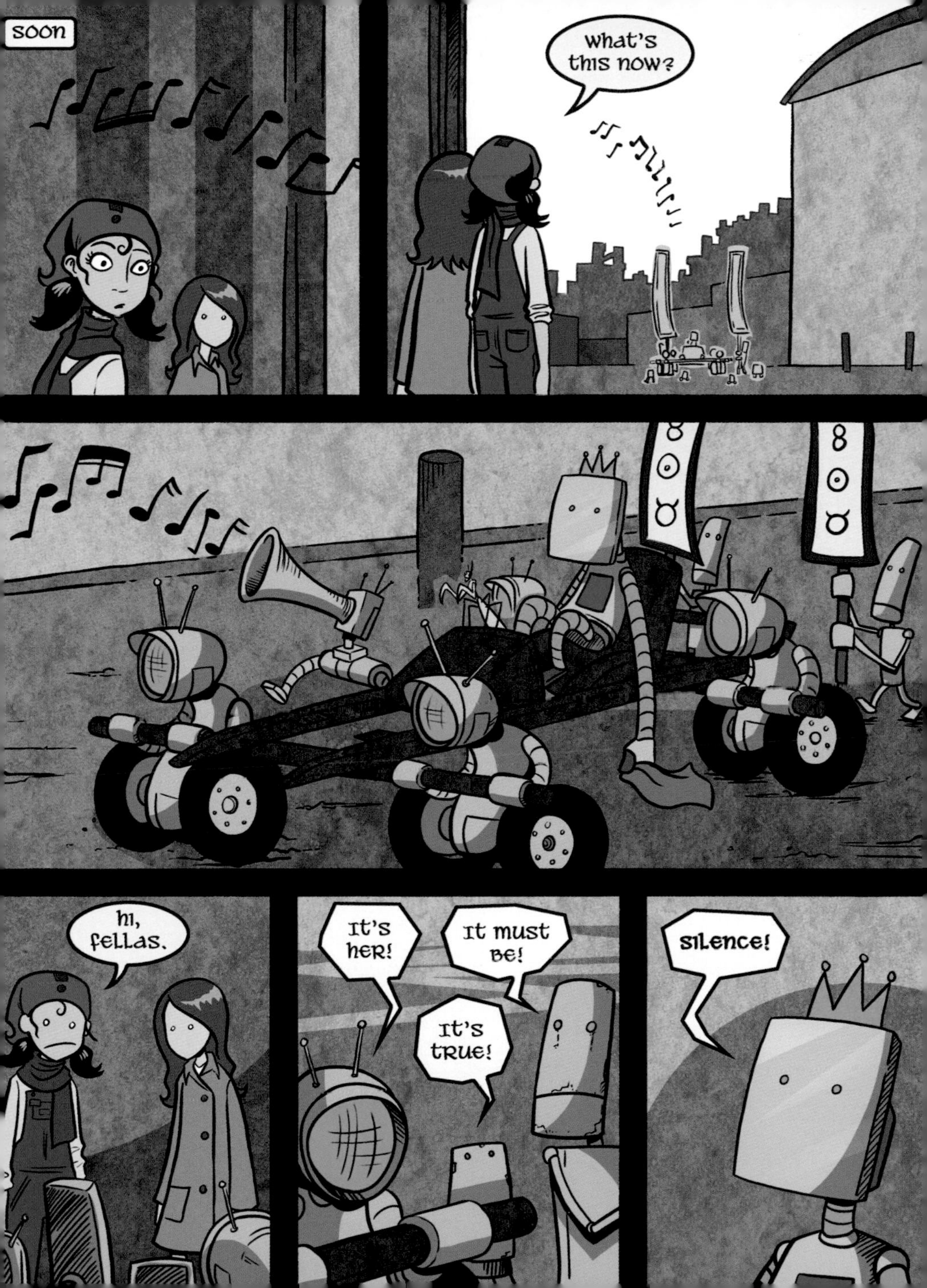
soon
What's this now?
hi, fellas.
It's her!
It must be!
It's true!
silence!

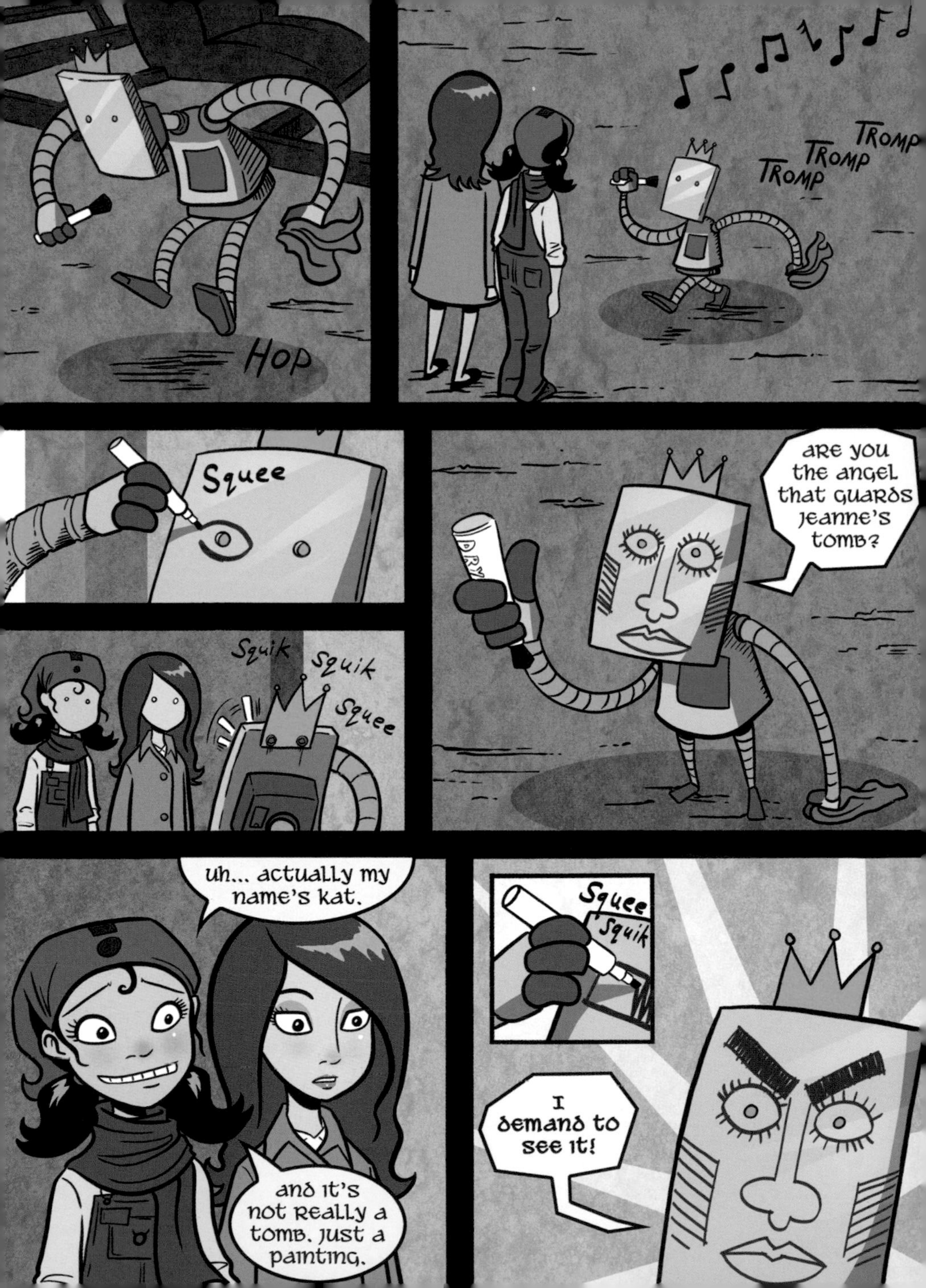
HOP
TROMP
TROMP
TROMP
Squee
are you the angel that guards Jeanne's tomb?
Squik
Squik
Squee
uh... actually my name's Kat.
and it's not really a tomb. just a painting.
Squee
Squik
I demand to see it!

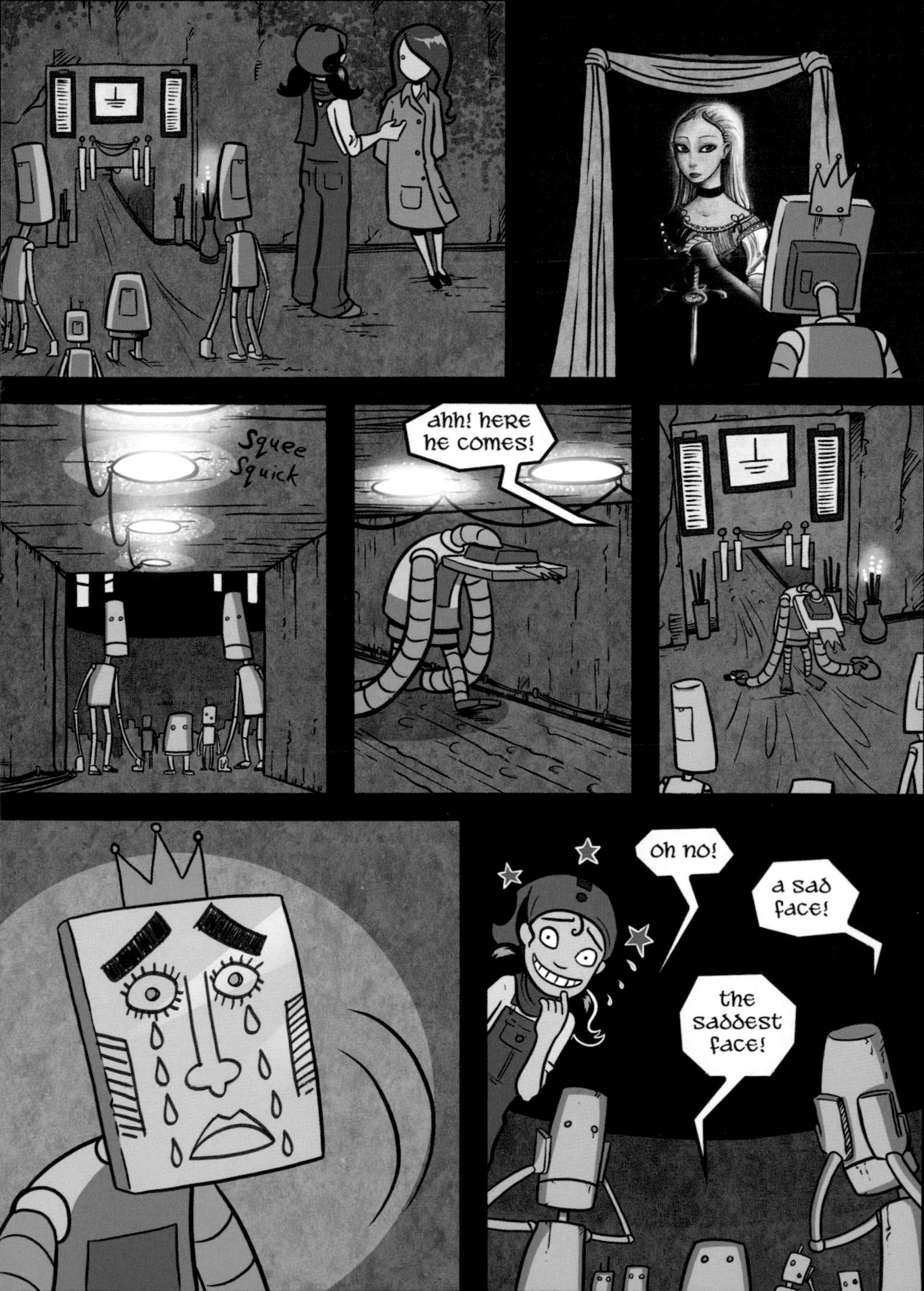
Squee
Squick
ahh! here he comes!
oh no!
a sad face!
the saddest face!

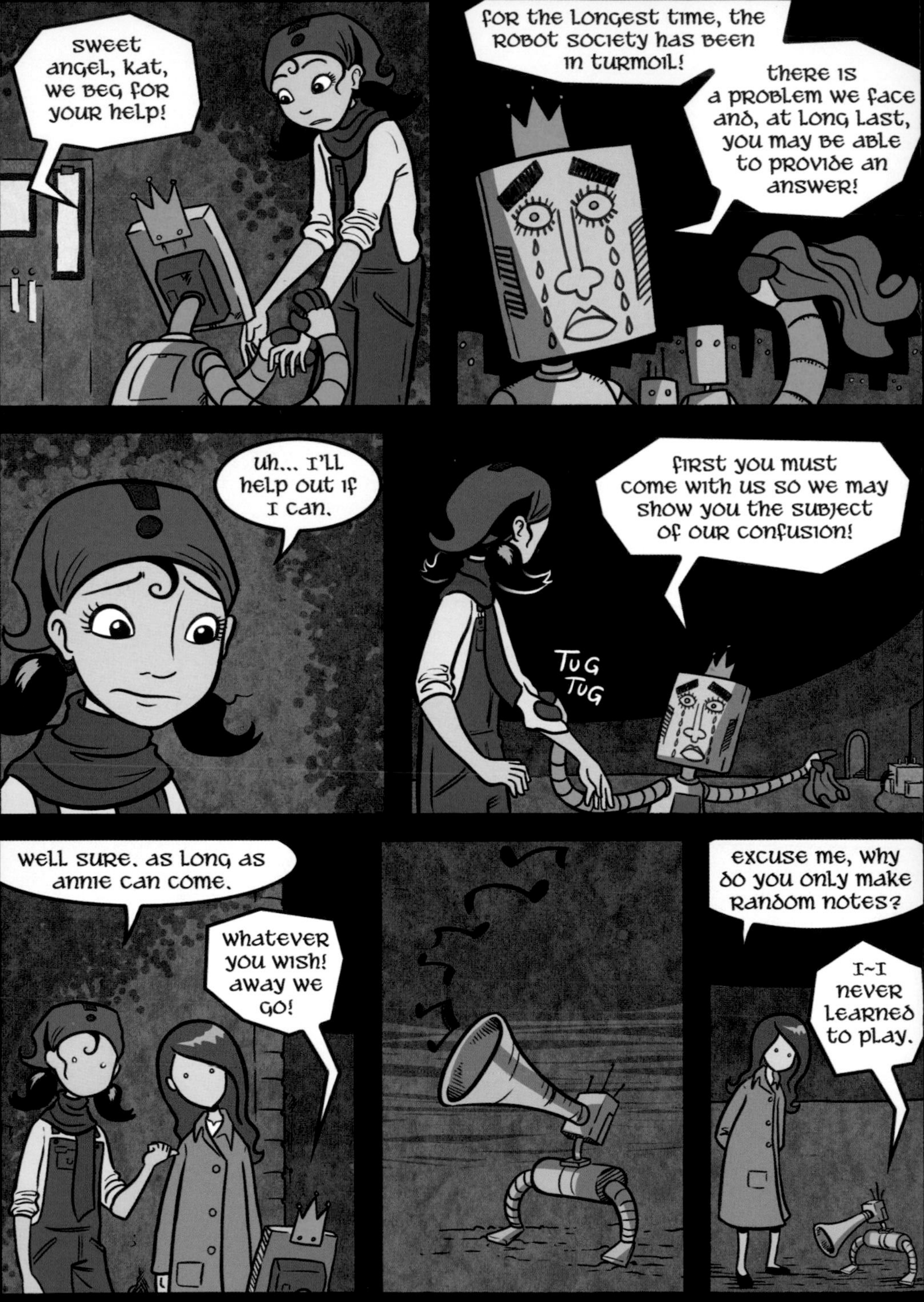
sweet angel, kat, we beg for your help!
for the longest time, the robot society has been in turmoil!
there is a problem we face and, at long last, you may be able to provide an answer!
uh... I'll help out if I can.
first you must come with us so we may show you the subject of our confusion!
TUG TUG
well sure. as long as annie can come.
whatever you wish! away we go!
excuse me, why do you only make random notes?
I-I never learned to play.

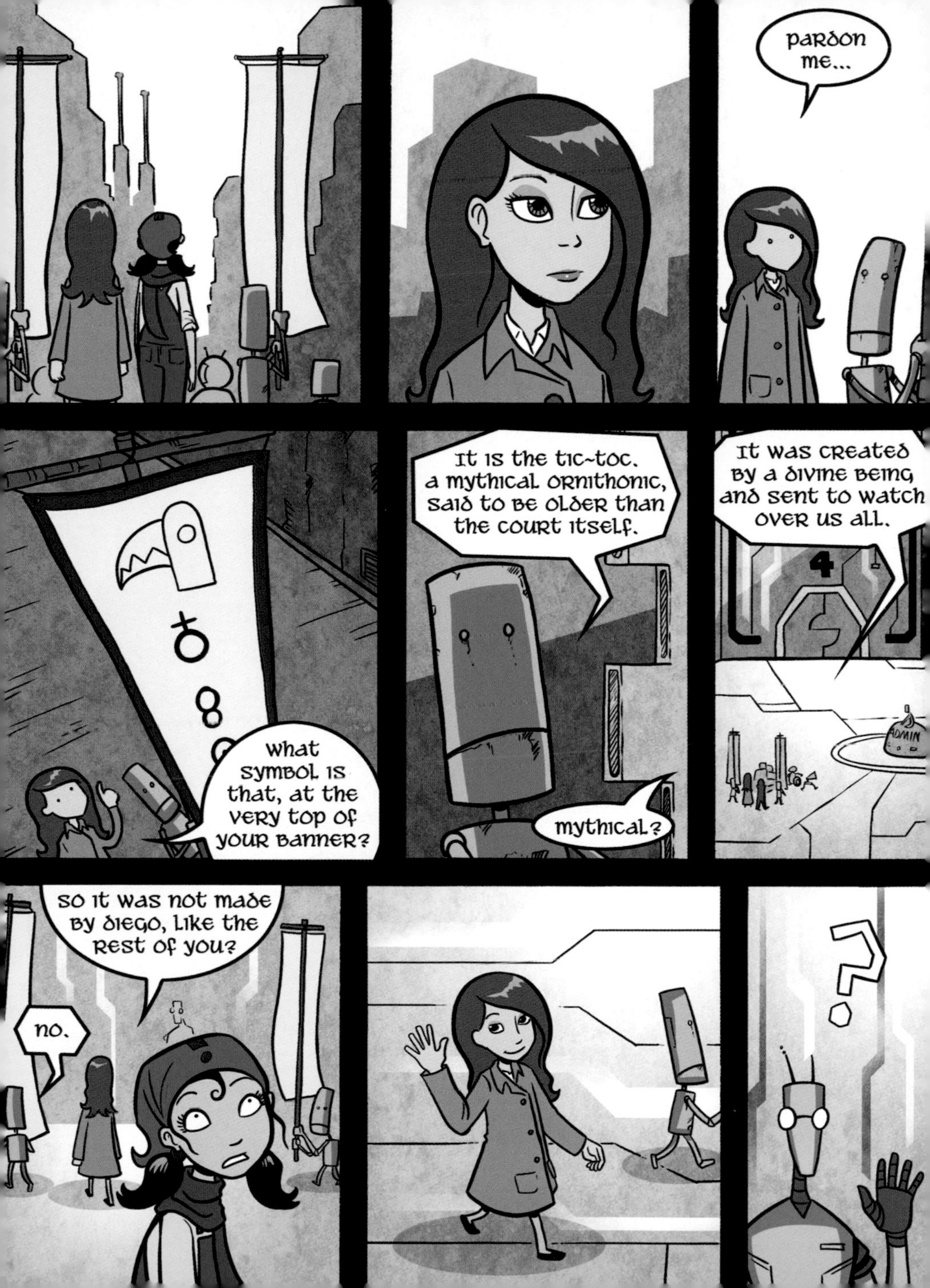
pardon me...
What symbol is that, at the very top of your banner?
It is the tic~toc. a mythical ornithonic, said to be older than the court itself.
mythical?
It was created by a divine being and sent to watch over us all.
4
ADMIN
so it was not made by diego, like the rest of you?
no.
?

and this is the last remaining original model with a memory intact.

what is all this?

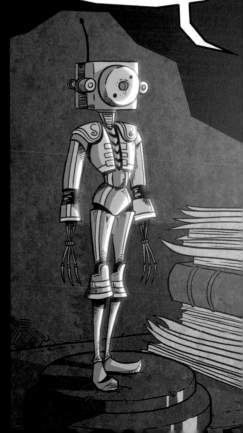

the only known collection of diego's original work before the discovery of jeanne's tomb.

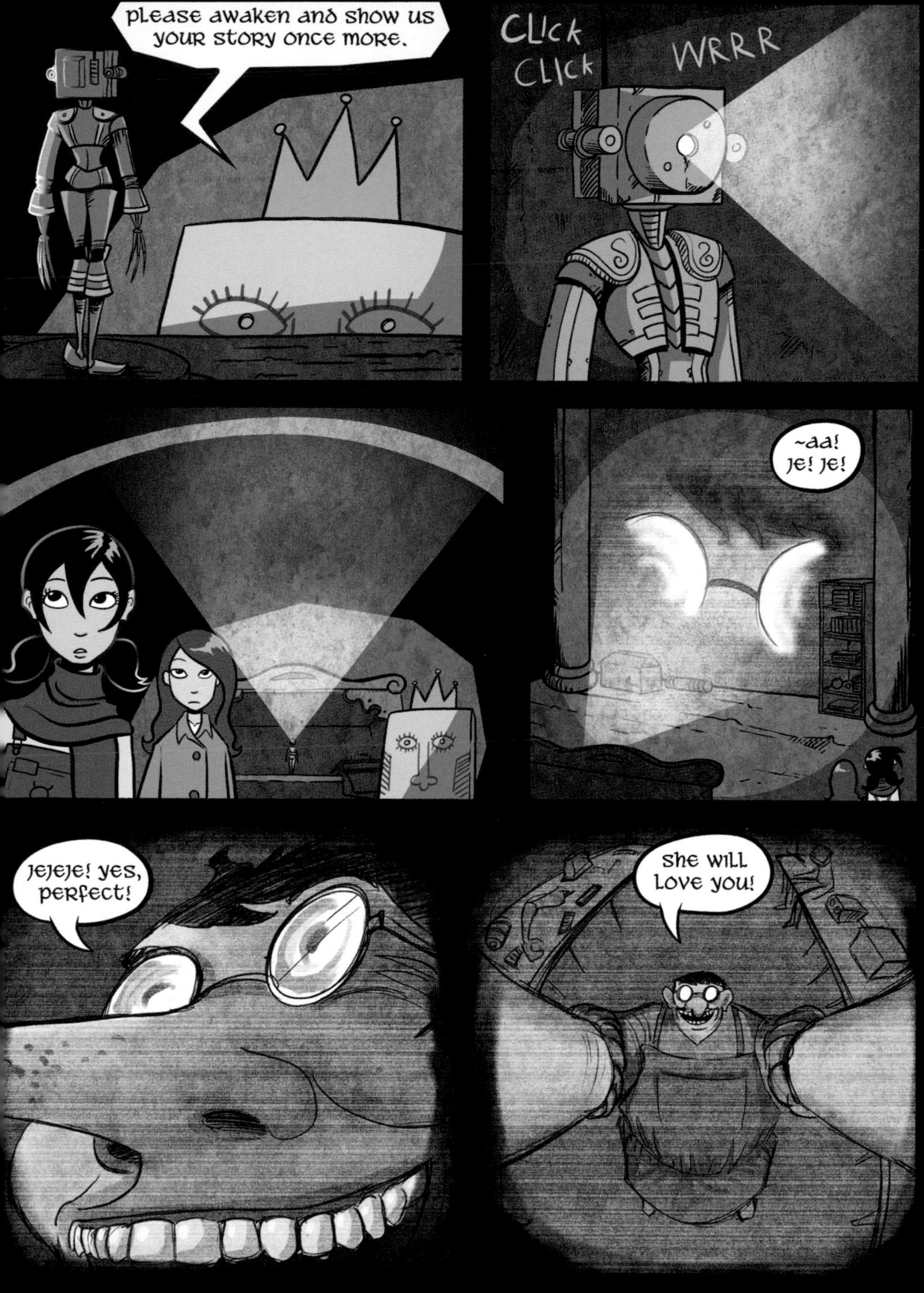
please awaken and show us your story once more.
CLICK CLICK
WRRR
~aa! JE! JE!
JEJEJE! YES, PERFECT!
SHE WILL LOVE YOU!

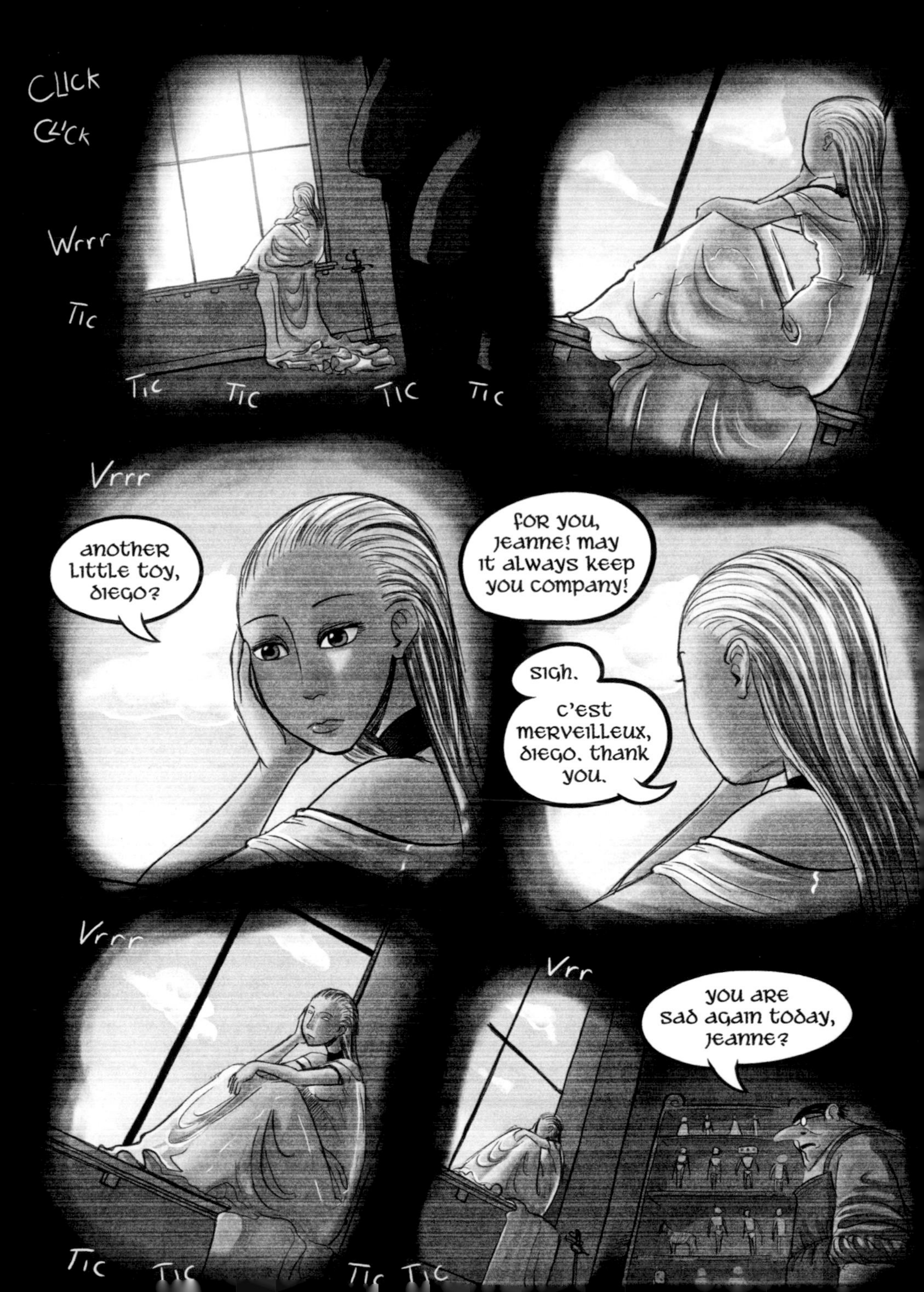
CLICK
CLICK
Wrrr
TIC
TIC TIC TIC TIC
Vrrr
another little toy, diego?
for you, jeanne! may it always keep you company!
sigh.
c'est merveilleux, diego. thank you.
Vrrr
Vrr
you are sad again today, jeanne?
TIC TIC TIC TIC

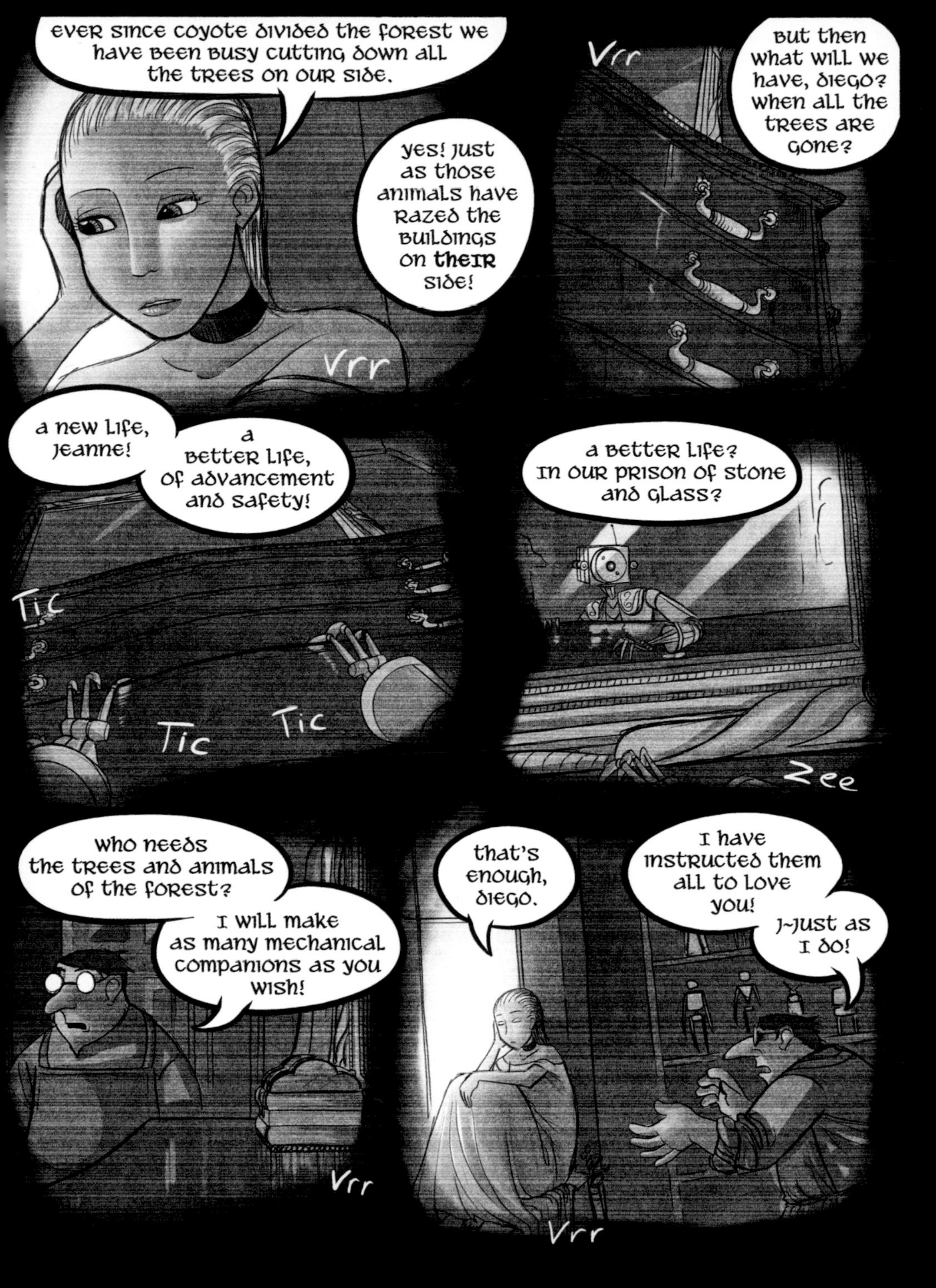
EVER SINCE COYOTE DIVIDED THE FOREST WE HAVE BEEN BUSY CUTTING DOWN ALL THE TREES ON OUR SIDE.
YES! JUST AS THOSE ANIMALS HAVE RAZED THE BUILDINGS ON THEIR SIDE!
Vrr
Vrr
BUT THEN WHAT WILL WE HAVE, DIEGO? WHEN ALL THE TREES ARE GONE?
A NEW LIFE, JEANNE!
A BETTER LIFE, OF ADVANCEMENT AND SAFETY!
Tic
Tic
Tic
A BETTER LIFE? IN OUR PRISON OF STONE AND GLASS?
Zee
WHO NEEDS THE TREES AND ANIMALS OF THE FOREST?
I WILL MAKE AS MANY MECHANICAL COMPANIONS AS YOU WISH!
Vrr
THAT'S ENOUGH, DIEGO.
I HAVE INSTRUCTED THEM ALL TO LOVE YOU!
J-JUST AS I DO!
Vrr

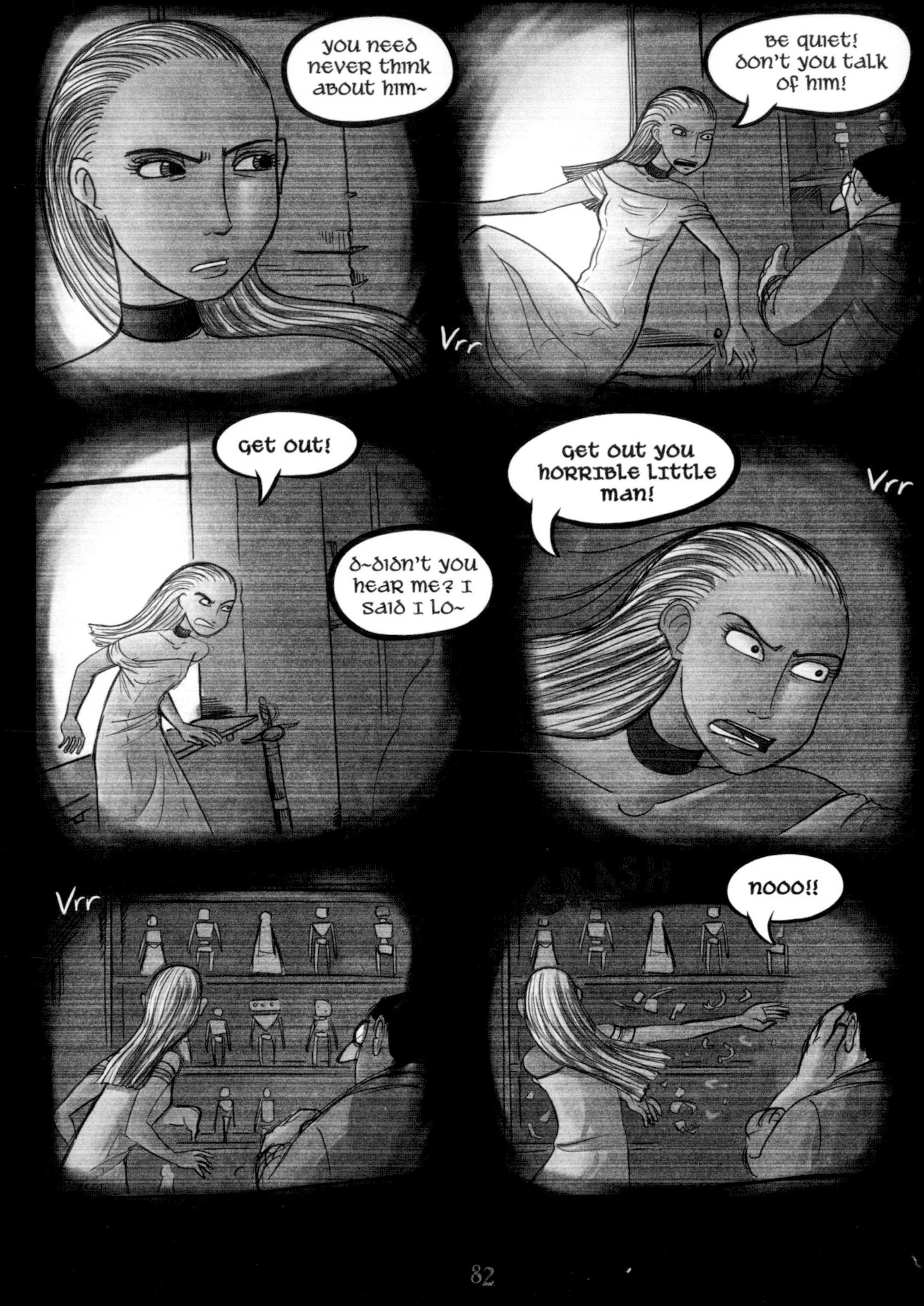
you need never think about him~
Vrr
be quiet! don't you talk of him!
get out!
d~didn't you hear me? I said I lo~
get out you horrible little man!
Vrr
Vrr
nooo!!

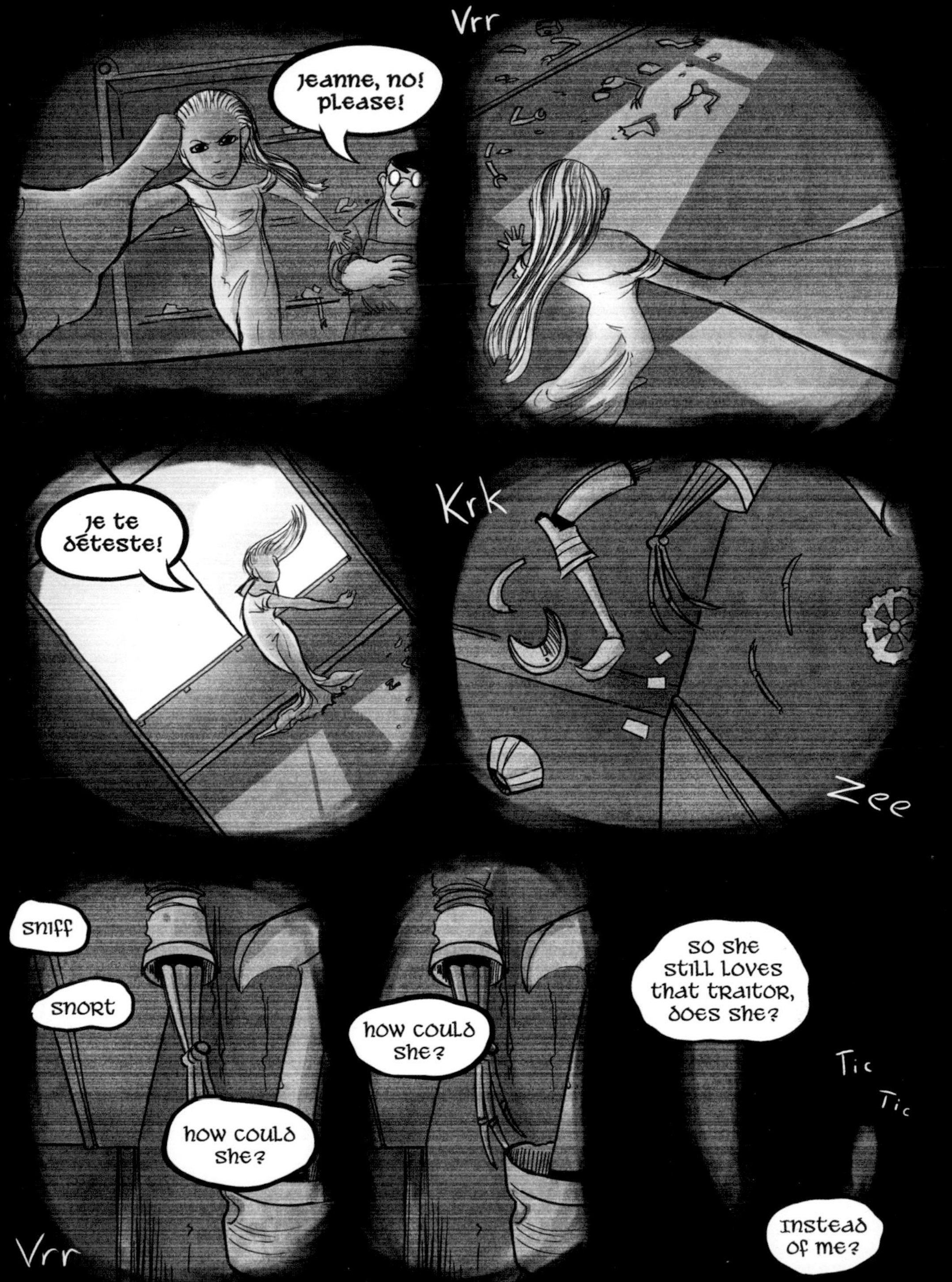
Vrr
Jeanne, no! please!
Je te déteste!
Krk
Zee
sniff
snort
how could she?
how could she?
so she still loves that traitor, does she?
Tic
Tic
instead of me?
Vrr

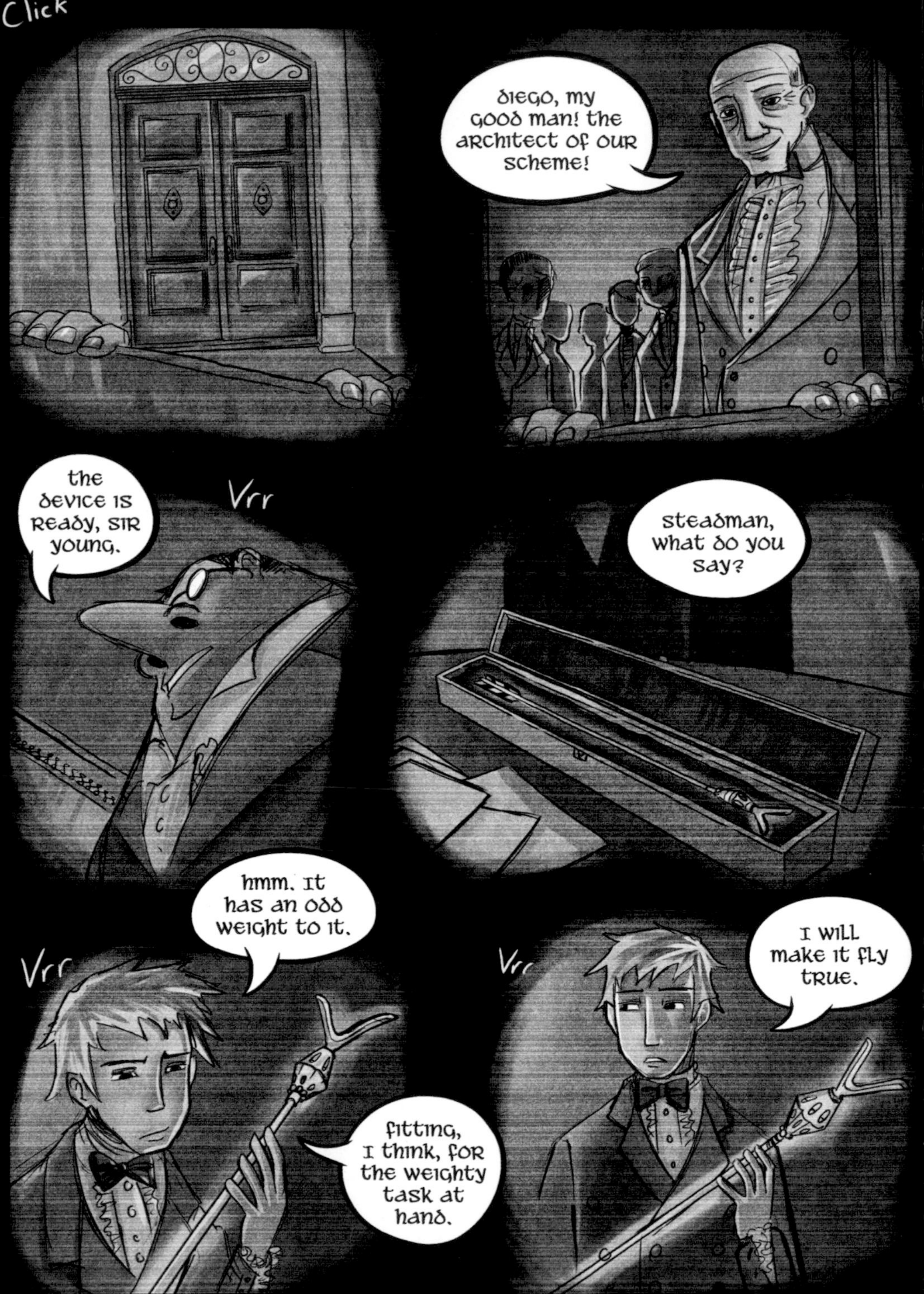
Click
Diego, my good man! the architect of our scheme!
the device is ready, sir young.
Vrr
steadman, what do you say?
hmm. it has an odd weight to it.
Vrr
fitting, I think, for the weighty task at hand.
Vrr
I will make it fly true.

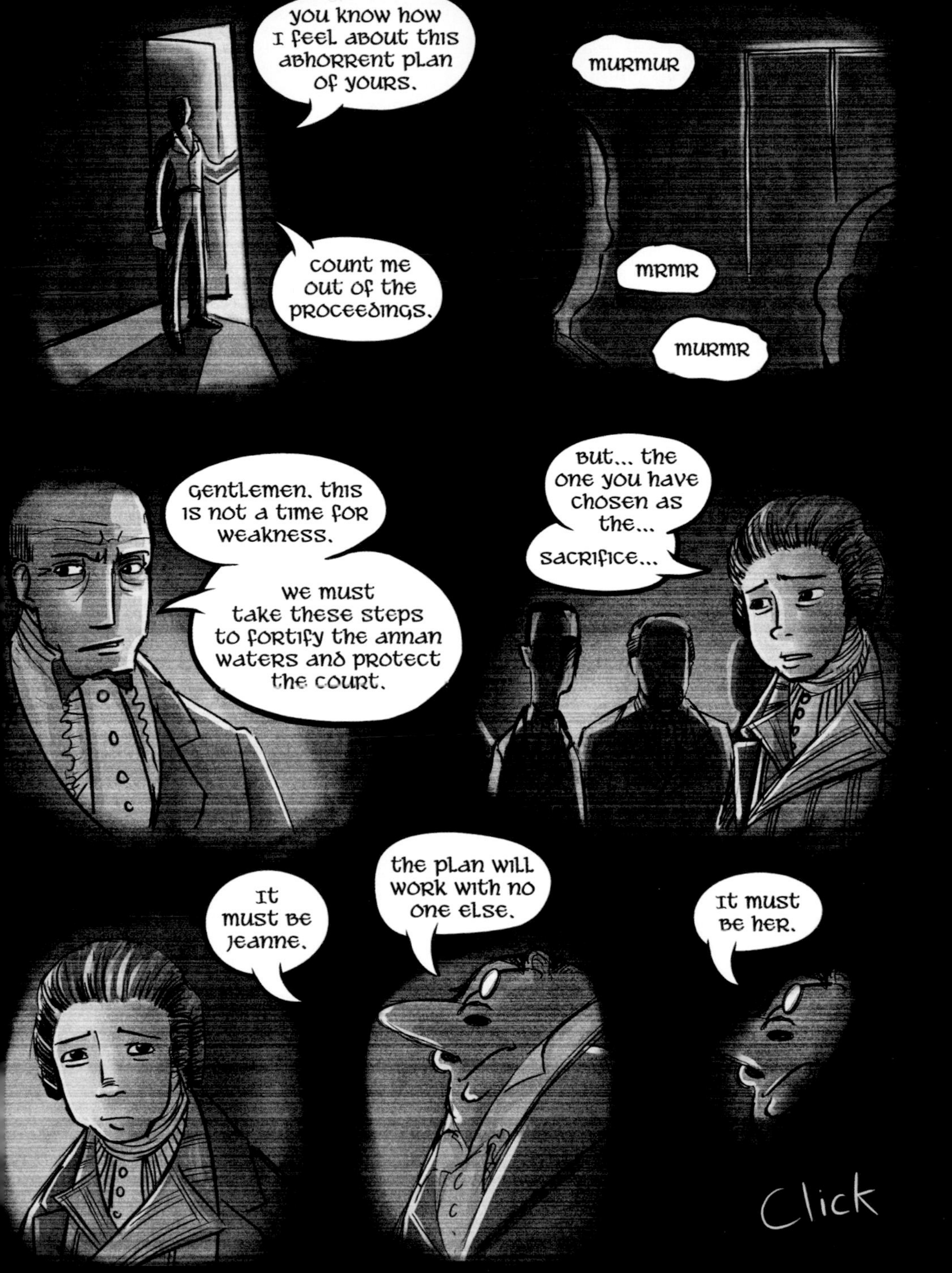
you know how I feel about this abhorrent plan of yours.
count me out of the proceedings.
murmur
mrmr
murmr
gentlemen, this is not a time for weakness.
we must take these steps to fortify the annan waters and protect the count.
but... the one you have chosen as the...
sacrifice...
it must be jeanne.
the plan will work with no one else.
it must be her.
Click

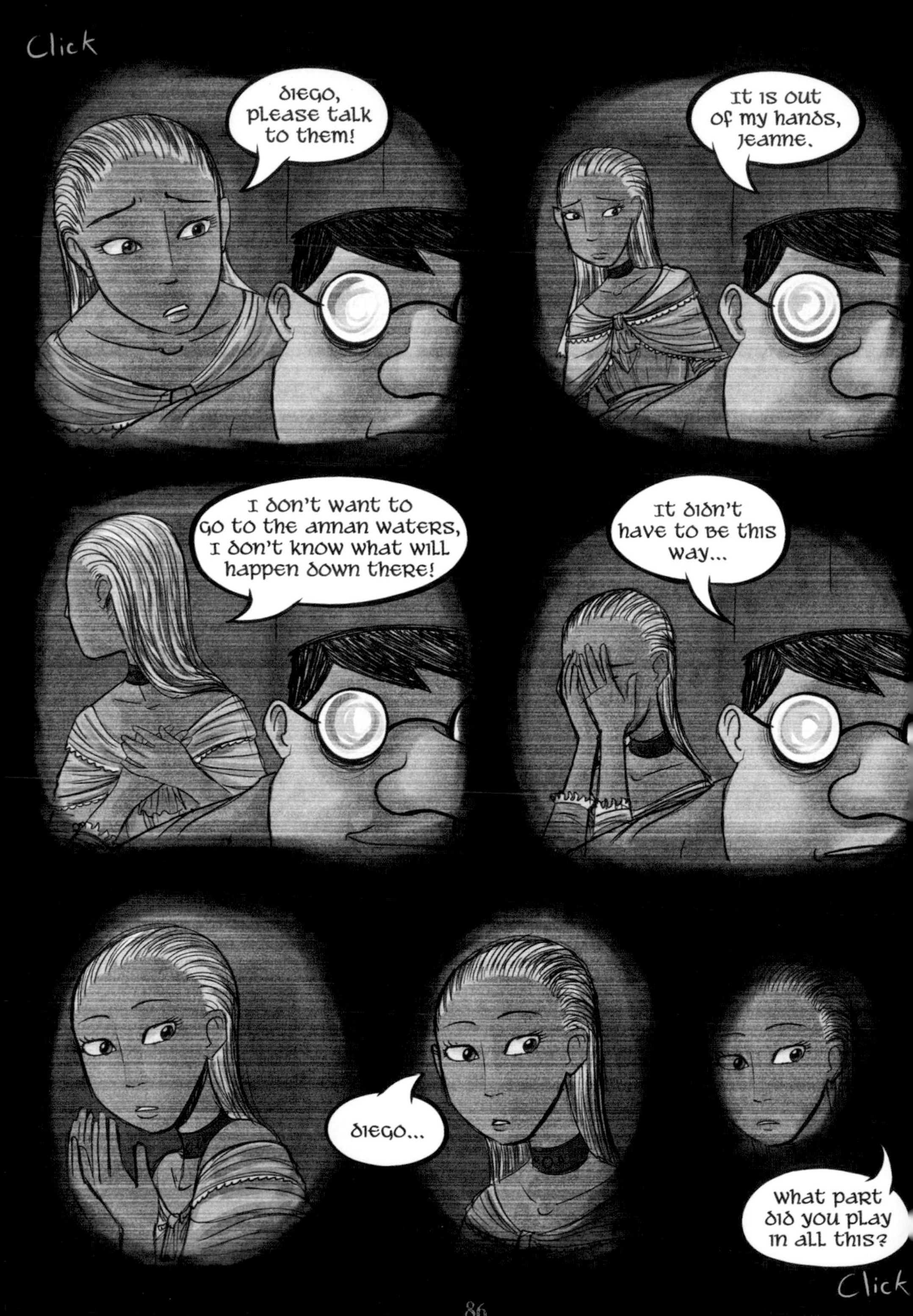
Click
Diego, please talk to them!
It is out of my hands, Jeanne.
I don't want to go to the Annan Waters, I don't know what will happen down there!
It didn't have to be this way...
Diego...
What part did you play in all this?
Click

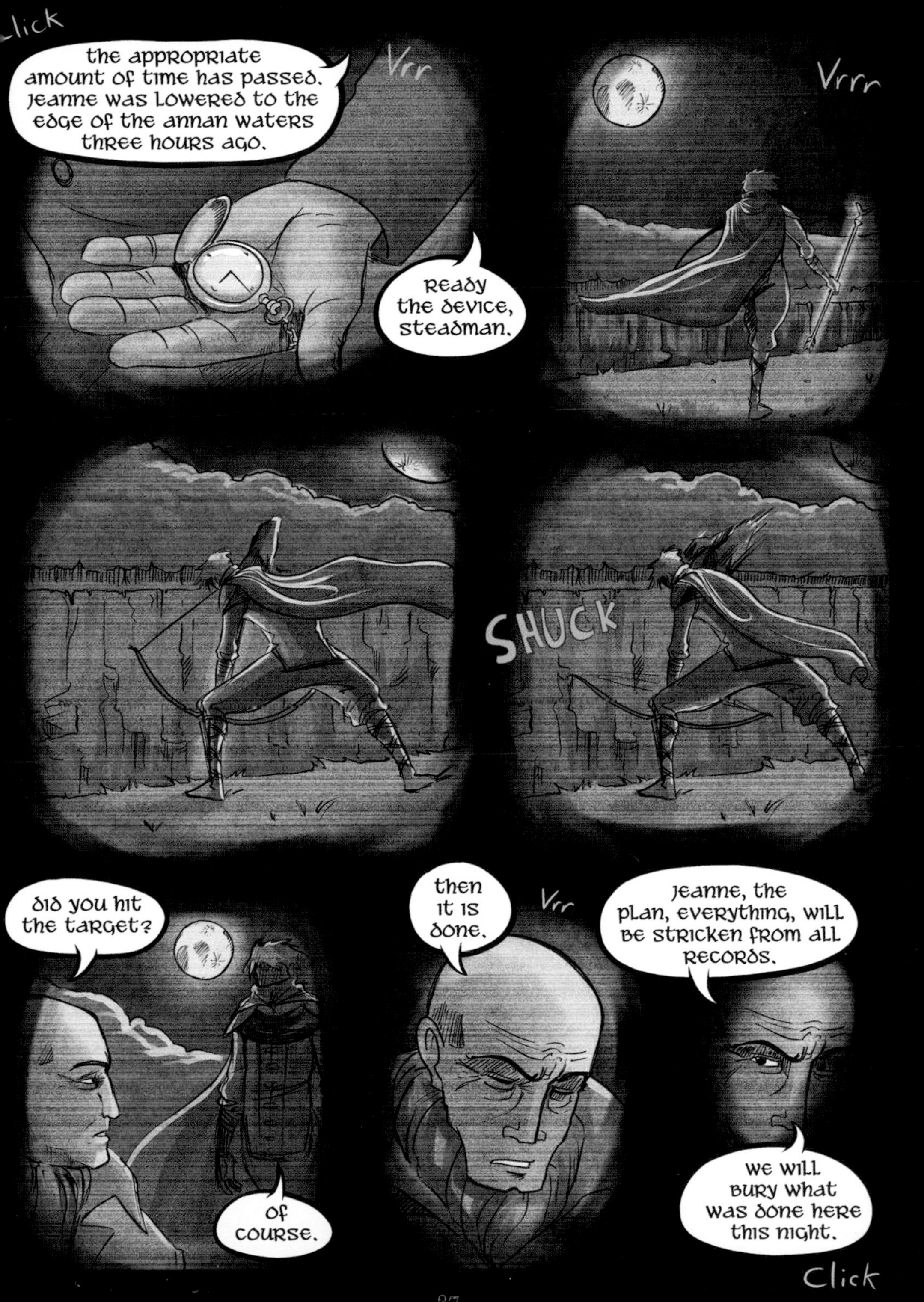

Click
the appropriate amount of time has passed. Jeanne was lowered to the edge of the annan waters three hours ago.
Vrr
Ready the device, steadman.
Vrrr
SHUCK
Did you hit the target?
Of course.
Vrr
Then it is done.
Jeanne, the plan, everything, will be stricken from all records.
We will bury what was done here this night.
Click

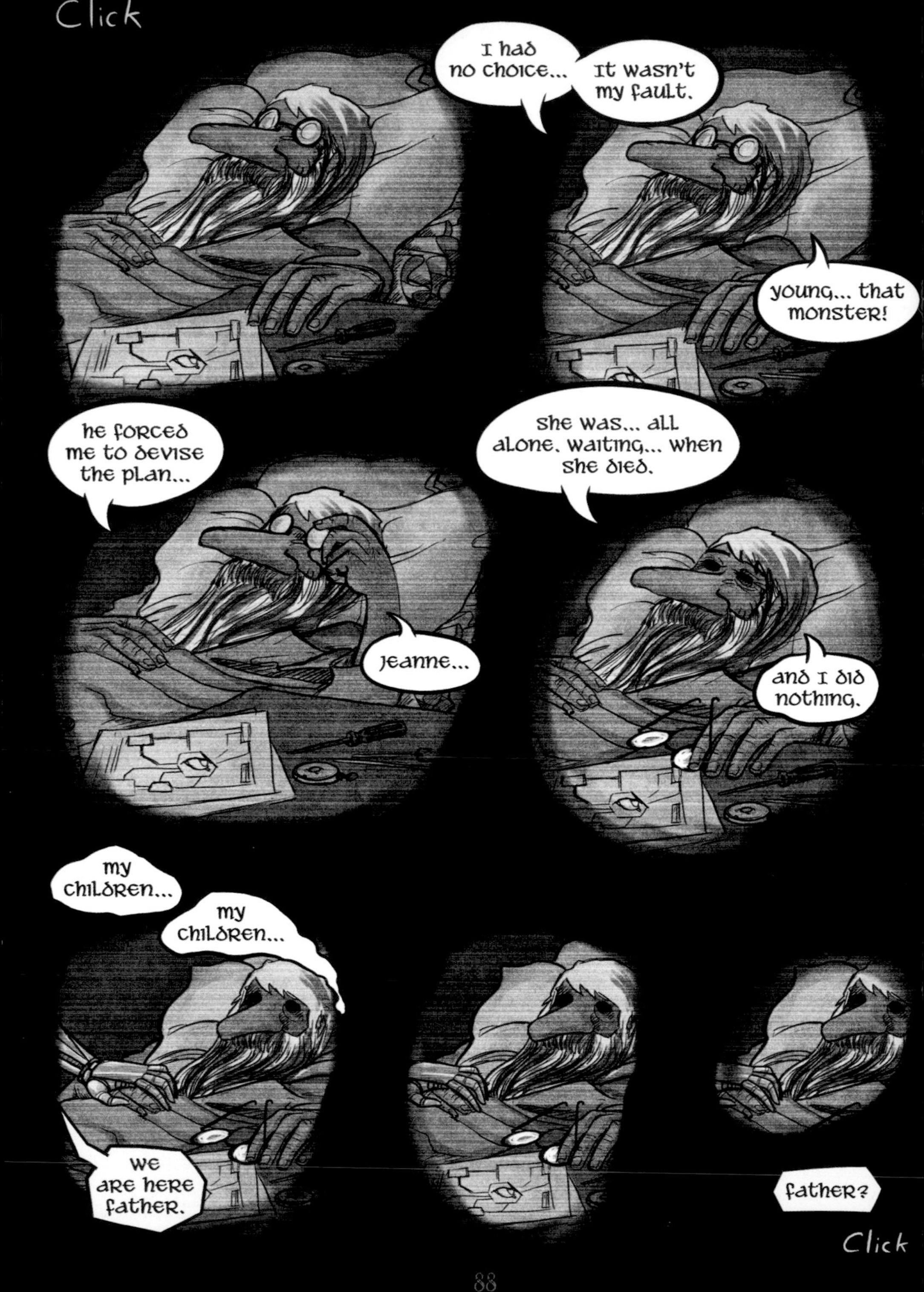
Click
I had no choice...
It wasn't my fault.
young... that monster!
he forced me to devise the plan...
Jeanne...
she was... all alone, waiting... when she died.
and I did nothing.
my children...
my children...
we are here father.
father?
Click

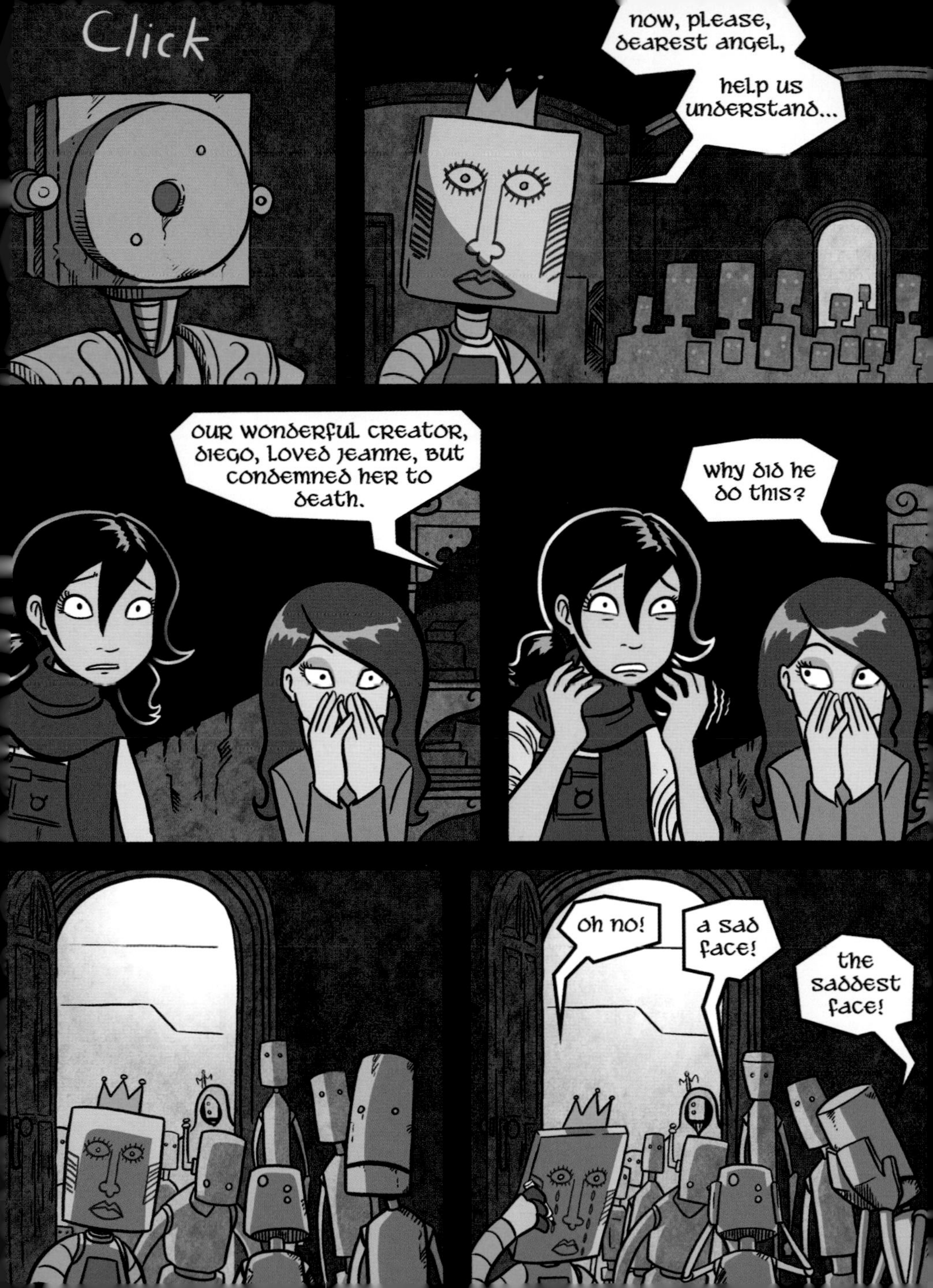
Click
now, please, dearest angel,
help us understand...
our wonderful creator, diego, loved jeanne, but condemned her to death.
why did he do this?
oh no!
a sad face!
the saddest face!

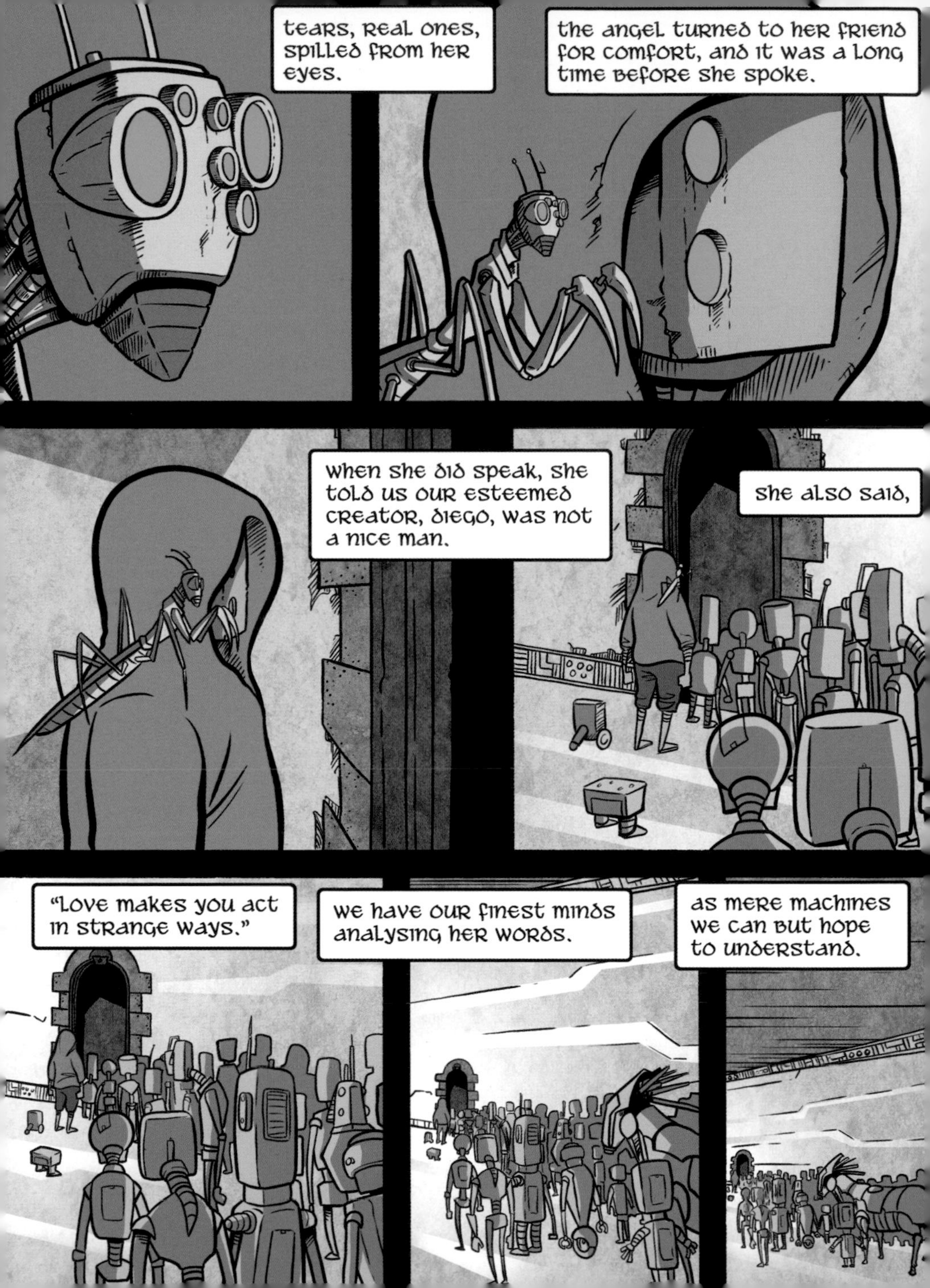
tears, real ones, spilled from her eyes.
the angel turned to her friend for comfort, and it was a long time before she spoke.
when she did speak, she told us our esteemed creator, diego, was not a nice man.
she also said,
"love makes you act in strange ways."
we have our finest minds analysing her words.
as mere machines we can but hope to understand.

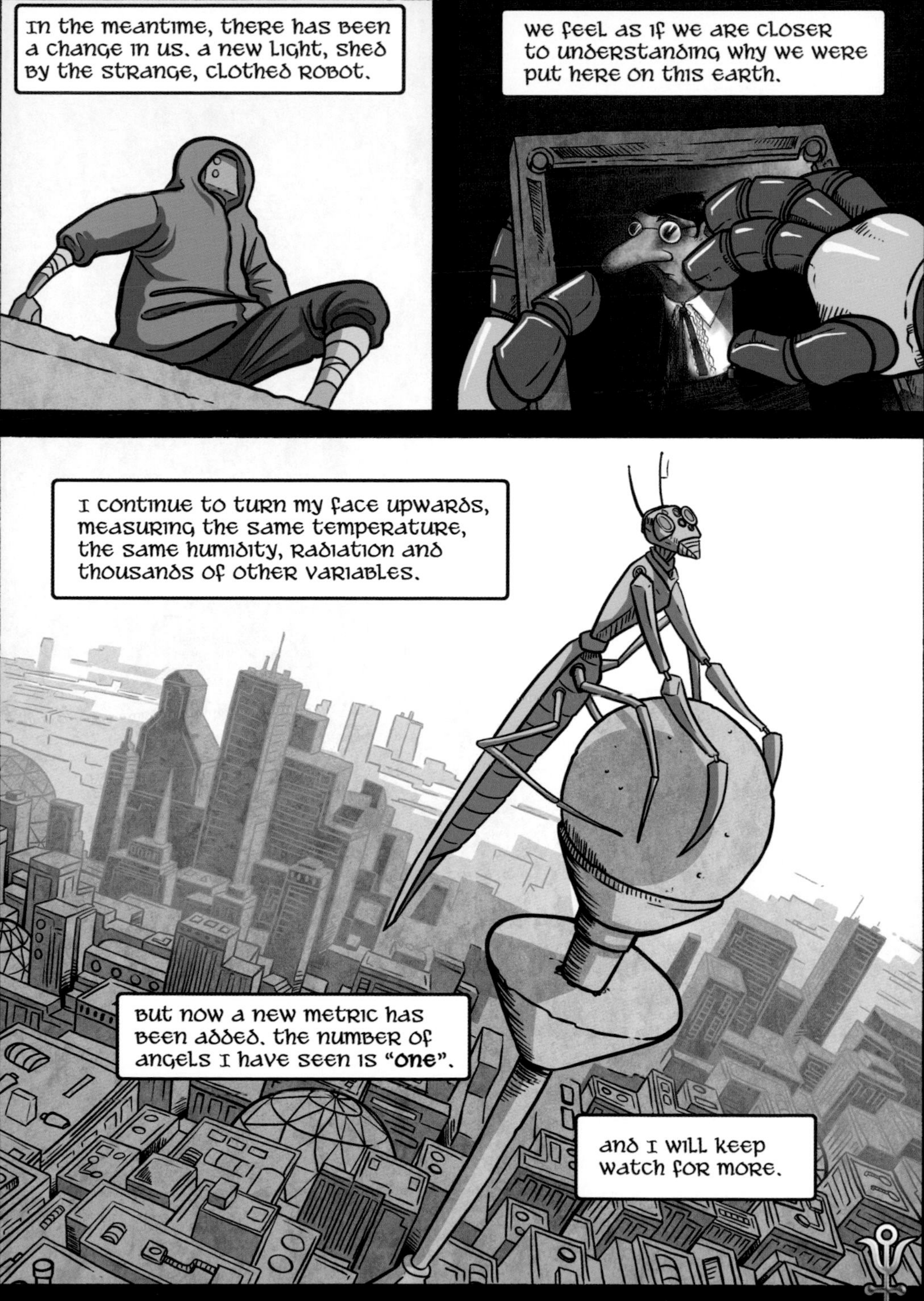
In the meantime, there has been a change in us. a new light, shed by the strange, clothed robot.
we feel as if we are closer to understanding why we were put here on this earth.
I continue to turn my face upwards, measuring the same temperature, the same humidity, radiation and thousands of other variables.
But now a new metric has been added. the number of angels I have seen is "one".
and I will keep watch for more.

Robot Handling
Section H: Miscellaneous

COURT ROBOTS MAY SOMETIMES BECOME ATTRACTED TO YOU.
If you find yourself in this situation, please observe
the following steps.

1: Spurn all advances. The robot may try to ply you with tacky gifts and/or poorly constructed poetry. Make it clear they have failed to impress you.	
2: Define boundaries. Remind the robot you are a higher order of being, while it is merely an appliance. Romantic longing leads to an inefficient appliance.	
3: Set an example. If possible, ensure this behaviour is not repeated by making a mockery of it in front of its robot peers.	

Gunnerkrigg Court

Chapter 26:
The Old Dog's Tricks

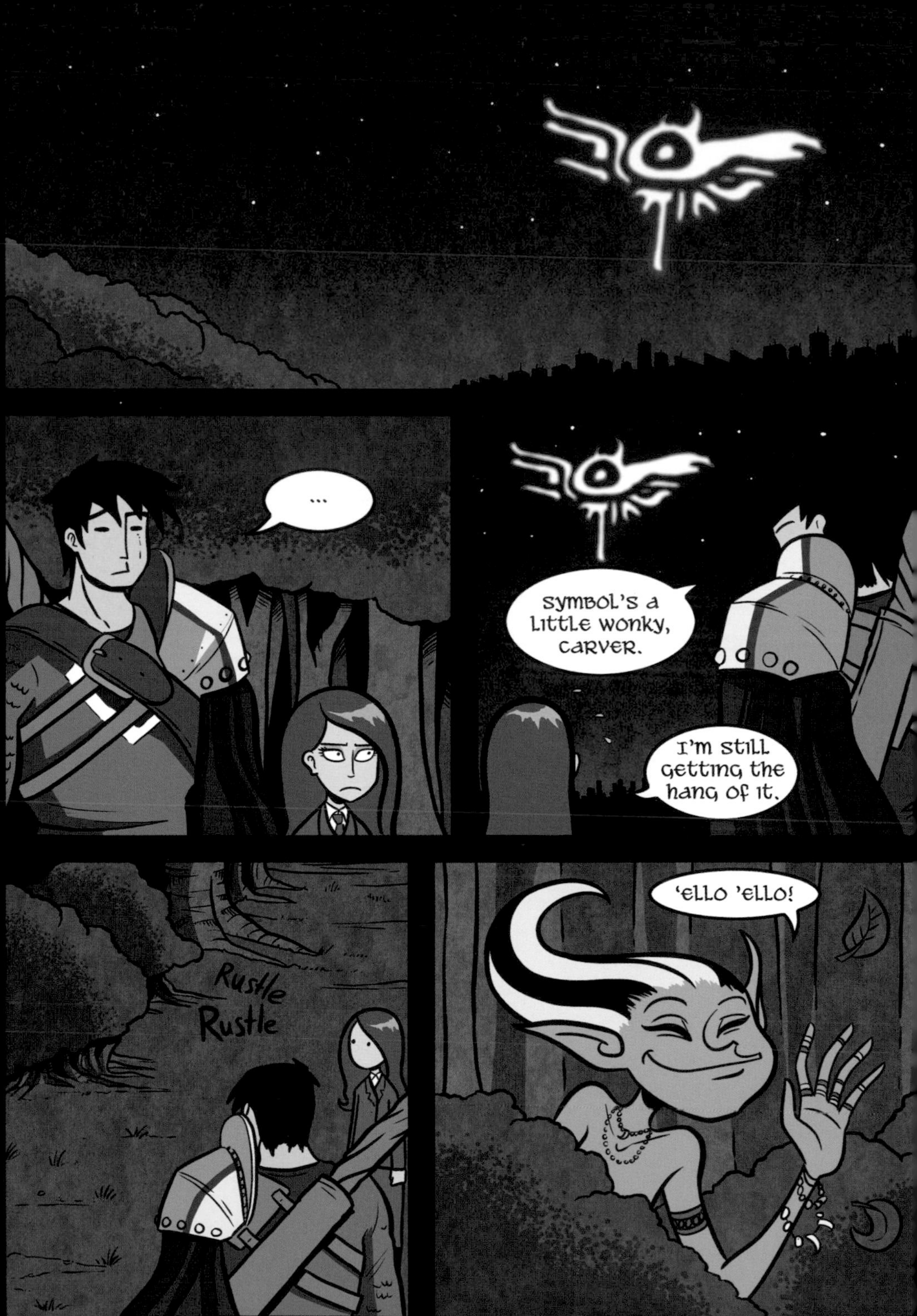
...
Symbol's a little wonky, Carver.
I'm still getting the hang of it.
Rustle
Rustle
'ello 'ello!

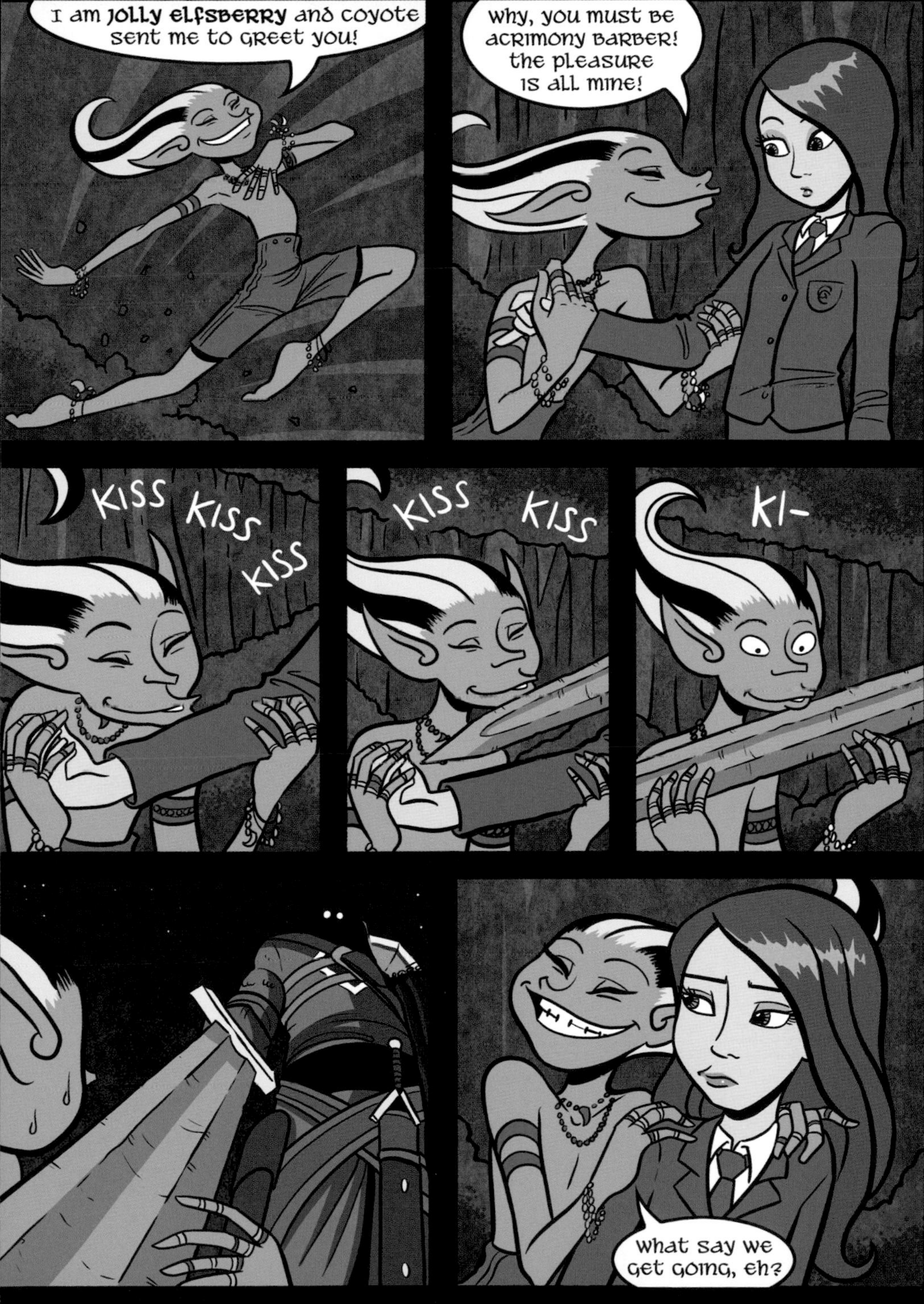
I am JOLLY ELFSBERRY and coyote sent me to greet you!
Why, you must be acrimony barber! the pleasure is all mine!
KISS KISS KISS
KISS KISS
KI-
What say we get going, eh?

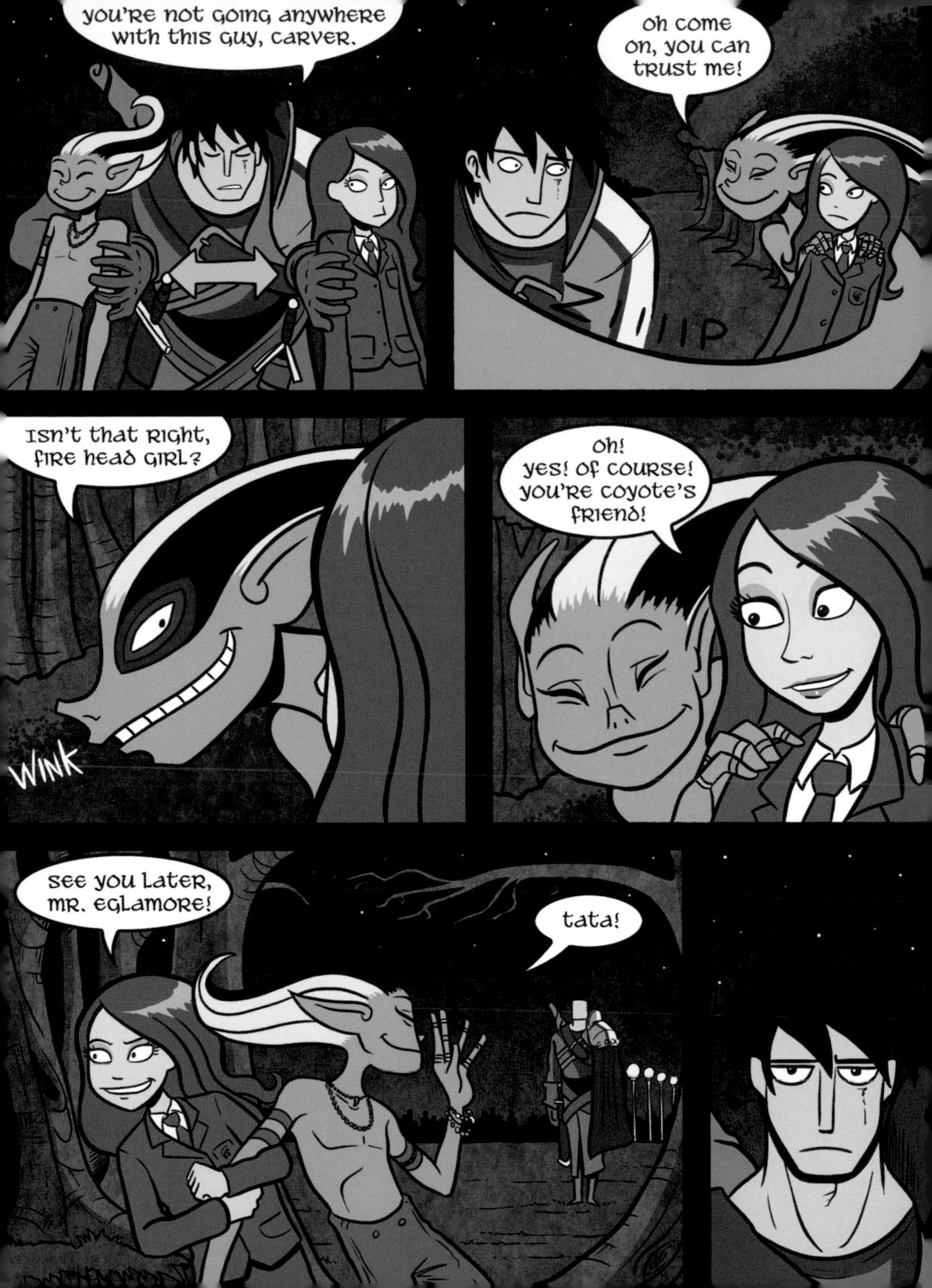
you're not going anywhere with this guy, carver.
oh come on, you can trust me!
ZIIIP
isn't that right, fire head girl?
WINK
oh! yes! of course! you're coyote's friend!
see you later, mr. eglamore!
tata!

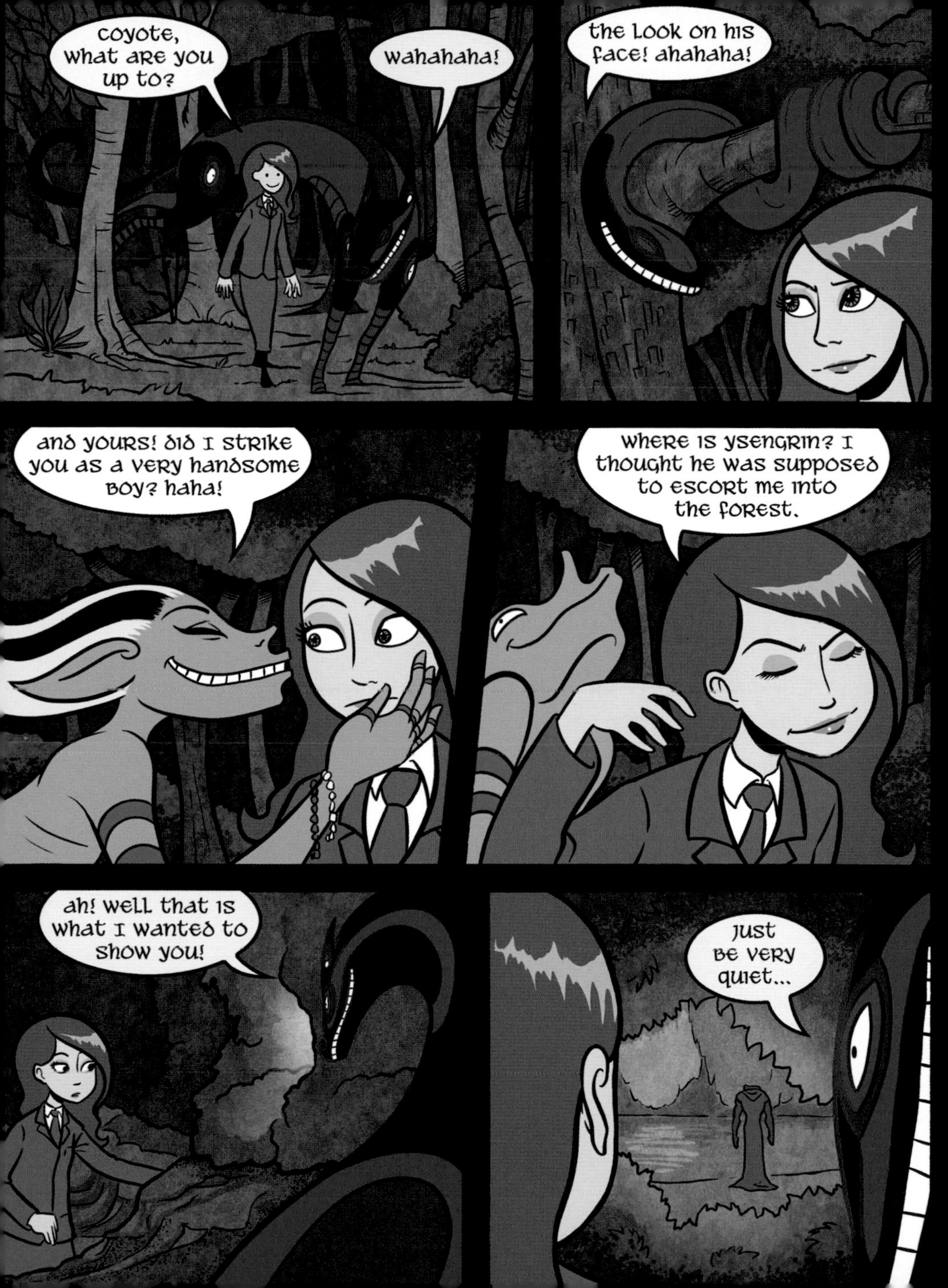
coyote, what are you up to?
wahahaha!
the look on his face! ahahaha!
and yours! did I strike you as a very handsome boy? haha!
where is ysengrin? I thought he was supposed to escort me into the forest.
ah! well that is what I wanted to show you!
just be very quiet...

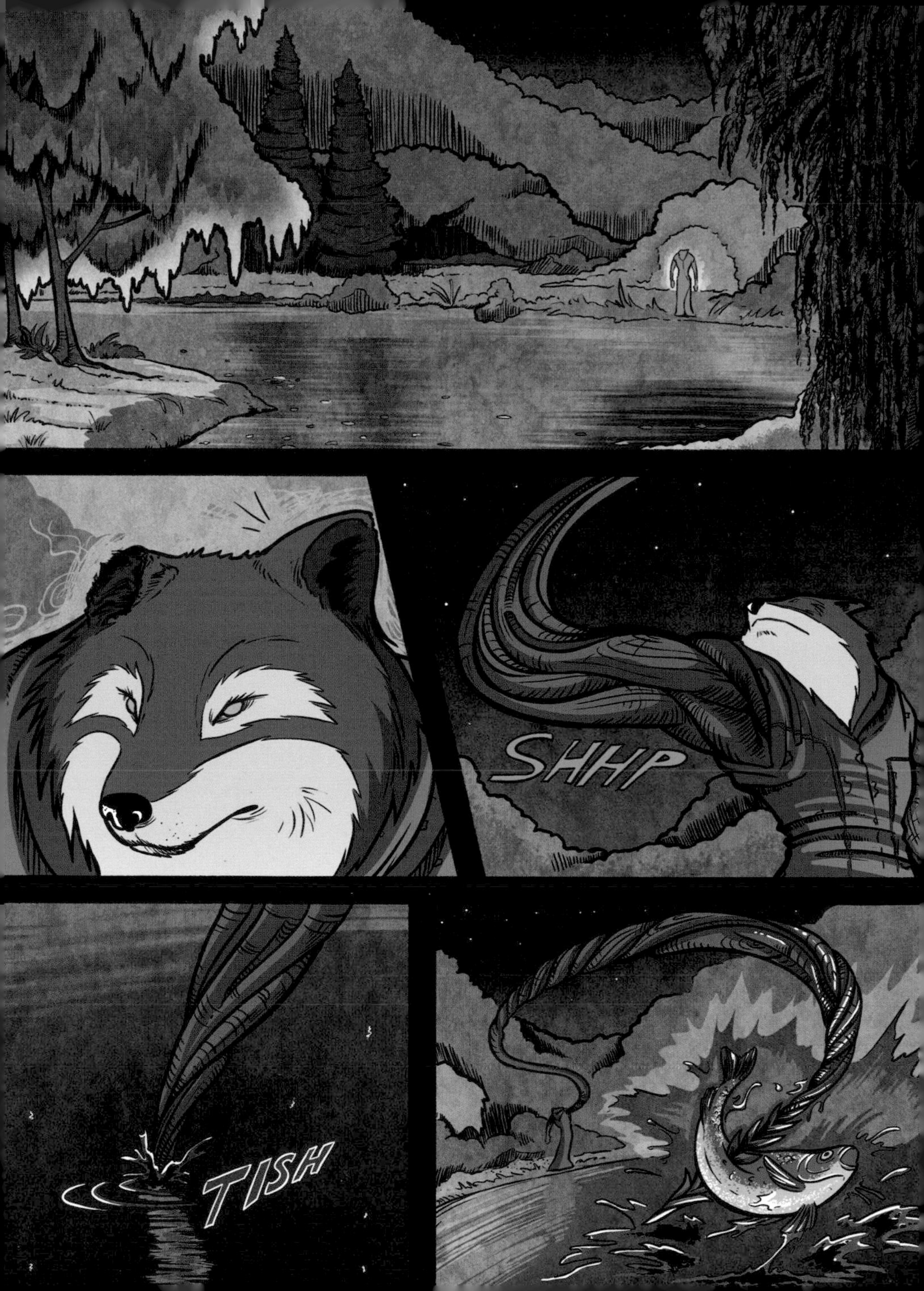
SHHP
TISH

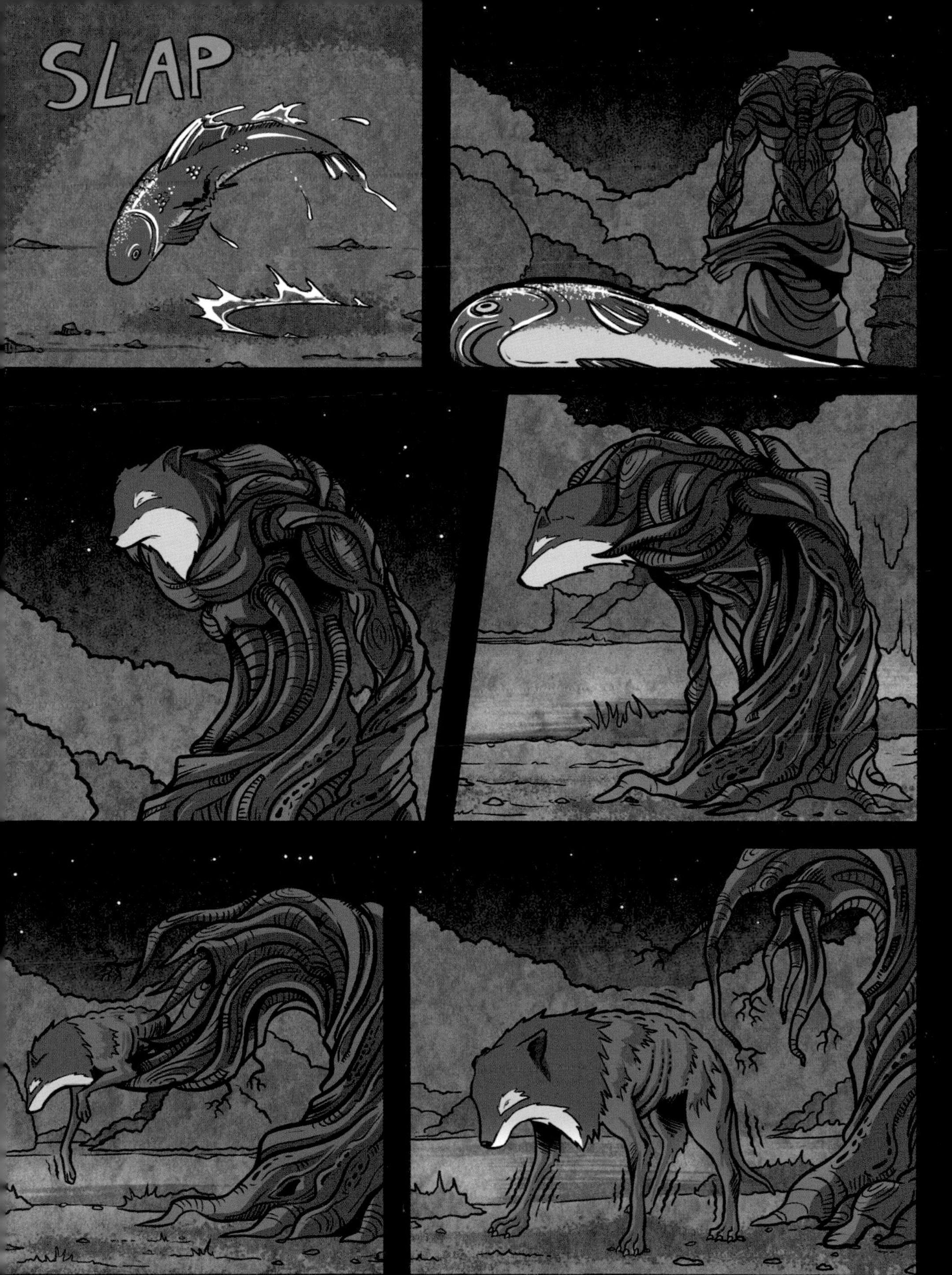
SLAP

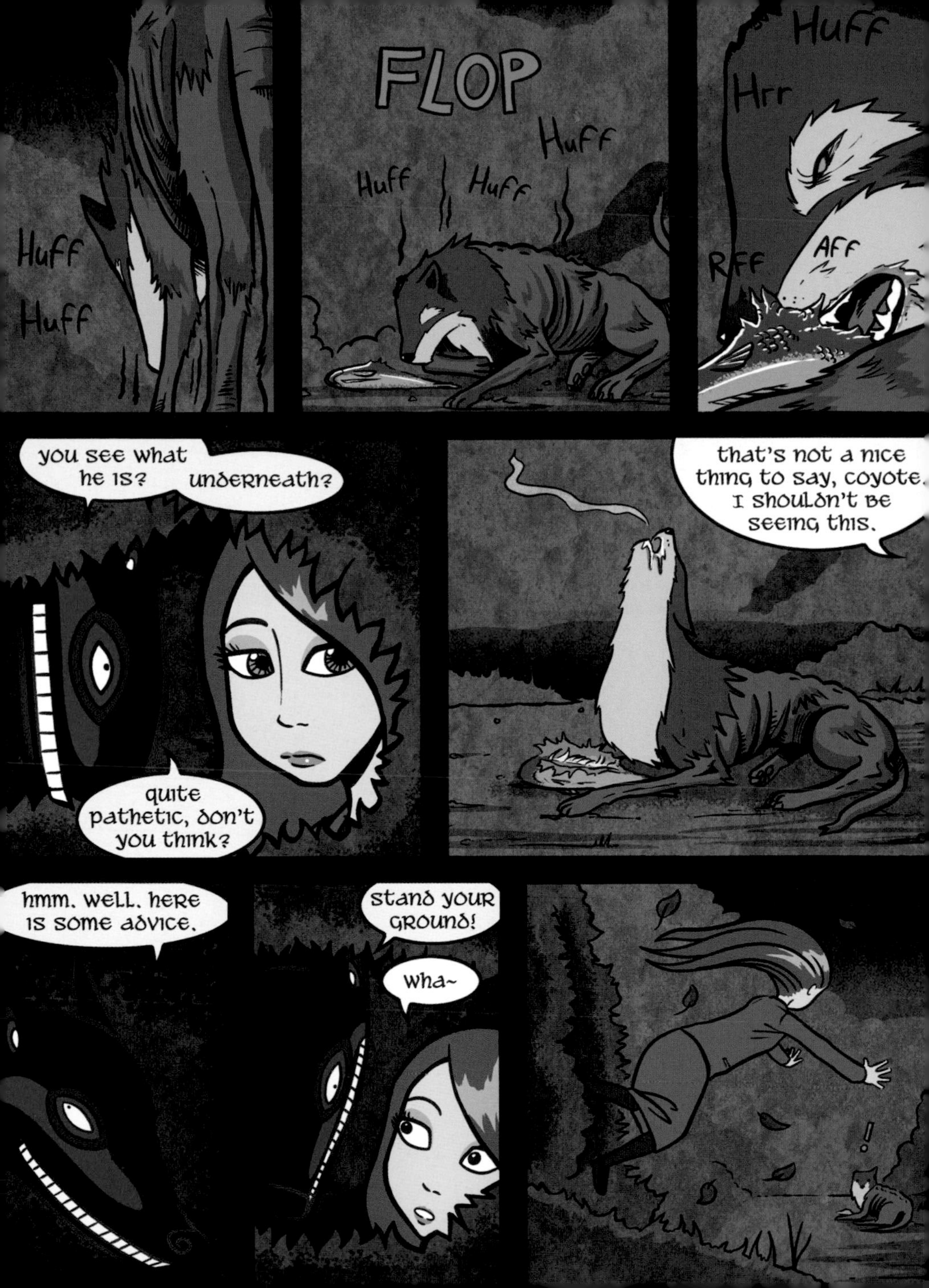
Huff
Huff
FLOP
Huff
Huff
Huff
Huff
Hrr
RFF
AFF
you see what he is? underneath?
quite pathetic, don't you think?
that's not a nice thing to say, coyote. I shouldn't be seeing this.
hmm. well. here is some advice.
stand your ground!
Wha~
!

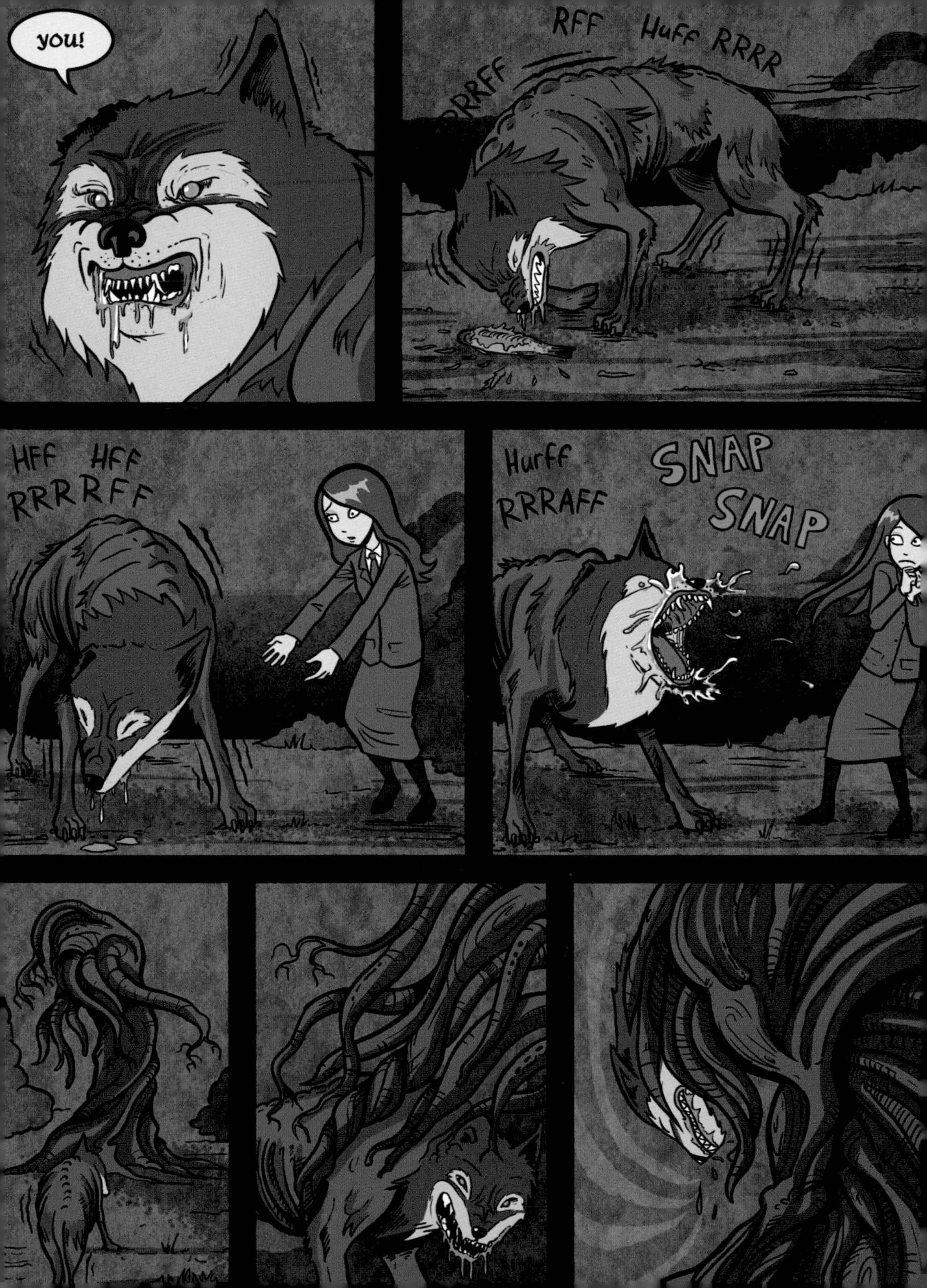
YOU!
RFF Huff RRRR
RRRFF
HFF HFF
RRRRFF
Hurff
RRRAFF
SNAP
SNAP

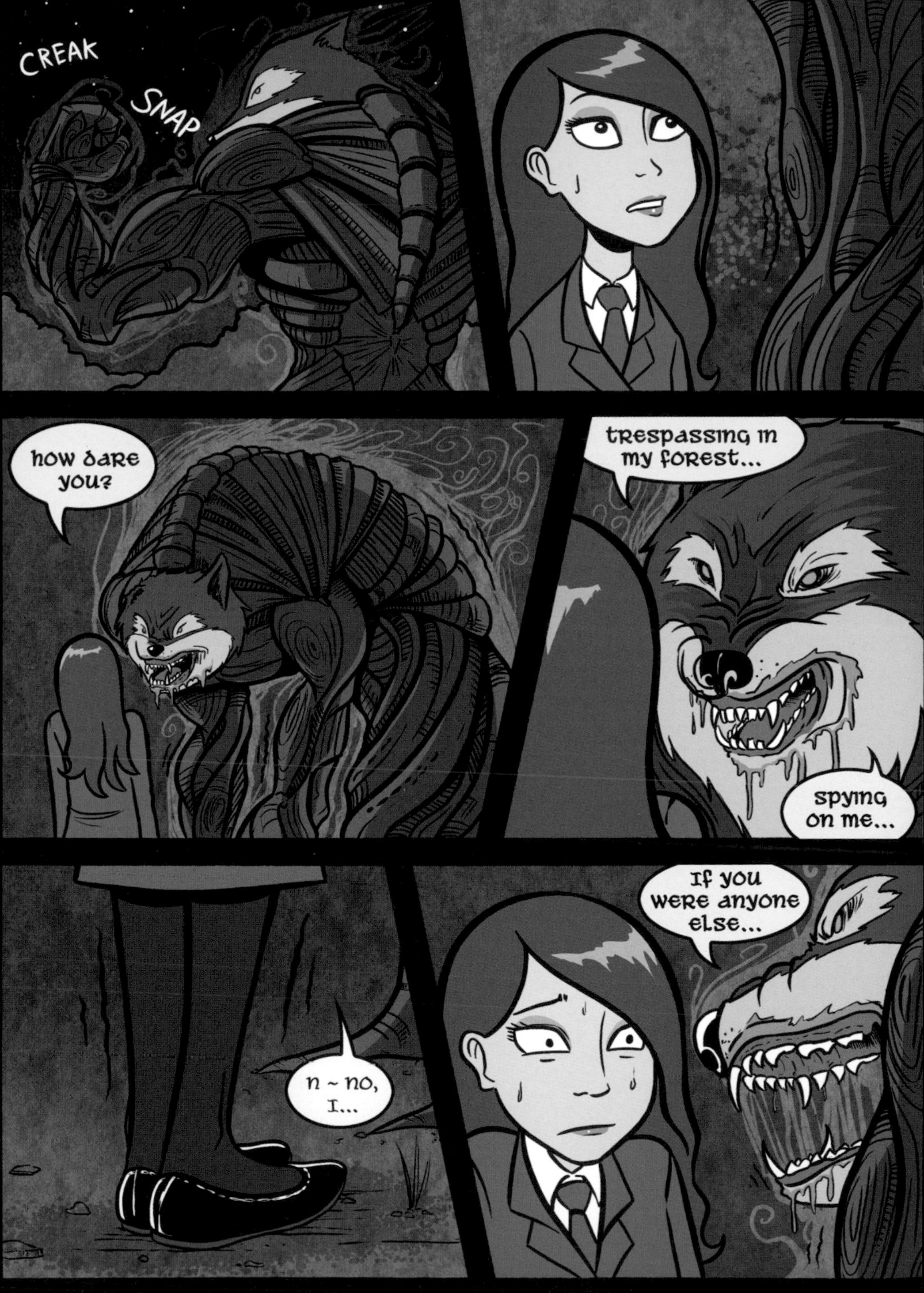
CREAK
SNAP
how dare you?
trespassing in my forest...
spying on me...
If you were anyone else...
n ~ no, I...

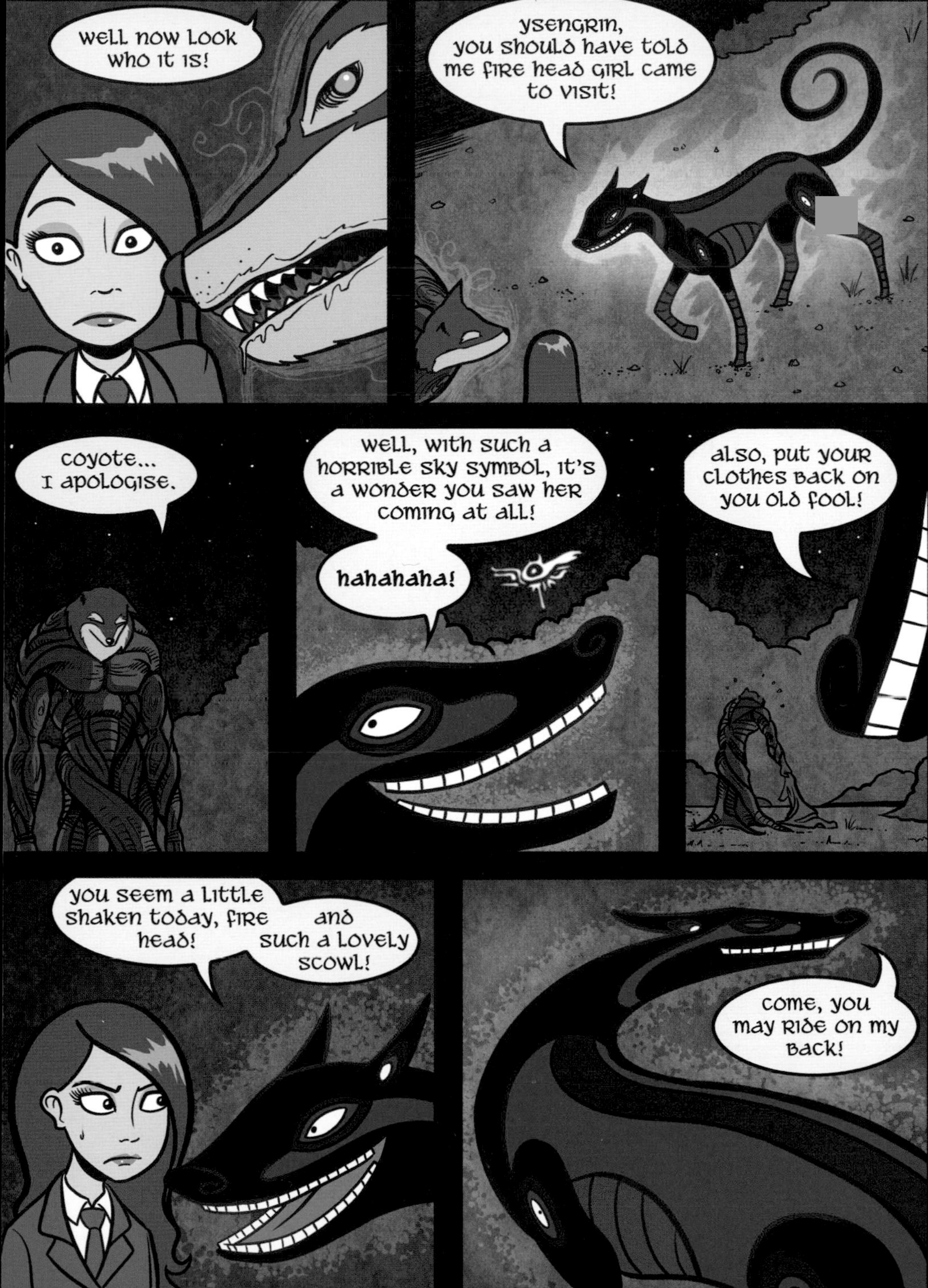
well now look who it is!
ysengrin, you should have told me fire head girl came to visit!
coyote... I apologise.
well, with such a horrible sky symbol, it's a wonder you saw her coming at all!
hahahaha!
also, put your clothes back on you old fool!
you seem a little shaken today, fire head!
and such a lovely scowl!
come, you may ride on my back!

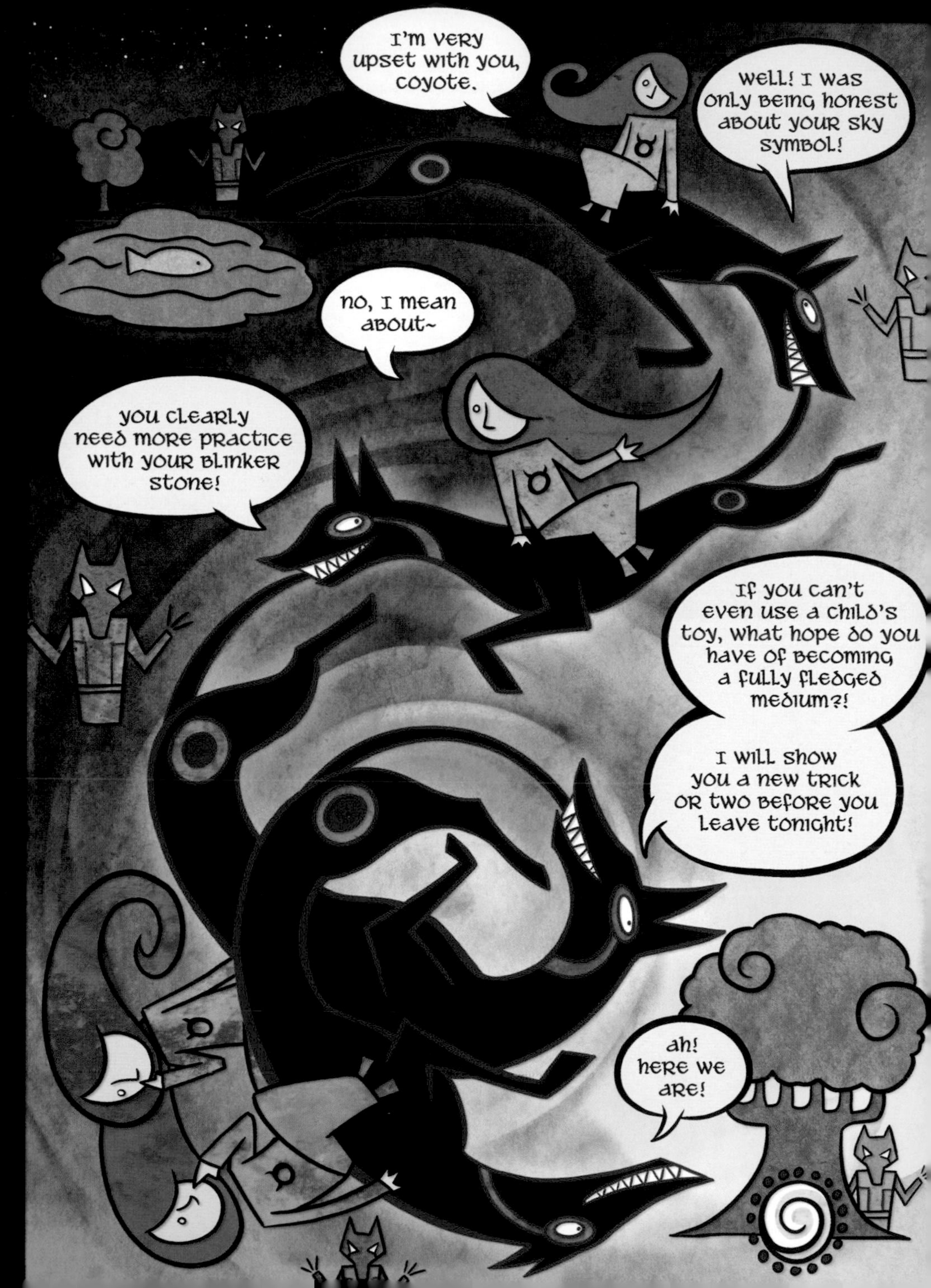
I'm very upset with you, coyote.
well! I was only being honest about your sky symbol!
no, I mean about~
you clearly need more practice with your blinker stone!
If you can't even use a child's toy, what hope do you have of becoming a fully fledged medium?!
I will show you a new trick or two before you leave tonight!
ah! here we are!

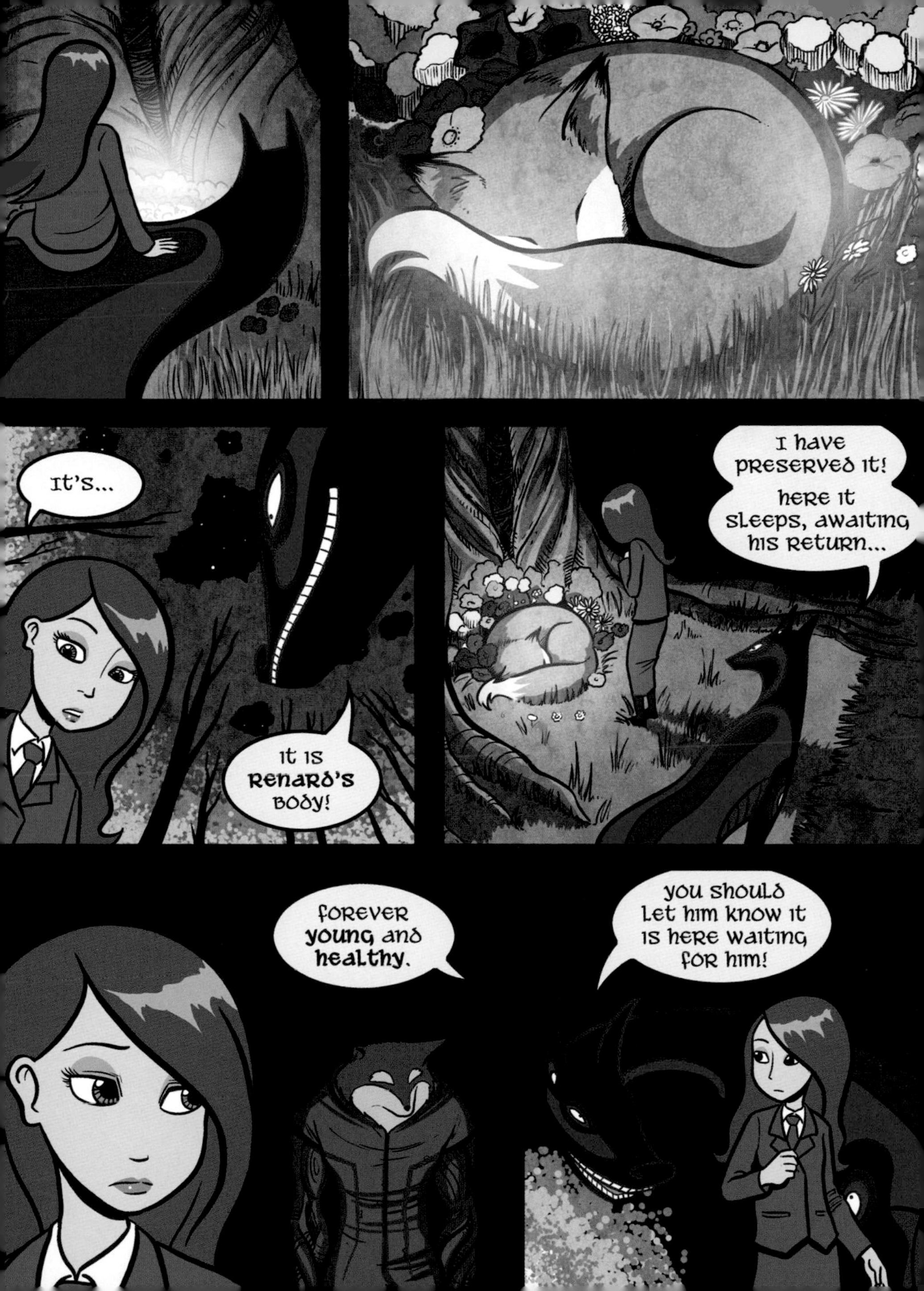
It's...
it is Renard's body!
I have preserved it!
here it sleeps, awaiting his return...
forever young and healthy.
you should let him know it is here waiting for him!

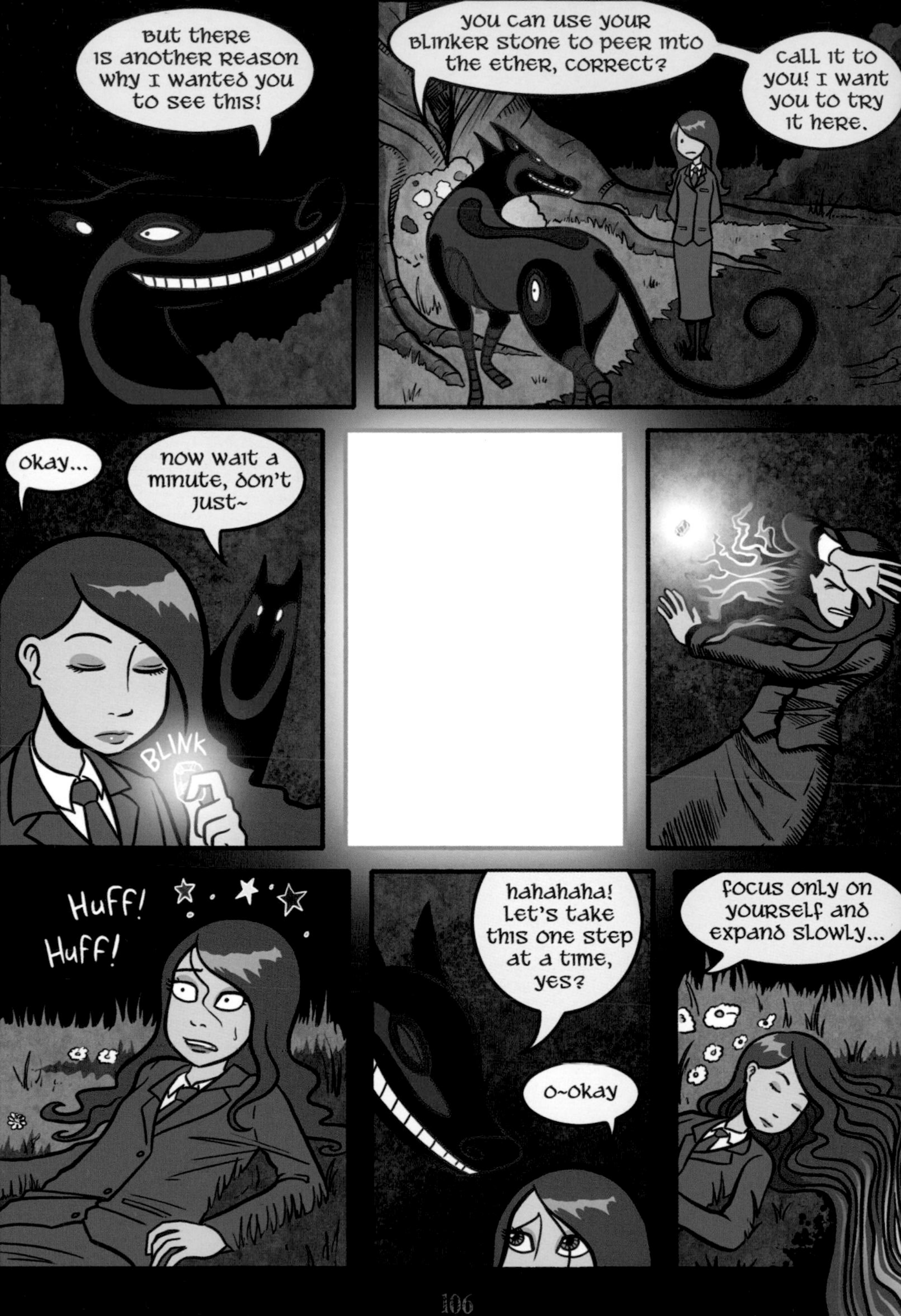
But there is another reason why I wanted you to see this!
you can use your Blinker stone to peer into the ether, correct?
Call it to you! I want you to try it here.
okay...
now wait a minute, don't just~
BLINK
Huff! Huff!
hahahaha! Let's take this one step at a time, yes?
O~okay
focus only on yourself and expand slowly...

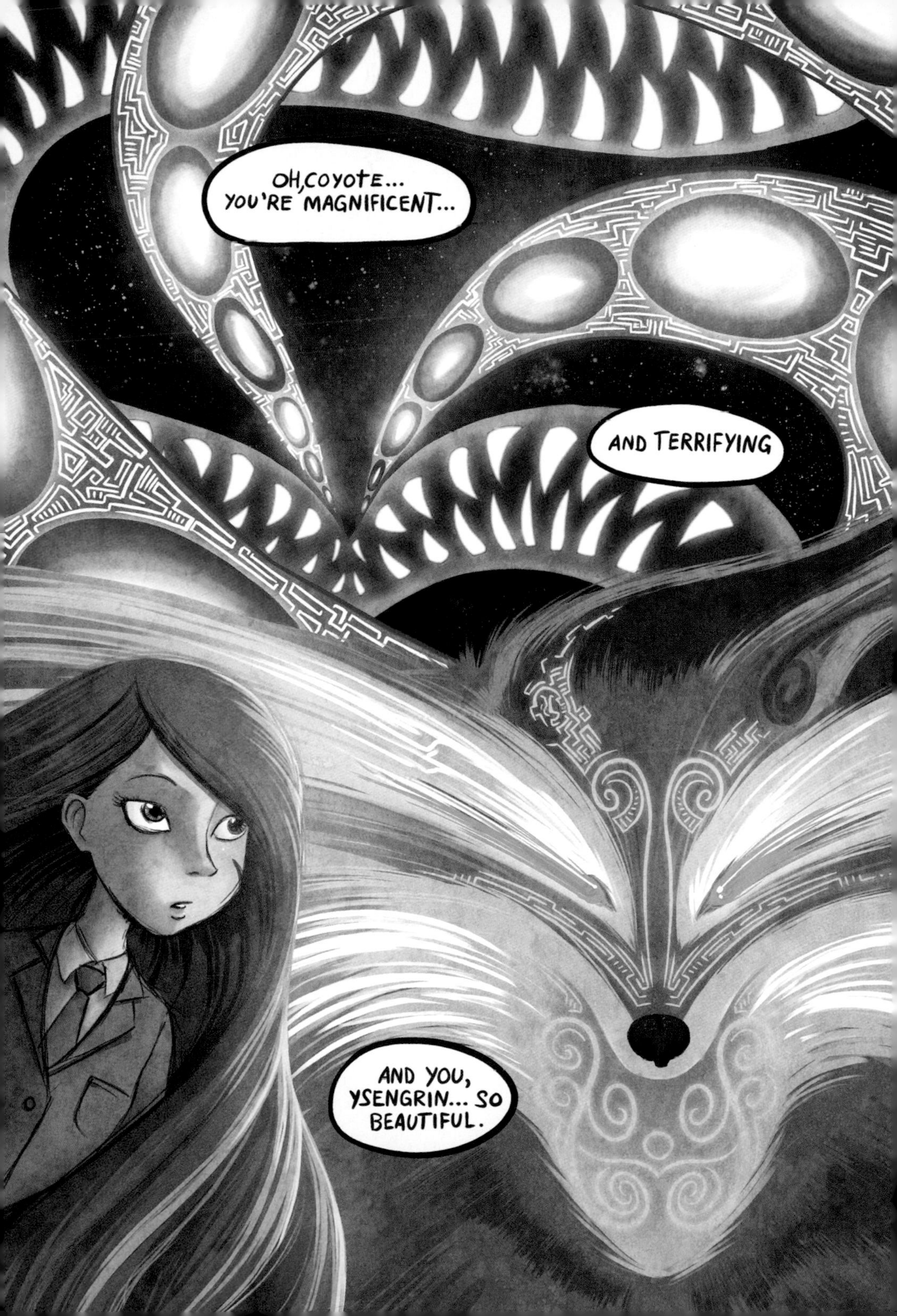
OH, COYOTE... YOU'RE MAGNIFICENT...
AND TERRIFYING
AND YOU, YSENGRIN... SO BEAUTIFUL.

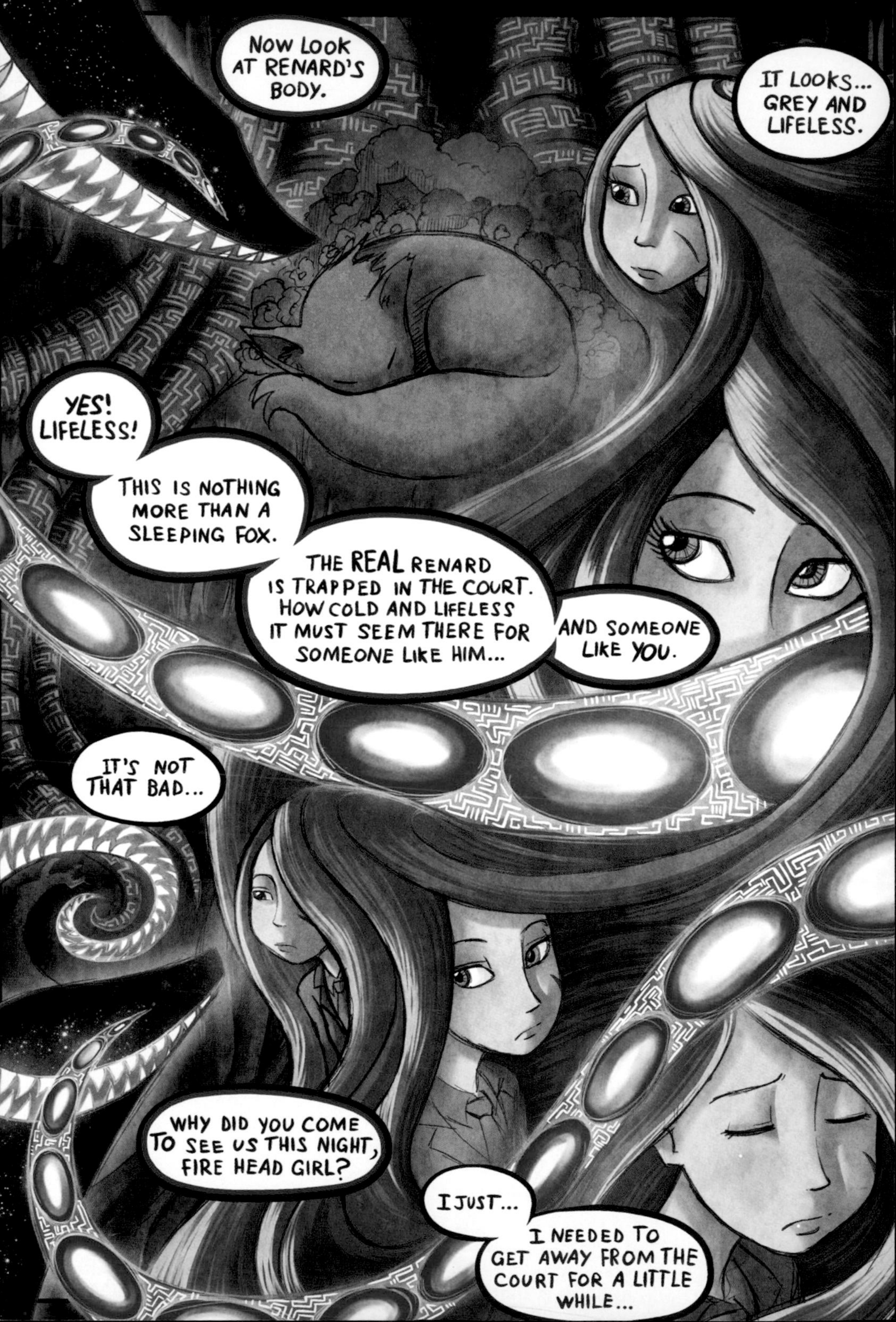

NOW LOOK AT RENARD'S BODY.
IT LOOKS... GREY AND LIFELESS.
YES! LIFELESS!
THIS IS NOTHING MORE THAN A SLEEPING FOX.
THE REAL RENARD IS TRAPPED IN THE COURT. HOW COLD AND LIFELESS IT MUST SEEM THERE FOR SOMEONE LIKE HIM...
AND SOMEONE LIKE YOU.
IT'S NOT THAT BAD...
WHY DID YOU COME TO SEE US THIS NIGHT, FIRE HEAD GIRL?
I JUST...
I NEEDED TO GET AWAY FROM THE COURT FOR A LITTLE WHILE...

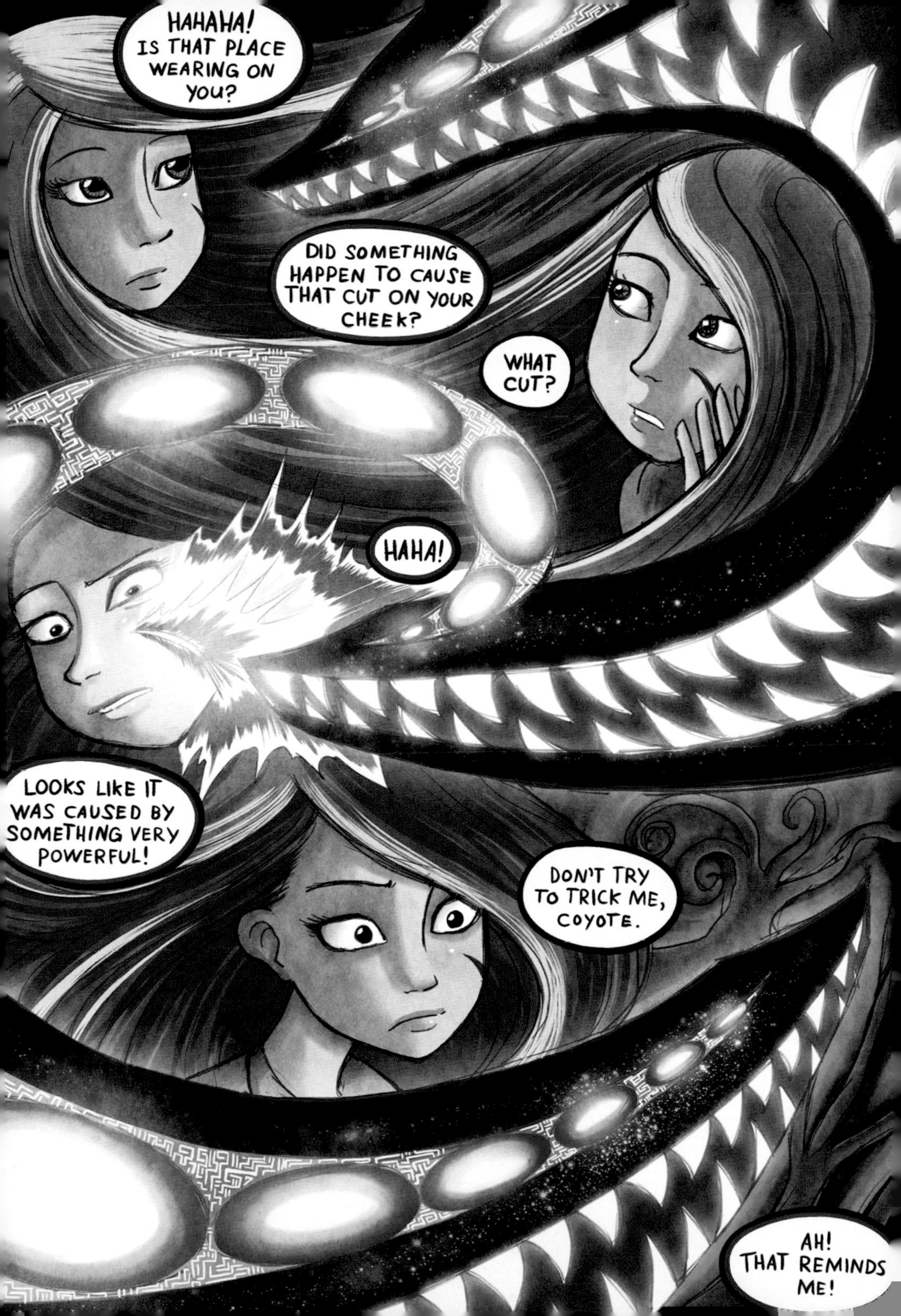
HAHAHA! IS THAT PLACE WEARING ON YOU?
DID SOMETHING HAPPEN TO CAUSE THAT CUT ON YOUR CHEEK?
WHAT CUT?
HAHA!
LOOKS LIKE IT WAS CAUSED BY SOMETHING VERY POWERFUL!
DON'T TRY TO TRICK ME, COYOTE.
AH! THAT REMINDS ME!

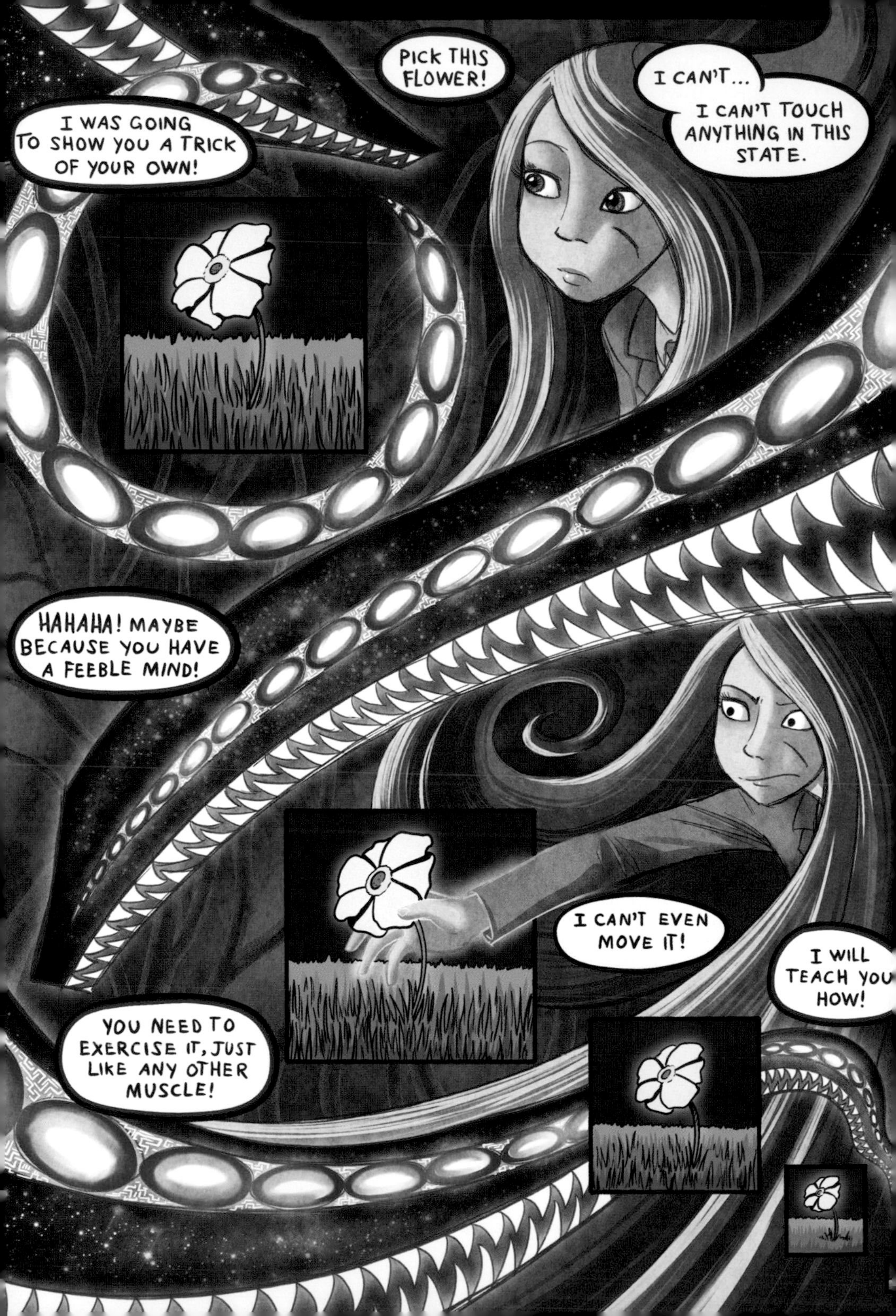
PICK THIS FLOWER!
I WAS GOING TO SHOW YOU A TRICK OF YOUR OWN!
I CAN'T...
I CAN'T TOUCH ANYTHING IN THIS STATE.
HAHAHA! MAYBE BECAUSE YOU HAVE A FEEBLE MIND!
I CAN'T EVEN MOVE IT!
YOU NEED TO EXERCISE IT, JUST LIKE ANY OTHER MUSCLE!
I WILL TEACH YOU HOW!

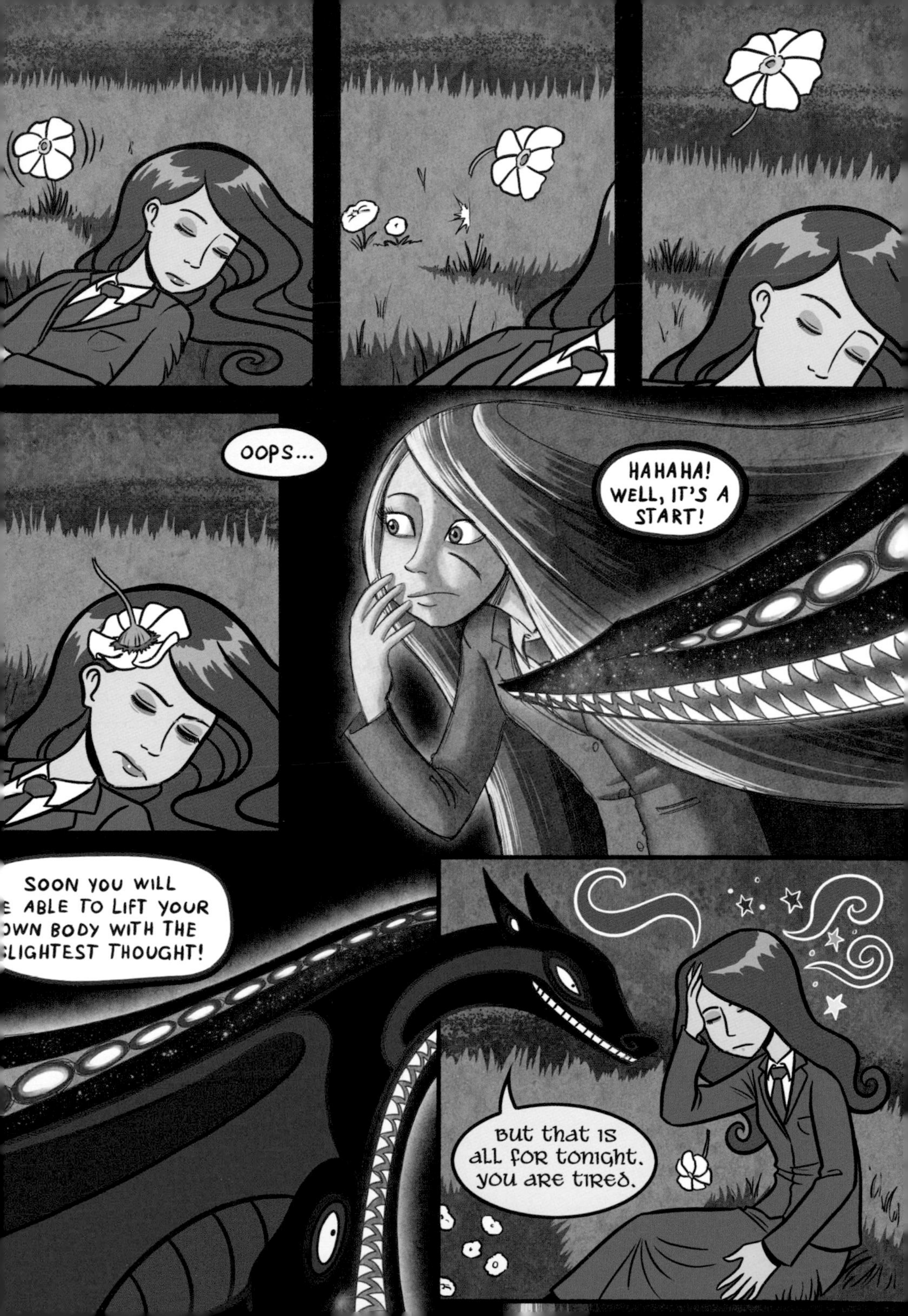
OOPS...
HAHAHA! WELL, IT'S A START!
SOON YOU WILL
E ABLE TO LIFT YOUR
OWN BODY WITH THE
LIGHTEST THOUGHT!
But that is all for tonight. you are tired.

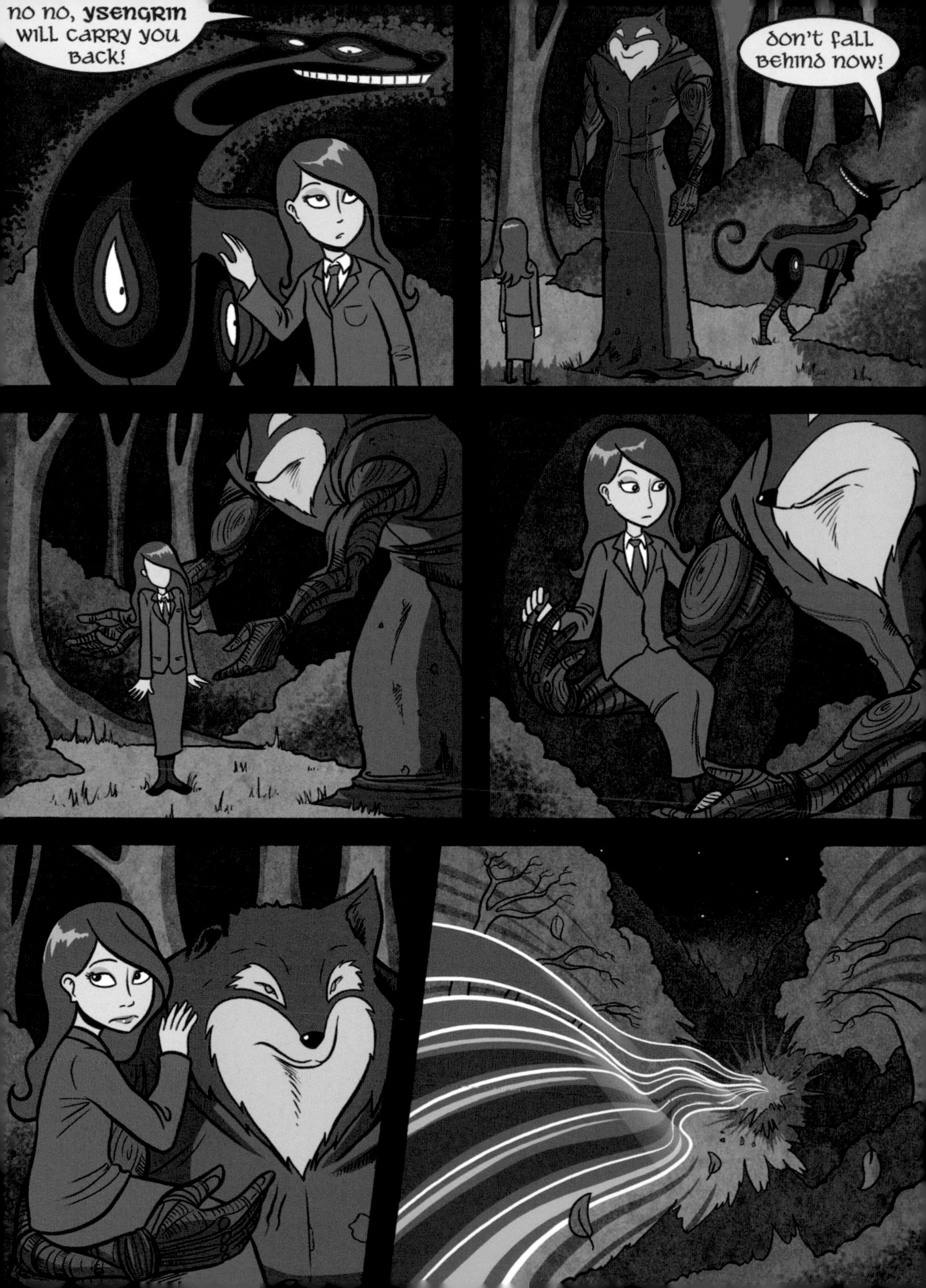
no no, YSENGRIN WILL CARRY YOU BACK!
don't fall behind now!

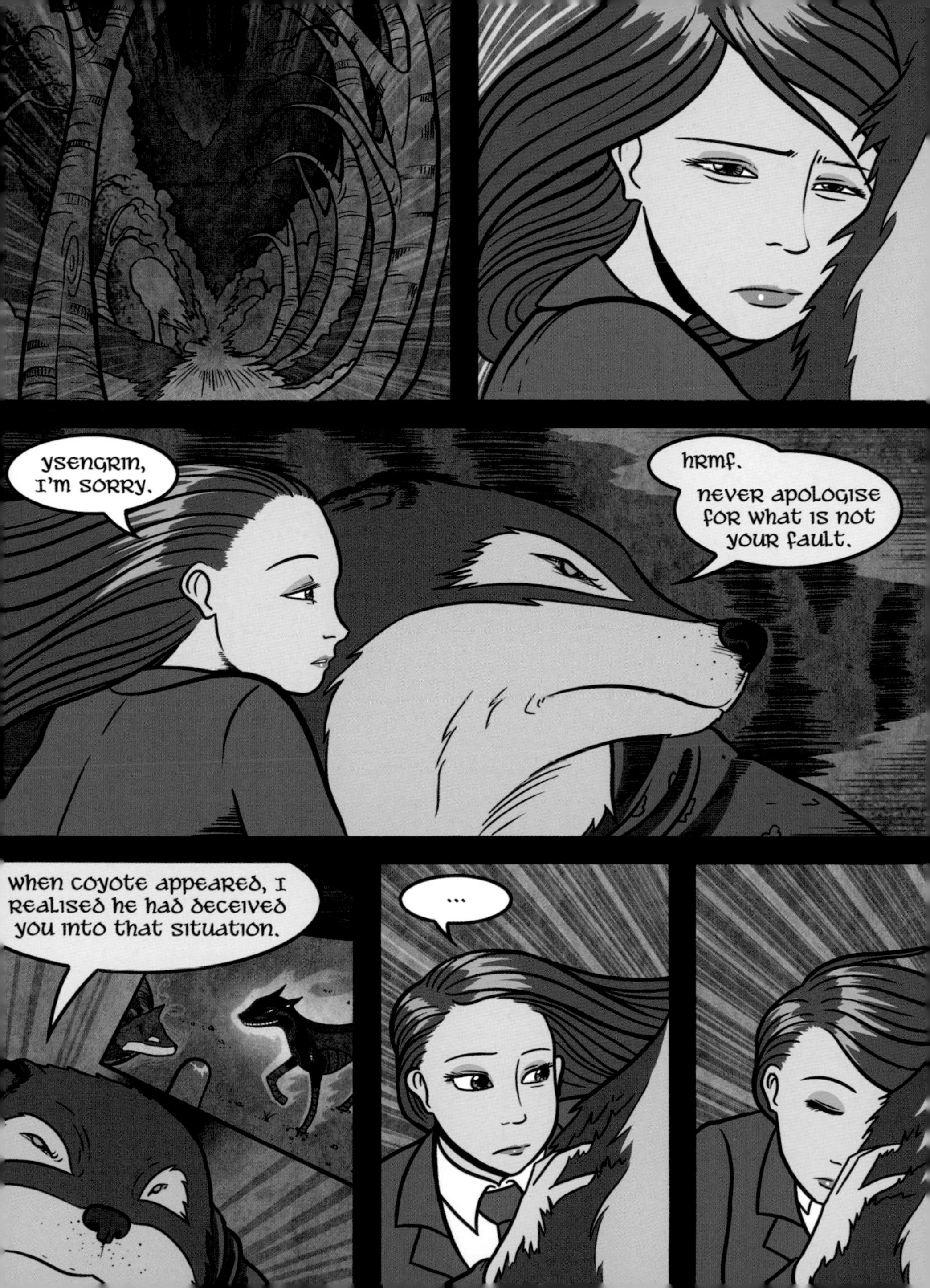
ysengrin, I'm sorry.
hrmf.
never apologise for what is not your fault.
when coyote appeared, I realised he had deceived you into that situation.
...

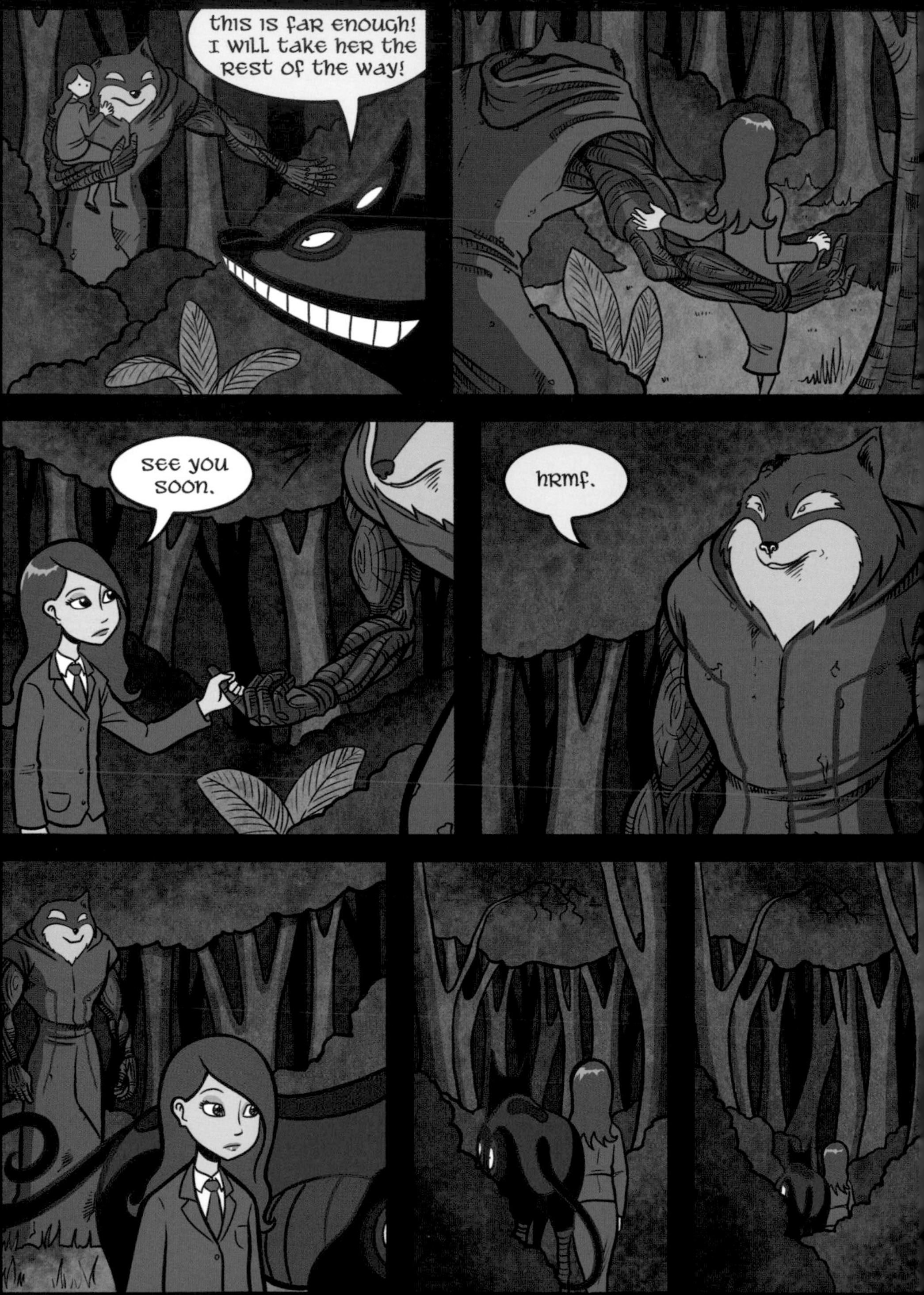
this is far enough! I will take her the rest of the way!
see you soon.
hrmf.

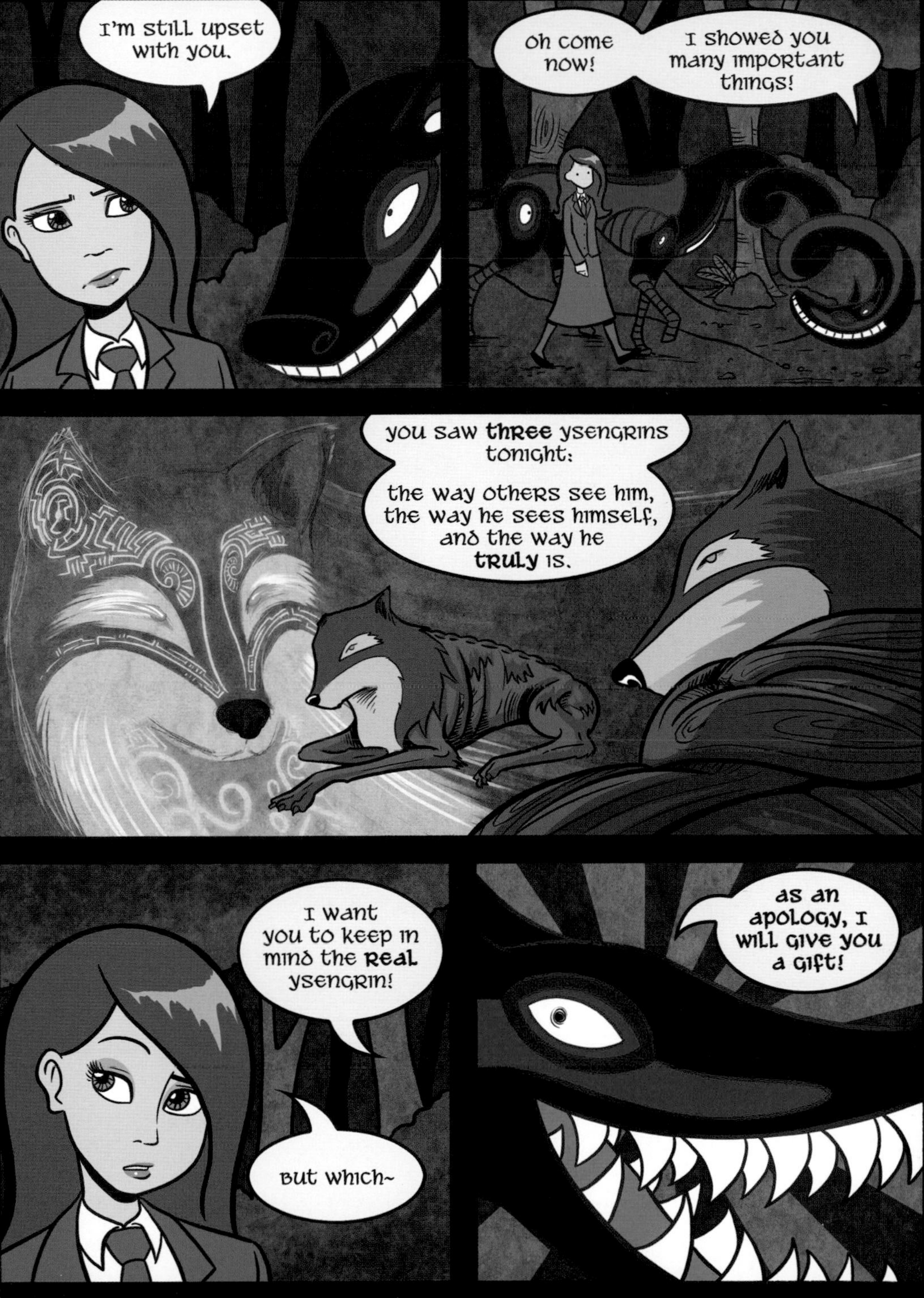
I'm still upset with you.
Oh come now!
I showed you many important things!
you saw three ysengrins tonight:
the way others see him, the way he sees himself, and the way he truly is.
I want you to keep in mind the real ysengrin!
But which~
as an apology, I will give you a gift!

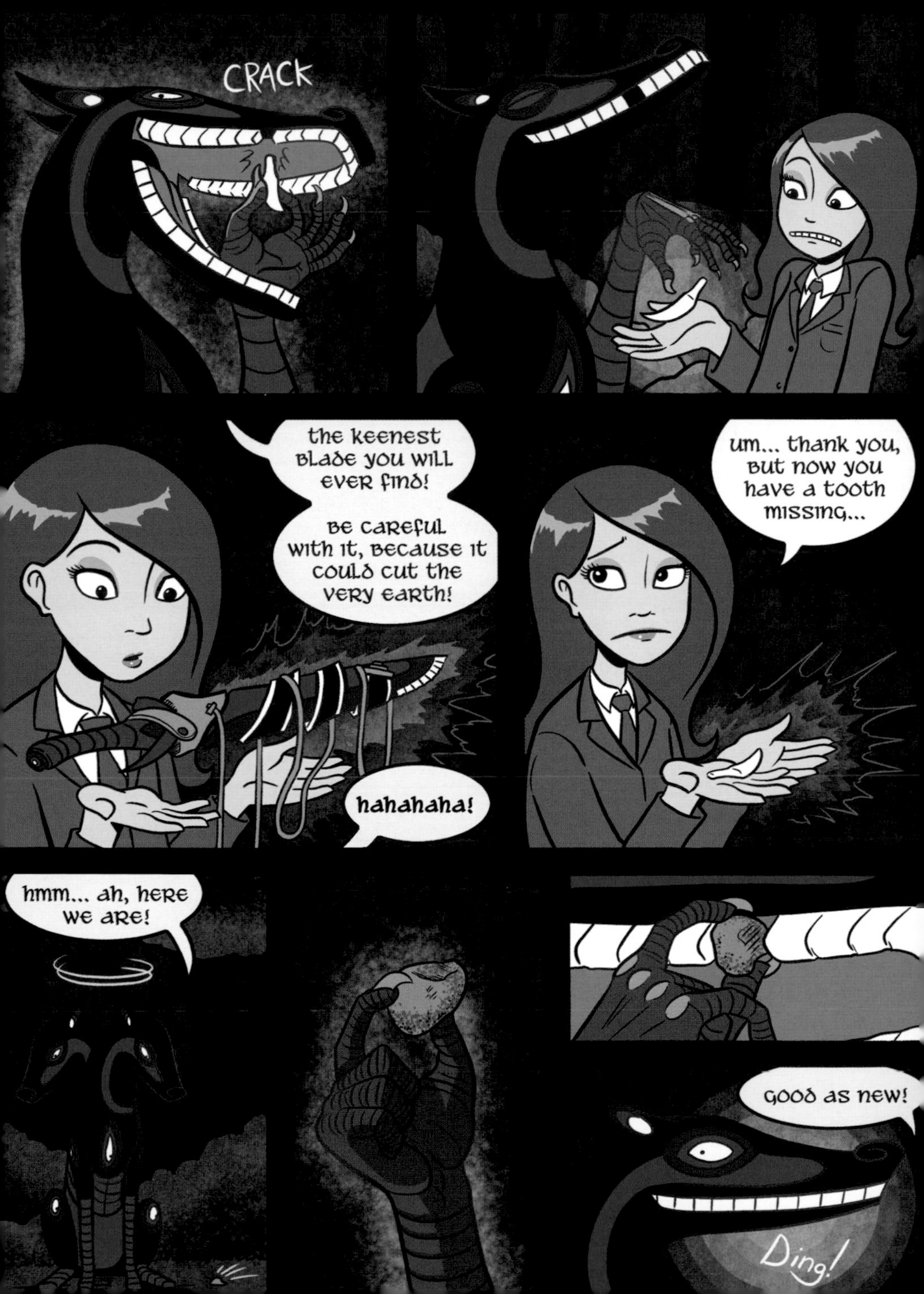
CRACK
the keenest blade you will ever find!
be careful with it, because it could cut the very earth!
hahahaha!
um... thank you, but now you have a tooth missing...
hmm... ah, here we are!
good as new!
Ding!

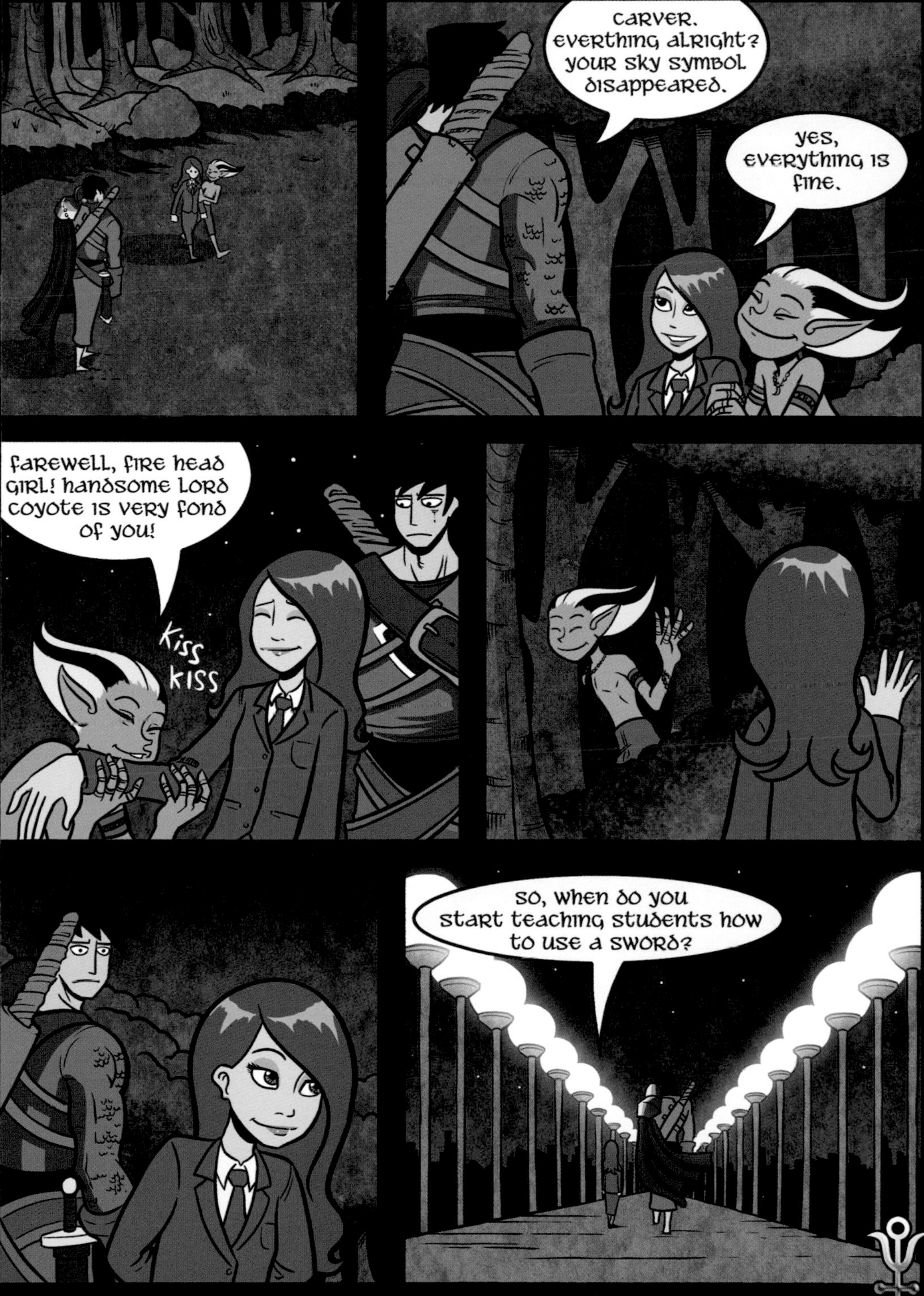
carver. everthing alright? your sky symbol disappeared.
yes, everything is fine.
farewell, fire head girl! handsome lord coyote is very fond of you!
kiss kiss
so, when do you start teaching students how to use a sword?

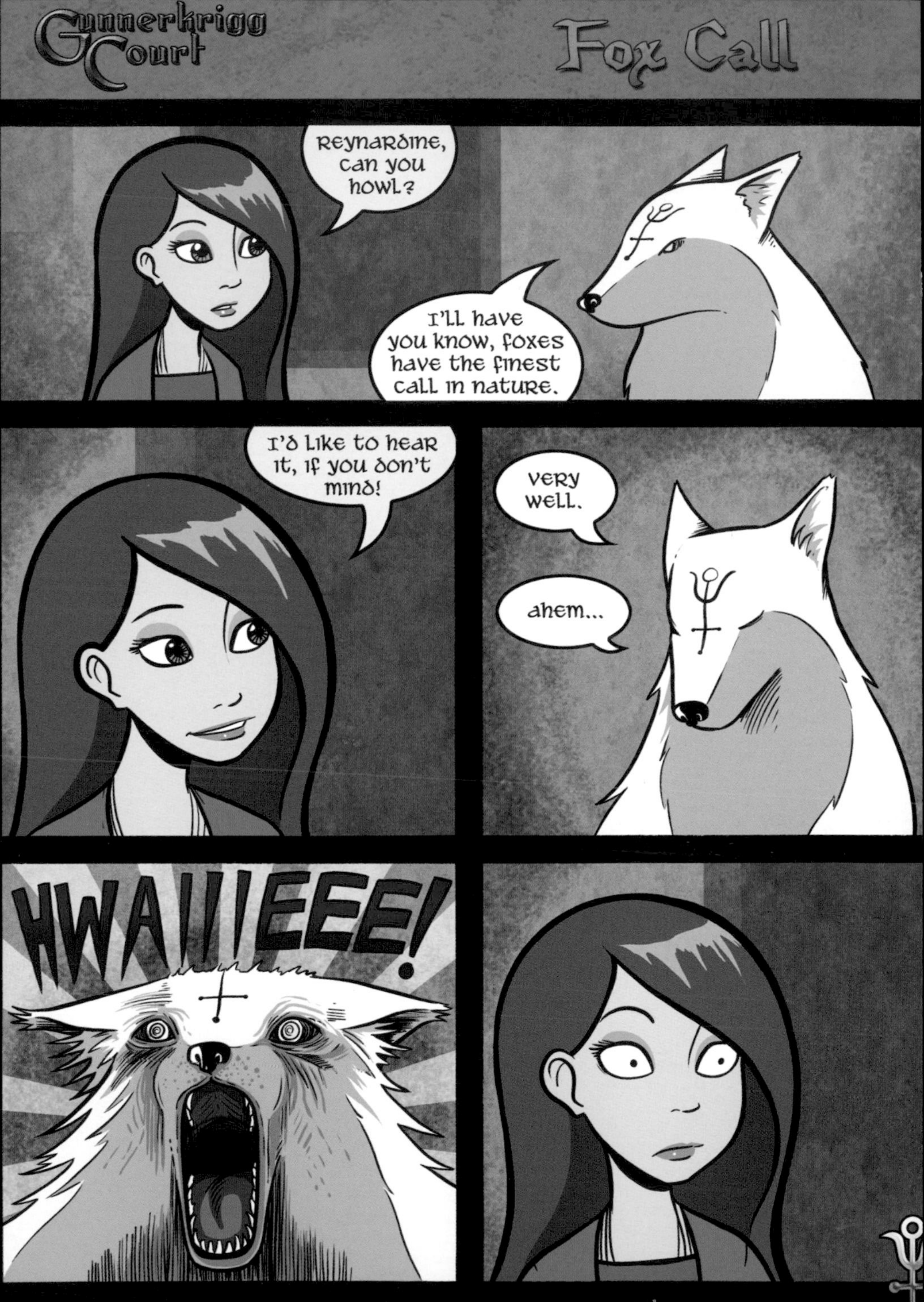
Gunnerkrigg Court
Fox Call
Reynardine, can you howl?
I'll have you know, foxes have the finest call in nature.
I'd like to hear it, if you don't mind!
Very well.
ahem...
HWAIIEEE!

Gunnerkrigg Court

Chapter 27:

Spring Heeled

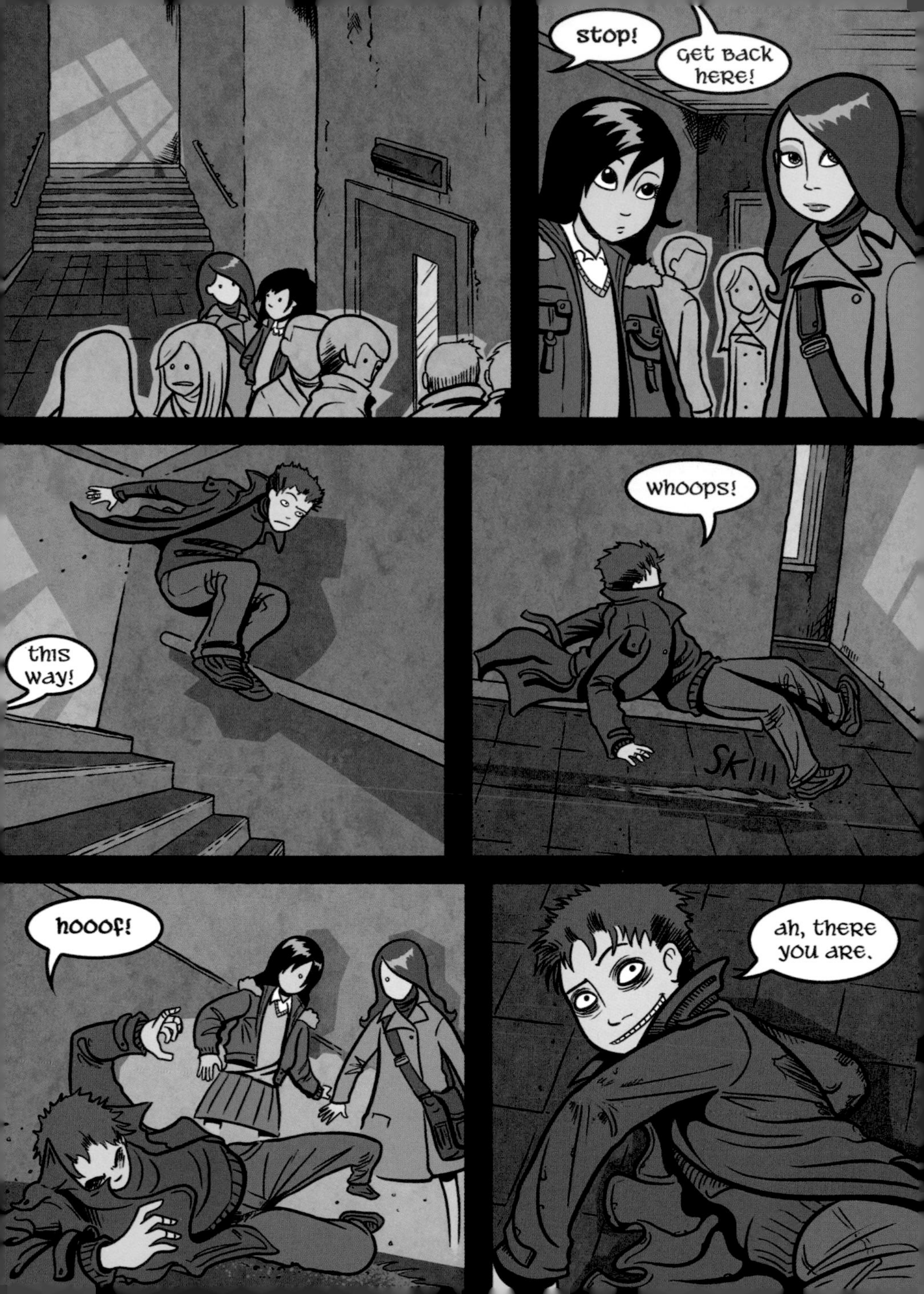
stop!
get back here!
this way!
whoops!
SKIII
hooof!
ah, there you are.

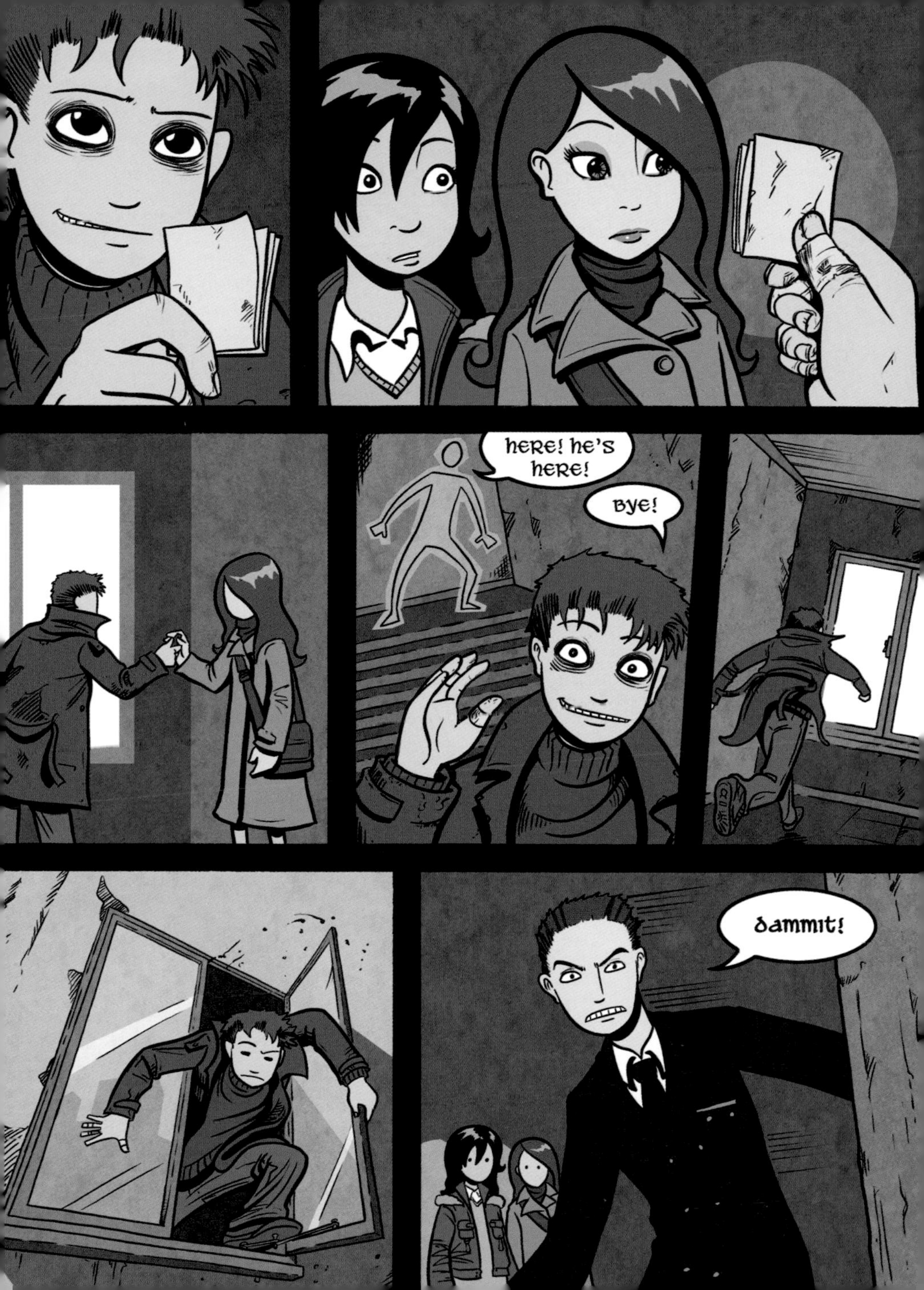
here! he's here!
bye!
dammit!

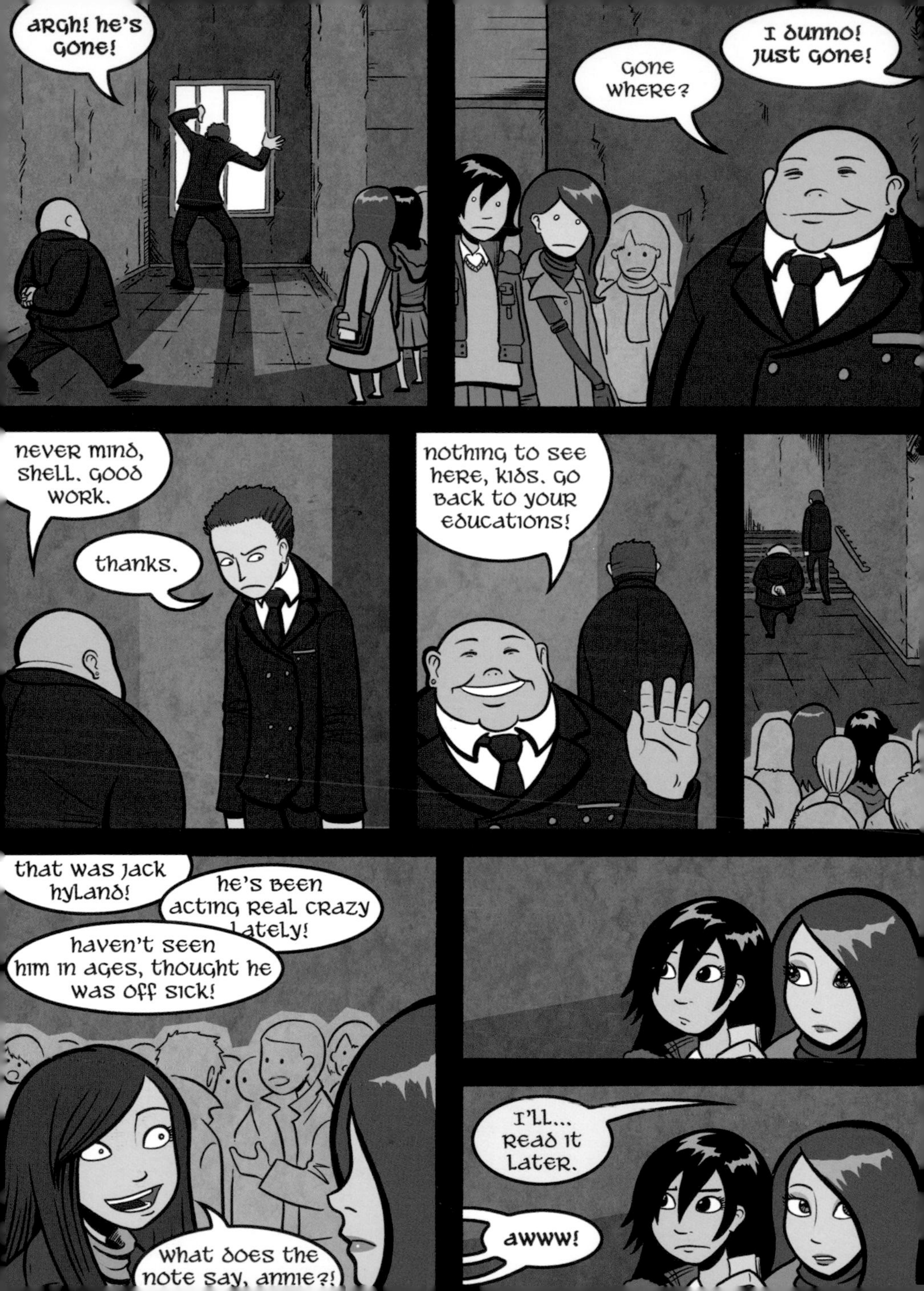
argh! he's gone!
gone where?
I dunno! just gone!
never mind, shell. good work.
thanks.
nothing to see here, kids. go back to your educations!
that was jack hyland!
he's been acting real crazy lately!
haven't seen him in ages, thought he was off sick!
what does the note say, annie?!
I'll... read it later.
awww!

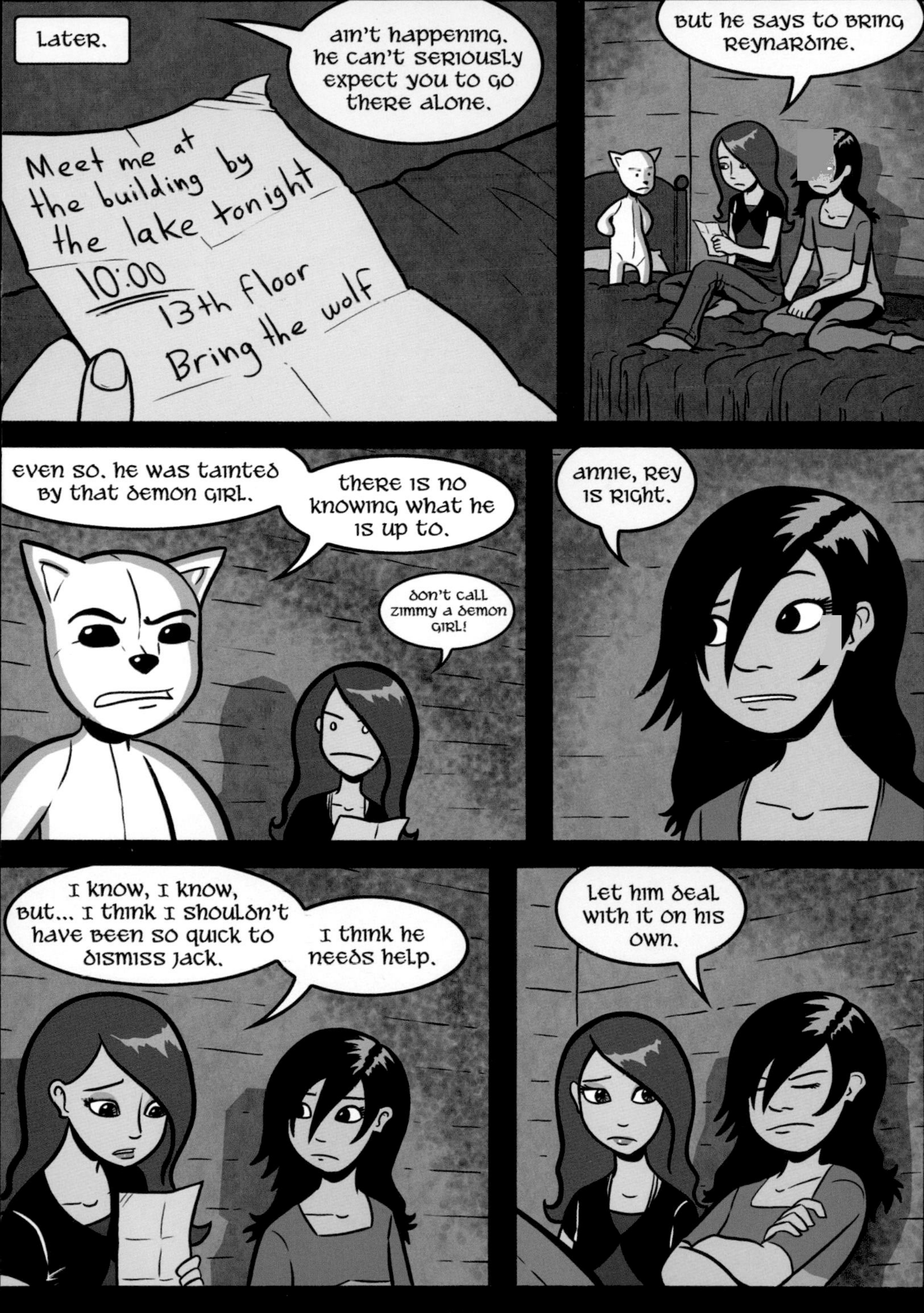
Later.
Meet me at the building by the lake tonight
10:00
13th floor
Bring the wolf
ain't happening. he can't seriously expect you to go there alone.
But he says to bring Reynardine.
even so. he was tainted by that demon girl.
there is no knowing what he is up to.
don't call zimmy a demon girl!
annie, rey is right.
I know, I know, but... I think I shouldn't have been so quick to dismiss jack.
I think he needs help.
Let him deal with it on his own.

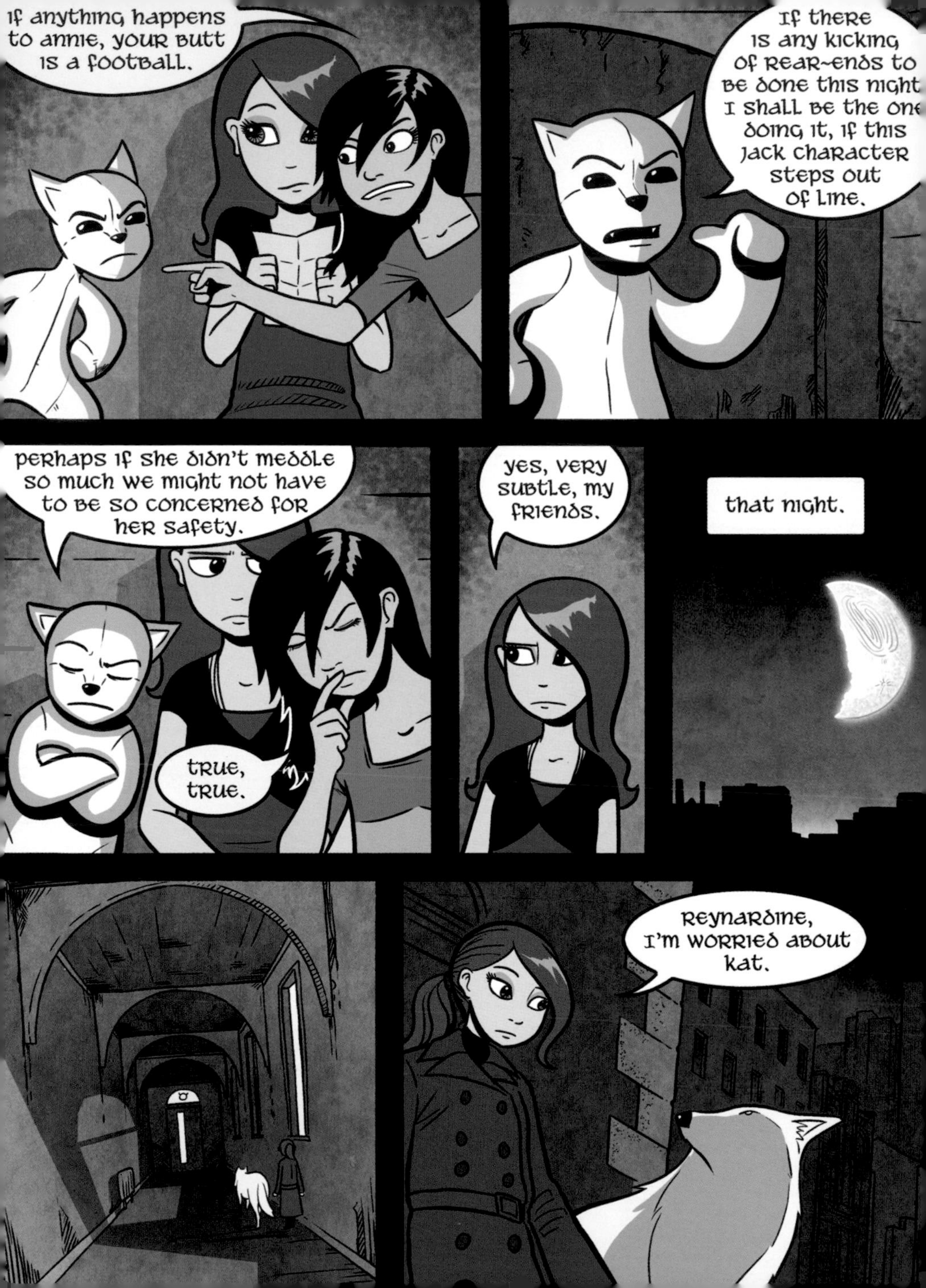
If anything happens to annie, your butt is a football.
If there is any kicking of rear~ends to be done this night I shall be the one doing it, if this jack character steps out of line.
perhaps if she didn't meddle so much we might not have to be so concerned for her safety.
true, true.
yes, very subtle, my friends.
that night.
Reynardine, I'm worried about kat.

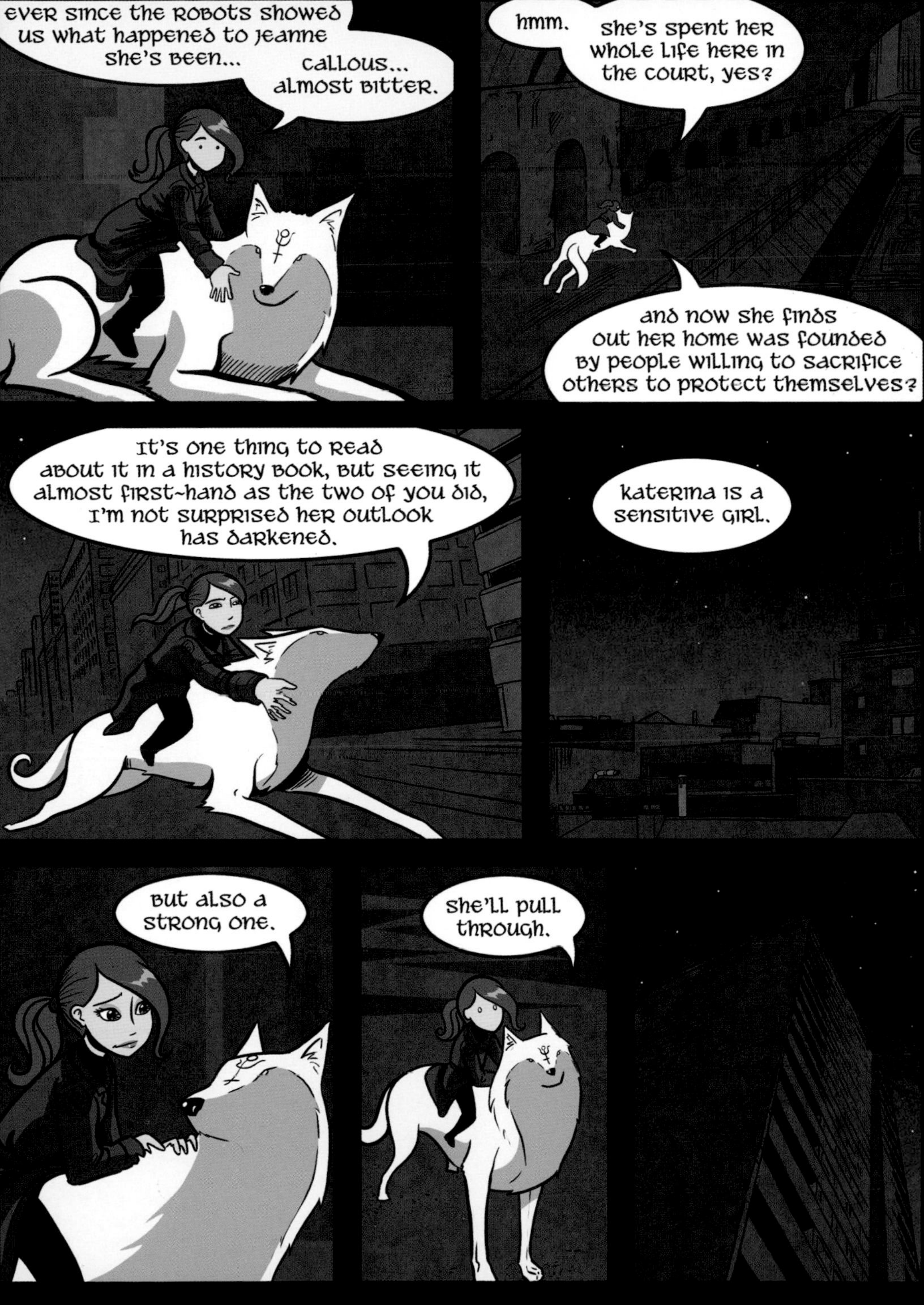
ever since the robots showed us what happened to jeanne she's been... callous... almost bitter.
hmm.
she's spent her whole life here in the court, yes?
and now she finds out her home was founded by people willing to sacrifice others to protect themselves?
it's one thing to read about it in a history book, but seeing it almost first-hand as the two of you did, I'm not surprised her outlook has darkened.
katerina is a sensitive girl.
but also a strong one.
she'll pull through.

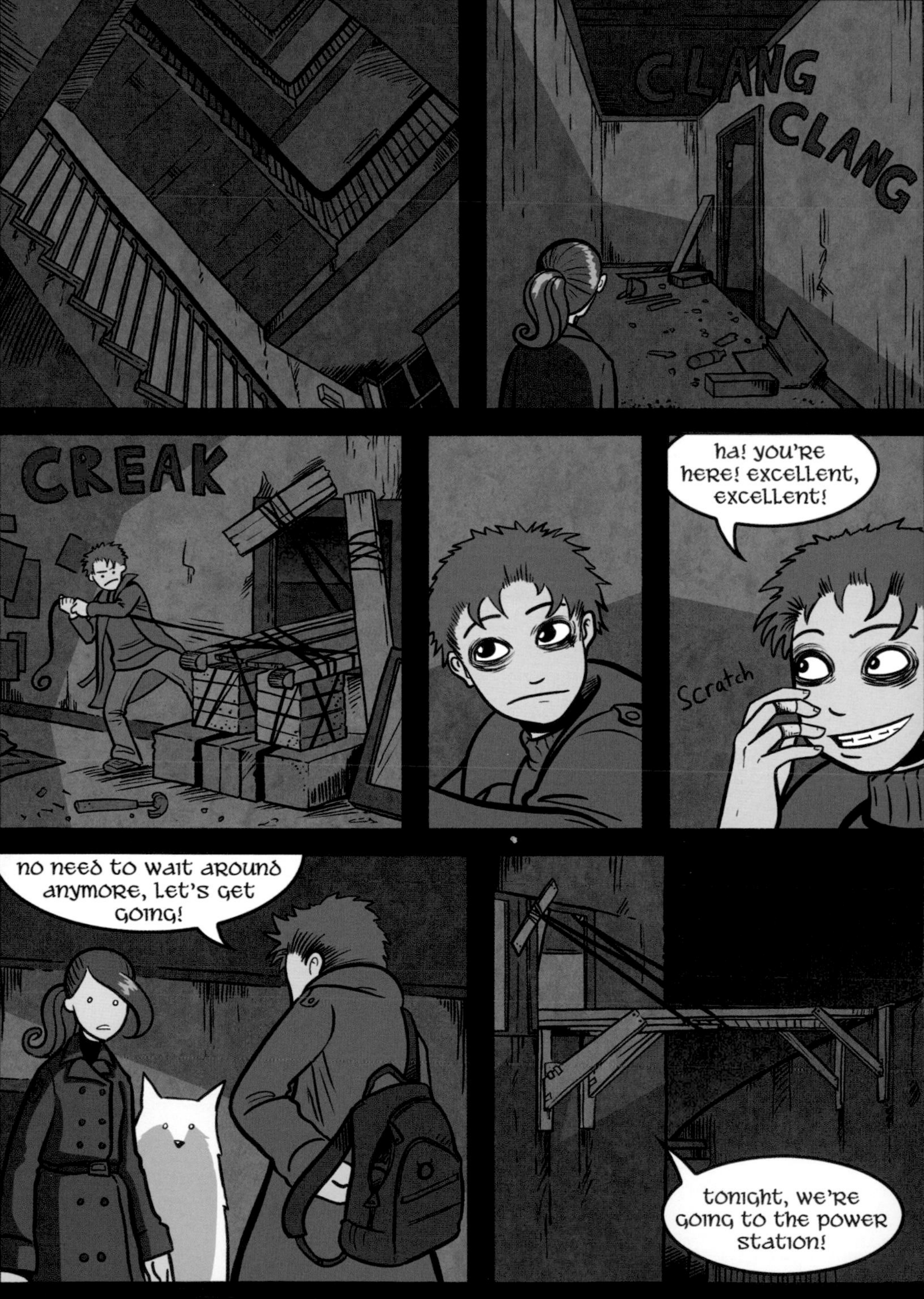
CLANG
CLANG
CLANG
CREAK
ha! you're here! excellent, excellent!
Scratch
no need to wait around anymore, let's get going!
tonight, we're going to the power station!

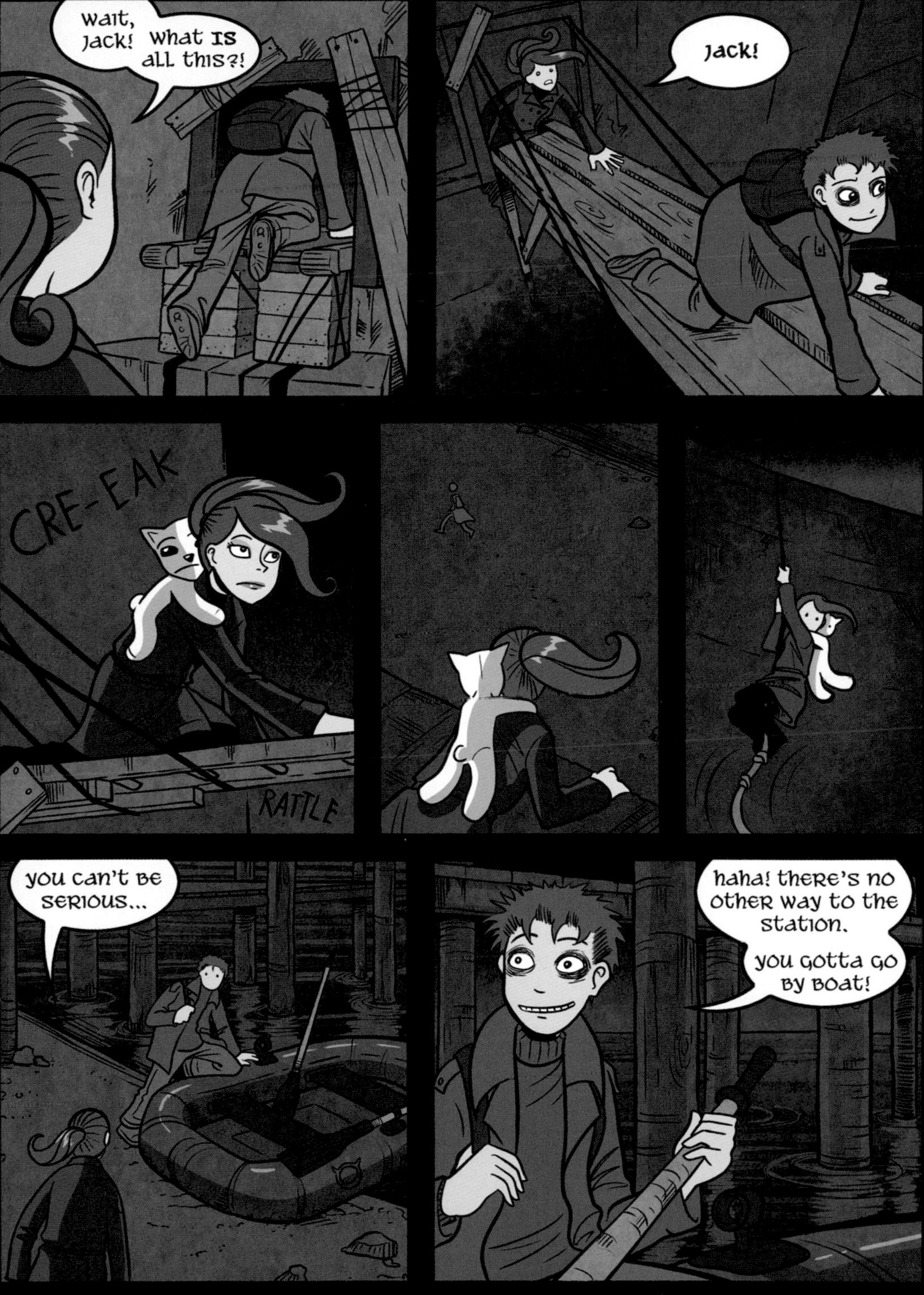
wait, Jack! what IS all this?!
Jack!
CRE-EAK
RATTLE
you can't be serious...
haha! there's no other way to the station.
you gotta go by boat!

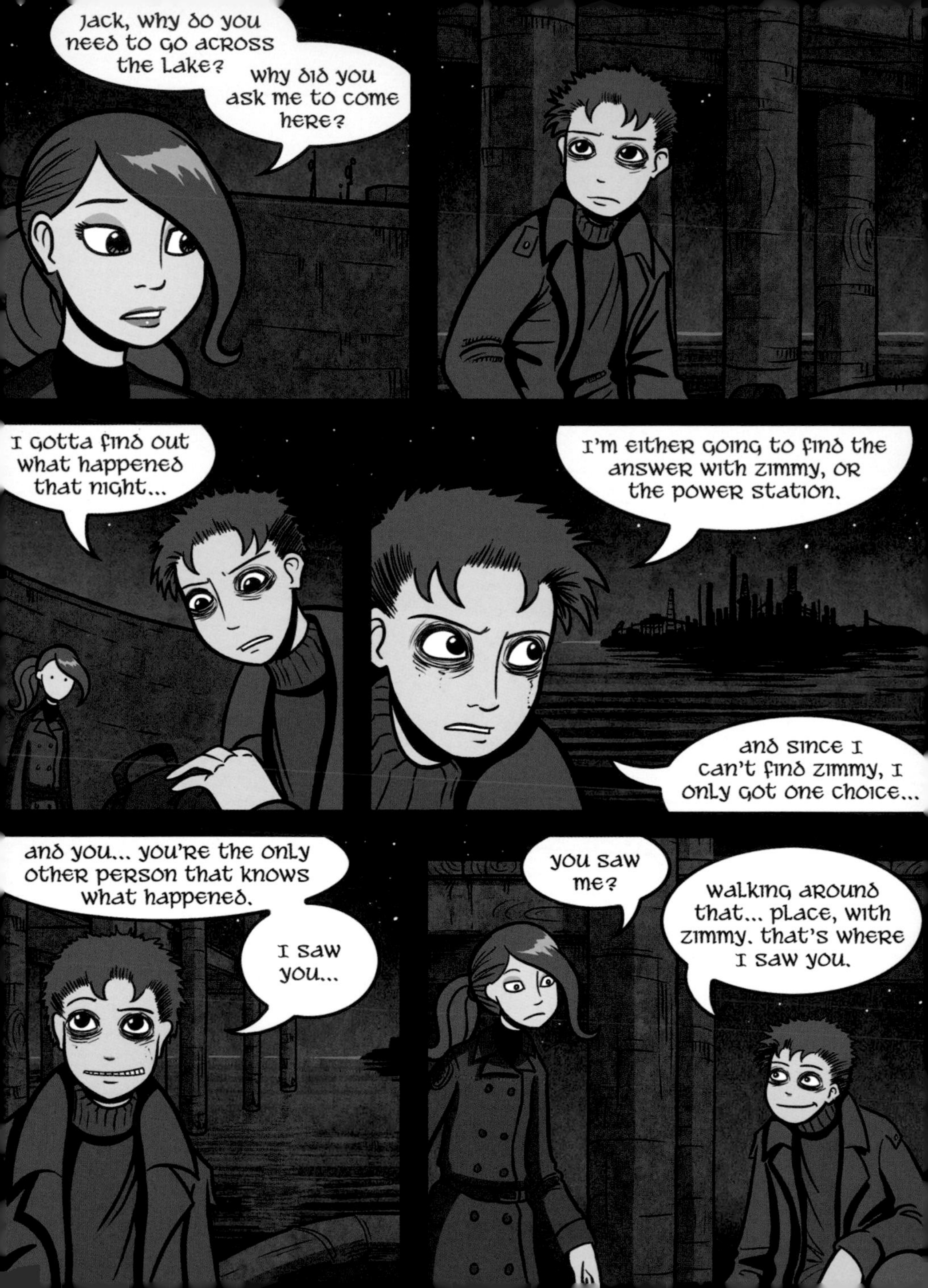
Jack, why do you need to go across the lake?
Why did you ask me to come here?
I gotta find out what happened that night...
I'm either going to find the answer with Zimmy, or the power station.
And since I can't find Zimmy, I only got one choice...
And you... you're the only other person that knows what happened.
I saw you...
You saw me?
Walking around that... place, with Zimmy. That's where I saw you.

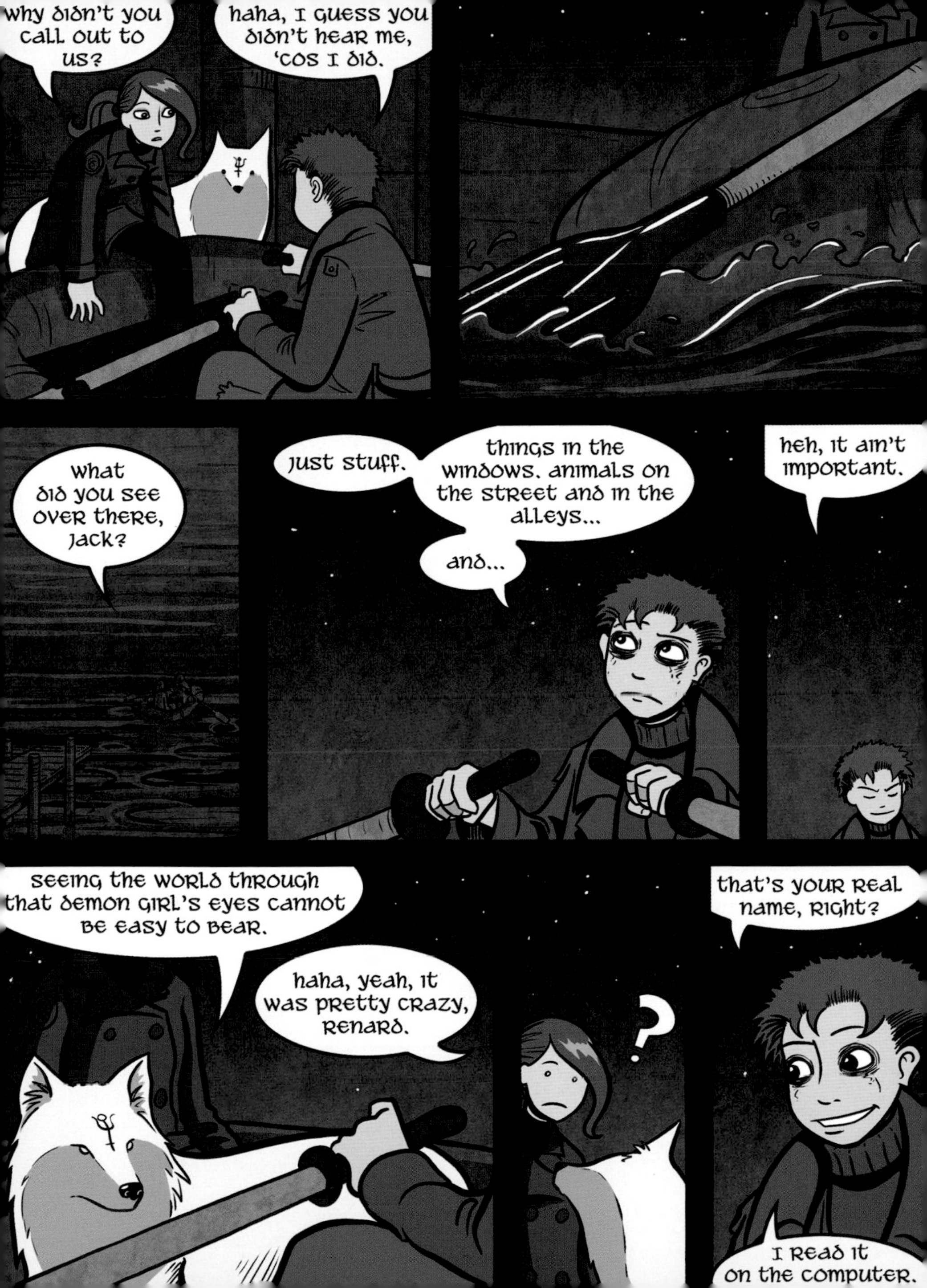
why didn't you call out to us?
haha, I guess you didn't hear me, 'cos I did.
what did you see over there, jack?
just stuff.
things in the windows. animals on the street and in the alleys...
and...
heh, it ain't important.
seeing the world through that demon girl's eyes cannot be easy to bear.
haha, yeah, it was pretty crazy, Renard.
?
that's your real name, right?
I read it on the computer.

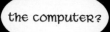

the computer?

yeah, the school network is easy to root around in.

but it's a closed system. completely shut off from the rest of the court.

I couldn't find anything about the power station, or anything outside the school.

they got basic stuff on the school network.

information on all the students, like.

I read all about you two.

how **you** tried to kill her.

and about how your dad ditched you.

haha, don't worry about it. none of my business really.

I was looking for information on zimmy, but everything on students from chester and foley is blocked off.

oh, hey! did you know you got a kid in your class that can talk to animals?!

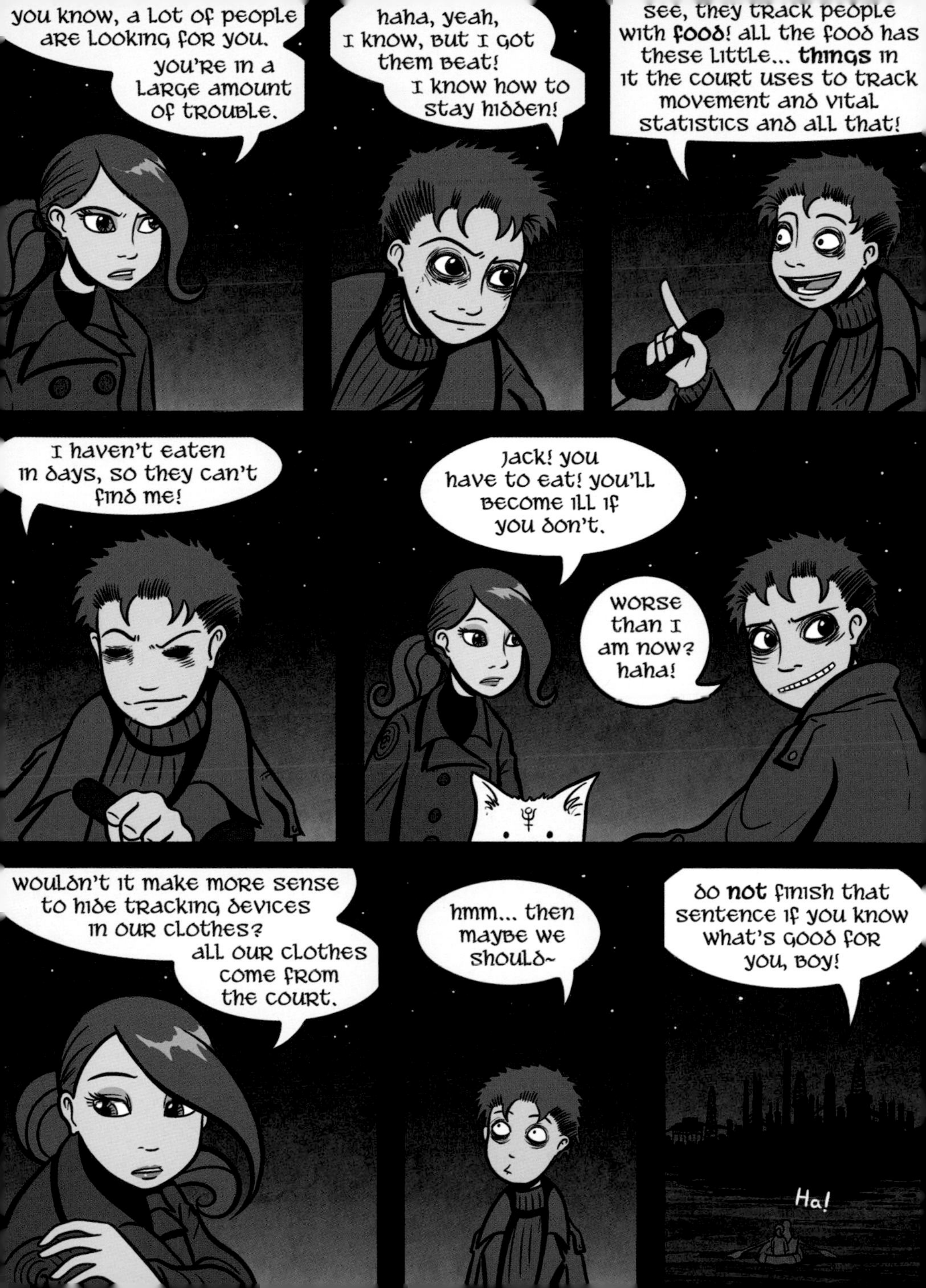
you know, a lot of people are looking for you.
you're in a large amount of trouble.
haha, yeah, I know, but I got them beat!
I know how to stay hidden!
see, they track people with food! all the food has these little... things in it the court uses to track movement and vital statistics and all that!
I haven't eaten in days, so they can't find me!
Jack! you have to eat! you'll become ill if you don't.
worse than I am now? haha!
wouldn't it make more sense to hide tracking devices in our clothes?
all our clothes come from the court.
hmm... then maybe we should~
do not finish that sentence if you know what's good for you, boy!
Ha!

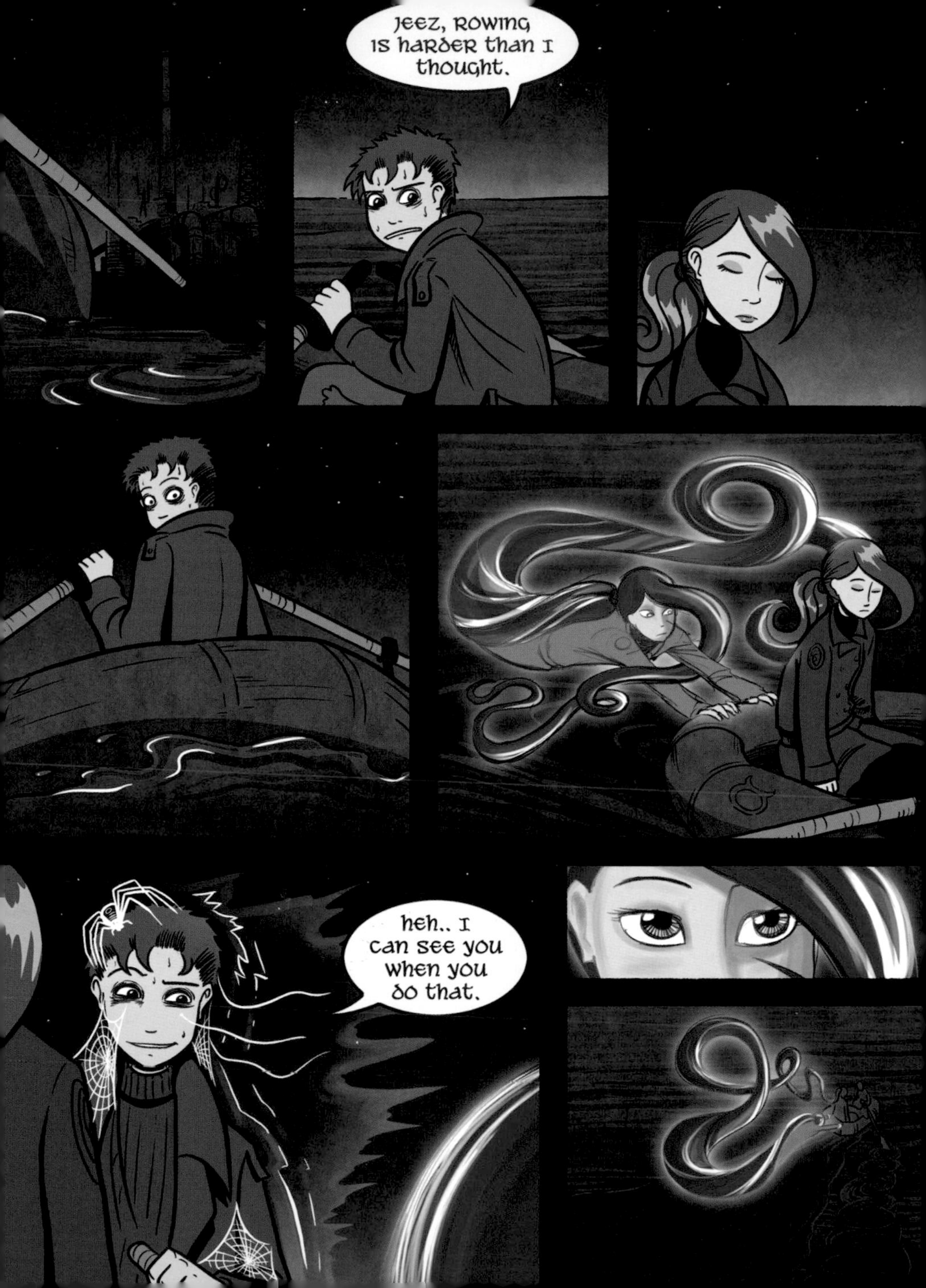
JEEZ, ROWING IS HARDER THAN I THOUGHT.
heh.. I can see you when you do that.

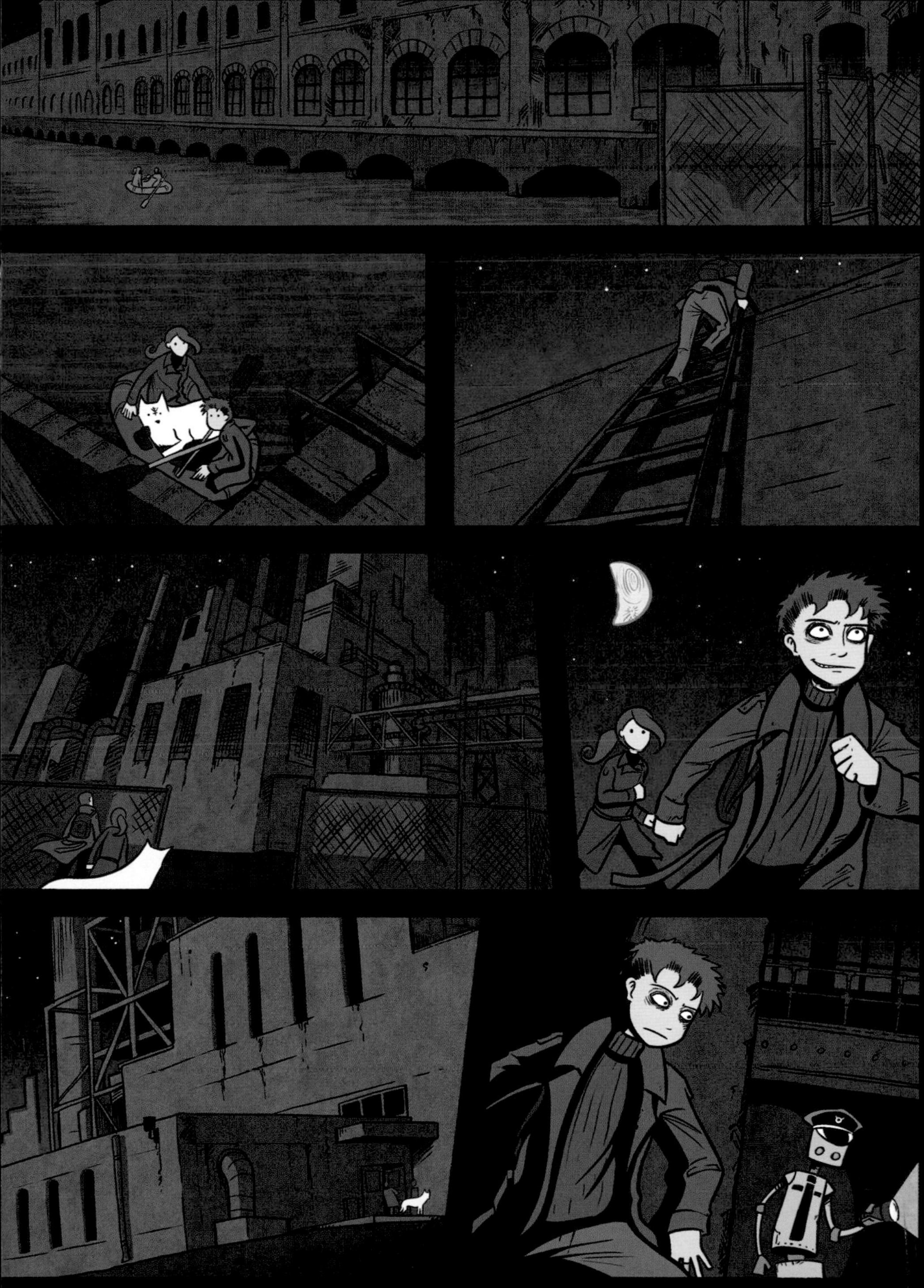

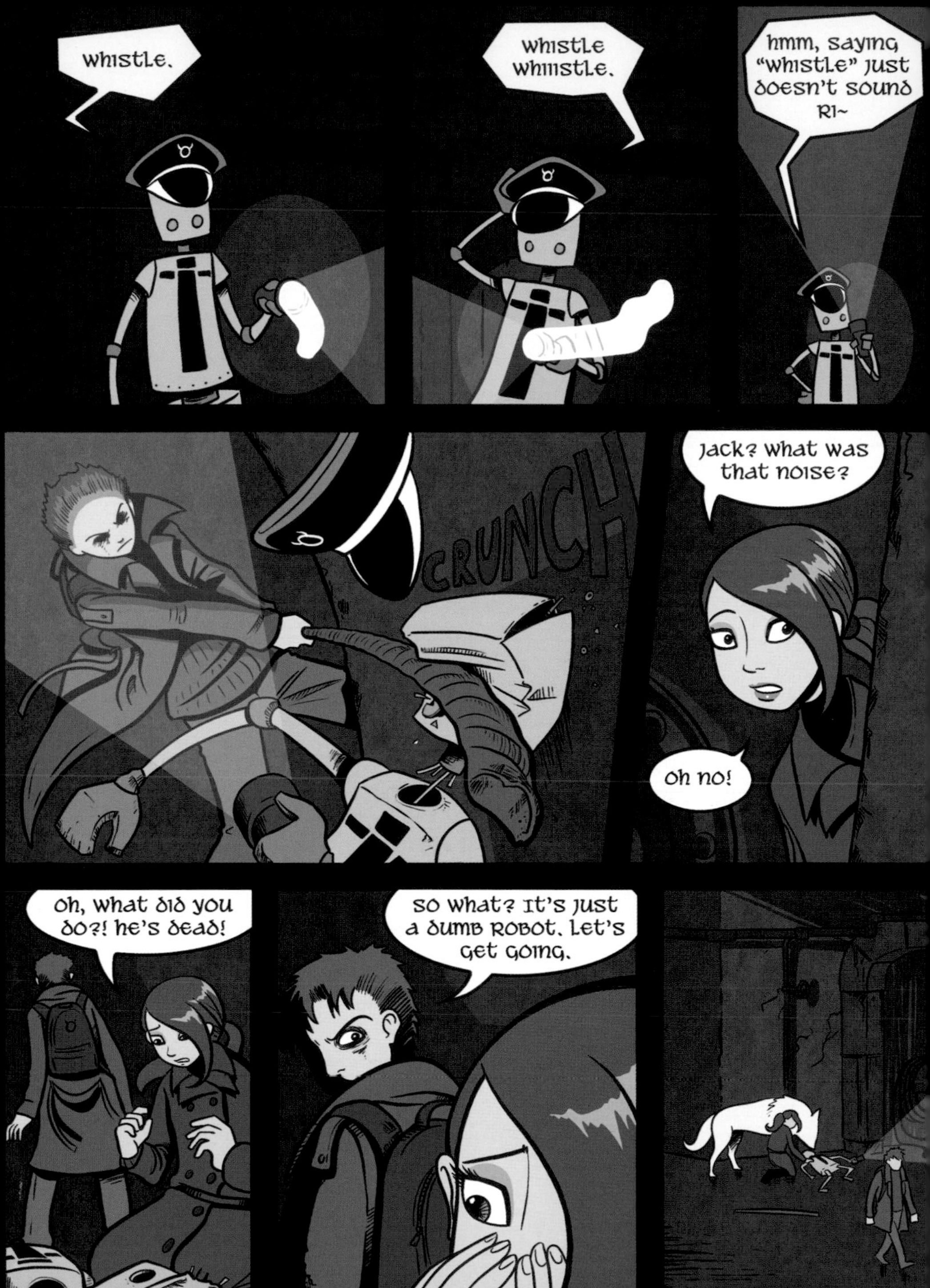
whistle.
whistle whiiistle.
hmm, saying "whistle" just doesn't sound ri~
CRUNCH
Jack? what was that noise?
oh no!
oh, what did you do?! he's dead!
so what? It's just a dumb robot. Let's get going.

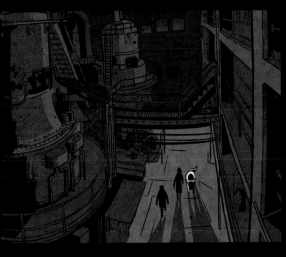

hang on.

STICK

now what are you doing?

STICK

security.

anyone comes this way, I'll know about it.

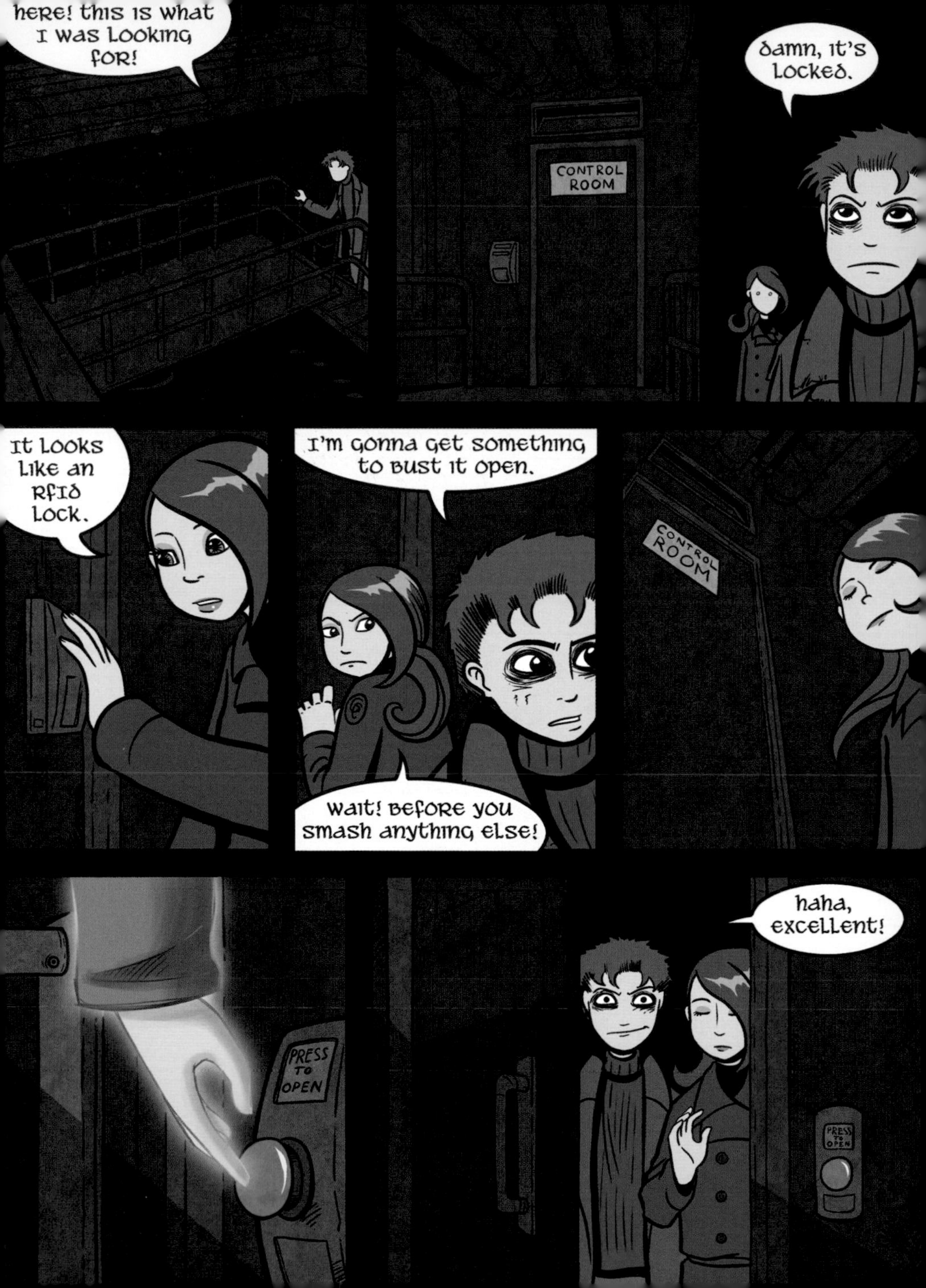
here! this is what I was looking for!
CONTROL ROOM
damn, it's locked.
It looks like an RFID lock.
I'm gonna get something to bust it open.
Wait! Before you smash anything else!
CONTROL ROOM
PRESS TO OPEN
haha, excellent!
PRESS TO OPEN

Vrrr-
rrr
krk-krrrr

this is all gibberish to me...

this place is called... an **ether station**?

I cannot imagine a hell-hole further removed from the ether than this.

ARRAY

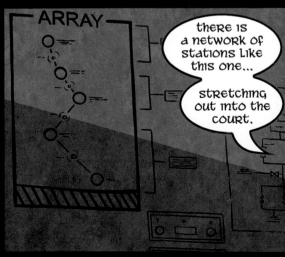

there is a network of stations like this one...

stretching out into the court.

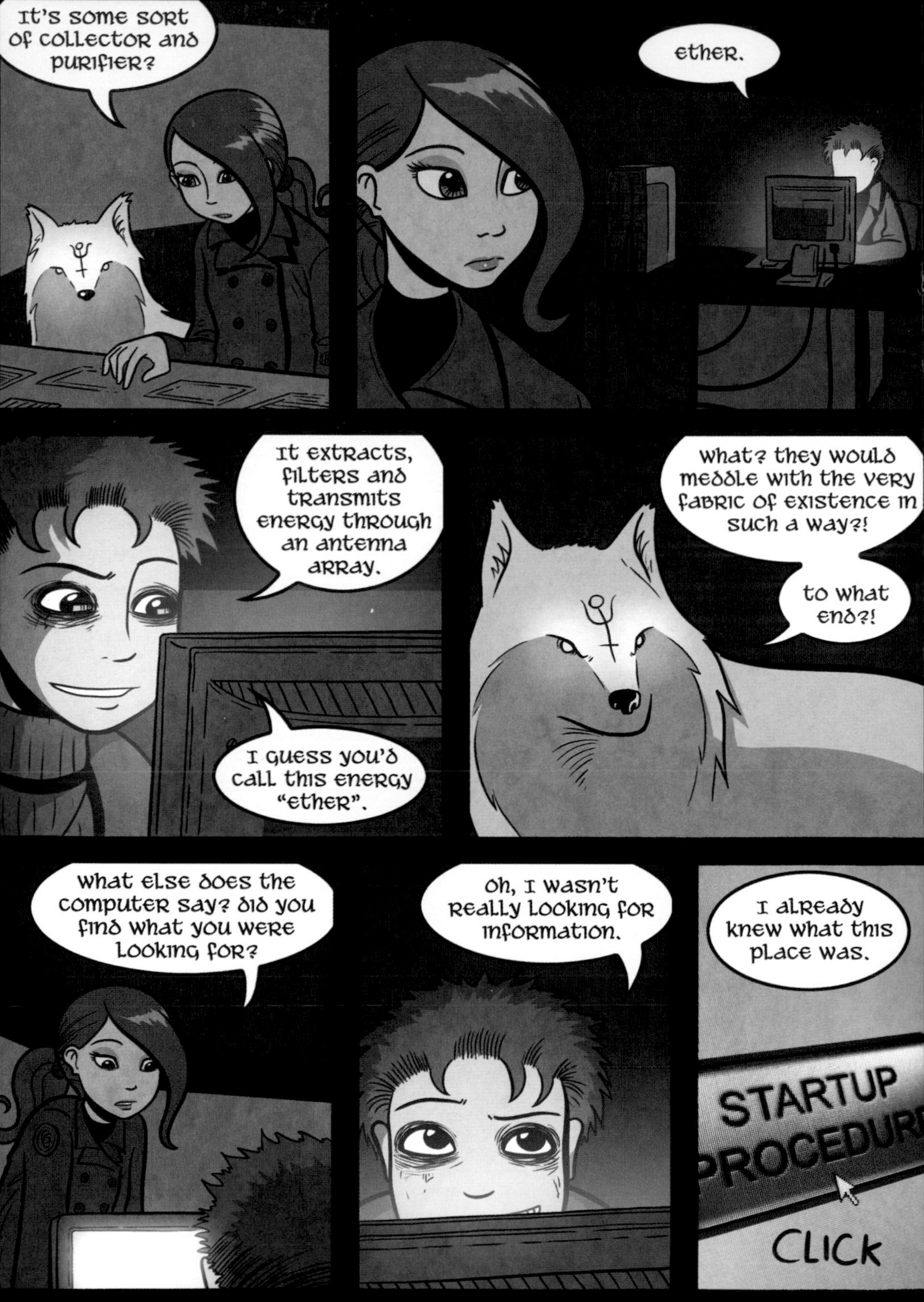
It's some sort of collector and purifier?
ether.
It extracts, filters and transmits energy through an antenna array.
I guess you'd call this energy "ether".
What? they would meddle with the very fabric of existence in such a way?!
to what end?!
What else does the computer say? did you find what you were looking for?
Oh, I wasn't really looking for information.
I already knew what this place was.
STARTUP PROCEDUR
CLICK

Blink
Click
Blink
Click click
NMMMMMMN
VOOOOOOOOOC
OOOOOOOOOOOOOOOOOOOOOC
Jack!

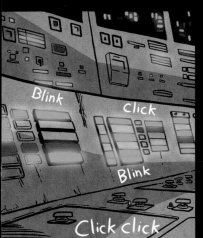

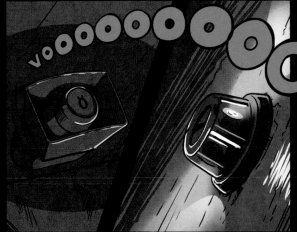

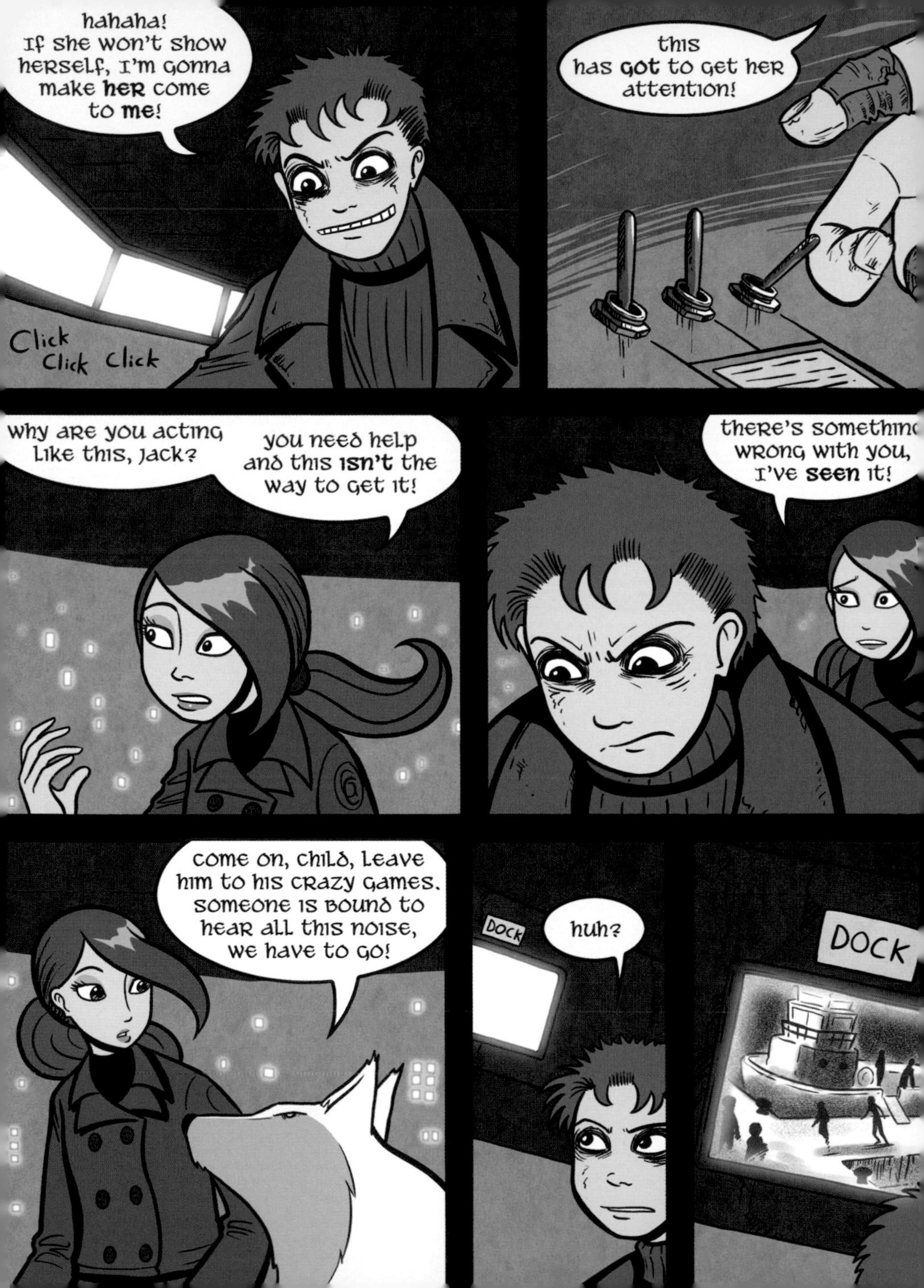
hahaha! If she won't show herself, I'm gonna make **her** come to **me**!
Click Click Click
this has **got** to get her attention!
why are you acting like this, Jack?
you need help and this **isn't** the way to get it!
there's somethin wrong with you, I've **seen** it!
come on, child, leave him to his crazy games. someone is bound to hear all this noise, we have to go!
DOCK
huh?
DOCK

how'd they get here so fast?!

they must've tracked **you** to get to me!

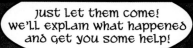
JUST LET THEM COME! WE'LL EXPLAIN WHAT HAPPENED AND GET YOU SOME HELP!

I don't need their help!

I just need to see her again...

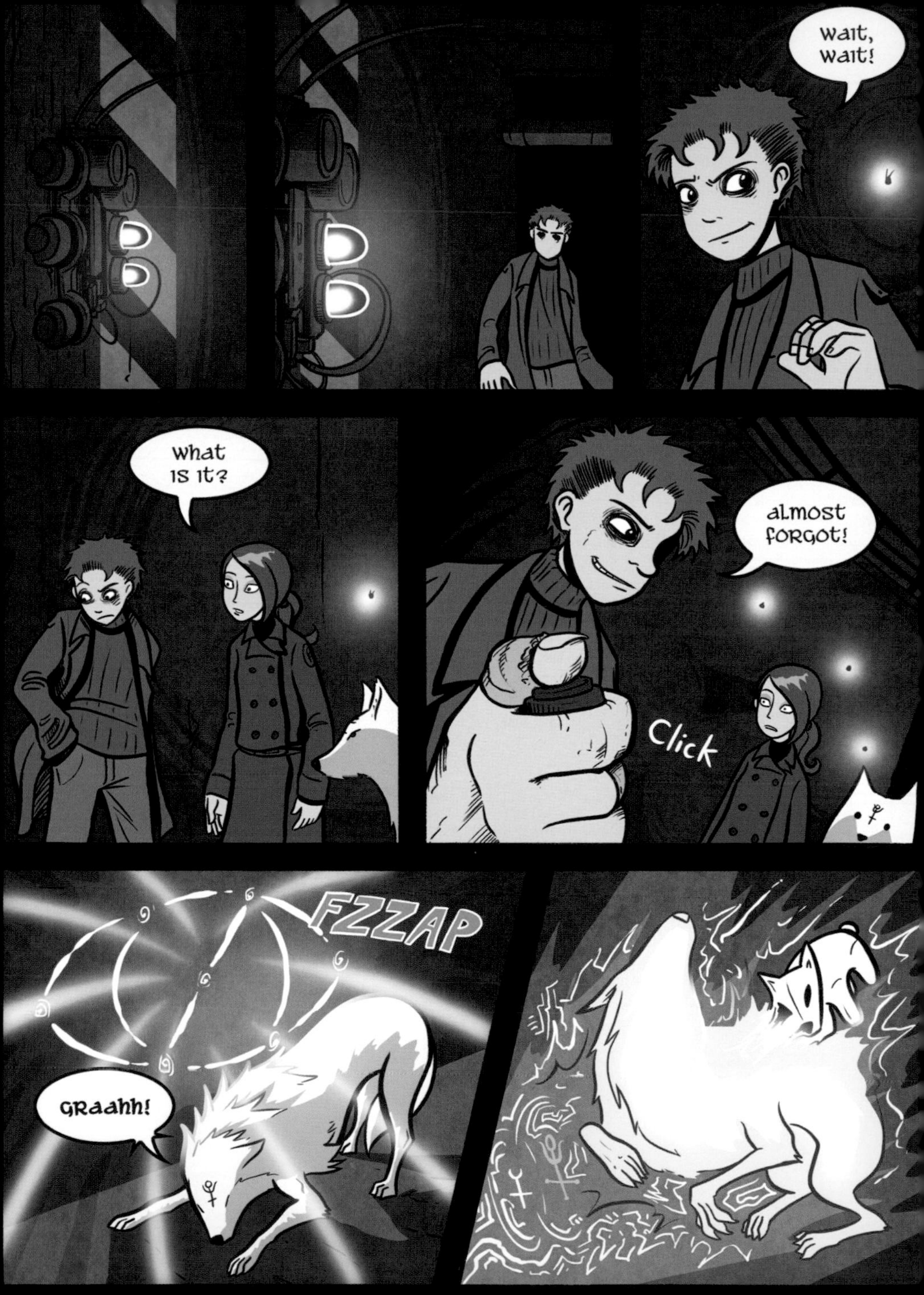
wait, wait!
what is it?
almost forgot!
Click
FZZAP
GRaahh!

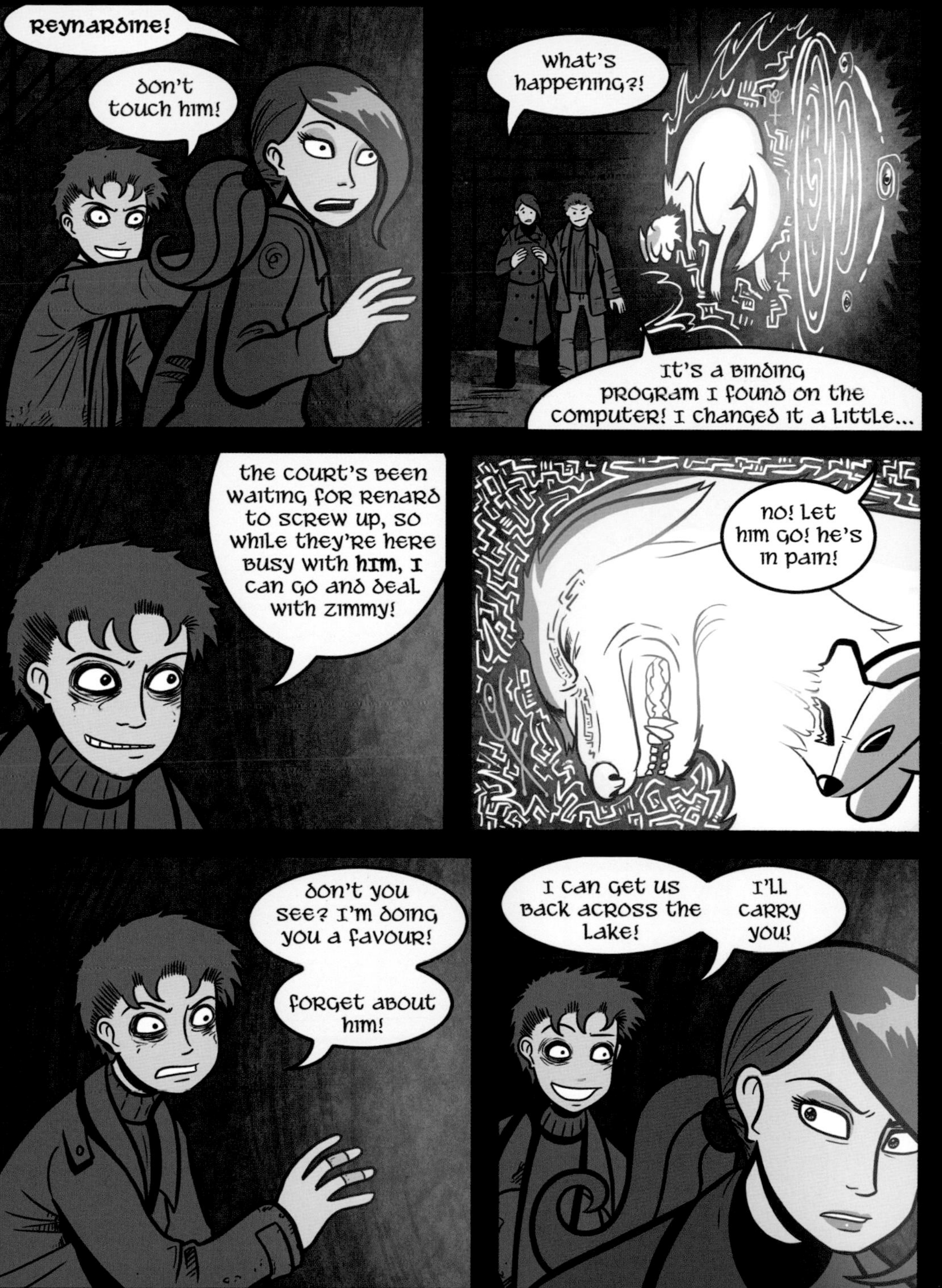
Reynardine!
don't touch him!
What's happening?!
It's a binding program I found on the computer! I changed it a little...
the court's been waiting for Renard to screw up, so while they're here busy with **him**, I can go and deal with Zimmy!
no! Let him go! he's in pain!
don't you see? I'm doing you a favour!
forget about him!
I can get us back across the lake!
I'll carry you!

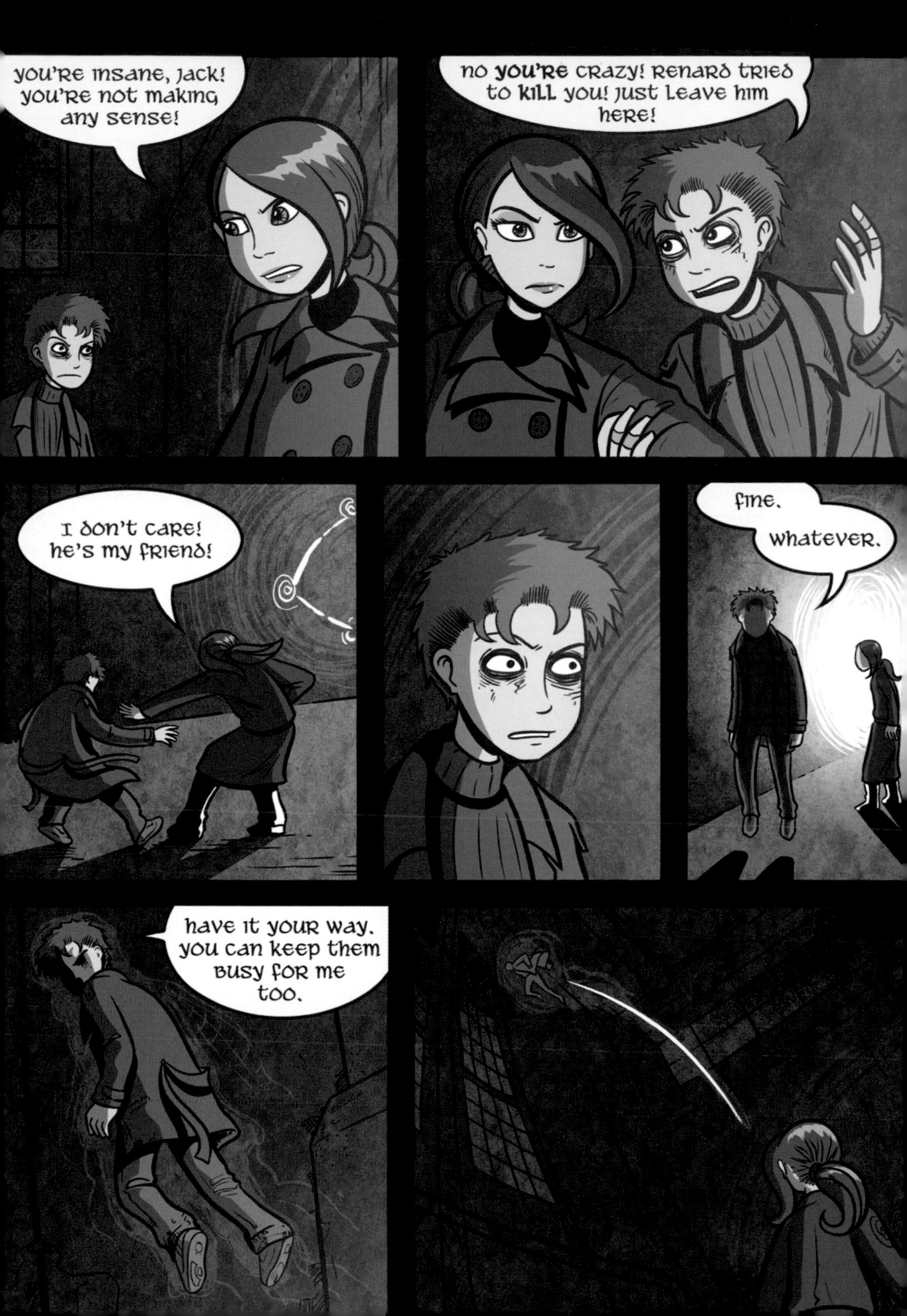
you're insane, jack! you're not making any sense!
no **you're** crazy! renard tried to **kill** you! just leave him here!
I don't care! he's my friend!
fine.
whatever.
have it your way. you can keep them busy for me too.

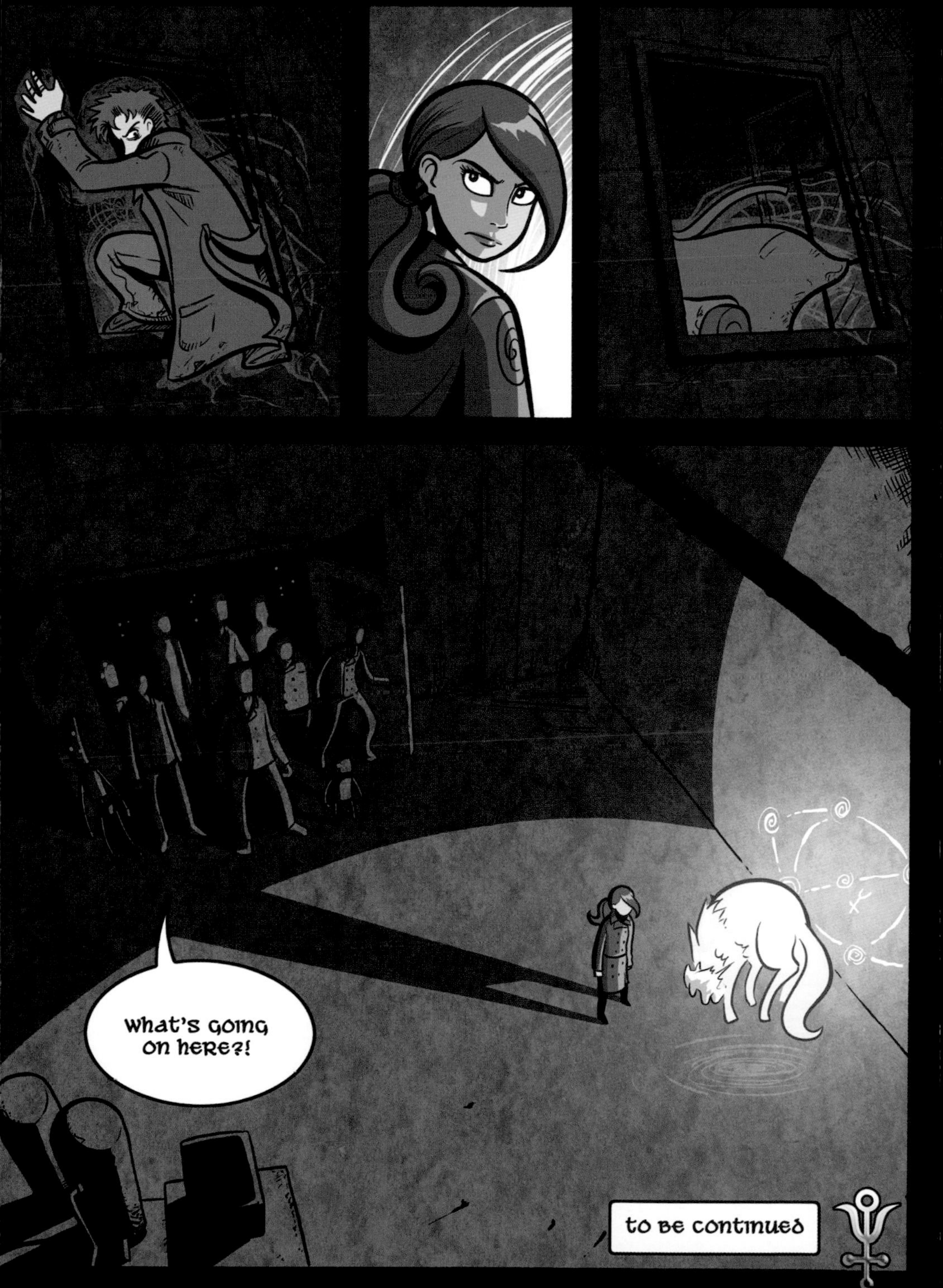
What's going on here?!
to be continued

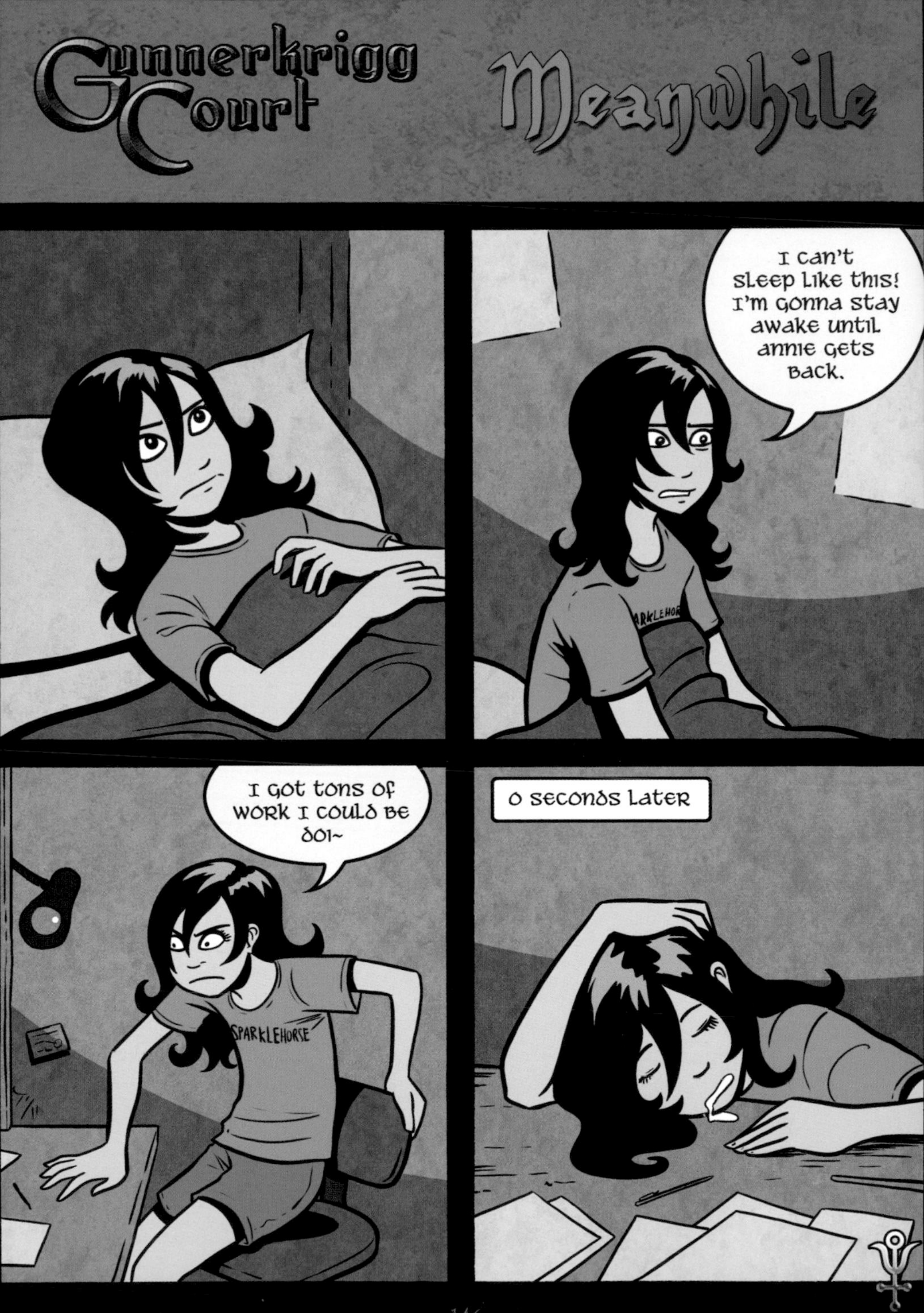
Gunnerkrigg Court
Meanwhile
I can't sleep like this! I'm gonna stay awake until annie gets back.
SPARKLEHORSE
I got tons of work I could be doi~
SPARKLEHORSE
0 seconds later

Gunnerkrigg Court

Chapter 28:

Spring Heeled

Part 2

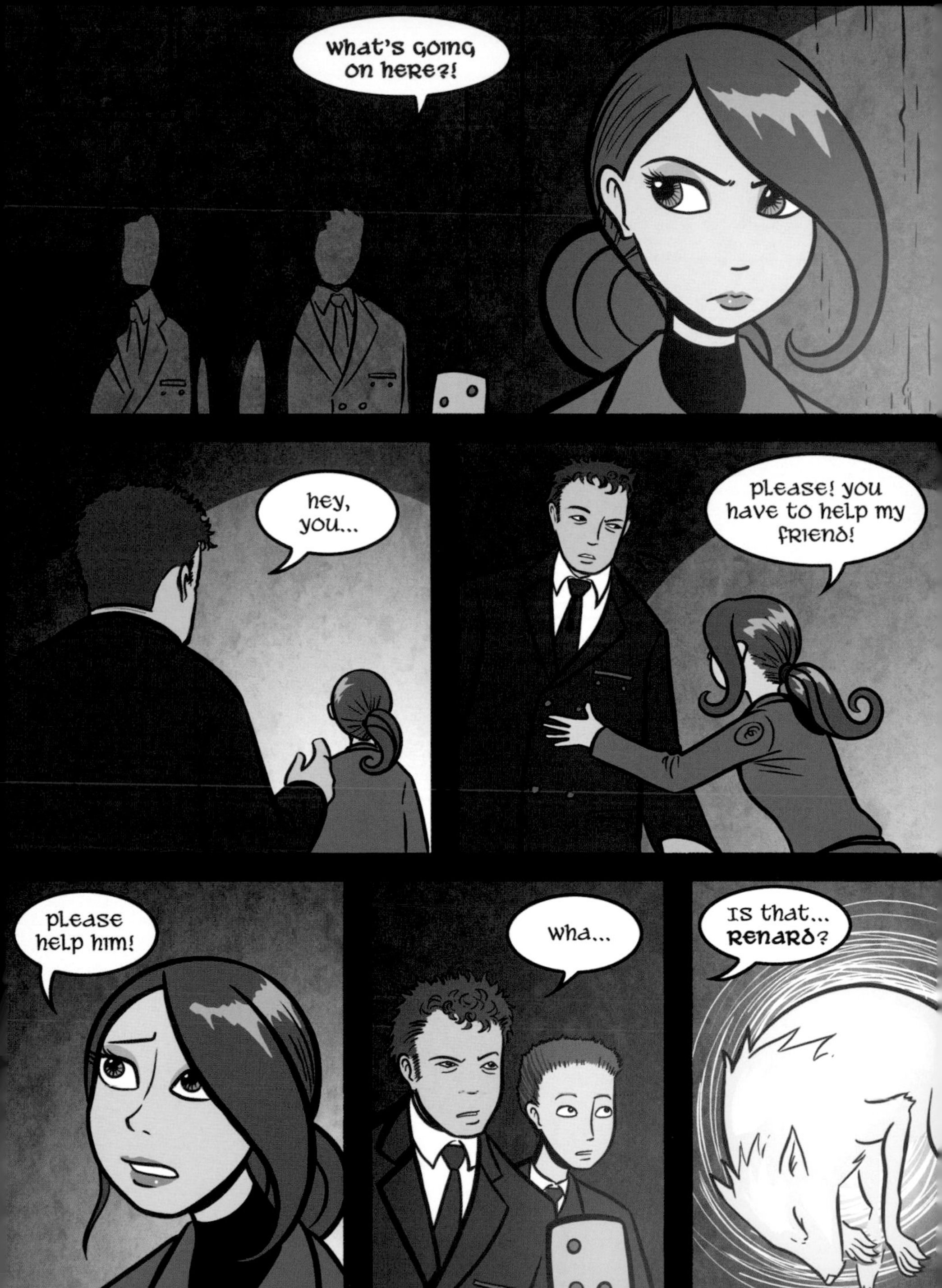
what's going on here?!
hey, you...
please! you have to help my friend!
please help him!
wha...
Is that... RENARD?

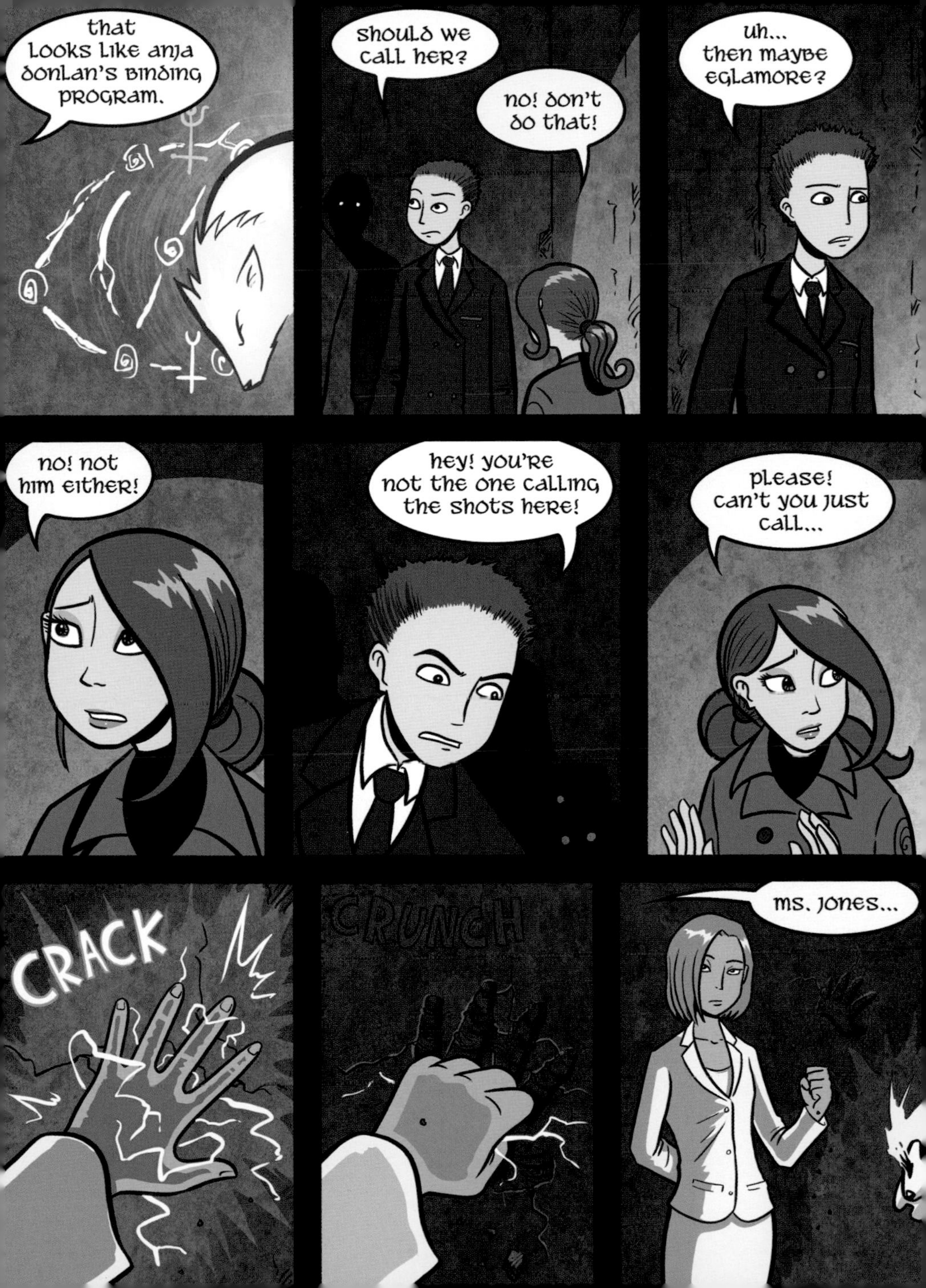
that looks like anja donlan's binding program.
should we call her?
no! don't do that!
uh... then maybe eglamore?
no! not him either!
hey! you're not the one calling the shots here!
please! can't you just call...
CRACK
CRUNCH
ms. jones...

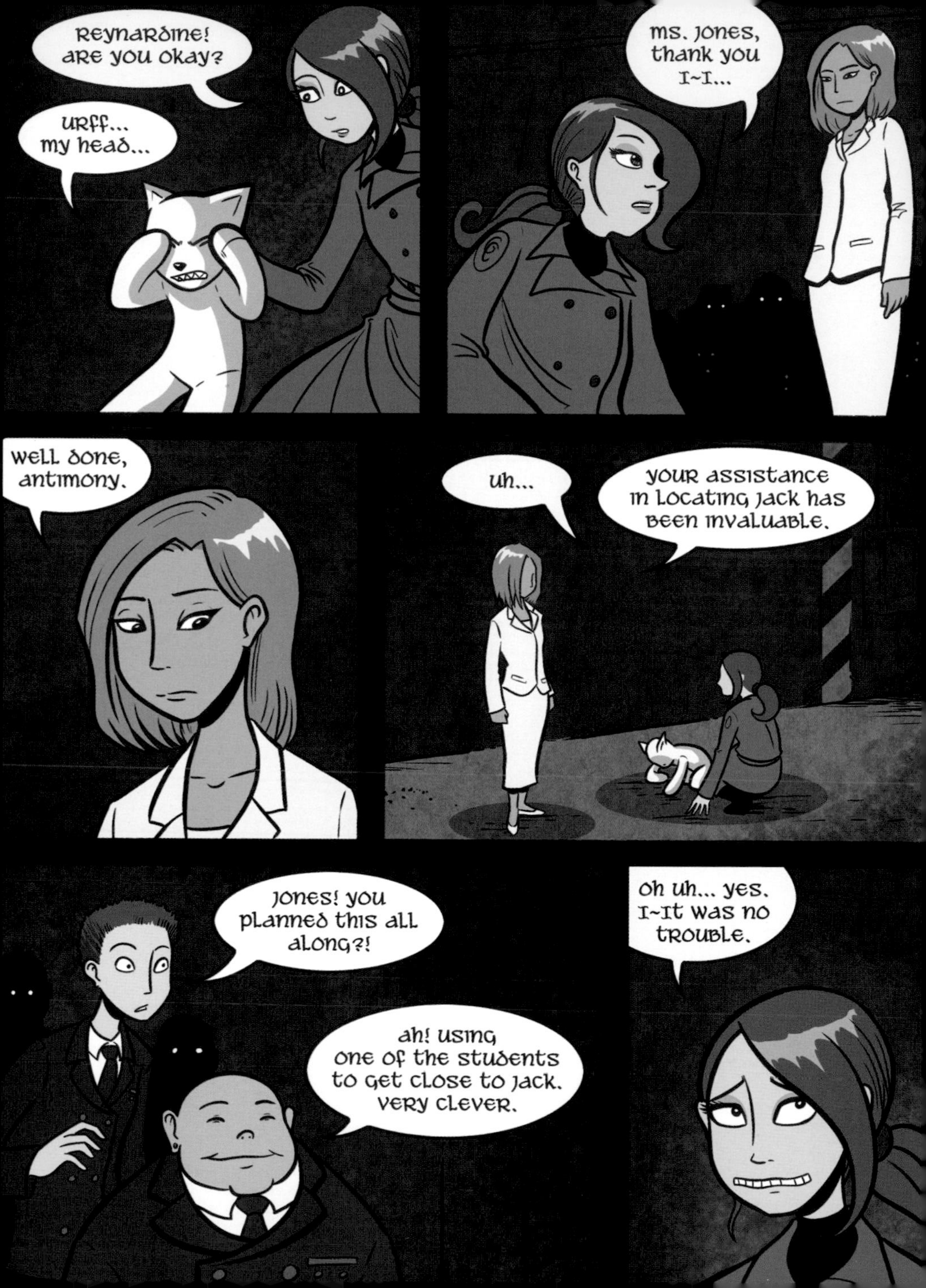
Reynardine! are you okay?
Urff... my head...
Ms. Jones, thank you I-I...
Well done, Antimony.
Uh...
Your assistance in locating Jack has been invaluable.
Jones! You planned this all along?!
Ah! Using one of the students to get close to Jack. Very clever.
Oh uh... yes. I-It was no trouble.

SO WHERE IS YOUNG HYLAND NOW?

HE'S BEEN HIDING IN A BUILDING NEXT TO THE LAKE. I THINK HE'S GOING BACK THERE.

AND I THINK... UH...

I THINK HE CAN FLY.

THAT'S CRAZY!

IF SHE SAYS HE CAN FLY, THEN HE CAN FLY.

AH... OF COURSE.

WE WILL HAVE TO RETURN TO THE BOAT, AATA, PLEASE HAVE SOME OF YOUR PEOPLE MAN THE ETHER STATION.

I'M QUALIFIED TO OPERATE THIS FACILITY.

AS AM I.

SHALL WE SHUT IT ALL DOWN?

NO, JACK STARTED IT FOR A REASON, AND I WOULD LIKE TO FIND OUT WHY.

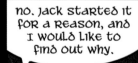

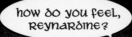

how do you feel, reynardine?

a little... better. if jones could just...

clutch me to her chest!

you're fine.

ahaha!

so, you feel jack was affected by his encounter with zimmy?

yes. I don't know him very well, but... he destroyed a robot without a second thought.

it's like he's a different person.

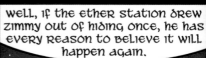

well, if the ether station drew zimmy out of hiding once, he has every reason to believe it will happen again.

are we going to stop him?

it will be far more interesting to see what happens if we don't.

juliette, allow the station to enter the collection stage.

yes, jones.

zimmy... the station... i don't understand.

the court found a way to extract etheric energies from the earth.

this particular station uses a form of evaporation to extract it from the water in the lake.

the energy is then used in further experiments. unfortunately, many of the details are kept secret. even from me.

and zimmy...

well, try to imagine a station such as this one in the mind of a person.

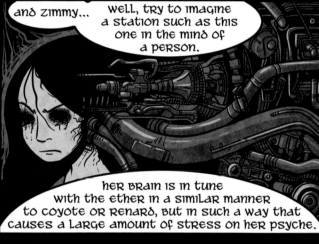

her brain is in tune with the ether in a similar manner to coyote or renard, but in such a way that causes a large amount of stress on her psyche.

and gamma helps ease the stress?

exactly. in much the same way a heat sink absorbs and dissipates heat from an overloaded computer processor.

further stress on zimmy's mind, or even distance from gamma, can lead to distortions that present themselves in the physical world.

153

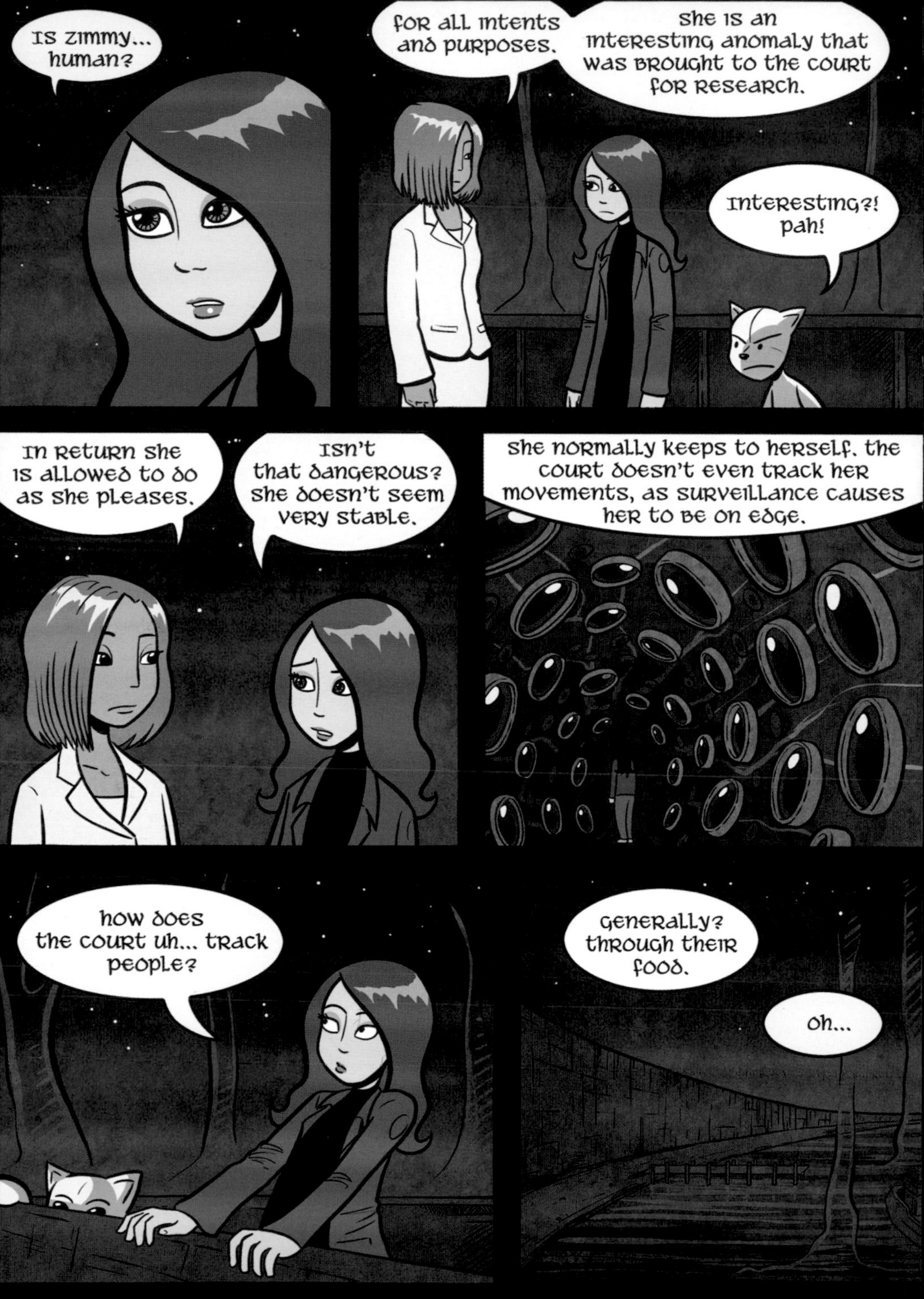
Is Zimmy... human?
For all intents and purposes.
She is an interesting anomaly that was brought to the court for research.
Interesting?! Pah!
In return she is allowed to do as she pleases.
Isn't that dangerous? She doesn't seem very stable.
She normally keeps to herself. The court doesn't even track her movements, as surveillance causes her to be on edge.
How does the court uh... track people?
Generally? Through their food.
Oh...

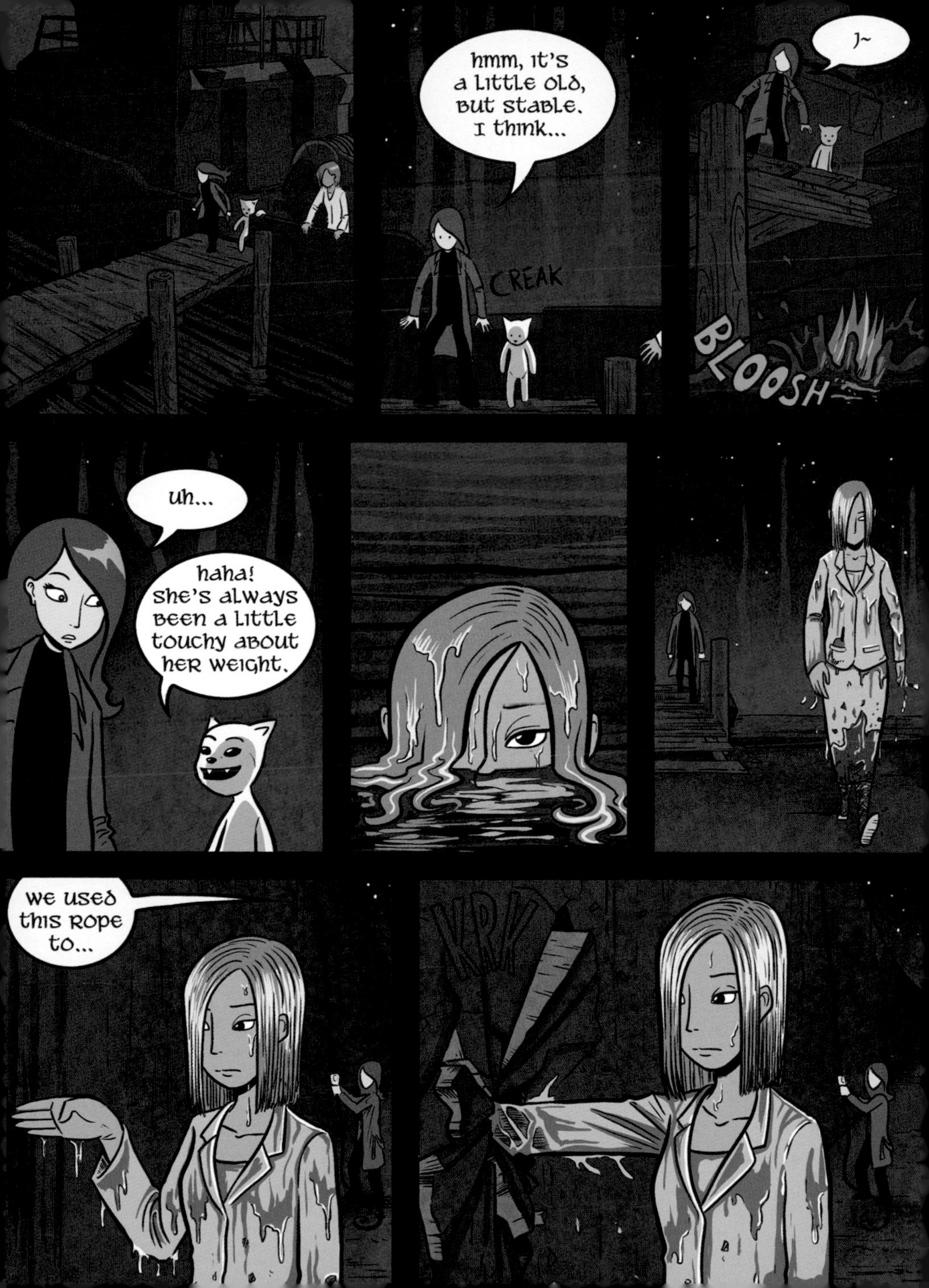
hmm, it's a little old, but stable. I think...
CREAK
J~
BLOOSH
uh...
haha! she's always been a little touchy about her weight.
we used this rope to...

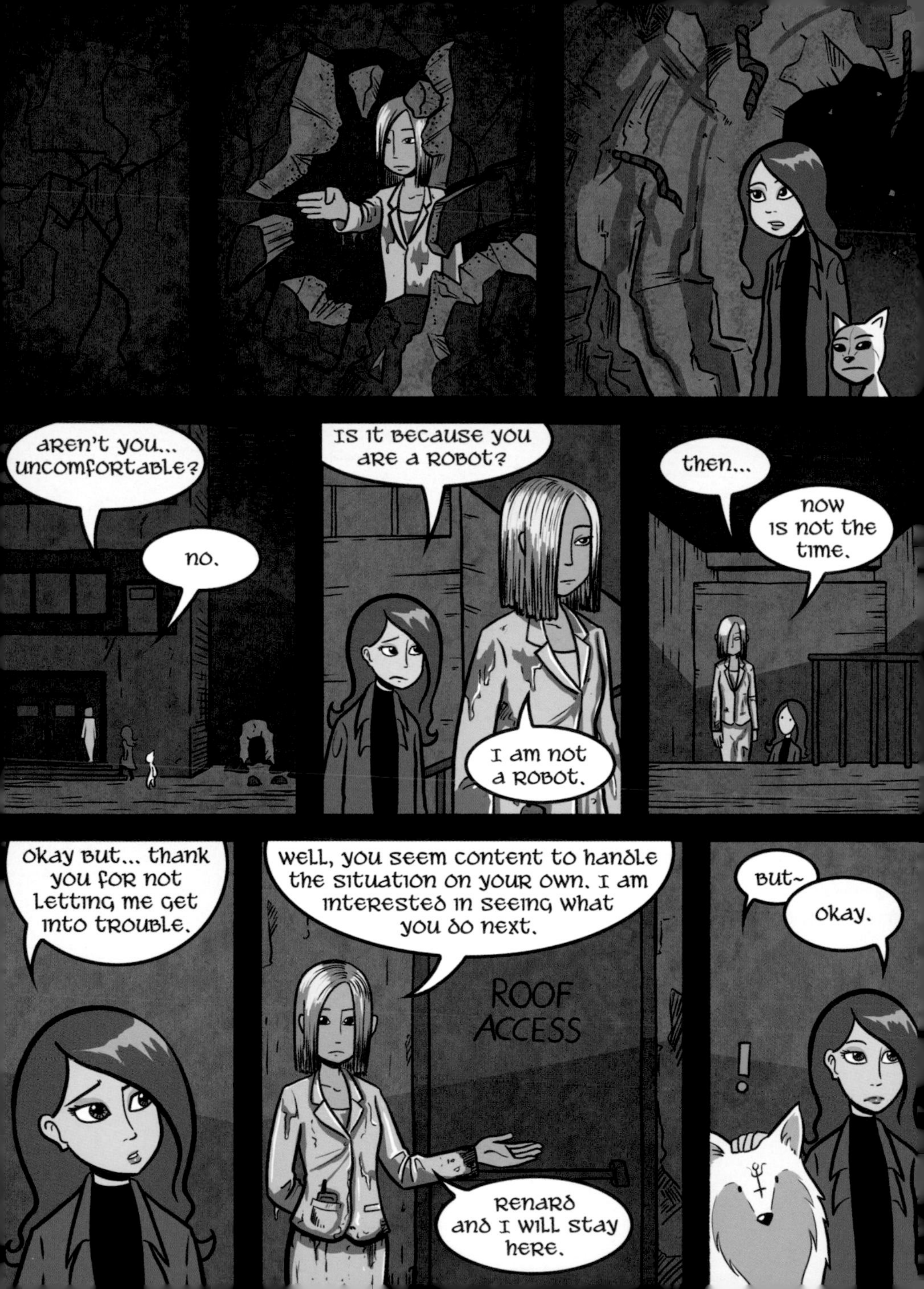
aren't you... uncomfortable?
no.
is it because you are a robot?
I am not a robot.
then...
now is not the time.
okay but... thank you for not letting me get into trouble.
well, you seem content to handle the situation on your own. I am interested in seeing what you do next.
ROOF ACCESS
Renard and I will stay here.
but~
okay.
!

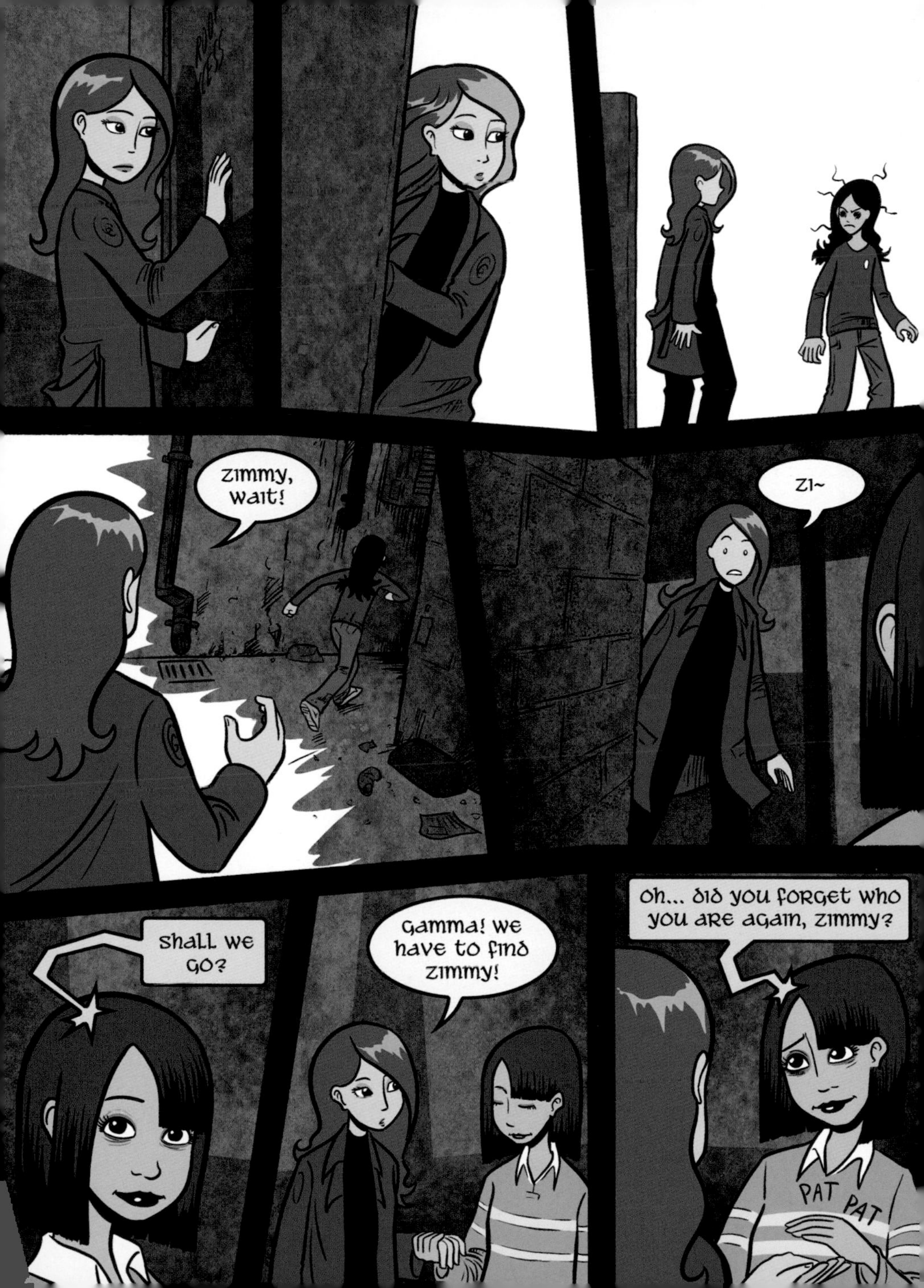
Zimmy, wait!
Zi~
Shall we go?
Gamma! We have to find Zimmy!
Oh... did you forget who you are again, Zimmy?
PAT PAT

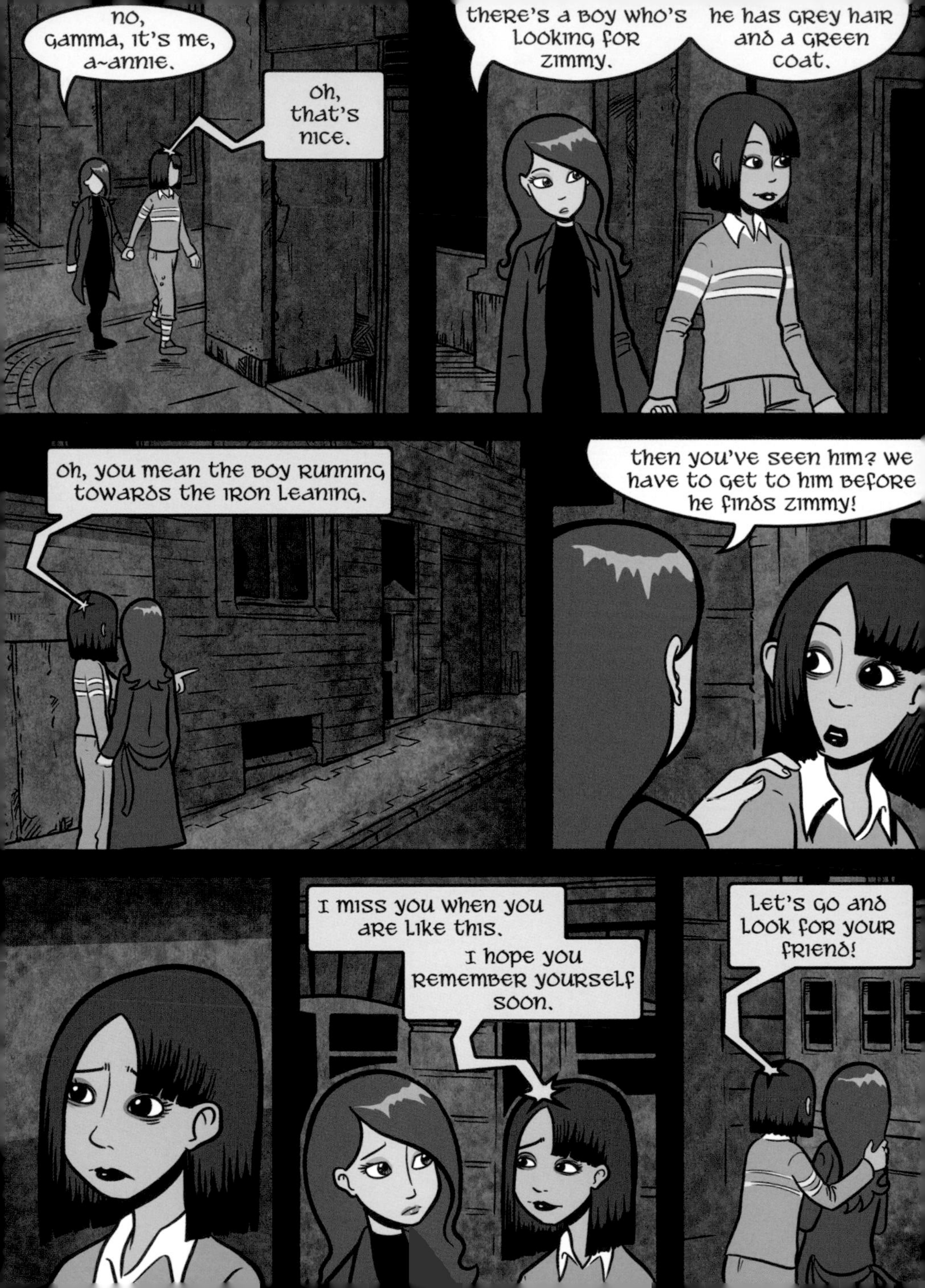
no, Gamma, it's me, a~annie.
oh, that's nice.
there's a boy who's looking for zimmy.
he has grey hair and a green coat.
oh, you mean the boy running towards the iron leaning.
then you've seen him? we have to get to him before he finds zimmy!
I miss you when you are like this.
I hope you remember yourself soon.
let's go and look for your friend!

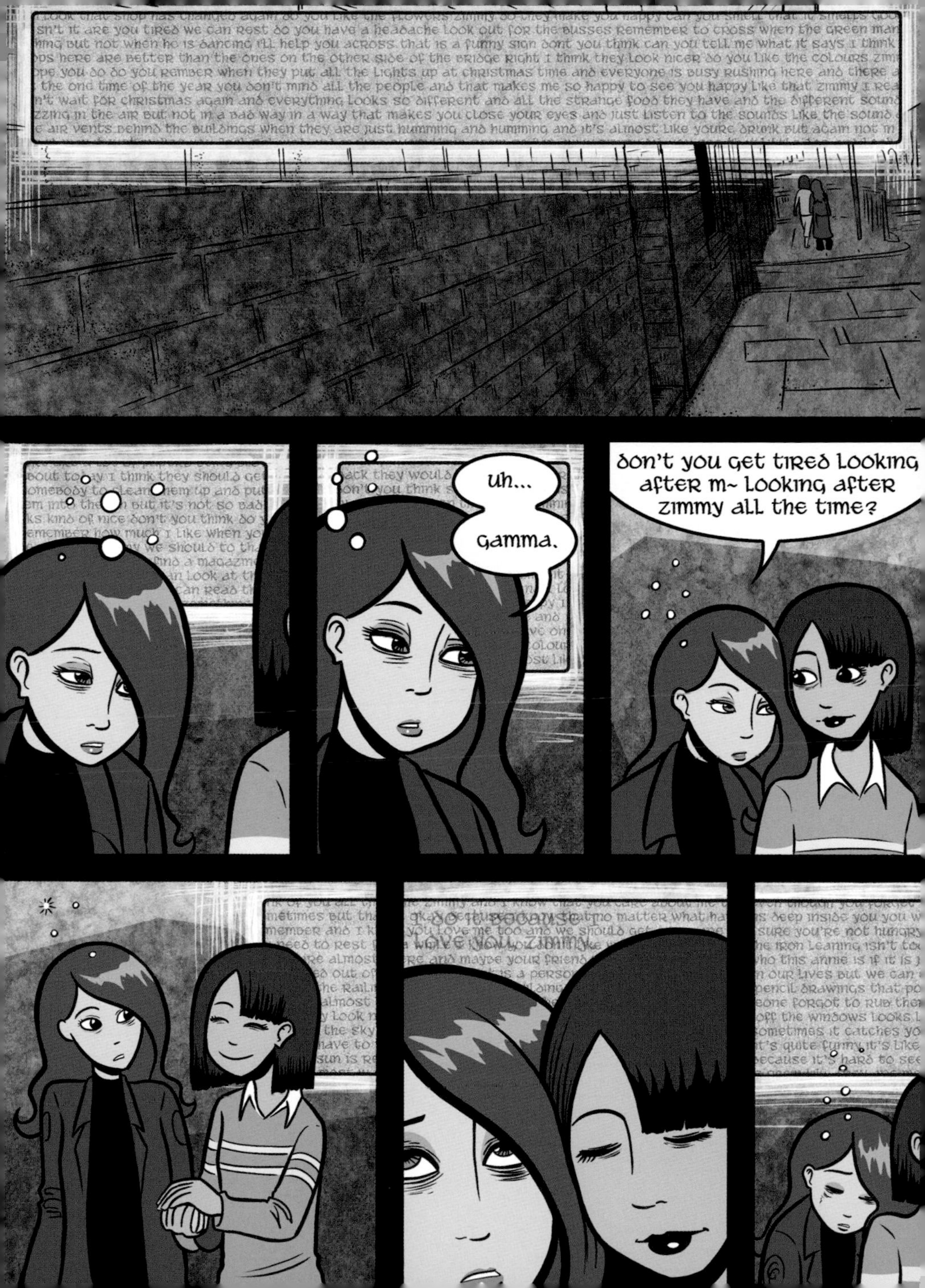
sn't it are you tired we can rest do you have a headache look out for the busses remember to cross when the green man
ning but not when he is dancing i'll help you across that is a funny sign dont you think can you tell me what it says i think
ops here are better than the ones on the other side of the bridge right i think they look nicer do you like the colours zimm
ope you do do you rember when they put all the lights up at christmas time and everyone is busy rushing here and there a
the one time of the year you don't mind all the people and that makes me so happy to see you happy like that zimmy i rea
n't wait for christmas again and everything looks so different and all the strange food they have and the different sound
zzing in the air but not in a bad way in a way that makes you close your eyes and just listen to the sounds like the sound
e air vents behind the buildings when they are just humming and humming and it's almost like youre drunk but again not m
uh...
gamma.
don't you get tired looking after m~ looking after zimmy all the time?
so it's because
love you, zimmy.

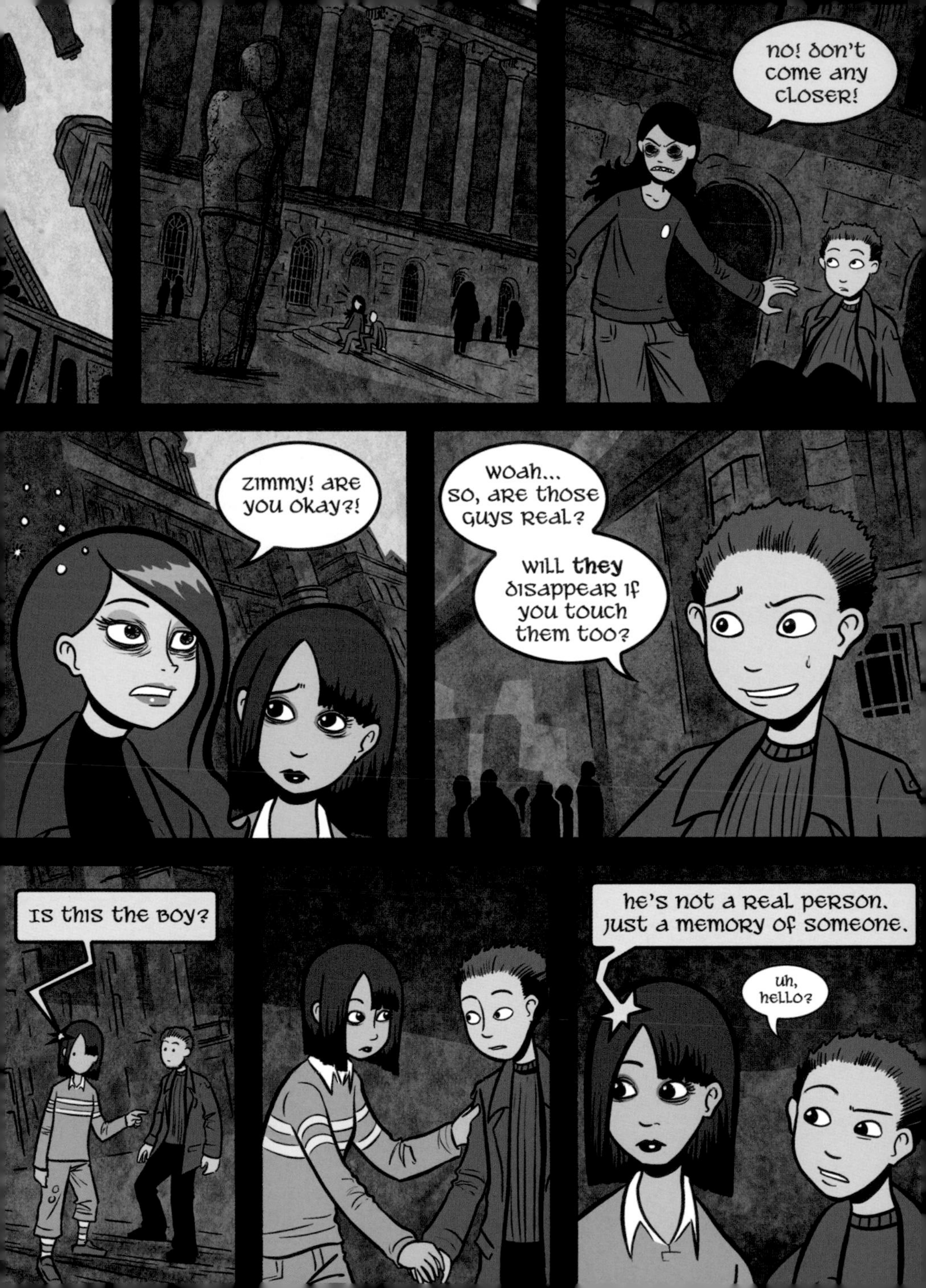
no! don't come any CLOSER!
ZIMMY! ARE YOU OKAY?!
WOAH... SO, ARE THOSE GUYS REAL?
WILL **they** DISAPPEAR IF YOU TOUCH THEM TOO?
IS THIS THE BOY?
HE'S NOT A REAL PERSON. JUST A MEMORY OF SOMEONE.
UH, HELLO?

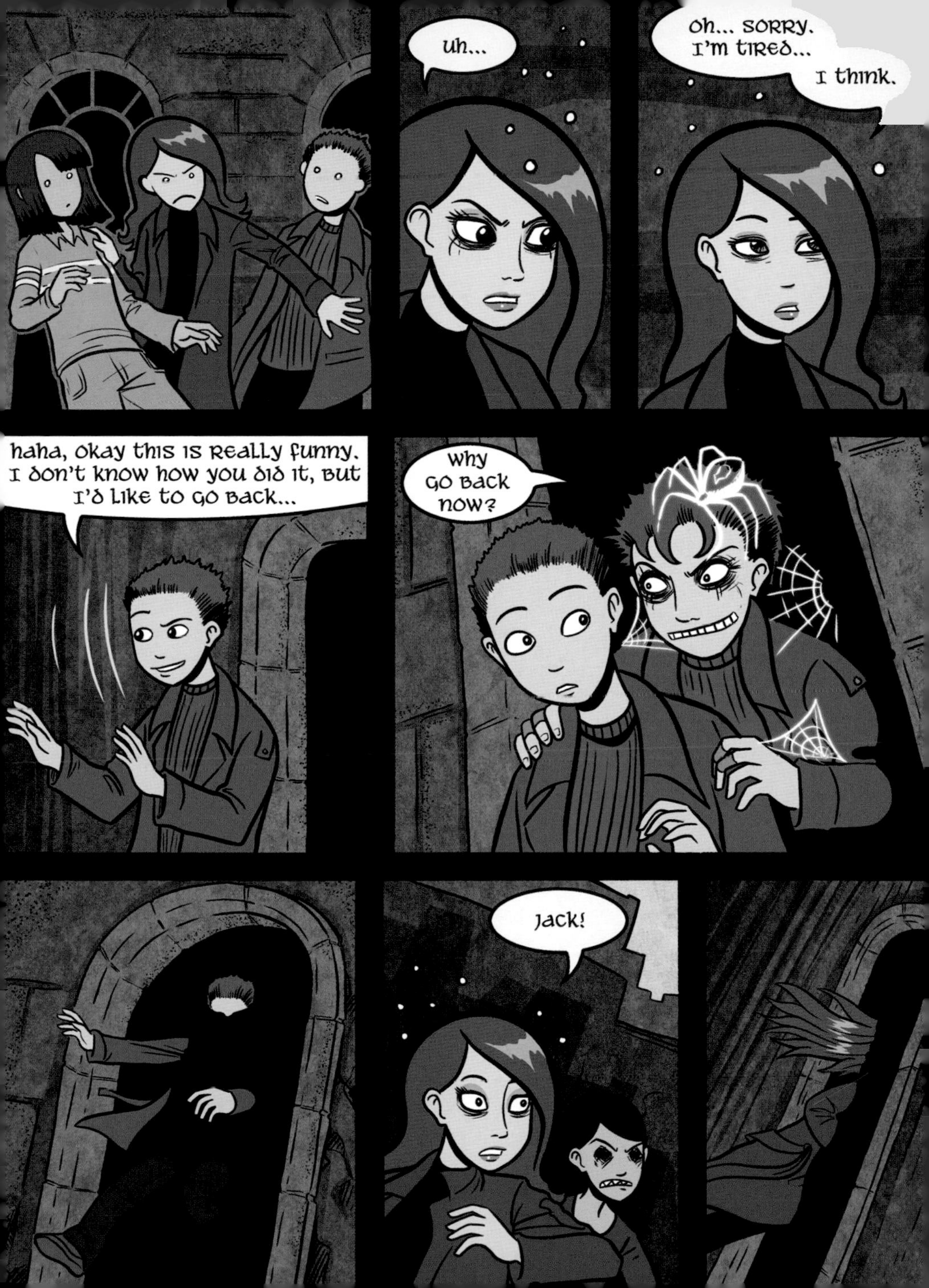
uh...
Oh... SORRY. I'm TIRED...
I think.
haha, okay this is really funny. I don't know how you did it, but I'd like to go back...
Why go back now?
Jack!

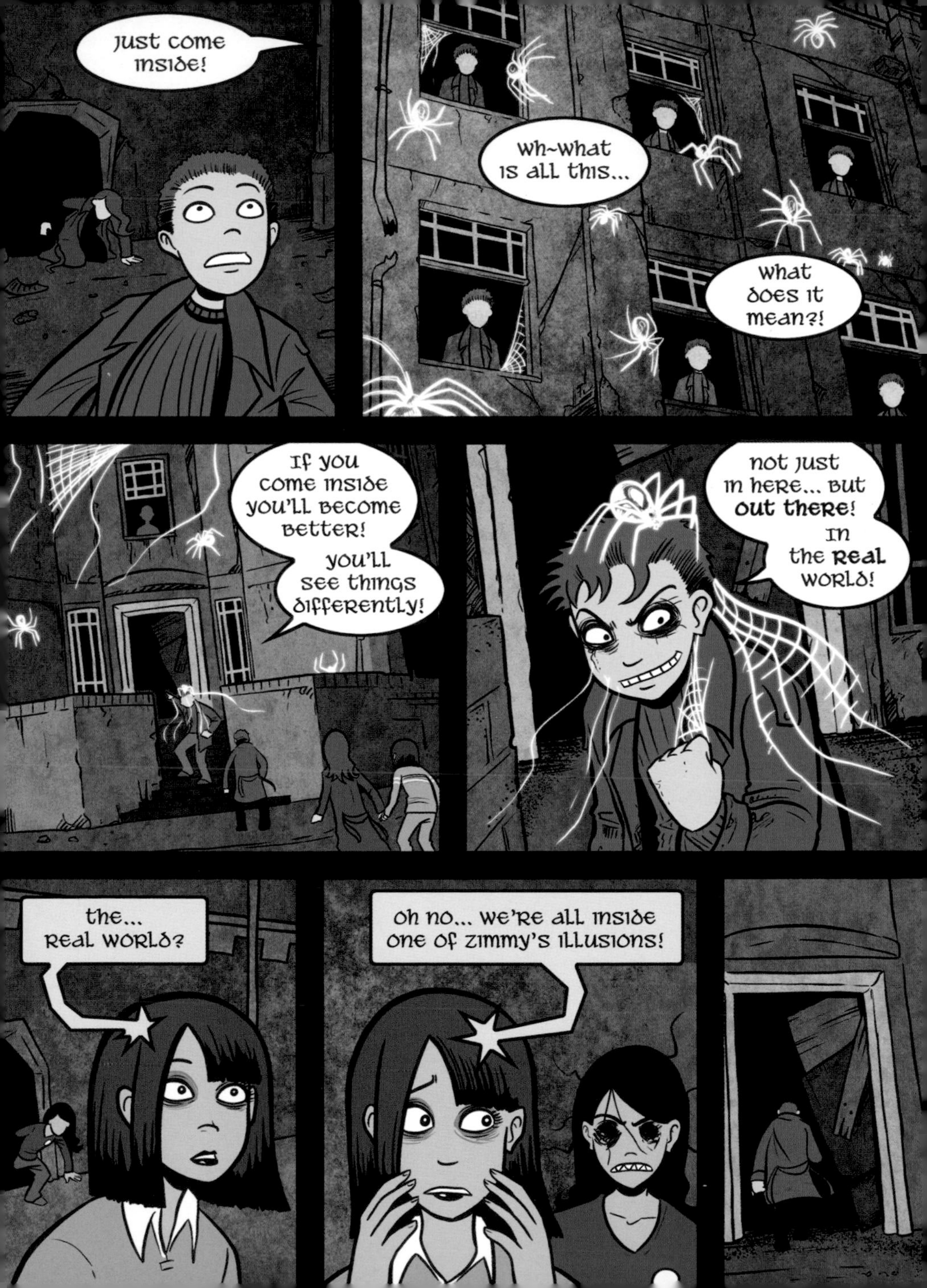
JUST COME INSIDE!
WH~WHAT IS ALL THIS...
WHAT DOES IT MEAN?!
IF YOU COME INSIDE YOU'LL BECOME BETTER!
YOU'LL SEE THINGS DIFFERENTLY!
NOT JUST IN HERE... BUT OUT THERE!
IN THE REAL WORLD!
THE... REAL WORLD?
OH NO... WE'RE ALL INSIDE ONE OF ZIMMY'S ILLUSIONS!

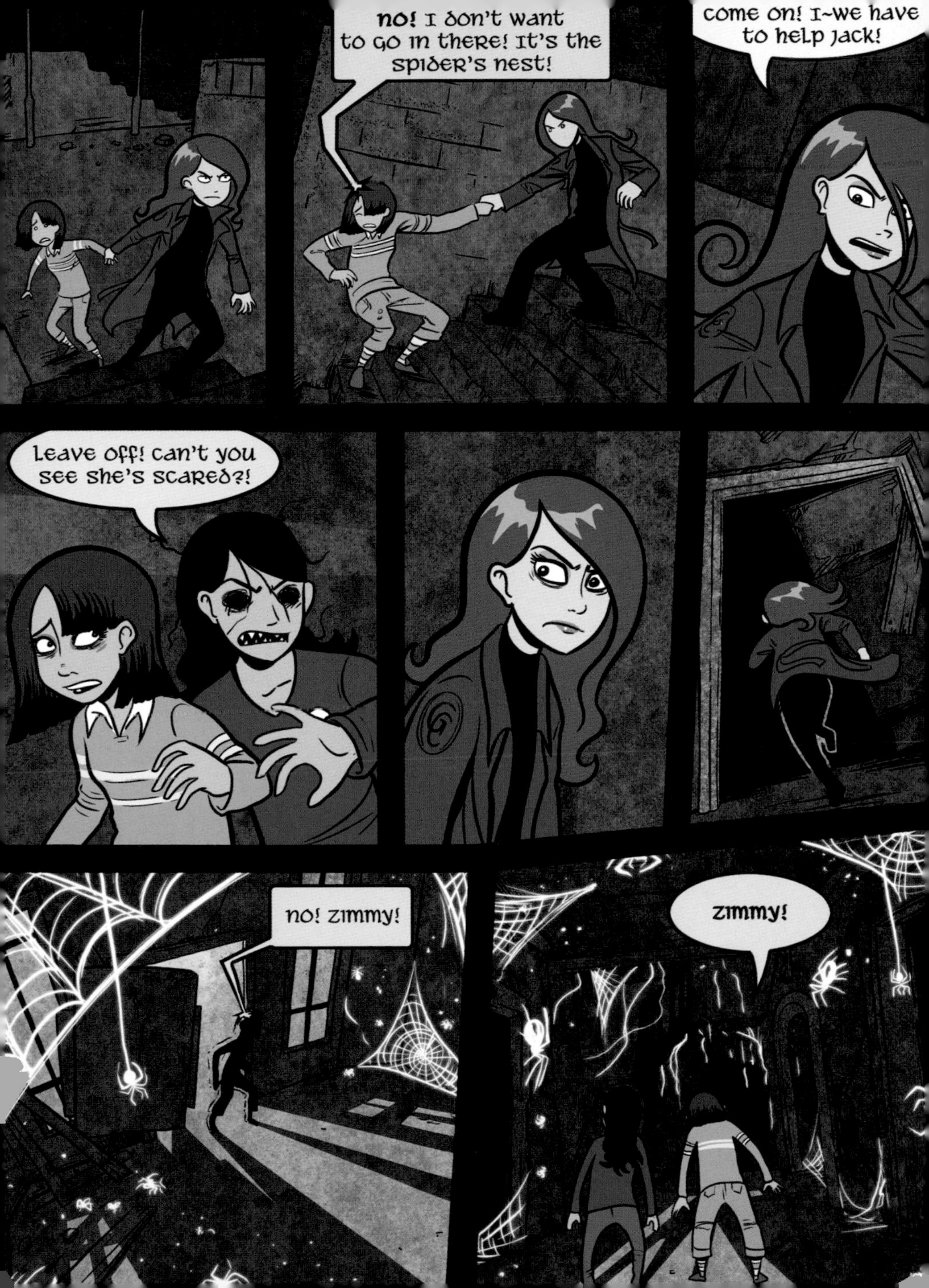
no! I don't want to go in there! It's the spider's nest!
come on! I~we have to help Jack!
Leave off! can't you see she's scared?!
no! zimmy!
zimmy!

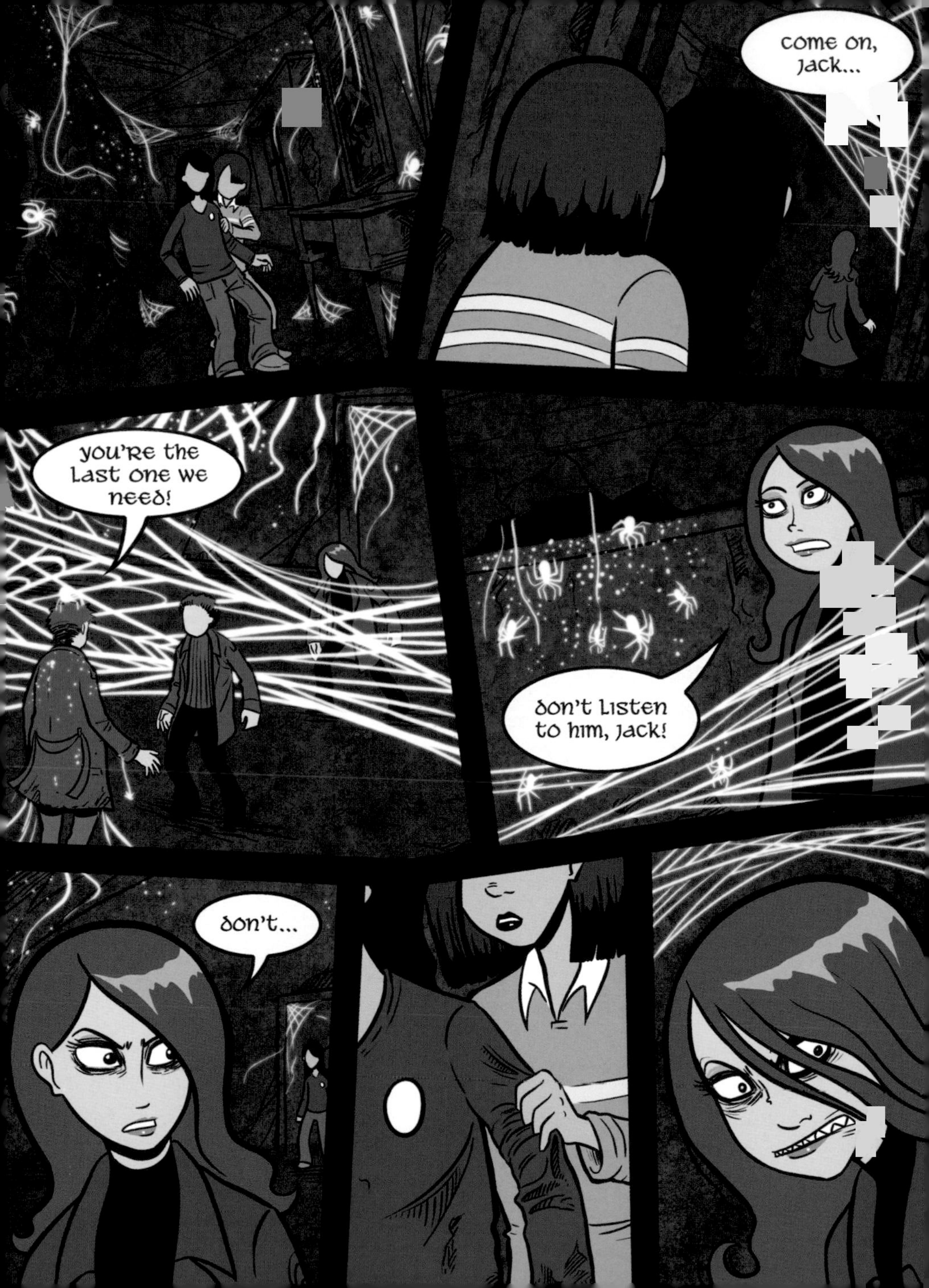
come on, jack...
you're the last one we need!
don't listen to him, jack!
don't...

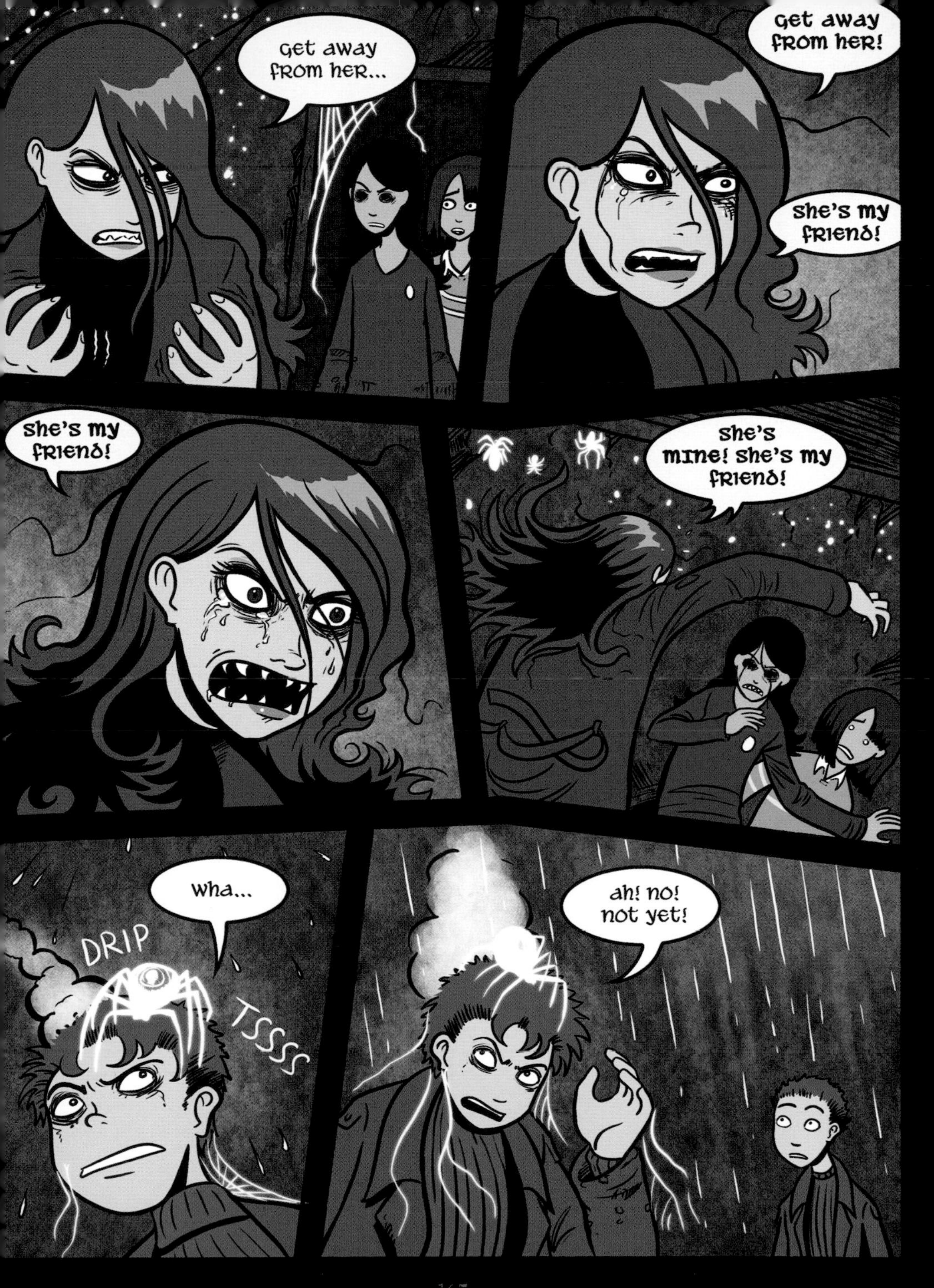
get away from her...
get away from her!
she's my friend!
she's my friend!
she's mine! she's my friend!
wha...
DRIP
TSSSS
ah! no! not yet!

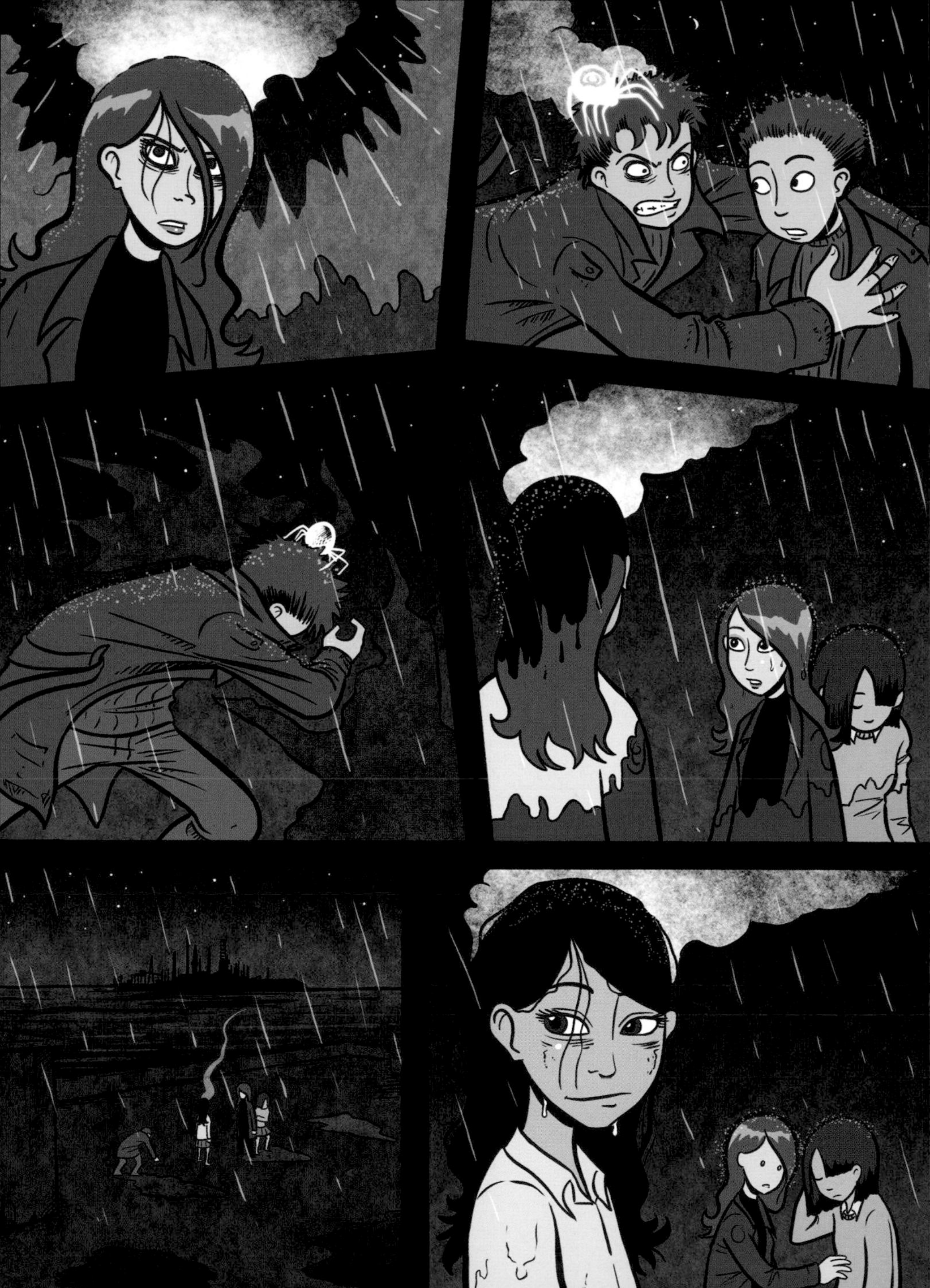

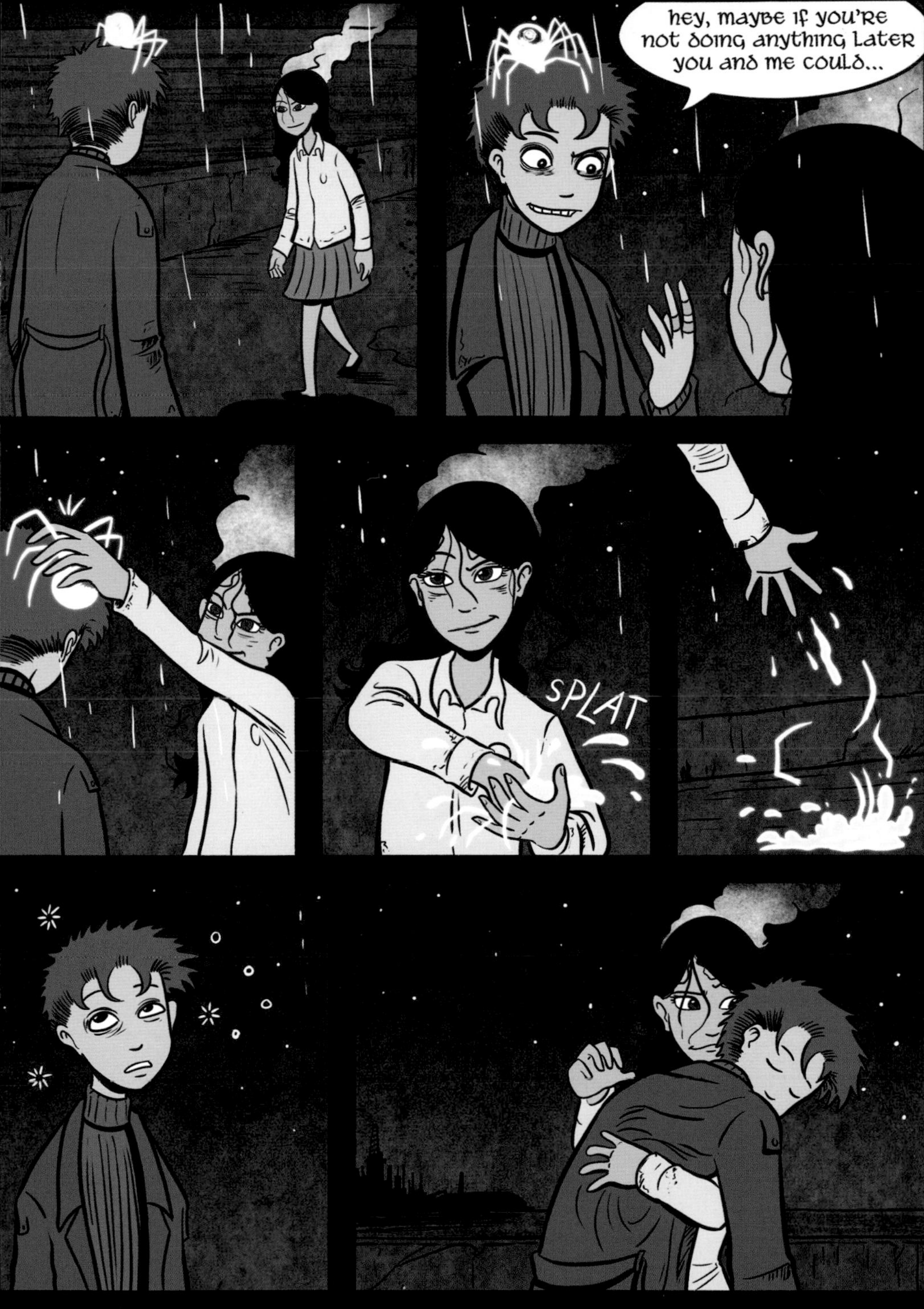
hey, maybe if you're not doing anything later you and me could...
SPLAT

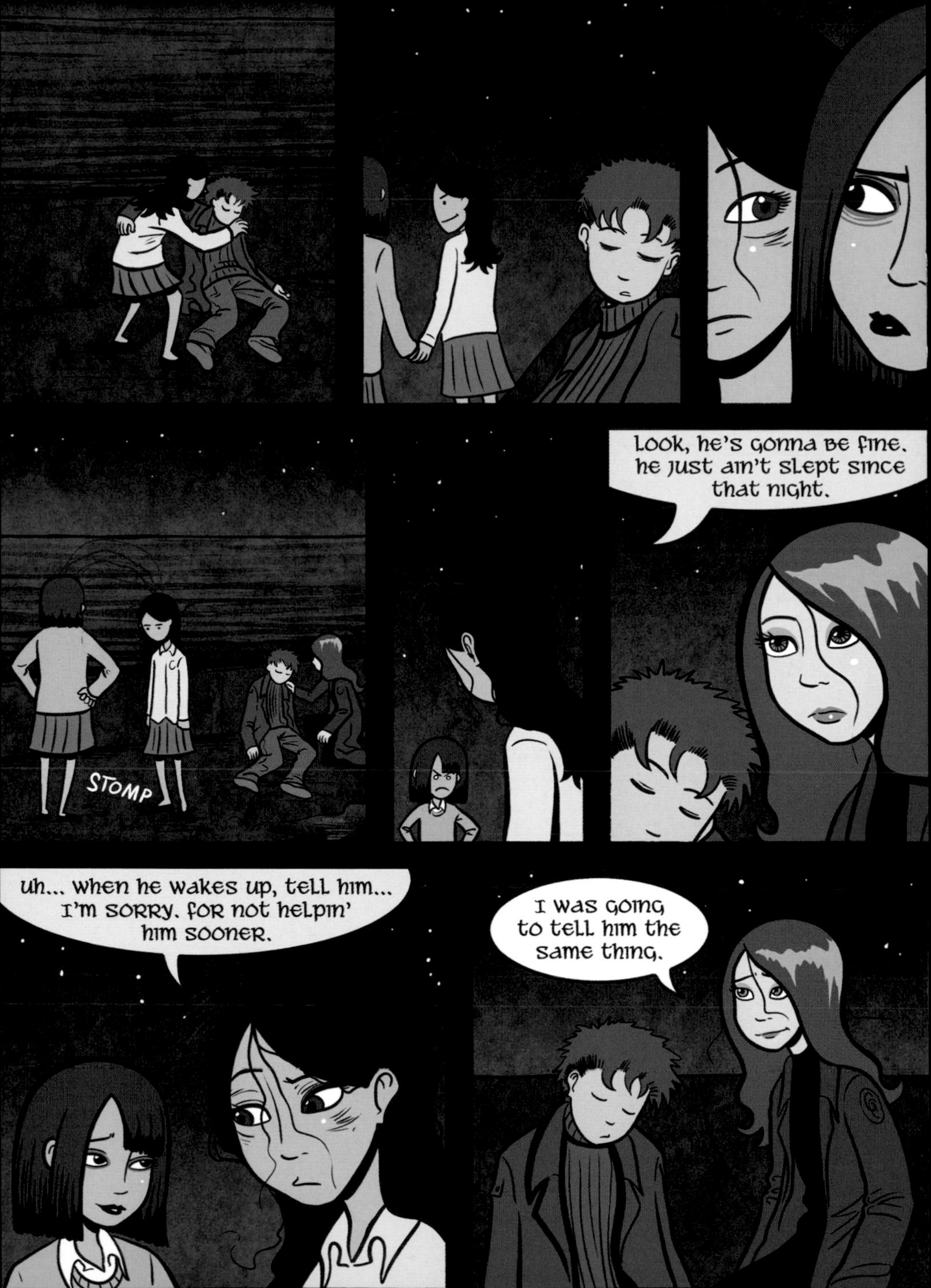
LOOK, HE'S GONNA BE FINE. HE JUST AIN'T SLEPT SINCE THAT NIGHT.
STOMP
UH... WHEN HE WAKES UP, TELL HIM... I'M SORRY. FOR NOT HELPIN' HIM SOONER.
I WAS GOING TO TELL HIM THE SAME THING.

WHAT ABOUT YOU? WILL YOU BE OKAY WITH THOSE... THINGS?

OH, DON'T WORRY 'BOUT THEM **WHITELEGS**. THEY'RE ALWAYS TRYIN' TO HITCH A RIDE OUTTA HERE.

YOUR BOYFRIEND THERE WAS JUST IN THE WRONG PLACE, Y'KNOW? BUT HE PUT UP A FIGHT. HE DIDN'T GO **COMPLETELY** MENTAL.

GAMMA THINKS HE MIGHT BE ABLE TO DO SOME OF THAT STUFF YOU GUYS DO, Y'KNOW, THAT MAGICAL CRAP.

DON'T UNDERSTAND IT MYSELF.

THANK YOU, ZIMMY. AND GAMMA.

ALSO; NOT MY BOYFRIEND.

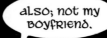

HEH, RIGHT.

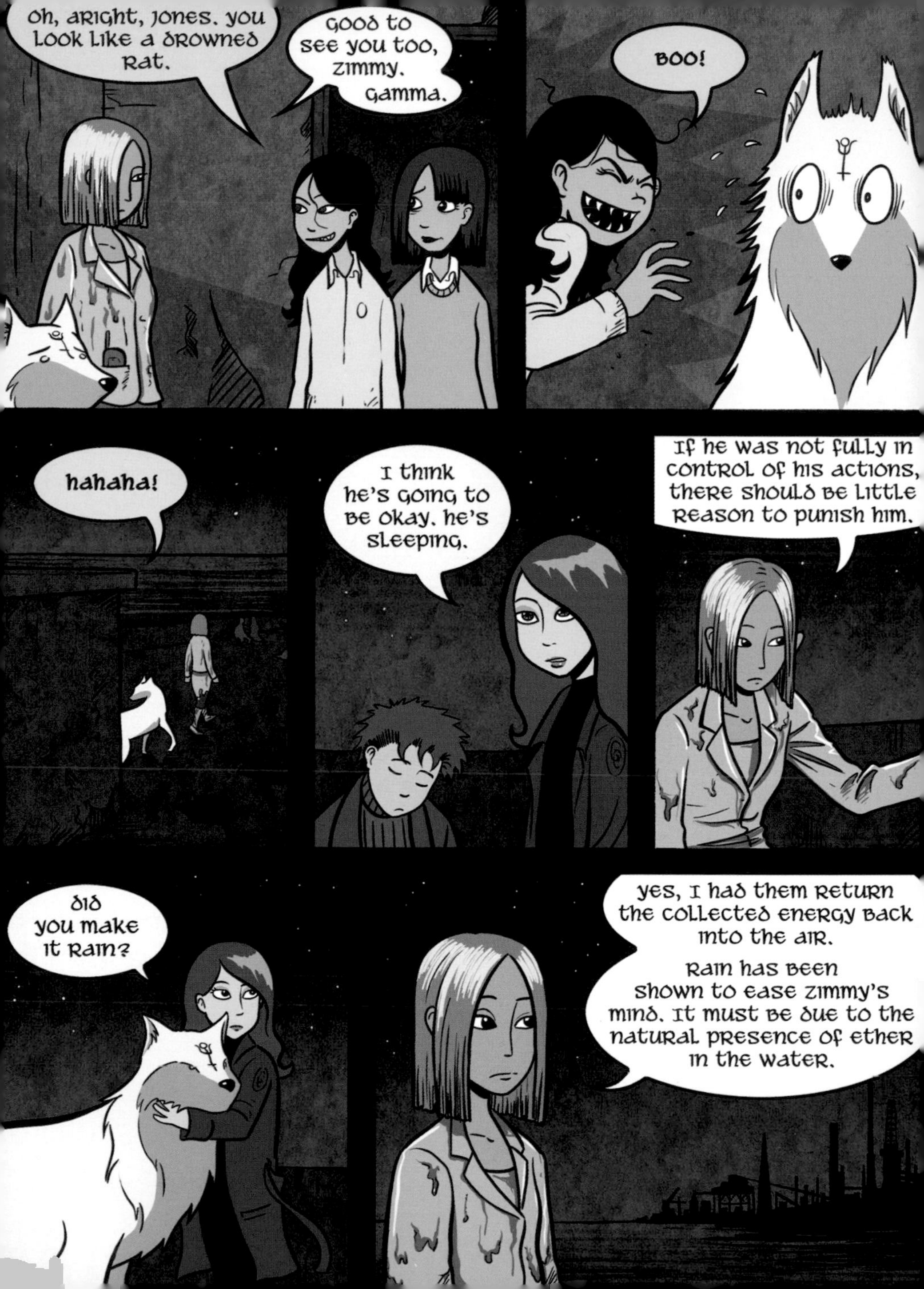
oh, aRight, jones. you Look Like a drowned Rat.
Good to see you too, zimmy. Gamma.
BOO!
hahaha!
I think he's going to be okay. he's sleeping.
If he was not fully in control of his actions, there should be little reason to punish him.
did you make it rain?
yes, I had them return the collected energy back into the air.
Rain has been shown to ease zimmy's mind. It must be due to the natural presence of ether in the water.

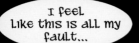

I feel like this is all my fault...

If you knew about Jack's condition, you should have told someone about it.

I don't want you to lose your initiative, Antimony, but you should know you don't have to deal with **everything** by yourself.

On the other hand, Zimmy keeps people at arm's length because she knows she is a danger to those around her.

She can hardly be blamed for what she is.

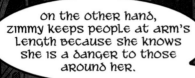

A demon is what she is.

A label commonly applied to what is feared and misunderstood.

Don't forget, you are known as "the demon Renard" to many people.

...

Now, as for the matter of you being in trouble, Antimony...

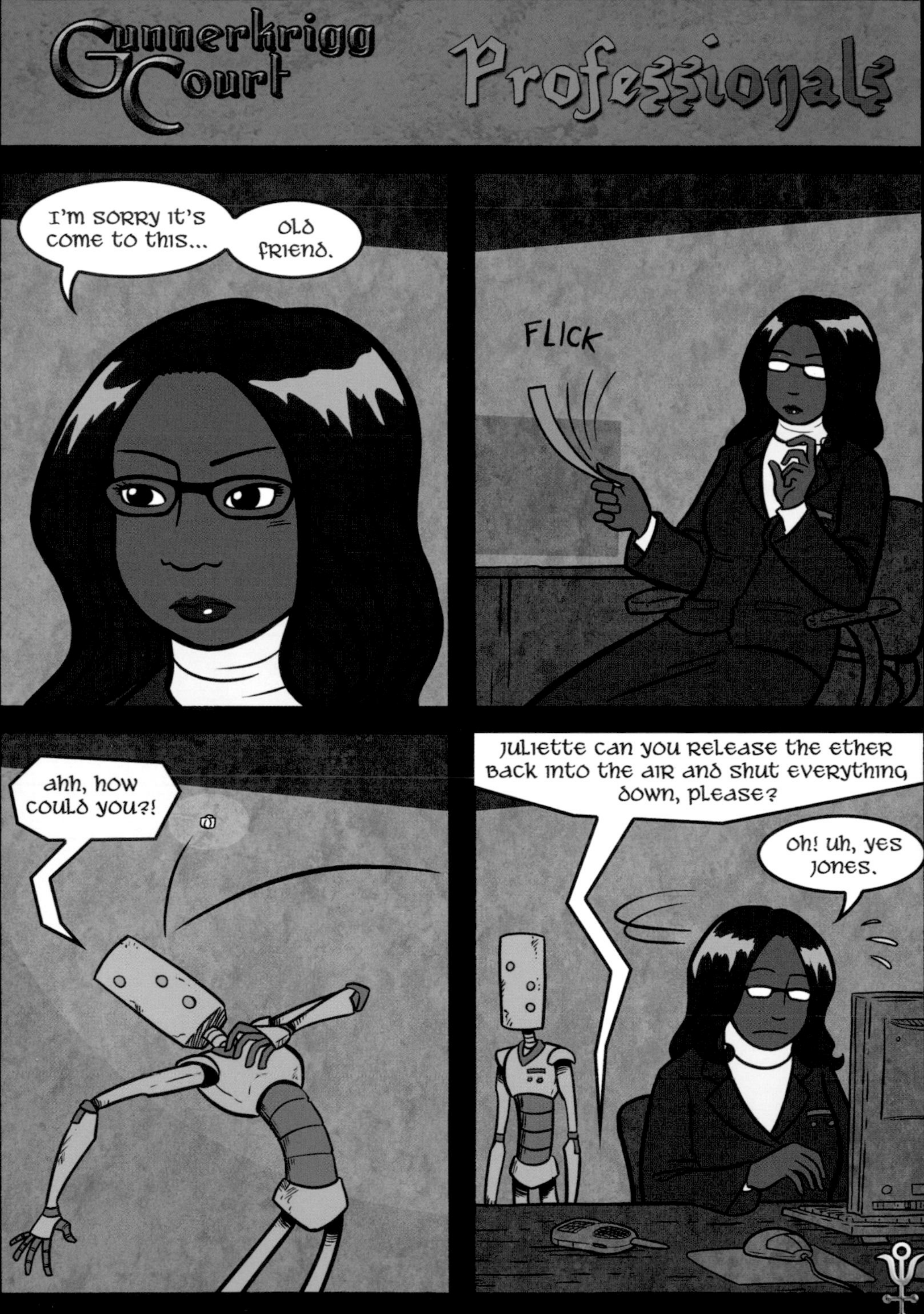
Gunnerkrigg Court
Professionals
I'M SORRY IT'S COME TO THIS...
OLD FRIEND.
FLICK
AHH, HOW COULD YOU?!
JULIETTE CAN YOU RELEASE THE ETHER BACK INTO THE AIR AND SHUT EVERYTHING DOWN, PLEASE?
OH! UH, YES JONES.

Gunnerkrigg Court

Chapter 29:

A Bad Start

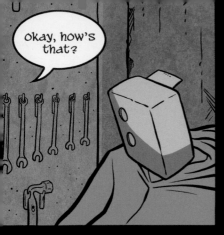

okay, how's that?

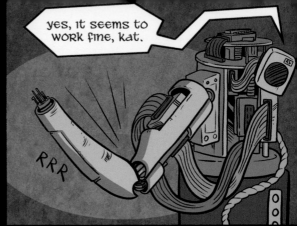

yes, it seems to work fine, kat.

RRR

hmm...

no. it's no good.

it's fine, really.

it's **not** fine!

it's too... complicated, too clunky!

the whole rig's a mess.

Clatter

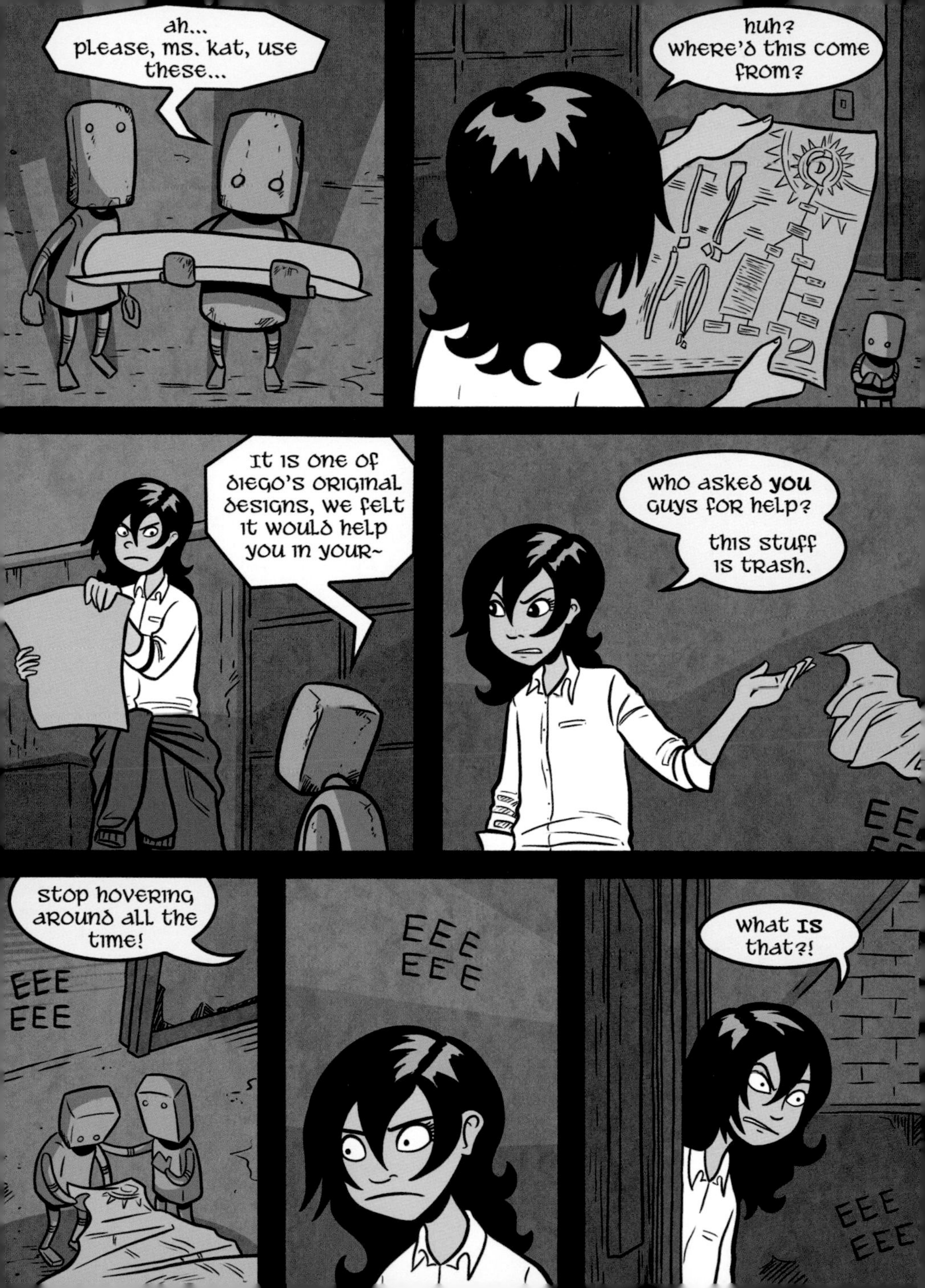

ah...
please, ms. kat, use these...
huh? where'd this come from?
It is one of diego's original designs, we felt it would help you in your~
who asked **you** guys for help?
this stuff is trash.
EEE
stop hovering around all the time!
EEE EEE
EEE EEE
What **IS** that?!
EEE EEE

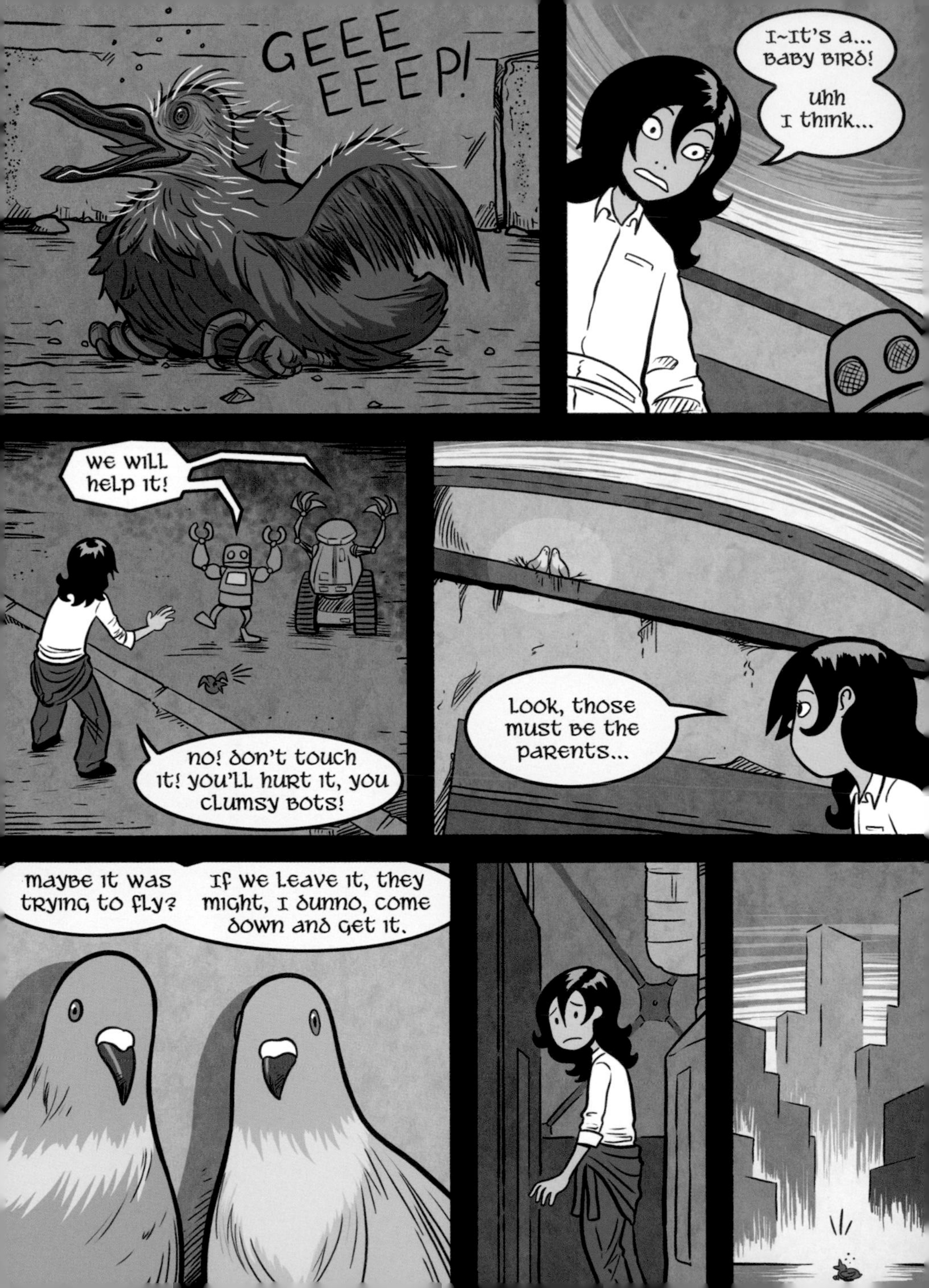
GEEE EEEP!
I~It's a... Baby bird!
uhh I think...
we will help it!
no! don't touch it! you'll hurt it, you clumsy bots!
Look, those must be the parents...
maybe it was trying to fly?
If we leave it, they might, I dunno, come down and get it.

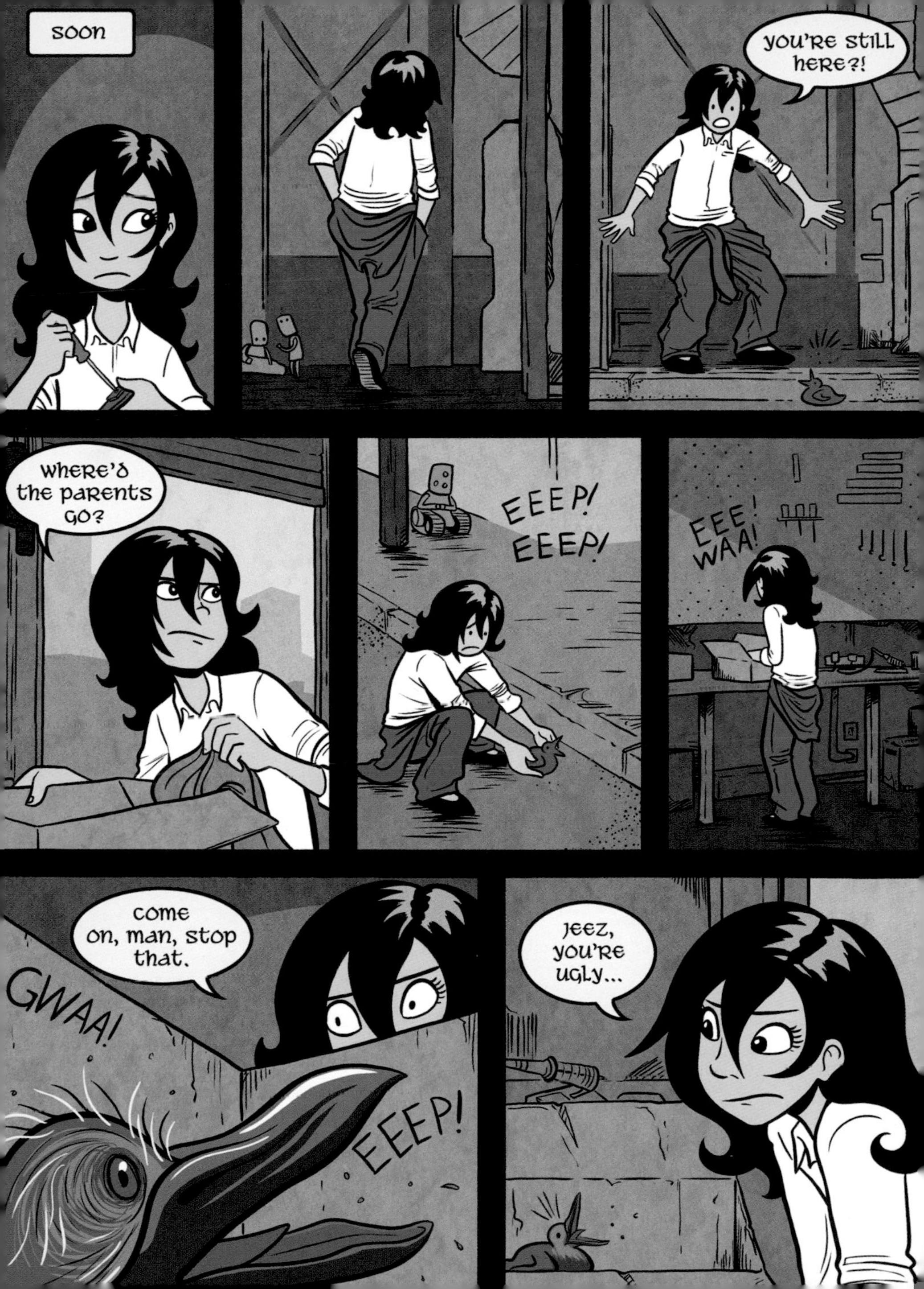
soon
you're still here?!
where'd the parents go?
EEEP! EEEP!
EEE! WAA!
come on, man, stop that.
GWAA!
EEEP!
jeez, you're ugly...

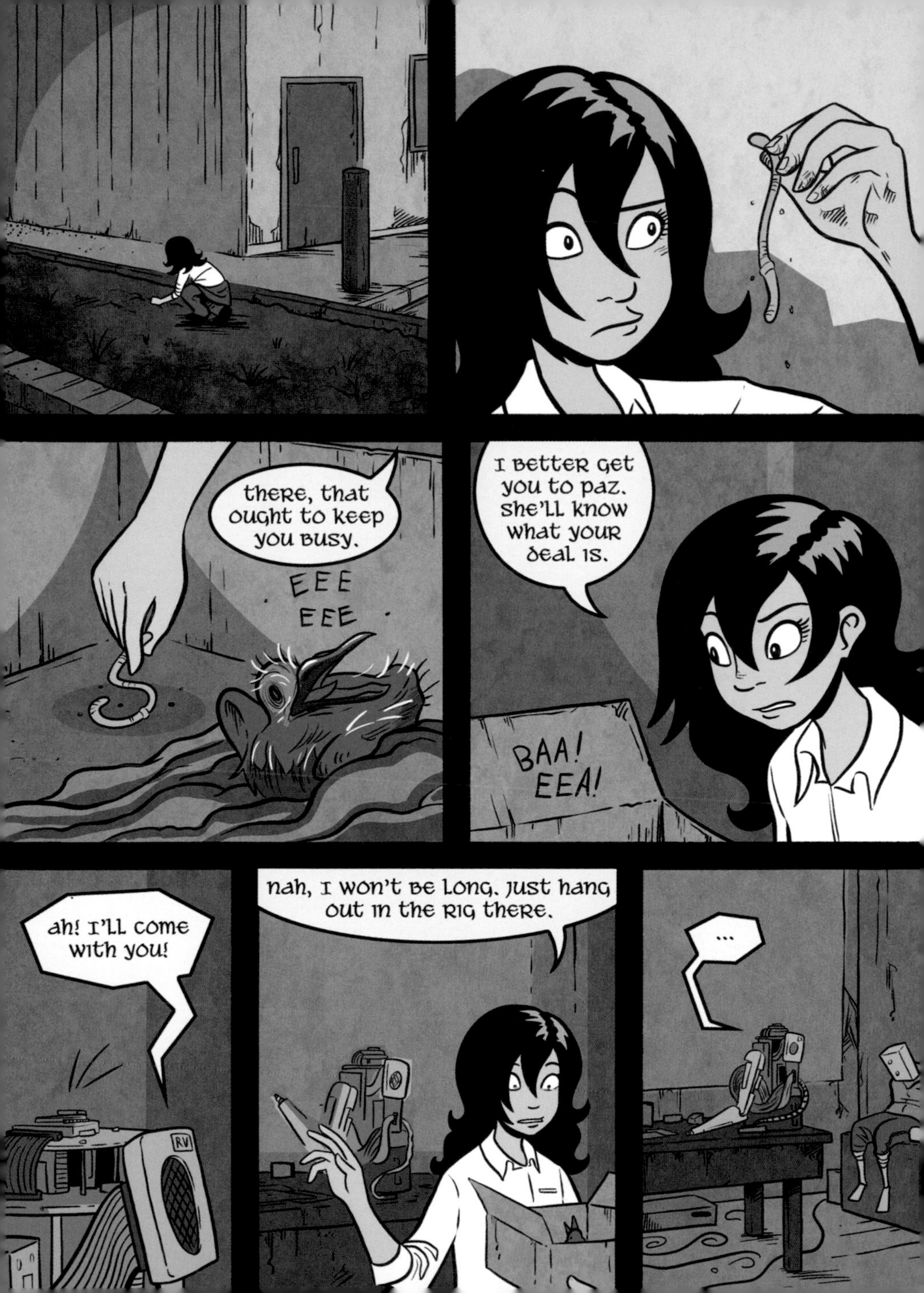
there, that ought to keep you busy.
EEE EEE
I better get you to paz. she'll know what your deal is.
BAA! EEA!
ah! I'll come with you!
nah, I won't be long. just hang out in the rig there.
...
RV

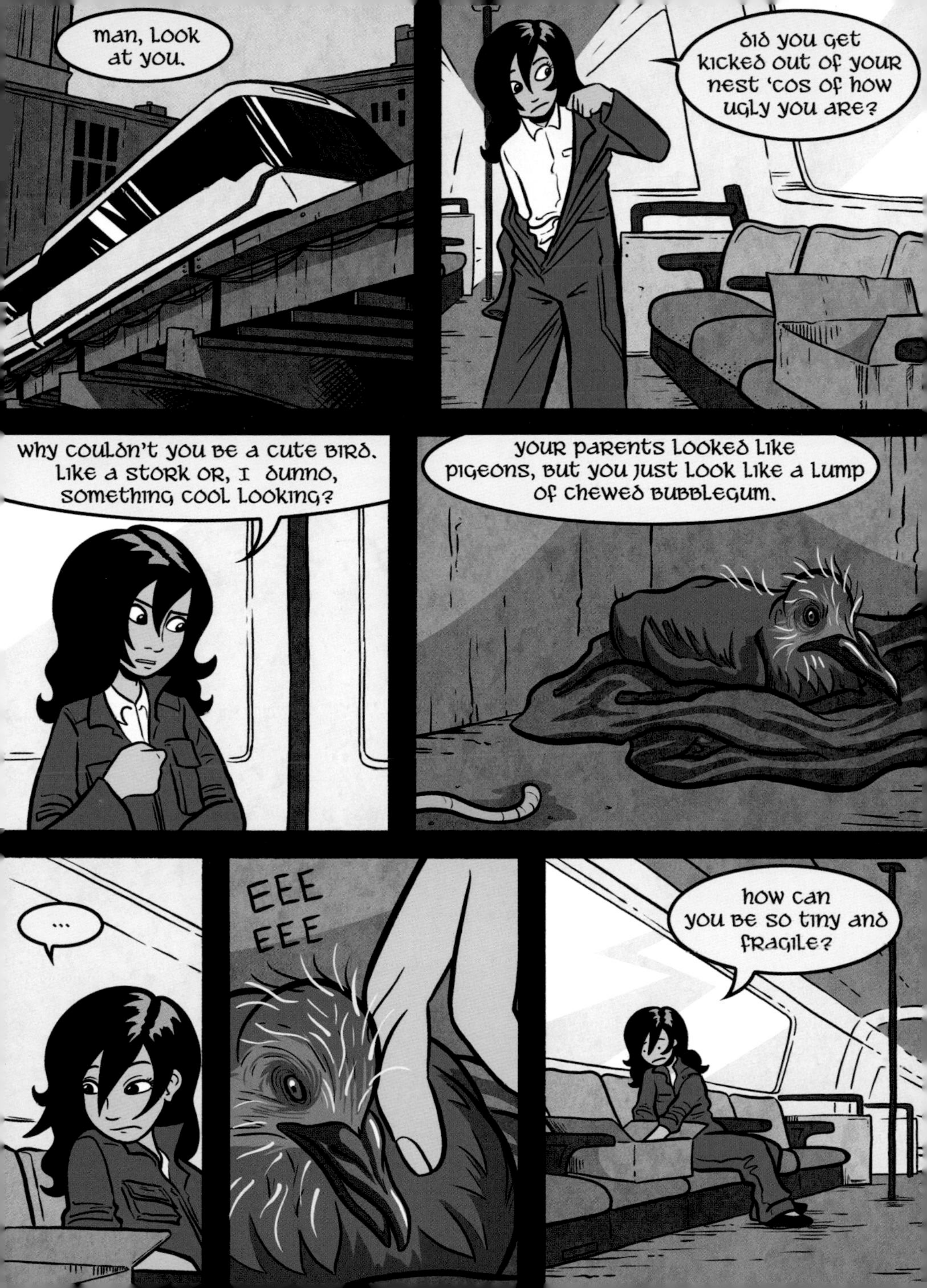
man, look at you.
did you get kicked out of your nest 'cos of how ugly you are?
why couldn't you be a cute bird. like a stork or, I dunno, something cool looking?
your parents looked like pigeons, but you just look like a lump of chewed bubblegum.
...
EEE EEE
how can you be so tiny and fragile?

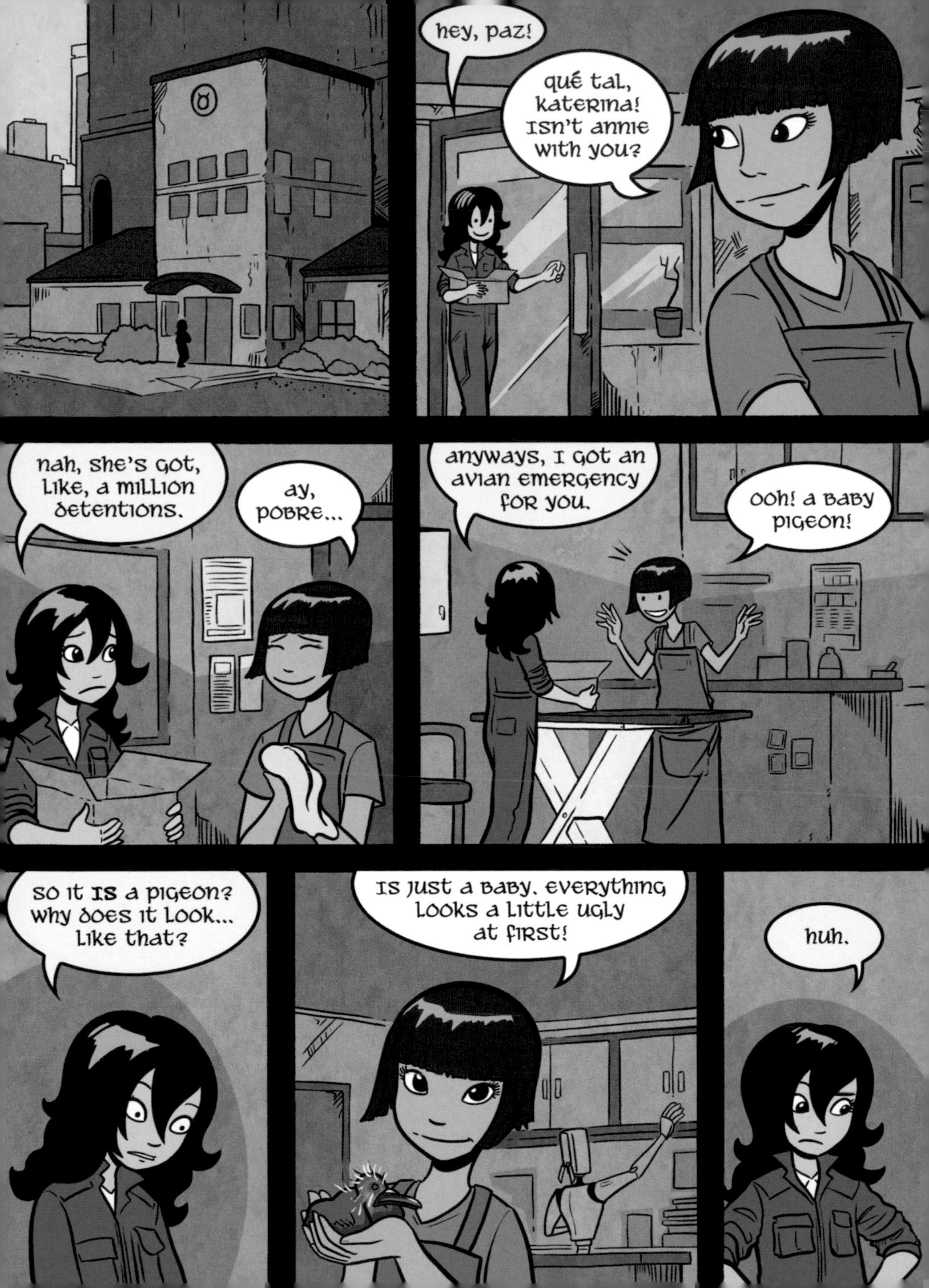
hey, paz!
qué tal, katerina! isn't annie with you?
nah, she's got, like, a million detentions.
ay, pobre...
anyways, I got an avian emergency for you.
ooh! a baby pigeon!
so it IS a pigeon? why does it look... like that?
is just a baby. everything looks a little ugly at first!
huh.

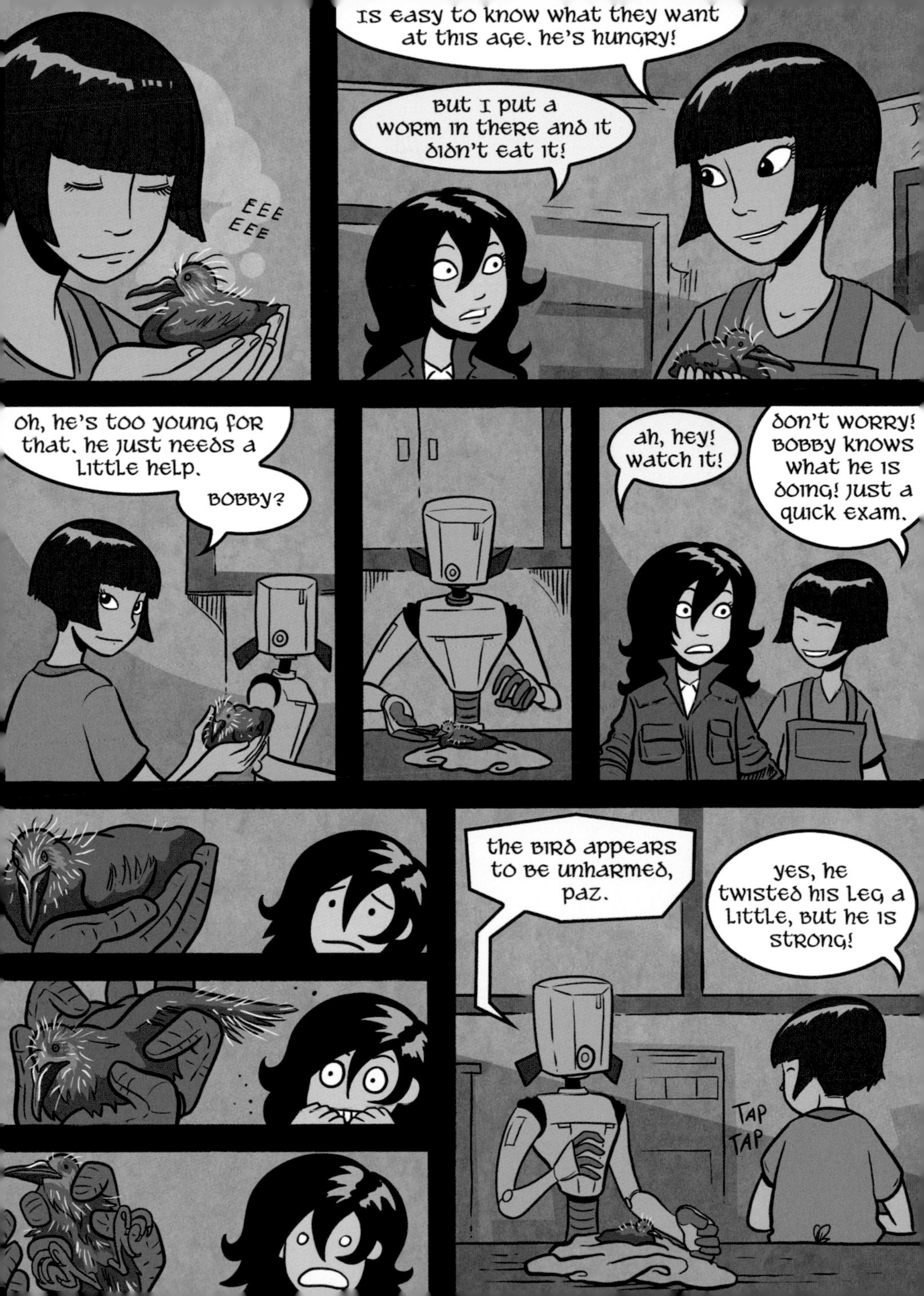
EEE EEE
IS EASY TO KNOW WHAT THEY WANT AT THIS AGE. HE'S HUNGRY!
BUT I PUT A WORM IN THERE AND IT DIDN'T EAT IT!
OH, HE'S TOO YOUNG FOR THAT. HE JUST NEEDS A LITTLE HELP.
BOBBY?
AH, HEY! WATCH IT!
DON'T WORRY! BOBBY KNOWS WHAT HE IS DOING! JUST A QUICK EXAM.
THE BIRD APPEARS TO BE UNHARMED, PAZ.
YES, HE TWISTED HIS LEG A LITTLE, BUT HE IS STRONG!
TAP TAP

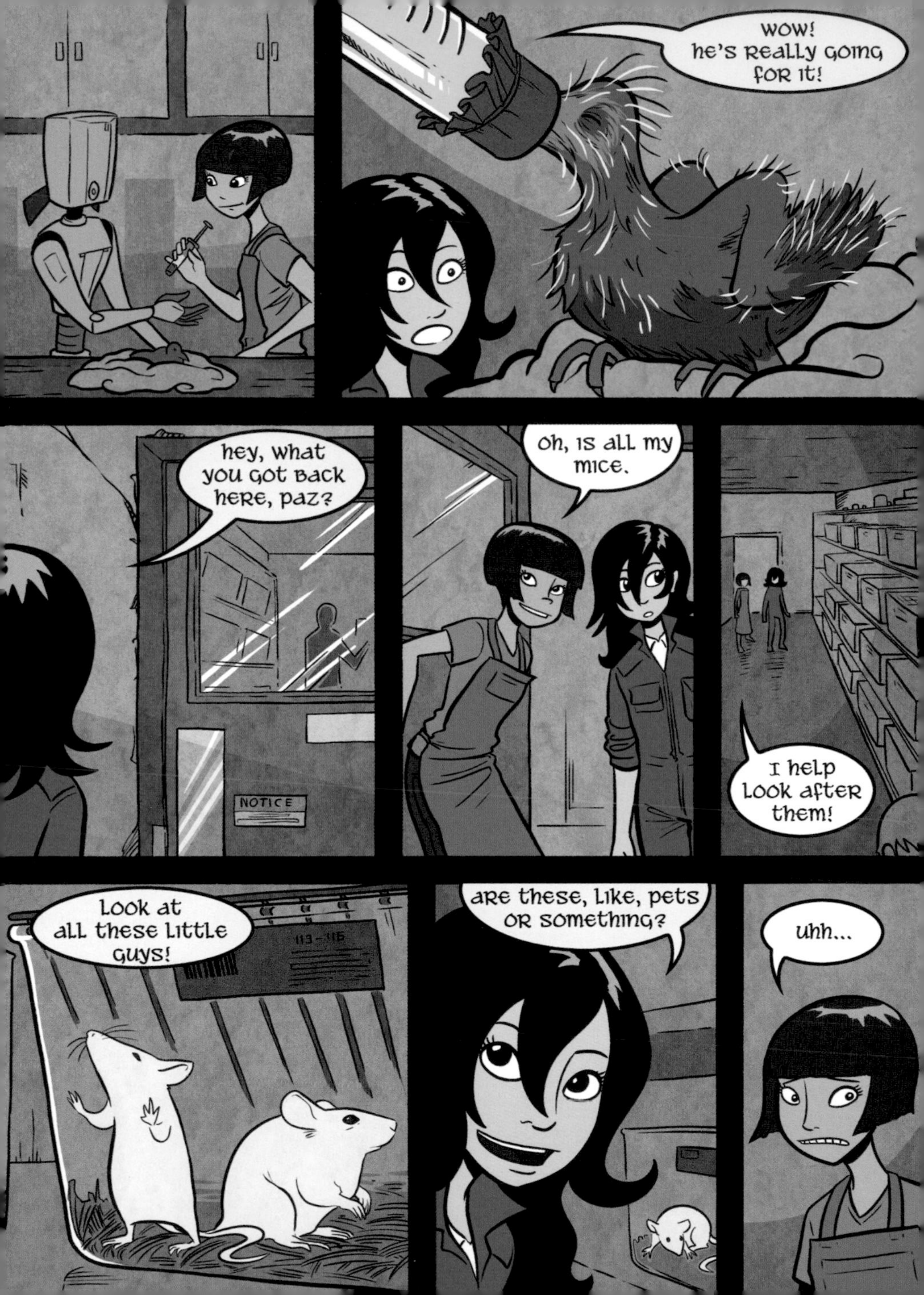
WOW! he's Really Going for it!
hey, what you got Back here, paz?
Oh, is all my mice.
I help look after them!
NOTICE
look at all these little guys!
113-115
are these, like, pets or something?
uhh...

BWOOO hoo~hoo!

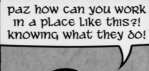

paz how can you work in a place like this?! knowing what they do!

they are not **all** used for testing! and many of the tests are non~invasive! they study behaviour and learning patterns...

that doesn't make it better! this place... the whole court... they just do what's best for themselves.

they don't care what happens to anyone else.

kat... I know is not perfect. I wish for a day when we didn't need to keep these mice... but until then, I try to make life comfortable for them.

and there are very strict rules and limitations. is all very tightly self~regulated.

self~regulated?! that just means they can do what they want!

no! you see, to do that, they would have to get through **me** first.

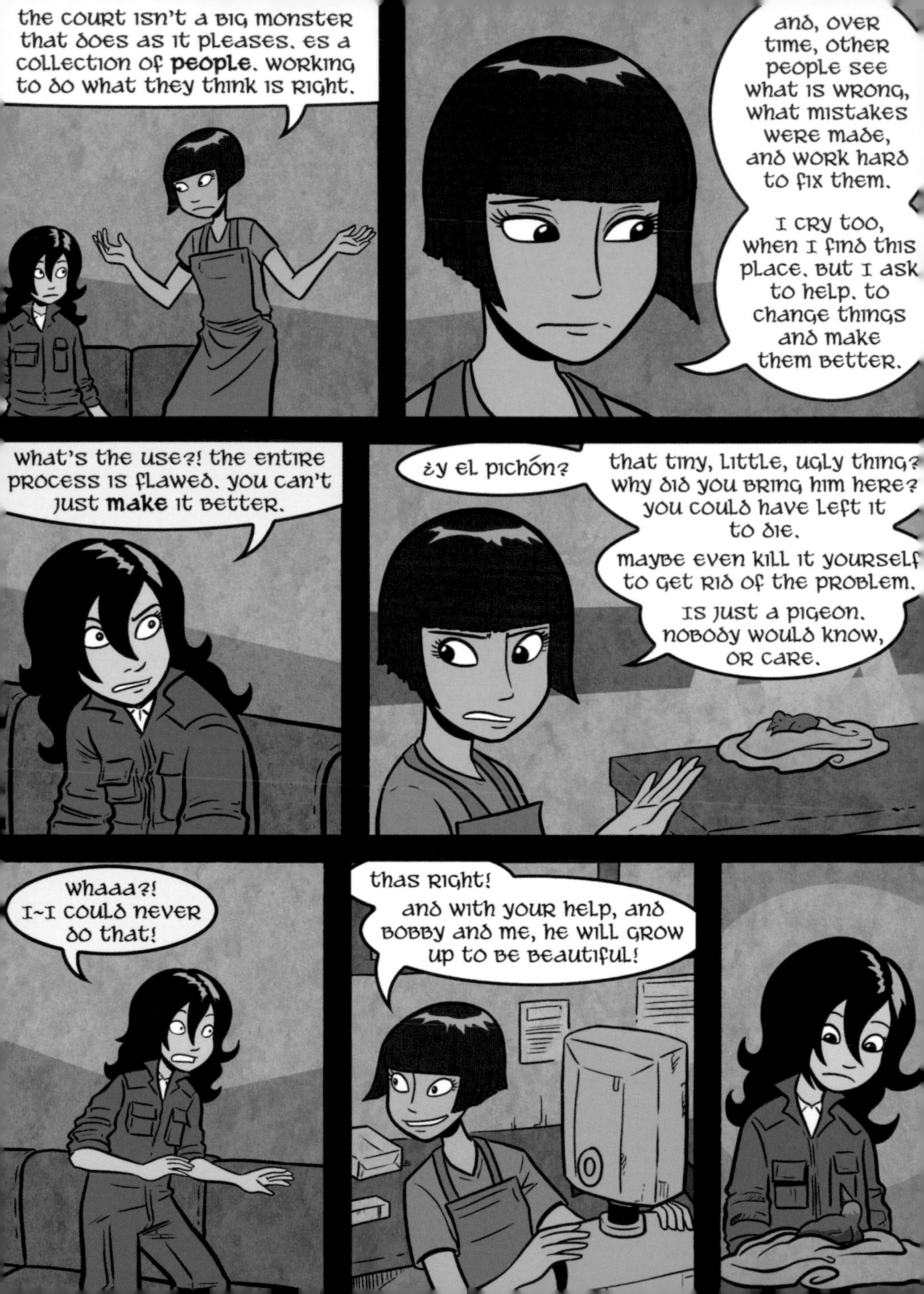
the court isn't a big monster that does as it pleases. es a collection of **people**. working to do what they think is right.
and, over time, other people see what is wrong, what mistakes were made, and work hard to fix them.
I cry too, when I find this place. but I ask to help. to change things and make them better.
what's the use?! the entire process is flawed. you can't just **make** it better.
¿y el pichón?
that tiny, little, ugly thing? why did you bring him here? you could have left it to die.
maybe even kill it yourself to get rid of the problem.
is just a pigeon. nobody would know, or care.
Whaaa?! I-I could never do that!
thas right!
and with your help, and bobby and me, he will grow up to be beautiful!

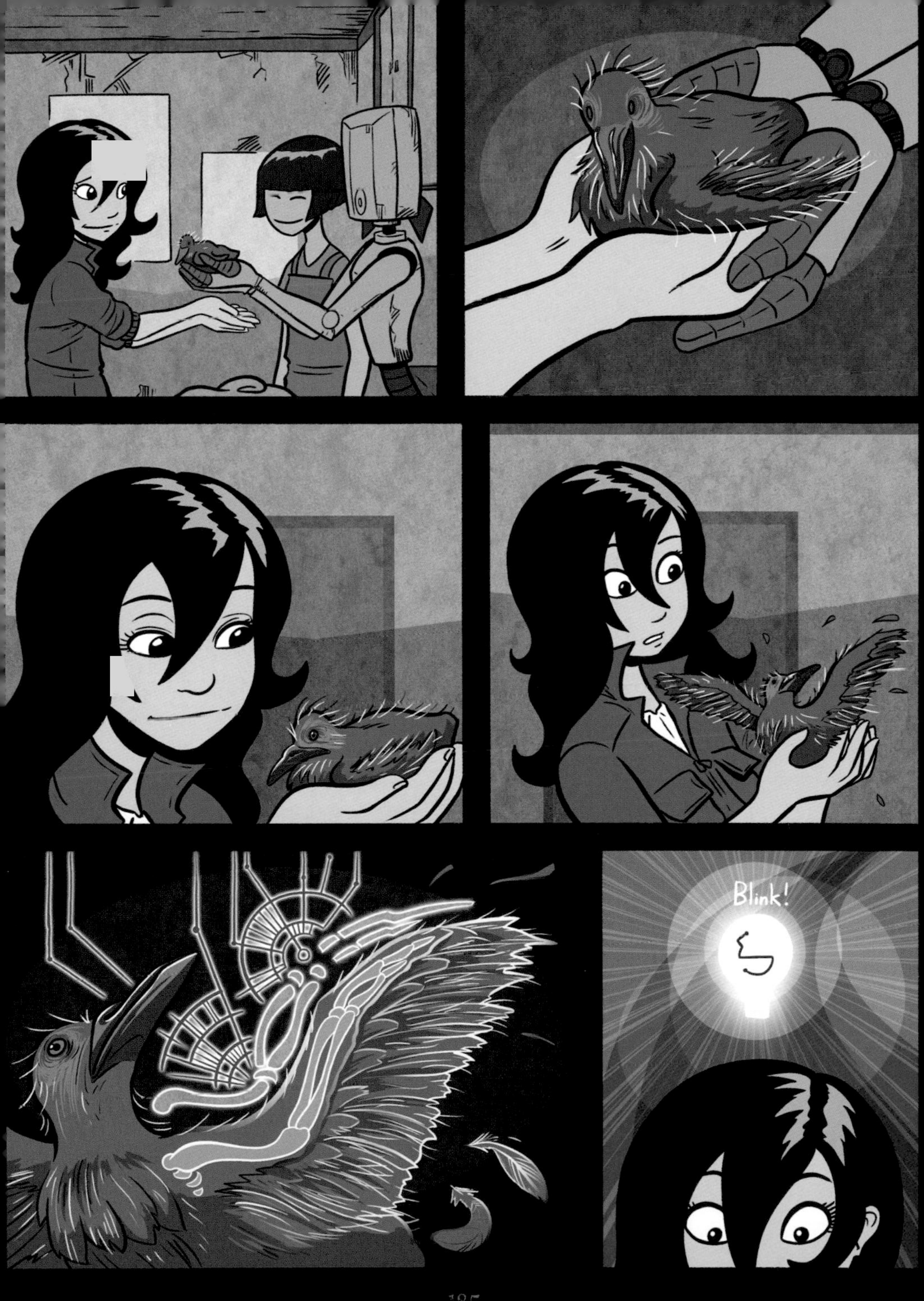
Blink!

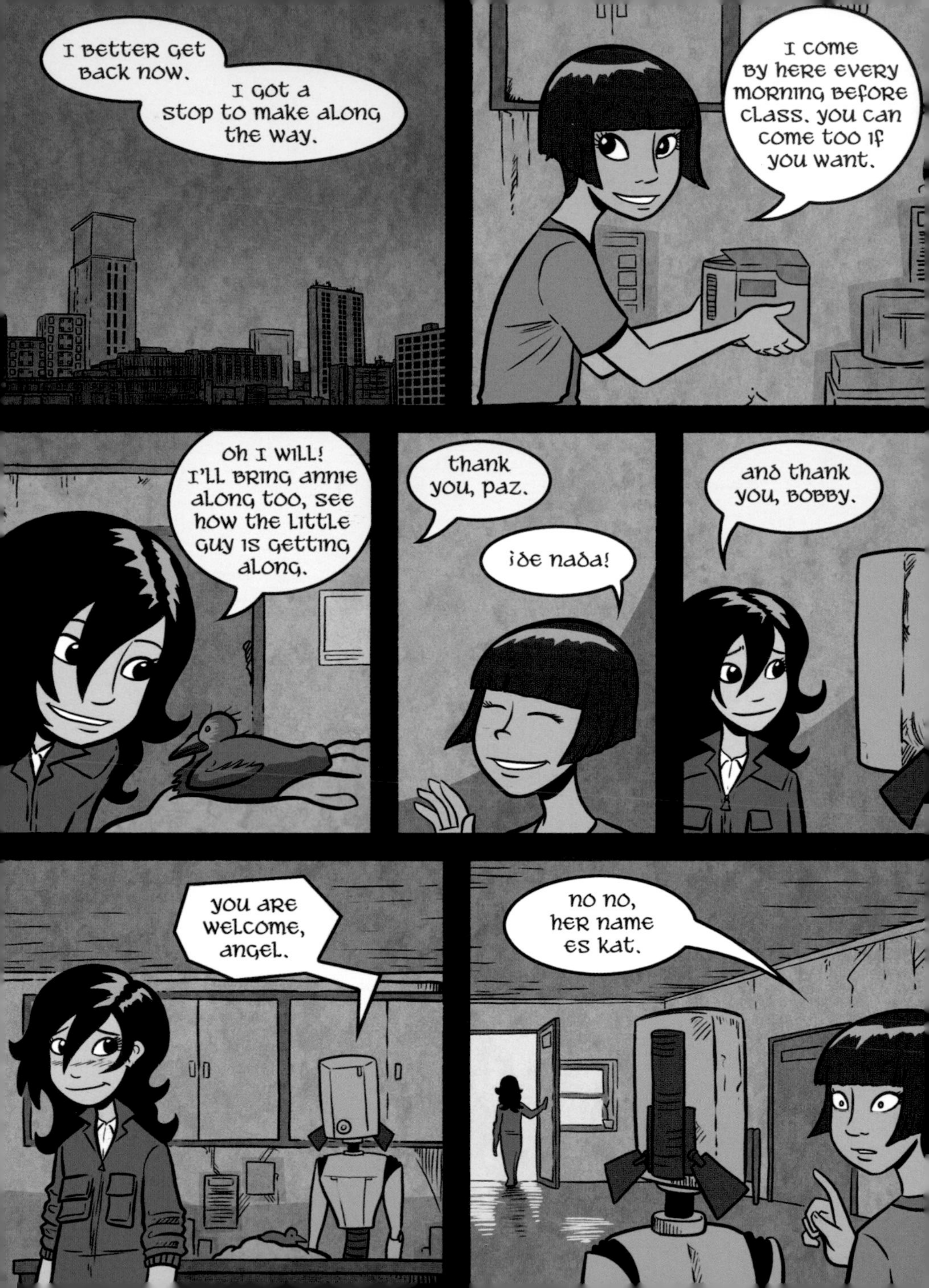
I better get back now.
I got a stop to make along the way.
I come by here every morning before class. you can come too if you want.
Oh I will! I'll bring annie along too, see how the little guy is getting along.
thank you, paz.
¡de nada!
and thank you, bobby.
you are welcome, angel.
no no, her name es kat.

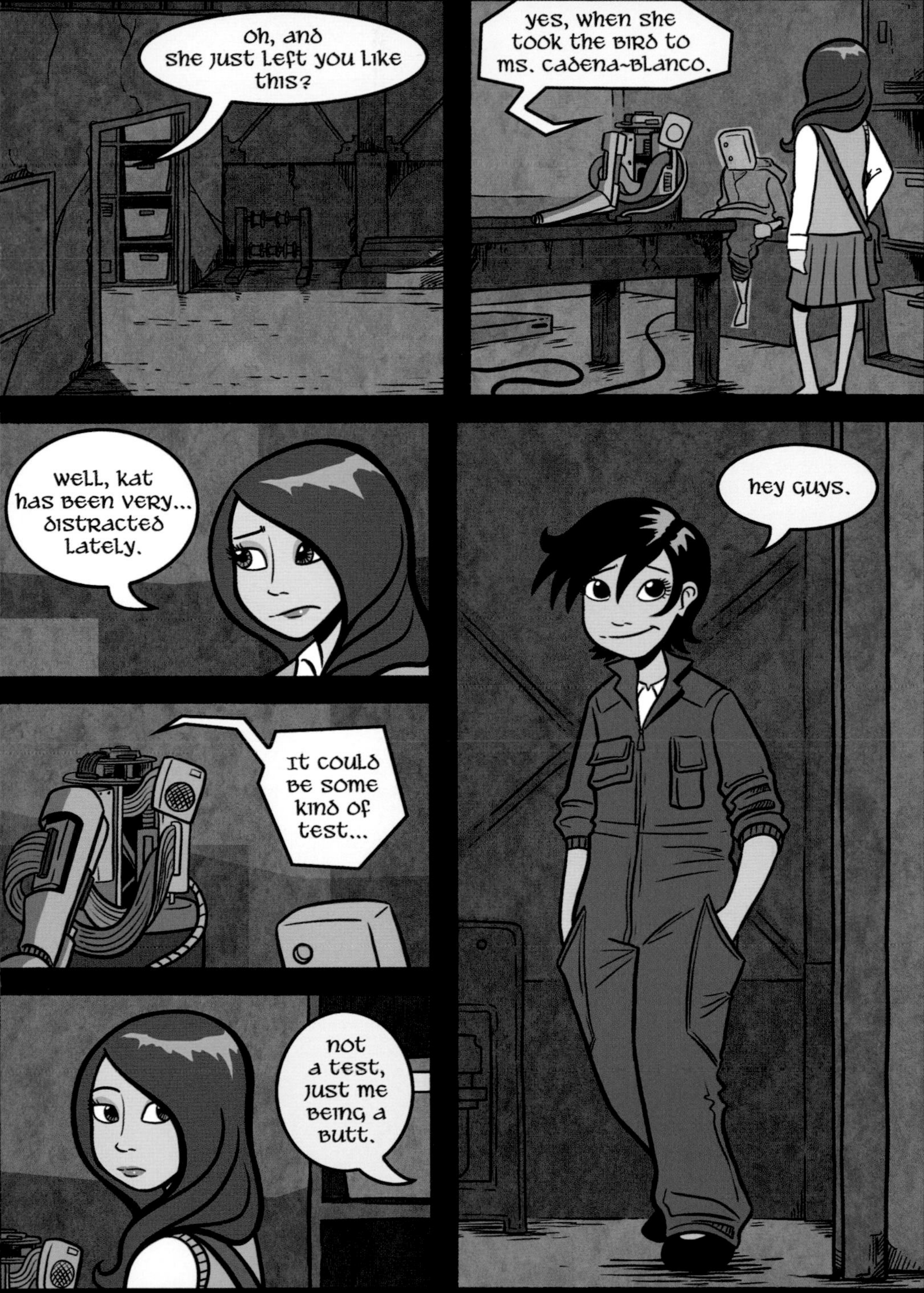

oh, and she just left you like this?
yes, when she took the bird to ms. cadena-blanco.
well, kat has been very... distracted lately.
it could be some kind of test...
not a test, just me being a butt.
hey guys.

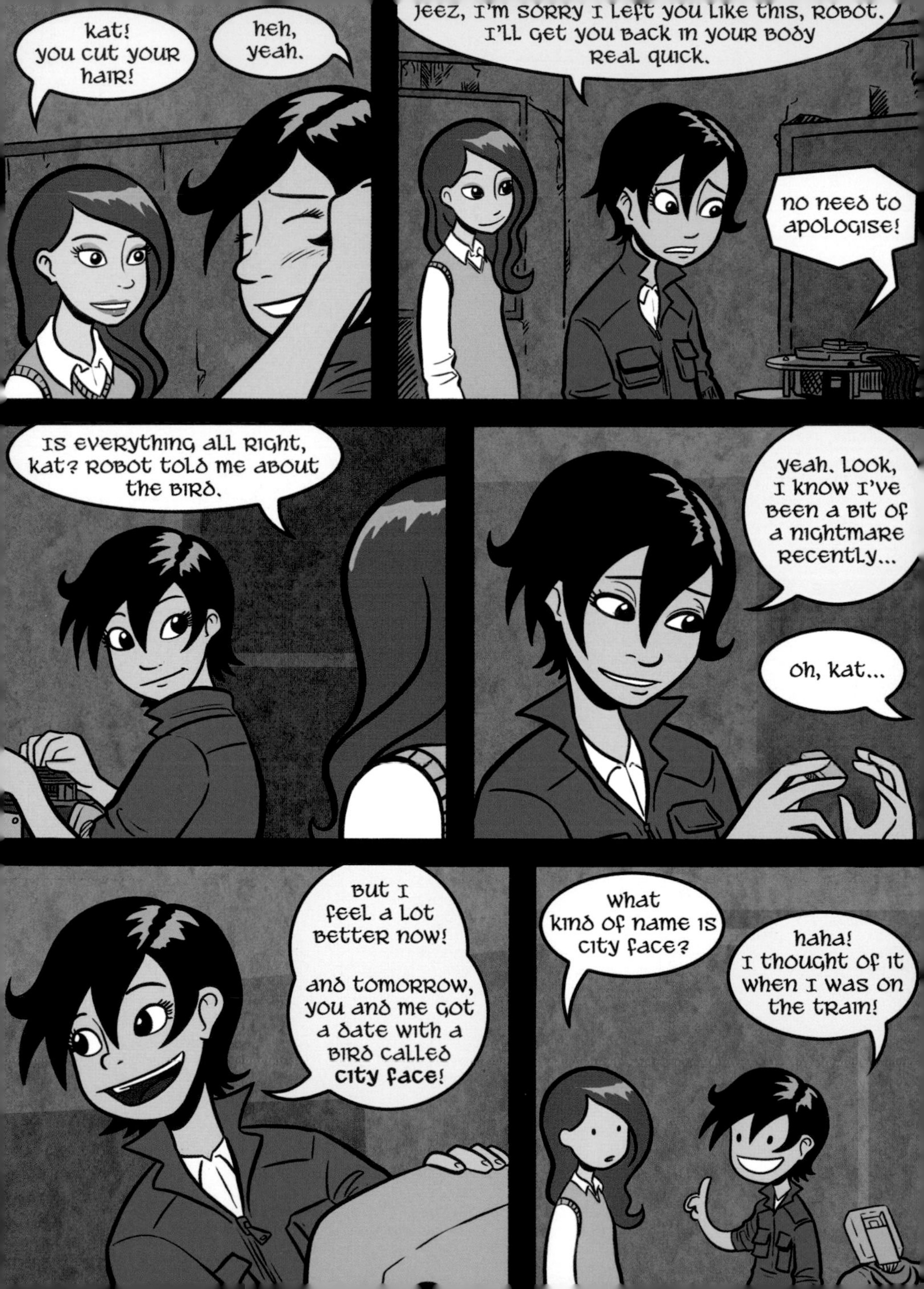
kat! you cut your hair!
heh, yeah.
jeez, I'm sorry I left you like this, robot. I'll get you back in your body real quick.
no need to apologise!
Is everything all right, kat? robot told me about the bird.
yeah. look, I know I've been a bit of a nightmare recently...
oh, kat...
but I feel a lot better now!
and tomorrow, you and me got a date with a bird called city face!
what kind of name is city face?
haha! I thought of it when I was on the train!

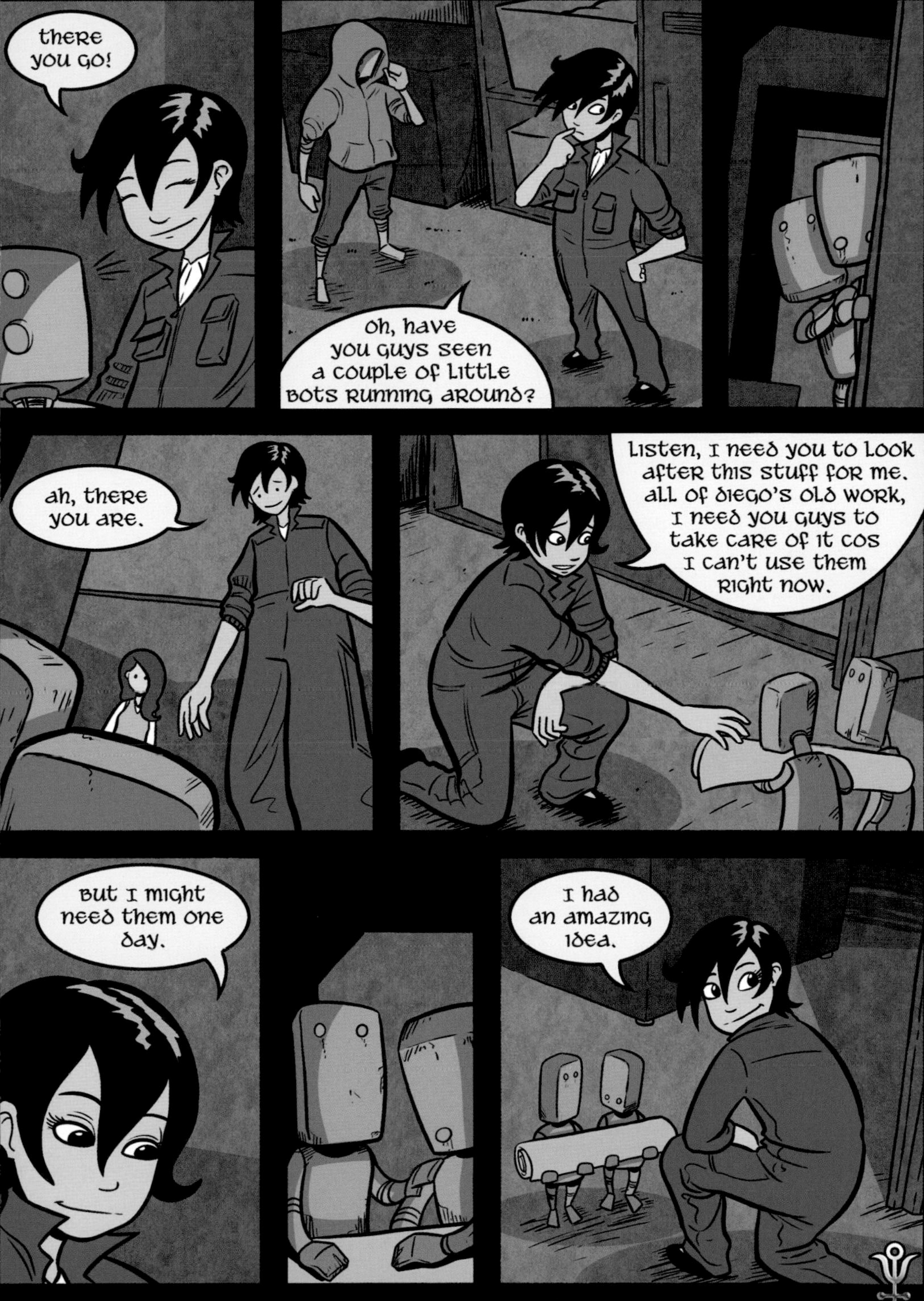
there you go!
oh, have you guys seen a couple of little bots running around?
ah, there you are.
listen, I need you to look after this stuff for me. all of diego's old work, I need you guys to take care of it cos I can't use them right now.
but I might need them one day.
I had an amazing idea.

Gunnerkrigg Court

Pigeon Facts

With Bobby

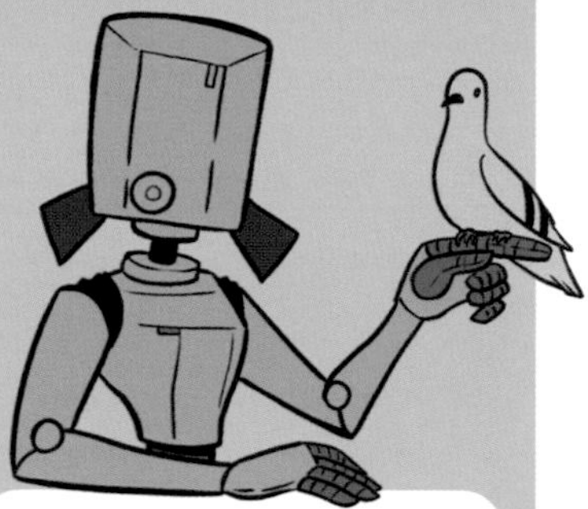

Dear Friend

Cher Ami, a registered homing pigeon, was awarded the *Croix de Guerre* military decoration in the First World War. He flew through enemy territory, receiving a bullet in the chest and losing most of one leg, to deliver a message that saved the lives of 200 American soldiers.

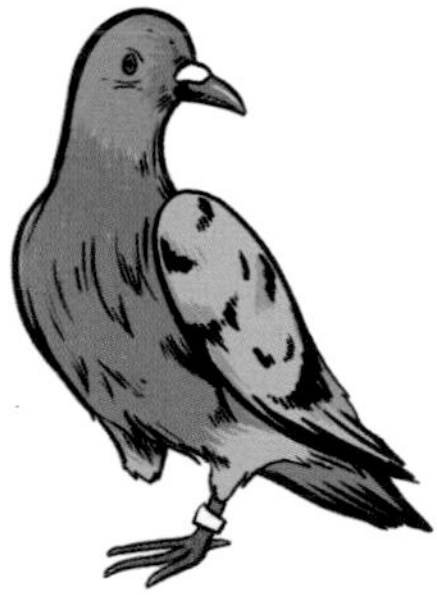

What's in a name?

"Pigeon" is the common name for birds in the Columbidae family. Another name is "dove".

Rock Pigeon

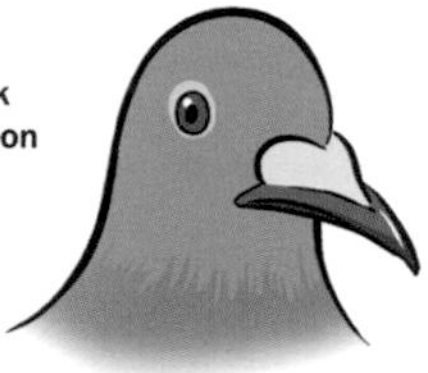

Dove

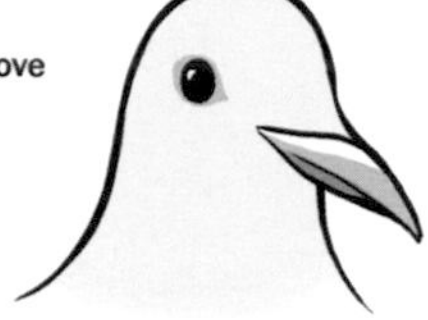

Smarter than your average bird

Pigeons are very intelligent, being one of only six animal species able to recognise their reflections as images of themselves and capable of abstract conceptualisation.

Arch Angel

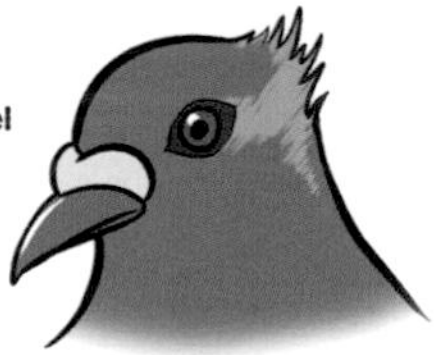

Carneau

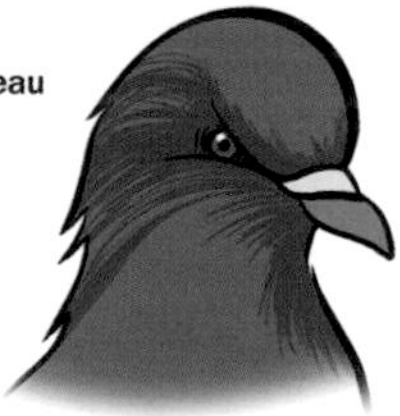

GPS enabled

Pigeons are able to navigate vast distances using the geomagnetic activity of the planet, but they have also been proven to navigate using human roads and transportation routes.

Kormoner Tumbler

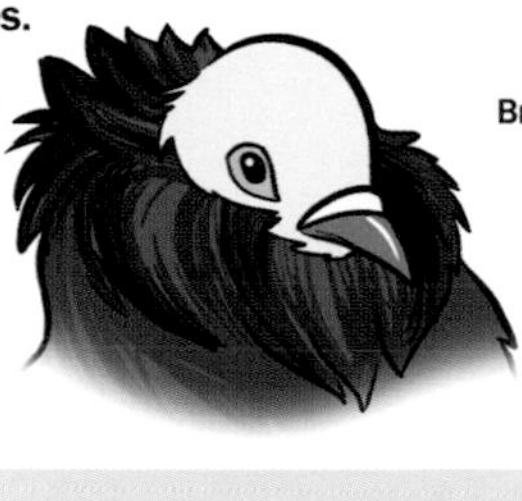

Bronzewing

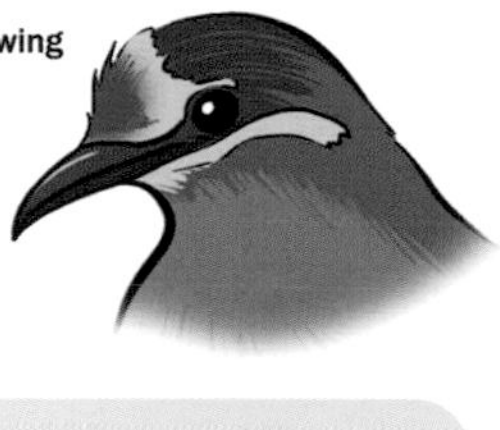

Bobby's fun corner

Please try to extract the word PIGEON from this scramble of letters:

ENOGIP

Answer: PIGEON

One day I saw a pigeon fall from a tree, its body twisted and broken after an attack somewhere above. It writhed on the floor in silence and eventually died. It had no expression, just as I have no expression. I have never relayed this story to anyone.

Gunnerkrigg Court

Chapter 30:

The Coward Heart

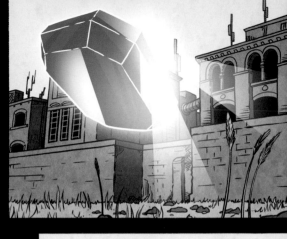

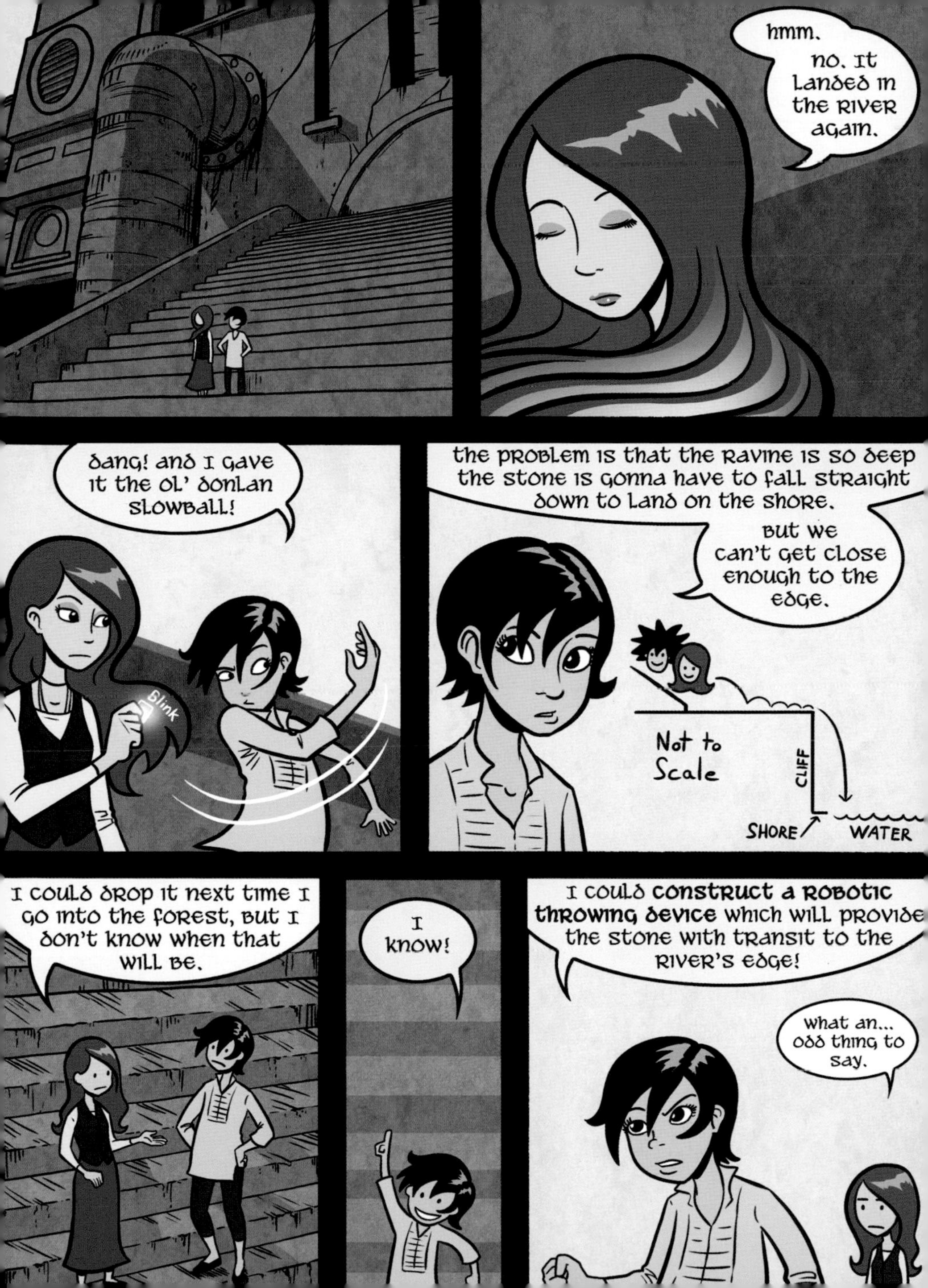
hmm.
no. It Landed in the River again.
dang! and I gave it the ol' donlan slowball!
Blink
the problem is that the ravine is so deep the stone is gonna have to fall straight down to land on the shore.
but we can't get close enough to the edge.
Not to Scale
CLIFF
SHORE
WATER
I could drop it next time I go into the forest, but I don't know when that will be.
I know!
I could **construct a robotic throwing device** which will provide the stone with transit to the river's edge!
what an... odd thing to say.

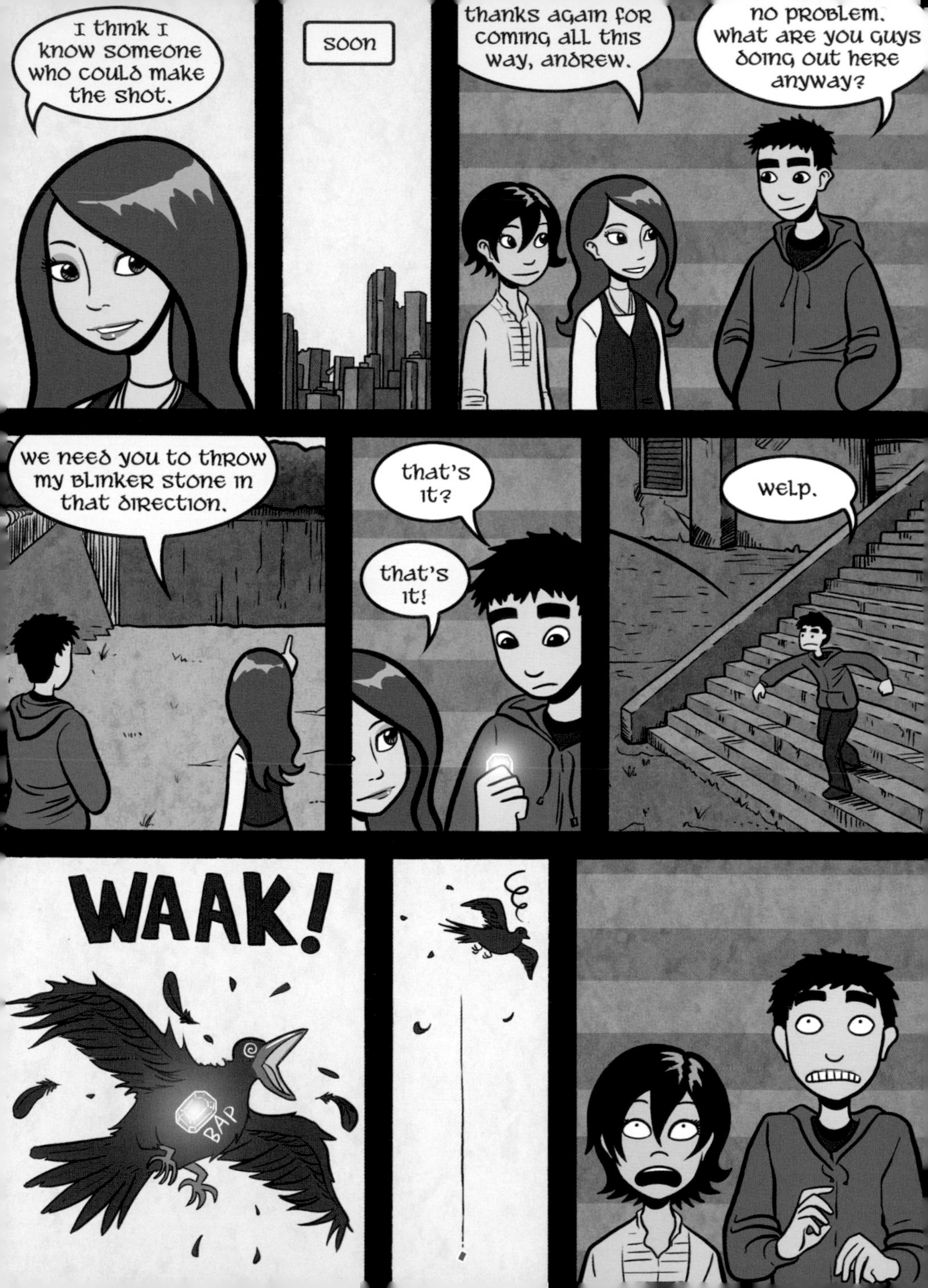
I think I know someone who could make the shot.
soon
thanks again for coming all this way, andrew.
no problem. what are you guys doing out here anyway?
we need you to throw my blinker stone in that direction.
that's it?
that's it!
welp.
WAAK!
BAP

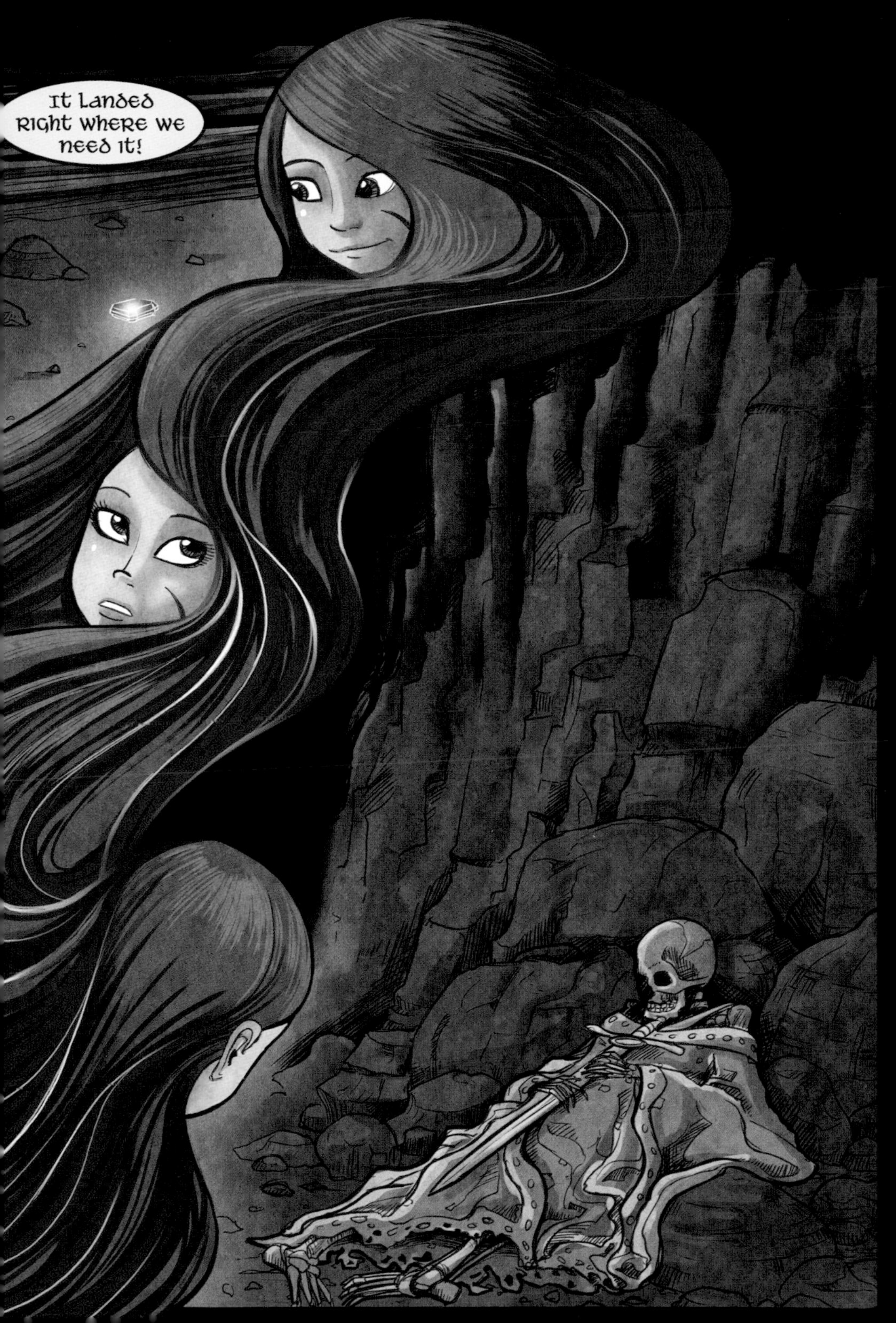
It Landed Right where we need it!

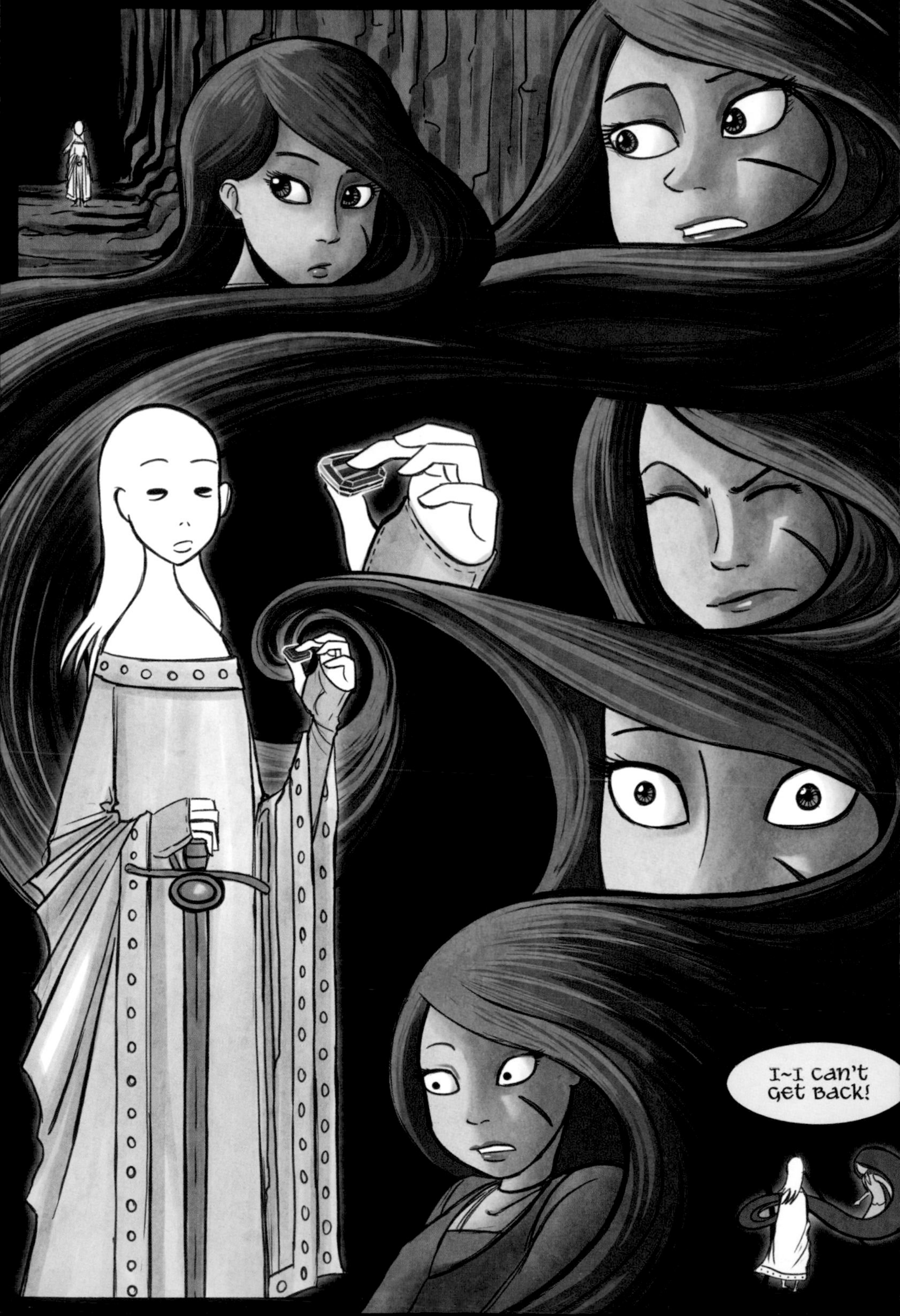
I~I can't get back!

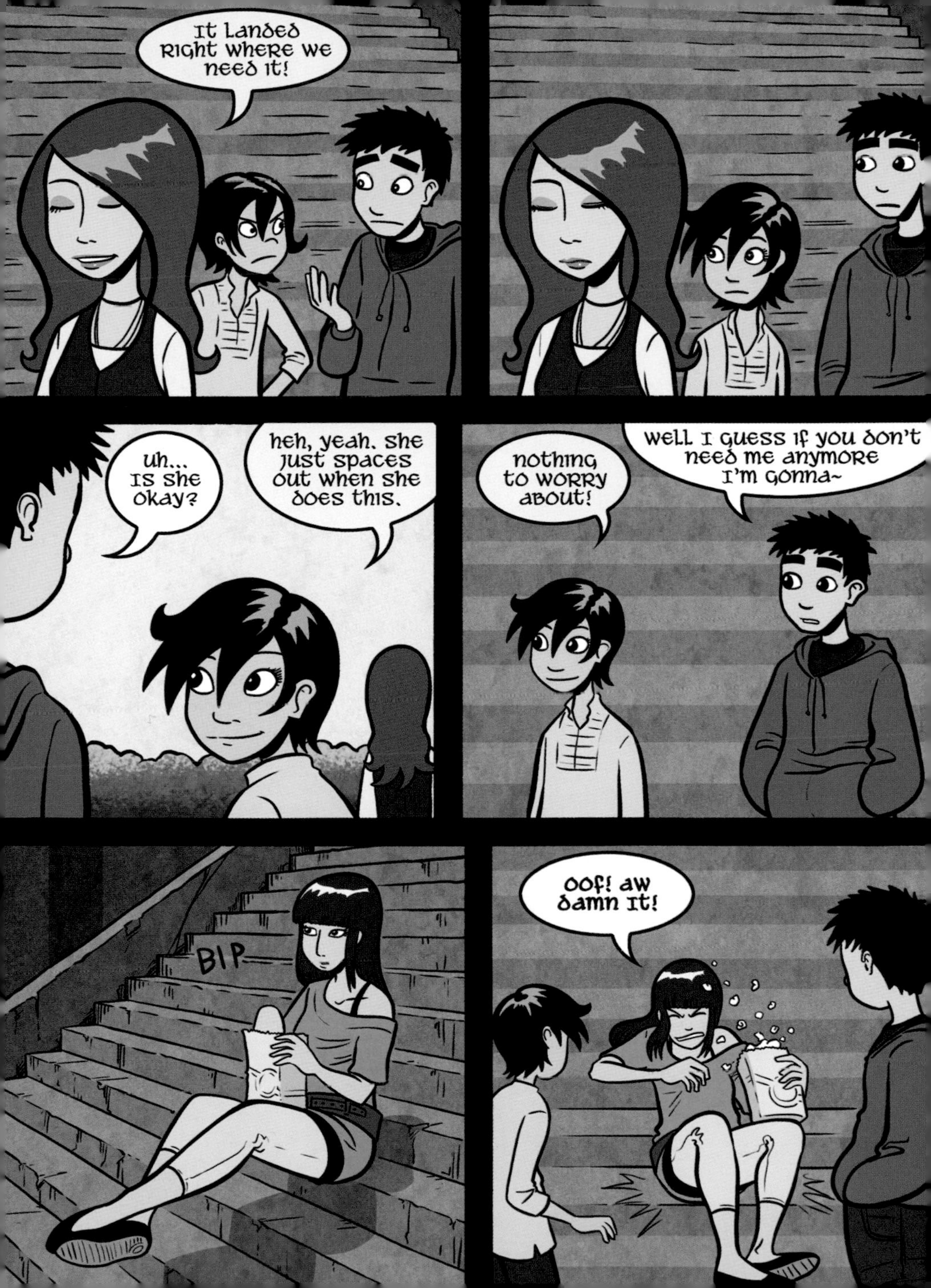

It Landed Right where we need it!
uh... Is she okay?
heh, yeah. she just spaces out when she does this.
nothing to worry about!
well I guess if you don't need me anymore I'm gonna~
BIP
oof! aw damn it!

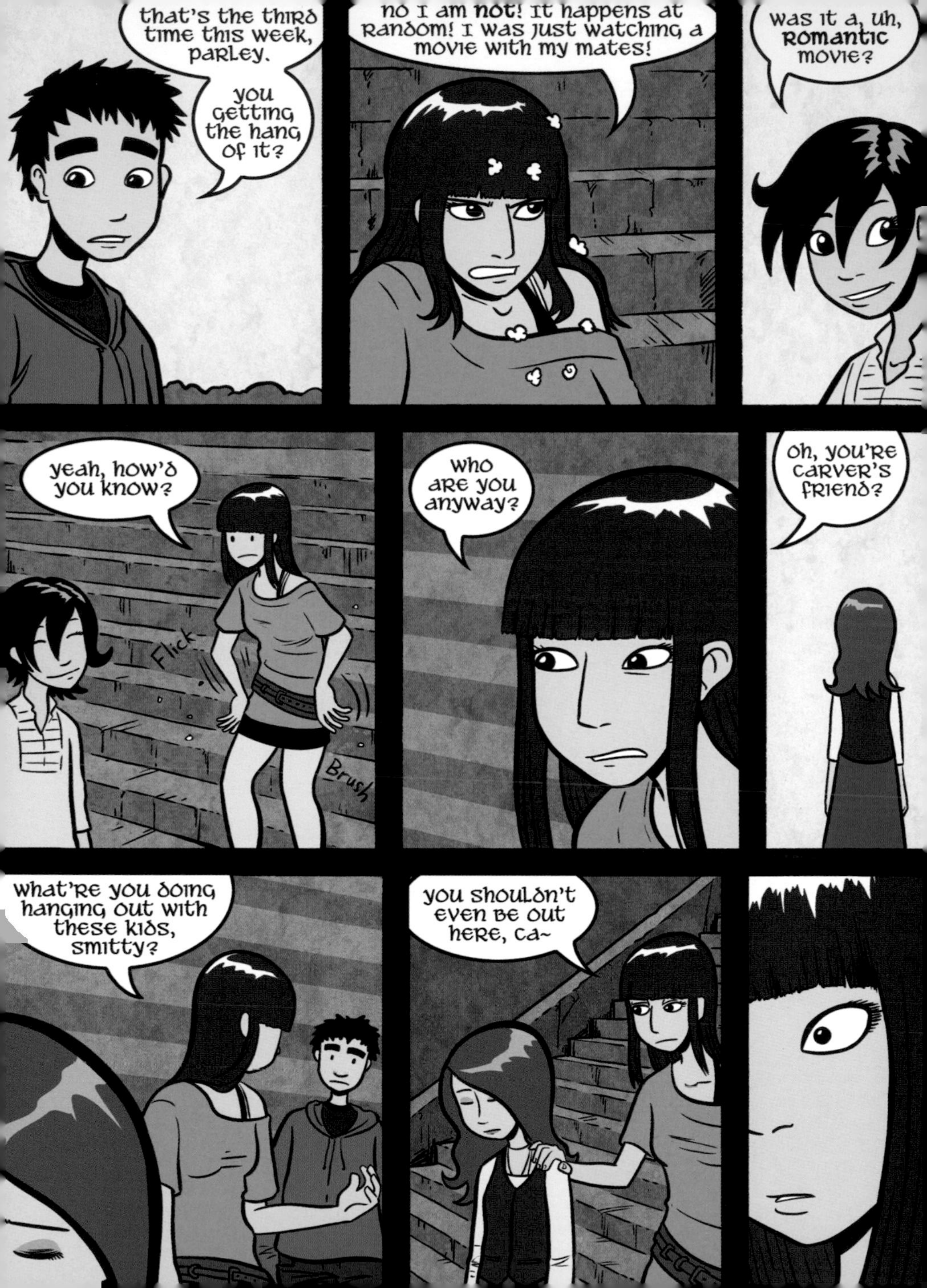
that's the third time this week, parley.
you getting the hang of it?
no I am not! It happens at random! I was just watching a movie with my mates!
was it a, uh, romantic movie?
yeah, how'd you know?
Flick
Brush
who are you anyway?
oh, you're carver's friend?
what're you doing hanging out with these kids, smitty?
you shouldn't even be out here, ca~

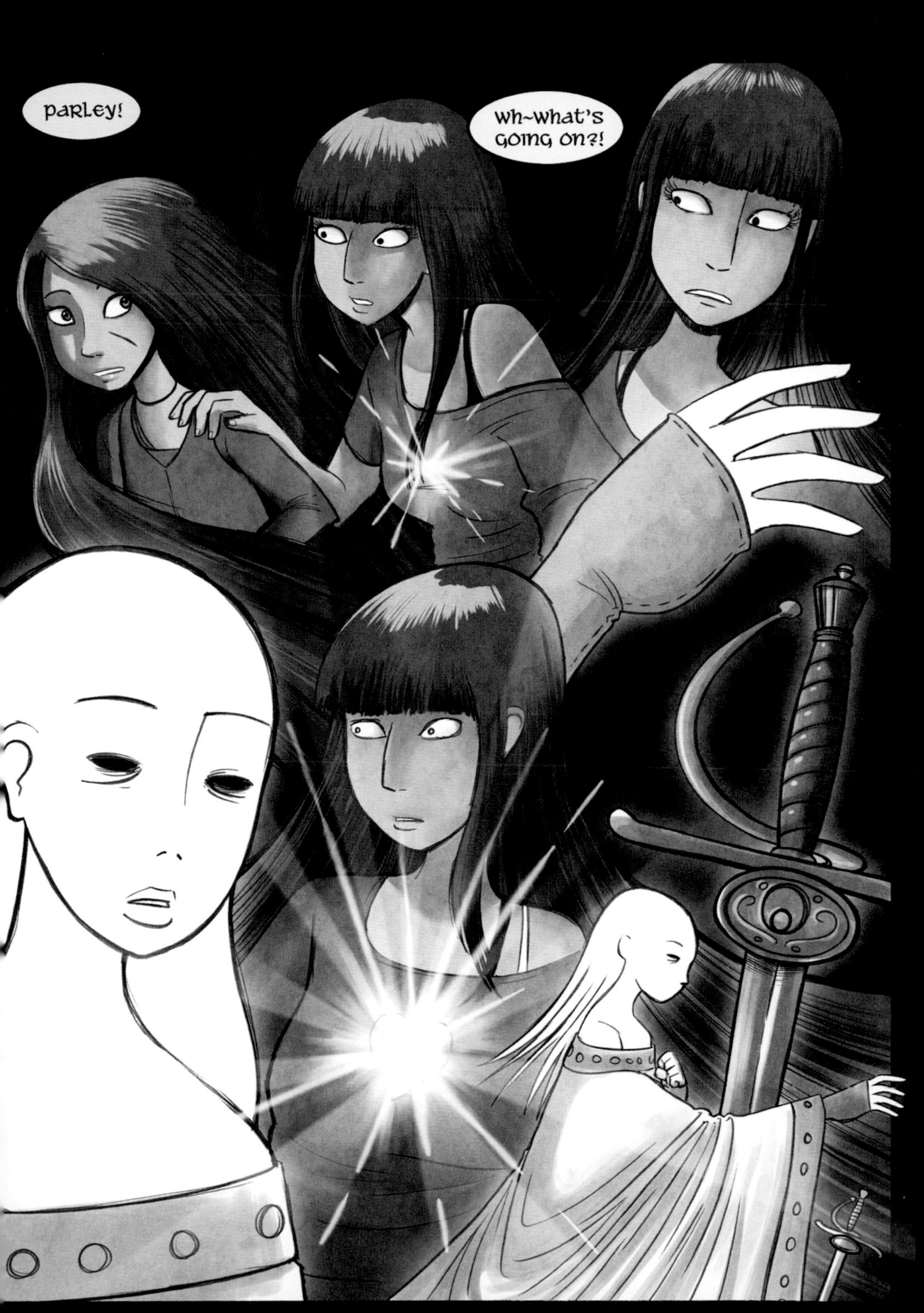
Parley!
Wh~What's going on?!

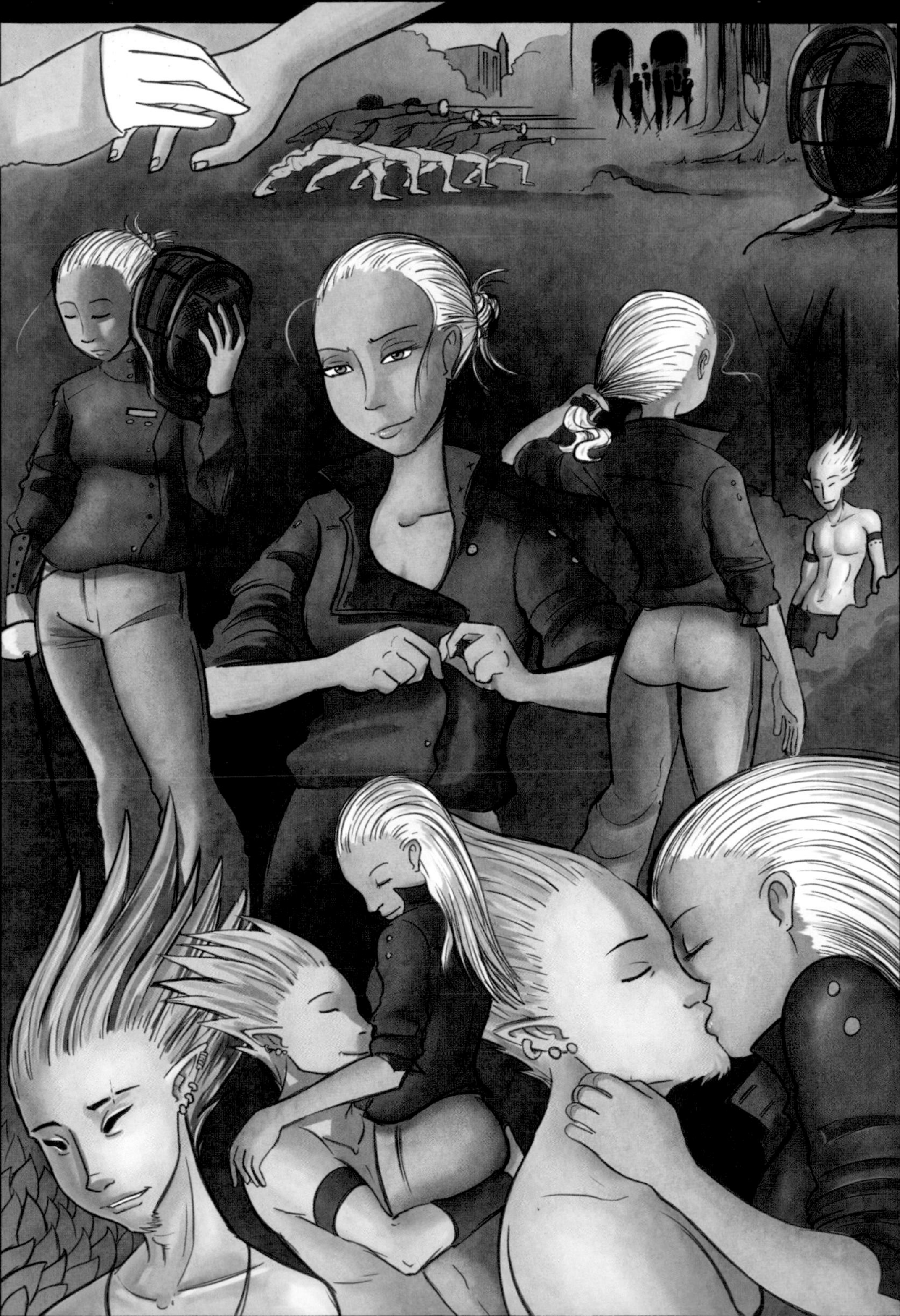

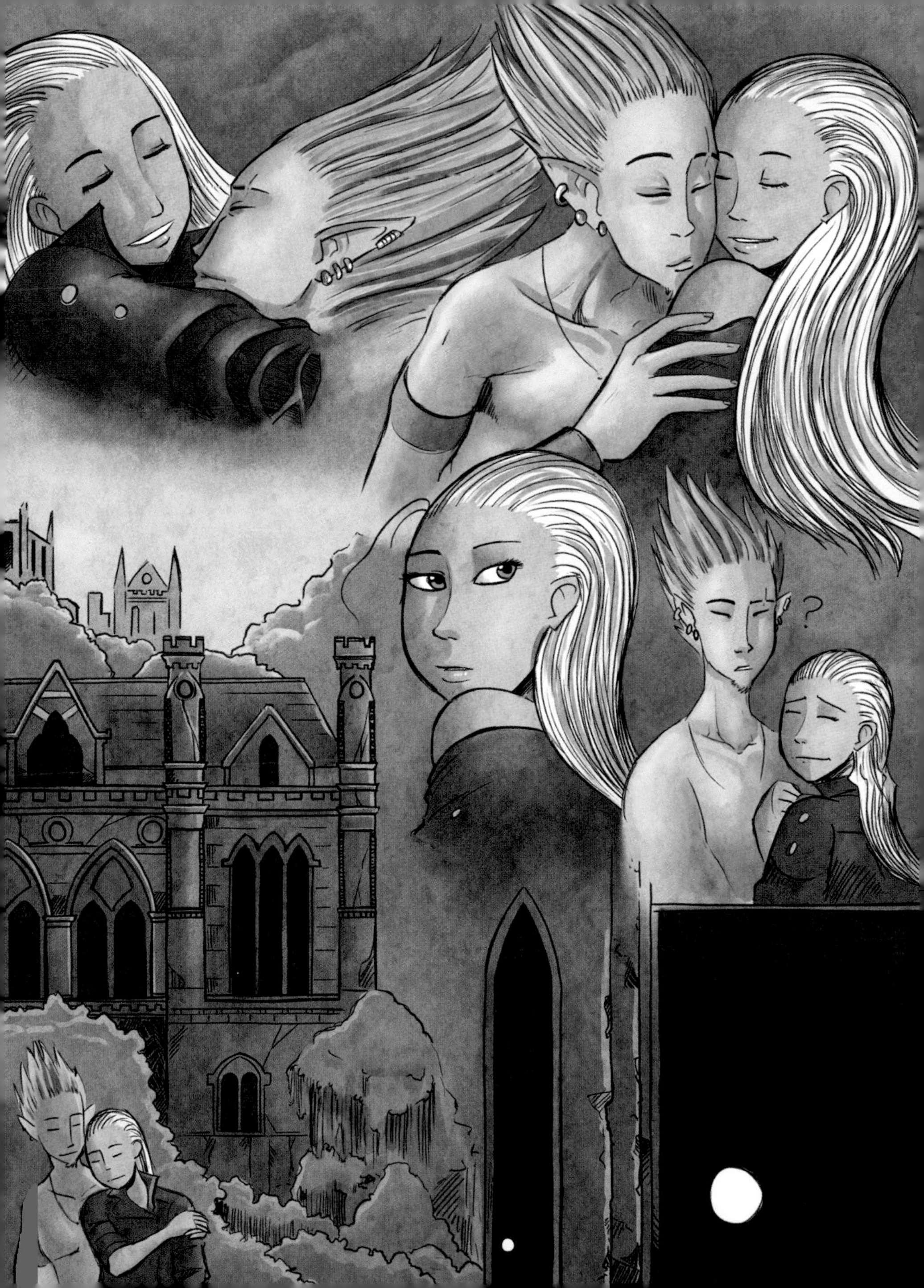
?

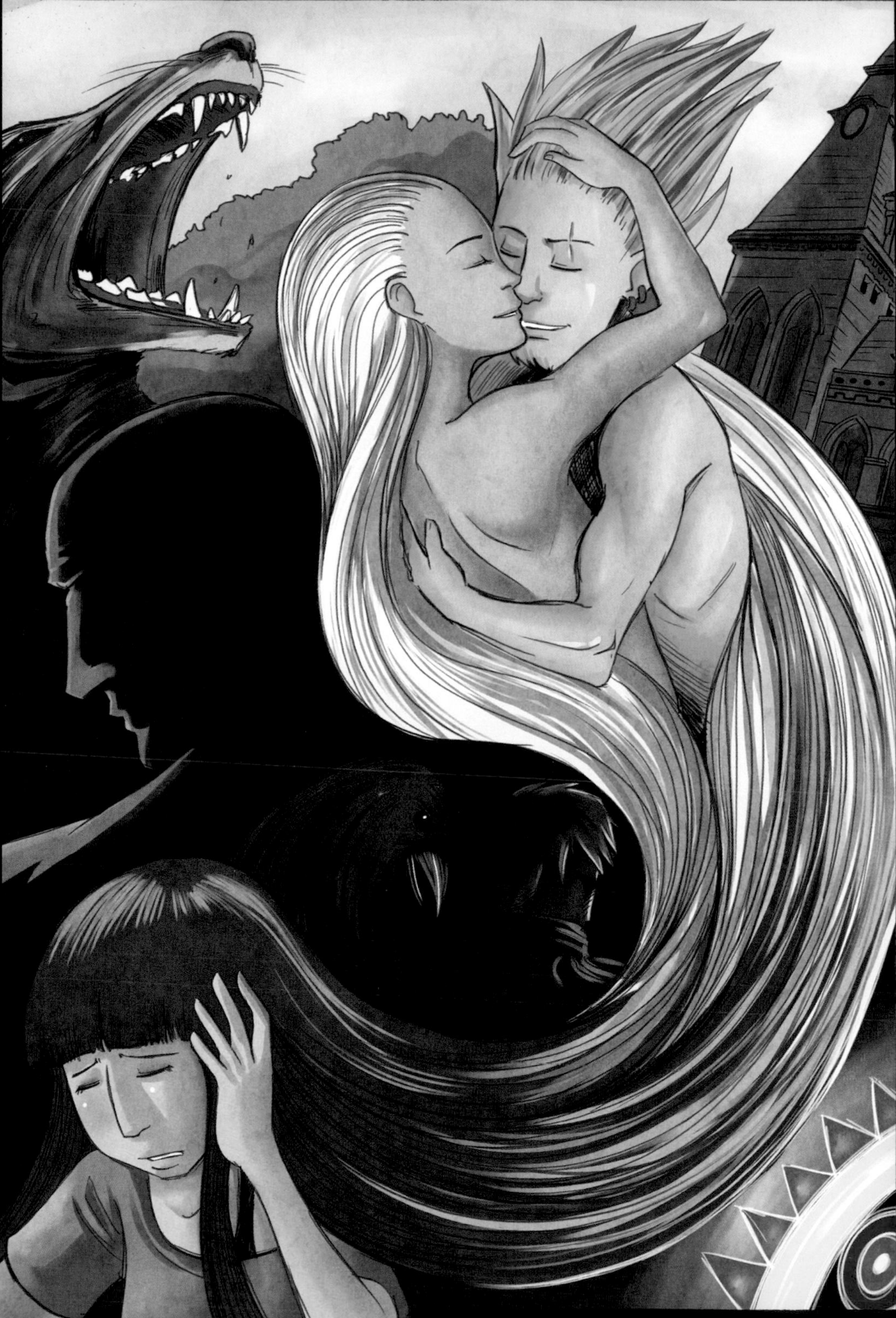

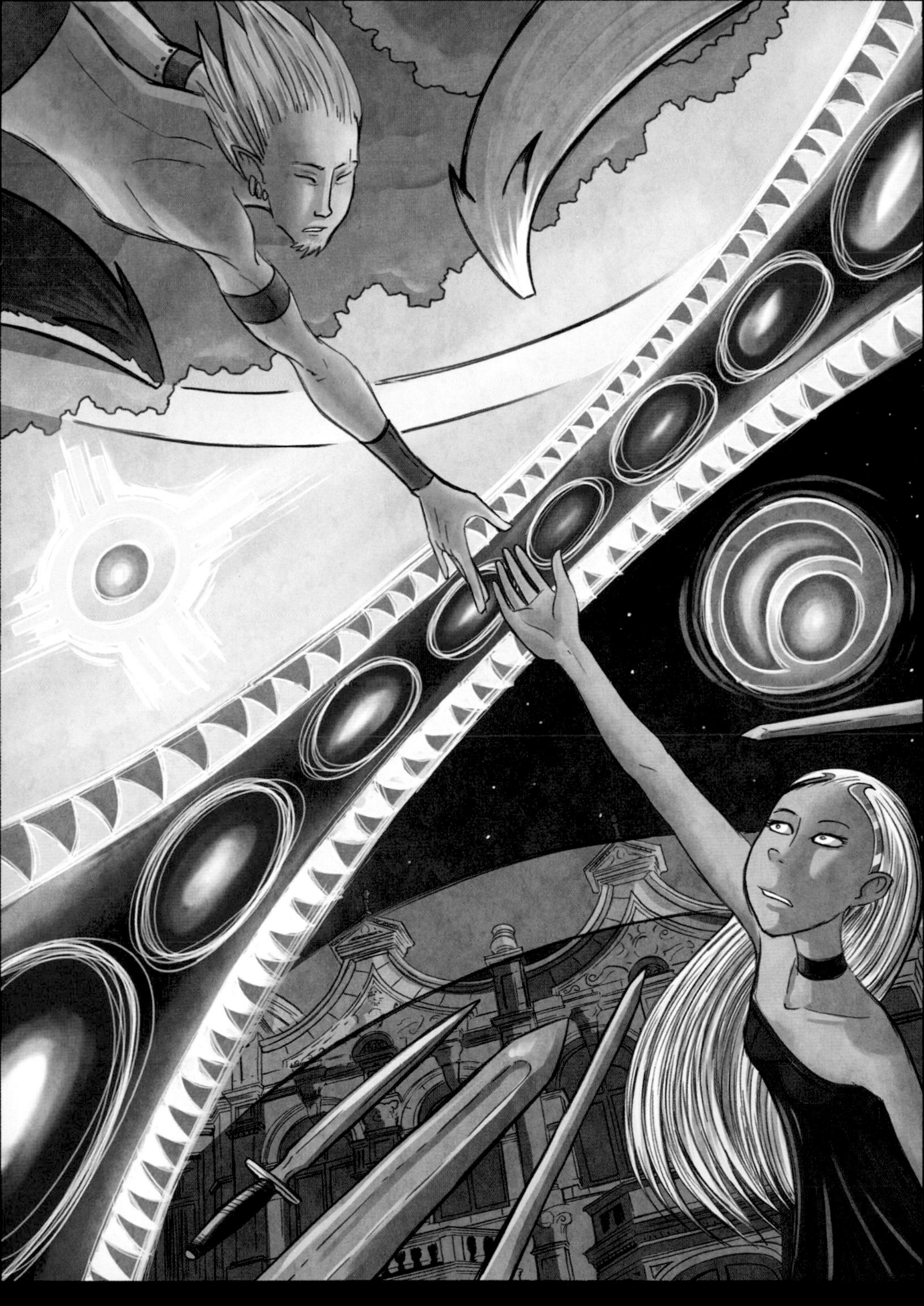

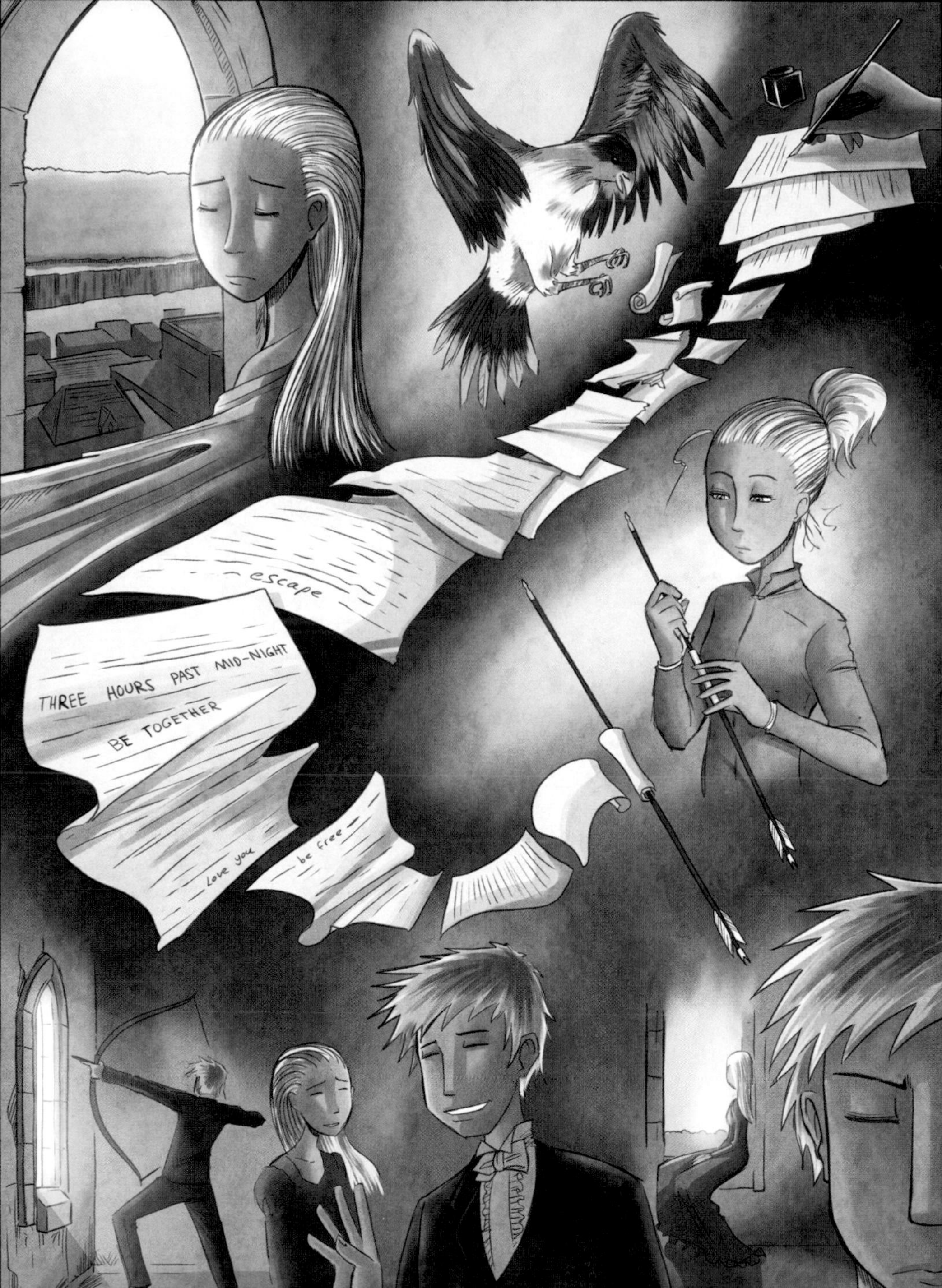
escape
THREE HOURS PAST MID-NIGHT
BE TOGETHER
love you
be free

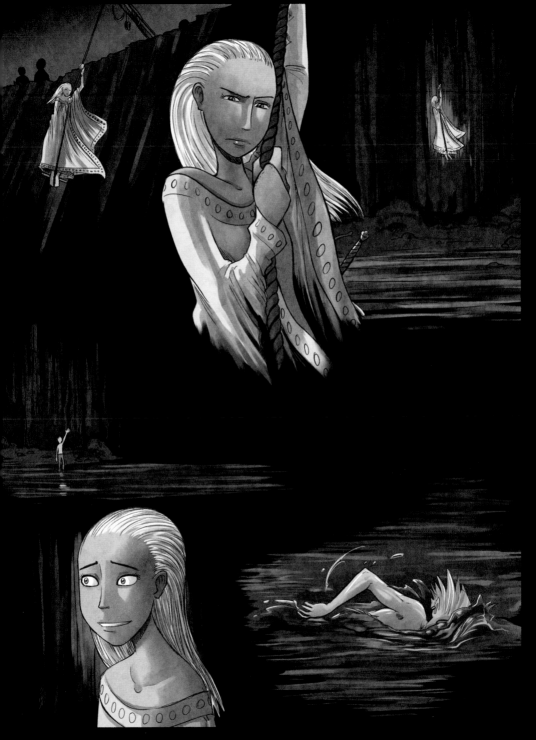

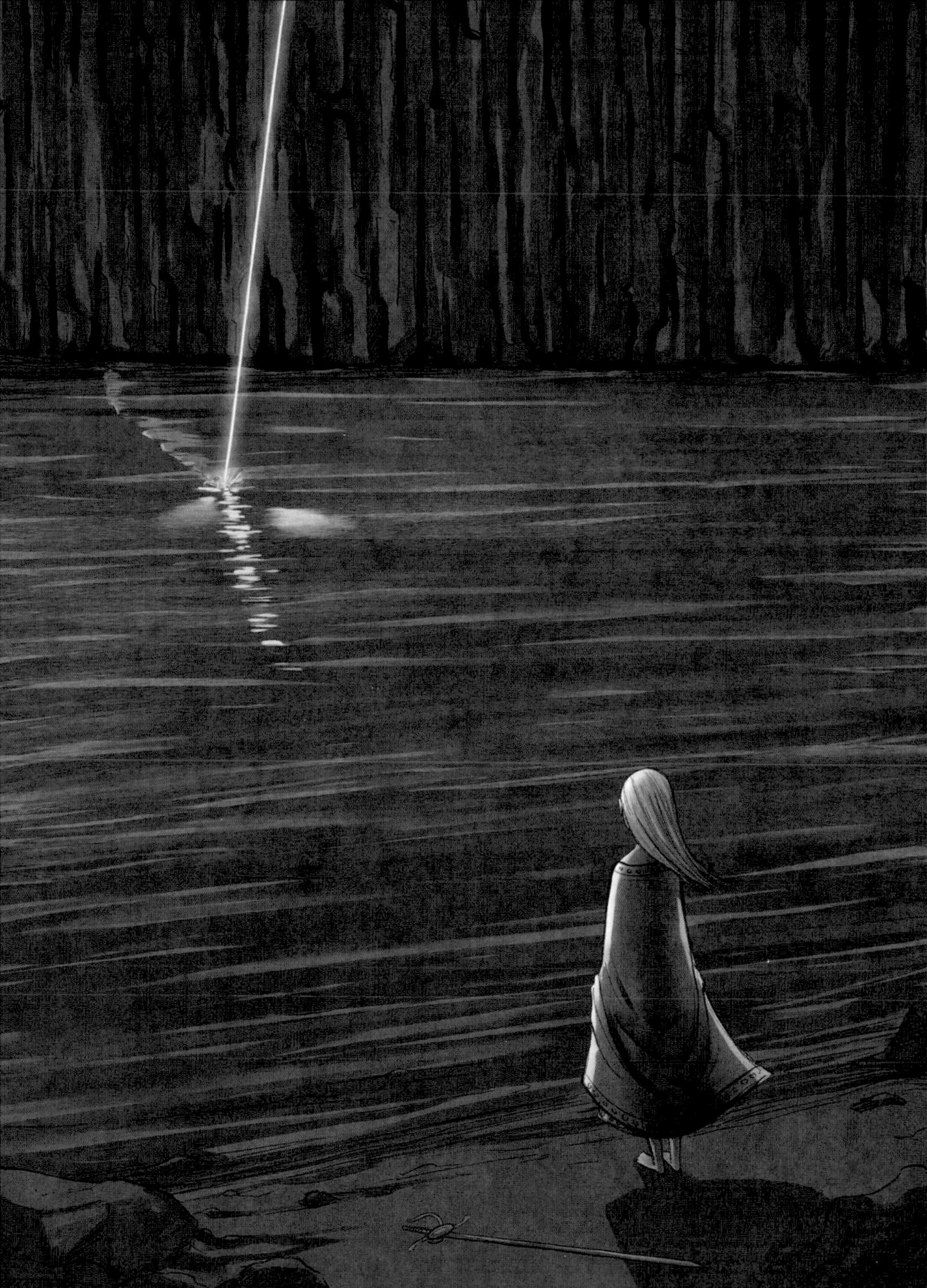

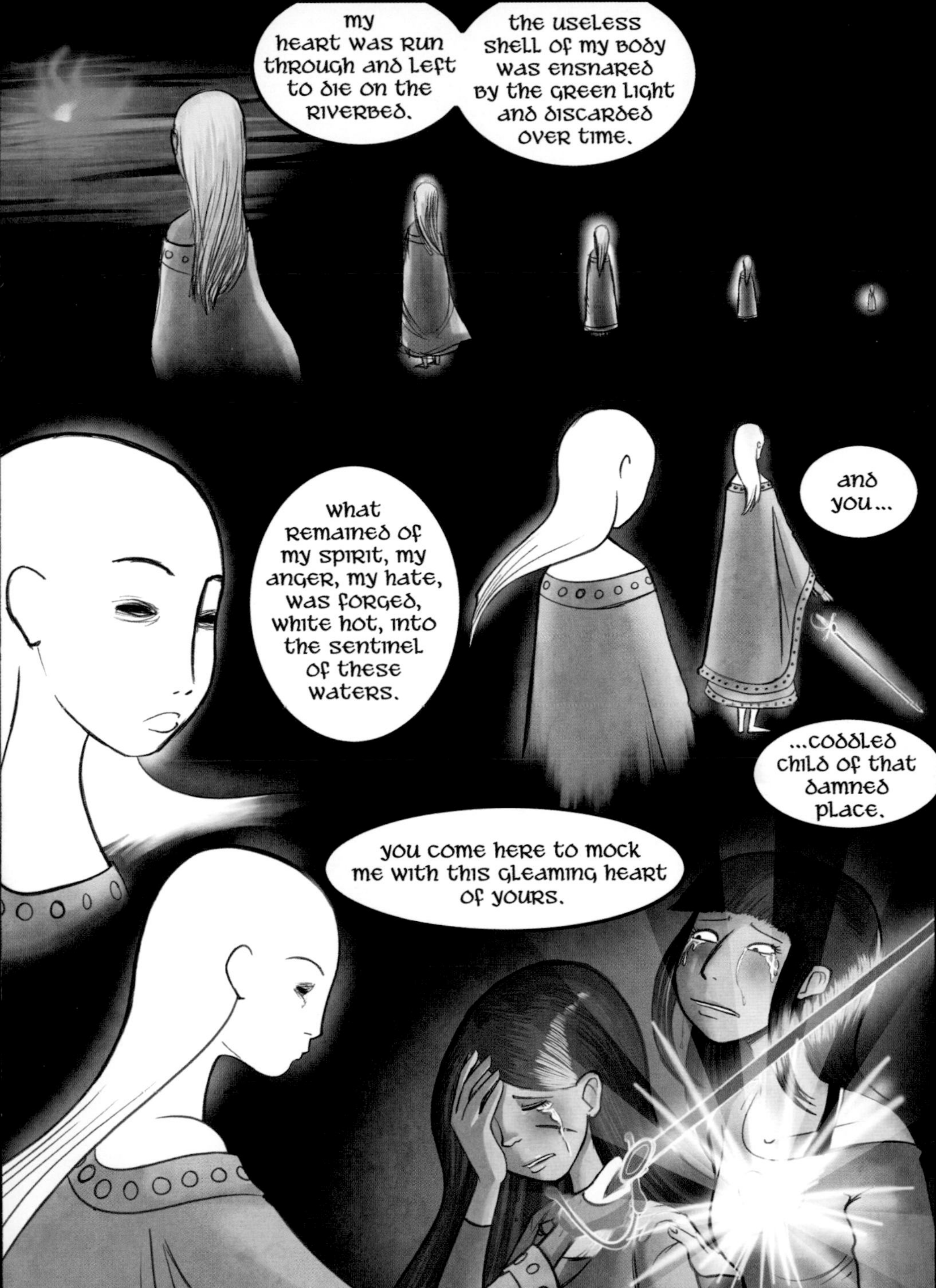
my heart was run through and left to die on the riverbed.
the useless shell of my body was ensnared by the green light and discarded over time.
what remained of my spirit, my anger, my hate, was forged, white hot, into the sentinel of these waters.
and you...
...coddled child of that damned place.
you come here to mock me with this gleaming heart of yours.

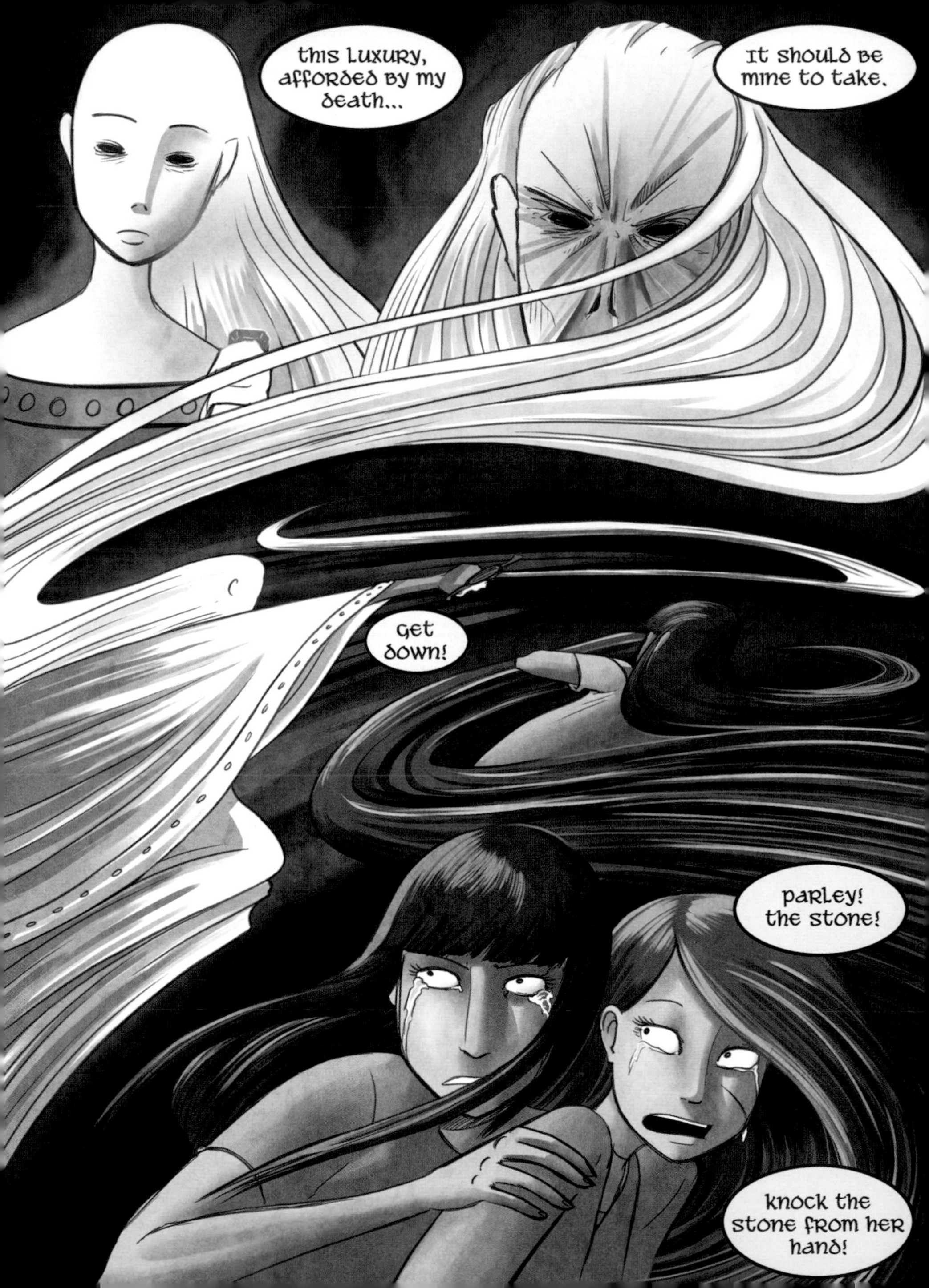
this luxury, afforded by my death...
It should be mine to take.
get down!
parley! the stone!
knock the stone from her hand!

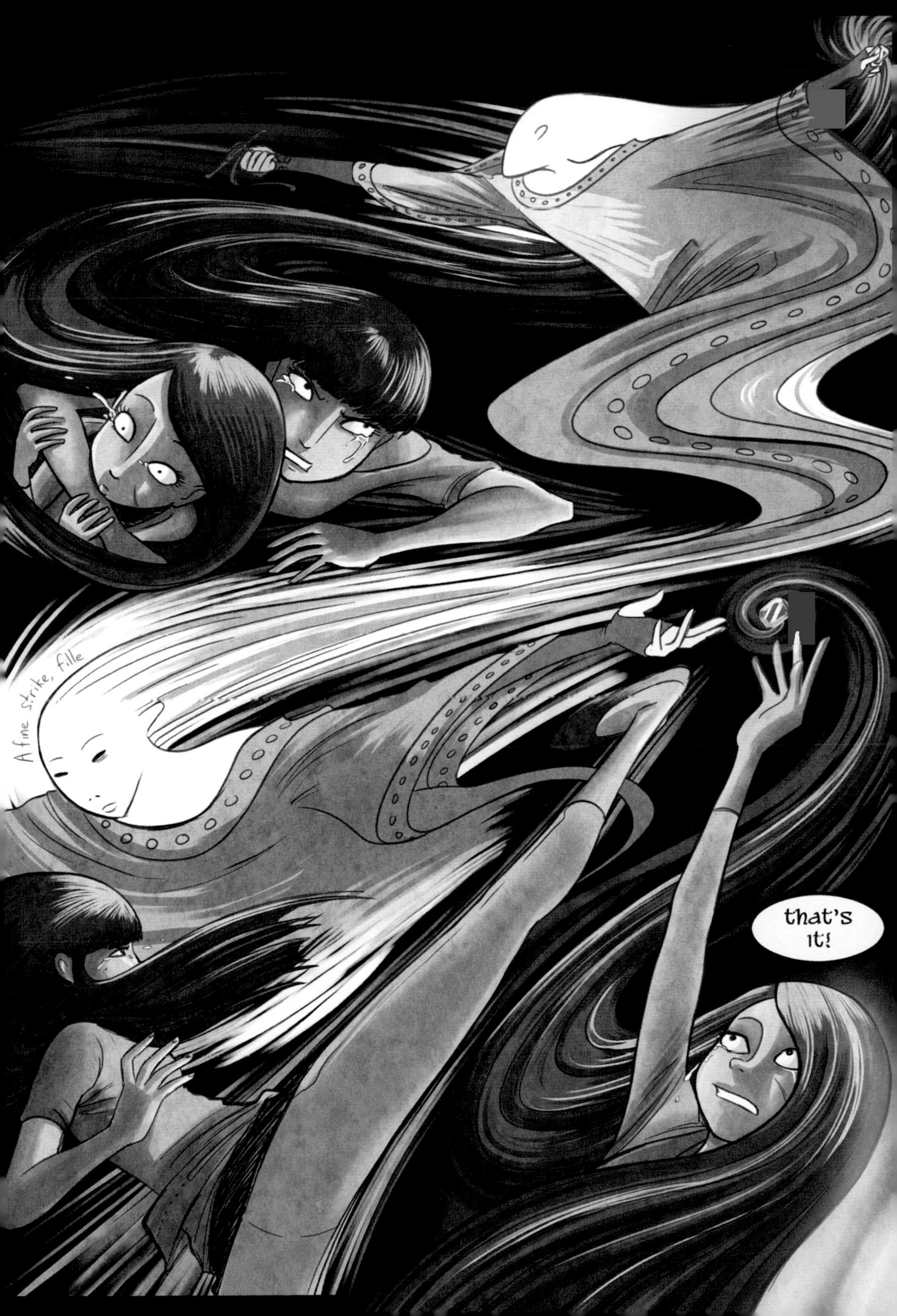
A fine strike, fille
that's it!

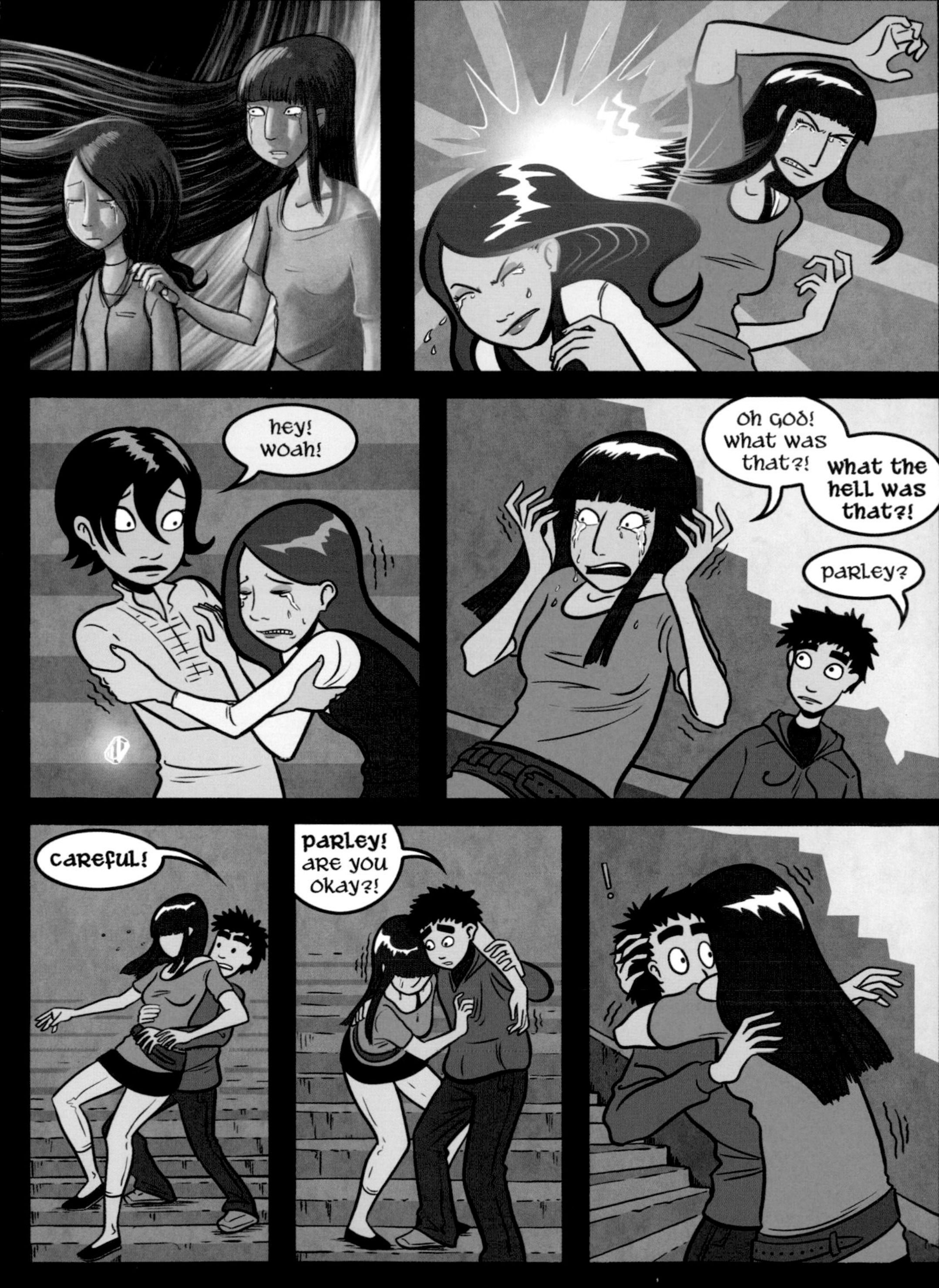
hey! woah!
oh God! what was that?!
what the hell was that?!
parley?
careful!
parley! are you okay?!
!

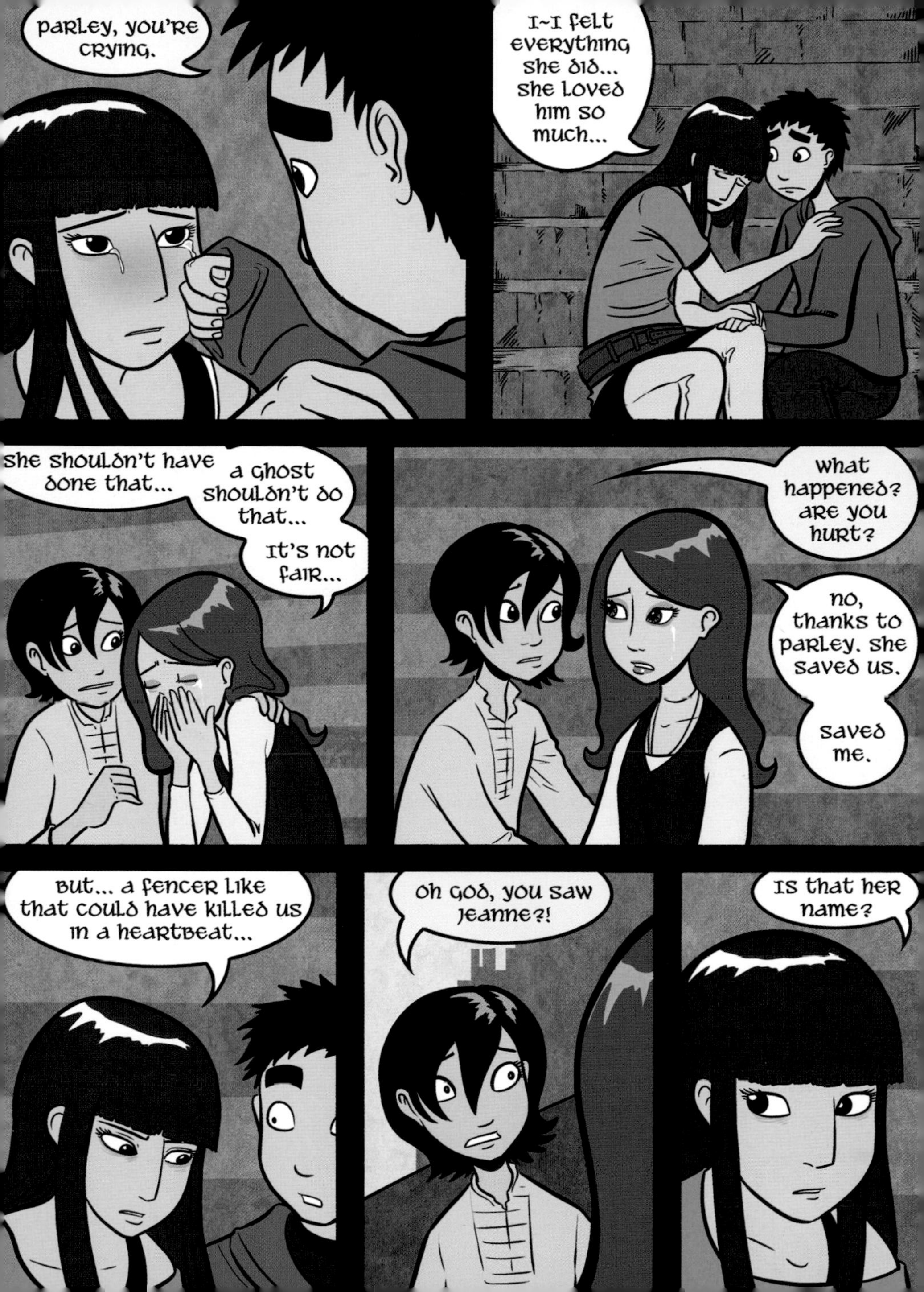
parley, you're crying.
I~I felt everything she did... she loved him so much...
she shouldn't have done that...
a ghost shouldn't do that...
It's not fair...
what happened? are you hurt?
no, thanks to parley. she saved us.
saved me.
but... a fencer like that could have killed us in a heartbeat...
oh god, you saw jeanne?!
Is that her name?

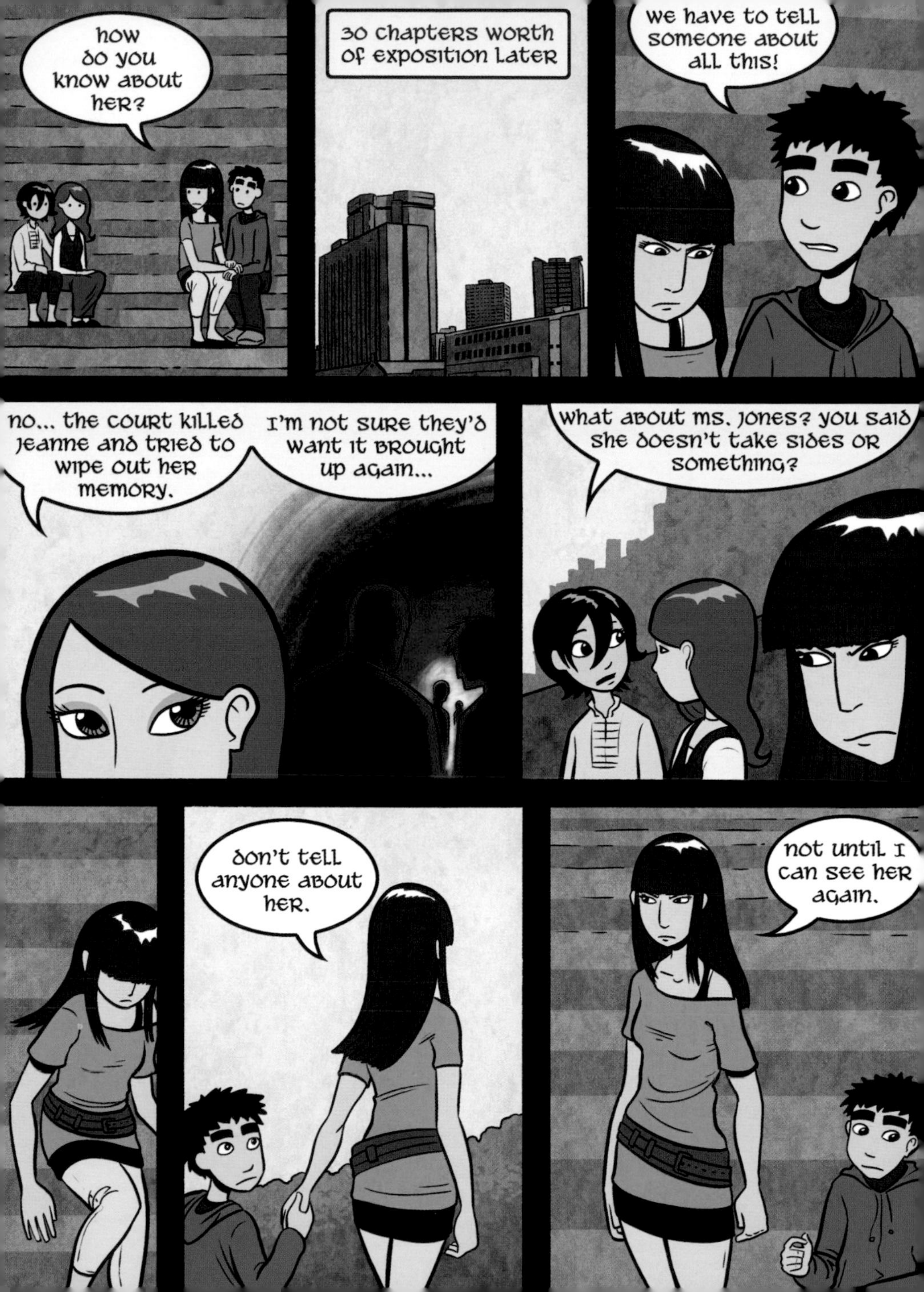
how do you know about her?
30 chapters worth of exposition later
we have to tell someone about all this!
no... the court killed jeanne and tried to wipe out her memory.
I'm not sure they'd want it brought up again...
what about ms. jones? you said she doesn't take sides or something?
don't tell anyone about her.
not until I can see her again.

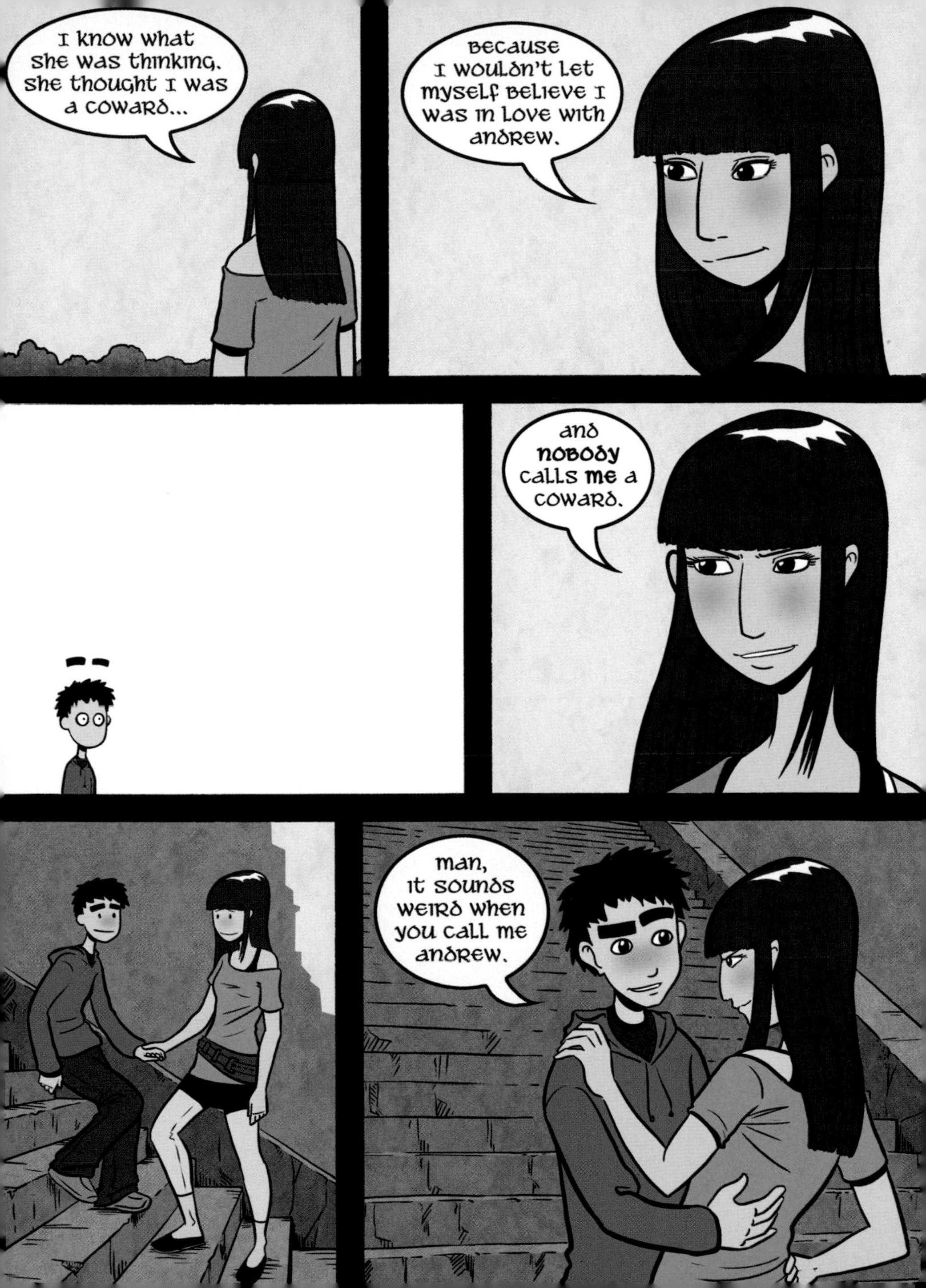
I know what she was thinking. she thought I was a coward...
Because I wouldn't let myself believe I was in love with andrew.
and nobody calls me a coward.
--
man, it sounds weird when you call me andrew.

so.

I think that device is keeping Jeanne stuck down there.

yeah, maybe if we can get it somehow, she can... move on.

well I think I can get us down there. I just gotta...

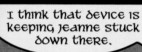

BIP

BIP

woops!

haha, I think I get it now.

BIP
BIP
BIP
BIP

man, I wonder how that works.

that's incredible, parley...

perhaps we can find some information on this steadman person.

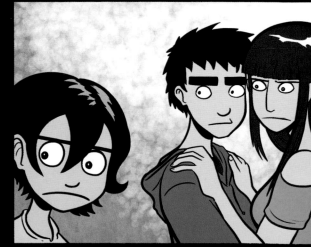

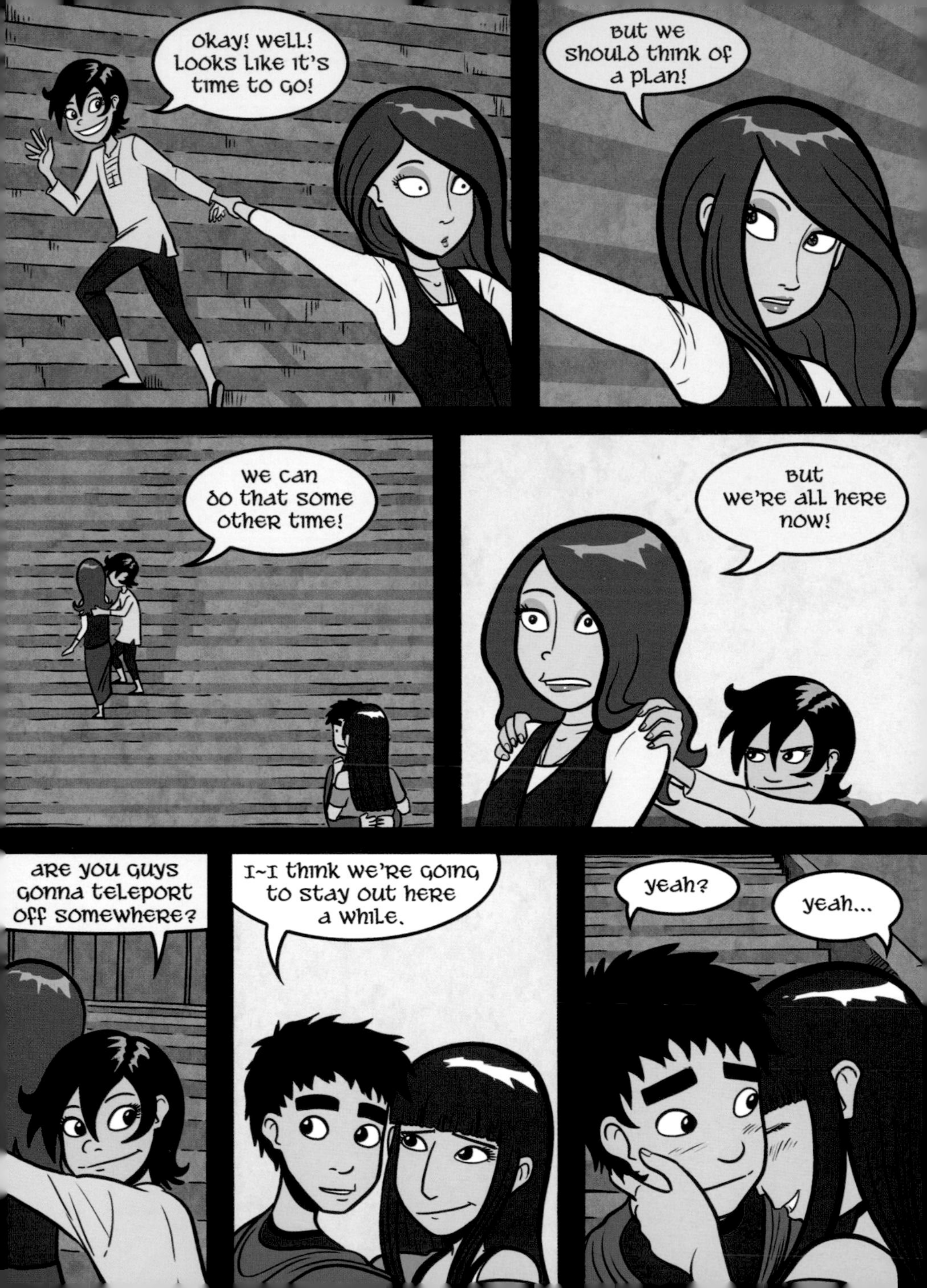
Okay! Well! Looks like it's time to go!
But we should think of a plan!
We can do that some other time!
But we're all here now!
Are you guys gonna teleport off somewhere?
I-I think we're going to stay out here a while.
Yeah?
Yeah...

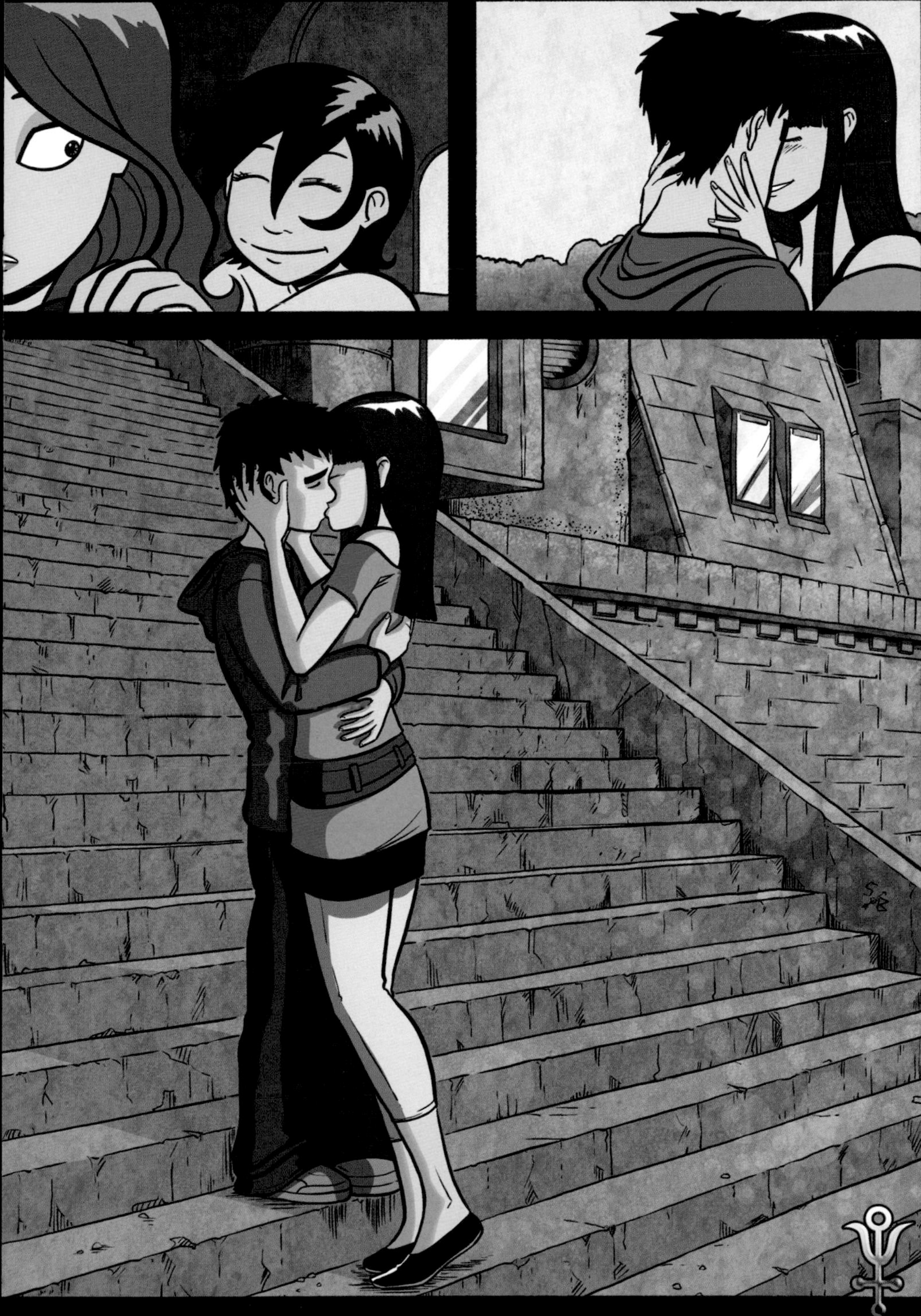

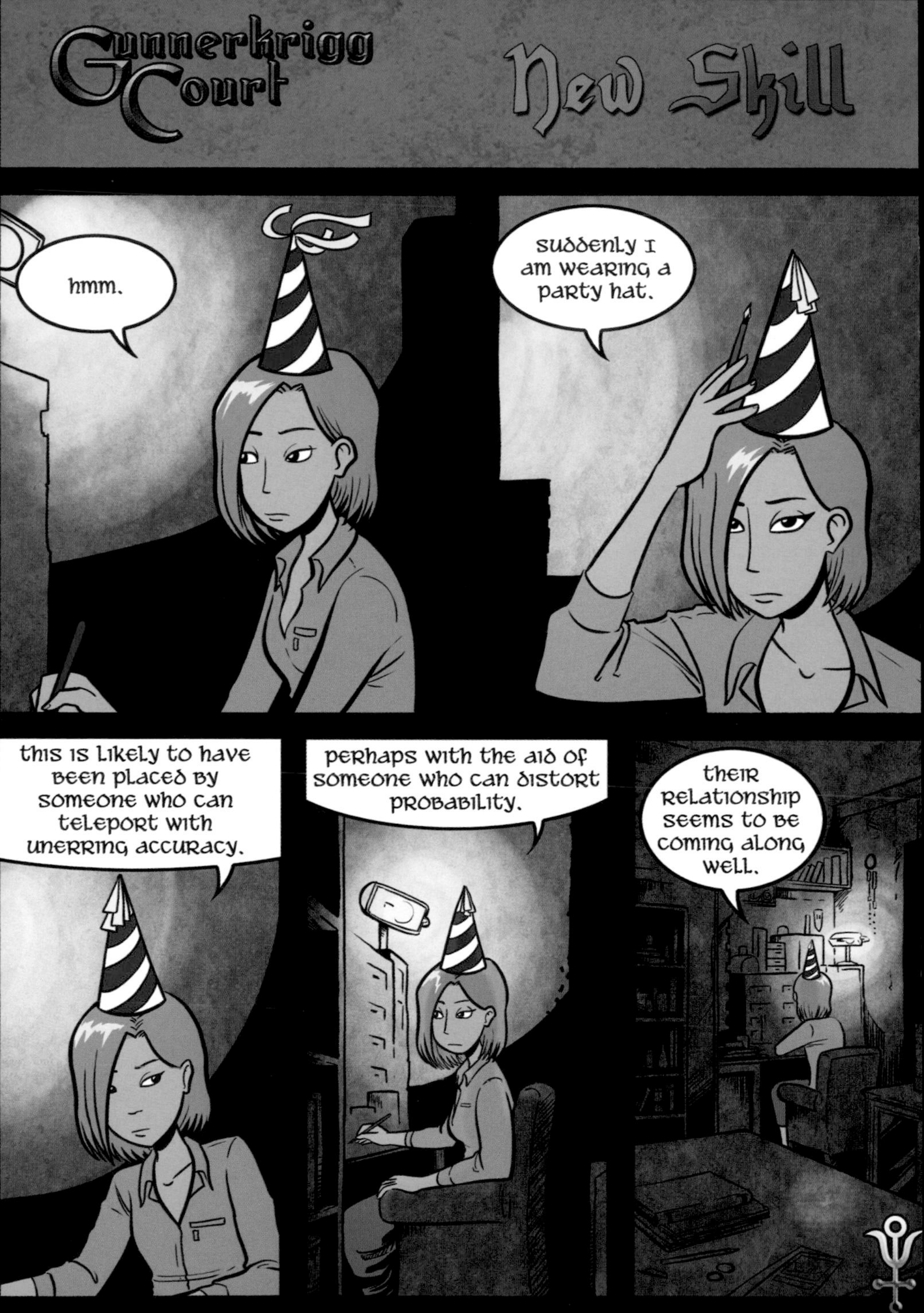
Gunnerkrigg Court
New Skill
hmm.
suddenly I am wearing a party hat.
this is likely to have been placed by someone who can teleport with unerring accuracy.
perhaps with the aid of someone who can distort probability.
their relationship seems to be coming along well.

Gunnerkrigg Court

Chapter 31:

Fire Spike

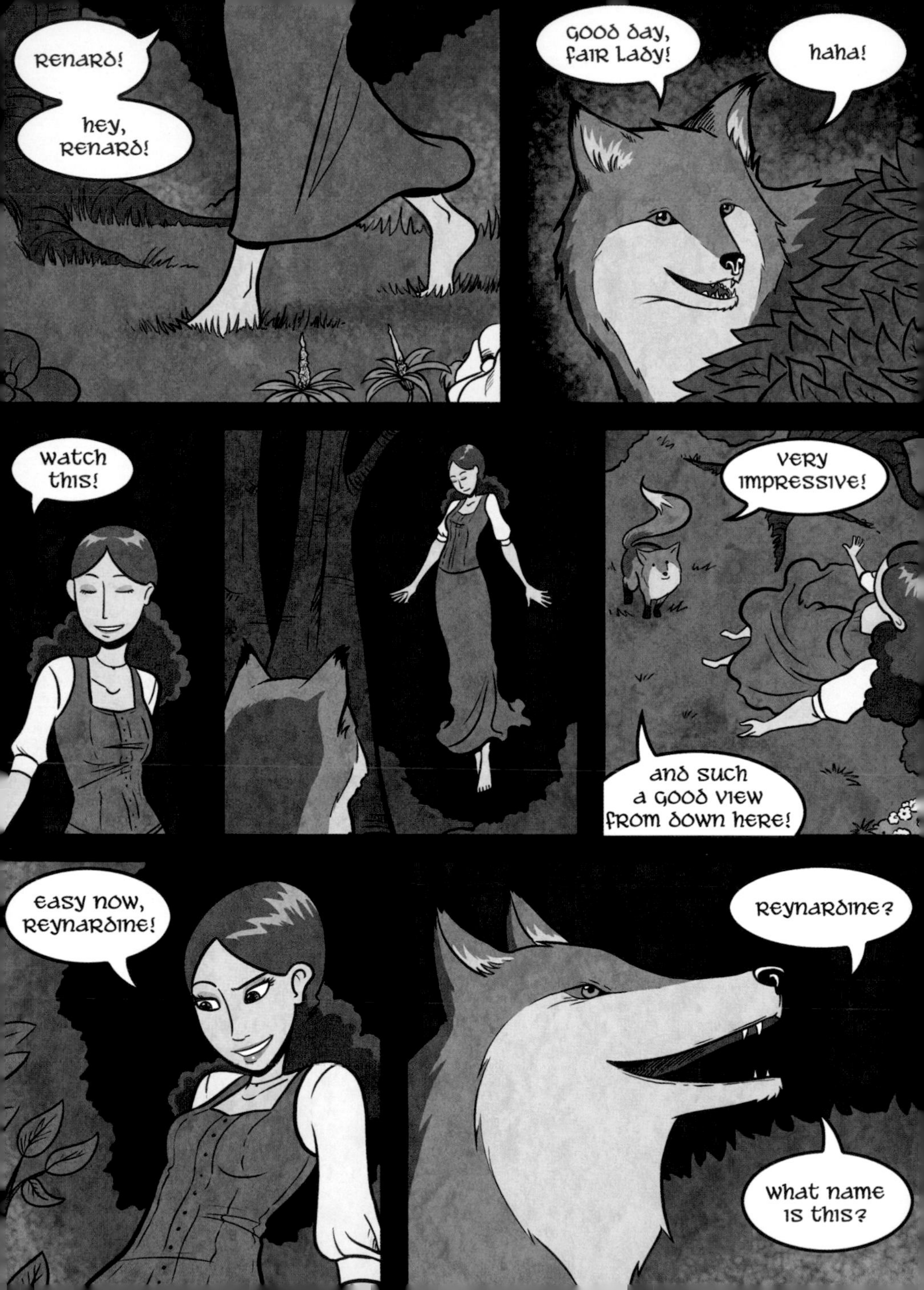
RENARD!
hey, RENARD!
GOOD day, fair Lady!
haha!
watch this!
VERY IMPRESSIVE!
and such a GOOD VIEW from down here!
easy now, REYNARDINE!
REYNARDINE?
what name is this?

IT'S THE name of a demon who steals the hearts of young girls.

then...

have I captured your heart?

SURMA, I... I LOVE YOU!

watch how high I can go!

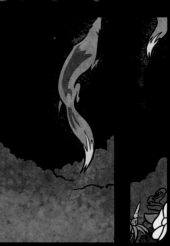

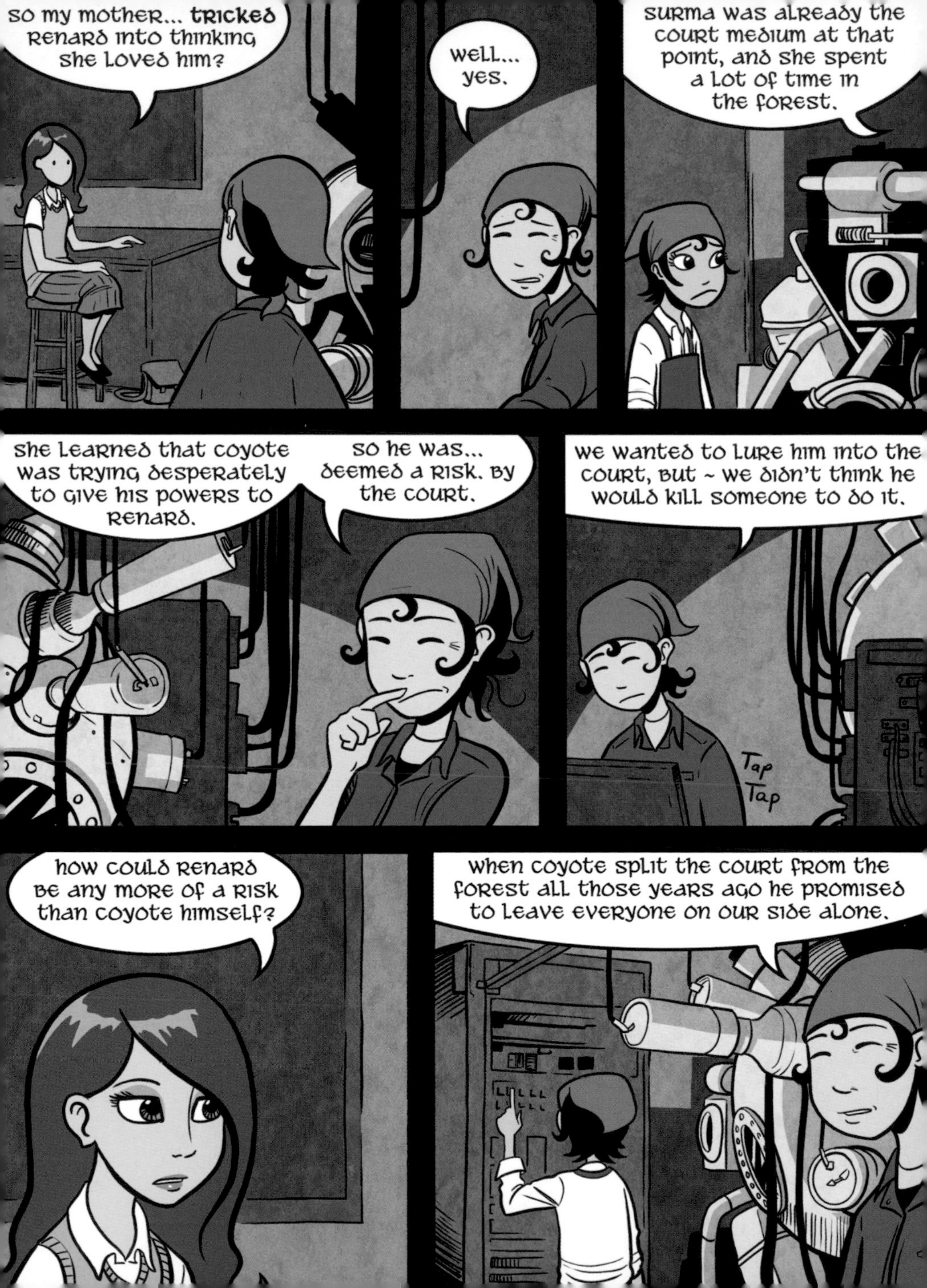
so my mother... tricked Renard into thinking she loved him?
well... yes.
Surma was already the court medium at that point, and she spent a lot of time in the forest.
she learned that coyote was trying desperately to give his powers to Renard.
so he was... deemed a risk. By the court.
we wanted to lure him into the court, but ~ we didn't think he would kill someone to do it.
Tap Tap
how could Renard be any more of a risk than coyote himself?
when coyote split the court from the forest all those years ago he promised to leave everyone on our side alone.

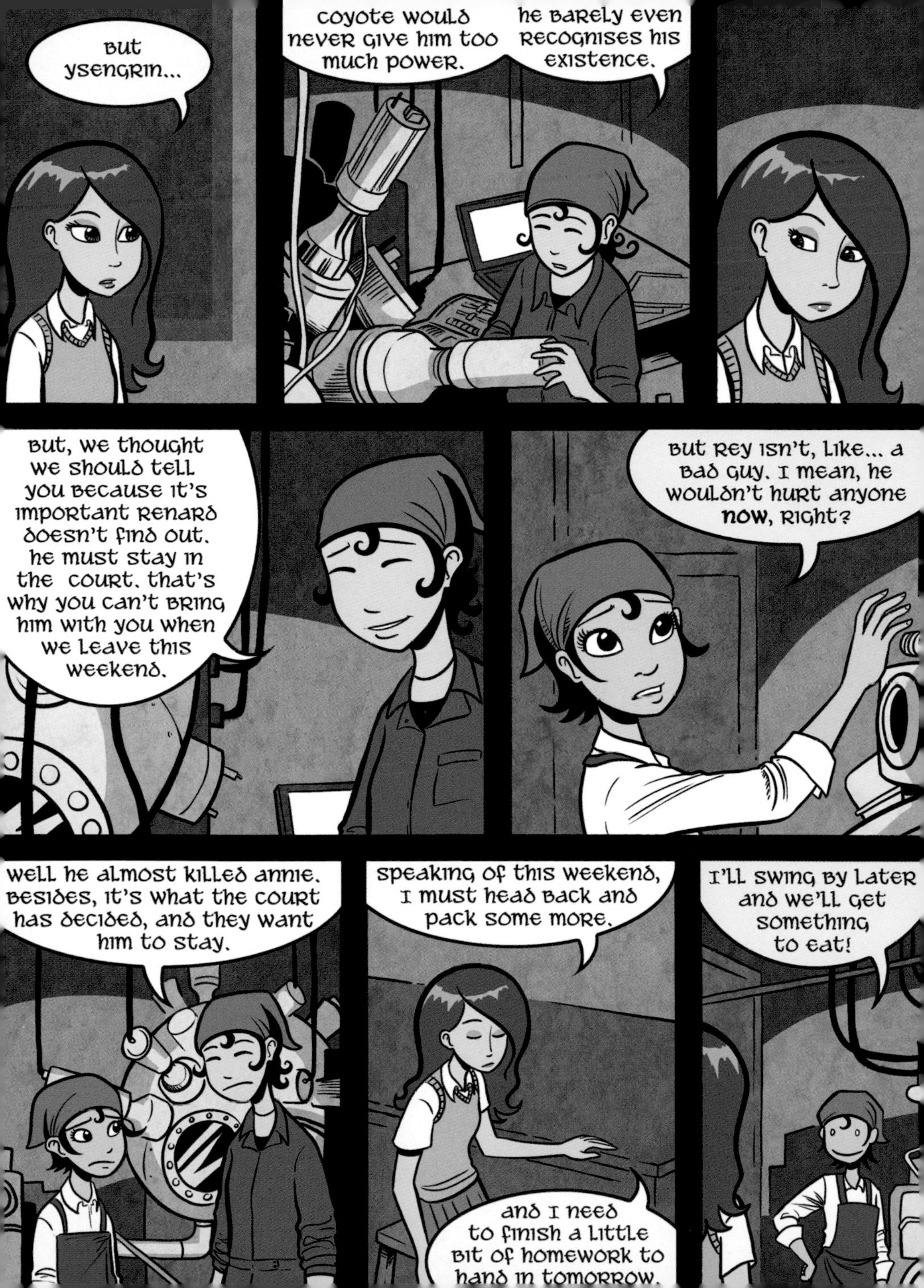
But Ysengrin...
Coyote would never give him too much power.
He barely even recognises his existence.
But, we thought we should tell you because it's important Renard doesn't find out. He must stay in the court. That's why you can't bring him with you when we leave this weekend.
But Rey isn't, like... a bad guy. I mean, he wouldn't hurt anyone **now**, right?
Well he almost killed Annie. Besides, it's what the court has decided, and they want him to stay.
Speaking of this weekend, I must head back and pack some more.
And I need to finish a little bit of homework to hand in tomorrow.
I'll swing by later and we'll get something to eat!

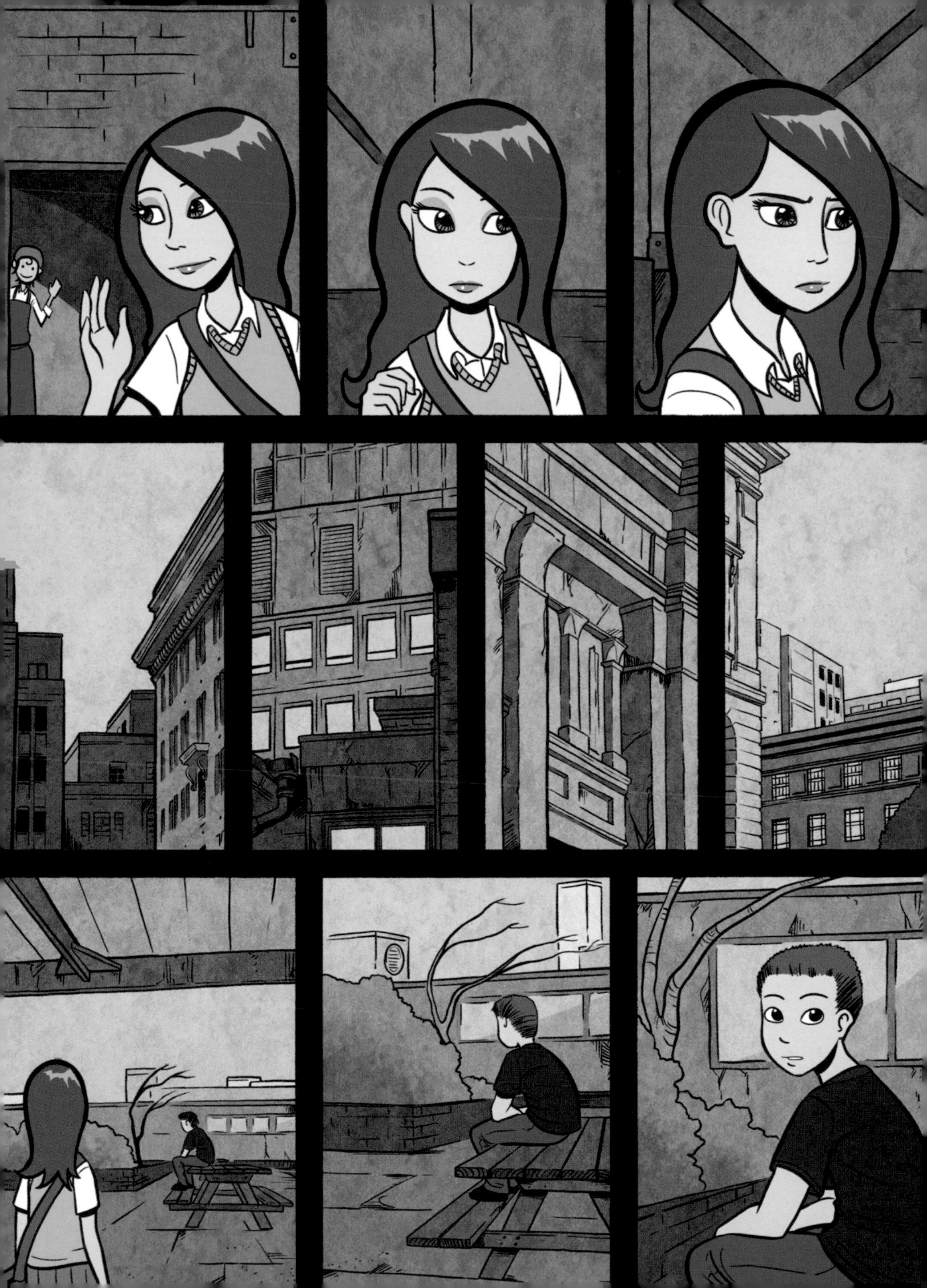

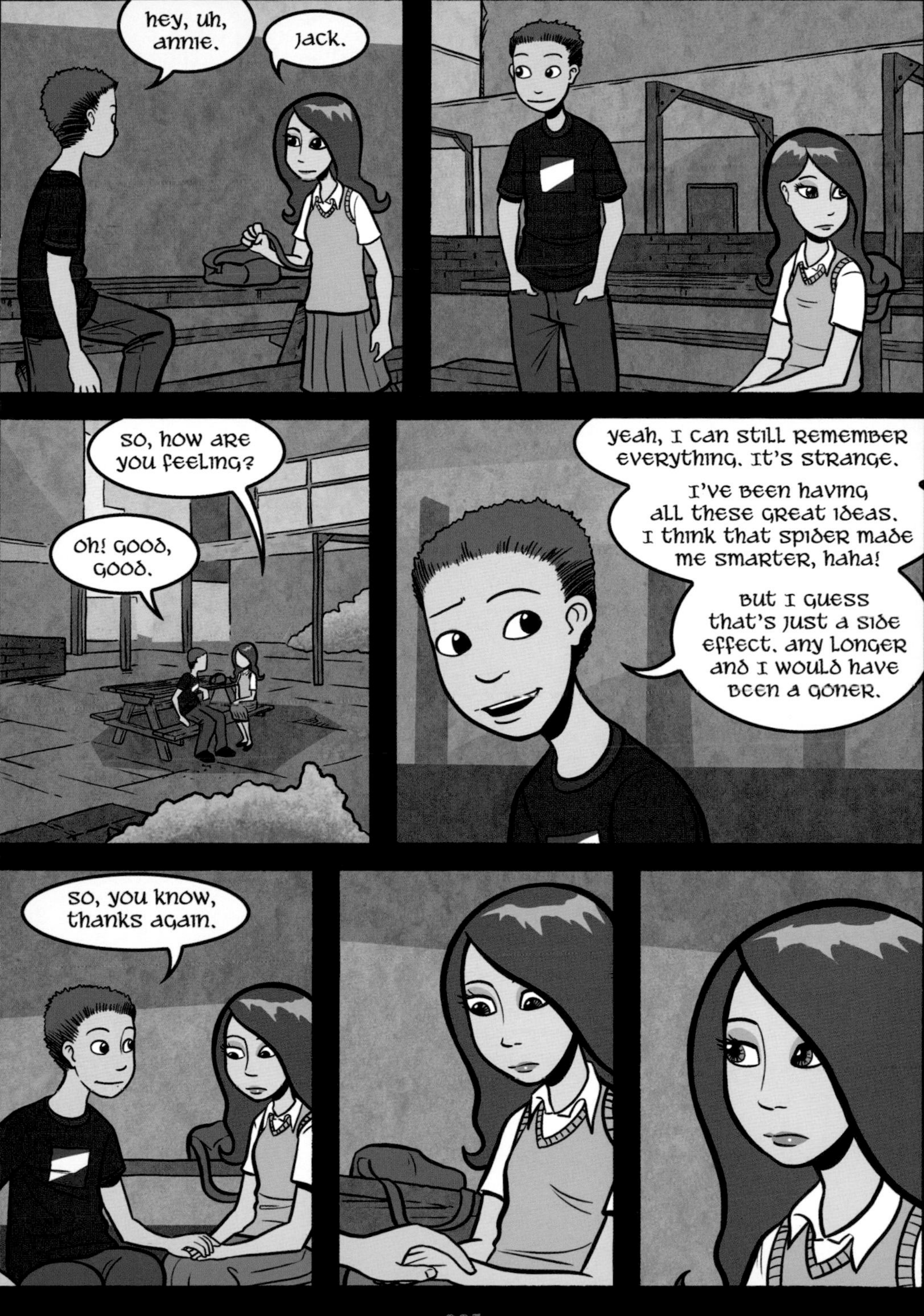
hey, uh, annie.
Jack.
so, how are you feeling?
oh! good, good.
yeah, I can still remember everything. It's strange.
I've been having all these great ideas. I think that spider made me smarter, haha!
But I guess that's just a side effect. any longer and I would have been a goner.
so, you know, thanks again.

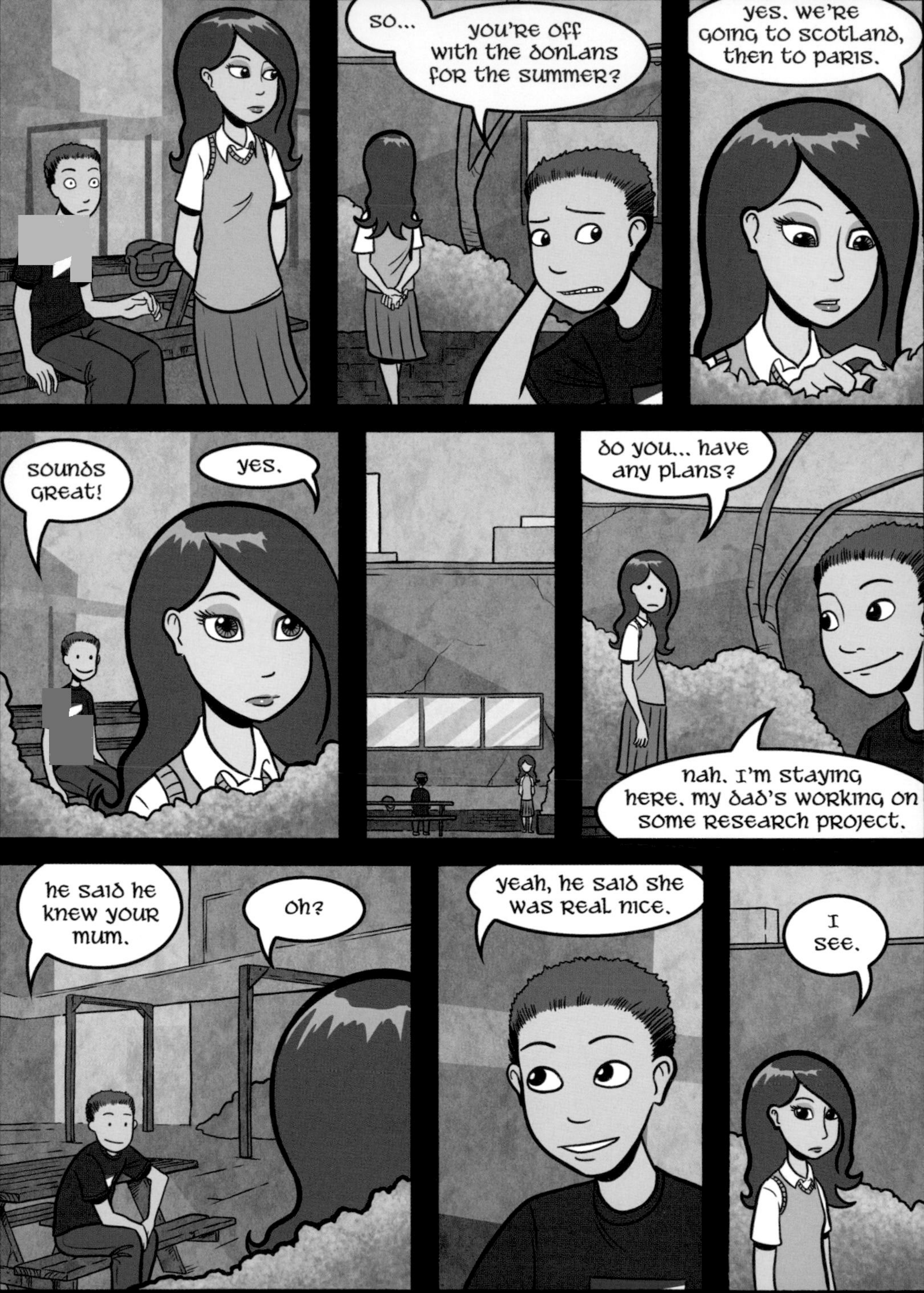
so...
you're off with the donlans for the summer?
yes. we're going to scotland, then to paris.
sounds great!
yes.
do you... have any plans?
nah. I'm staying here. my dad's working on some research project.
he said he knew your mum.
oh?
yeah, he said she was real nice.
I see.

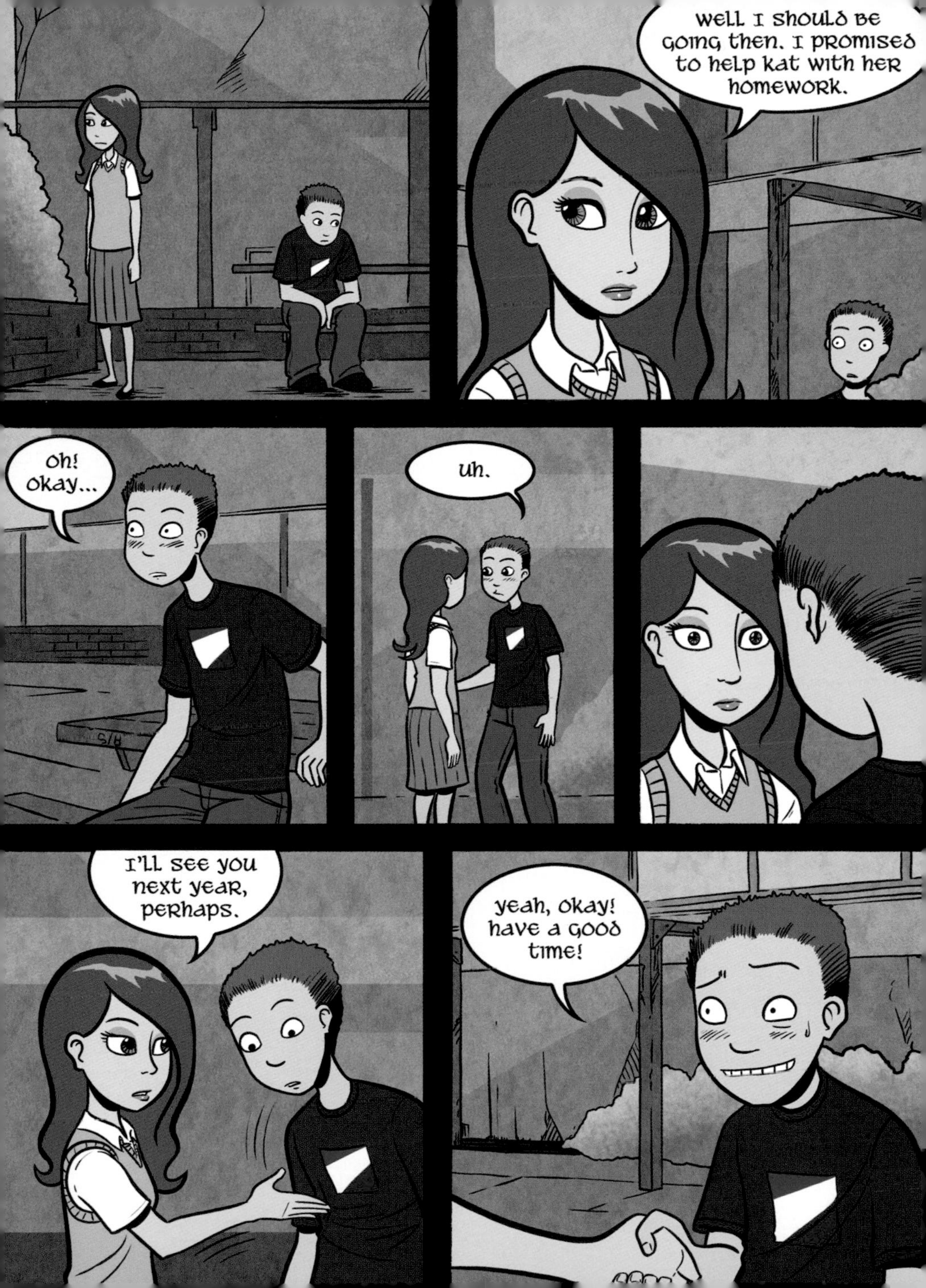
WELL I SHOULD BE GOING THEN. I PROMISED TO HELP KAT WITH HER HOMEWORK.
OH! OKAY...
UH.
I'LL SEE YOU NEXT YEAR, PERHAPS.
YEAH, OKAY! HAVE A GOOD TIME!

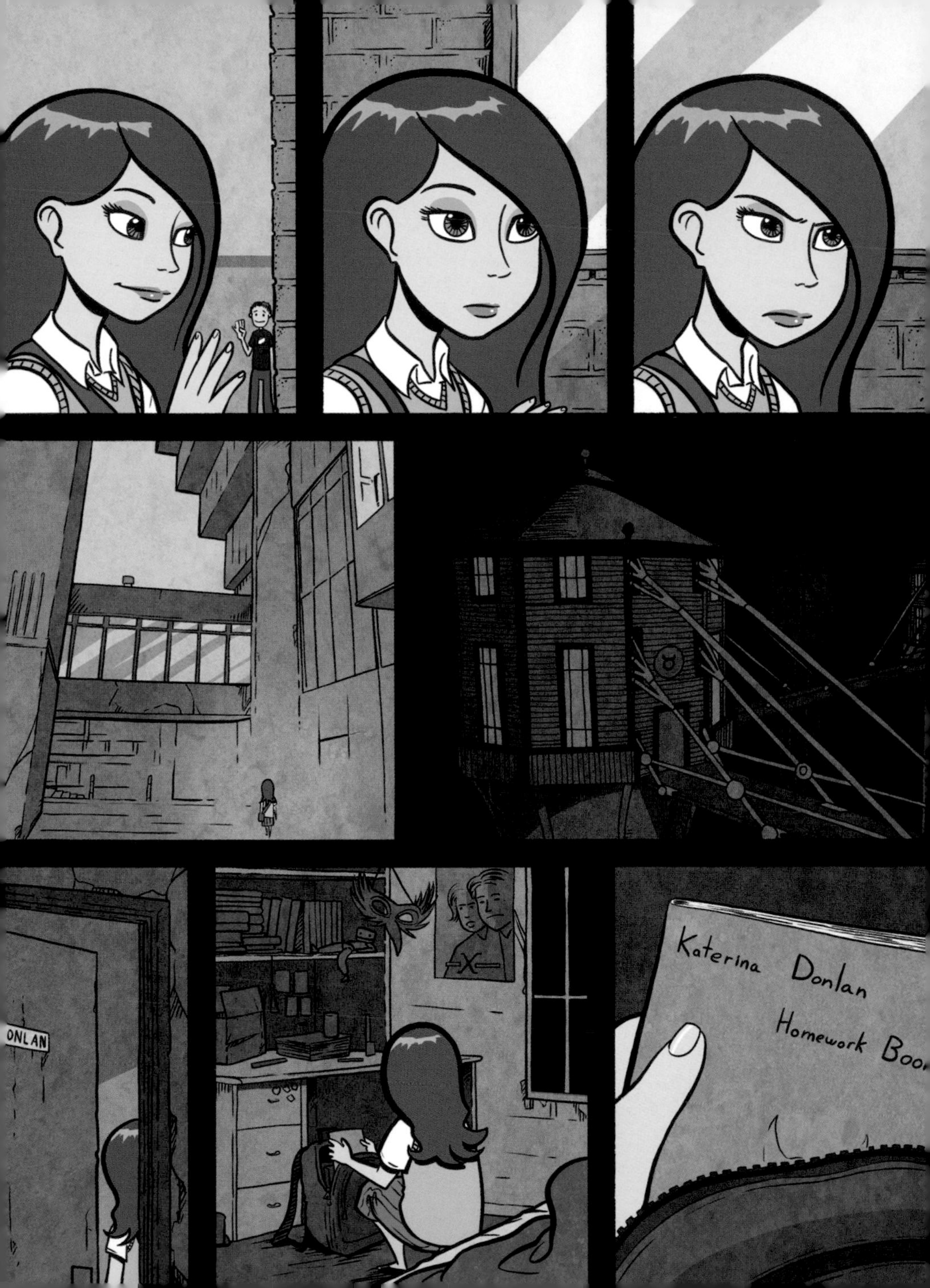
ONLAN
Katerina Donlan
Homework Boo

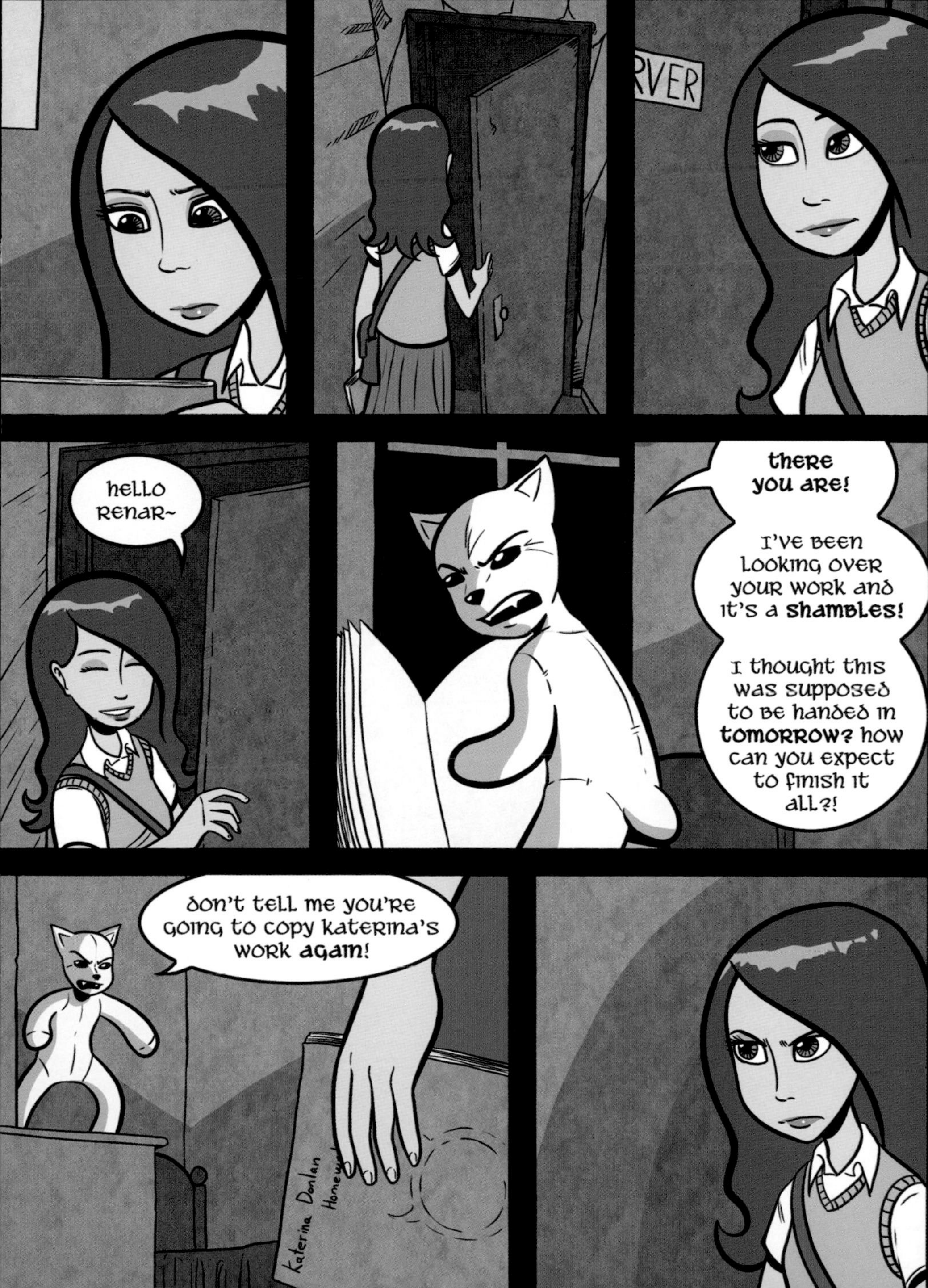
RVER
hello Renar~
there you are!
I've been looking over your work and it's a shambles!
I thought this was supposed to be handed in tomorrow? how can you expect to finish it all?!
don't tell me you're going to copy katerina's work again!
Katerina Donlan Homework

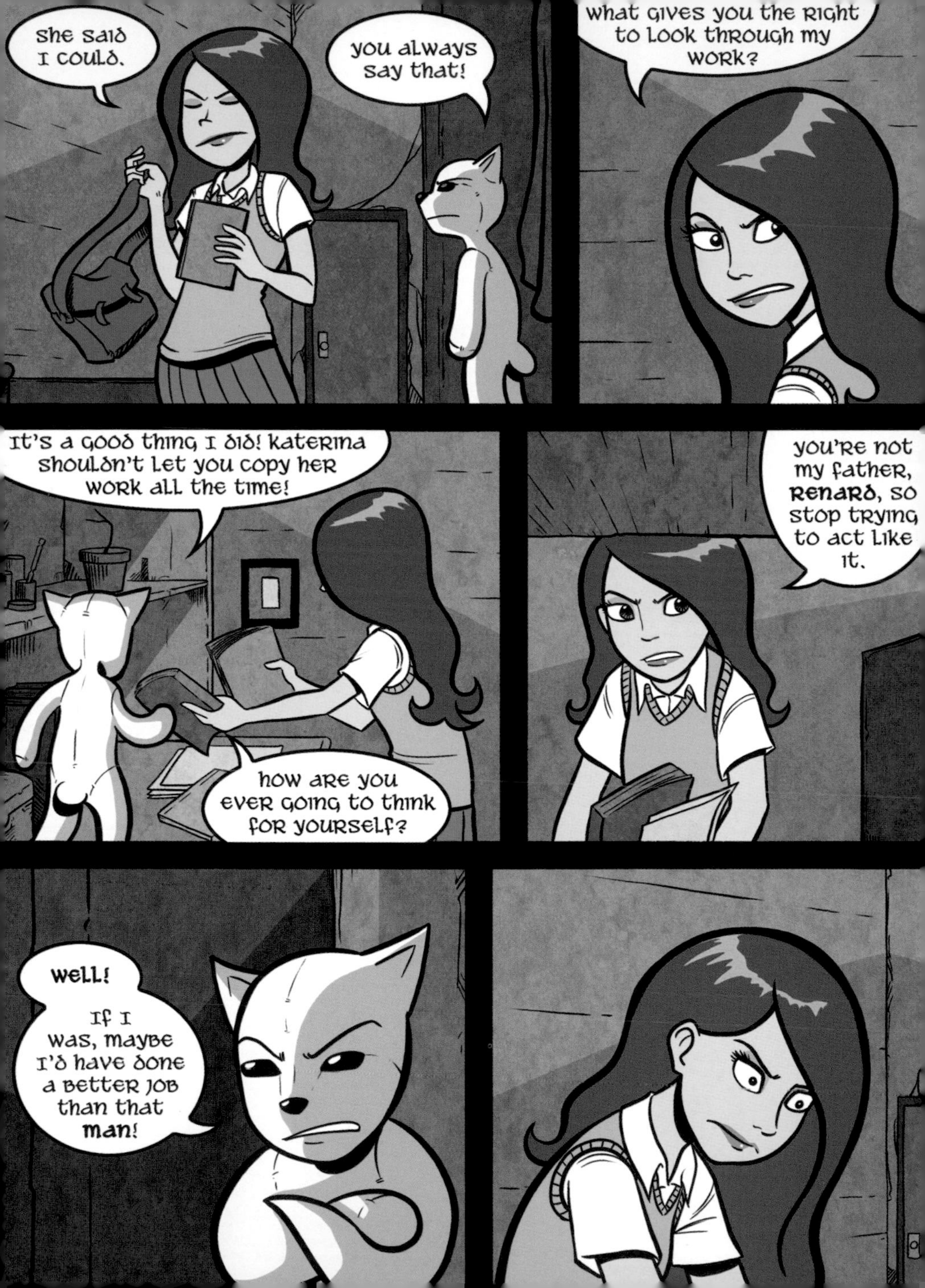
She said I could.
You always say that!
What gives you the right to look through my work?
It's a good thing I did! Katerina shouldn't let you copy her work all the time!
How are you ever going to think for yourself?
You're not my father, RENARD, so stop trying to act like it.
WELL!
If I was, maybe I'd have done a better job than that man!

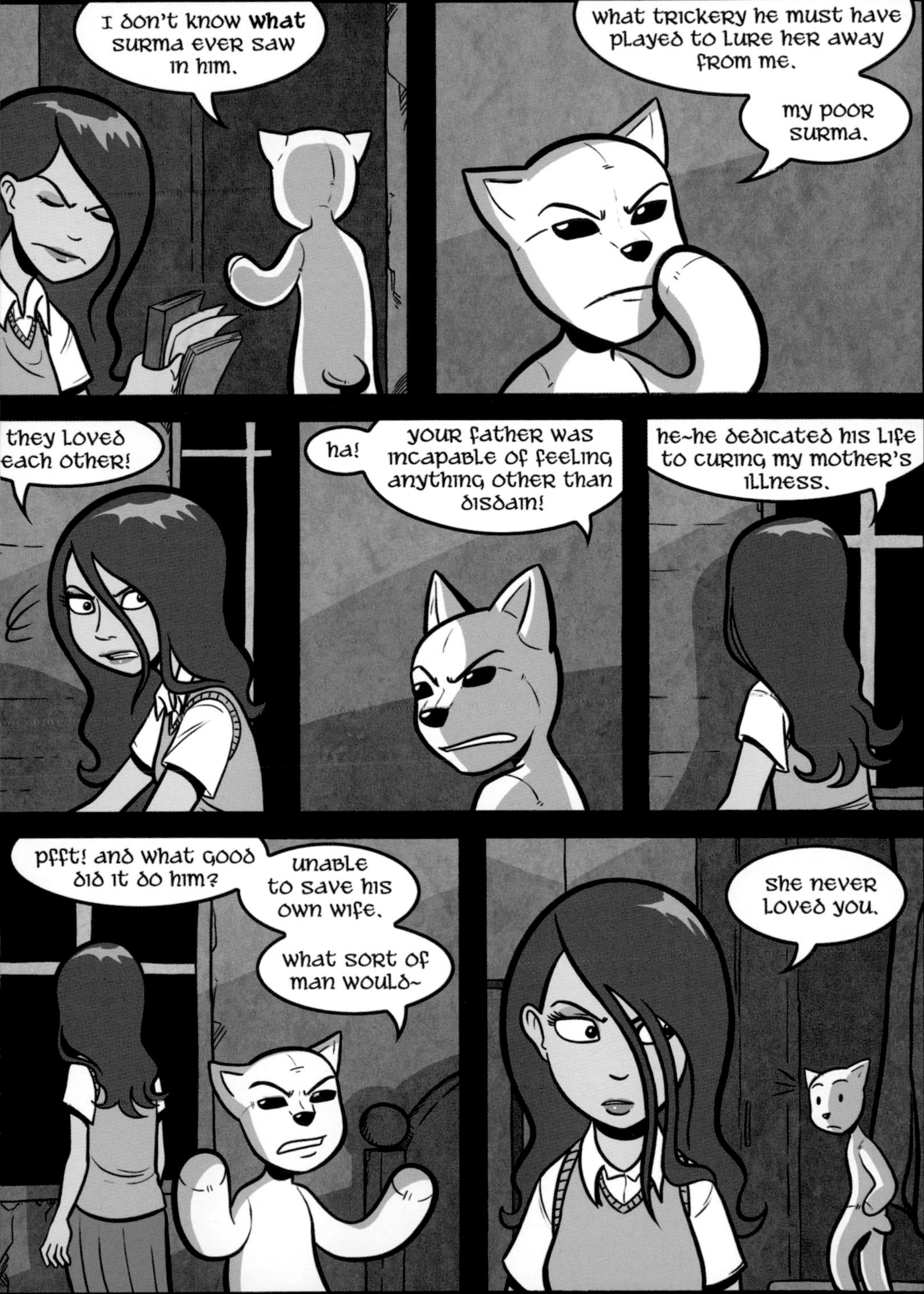
I don't know what surma ever saw in him.
what trickery he must have played to lure her away from me.
my poor surma.
they loved each other!
ha!
your father was incapable of feeling anything other than disdain!
he-he dedicated his life to curing my mother's illness.
pfft! and what good did it do him?
unable to save his own wife.
what sort of man would-
she never loved you.

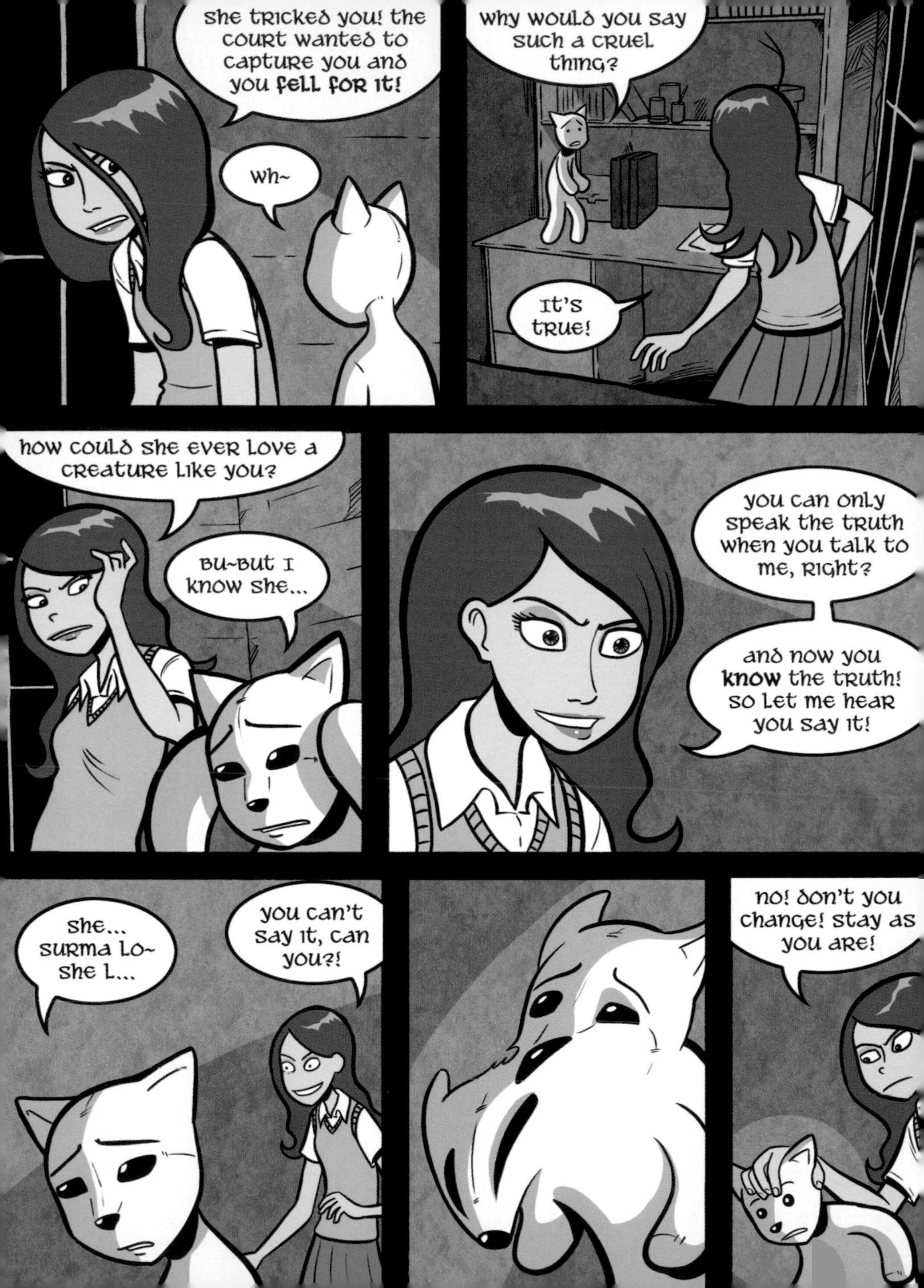
she tricked you! the court wanted to capture you and you fell for it!
wh~
why would you say such a cruel thing?
it's true!
how could she ever love a creature like you?
bu~but I know she...
you can only speak the truth when you talk to me, right?
and now you know the truth! so let me hear you say it!
she... surma lo~ she l...
you can't say it, can you?!
no! don't you change! stay as you are!

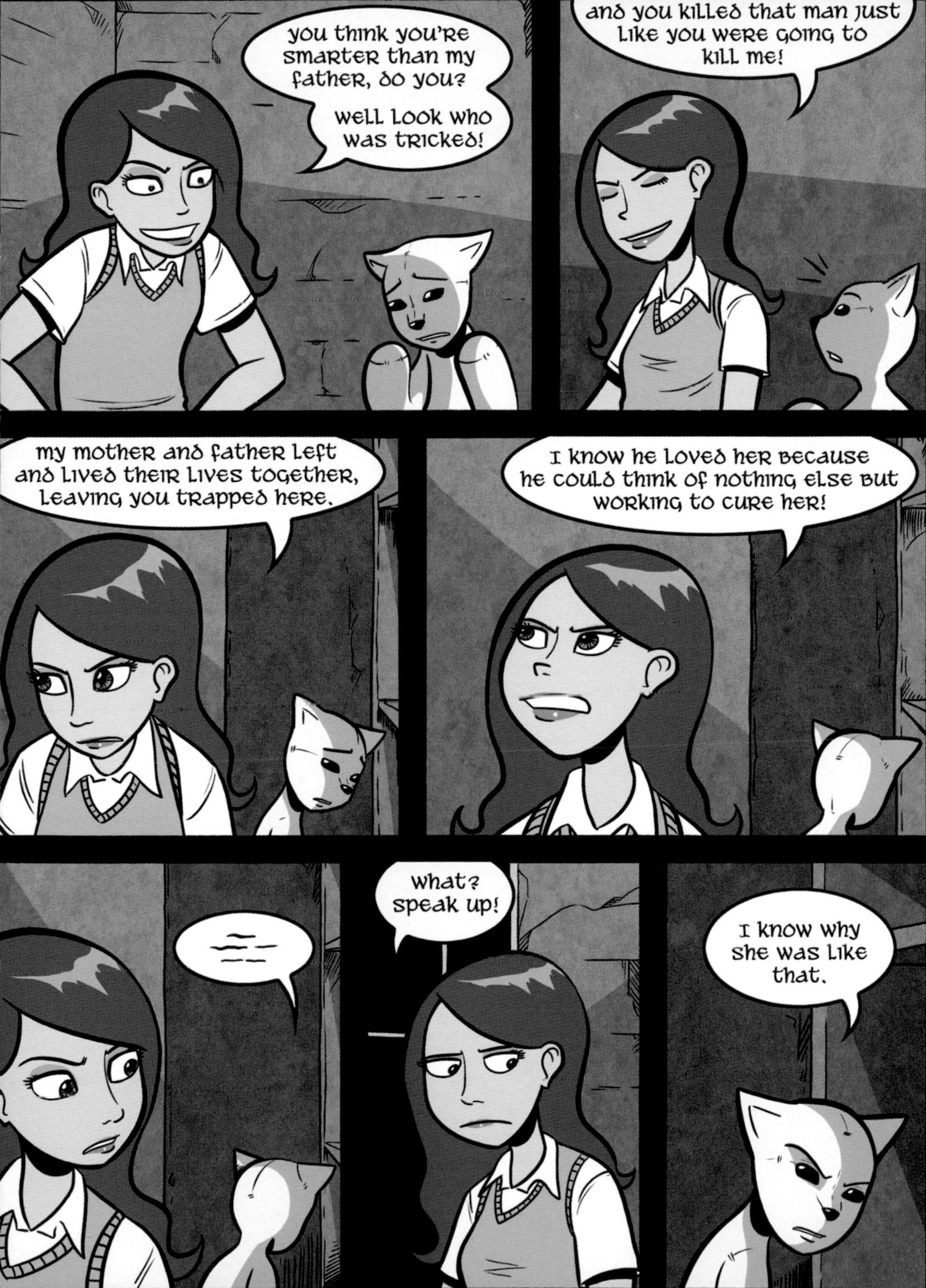

you think you're smarter than my father, do you?
well look who was tricked!
and you killed that man just like you were going to kill me!
my mother and father left and lived their lives together, leaving you trapped here.
I know he loved her because he could think of nothing else but working to cure her!
what? speak up!
I know why she was like that.

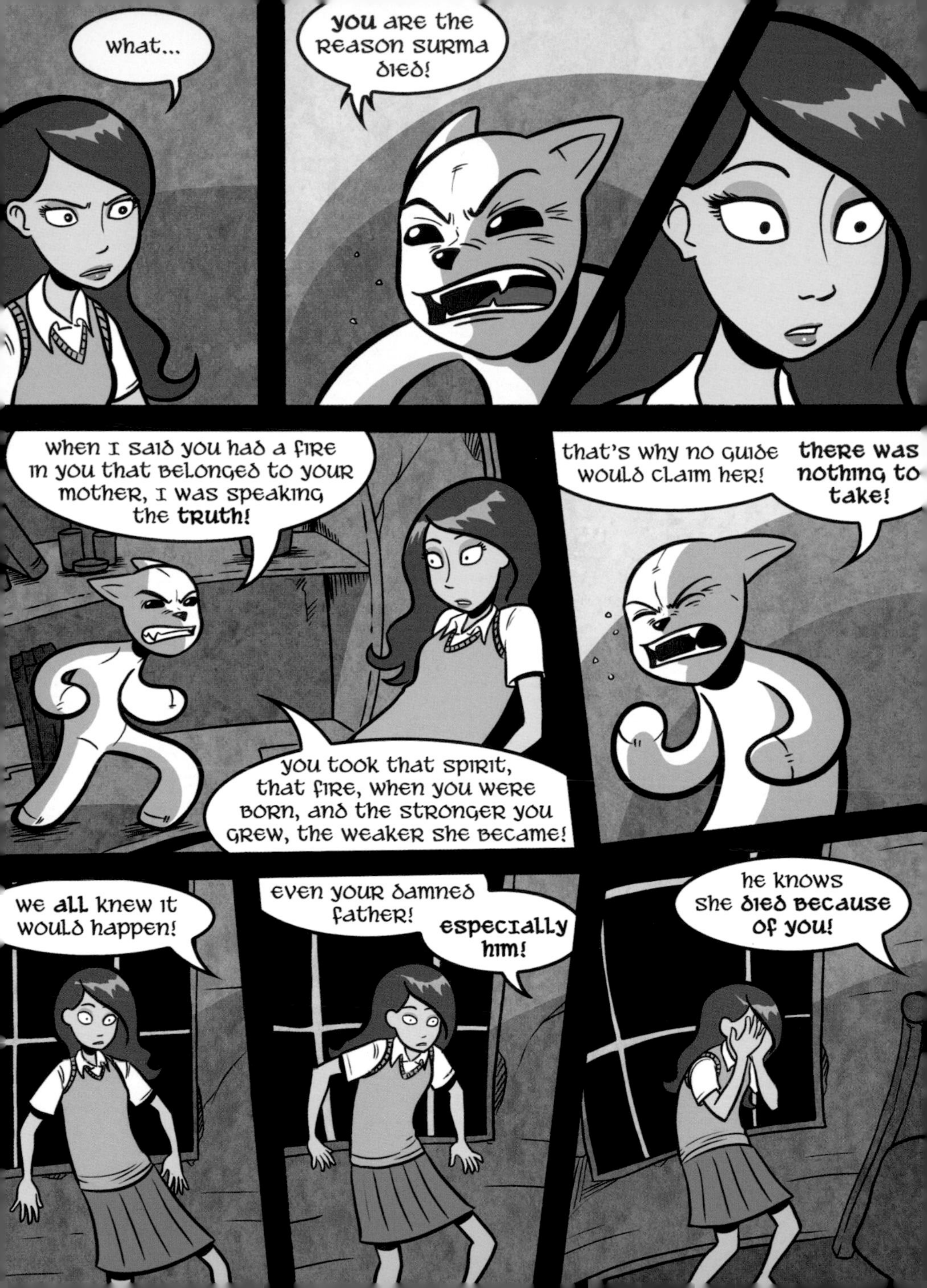
what...
you are the reason surma died!
when I said you had a fire in you that belonged to your mother, I was speaking the truth!
you took that spirit, that fire, when you were born, and the stronger you grew, the weaker she became!
that's why no guide would claim her!
there was nothing to take!
we all knew it would happen!
even your damned father!
especially him!
he knows she died because of you!

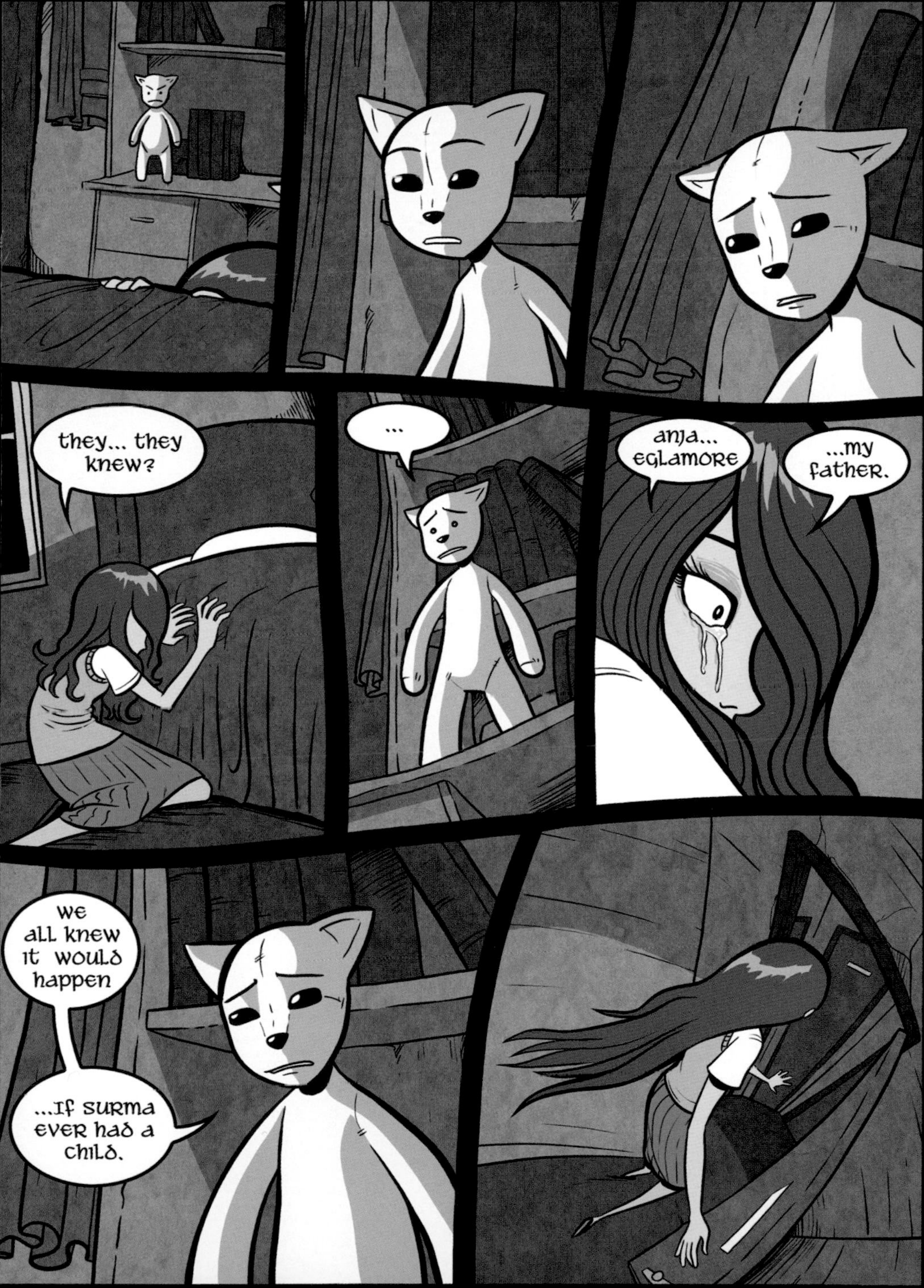
they... they knew?
...
anja... eglamore
...my father.
we all knew it would happen
...if surma ever had a child.

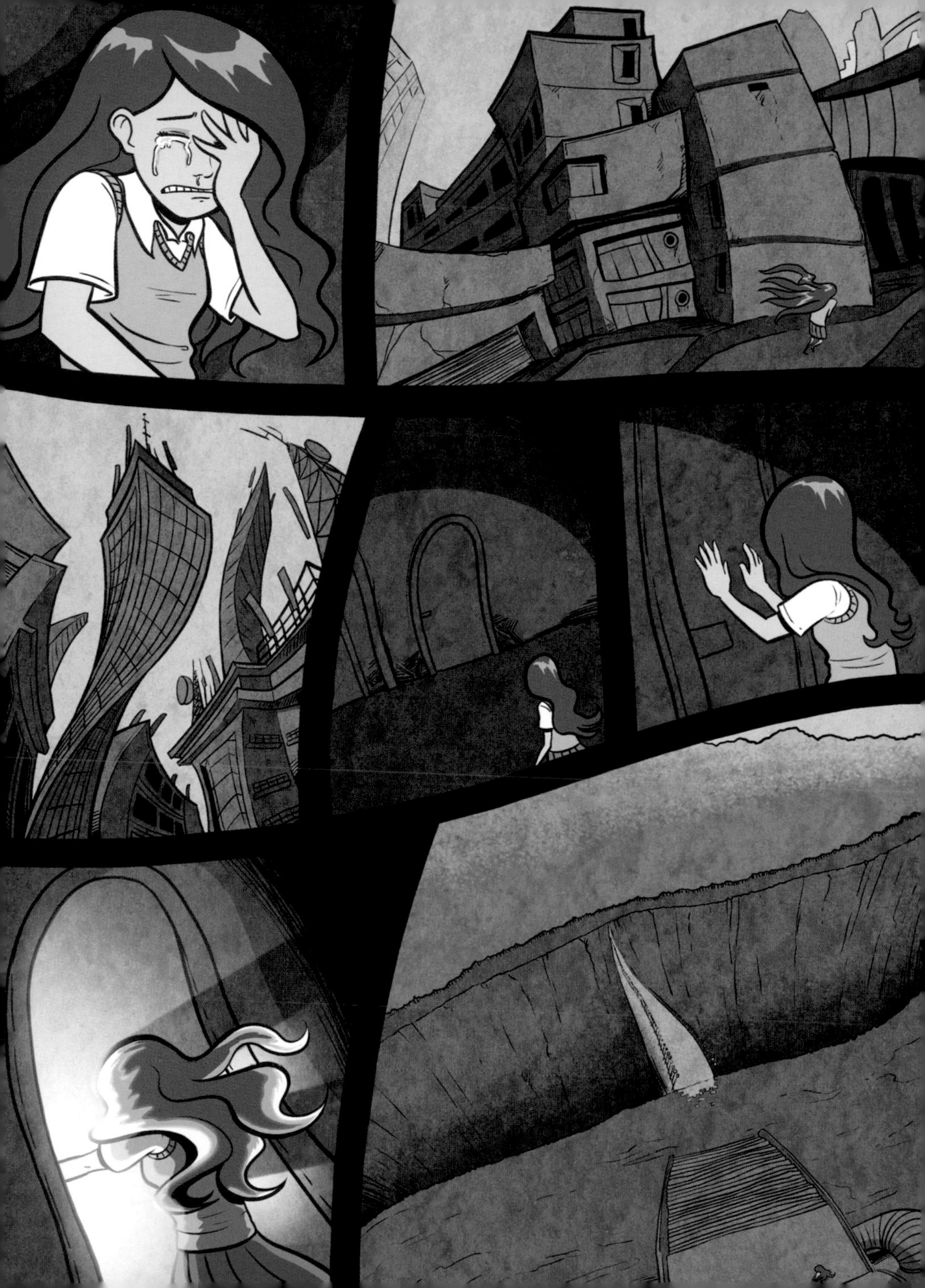

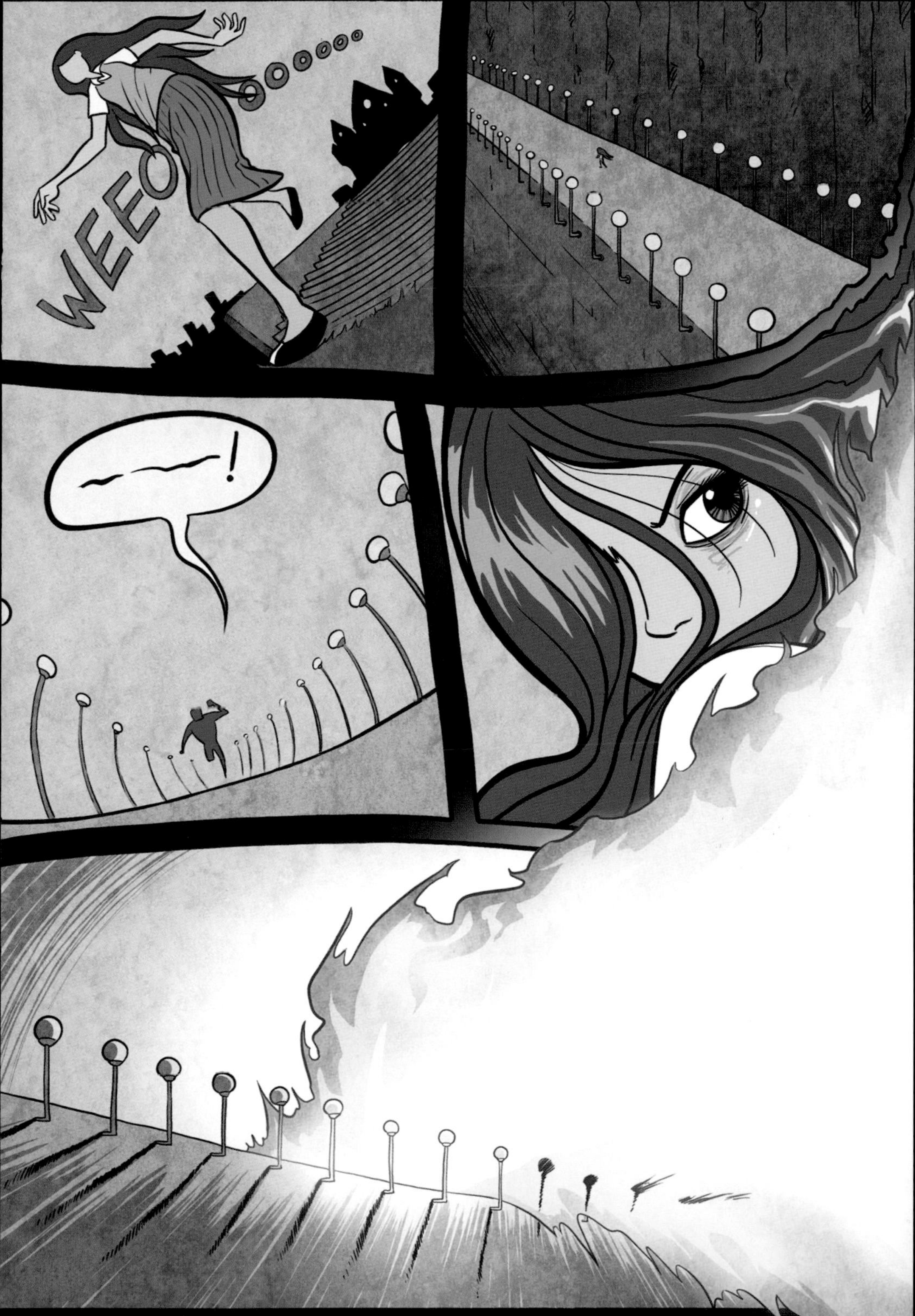
WEEOOOOOOOOO

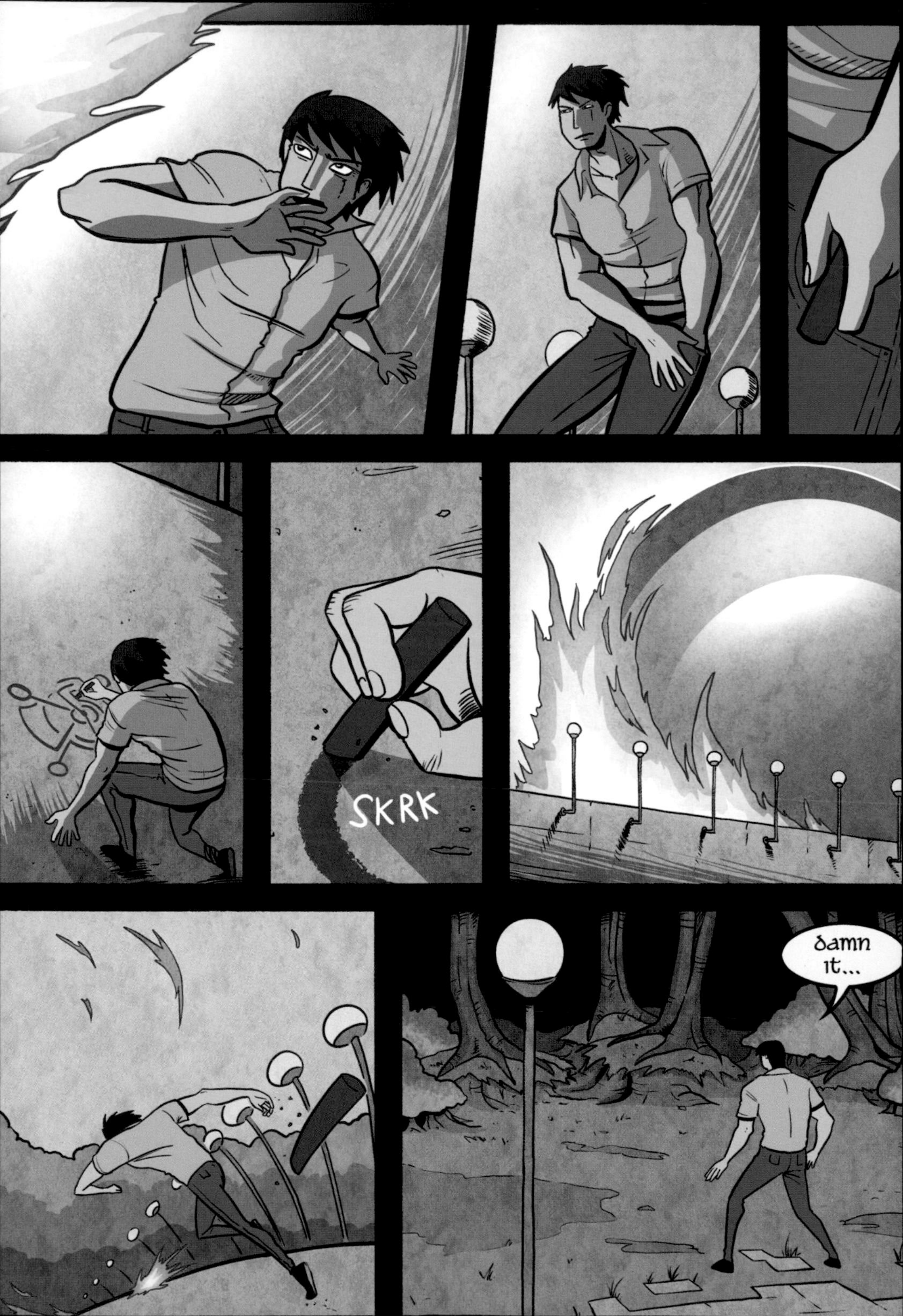
SKRK
damn it...

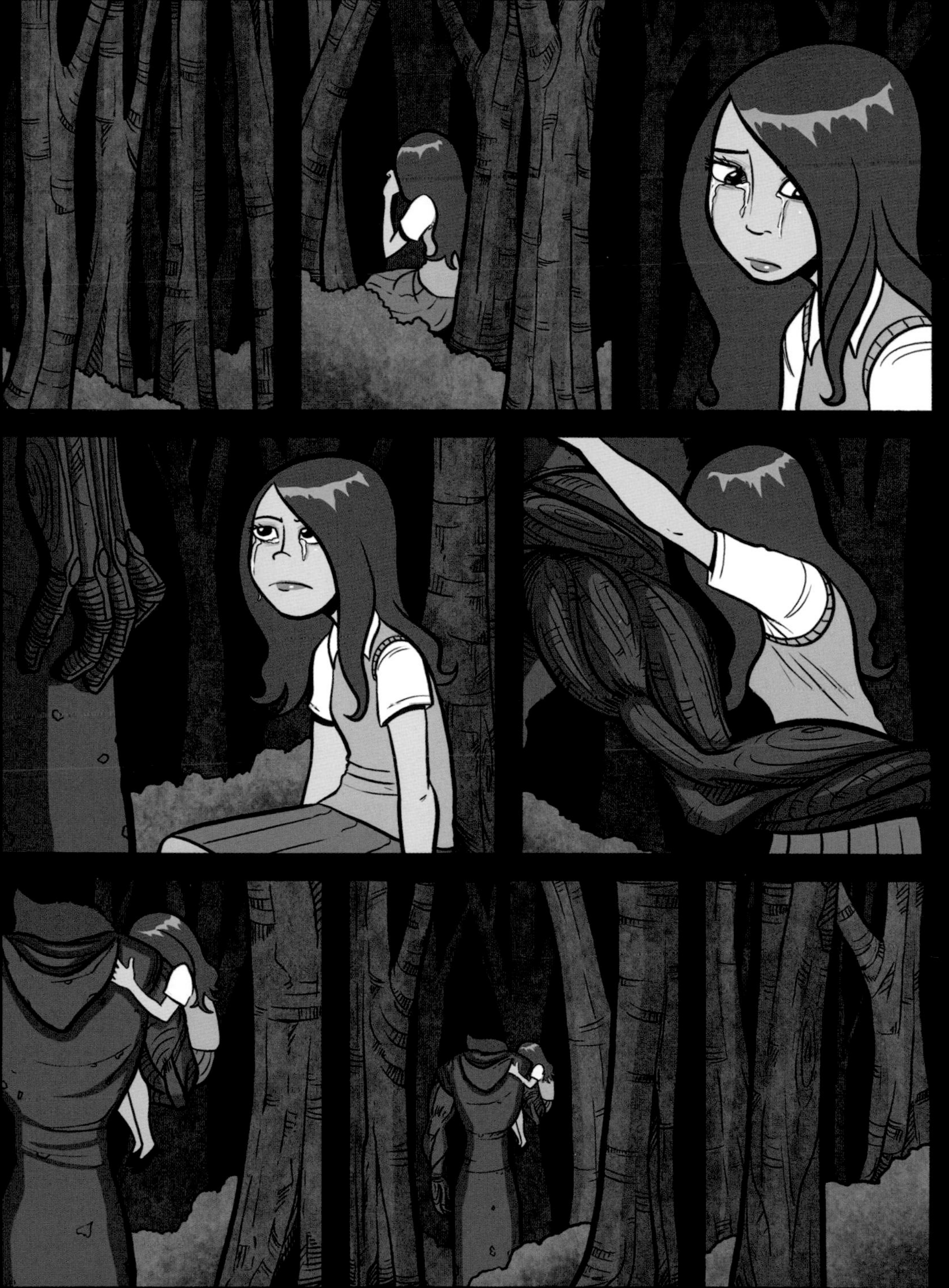

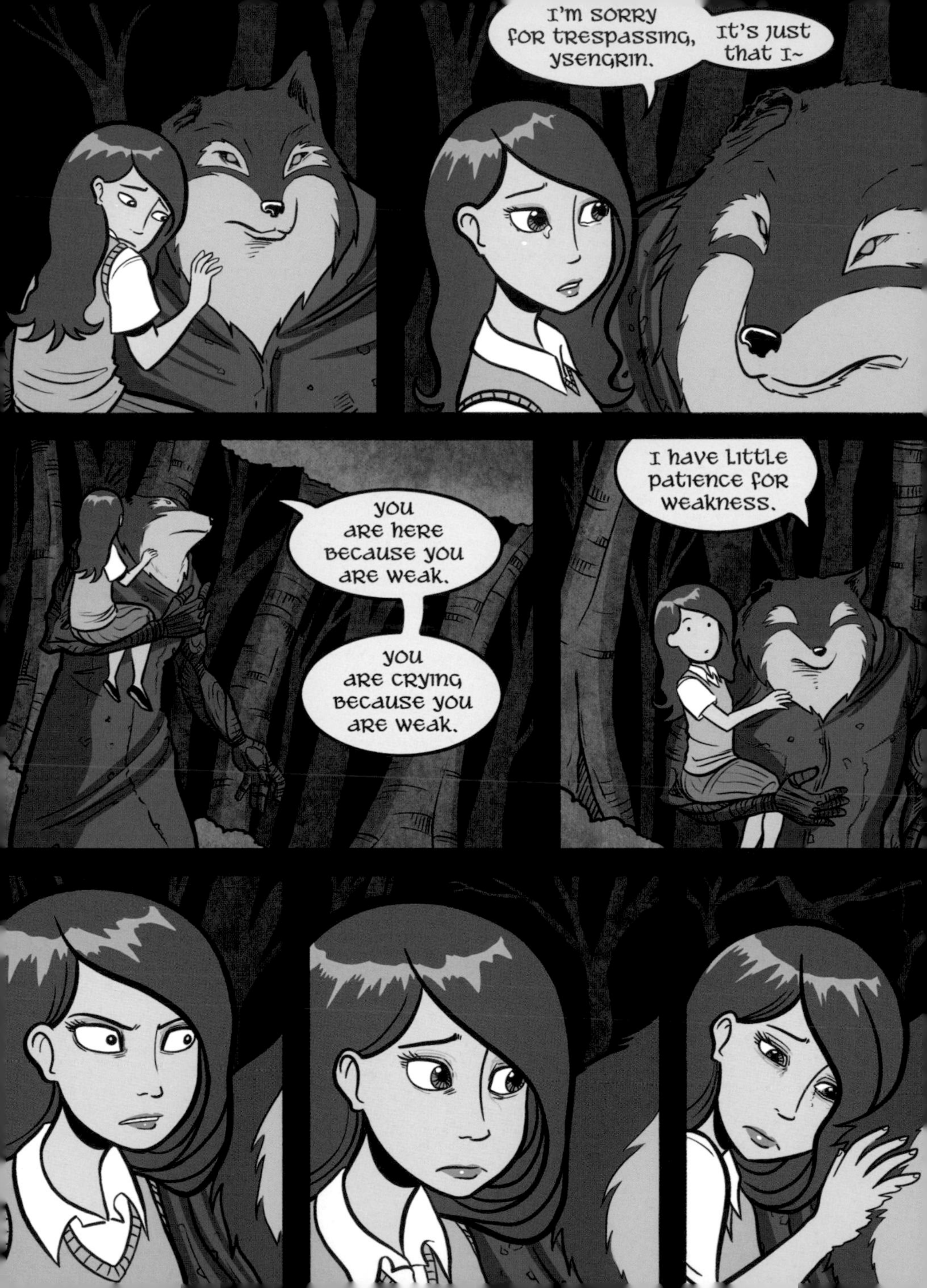
I'M SORRY FOR TRESPASSING, YSENGRIN.
IT'S JUST THAT I~
YOU ARE HERE BECAUSE YOU ARE WEAK.
YOU ARE CRYING BECAUSE YOU ARE WEAK.
I HAVE LITTLE PATIENCE FOR WEAKNESS.

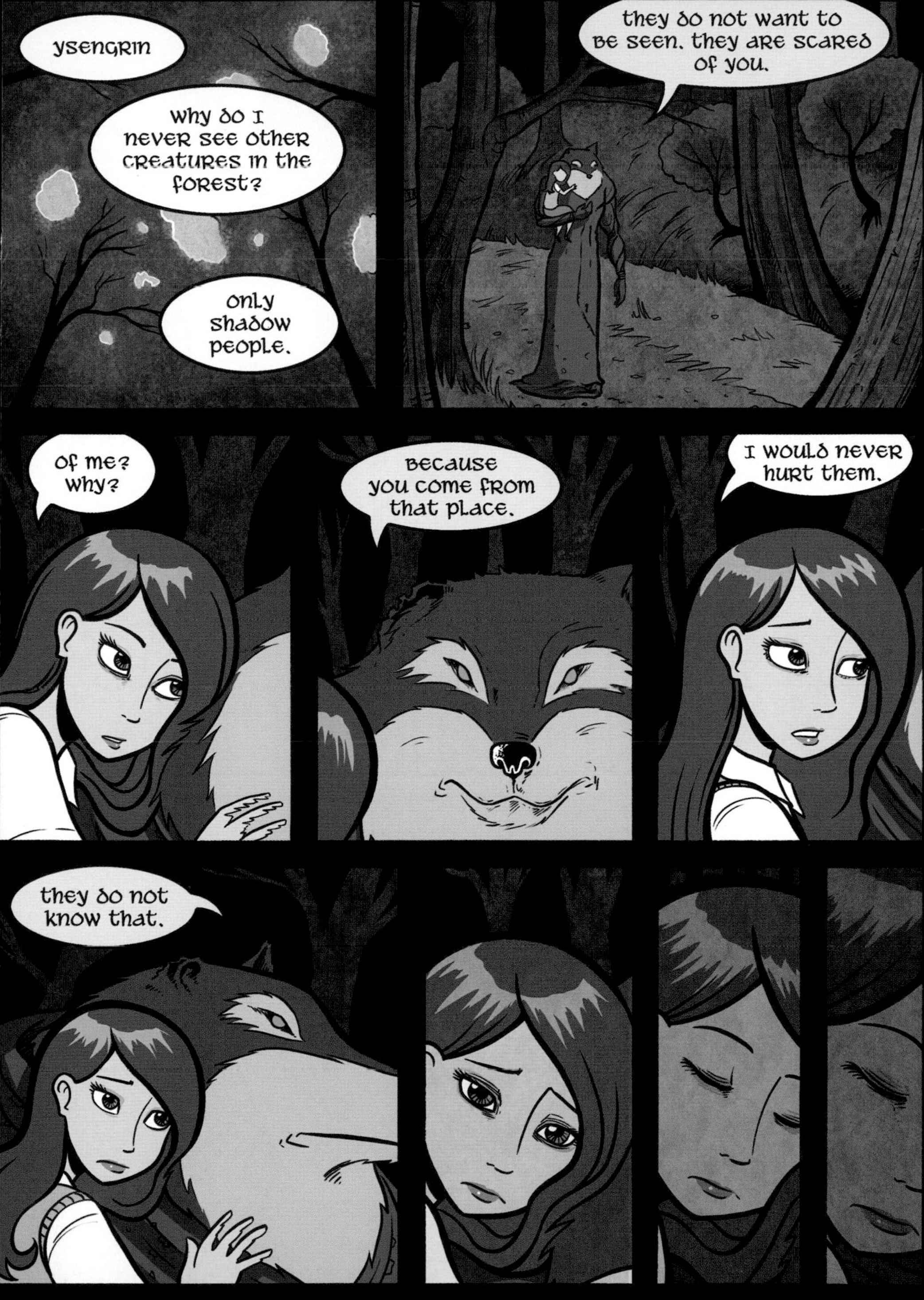
ysengrin
why do I never see other creatures in the forest?
only shadow people.
they do not want to be seen. they are scared of you.
of me? why?
because you come from that place.
I would never hurt them.
they do not know that.

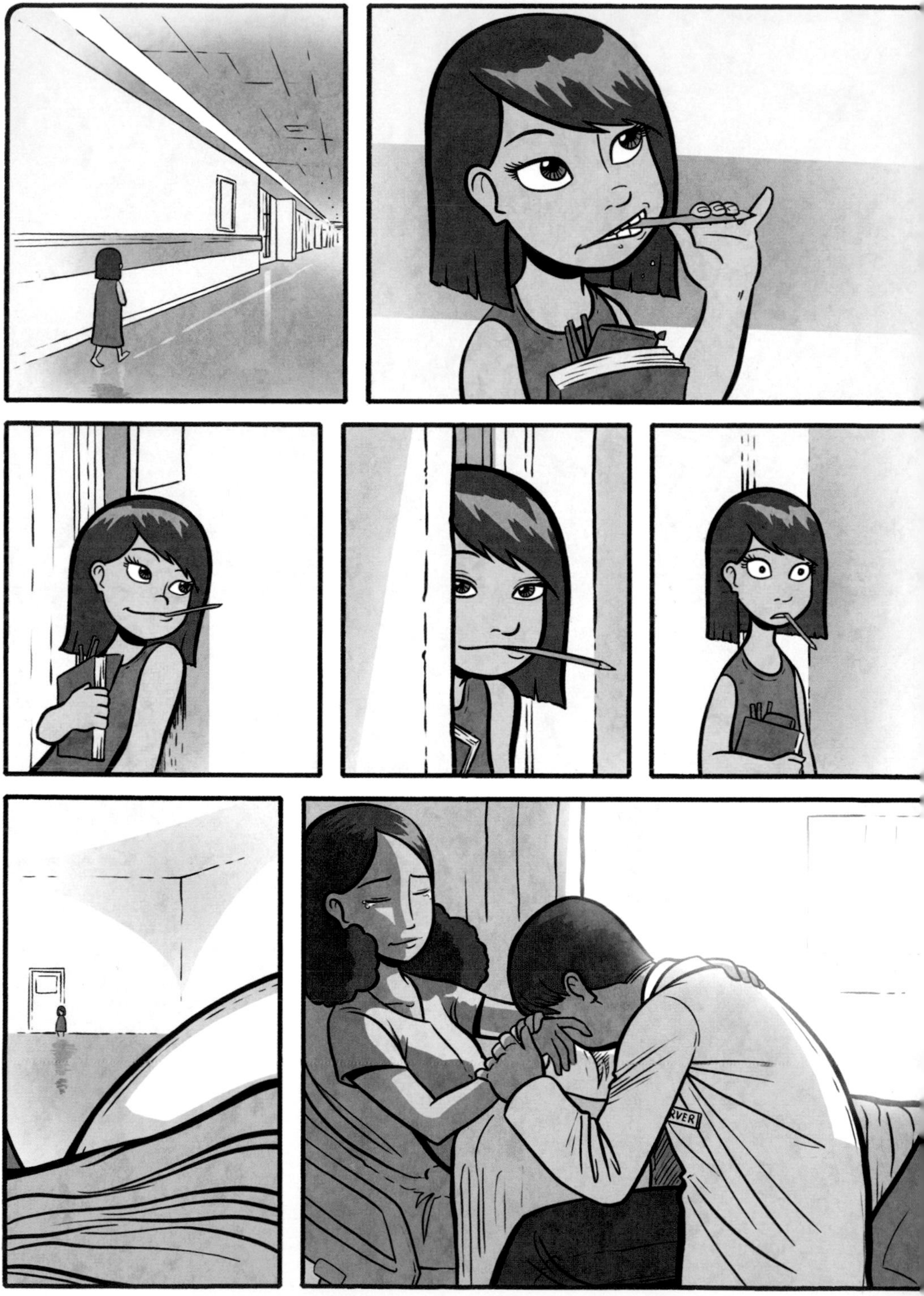

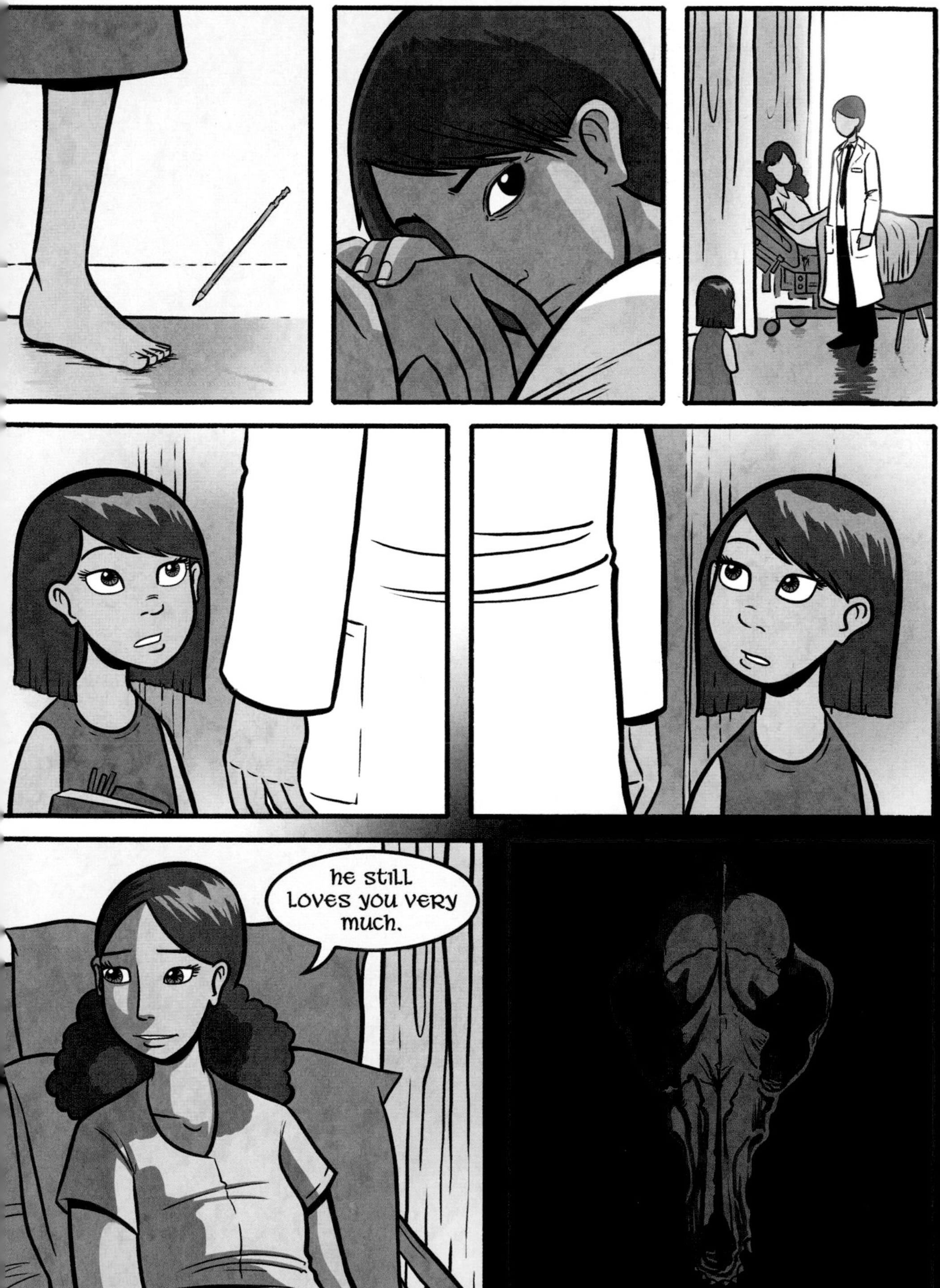
he still loves you very much.

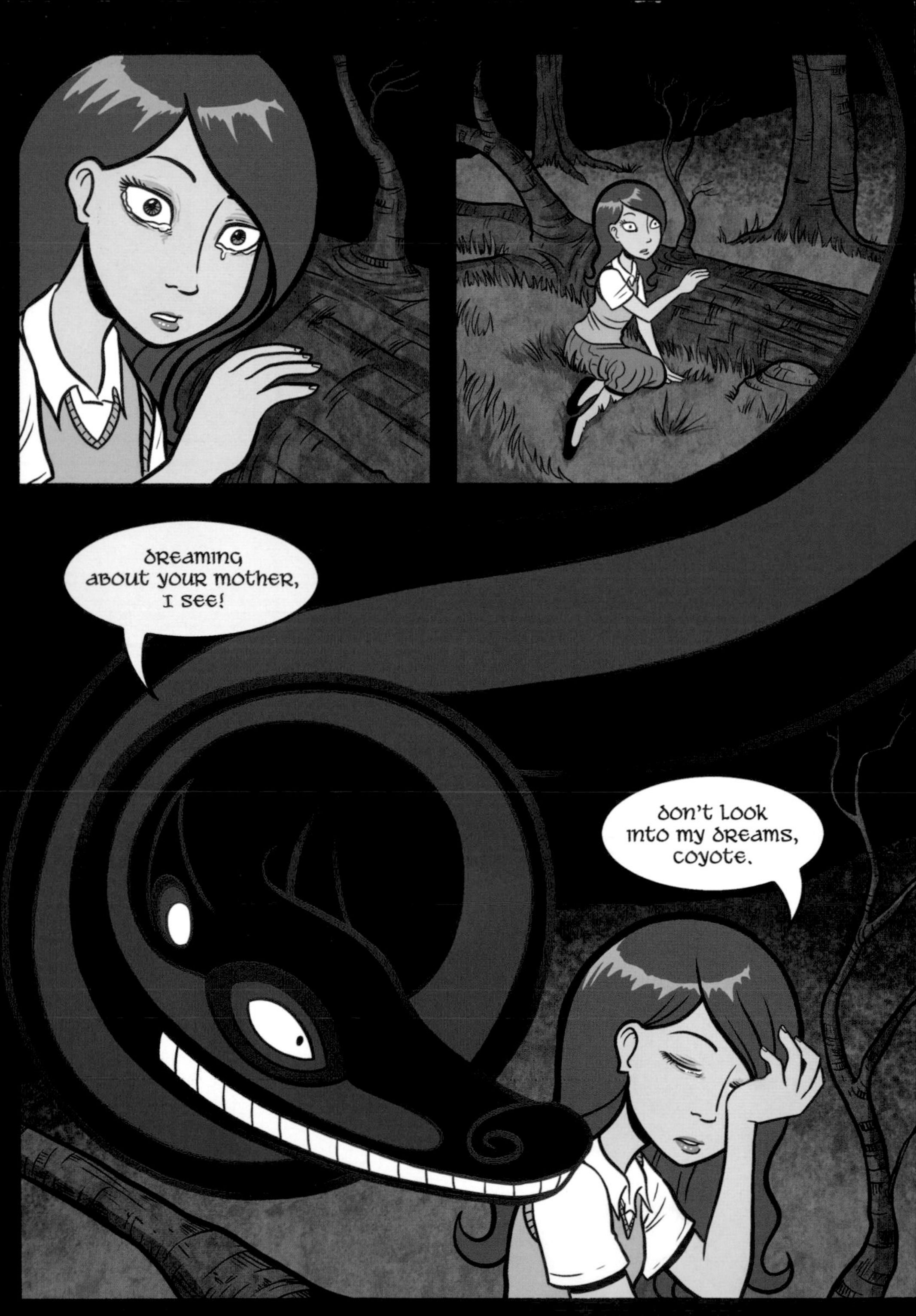
Dreaming about your mother, I see!
Don't look into my dreams, coyote.

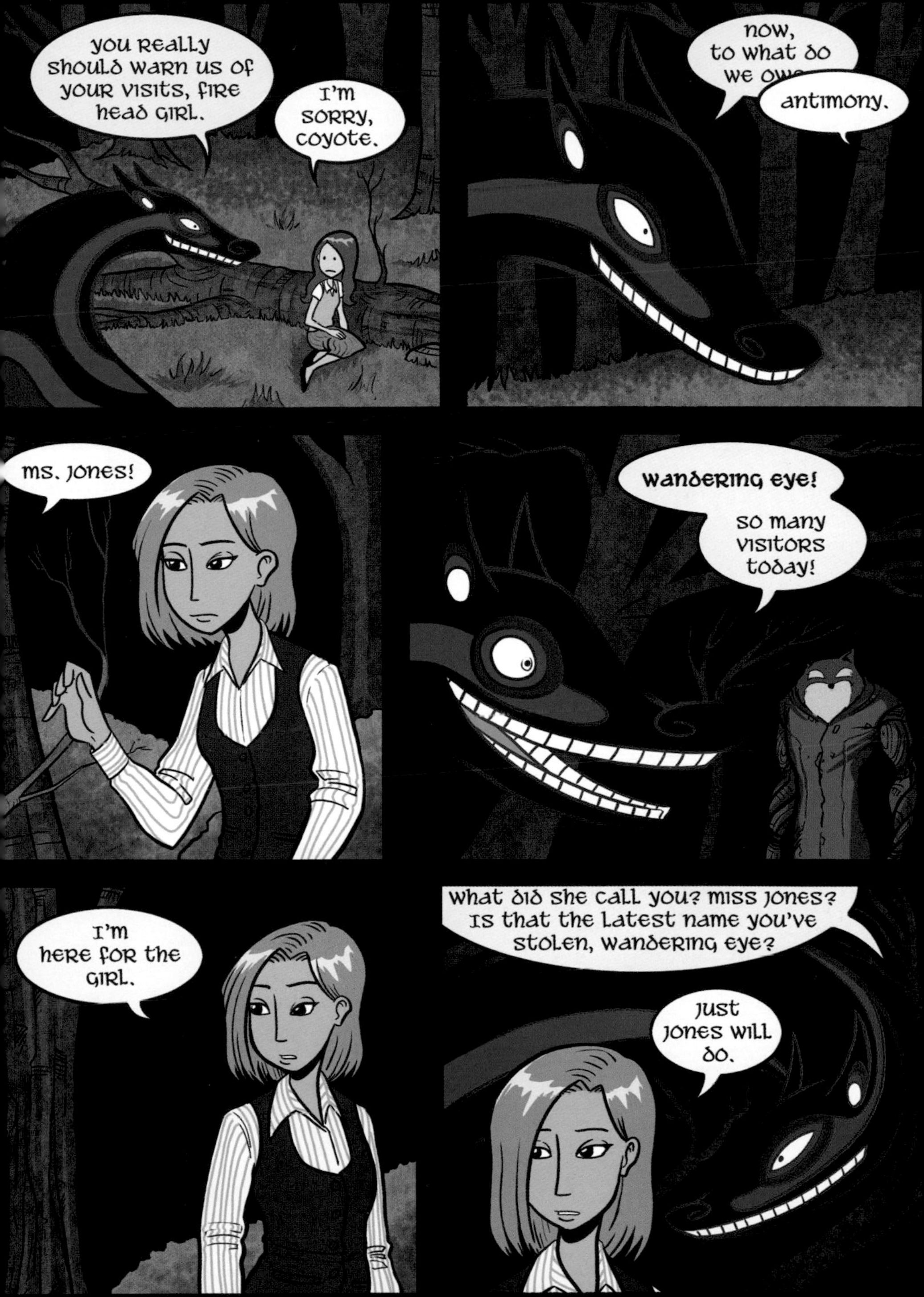

you really should warn us of your visits, fire head girl.
I'm sorry, coyote.
now, to what do we owe
antimony.
ms. jones!
wandering eye!
so many visitors today!
I'm here for the girl.
what did she call you? miss jones? is that the latest name you've stolen, wandering eye?
just jones will do.

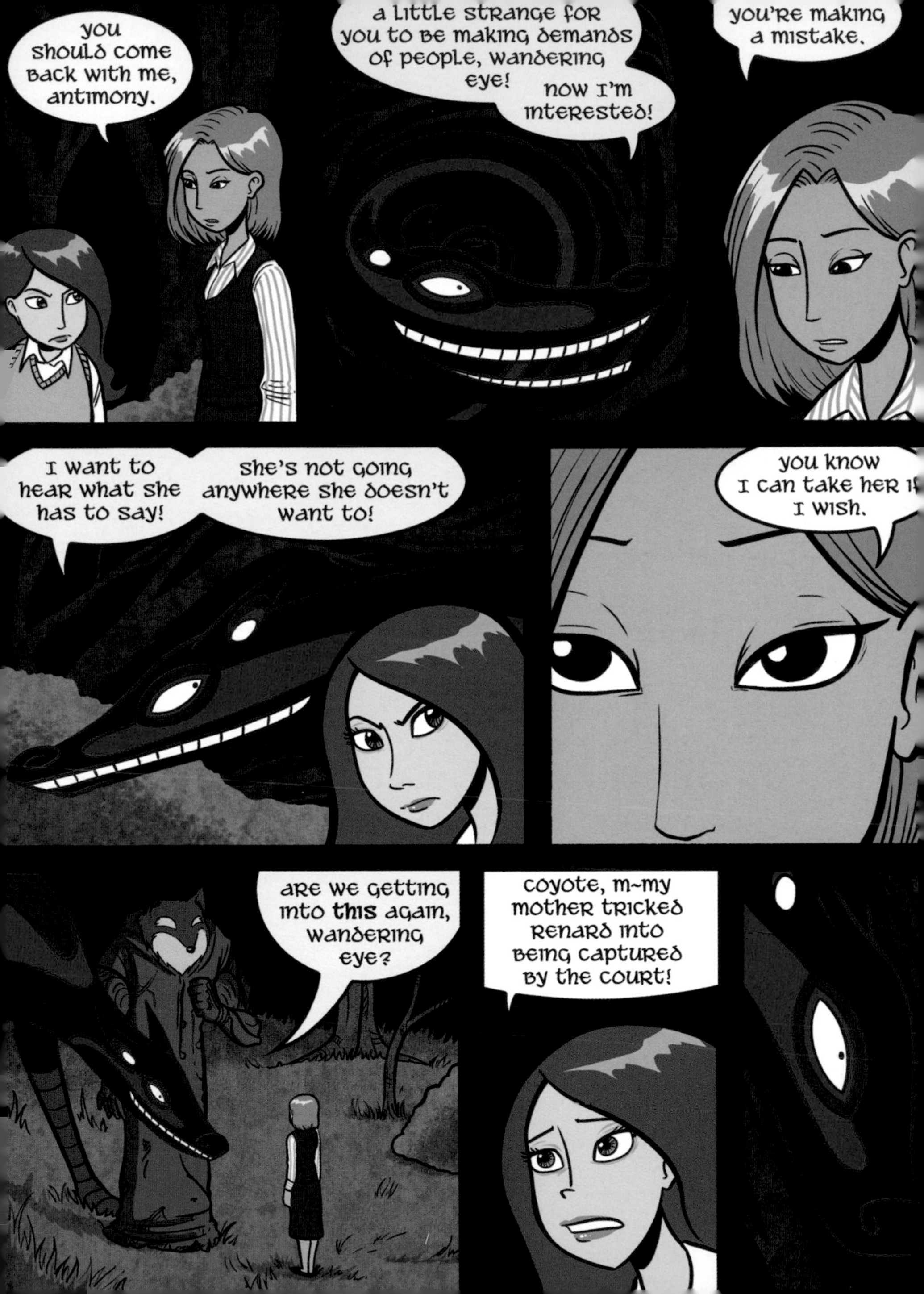
you should come back with me, antimony.
a little strange for you to be making demands of people, wandering eye!
now I'm interested!
you're making a mistake.
I want to hear what she has to say!
she's not going anywhere she doesn't want to!
you know I can take her if I wish.
are we getting into this again, wandering eye?
coyote, m-my mother tricked renard into being captured by the court!

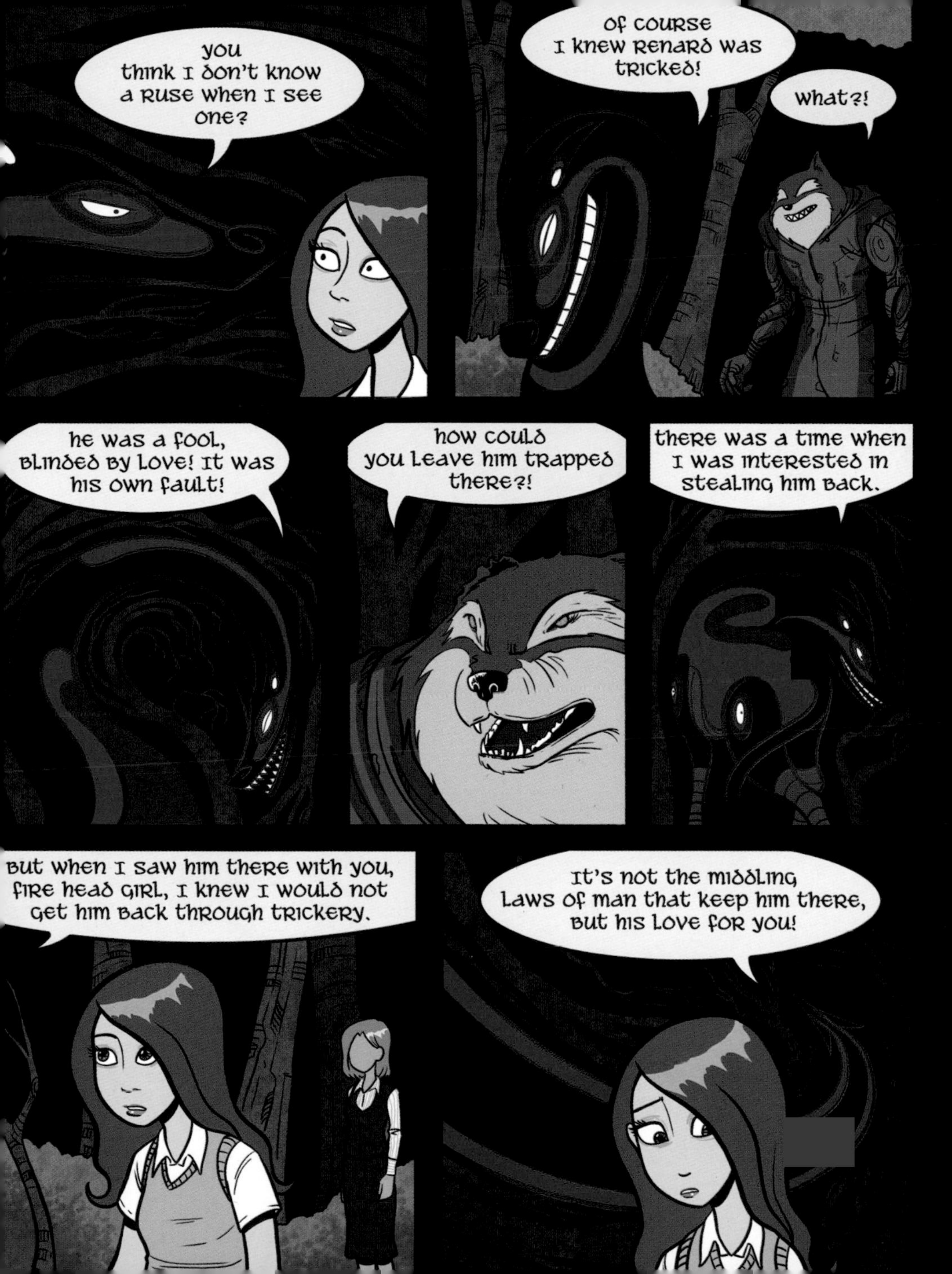
you think I don't know a ruse when I see one?
Of course I knew Renard was tricked!
What?!
he was a fool, blinded by love! It was his own fault!
how could you leave him trapped there?!
there was a time when I was interested in stealing him back.
but when I saw him there with you, fire head girl, I knew I would not get him back through trickery.
It's not the middling laws of man that keep him there, but his love for you!

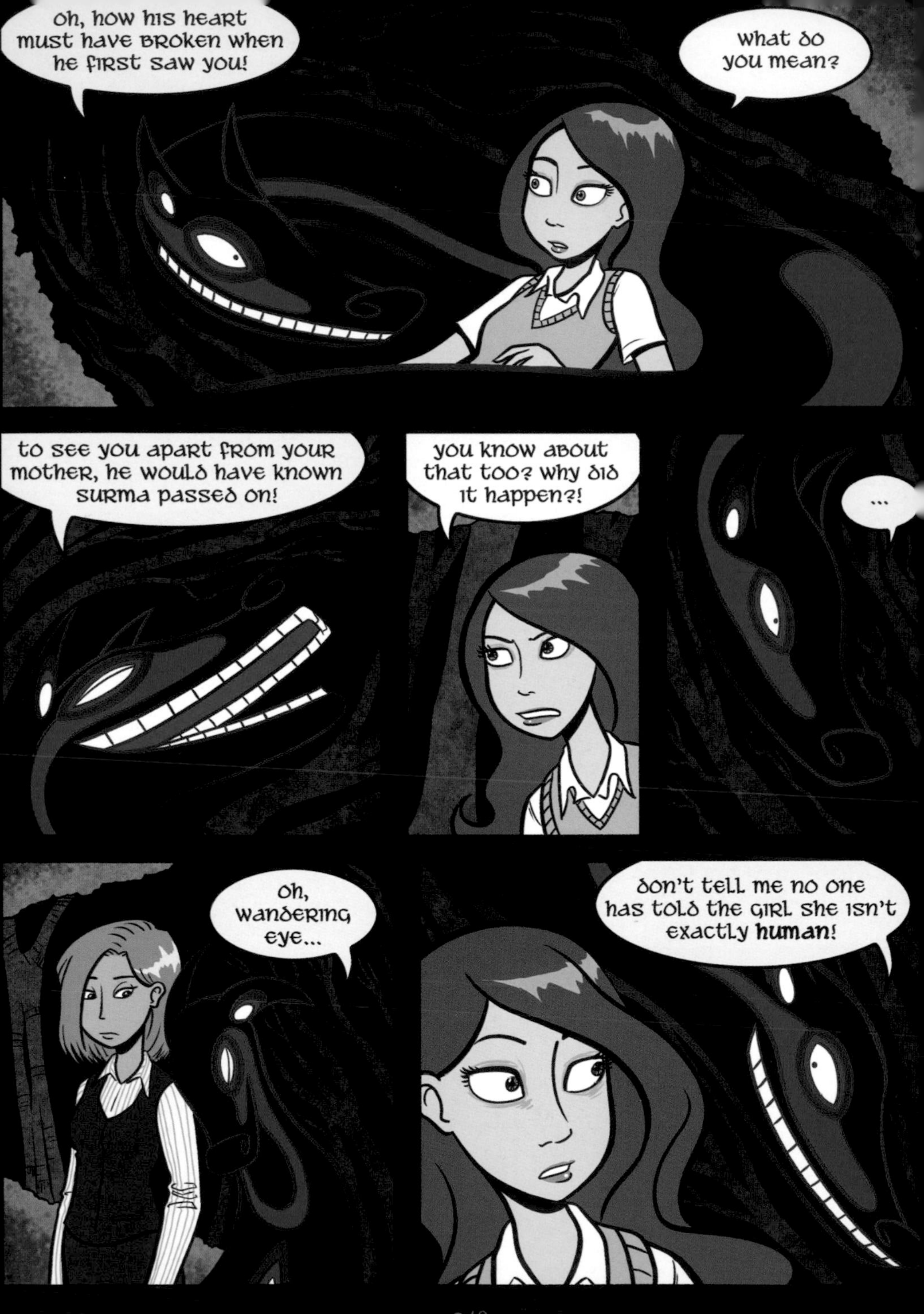
oh, how his heart must have broken when he first saw you!
what do you mean?
to see you apart from your mother, he would have known surma passed on!
you know about that too? why did it happen?!
...
oh, wandering eye...
don't tell me no one has told the girl she isn't exactly **human**!

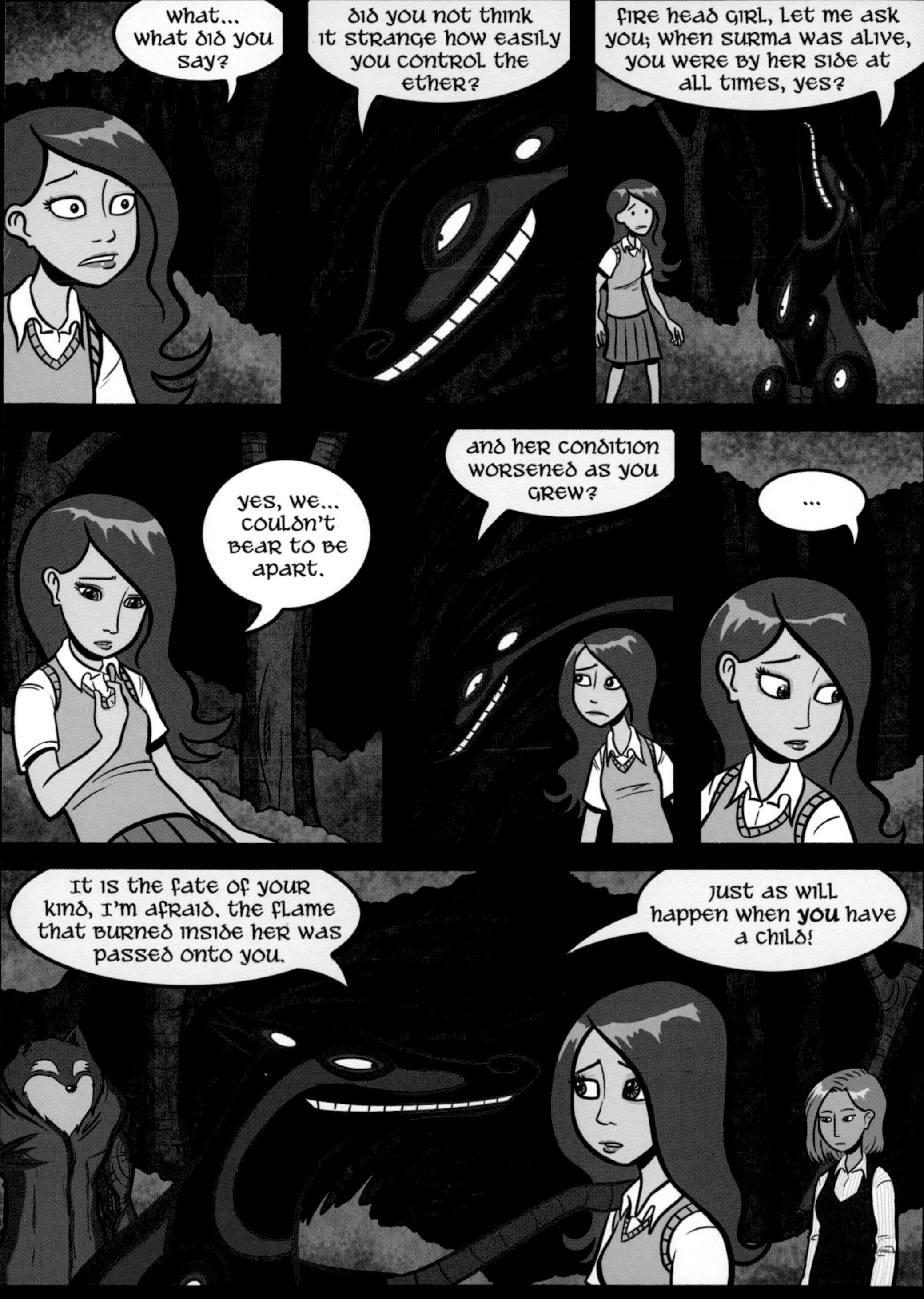
What... what did you say?
Did you not think it strange how easily you control the ether?
Fire head girl, let me ask you; when Surma was alive, you were by her side at all times, yes?
Yes, we... couldn't bear to be apart.
And her condition worsened as you grew?
...
It is the fate of your kind, I'm afraid. The flame that burned inside her was passed onto you.
Just as will happen when **you** have a child!

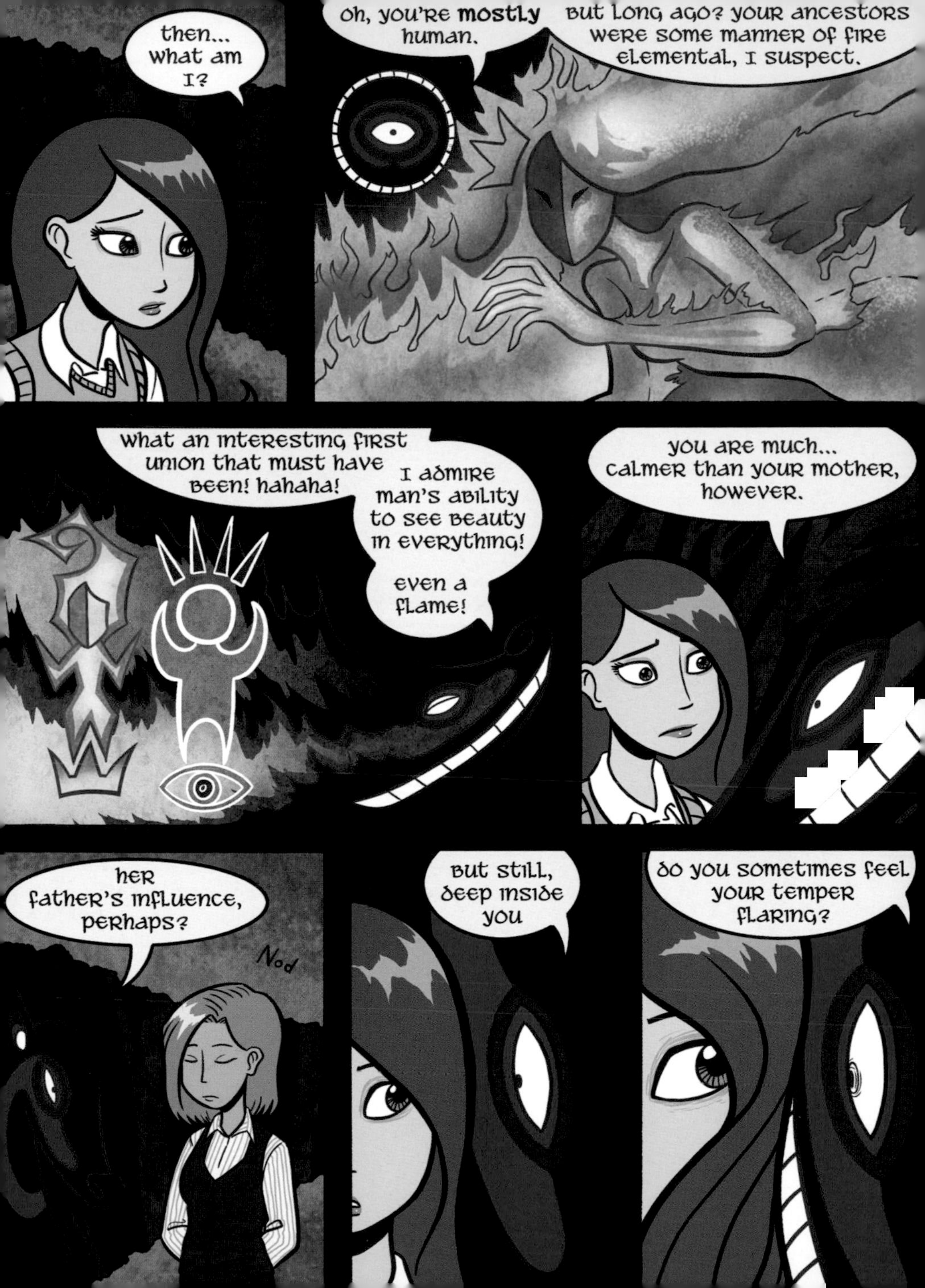
then... what am I?
Oh, you're **mostly** human.
But long ago? Your ancestors were some manner of fire elemental, I suspect.
What an interesting first union that must have been! Hahaha!
I admire man's ability to see beauty in everything!
Even a flame!
You are much... calmer than your mother, however.
Her father's influence, perhaps?
Nod
But still, deep inside you
Do you sometimes feel your temper flaring?

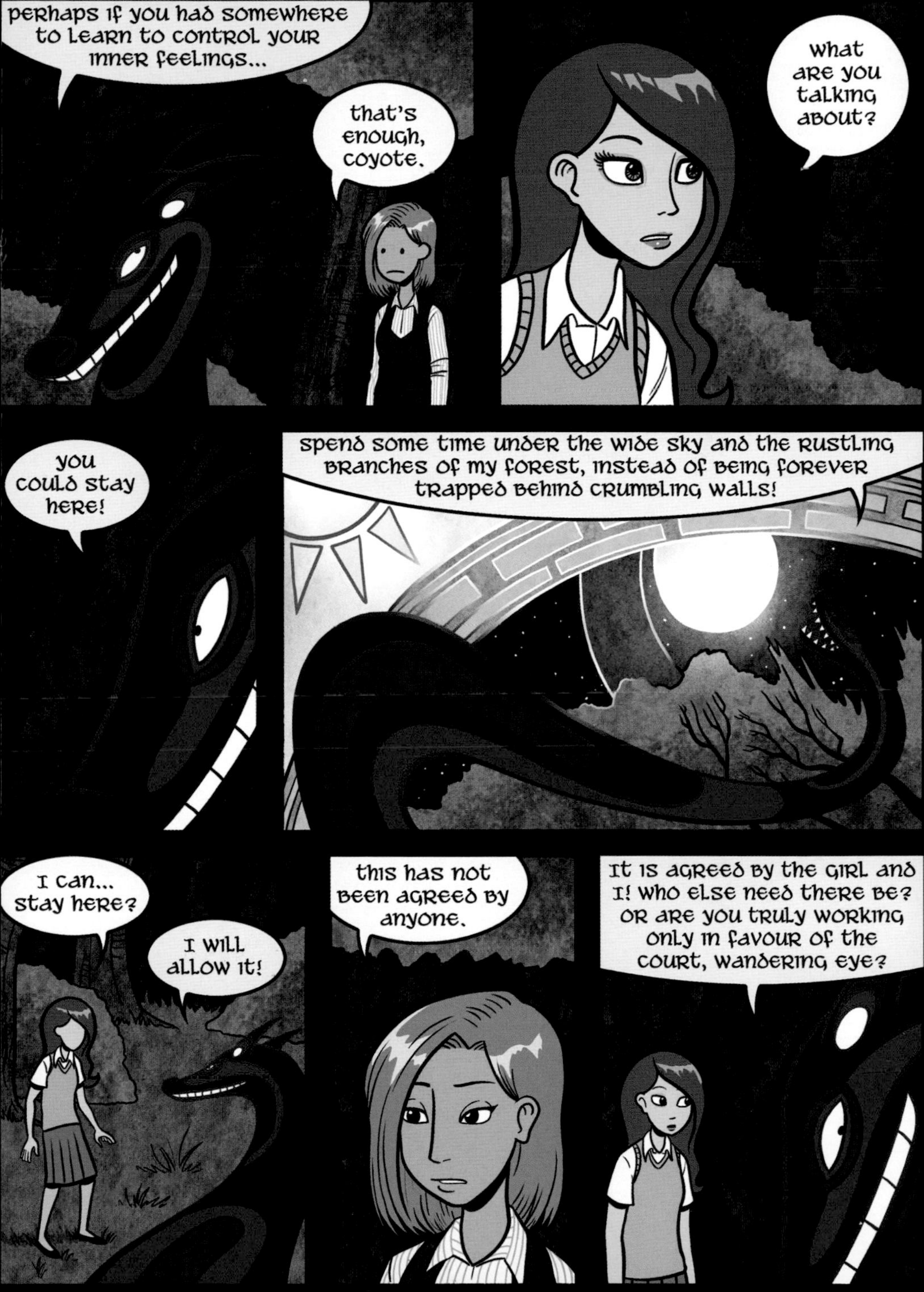
perhaps if you had somewhere to learn to control your inner feelings...
that's enough, coyote.
what are you talking about?
you could stay here!
spend some time under the wide sky and the rustling branches of my forest, instead of being forever trapped behind crumbling walls!
I can... stay here?
I will allow it!
this has not been agreed by anyone.
It is agreed by the girl and I! who else need there be? or are you truly working only in favour of the court, wandering eye?

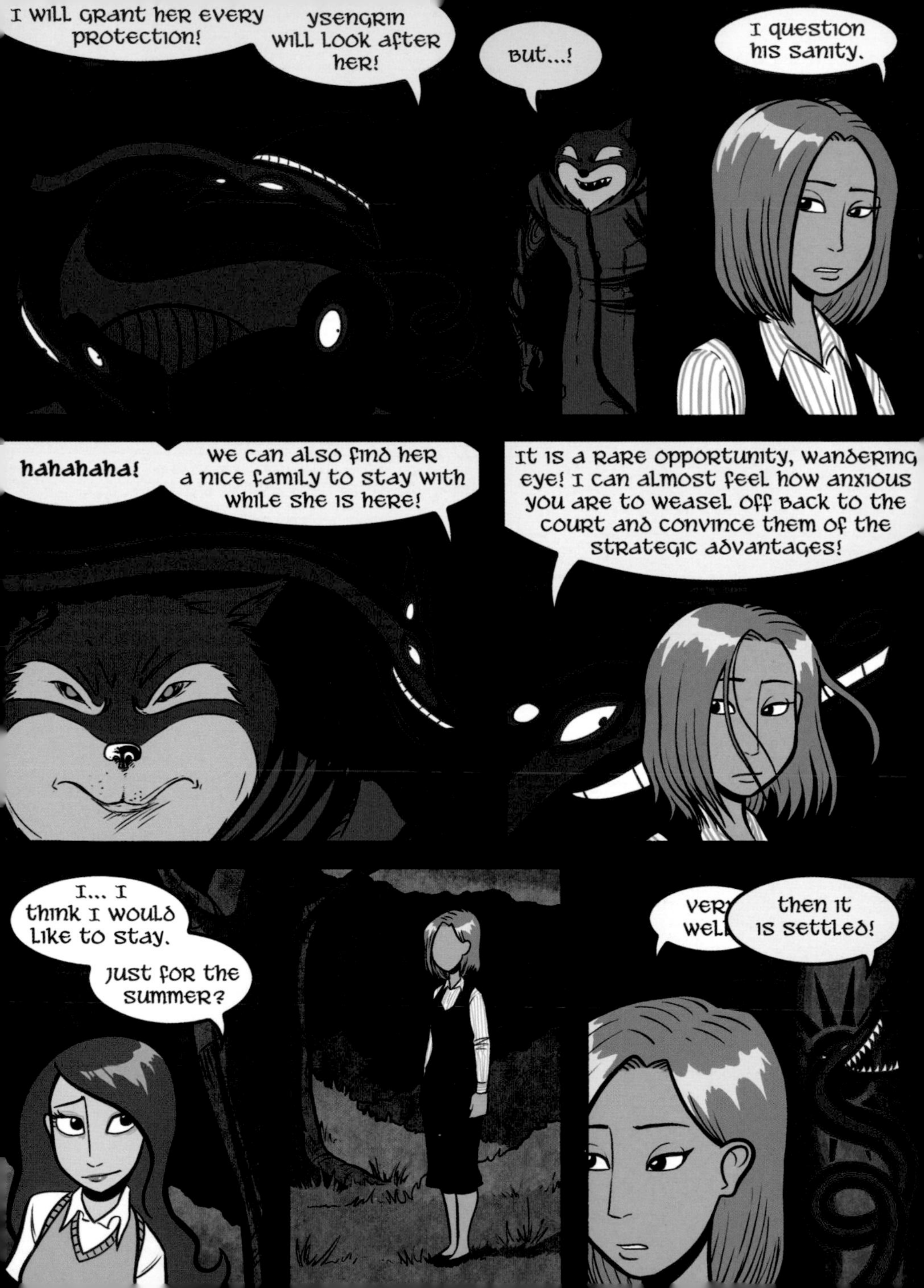
I WILL GRANT HER EVERY PROTECTION!
YSENGRIN WILL LOOK AFTER HER!
BUT...!
I QUESTION HIS SANITY.
HAHAHAHA!
WE CAN ALSO FIND HER A NICE FAMILY TO STAY WITH WHILE SHE IS HERE!
IT IS A RARE OPPORTUNITY, WANDERING EYE! I CAN ALMOST FEEL HOW ANXIOUS YOU ARE TO WEASEL OFF BACK TO THE COURT AND CONVINCE THEM OF THE STRATEGIC ADVANTAGES!
I... I THINK I WOULD LIKE TO STAY.
JUST FOR THE SUMMER?
THEN IT IS SETTLED!

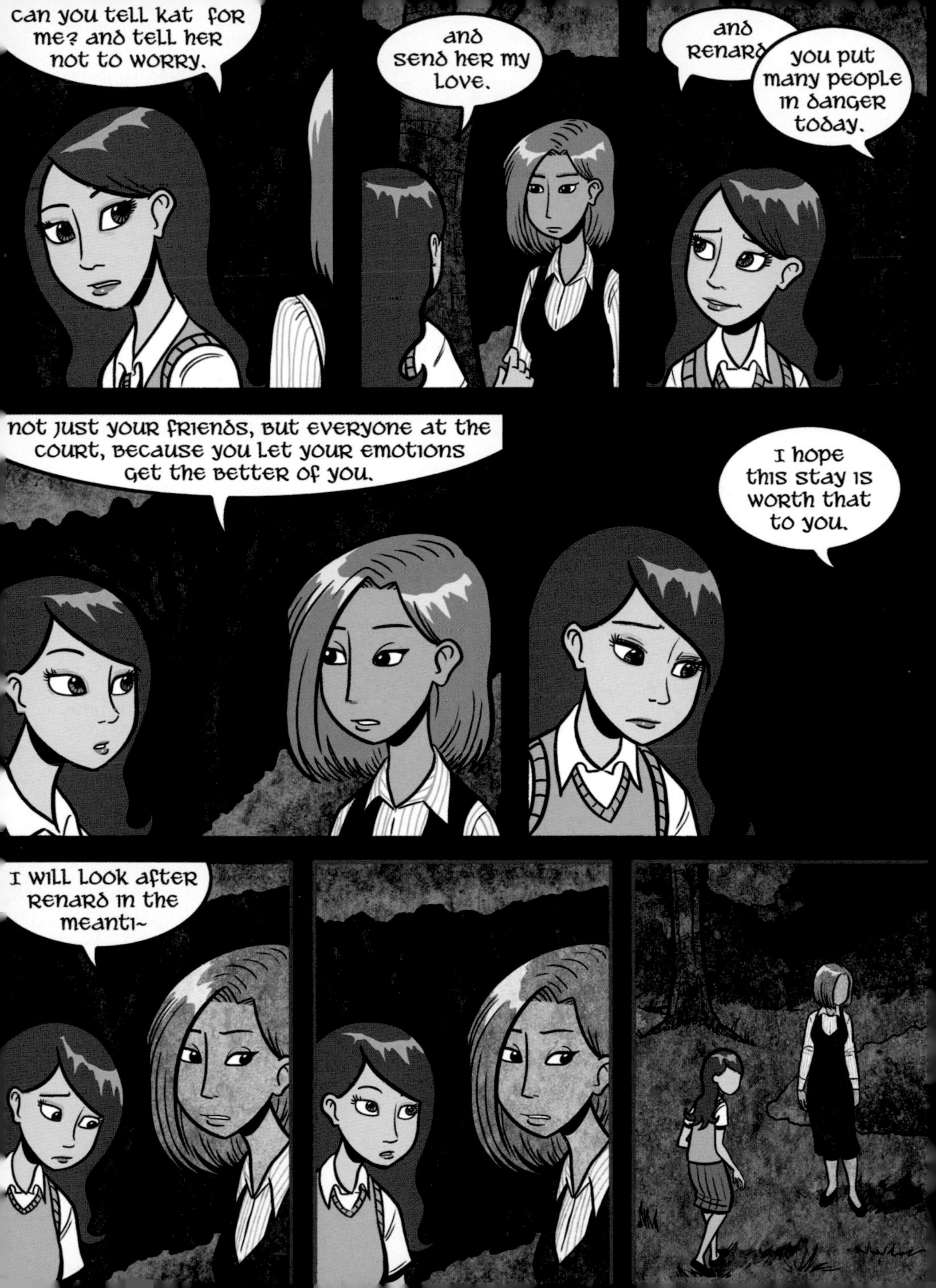
can you tell kat for me? and tell her not to worry.
and send her my love.
and Renard
you put many people in danger today.
not just your friends, but everyone at the court, because you let your emotions get the better of you.
I hope this stay is worth that to you.
I will look after Renard in the meanti~

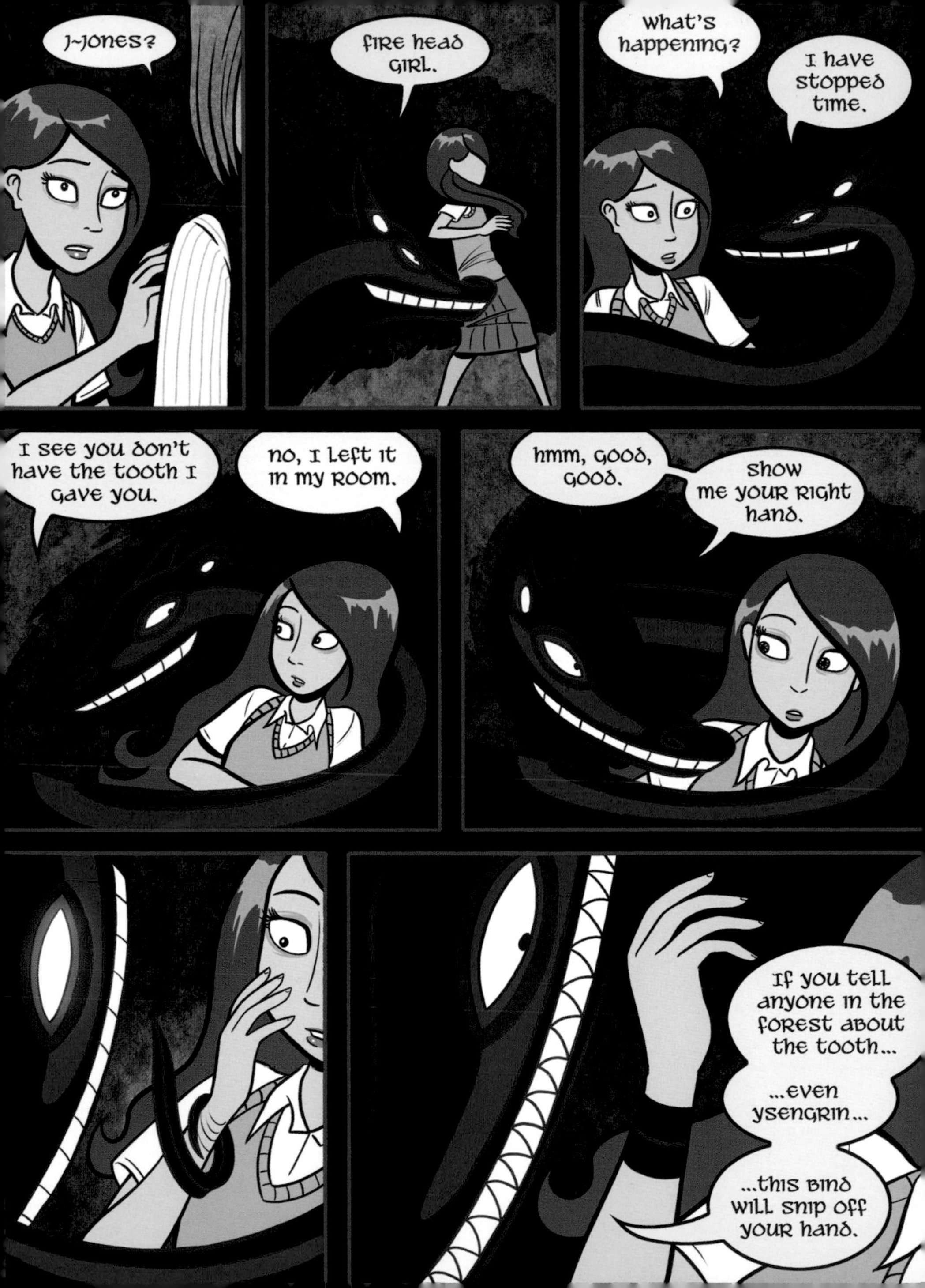
J-JONES?
FIRE HEAD GIRL.
WHAT'S HAPPENING?
I HAVE STOPPED TIME.
I SEE YOU DON'T HAVE THE TOOTH I GAVE YOU.
NO, I LEFT IT IN MY ROOM.
HMM, GOOD, GOOD.
SHOW ME YOUR RIGHT HAND.
IF YOU TELL ANYONE IN THE FOREST ABOUT THE TOOTH...
...EVEN YSENGRIN...
...THIS BIND WILL SNIP OFF YOUR HAND.

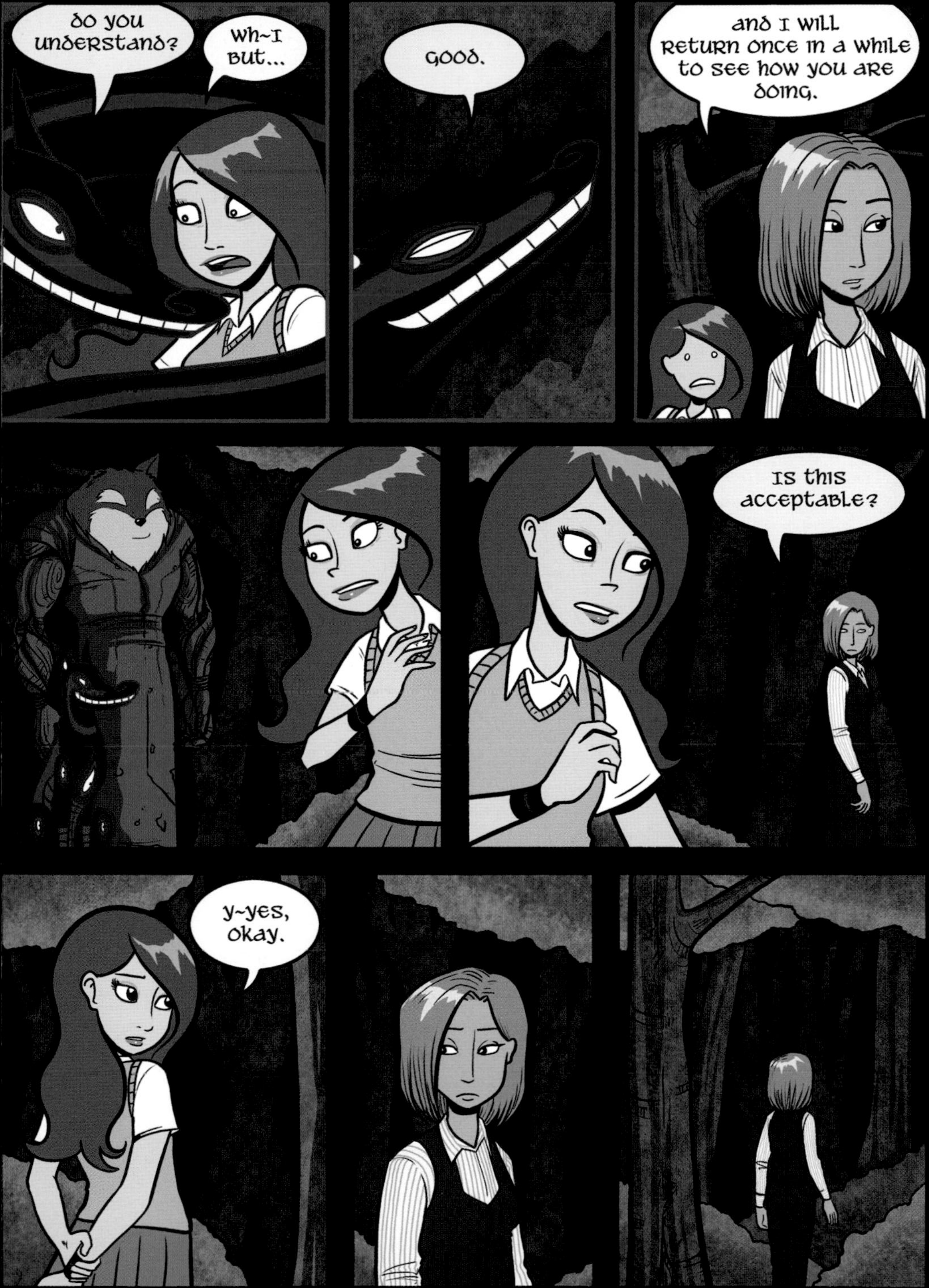
do you understand?
wh~I but...
good.
and I will return once in a while to see how you are doing.
Is this acceptable?
y~yes, okay.

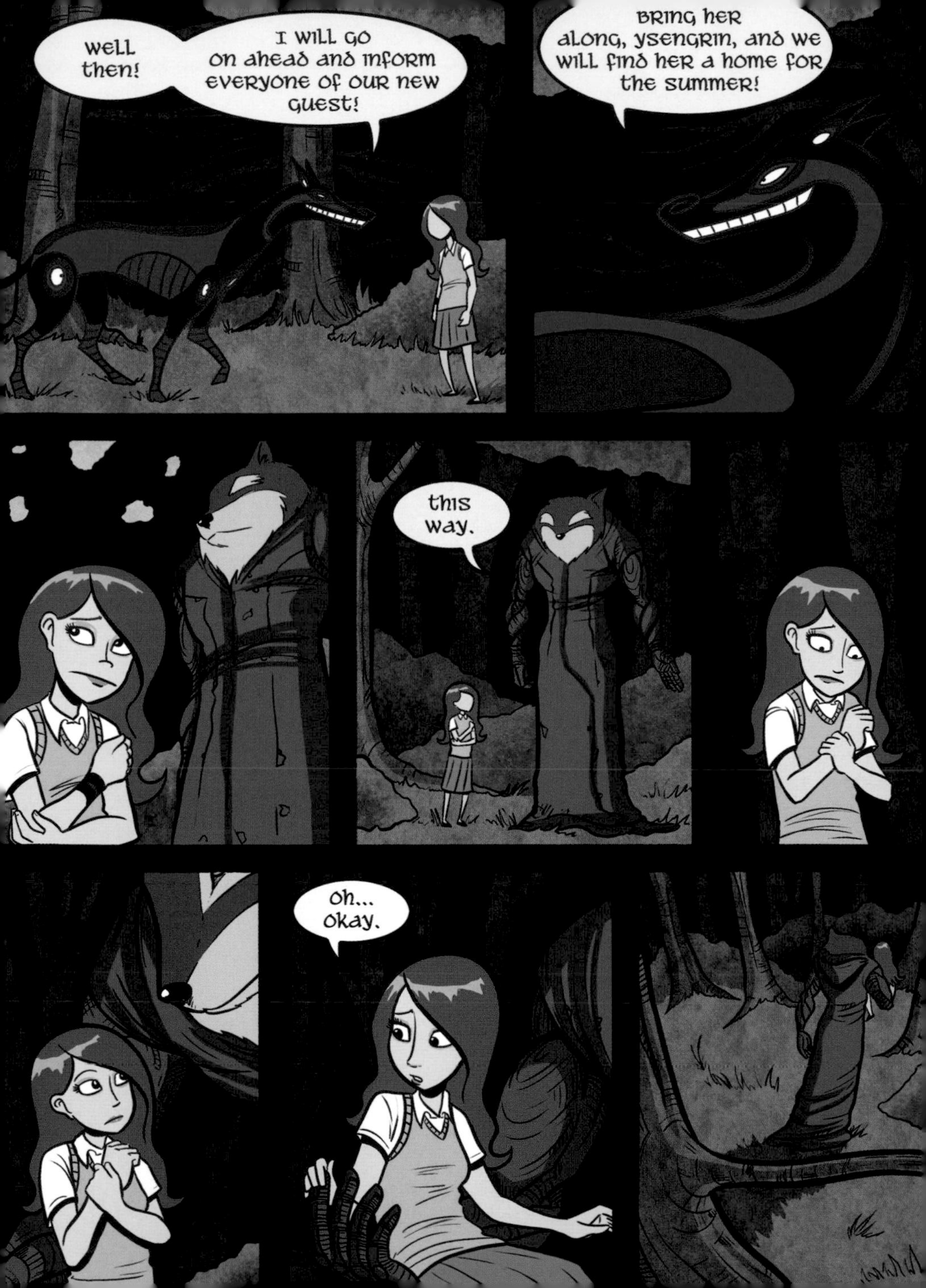

WELL then!
I WILL GO on ahead and inform everyone of our new guest!
BRING her along, ysengrin, and we WILL find her a home for the summer!
this way.
oh... okay.

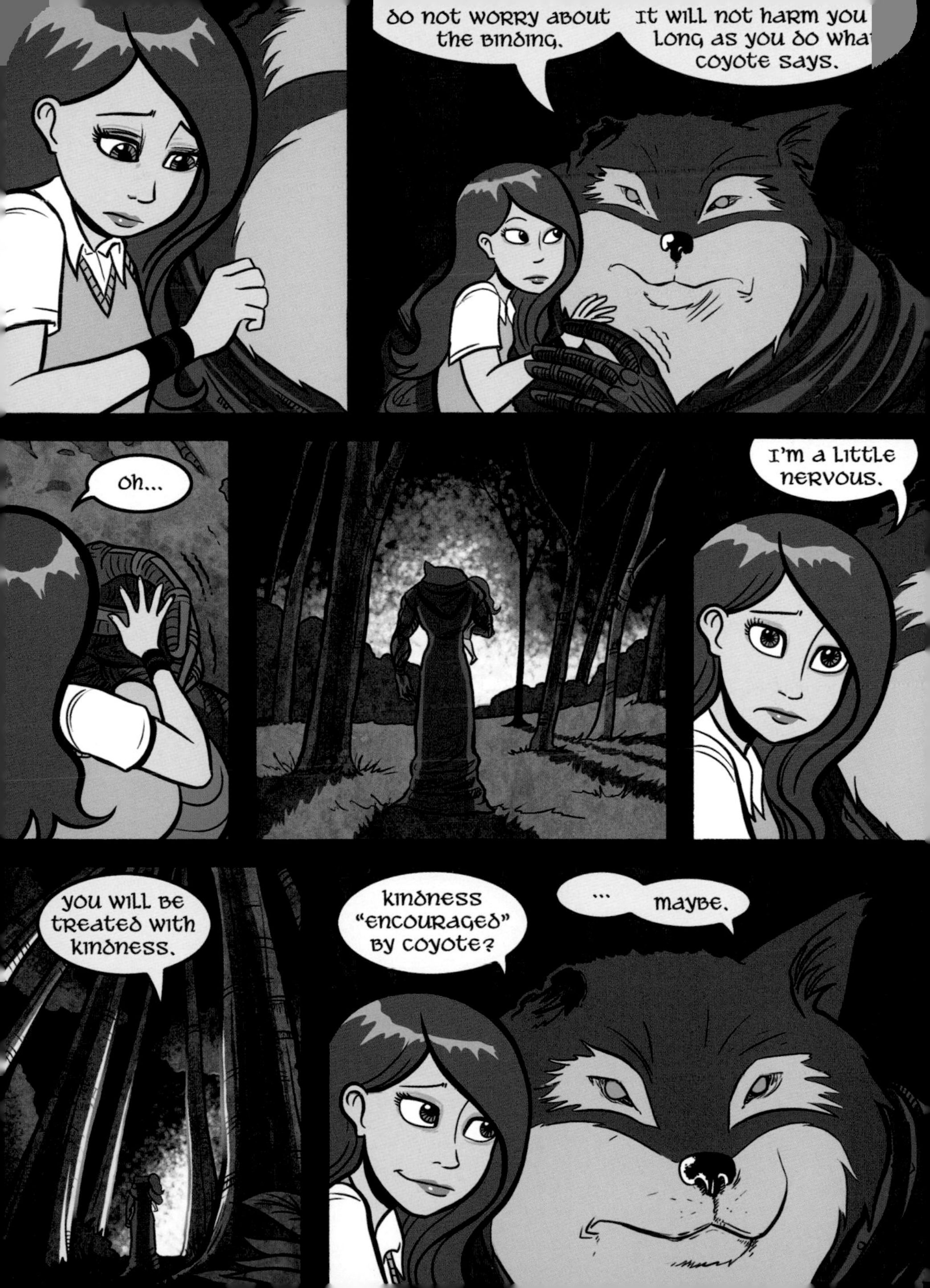
do not worry about the binding.
It will not harm you long as you do wha
coyote says.
oh...
I'm a little nervous.
you will be treated with kindness.
kindness "encouraged" by coyote?
...
maybe.

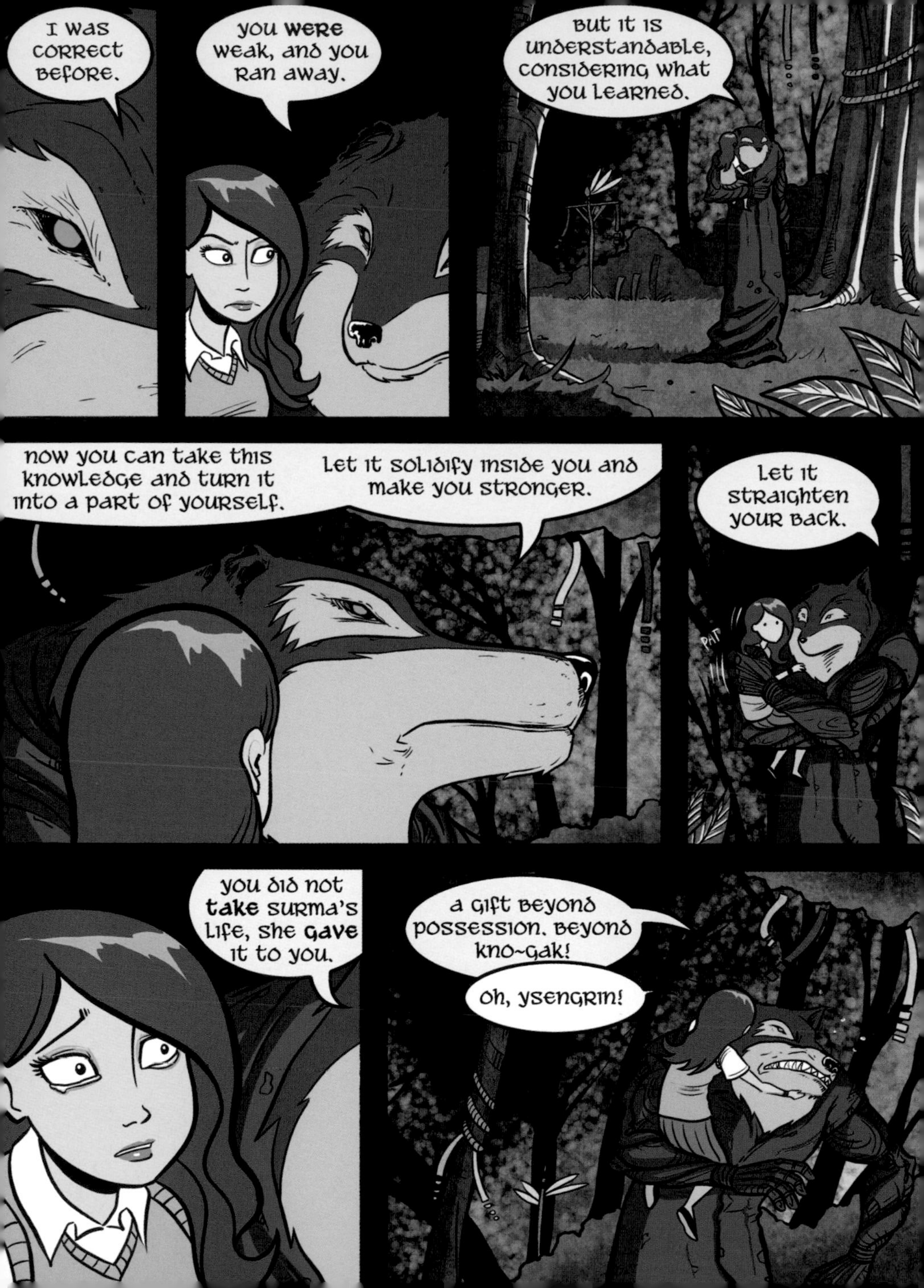
I was correct before.
you were weak, and you ran away.
But it is understandable, considering what you learned.
now you can take this knowledge and turn it into a part of yourself.
Let it solidify inside you and make you stronger.
Let it straighten your back.
PAT
you did not take surma's life, she gave it to you.
a gift beyond possession. beyond kno~gak!
Oh, ysengrin!

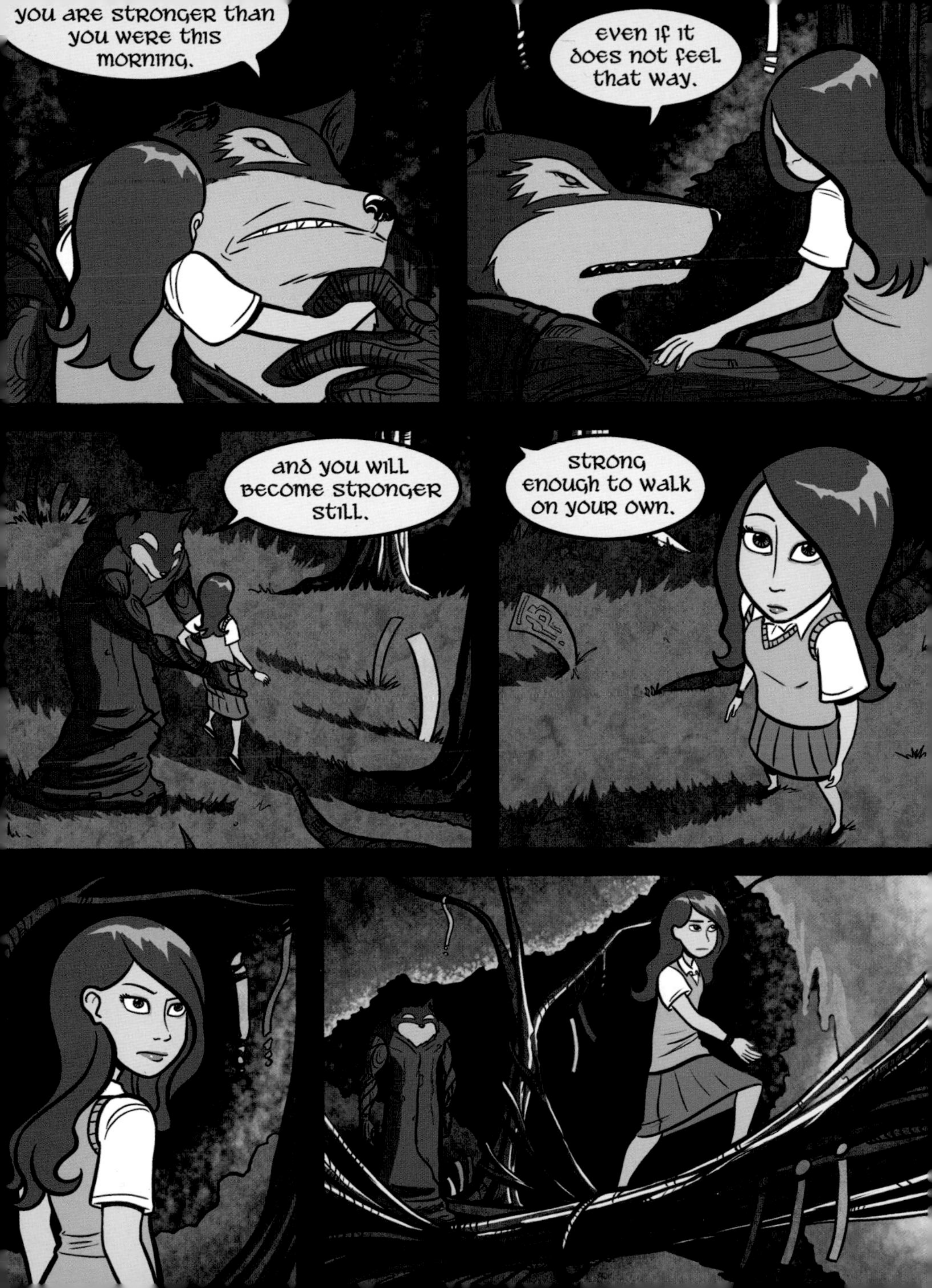
YOU ARE STRONGER THAN YOU WERE THIS MORNING.
EVEN IF IT DOES NOT FEEL THAT WAY.
AND YOU WILL BECOME STRONGER STILL.
STRONG ENOUGH TO WALK ON YOUR OWN.

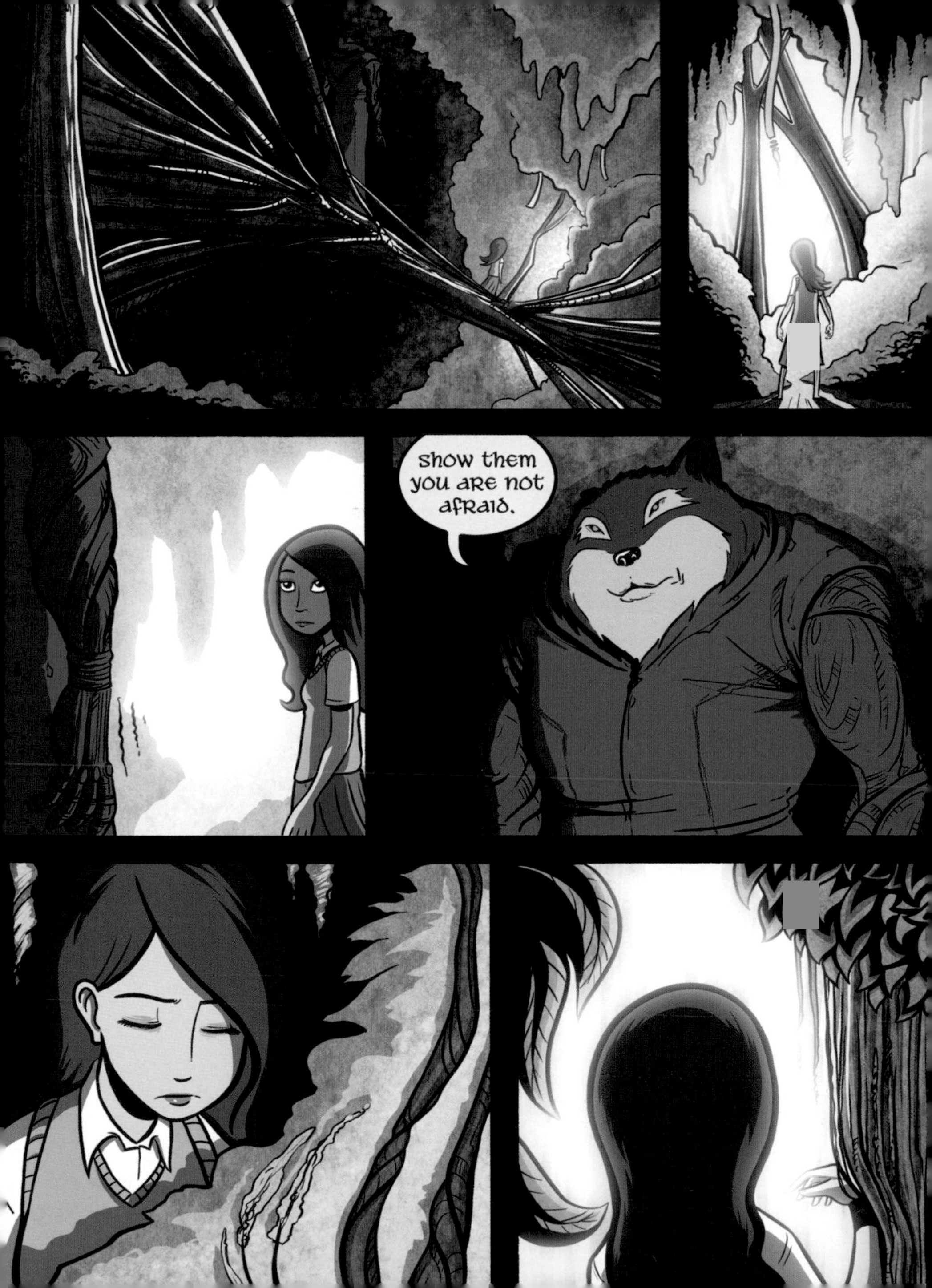
show them you are not afraid.

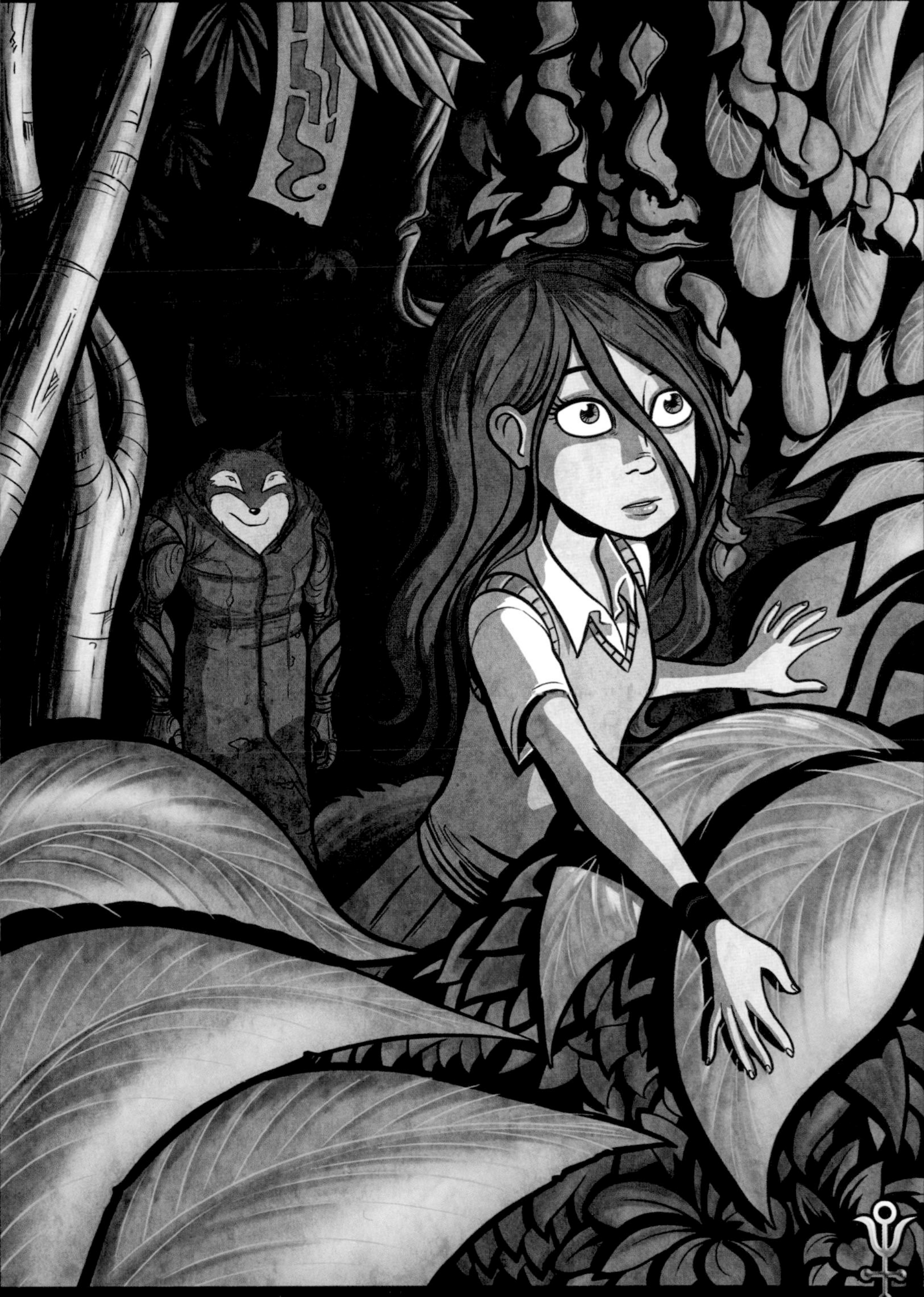

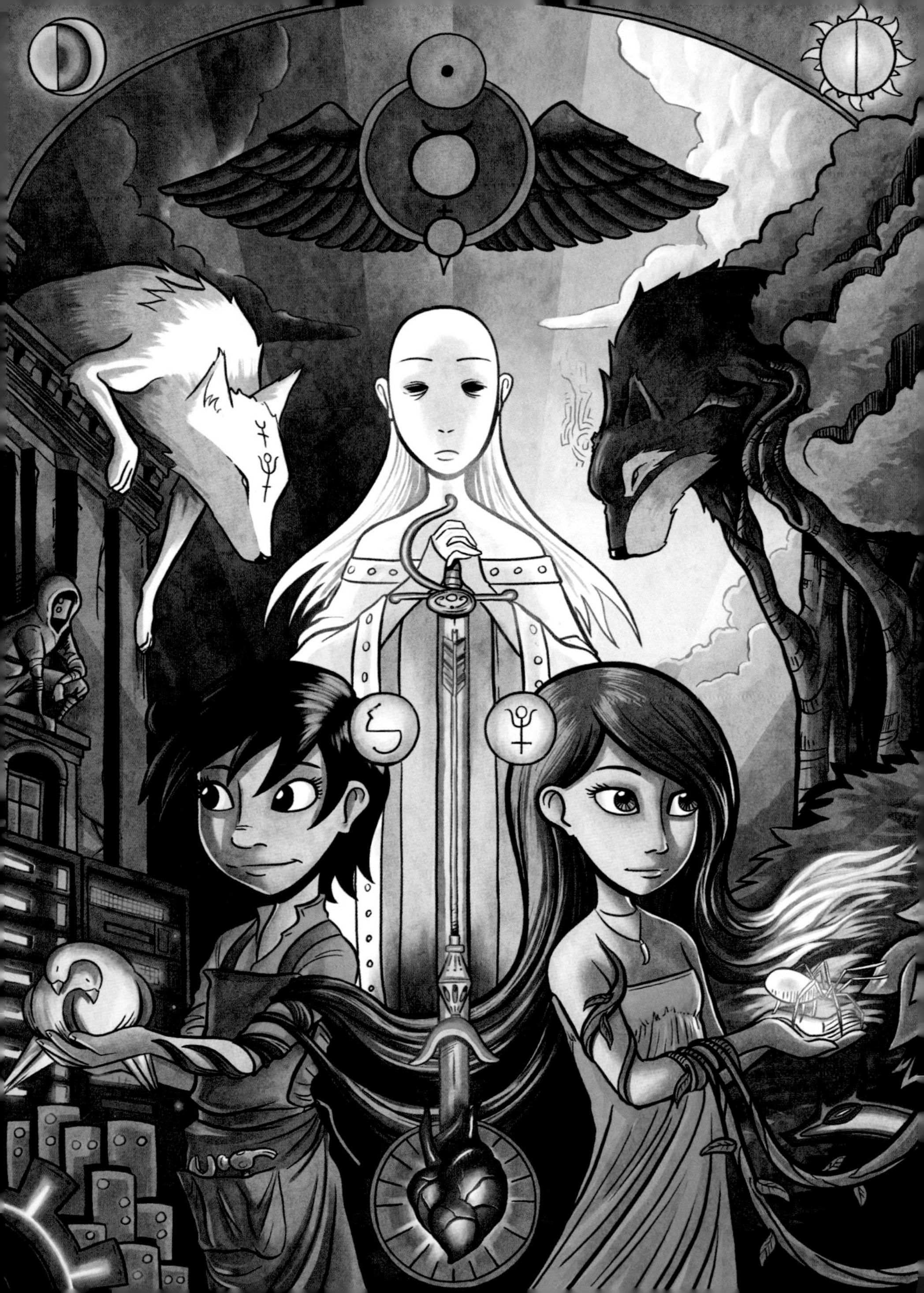

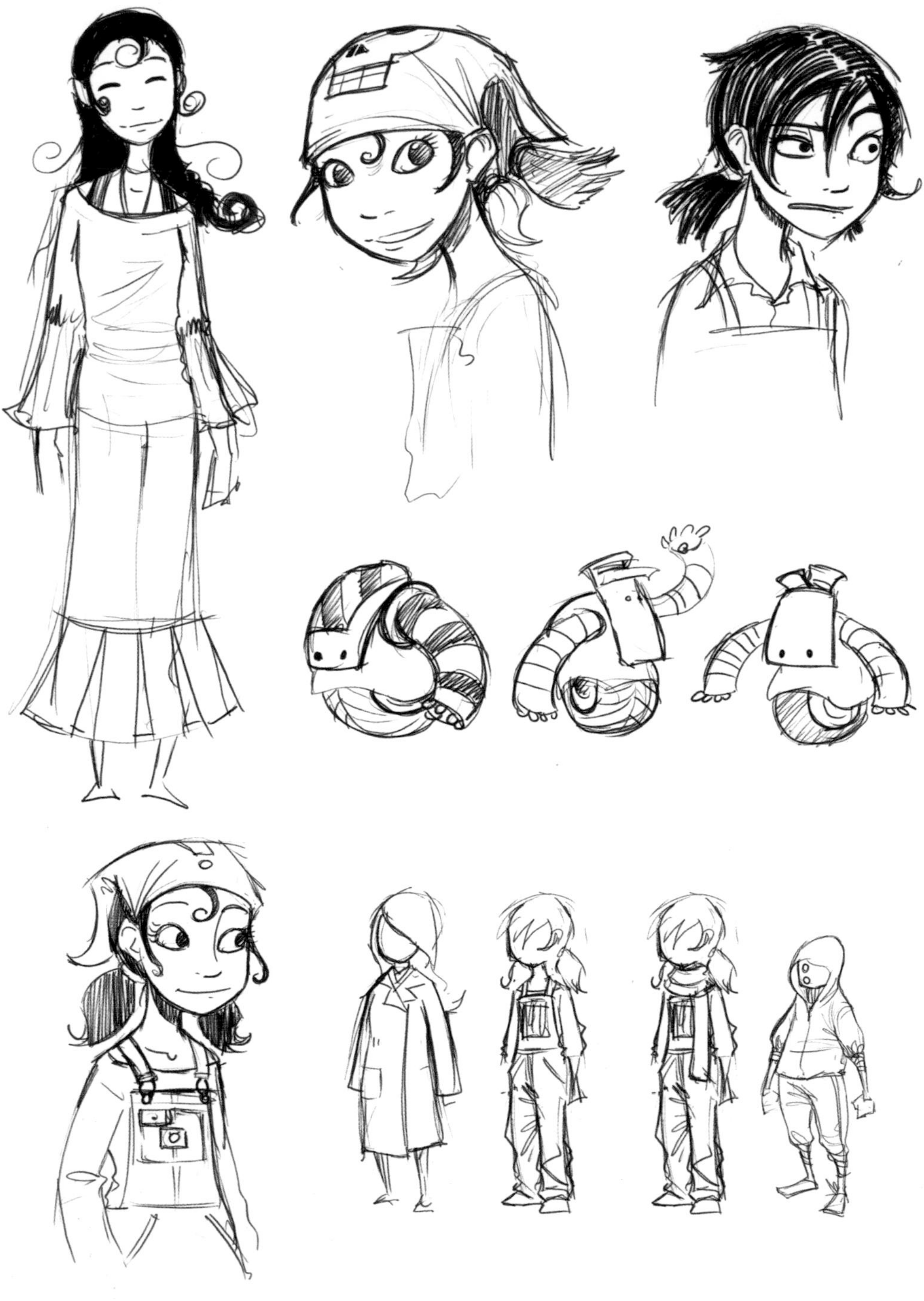

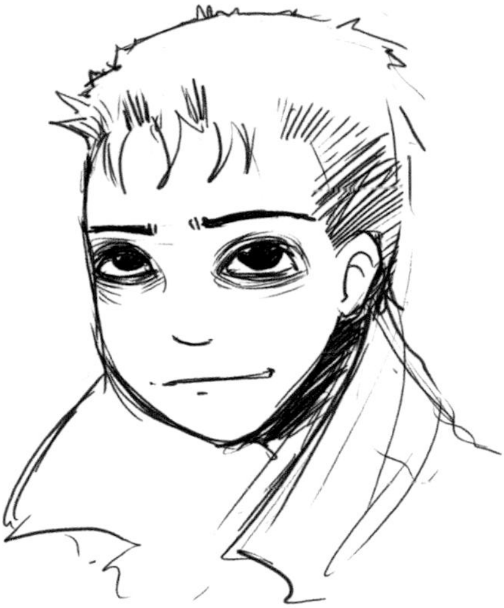
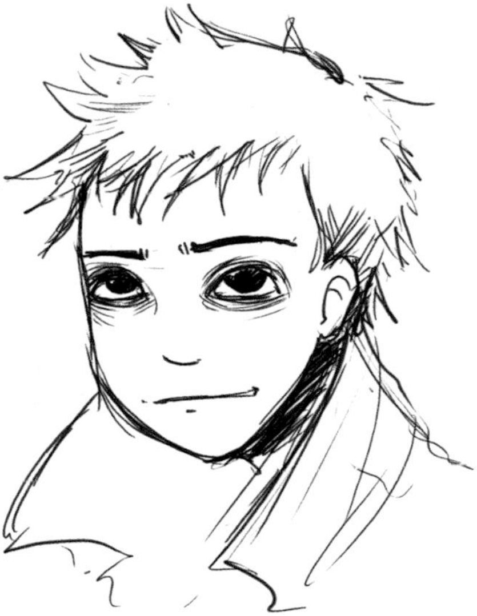
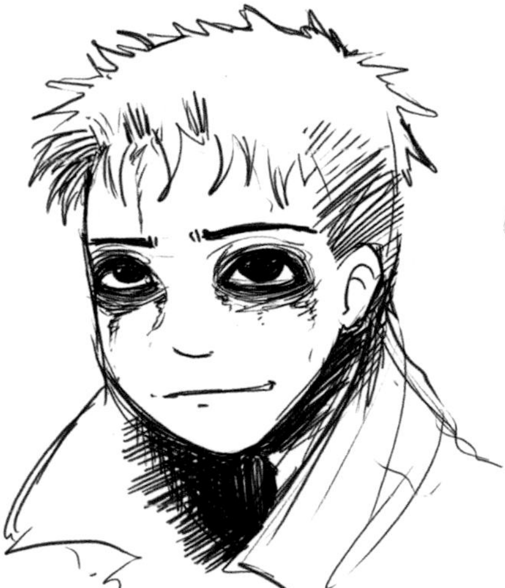
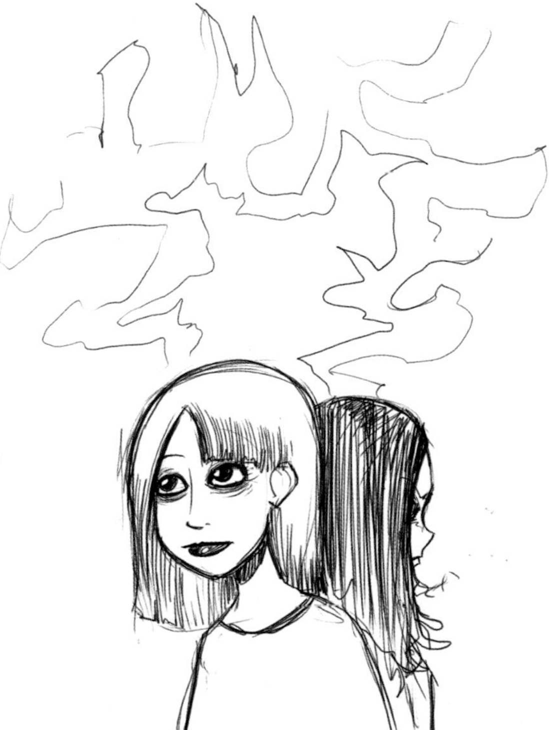

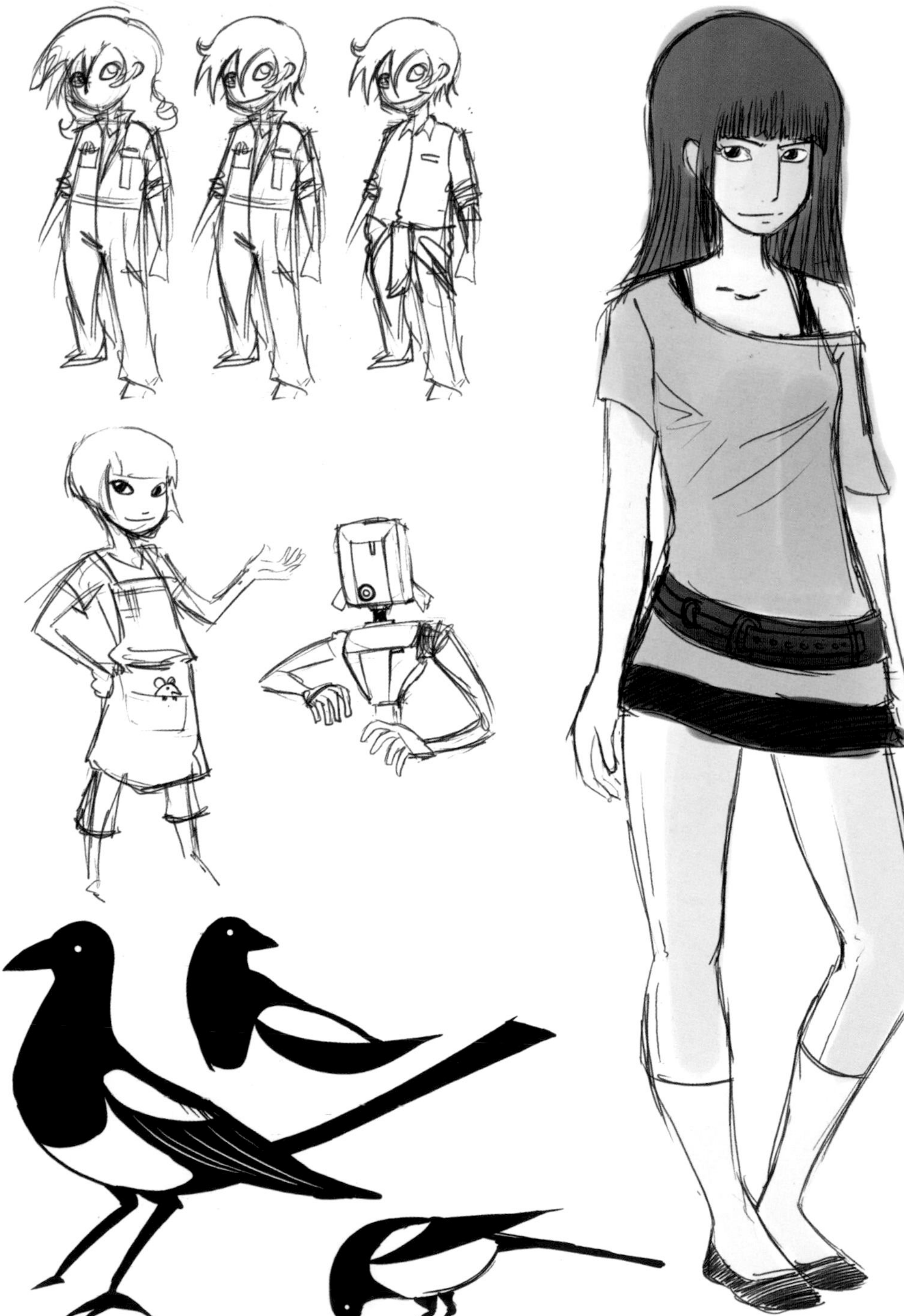

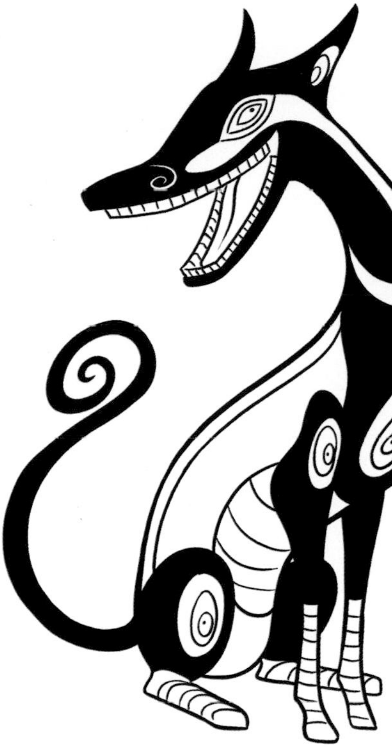

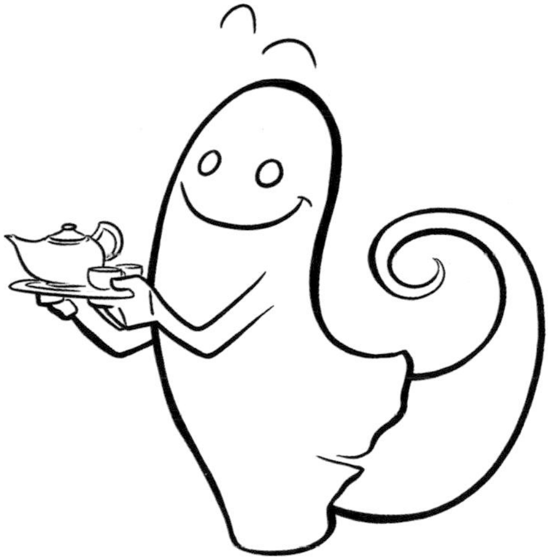

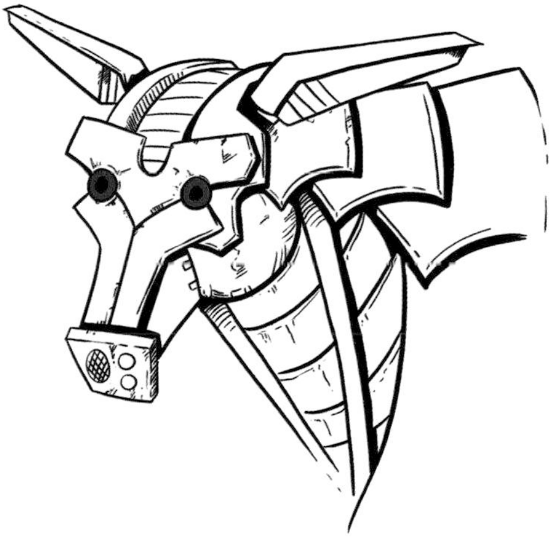

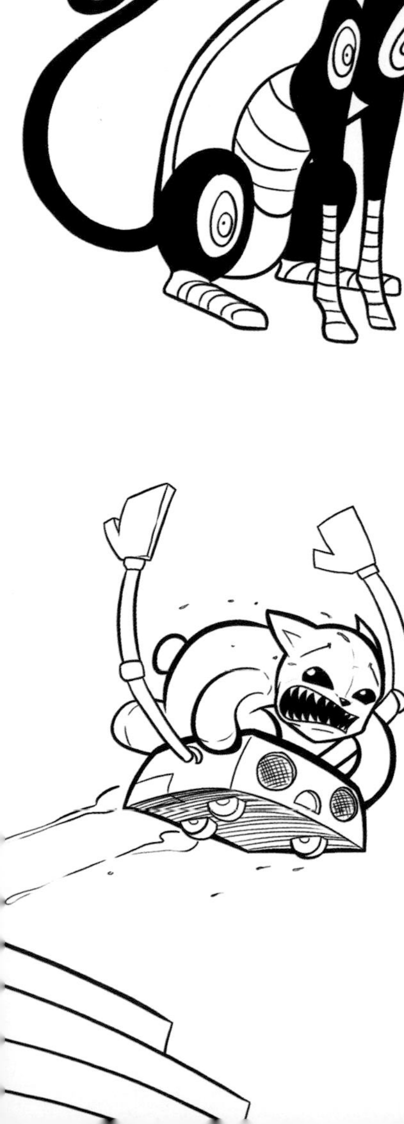

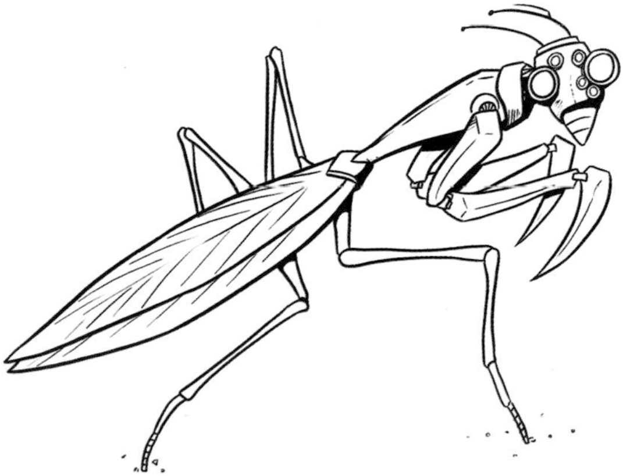

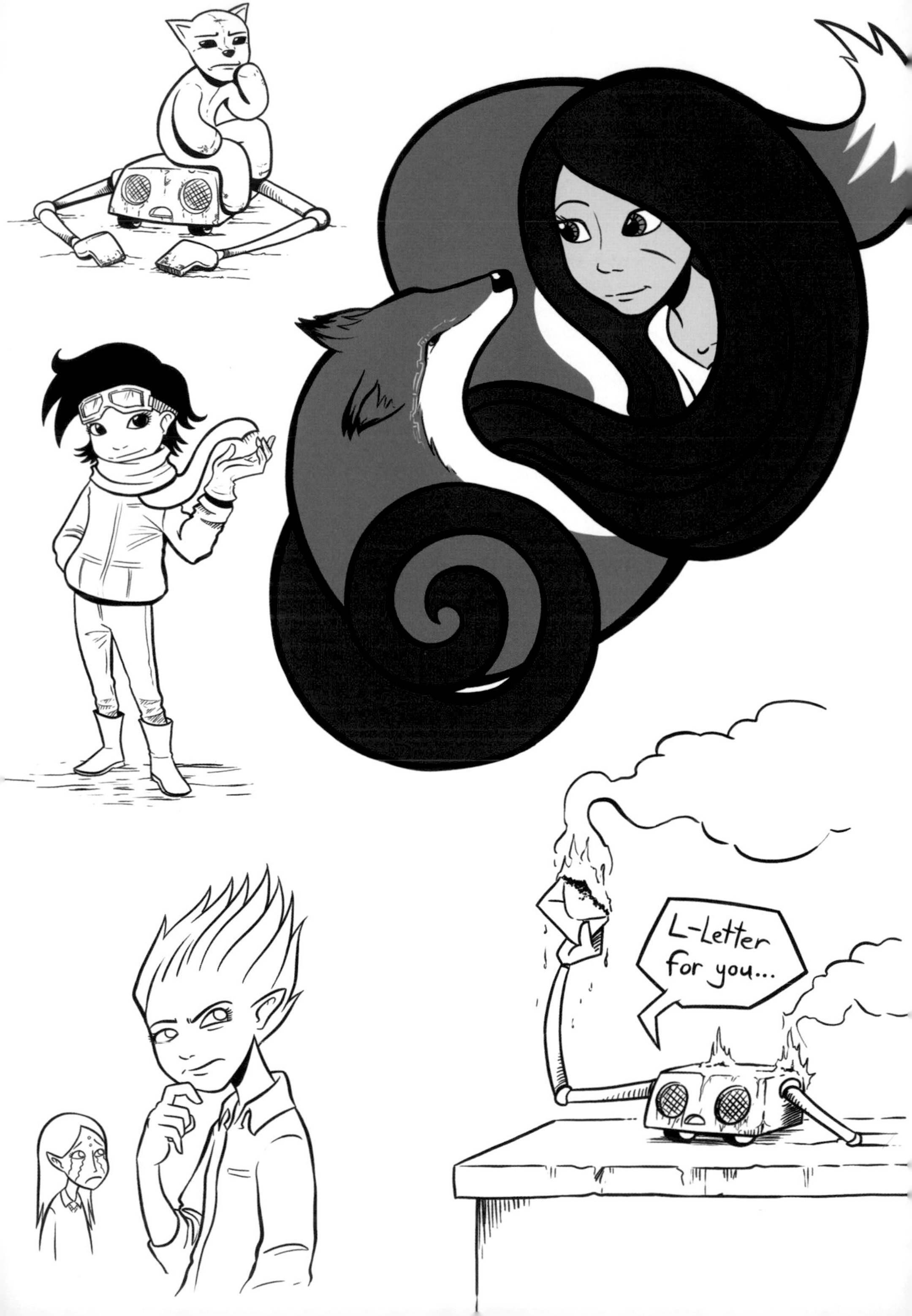
L-Letter for you...

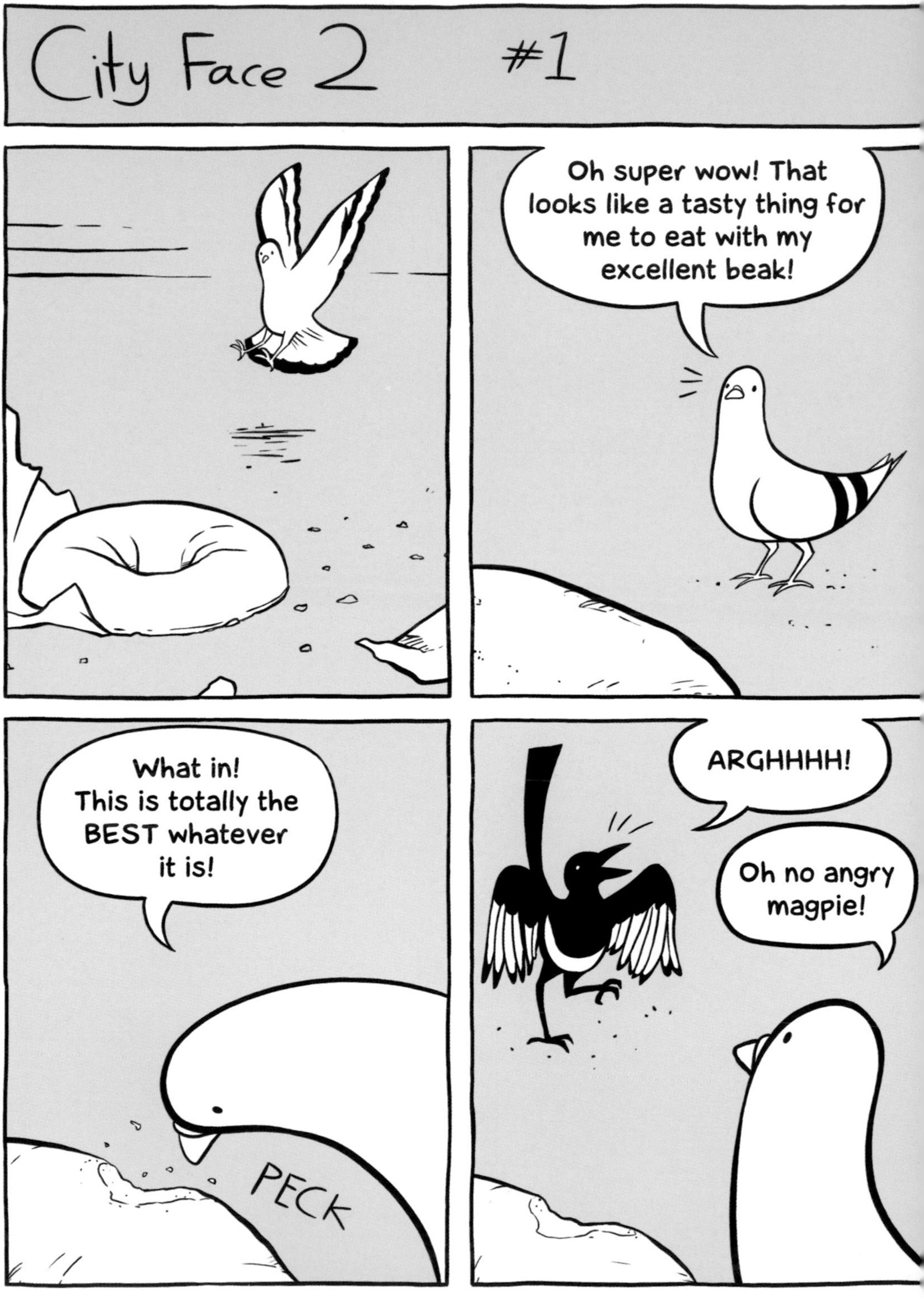
City Face 2 #1
Oh super wow! That looks like a tasty thing for me to eat with my excellent beak!
What in! This is totally the BEST whatever it is!
PECK
ARGHHHH!
Oh no angry magpie!

City Face 2 #2

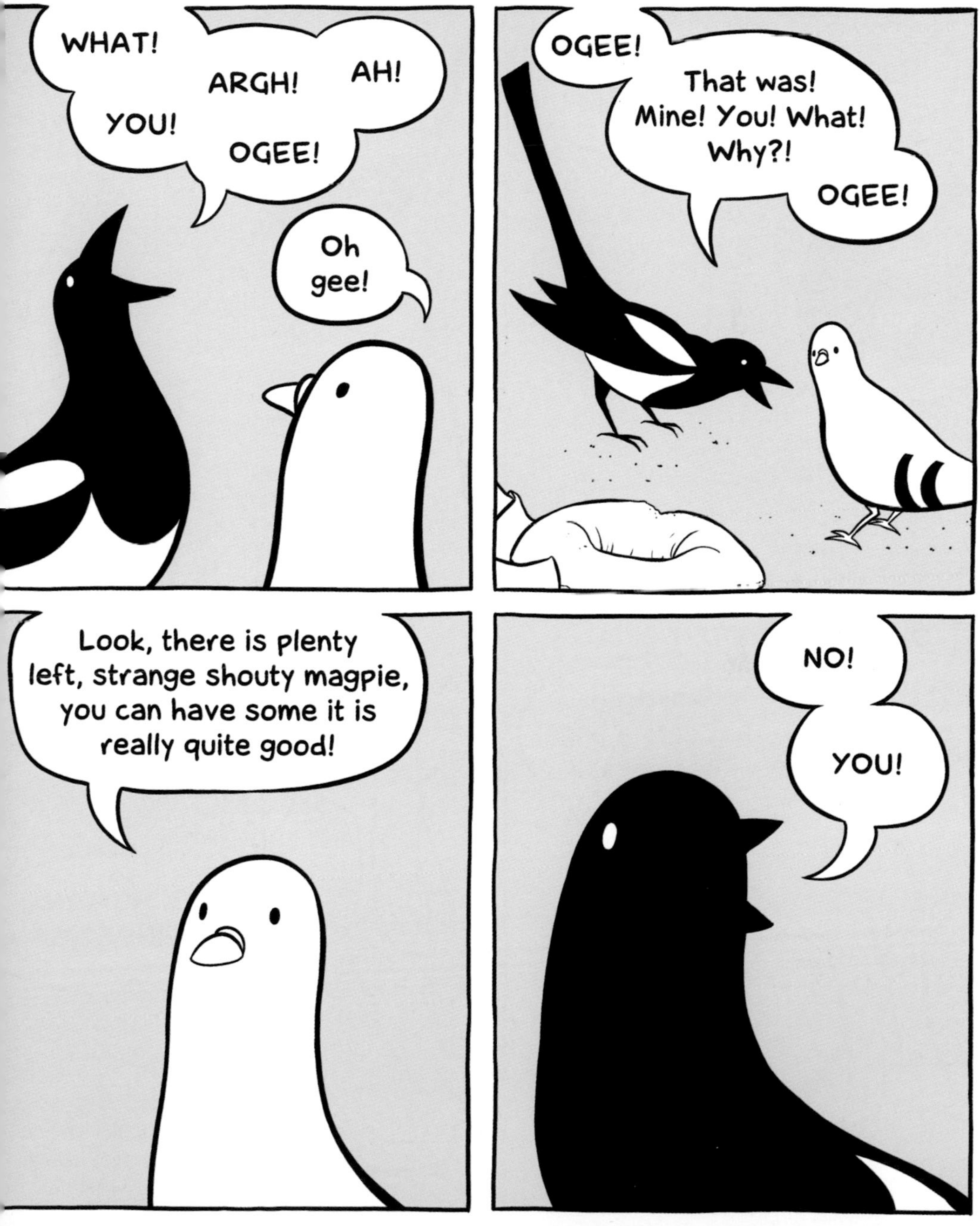
WHAT! ARGH! AH! YOU! OGEE!
Oh gee!
OGEE!
That was! Mine! You! What! Why?! OGEE!
Look, there is plenty left, strange shouty magpie, you can have some it is really quite good!
NO!
YOU!

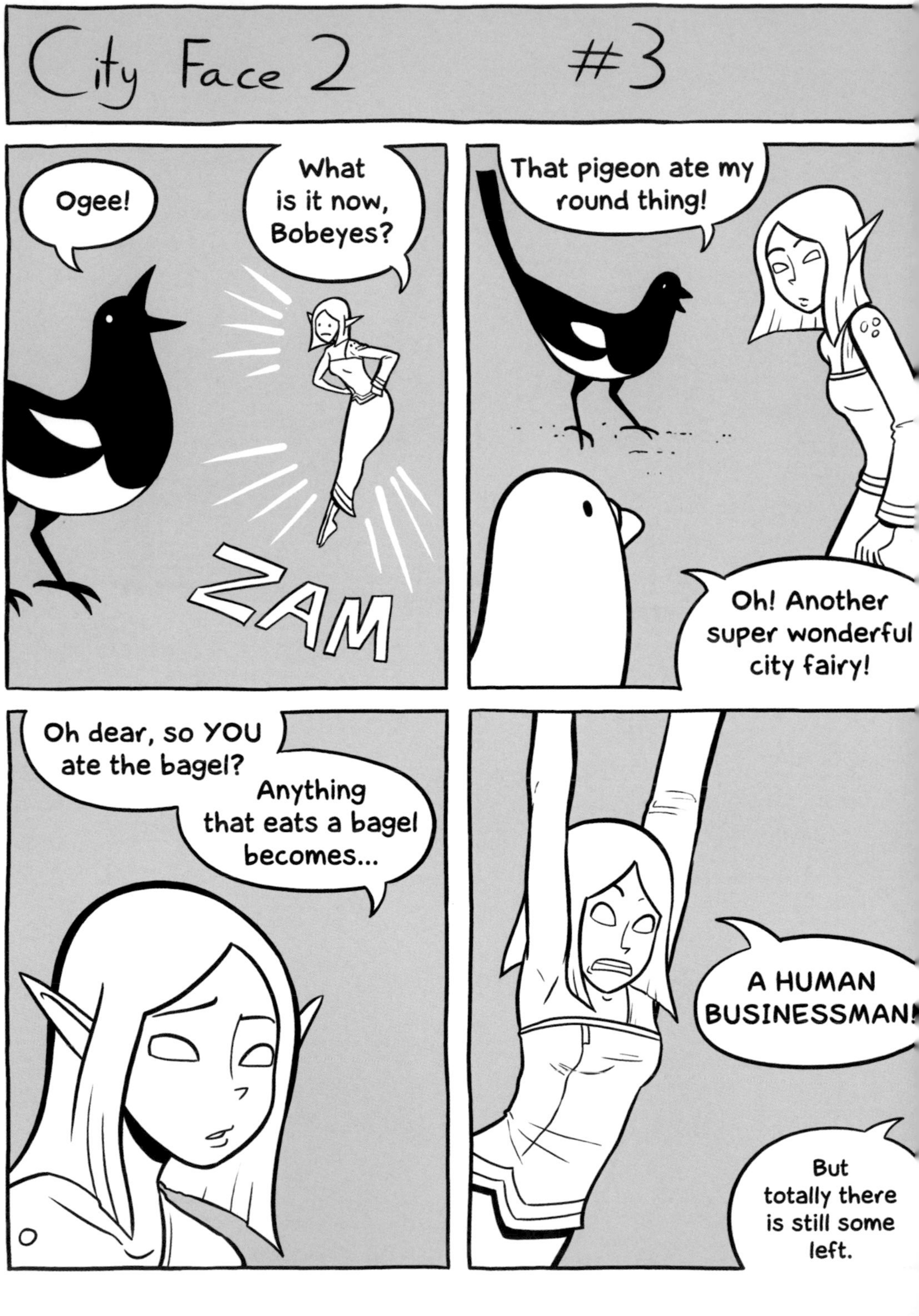
City Face 2 #3
Ogee!
What is it now, Bobeyes?
ZAM
That pigeon ate my round thing!
Oh! Another super wonderful city fairy!
Oh dear, so YOU ate the bagel?
Anything that eats a bagel becomes...
A HUMAN BUSINESSMAN!
But totally there is still some left.

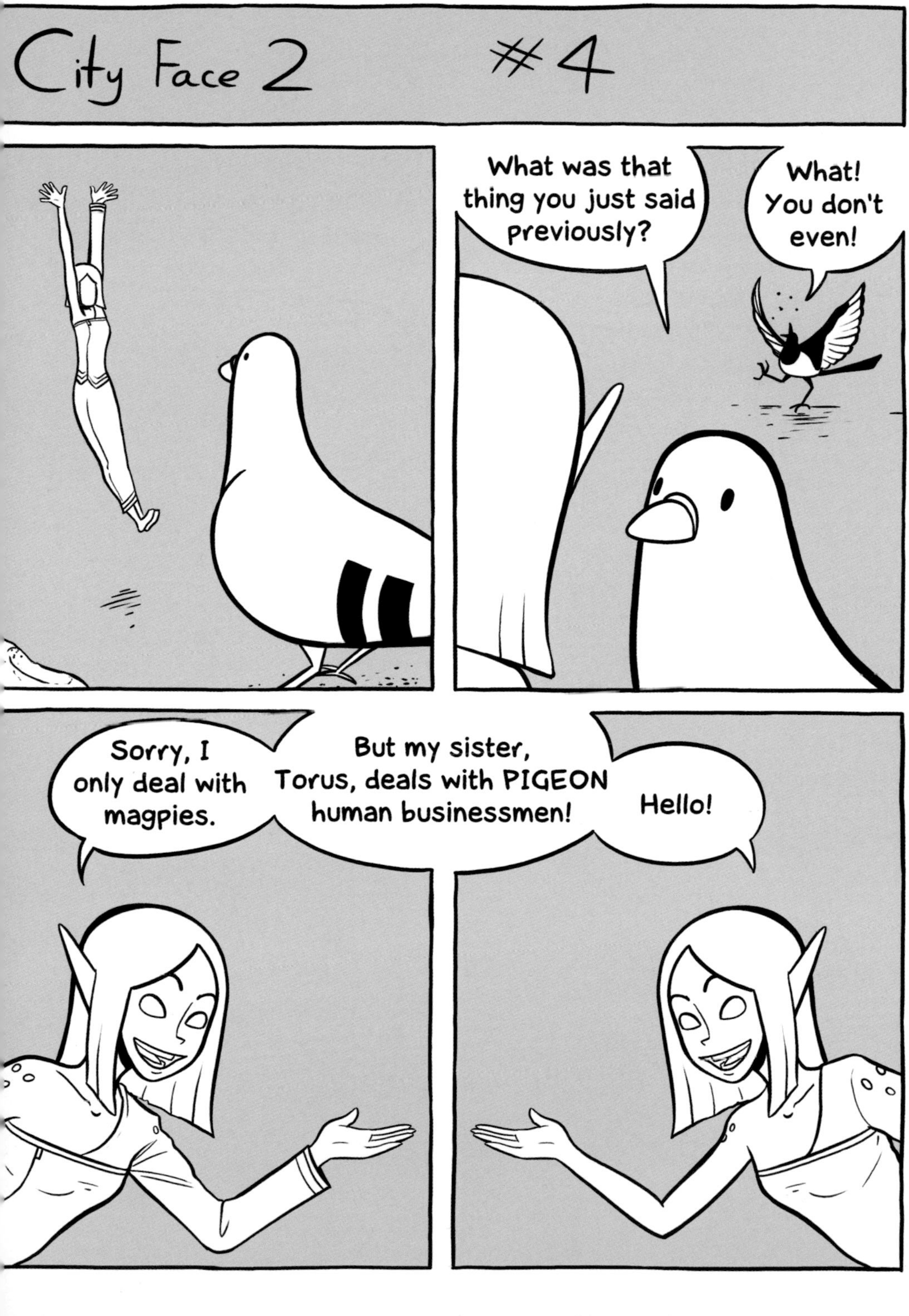
City Face 2
#4
What was that thing you just said previously?
What! You don't even!
Sorry, I only deal with magpies.
But my sister, Torus, deals with PIGEON human businessmen!
Hello!

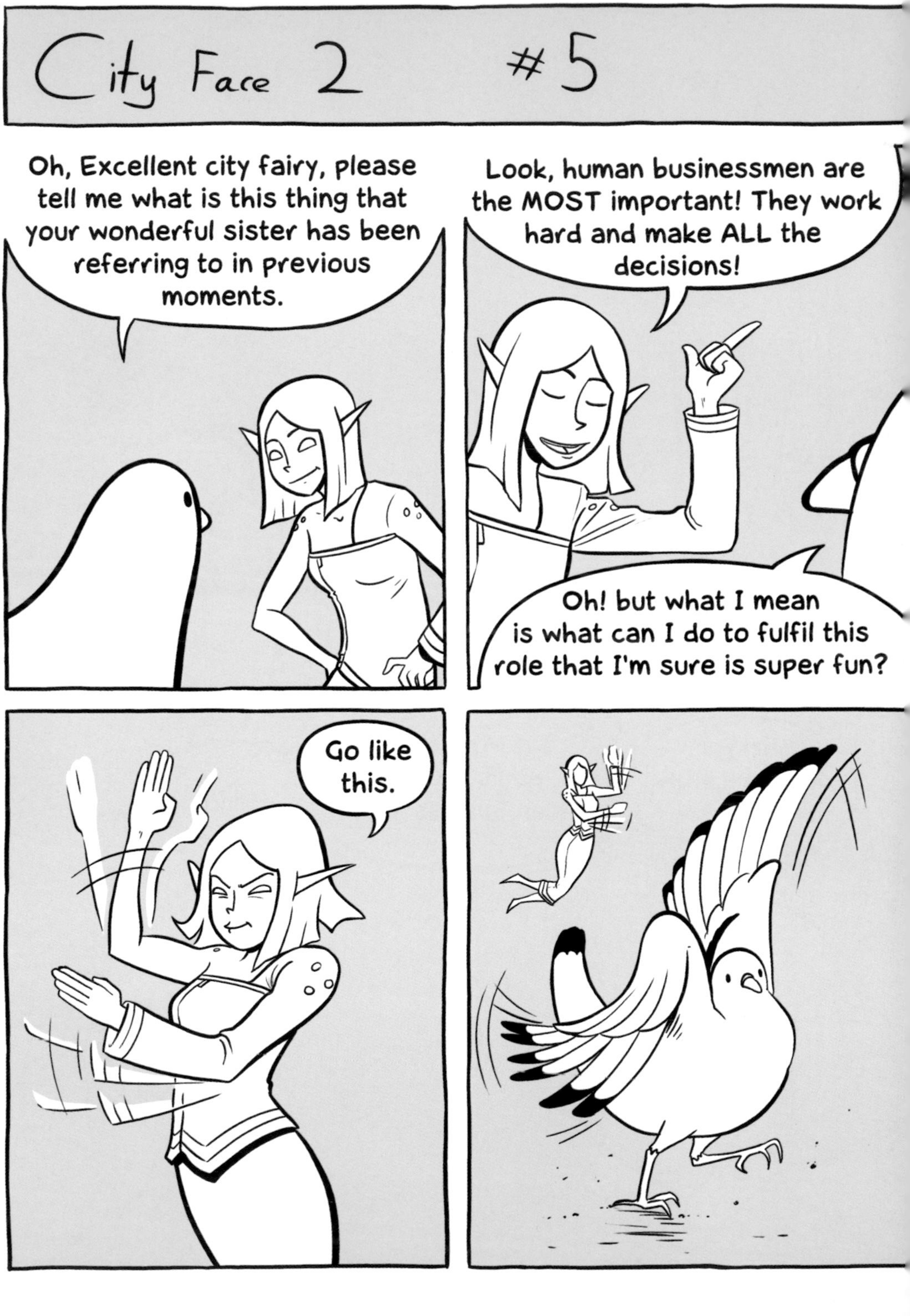
City Face 2 #5
Oh, Excellent city fairy, please tell me what is this thing that your wonderful sister has been referring to in previous moments.
Look, human businessmen are the MOST important! They work hard and make ALL the decisions!
Oh! but what I mean is what can I do to fulfil this role that I'm sure is super fun?
Go like this.

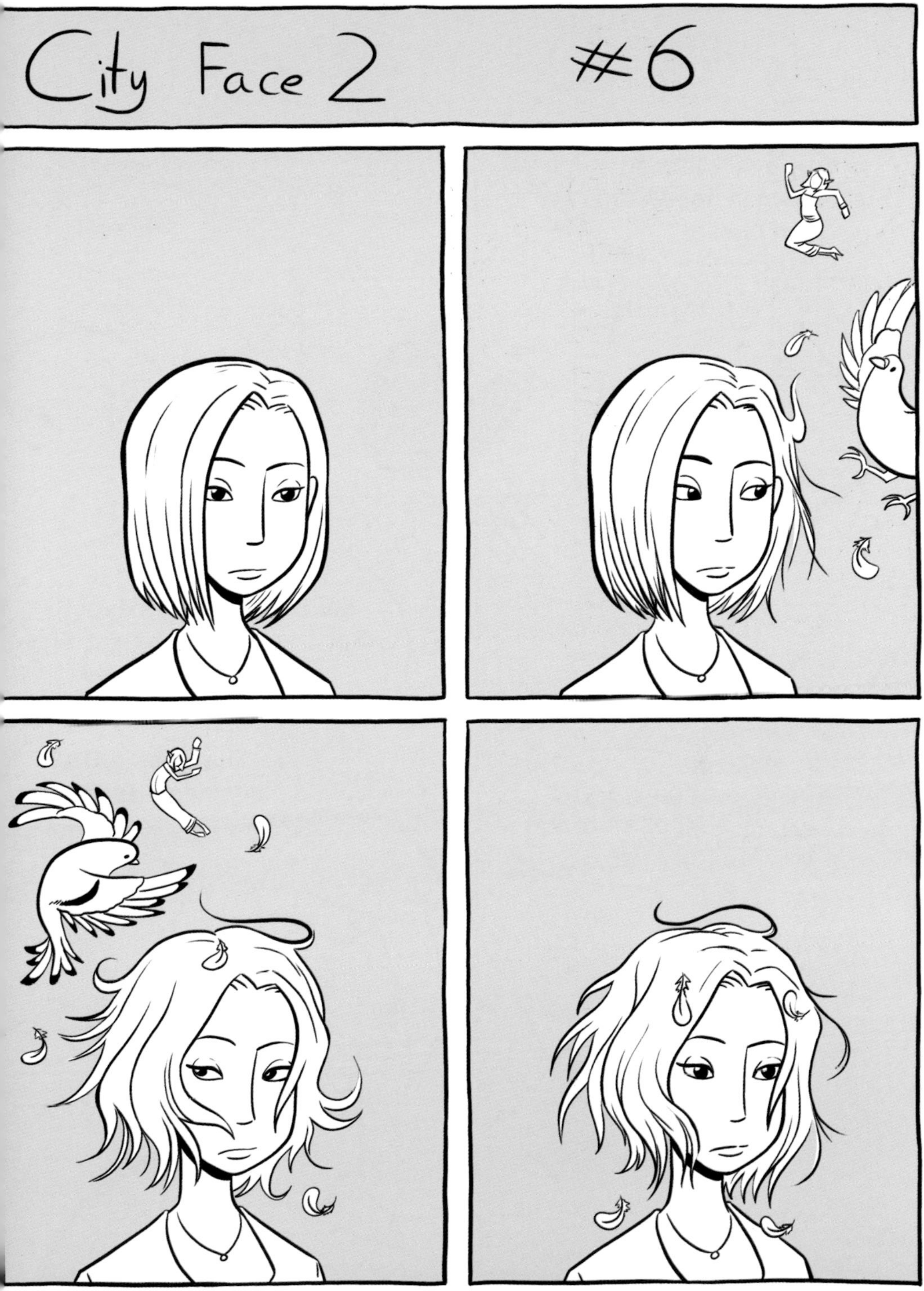
City Face 2
#6

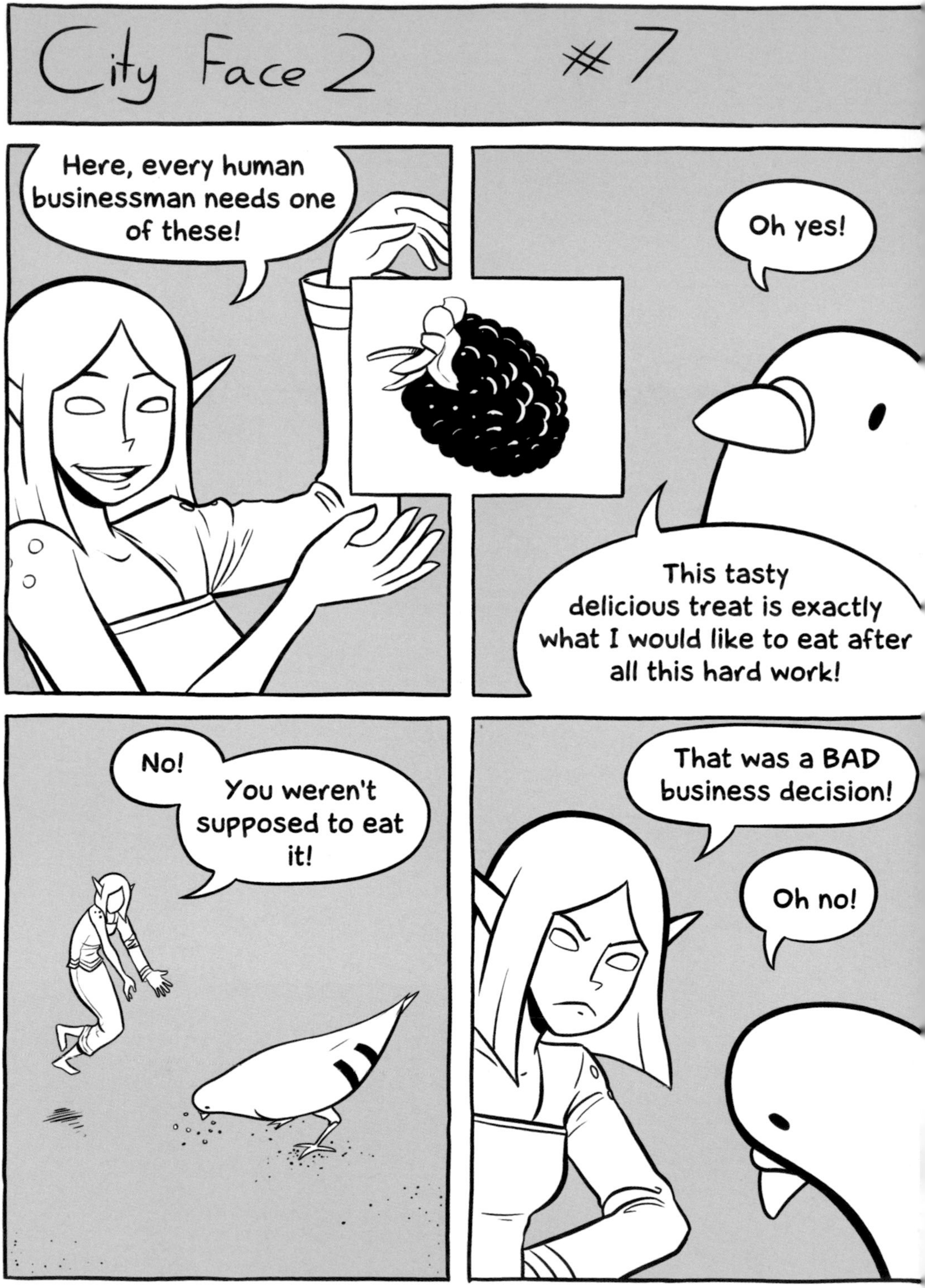
City Face 2 #7
Here, every human businessman needs one of these!
Oh yes!
This tasty delicious treat is exactly what I would like to eat after all this hard work!
No!
You weren't supposed to eat it!
That was a BAD business decision!
Oh no!

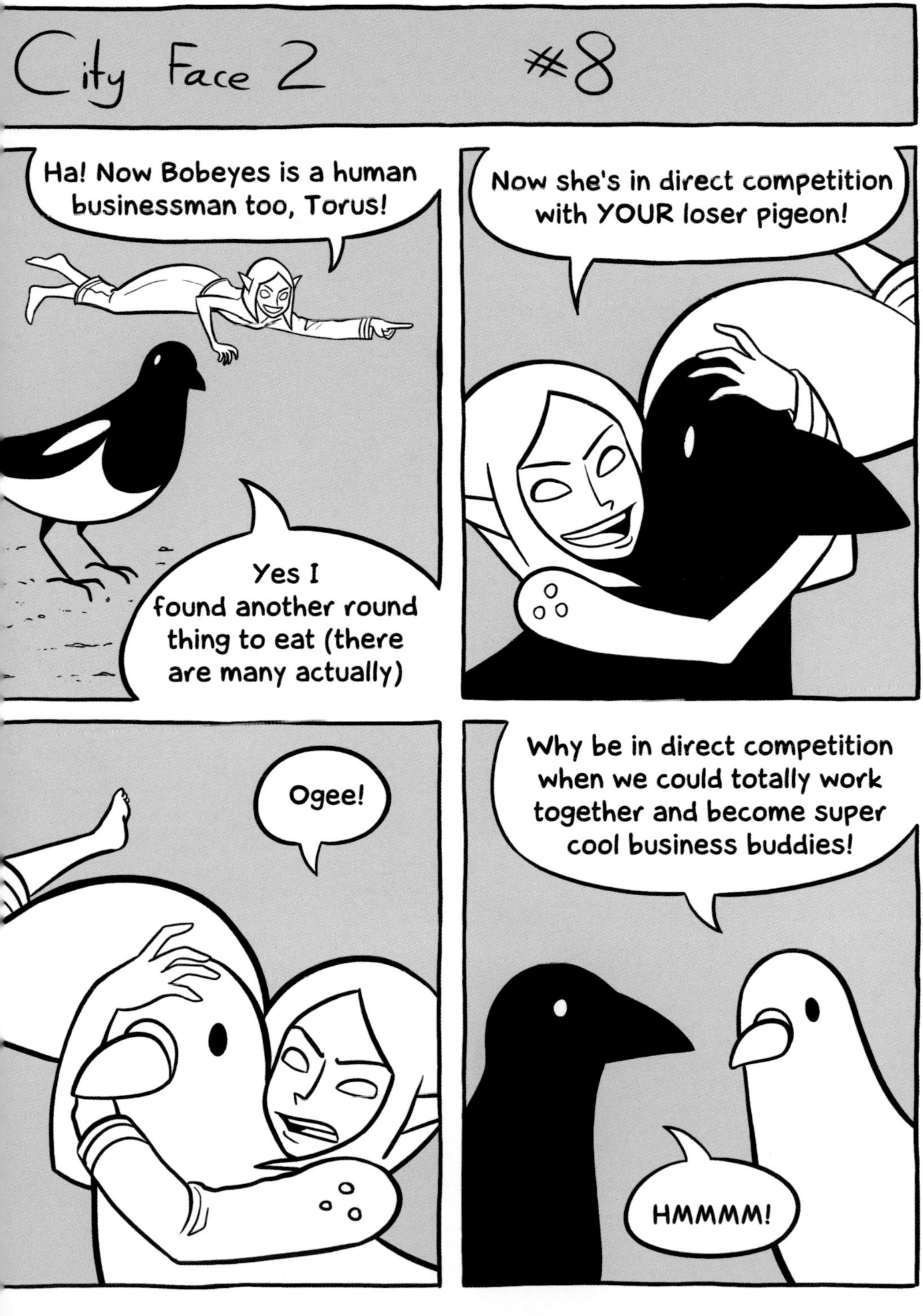
City Face 2 #8
Ha! Now Bobeyes is a human businessman too, Torus!
Yes I found another round thing to eat (there are many actually)
Now she's in direct competition with YOUR loser pigeon!
Ogee!
Why be in direct competition when we could totally work together and become super cool business buddies!
HMMMM!

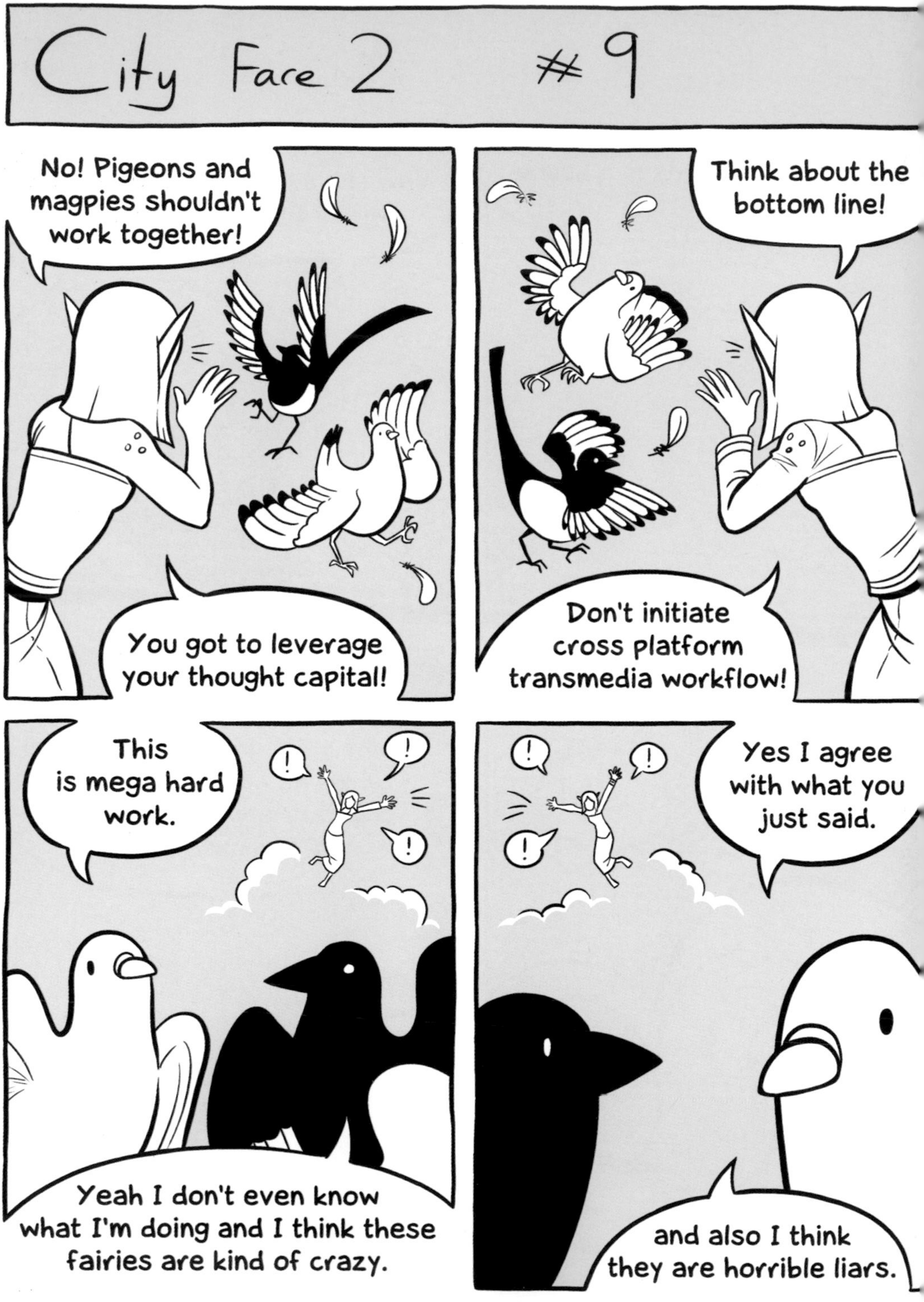
City Fare 2 #9
No! Pigeons and magpies shouldn't work together!
You got to leverage your thought capital!
Think about the bottom line!
Don't initiate cross platform transmedia workflow!
This is mega hard work.
!
!
!
Yeah I don't even know what I'm doing and I think these fairies are kind of crazy.
Yes I agree with what you just said.
!
!
!
and also I think they are horrible liars.

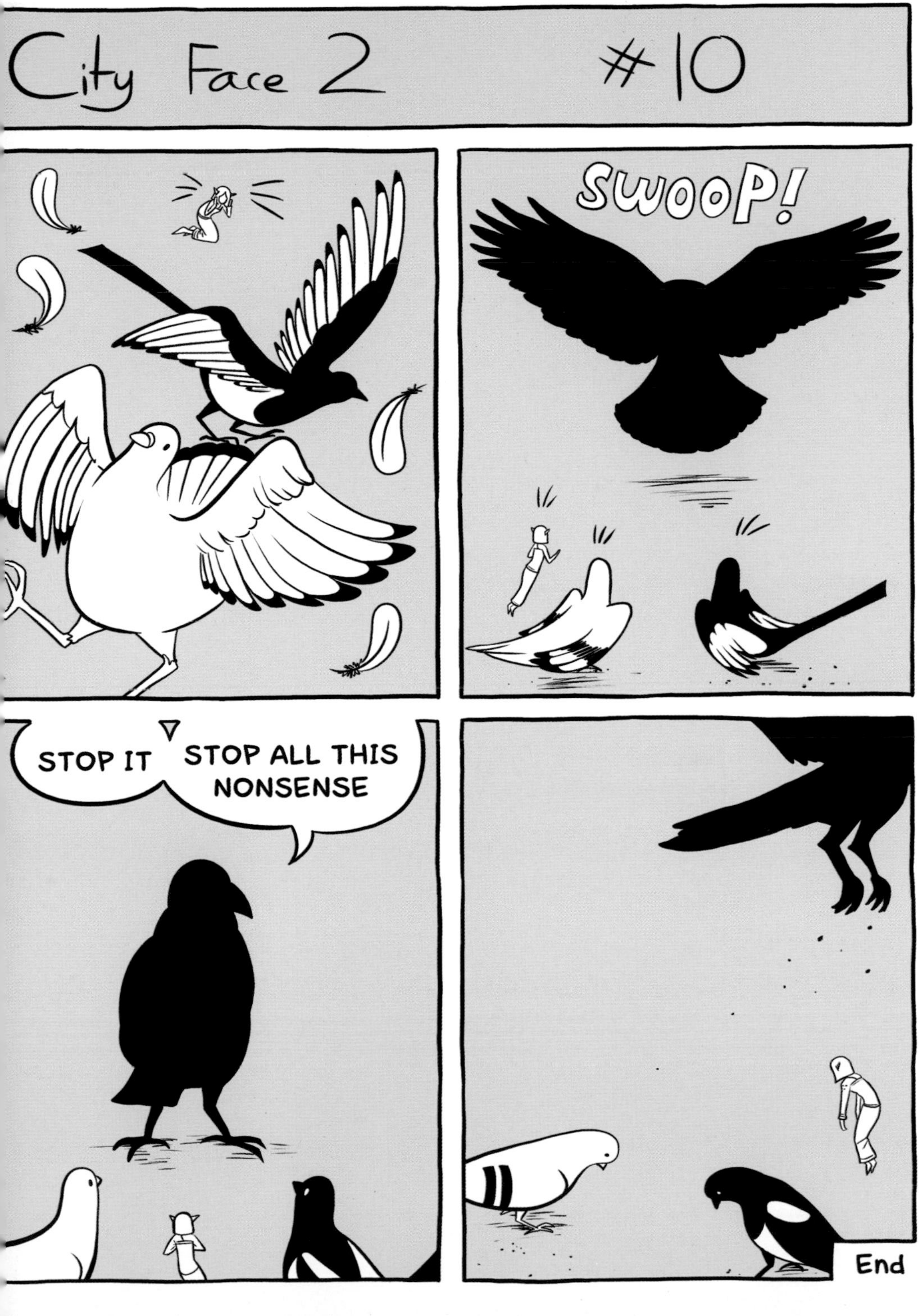
City Face 2
#10
SWOOP!
STOP IT
STOP ALL THIS NONSENSE
End

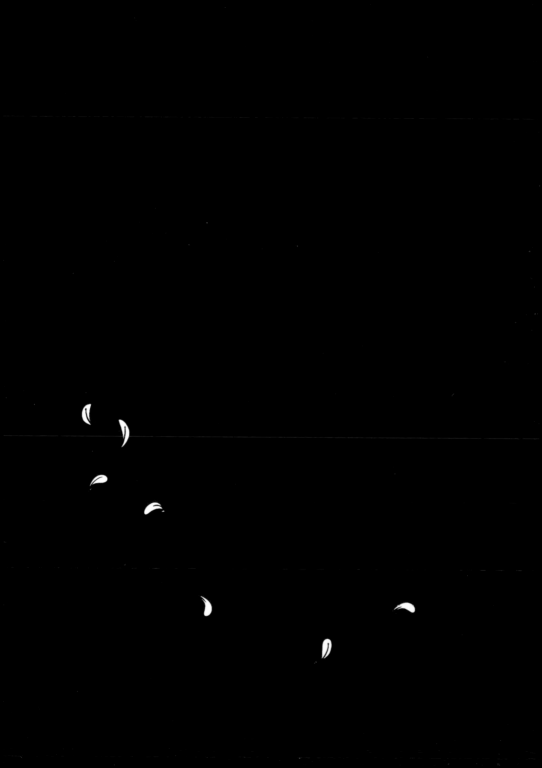

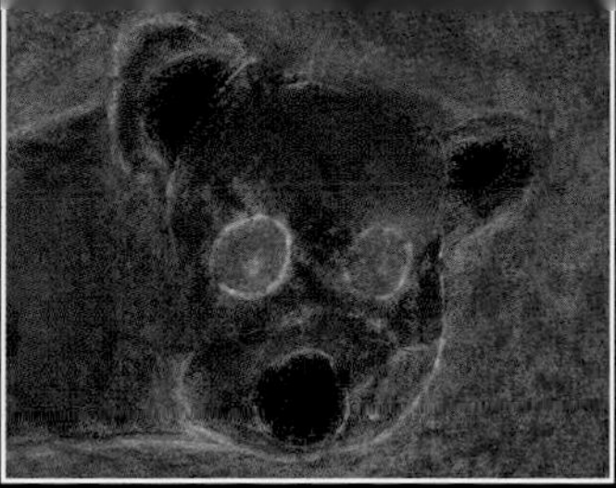

About the Author

Tom still lives in Birmingham, in the United Kingdom. He can still be found in one of three places:

1) Still at work.
2) Still at home.
3) Still waiting for the bus to take him to work, or home.

While waiting patiently for the National Express bus service *(formerly Travel West Midlands)*, he has had a lot of time to think about making a book. He is still happy to find that this has happened.

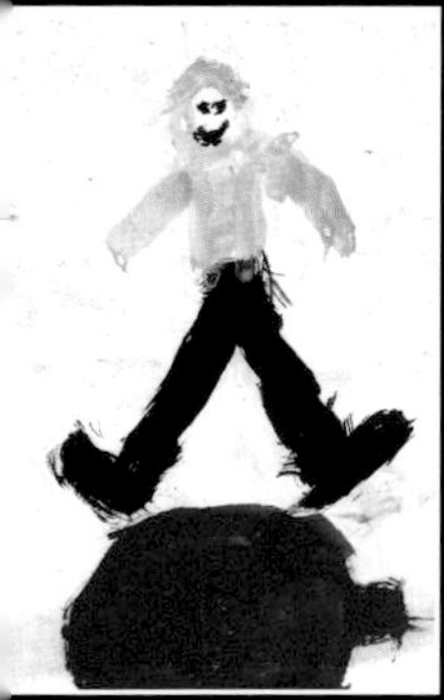

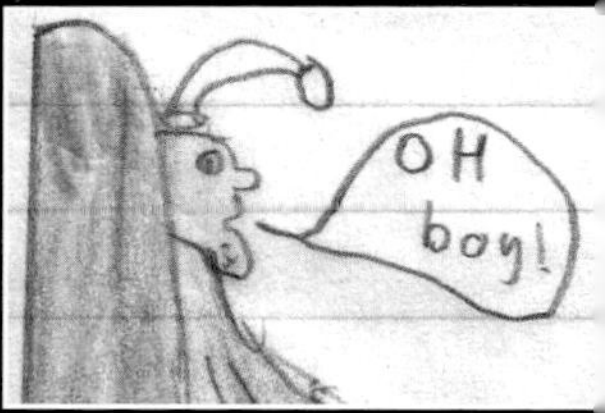
OH boy!

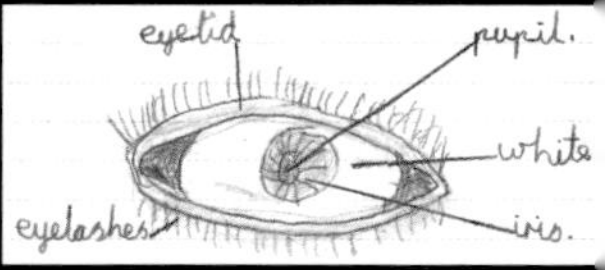
eyelid
pupil.
white
eyelashes
iris.

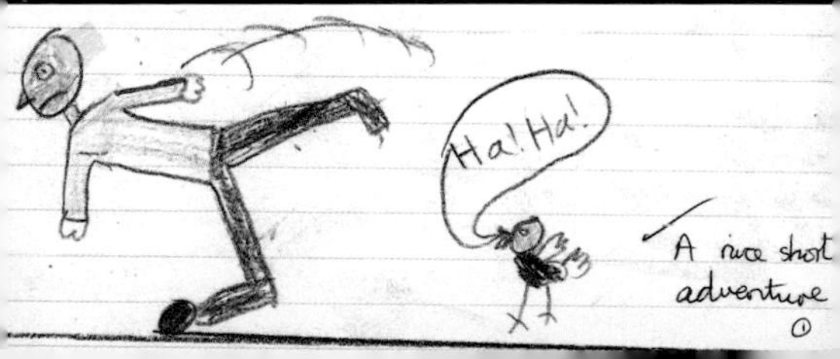
Ha! Ha!
A nice short adventure

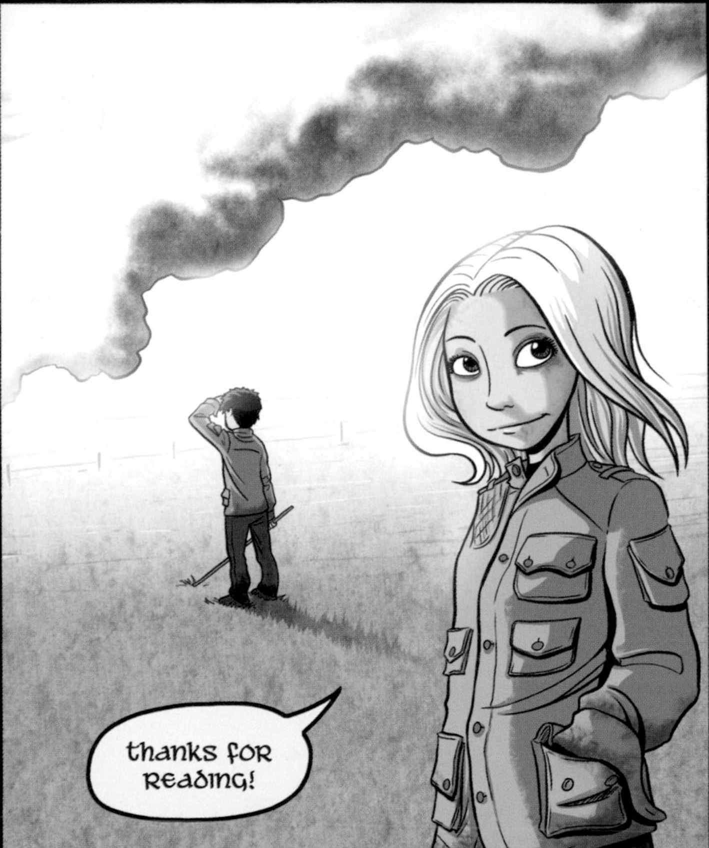
thanks for reading!

www.gunnerkrigg.com

G-12

EMMA S. CLARK MEMORIAL LIBRARY
SETAUKET, NEW YORK 11733
To view your account,

renew or request an item,

visit www.emmaclark.org